A
LIGHT
IN THE
FLAME

Also From Jennifer L. Armentrout

Fall With Me
Dream of You (a 1001 Dark Nights Novel)
Forever With You
Fire in You

By J. Lynn
Wait for You
Be with Me
Stay with Me

The Blood and Ash Series
From Blood and Ash
A Kingdom of Flesh and Fire
The Crown of Gilded Bones
The War of Two Queens

The Flesh and Fire Series
A Shadow in the Ember
A Light in the Flame

The Covenant Series
Half-Blood
Pure
Deity
Elixir
Apollyon
Sentinel

The Lux Series
Shadows
Obsidian
Onyx
Opal
Origin
Opposition
Oblivion

A
LIGHT
IN THE
FLAME

#1 NEW YORK TIMES BESTSELLING AUTHOR

JENNIFER L.
ARMENTROUT

**To see a full version of the map, visit
https://theblueboxpress.com/alitfmap/**

A Light in the Flame
A Flesh and Fire Novel
By Jennifer L. Armentrout

Copyright 2022 Jennifer L. Armentrout
ISBN: 9781957568041

Published by Blue Box Press, an imprint of Evil Eye Concepts, Incorporated

Cover design by Hang Le

Acknowledgments

Behind every book is a team of people who helped make it possible. Thank you to Blue Box Press—Liz Berry, Jillian Stein, MJ Rose, Chelle Olson, Kim Guidroz, Jessica Saunders, and the amazing editing and proofreading teams. I'd also like to thank the wonderful team at Social Butterfly. And Michael Perlman and the entire team at S&S for their hardcover distribution support and expertise. Also, to Hang Le for her incredible talent at design; my agents Kevan Lyon and Taryn Fagerness; my assistant, Malissa Coy; shop manager Jen Fisher; and the brain behind ApollyCon and more: Steph Brown. Also, the JLAnders mods, Vonetta Young and Mona Awad. Thank you all for being the most amazing, supportive team an author could want, for making sure these books are read all across the world, creating merch, helping with plot issues, and more.

I also need to thank those who've helped keep my head above water, either by helping me work my way out of a plot corner or just by being there to make me laugh, be an inspiration, or to get me in or out of trouble—KA Tucker, Kristen Ashley, JR Ward, Sarah J. Maas, and Brigid Kemmerer (one of these days I will be able to spell your last name without looking it up). Also, Kayleigh Gore for always being down to randomly read an out-of-context chapter, Steve Berry for story times, Andrea Joan, Stacey Morgan, Margo Lipschultz, and so many more.

A big thank you to JLAnders for always creating a fun and often hilarious place to chill. And to the ARC team for your honest reviews and support.

Most importantly, none of this would be possible without you, the reader. I hope you realize how much you mean to me.

Dedication

To you, the reader. Without you, none of this would be possible.
Thank you.

ILISEEUM

ABYSS

VALE

PILLARS OF ASPHODEL

RED RIVER

DYING WOODS

VATHI

RED WOODS

CITY OF LETHE

SHADOWLANDS

BLACKBAY

HOUSE OF HAIDES

N

W   E

S

THYIA PLAINS

SIRTA

KITHREIA

LOTHO

CALLASTA ISLES

TRITON ISLES

TREES OF AIOS

DALOS

COR PALACE

Pronunciation Guide

Characters

Aios – a-uh-us
Andreia – ahn-dray-ah
Attes – AT-tayz
Aurelia – au-REL-ee-ah
Baines – baynz
Bele – bell
Dorcan – dohr-can
Dyses – DEYE-seez
Ector – ehktohr
Ehthawn – EE-thawn
Embris – EM-bris
Erlina – Er-LEE-nah
Ernald – ER-nald
Eythos – EE-thos
Ezmeria – ez-MARE-ee-ah
Gemma – jeh-muh
Halayna – ha-LAY-nah
Hanan – hay-nan
Holland – HAA-luhnd
Jadis – JAY-dis
Kayleigh – KAY-lee
Keella – kee-lah
King Saegar – [king] SAY-gar
Kolis – CO-lis
Kyn – kin
Lailah – lay-lah
Lathan – LEY-THahN
Loimus – loy-moos
Madis – mad-is
Maia – MY-ah
Marisol – MARE-i-soul
Mycella – MY-cell-AH
Nektas – NEC-tas
Nyktos – NIK-toes
Odetta – OH-det-ah

Orphine – OR-feen
Peinea – pain-ee-yah
Penellaphe – pen-NELL-uh-fee
Phanos – FAN-ohs
Polemus – pol-he-mus
Rhahar – RUH-har
Rhain – rain
Saion – SI-on
Sera – SEE-ra
Seraphena – SEE-ra-fee-na
Sotoria – so-TOR-ee-ah
Taric – tae-ric
Tavius – TAY-vee-us
Thad – thad
Theon – thEE-awn
Veses – VES-ees

Places
Cauldra Manor – call-drah [manor]
Dalos – day-los
Iliseeum – AH-lee-see-um
Kithreia – kith-REE-ah
Lasania – la-SAN-ee-uh
Lotho – LOW-tho
Massene – ma-see-nuh
Pillars of Asphodel – [pillars of] AS-foe-del
Sirta – SIR-ta
Triton Isles – TRY-ton [Isles]
Vathi – VAY-thee

Terms
Arae – air-ree
benada – ben-NAH-dah
Cimmerian – sim-MARE-ee-in
dakkai – di-ah-kee
eather – ee-thor
graeca – gray-cee
imprimen – IM-prim-en

kardia — CAR-dee-ah
kiyou wolf/wolves — ki-you [wolf/wolves]
meeyah Liessa — MEE-yah LEE-sa
sekya — sek-yah
sparanea — SPARE-ah-nay-ah

I

"*You are the heir to the lands and seas, skies and realms. A Queen instead of a King. You are the Primal of Life*," Nyktos—the Asher, the One who is Blessed, the Guardian of Souls and the Primal God of Common Men and Endings—rasped. Those lips of his that had whispered heated words against my skin and had also spoken cold, brutal truths were now parted. Wide, silver eyes churning with streams of luminous eather—the essence of the gods—fixed on mine. A sort of awe and wonder softened the cold lines of his high, broad cheekbones, his blade-straight nose, and cut jaw.

Wavy, reddish-brown hair fell against golden-bronze cheeks as he lowered himself to one knee, placing his left hand flat on the throne room floor and his right palm over his chest.

Nyktos was *bowing* to *me*.

I recoiled from him. "What are you doing?"

"The Primal of Life is the most powerful being in all the realms, usurping all other Primals and gods," Sir Holland said. Except he was no longer the man I once knew as a knight of the Royal Guard of Lasania, or a mere mortal. He was one of the Arae—an actual, godsforsaken *Fate*, neither god nor mortal. Able to see the past, present, and future of all, the Arae weren't beholden to any Primal Court.

Fates were as terrifying as any Primal, and I couldn't even begin to count how many times I'd kicked him.

"He is showing you the respect you are owed, Sera," Holland added as I continued staring at Nyktos.

"But I'm not the Primal of Life." I stated the obvious.

"You carry the only true embers of life inside you," Nyktos said, and that deep, softly spoken voice sent a myriad of shivers over my skin. "For all intents and purposes, you *are* the Primal of Life."

"He speaks the truth." The goddess Penellaphe drew closer, coming to stand beneath the open ceiling. The star-strewn sky cast a soft glow over her warm, light brown skin. "Denying it isn't a luxury which can be afforded."

"But I'm just a mortal—" My lungs felt as if they'd been filled with tiny holes, and Nyktos was *still* bowing to me. "Can you please stand or sit? Anything other than kneel? It's really weirding me out."

Nyktos's head tilted, sending several strands of hair against his cheek. "You are the *true* Primal of Life, just as my father was. As Holland said, it's a show of respect."

"But I don't des—" I cut myself off, my heart thumping and chest squeezing. The eather in his eyes stilled. "Can you just not do that? Please."

The Primal rose quickly, the wisps of essence in his eyes brightening so vividly they were almost painful to look upon. He towered over me, his stare seeming to peel away the layers of my very being, seeing...*sensing* what I felt.

I stiffened, my skin becoming hot and prickly. "You'd better not be reading my emotions."

Nyktos arched a dark brow. "Your accusatory tone is unnecessary."

"And your response wasn't a declaration of innocence," I retorted. Penellaphe's eyes flared wide.

"No." His voice had dropped, but it still somehow thundered through me. "It was not."

"Then don't do it," I snapped. "It's rude."

Nyktos's mouth opened, likely to point out that I was the last person who should speak on rude behavior.

"You have never been just a mortal, Seraphena." Holland stepped in smoothly, just as he'd done dozens of times in the past whenever I'd descended into a rant spiral. "You are the possibility of a future for all."

He'd said a version of that before during training, but it took on a whole different meaning now. "But I haven't completed any Culling, and you just said that I would..." Closing my eyes, I didn't finish the sentence.

Everyone here knew what had been said.

Breathe in. My mortal body and mind wouldn't be able to handle the power of the embers once I began the Ascension. The only chance I had of surviving wasn't even a hope. *Hold.* Because it required the blood of the Primal that one of the embers of life belonged to—that and sheer will powered by *love.*

The love of the Primal I'd spent the entirety of my life planning to kill. It didn't matter that I'd believed it was the only way to save my kingdom.

The irony of it all made me want to laugh, except I was going to die. Likely in less than five months and before I turned twenty-one, taking the last true embers of life with me. The mortal realm would be hit first and the hardest. Eventually, the Rot would spread beyond the Shadowlands to all of Iliseeum.

I exhaled long and slow, just like Holland had taught me many years ago, when everything became too heavy, too much, and the weight of it all choked the air from me. My impending death wasn't something new. I'd always known. Whether I failed or succeeded when it came to fulfilling my destiny, I knew I would die in the process.

But it felt different now.

I'd finally had a taste of being something other than a means to an end, a weapon to be used and then discarded. I'd had a taste of *realness.* I'd finally felt like a fully formed person, not a specter soaked in blood. Not a liar and a monster who could kill without all that much remorse.

But that was who I was underneath it all, and Nyktos now knew that, too. There was no more hiding that truth—or any truths.

My lungs started to burn as tiny bursts of light danced across my vision. The breathing exercises weren't working. A tremor hit my hands, and panic unfurled in my chest. There was no air—

Fingertips touched my cheek. *Warm* fingertips. My eyes flew open, locking on features so finely pieced together I should've known the first time I saw him that he was more than a god. His touch startled me, not only because it was warm instead of shockingly cold as it had been before he took my blood into him, but because I still wasn't used to *touching.* I wasn't sure I ever would be when it had always been so rare that anyone allowed their skin to contact mine.

But he touched me. After everything, Nyktos touched *me.*

"Are you all right?" he asked, his voice low.

My tongue was heavy and useless, having nothing to do with my too-tight chest and everything to do with his concern. I didn't want it. Not now. It was wrong on so many different levels.

Nyktos stepped in close, lowering his head until his lips were mere inches from mine. A shiver followed his hand as he curled his fingers around the nape of my neck. His thumb gently pressed against my wildly thrumming pulse. He tilted my head as if lining up our mouths for a kiss as he'd done in his office before meeting with Holland and Penellaphe. But that would never happen again. He'd told me that himself.

"Breathe," Nyktos whispered.

It was as if he'd compelled the very air itself to enter my body, and it tasted of his scent—citrus and fresh air. The darts of lights cleared, and my lungs expanded with breath. The shaking continued in my hands as his thumb swept across my pulse, now racing for entirely different reasons. He stood so close to me that there was no stopping the flood of memories—the feel of his mouth against my throat, and his hands on my bare skin. The pain-tinged pleasure of his bite as he fed from me. Him moving *inside* me, creating the kind of pleasure that wouldn't be forgotten and warmed my blood even now.

I'd been Nyktos's *first*.

And he...he would be my *last*, no matter what happened from this point forward.

Sorrow crept in, cooling my heated blood and settling in my chest with a different, thicker kind of pressure. At least I no longer felt as if I couldn't catch my breath.

"She has trouble slowing her heart and breathing sometimes," Holland shared quietly—*and* unnecessarily.

"I've noticed." Nyktos's thumb continued those featherlight sweeps while I inwardly cringed. He probably thought...only the gods knew what he thought.

I didn't want to know.

Face heating, I backed away from Nyktos's touch, hitting the edge of the dais. His hand hovered in midair for a few seconds, and then his fingers curled inward. He dropped his arm as I turned to the raised platform. I focused on the hauntingly beautiful thrones sculpted from massive chunks of shadowstone. Their backs had been carved into large and widespread wings that touched at the tips, connecting the seats. I wiped damp palms against the patches of dried blood on my breeches.

"You are both positive that no one else knows what she is?" Nyktos asked.

"Besides your father? Embris knows the prophecy," Penellaphe answered, referencing the Primal God of Wisdom, Loyalty, and Duty as I pulled myself together. I faced them. This was too important for me to miss while having a mini breakdown. "And so does Kolis. Neither knows more than that."

The eather stirred once more in Nyktos's eyes at the mention of the Primal Kolis, who every mortal—including myself until recently—believed to be the Primal of Life and the King of Gods. But Kolis was the *true* Primal of Death. The one who'd impaled gods on the Rise surrounding the House of Haides just to remind Nyktos that all life was easily extinguished—or so I assumed. And it was a logical assumption. Nyktos's father had been the true Primal of Life, and Kolis had stolen Eythos's embers.

I fought the shudder, thinking over the prophecy Penellaphe had shared. The part about the desperation of golden crowns could be related to my ancestor King Roderick and the deal he'd made that'd started all of this. But prophecies were only possibilities, and they were... "Prophecies are fucking pointless," I muttered aloud.

Penellaphe turned her head to me, raising a brow.

I grimaced. "I'm sorry. That came out worse than I intended."

"I'm curious exactly how you intended that statement," Nyktos wondered. I shot him an arch stare. "But I do not disagree."

I stopped glaring at him like I wanted to stab him.

"I understand the sentiment," Penellaphe said with a bemused expression. "Prophecies can often be confusing, even to those who receive them. And, sometimes, only bits and pieces of a prophecy are known by one—the beginning or the end—while the middle is known to another and vice versa. But some visions have come to pass, both in Iliseeum and in the mortal realm. It's hard to see this since the destruction of the Gods of Divination and the passing of the last of the oracles."

"Gods of Divination?" I'd heard of the oracles, rare mortals who had lived long before my birth and were able to communicate directly with the gods without having to summon them.

"They were gods able to see what was hidden to others—their truths—both past and future," Penellaphe explained. "They called Mount Lotho home and served in Embris's Court. The oracles would speak to them, and they were the only gods truly welcomed by the Arae."

"Not the only gods welcomed," Holland corrected softly.

Penellaphe's rosy blush momentarily distracted me because there was definitely something going on there.

"Penellaphe's mother was a God of Divination," Holland continued. "That is why she was able to share a vision. Only those gods and the oracles could receive the visions the Ancients—the first Primals—dreamt."

"I don't have her other skills—the ability to see what is hidden or known," Penellaphe added. "Nor have I received any other visions."

"The consequences of what Kolis did when he stole the embers of life were far-reaching. Hundreds of gods were lost in the shockwave of energy," Nyktos explained. "The Gods of Divination took the hardest hit. They were all but destroyed, and no other mortal was born an oracle."

Sorrow crept into Penellaphe's expression. "And with that, what other visions the Ancients dreamt, and may only be known to them, have now been lost."

"Dreamt?" I lifted my brows.

"Prophecies are the dreams of the Ancients," she explained.

I pressed my lips together. Most of the Ancients, being the oldest of the Primals, had passed on to Arcadia. "Uh. I did not know prophecies were dreams."

"I don't think that piece of knowledge will help change Sera's opinion of them," Holland said wryly.

Nyktos huffed out a dry laugh.

"No, I imagine not." Penellaphe smiled, but it faded quickly. "Many gods and mortals have been born without hearing or seeing even one prophecy or vision, but they were far more common at one time."

"The vision you had?" I asked. "Do you know which Ancient dreamt it?"

She shook her head. "That is not known to those who receive them."

Well, of course not. But it didn't matter since the Ancients had entered Arcadia ages ago. "Prophecies aside, I Ascended Bele when I brought her back to life." Bele wasn't a Primal—at least not technically. Her brown eyes had turned the silver of a Primal, and the gods here in the Shadowlands believed that she would now be more powerful, but none knew exactly what it all meant. "That was felt, right?"

"It was," Penellaphe confirmed. "It wasn't as strong as when a Primal enters Arcadia, and the Fates raise another to take their place, but every god and Primal would've felt the shift of energy that occurred. Especially Hanan." Worry pinched her brow. As the Primal of the Hunt and Divine Justice, Hanan oversaw the Court that Bele had been born into. "He will know that another has risen to a power that could challenge his."

"But there is nothing that can be done about that." Nyktos crossed his arms over his chest.

"No," Penellaphe agreed softly. "There is not."

"Only those present when you brought her back know you Ascended Bele." Nyktos looked at me. "Neither Hanan nor any other Primal knows the full extent of what my father did when he placed the embers of life in the Mierel bloodline."

A whoosh went through my stomach at the reminder of the even bigger shock and blow that had been dealt. I didn't know how to come to terms with learning that I'd lived countless lives that I couldn't remember. That I had been Sotoria, the object of Kolis's love—*his obsession*—and the very thing that had started all of this.

I'd thought the stories of the mortal girl who'd been so frightened upon seeing a being from Iliseeum that she had fallen from the Cliffs of Sorrow were just some bizarre legend. But she'd been real. And Kolis had been the one who'd scared her so badly.

How could I be *her*? I ran from no one and nothing—well, except serpents. But I was a fighter. A—

"*You are a warrior, Seraphena,*" Holland had said. "*You always have been. Just like she learned to become.*"

Gods.

I pressed my fingers into my temple. I knew Eythos and Keella, the Primal of Rebirth, had done what they believed best. They'd captured Sotoria's soul before it passed to the Vale, preventing Kolis from bringing her back to life. Their actions had thus started a cycle of rebirth that had ended with *my* birth. But it felt like another violation. Another choice stripped away from her. Not me. We might have the same soul, but I wasn't her. I was…

You are just a vessel that would be empty if not for the ember of life you carry within you.

Nyktos's words had been harsh when he'd spoken them, but they were the truth. From birth, I had been nothing more than a blank canvas primed to become whatever the Primal of Death desired, or to be used in whatever manner my mother saw fit.

I sat on the edge of the dais, fighting the pressure as it threatened to return to my chest. "I saw Kolis not that long ago."

Nyktos's head jerked toward me.

I cleared my throat, unable to remember if I had told him this or not. "I was in the audience when Kolis arrived at the Sun Temple for the Rite. I was in the back and had my face covered, but I swear he looked directly at me." I forced a swallow. "Do I look like her? Like Sotoria?"

Penellaphe's hand went to the collar of her taupe gown. "If Kolis had seen you and you'd looked like Sotoria, he would've taken you right then."

The ragged breath I exhaled left a misty cloud behind as a sudden bone-deep chill entered the chamber. My gaze shot to Nyktos.

His skin had thinned, and deep, dark shadows blossomed beneath his flesh, reminding me of how he'd appeared in his true form. His skin had been a kaleidoscope of midnight and moonlight, his wings much like a draken's but made of a solid mass of eather—power.

He looked like he was about to go full Primal again. "Sotoria didn't belong to him then, and Seraphena doesn't belong to him now."

Seraphena.

I could count on one hand how many people called me by my full name, and none of them spoke it like he did. As if it were a prayer and a reckoning.

"I don't know what Sotoria originally looked like," Holland said after a few moments. "I didn't follow her threads of fate until after Eythos had come to ask what—if anything—could be done about his brother's betrayal. All that I do know is that she didn't appear the same with each rebirth. But it's possible that Kolis sensed traces of eather in you and believed you were a child of a mortal and a god—a godling or a god entering their Culling."

I nodded slowly, forcing my thoughts past the whole Sotoria thing. I had to. All of that was just too much. "But what I did has already drawn their attention. It's not like we can pretend it hasn't happened."

"I know," Nyktos remarked coolly. "I expect I will have numerous unwanted visitors."

"Being his Consort will offer you some level of protection," Penellaphe said, looking at Nyktos. "Until then, any Primal could make a move against her. Even a god. And it would be unlikely you'd have the other Primals' support if you retaliated. The politics of our Courts?" Penellaphe sent me a sympathetic grimace. "They are rather archaic."

That was one way to describe them. Cutthroat was another.

"But a coronation won't be without its risks," Penellaphe added. "Most of the gods and Primals from all nine Courts, including yours, will show for the ceremony. They *should* follow the customs, which prohibit…conflict at such events. But as you know, many like to push that line."

"Do I ever…" Nyktos muttered.

The goddess winced. "Kolis doesn't make a habit of joining such festivities, but…"

"He knows something is here. He already sent his dakkais and draken, as I'm sure you know." Nyktos pinned Holland with a hard stare, and the Arae arched a dark brow. "Kolis hasn't shown in the Shadowlands since he betrayed my father, but that doesn't mean he can't. I assume that if you know whether he can or cannot enter the Shadowlands," he said to Holland, "it's something you won't be able to answer."

"Unfortunately, you would be correct," Holland confirmed, and I wondered if knowing and not being able to say anything was more frustrating than having no knowledge at all.

Probably not, considering how annoyed I was.

Despite the temperature of the room returning to normal, a chill broke out across my skin as I thought of what could come. "What will happen if Kolis enters the Shadowlands?"

"Kolis can be unpredictable, but he's no fool," Nyktos said. "If he can enter the Shadowlands and comes to the coronation, he won't try something in front of the other Primals and gods. He believes he's the fair and rightful King of Gods, and he likes to keep up the façade, even though the Primals know better."

"But if he—" I started.

"I won't let him lay a finger on you," Nyktos swore, his eyes flashing.

My heart tripped. While that was a nice vow for him to make, I knew it stemmed from the knowledge that I carried the embers of life in me. And because Nyktos was decent. Protective. *Good.* "Thanks, but I'm not worried about what will happen to me."

Nyktos's jaw hardened. "Of course, not."

I ignored that. "What will Kolis do if he realizes you're shielding someone who carries the embers of life?" I demanded. "Or discovers that I carry Sotoria's soul? What will he do to the Shadowlands? To those living here? I want to know what my presence will cost you."

"Your presence will cost me *nothing.*" Shadows deepened once more beneath Nyktos's flesh.

"Bullshit," I said, and the silver of his irises shifted to iron. "I don't need to be protected from the truth. It's not like I'll be so frightened by it that I'll run off a nearby cliff."

Holland sighed.

"That's good to know," Nyktos replied dryly. "But I am more concerned about you running in a very opposite direction."

I lifted my chin. "I don't know what you mean."

"Bullshit," he parroted, and my eyes narrowed. He was right. I absolutely knew what he meant.

Whatever.

"Kolis already knows that there is something here with the power to create life," Penellaphe interjected, ignoring the furious glare Nyktos sent her. "But as Nyktos said, Kolis is no fool. He sent the dakkais as a warning. A way of showing Nyktos that he is very much aware."

"But that was after I brought Gemma back," I said. Gemma was one of the third sons and daughters given over during the Rite to serve the Primal of Life and his Court. A tradition honored and respected throughout all the kingdoms in the mortal realm.

An honor that had become nothing but a nightmare under Kolis's rule.

Gemma had been one of the few that Nyktos had secreted away from Kolis's Court with the aid of gods like Bele and others and then sheltered in the Shadowlands. He gave them sanctuary. A sliver of peace.

The things my mere existence threatened.

Gemma hadn't gone into detail about what her time spent in Kolis's Court had been like, but she hadn't needed to for me to know that being Kolis's favorite for a while wasn't anything pleasant. Whatever had been done to her was bad enough that when she'd spotted one of the gods from Kolis's Court in Lethe, she had panicked. So afraid of being sent back to him, she had run into the Dying Woods—where certain death awaited her.

"He hasn't responded to what I did to Bele," I continued. And then added, "As far as I know."

"Only because I imagine that act caught him off guard," Penellaphe mused. "Neither he nor anyone else would've expected that." She glanced at Nyktos. "He hasn't summoned you?"

"No."

"Is that the truth?" I demanded.

Nyktos nodded. "I can only delay in answering his summonses. I can't deny them."

"He's likely cautious right now," Penellaphe said. "And I imagine he's also very curious, considering exactly what could be hidden away in the Shadowlands, how it could be possible for embers of life to exist, and how he could make use of whatever this source of power is."

"Aid him in whatever twisted ideal of life he believes he's creating," Holland tacked on.

"You know what he's been doing to the Chosen who have gone missing?" Nyktos's gaze sharpened on him. "These things called Revenants?"

"I know that what he calls Revenants are not the *only* mockery of life he's managed to create." Holland's dark gaze locked on Nyktos. "And you've already seen what he's had a hand in creating. What some of the gods of his Court have been doing in the mortal realm."

Nyktos's brows pinched together, and then he glanced at me. "Your seamstress."

It took me a moment to realize he meant my mother's seamstress. "Andreia Joanis?" Before I found her dead, I'd seen the god Madis near her home in Stonehill, a district that faced the Stroud Sea. Her veins had darkened, staining her skin as if ink filled them, and her eyes…they had been burned. Nyktos had been following Madis that night, and he'd ended up there. He too had believed she was dead. "She came back to life or something. Sat up and opened her mouth. She had four fangs I do not recall her ever having before."

Holland barked out a short, guttural word in a language I didn't recognize as he turned his head, spitting on the ground.

My brows flew up. "Come again?"

"Craven?" Nyktos's eyes narrowed as he recognized whatever Holland had said.

The Fate nodded. "It is what becomes of a mortal when their life force—their blood—is stolen from them, and the loss isn't replenished. It does not matter who the mortal was before. The act rots them, in body and in mind, turning them into amoral creatures driven by an insatiable need for blood. Craven."

Nyktos had gone still. "The act of killing a mortal while feeding has been forbidden since the dawn of time."

"And that outcome is why," Holland said. "It is a balance."

I threw up my hands. "How in the hell is turning a mortal into something like that a balance?"

"The balance here demands that the life taken is then restored to serve as a reminder to the gods that their inability to control themselves has consequences. Maintaining balance isn't always as simple to understand as it is when, say, the Primal of Life restores a mortal's life." His eyes fixed on mine. Hard. All-seeing. "Another's life must be forsaken in their place."

I sucked in a sharp breath, my stomach hollowing. "The night I brought Lady Marisol back to life, my stepfather, the King of Lasania, died in his sleep." I hadn't even considered that it had anything to do with my actions. "Good gods. I killed my stepfather?"

"No," Nyktos cut in, his eyes narrowing on the Fate. "You didn't."

I stared at Nyktos. How could he be so sure of that? Because it sure sounded like I had.

"It was not intentional," Holland said. "But it was her time. You intervened, upset the balance, and it had to be righted."

"By whom?" I demanded. "Who decides how balance is restored?"

Holland looked back at me.

I stiffened. "You?"

"Not him," Nyktos answered. "The Arae in general. They are like…cosmic cleaners."

I had no idea what to say to that. Or how to feel—well, other than guilty. And I should feel that because while King Ernald hadn't exactly been the greatest leader, he hadn't been bad. Except I really didn't feel anything but passing shock and a touch of shame. Like when I killed and knew I would barely think of it later.

And that disturbed me.

I disturbed myself.

But I couldn't dig deeper into that at the moment because that hadn't been the only life I'd restored. "And if a god is brought back? Does balance demand the death of another god?"

"Luckily, no," Nyktos said. "It has only ever applied to mortals."

"That doesn't sound entirely fair," I muttered. It was a relief to know that I hadn't killed another god, but I had sentenced a nameless, faceless mortal to death when I brought Gemma back. "Would have been good to know that."

Holland eyed me. "Would that have changed your actions?"

I snapped my mouth shut. I couldn't answer that.

"But now you know what you already knew. Some lessons will always be painful to learn." His smile was sad and gentle. And, thankfully, brief. "Either way, if this Andreia had not been killed, she would've left her home and attacked the first person she came into contact with—man, woman, or child."

"Did Madis do that to her?" Nyktos asked.

"I believe Madis was attempting to…rectify what one of Kolis's creations left behind." Holland tipped his chin slightly. "And that is all I can say about those matters. I do not know much more. But revealing anything else could be considered interference."

"And he's already walking a very fine line," Penellaphe reminded us, but mostly Nyktos, whose glare had narrowed on the Fate. "But at this moment, what Kolis is doing isn't our greatest concern, nor should it be yours."

I wasn't sure I agreed with that.

"You asked what Kolis would do to get to the embers of life. He would find a way to obtain them. Perhaps he wouldn't use his cruelest methods to do so"—her brilliant blue eyes dimmed, becoming haunted—"but if he were to realize *who* you once were, he would stop at nothing to have you."

"Penellaphe," Nyktos warned.

"It's the truth," she said, turning to him. "You cannot hide that from her. You may not be able to even try to do so."

"You have no idea what I am capable of doing when necessary," Nyktos told her.

"True," she said, her voice gentling. "But you know *exactly* what Kolis is capable of. As do I. He would burn through the Shadowlands to obtain his *graeca*."

In old Primal language, *graeca* meant life. But as Aios had said, it was also interchangeable with the word *love*.

Gemma had been the first I'd heard use the word *graeca*. She'd said that Kolis had often spoken of his *graeca* and that she believed it was related to whatever he was doing with the missing Chosen who returned as something different and not quite right. Something cold. Lifeless. *Hungry*.

I barely suppressed a shudder. "And what would he do to Nyktos if he attempted to shield me from Kolis?"

"You do not need to worry about that." Nyktos twisted toward me.

"Are you serious?" I exclaimed. "We're talking about the same person who killed your mother and father. Who impaled gods on the wall of your Rise to remind you that all life was fragile."

"It's not like I've forgotten that." Bright wisps of eather flared in his eyes again. "Whatever he will or won't do doesn't change anything. I will handle Kolis."

I shook my head, my frustration growing. "He could kill you—"

"No, he cannot," Holland interrupted. My head swung to him. "As I've said, there must always be balance. In everything—even among the Primals. Life cannot exist without Death, and they should not be one and the same."

"Wait." I dropped my hands to my knees. "You mean like a...a Primal of both Life and Death? Is that possible? Because you said *should not*. You didn't say *could not*."

"Anything is possible," Holland replied. "Even the impossible."

Struggling for patience, I stared at him. "That was such a remarkably helpful statement. Thank you."

Holland laughed.

"What he means to say is that such a thing, a Primal of both Life and Death, is not meant to exist," Nyktos said. "It would be unthinkable for the embers of both to thrive in one being. But if they could?" He gave a short laugh with a raise of his dark brows. "The kind of power they'd wield? It would be truly absolute. They could unravel realms in the same breath they created new ones."

"There would be no stopping such a being," Holland added. "There could be no balance. Therefore, the Fates ensured long ago that such power must be split and that an absence of either ember would cause a collapse of all the realms. It wouldn't be like the Rot—a slow death. It would be sudden and absolute for all. Kolis cannot Ascend another Primal to take the place of a fallen. By killing Nyktos, he'd doom himself. He understands that much, at least."

Yeah, except I had technically done that with Bele, paving the way for her to replace Hanan if he fell.

But knowing that Kolis wouldn't kill Nyktos was a relief. Still, how could he be sure what Kolis would or wouldn't do? He couldn't. Kolis didn't sound like the most rational Primal.

Frustration surged through me. "What does Kolis even want? What is his goal with these creations of his?"

Holland snorted. "That is a good question."

"One you know the answer to and can't share?" I countered.

"I actually don't know," he said. "Fates don't know the inner workings of one's mind."

Fates also weren't at all helpful.

"He wants to rule over all—Iliseeum and the mortal realm," Nyktos answered. "The Courts in Iliseeum would replace the kingdoms in the mortal realm. There would only be him and his sycophants, and mortals would be put in their place—or so he believes. Beneath those greater than them. And I imagine the mockery of life he has been creating is being done in an attempt to aid his cause."

So Kolis was creating an army of mortals controlled by hunger? Unnerved, I squeezed my knees until I felt the bones beneath my fingers.

"That can't be possible."

Holland opened his mouth.

"If you say that anything is possible, even the impossible, I might scream," I warned. The Fate closed his mouth. "Mortals would fight back, even those most loyal to the gods. He'd have to battle an entire realm, and then what would be left for him to rule over?"

"It wouldn't be easy, and it would end in the kind of death even I would have a hard time imagining," Nyktos said. "He would be left to rule over a kingdom of bones."

"But will that knowledge stop him?" Penellaphe asked quietly. "Has it?"

Didn't appear to have.

But Kolis wouldn't get what he wanted either. Not after I died. He'd rule over a kingdom of bones.

Unable to sit any longer, I stood and reached for the shadowstone dagger Nyktos had returned to me, only to realize that I'd left it in his office. I faced Holland. "How long does the mortal realm have?" I swallowed thickly. "Once I die."

"You won't die," Nyktos stated as if he had the authority to make such a claim.

He didn't.

"She will," Holland said quietly. "She will die without the love of the one who Ascends her—a love that cannot be ignored. A love that must be acknowledged." He looked at Nyktos. "And you have—"

"We heard you the first time," I snapped as the Primal thrust a hand through his hair.

"But you haven't," Holland returned. "You haven't heard *why* he cannot save you as he is now." He tilted his head to Nyktos. "Has she, Your Highness?"

Tension thickened the air as the Primal held the Arae's stare. "No. She has not."

Nothing could be gained from Nyktos's expression. Unease took root. "What are you two even talking about?"

A muscle throbbed in Nyktos's temple. "I cannot love," he bit out between clenched teeth, speaking to Holland. "I made sure that would never be a weakness someone could exploit."

Something told me that this was more than just him making such a claim. "And how can you ensure that?"

"Maia," he said, speaking of the Primal of Love, Beauty, and Fertility. "I had her remove my *kardia*."

Penellaphe gasped, her eyes widening with shock. "Good Fates," she whispered. "I have known none who've done that."

I was obviously missing something and also getting tired of asking questions. "What is a *kardia*?"

"It's the piece of the soul—the spark—that all living creatures are born and die with. It allows them to love another not of their blood irrevocably, selflessly." Penellaphe swallowed. "It must have been terribly painful to have that torn from you. To truly be unable to love."

2

"It was barely an inconvenience," Nyktos muttered, clearly not pleased with the topic, and I...

I was stunned.

I'd believed that Nyktos could never *allow* himself to love. Not when he saw it as a weakness and also as a weapon to be wielded against him—just as I had sought to use it. But I hadn't known that he was truly incapable of feeling love.

I was shocked that he would do that to himself, even though I understood *why* he would, after everything he'd been through. But I didn't understand because he was...

"You care about others," I said, shaking my head in confusion. "I know you do. How—?"

"Caring and loving are two vastly different things," Nyktos said. "I am not incapable of caring for or about another. The *kardia* is simply unable to sway me. Something one would think all Primals would ensure."

"Yeah. Namely, Kolis," I murmured, running my palm over my chest where the embers remained still. But my heart ached for Nyktos. I glanced at Holland, who had fallen silent, and irritation darted through me. "You couldn't give me a single hint that there was truly no point to any of what you trained me to do?"

"There is only so much I can do and say," Holland said quietly.

"Or *could*."

I knew that. The rules. Still, it was irritating. I cleared my throat. "So, like I asked before, how long does the mortal realm have?"

"It's hard to know," Holland shared. "What you know as the Rot in the mortal realm has made the Shadowlands into what it is now. But it would not happen that way with the rest of Iliseeum. It has only just begun to spread beyond these lands. It would take Iliseeum longer to suffer the truly catastrophic effects, but the mortal realm would have…a year? Maybe two or three if lucky. But it would not be easy to survive such an event."

Or be something anyone would want to survive.

The image of the Coupers filled my mind, the family lying together in that bed as they must have done a hundred times before. They had already been dying a slow death from starvation, and hundreds of thousands more would end up just like them when all the vegetation died. Then the livestock. The famine and sickness would be horrific, leading to wars and more violence.

Panic blossomed deep in my chest as I thought about the people of Lasania—my stepsister Ezra, Marisol, and the Ladies of Mercy, who did everything in their power to keep children from falling prey to the worst sort of humanity. Then I thought of the Massey family and all the other hardworking men and women beyond Lasania. So many who would have no chance. None.

"Can we not warn them?" I asked of Holland, my heart twisting. "Perhaps if we do, Ezra can work to—"

"*Queen* Ezmeria has already begun implementing much-needed changes in Lasania," Holland interrupted.

I gasped. "Queen?"

A small, fond smile tugged at his lips as he nodded.

"She married?" I whispered, hopeful. "Marisol?"

"Yes. She took the throne not long after you were taken into the Shadowlands."

I squeezed my eyes shut against the rush of relief. Ezra had done as I'd asked of her. She'd taken the throne from my mother. Gods, I would give any amount of coin to have seen the look on my mother's face. A choked laugh left me as I opened my eyes, becoming aware of Nyktos watching me in that close, intense way of his. "How did she do it? Did my—?" I stopped. None of that mattered at the moment. "I need to warn her."

"I would advise against that," Nyktos said.

"I wasn't asking you," I snapped before I could stop myself.

He simply continued eying me, seeming utterly unperturbed by my response.

"Sometimes, it is best to not know if or when the end is coming," Penellaphe advised.

"Didn't you say that knowledge is power?" I pointed out.

"*Sometimes*, it is," she reiterated. "But when it's not, all it does is unleash harm and pain."

"And fear." Holland's voice lowered in the way it had when he'd comforted me after I'd returned from my first session with the Mistresses of the Jade. I squirmed where I stood. "The truth will not help them. All it would do is cause panic."

If I had learned anything, it was that the truth led to a choice. And I now knew the truth about many things, which meant I had *choices* to make. To hide and be protected? Ignore what would become of the mortal realm and eventually Iliseeum? Live without purpose until I died?

Or fight back.

I glanced at Holland. He watched me in a way where I almost expected him to hand me a dagger to train with.

"There is something else," Penellaphe added. "A way I may be of assistance. At least…temporarily." She swallowed, focusing on me. "If anyone were to learn what you carry inside you, they may attempt to take you. Not just Kolis. I can help prevent that."

"You can?"

"A charm?" Nyktos surmised. He cocked his head. "I don't know of anything that could be placed on a person to prevent such a thing."

"You wouldn't, would you? Not as a Primal of Death." Penellaphe smiled. "But I am not just a goddess of Loyalty and Duty, I am also a goddess of Wisdom."

"Meaning," Nyktos said, a slow grin appearing, "you know more than I do, and I should shut the hell up?"

Penellaphe's eyes glimmered in the starlight. "Precisely."

Less than a handful of minutes later, I found myself seated on the dais with the male I'd seen in the hall with Penellaphe when she first arrived, *drawing* on my skin.

He sat beside me, his head bent as he wrote a series of unrecognizable letters in bold, black ink on my arm, his lion's mane of hair shielding his features. He'd started on my right side, drawing the letters so they traveled around the circumference of my wrist. He'd already completed about three lines.

As I leaned back and squinted, the letters almost looked like shapes.

And the shape reminded me of shackles.

"Will this fade?" I asked.

"They will fade as soon as I'm finished," the man said as the featherlight touch of his brush tickled. All that I knew about him was that he was a *viktor*—a not-so-quite-mortal being, born to protect someone of importance or a harbinger of great change. "But Primals and some powerful gods will be able to sense the charm."

Speaking of Primals…

My gaze flicked up to where Nyktos stood close behind the man.

Too close.

He was practically breathing down the man's neck. "How does this charm work?"

"It will prevent her from being taken against her will from wherever the charm was placed," he explained, tilting his head as he finished another line. The weathered lines of his sunbaked face added a rugged handsomeness to his features. "If anyone attempts it, the charm will retaliate."

I raised a brow. "With what?"

"With a jolt of energy as painful as taking a direct hit of eather to the chest," he said. "It'd knock even a Primal on their ass and keep knocking them down if they got up and tried again."

"Nice."

Bright blue eyes met mine as he grinned.

"And how did you learn of this charm?" Nyktos pressed.

"I saw it done once by a god from the Thyia Plains," he shared, referencing the Primal Keella's Court. "But I didn't know what they were doing for the mortal. Penellaphe knew what the letters meant and how they worked. That each letter forms a symbol of protection, one powered by essence."

I wondered if they were like the wards Nyktos had put in place to protect my family.

Then it struck me that it could be someone like this man, another *viktor*, who had given my family the knowledge of how to kill a Primal—something no mere mortal should ever know. It made sense that perhaps a member of my family had been guided by one aware of their purpose.

"The charm only prevents you from being taken." He lowered my right arm to my lap and then picked up my left one. "And the only way the charm can be nullified is if you give your permission."

I nodded, glancing from Nyktos to where Holland stood several feet away with his back to us, almost as if he were pretending to be unaware of what was going on, even though this must have been the reason he and Penellaphe had arrived with this man.

"Thank you for doing this, Ward," I said, remembering hearing Penellaphe call him that when they first showed up.

"Ward is actually my surname," he responded. "Vikter is my name."

I belted out a quick, sharp laugh. "You're a *viktor* named Vikter?"

"He is *the viktor*," Penellaphe said, sitting beside me on the dais. "The first."

"Oh." I bit down on my lip. "So they're named after you?"

"I believe so."

"He's not a fan of that."

Vikter smiled. "It makes communication somewhat difficult in Mount Lotho when so many of the other *viktors* are in residence, and someone calls your name," he said. Behind him, Nyktos smirked. "It can take the others a while to forget who they become and remember who they were before they were reborn."

"Others?" I watched him dip the brush into an ink bottle resting on his knee. How it stayed balanced there, I had no idea. "Do you remember the lives you've lived?"

"I remember everything."

"Because he was the first," Penellaphe added. "Before the Fates realized it would be easier for them not to recall the details of their lives."

I stared at Vikter, somewhat dumbfounded. I couldn't imagine living dozens or hundreds of lifetimes and remembering all those lives—all the experiences, and those I'd met, loved, and lost.

And, apparently, I had.

My chest rose sharply in an attempt to drag in a deeper breath. It barely worked.

Nyktos moved to Vikter's side, his gaze on me, and I was sure I projected my feelings.

I cleared my throat. "How did you end up becoming the first?"

Vikter chuckled roughly. "That is a long, convoluted story not as interesting as you may think it is."

"Vikter is far too humble," Penellaphe jumped in. "He saved the life of someone very important and paid a very steep price for doing so. The Fates decided to reward him and, later, realized they could give aid without upsetting the balance."

Vikter didn't acknowledge any of that, and I wondered if he felt that what they'd done was a reward. Sure, he was kind of immortal, but to live and die repeatedly also meant experiencing endless loss.

"There," Vikter said, lowering my hand to rest beside the other. His handwriting was truly beautiful, but it chilled my skin because of how much the designs looked like shackles. "Finished."

No sooner had he spoken than a sharp, prickling sensation danced over my skin. A burst of light appeared. I gasped as silvery light flowed across my wrists, lighting up each letter until both bands glowed. The sheen pulsed twice and then faded.

My wrists were clear of ink.

I shifted my attention to Vikter and then to Nyktos. His eyes met mine. "I can't see it. But I…I can feel it."

"Perfect." Vikter rose.

"Thank you," I said, touching my skin and feeling nothing.

"Yes." Nyktos moved to stand where Vikter had sat. "Thank you for your aid."

"My pleasure." Vikter bowed to Nyktos and then to me. "Be safe."

"You, too," I said.

The skin crinkled around Vikter's eyes as he smiled. I watched him turn, placing the brush and ink into a pouch. "I'll wait in the hall."

Penellaphe nodded, rising as I watched Vikter leave. "We should not linger much longer." She glanced up at the gray sky. "To do so…"

"Could be seen as interference," Nyktos said, his shoulders straightening. "Thank you for answering the summons and taking the risks you have."

Penellaphe inclined her chin as I slid off the dais and stood. "I wish there was more we could do." She glanced at me, sympathy etched into the beautiful, delicate lines of her features. "I truly do."

"What you have done is more than enough." I crossed my arms. "Thank you."

She stepped toward Nyktos, taking his hands into hers as she led him away. Sapphire eyes glimmered in the starlight as she looked up at him. A pinch of envy stung my skin. To be able to touch Nyktos so easily, so casually…

"Sera."

Aware that Nyktos watched closely as Penellaphe spoke to him, I turned to Holland, who'd finally made his way back to me. My throat immediately thickened. Royal Guard or Fate, Holland was one of the few people in my life who…knew me.

Holland smiled, but it was small. Pained. "I hope you're not too angry with me or feel that I deceived you. I couldn't tell you the truth."

"I understand."

A look of doubt settled into a face that had never shown any true signs of aging. "Truly? You're not angry?"

A short laugh escaped me. Holland knew me so well. "Am I annoyed that I didn't know the truth? Sure. Am I mad?" I shrugged. "I have far bigger things to be angry about at the moment."

"That you do." A long moment passed. "Don't give up, Sera."

"I'm not." And I wasn't. Mainly because I wasn't sure exactly *what* I would be giving up on at this point.

"Good." His voice lowered then, and I had no idea if Nyktos heard what he said next, as Penellaphe had managed to draw him farther away toward the doors. "That thread that broke off from all the possible strings that chart the course of your life? It was unexpected. Unpredictable. Fate is never truly written in bone and blood. It can be as ever-changing as your thoughts. Your heart." He paused, glancing at Nyktos. "His."

I started to laugh again, but the sound withered. "Sure. Fate can be as erratic as the mind and heart." The words scratched their way from my throat. "But not in this case. Not with his heart. You've known that."

"Love is powerful, Seraphena." Holland lifted his hand to my cheek, and the touch carried a ripple of energy that hadn't been there before. "More so than even the Arae could imagine."

My brows furrowed. I was sure love was just super-duper special, but Nyktos had *physically* removed the part of him capable of loving. So, I had no idea what he was talking about.

Which wasn't entirely abnormal.

I exhaled shakily. "Will I see you again?"

"I can't answer that," he said. When I opened my mouth to reply, he quickly added, "But what I can tell you is something you already know. What you've spent your life preparing to become? What I trained you for? It wasn't a waste." Those dark, shining eyes held mine. "You are *his* weakness."

Become *his* weakness.

Make *him* fall in love.

End *him*.

Not Nyktos.

Kolis.

I was a weapon meant to be used against Kolis. That was my true destiny. But what I didn't know was if that meant Kolis would recognize me as Sotoria and that I was already his weakness, or if it meant that carrying Sotoria's soul would make it easier for me to seduce him.

My stomach twisted and dipped sharply. The idea of seducing Kolis made me want to vomit. I didn't...I didn't want to have to go through with it.

"What are you thinking?"

I jolted at the sound of Nyktos's voice. I was so caught up in my thoughts I hadn't been aware of Nyktos guiding me to his office.

I really needed to be more aware of my surroundings.

Pushing limp strands of hair back from my face, I felt my stomach flip and flop for very different reasons as I faced him.

Nyktos stood in front of the closed doors, and dressed as he was in a loose, untucked white shirt and black breeches, he reminded me of...*Ash*. Rugged and still unearthly. A sense of wild brimming beneath the veneer of calm.

But he was Nyktos now. Not Ash. He'd never be Ash to me again.

"I'm thinking about a lot of things," I admitted. And there was a lot to think about: Kolis. His creations. What he wanted. Nyktos. What he'd done to himself. Ezra and her marriage to Marisol and seizing the Crown. Me. The knowledge that I'd inadvertently caused my stepfather's death. What was to come. Holland. What he'd shared before leaving.

Nyktos eyed me as he walked past the empty bookshelves along the wall. I wondered if there had ever been items on those shelves. Keepsakes. Mementos. He sat on the edge of the settee, his gaze never leaving me. It was odd to be in a position where I was standing over him.

"I cannot imagine what must be going on in your head," he said finally. "But you went from anger...to sadness. Tangy, bitter sorrow."

Shoulders tensing, I glared at him. "Don't read my emotions."

"It's hard not to. You project a lot," he reminded me. "And often. You were really projecting in the throne room."

"Sounds like you need to figure out how to block them then."

A ghost of a half-smile appeared but vanished quickly, and my heart seized again as I thought of what he'd done.

"When did you have this...*kardia* removed?" I asked.

"A while ago."

I eyed him. "Exactly what do you consider a while?"

"A while," he repeated.

"That's evasive."

"It's more like it doesn't matter when I had it done. Just that I did."

I stared at him, unsure why he was being so cagey about it. "No one else knows? Just Maia?"

He nodded. "Only she and Nektas know. Neither will speak a word of it."

I'd never met the Primal Goddess, but based on how close Nektas and Nyktos were, I didn't doubt the draken would stay silent on such a thing. "Did it hurt? And don't say it was barely an inconvenience. Obviously, that's not true."

Nyktos was silent for several moments. "The *kardia* is just a tiny part of the soul. Intangible. You would think that something unseen couldn't cause much pain, but it felt like my entire chest had been cracked open, and my heart dug out by a dakkai's claws and teeth," he stated dispassionately. "I nearly lost consciousness, and if I had been weak, I likely would've slipped into stasis—the deep sleep of the gods and Primals."

Horrified, I pressed my fist to my chest. "Why did you do it?" I asked, even though I already knew.

"I saw what the loss of love did to my father, and what love turned my uncle into," he said. "And I refused to repeat either of those mistakes or endanger another because of what I felt for them."

A knot lodged in my throat, and it took a moment for me to speak around it. "I'm sorry."

He stretched his neck from one side to the other. "You shouldn't be. I care more because I cannot love, and I believe caring for others is far more important than loving just one."

"You... You are right," I whispered. In a way, caring and kindness were purer without love. But I was still saddened. Shouldn't everyone have the chance to feel love for another, whatever it felt like?

Except Kolis.

Or Tavius.

Neither of them deserved that.

"What was Holland speaking to you about?" Nyktos asked.

"Nothing important." There was no way I would repeat any of that. I glanced at the desk as I rubbed my wrists, still not feeling the charm. A slender lamp cast a glow over the bare surface. Several moments ticked by, and I could feel his gaze on me—watching and likely seeing too much. "What are we going to do?"

"That's a loaded question," he remarked, exhaling deeply. "We'll continue as planned. In the meantime, I'm positive there will be guests."

"Unwanted visitors?"

He nodded. "Gods. Possibly even Primals. They'll be curious about what they felt when you Ascended Bele."

My lips tightened, and I started to pace in front of the bare shelves. "And I guess I'm supposed to remain hidden?"

"I know you don't like hiding."

I snorted. "What gave that away?"

"I don't like it either," he said, and I shot him a doubtful look. His eyebrows lowered and pulled closer together. "But, inevitably, they will see you, and even with the charm, we want to make it to the coronation before that happens."

"And if we don't?"

"None of them will think your arrival in the Shadowlands as my Consort, and the ripples of power they felt, are coincidental. Especially not when that unknown power was first felt in the mortal realm," he said, speaking of when I'd brought Marisol back to life. "And not when they meet you. They'll sense the aura of eather in you. If it hadn't been for Bele's Ascension, they might have assumed you were a godling. Now, they will question exactly what you are."

3

What you are.

Not *who* you are.

"And becoming your Consort will somehow stop them from questioning that?" I asked, rubbing my temple.

"No, but it will stop them from acting without concern for the consequences," Nyktos said. "Is your head hurting? I can have the tea made for you, if so."

"It's not that." At least, I hoped the dull ache had nothing to do with the Culling. The herbal mixture that helped with the Culling's side effects hadn't worn off this quickly before. "Wouldn't everything be easier if we canceled the coronation? There's really no point in holding it."

"In case you weren't listening in the throne room or to anything I said before that, you will be afforded a level of protection as my Consort—"

"I was listening, and I remember *everything* you've said to me," I snapped. Wisps of eather spilled into his irises as our eyes met. "But that doesn't explain the point behind doing it. You know what's going to happen in five months or less. Becoming your Consort won't stop that. I'm not going to survive the Culling. It is what it is. So, why would we welcome such a risk with a pointless coronation?"

Nyktos's fingers began tapping his knee. "Does the idea of your death not bother you at all?"

"Why don't you just read my emotions and find out?" I shot back.

A tight smile appeared. "You asked me not to. And contrary to what you may believe, I respect that request as much as possible."

"Whatever," I muttered.

"It's not whatever." His fingers continued drumming. "You didn't answer my question. Are you not bothered at all by the thought of your death?"

I crossed my arms, having no idea why we were even discussing this. "Dying from the Culling doesn't sound fun at all. So, yeah, it's bothersome."

Nyktos didn't even blink. "But?"

"But it *is* what it *is*," I repeated, returning to my pacing. "It's reality. I have to deal with it. So, I'm dealing with it. Like I'm dealing with the fact that I've spent my life planning to kill an innocent Primal. Just like I'm dealing with the fact that I've apparently lived the gods only know how many lives, all because I got scared in one of them and ran off a stupid cliff." My skin prickled. "Like how did I run off *a cliff*? It's not like it would've jumped out and surprised me. I had to know the edge was there, but I just kept running? What the hell?"

He raised an eyebrow. "I don't think it's possible to deal with that as quickly as you'd have me believe," he said. "And you didn't live all the lives because you fell from a cliff—whether you knew the edge was there or not. You lived them because of Kolis's obsession with Sotoria, and my father's potentially problematic method of intervention."

"Yeah, well, here I am, the end result of your father's potentially problematic method of intervention...*dealing with it*," I stated. "And no part of dealing with it has anything to do with how I feel about it."

"We'll have to disagree on that," he replied. "What was...done to you then and now wasn't and isn't fair or right. Neither is what has been thrust upon you."

"Unfair to me?" I nearly tripped as I stopped, staring at the shadowstone between the shelves. "What about to you? The last thing you need is knowing that..." I couldn't even bring myself to say it. "It's not fair to put my survival on you."

"We're not talking about me."

"Well, we're not talking about me either."

"Disagree."

Whatever incredibly lacking restraint I had that put a tether on my temper snapped as I spun on him. "Why do you even care how I feel about any of this? You don't trust me. You don't really even *like* me. The only reason I'm still standing here is because of the embers of life inside me."

Wisps of luminous silver began to swirl. He said nothing as his fingers finally stopped their damn thrumming upon his knee.

An ache pierced my chest, so painful and real that I almost looked down to see if a blade had been thrust there. I looked away, inhaling deeply. "Look, I get it. I do. This whole situation is messed up. You have every right to be furious with me. To hate me for what I planned. I would if I were you, so—wait. Can you even hate since you can't love?"

"Hate and love are not two sides of the same coin. One comes from the soul, and the other from the mind," he said. "Hate is a product of atrocities committed against someone or is birthed from what they have done to themselves and their hellish entitlements. There couldn't be two more different emotions."

"Oh. Okay, then," I murmured, wondering how he knew that when he couldn't love, but…whatever. What did I know?

"You think that's why I'm angry?" Swirling silver eyes locked with mine. "That it stems from your plans to kill me?"

"Is that a serious question?" I asked. "Uh. Yes."

"Don't get me wrong. Learning that you planned to seduce and kill me was annoying."

"Annoying?" I repeated, my brows lifting. "I would use a much more descriptive emotion than that, but okay."

Nyktos seemed to take a deep breath, and I supposed I should be grateful that patience didn't stem from the *kardia*. "What you plotted to do isn't something one easily forgets. But *what* enraged me is that you had to know what would've happened to you even if there *had* been a small chance you'd succeed. If one of my guards didn't get to you, Nektas would have. Your act would've meant your death—the final kind."

I shifted my weight from one foot to the other. "I…I know that. I've always known that. Even before I learned that the draken were bonded to you."

Nyktos tilted his head, and a lock of reddish-brown hair glided over his temple. "*That* is what infuriates me. From the first moment I saw you, you've behaved as if your life holds no value for you."

The back of my neck tightened. "Those shit, now super-dead gods killed a *babe*. If striking out at them had resulted in my death, then it would've been worth it."

"I'm not talking about that," he snapped, leaving me confused. The only time he'd seen me before was when he refused to take me as his Consort. I'd been quite well-behaved then. "You should value your life as much as you do the lives of others, Sera."

Heat crept to the front of my neck. "I do value my life."

Nyktos laughed, turning away. "That is a lie, and you know it."

Anger rose quickly. "Are your super special abilities some sort of lie detection?"

"Life would be so much easier if that were the case. But, no. Emotions can be faked, especially if someone is determined to hide their motives and how they truly feel."

It was on the tip of my tongue to tell him that nothing I had felt around him had been a farce. How much his words and his touch had…pleased me, and that what I'd felt then was real. I had finally felt *real*. But he wouldn't believe me. I didn't expect him to. He knew I had been groomed from a young age to carry out my duty. And I had been determined to do so…until I hadn't. But if I were in his place, I wouldn't believe a word I said either.

I looked down at the scuffed toes of my boots. "Then you can't possibly know what you claim to."

"Except all of your actions tell me what I need to know," he said. Several moments passed. "I mean no offense when I say that you don't value your life. I didn't mean it as an insult."

I snorted. "Sure sounded like one."

"I apologize if that was how it came across."

My head jerked. "You're seriously apologizing to me? Don't answer. It doesn't matter. Half of this conversation doesn't matter. What I was trying to say is that there is no reason to go through with this coronation. Whatever protection being crowned as your Consort offers cannot be worth it."

He slowly leaned forward. "Your safety is worth *everything*."

"Even the Shadowlands?"

His now-swirling eyes had never left mine, but, somehow, he'd moved without me even realizing, crossing the space between us. "*Yes*."

The breath I inhaled rattled through me, full of his citrusy scent. "You can't mean that."

"I mean it with every part of my being, Sera."

Sera. Not *liessa*. He hadn't called me that since I'd been in his bed, after I'd given him my blood. That had been a slip of the tongue then, something done in a moment of pleasure.

Nyktos loomed, a good head or two taller than I was. "You are…"

His jaw flexed, nostrils flaring. "What you carry inside you is far too important. They have to be part of the key to ending what Kolis has done. You may value those embers as little as you do your life, but I do not."

What I carried inside me. The embers were important. Not me. Never me.

I backed off, taking several steps. Did I expect him to say something else? That I mattered? To him? And that he cared for me, even though he couldn't love? After what I'd plotted? I didn't.

I just *wanted* it to be different.

Nyktos's chest rose sharply. "Sera—" A knock on the door interrupted us. His head cut in the direction of the sound. "What?" he barked.

My gaze flew to the entryway. I wouldn't have been surprised if whoever was there had simply backed away.

The doors opened to reveal Rhahar, his skin a warm, deep brown in the soft glow of the lamplight. Though nothing about his expression was warm as his gaze flickered over me. "There's a problem at the Pillars."

Most souls faced judgment at the Pillars of Asphodel. They were either rewarded with the Vale or sentenced to the Abyss. The Pillars couldn't judge some; their lives were far too complicated, and it required Nyktos's presence.

"How urgent?" Nyktos demanded as Rhahar's cousin drifted in behind him.

"Urgent enough to risk interrupting you," Saion replied blandly, a hand resting on the hilt of the sword strapped to his hip.

Nyktos cursed, shoving a hand over his head as he stalked to the credenza.

"Is everything okay?" I asked as Nyktos reached the cupboard.

Rhahar didn't look in my direction as he nodded, not elaborating. Pressure clamped down on my chest, even though his reaction didn't come as a surprise. My betrayal of Nyktos was a betrayal to all of them.

Breathing through the tightness in my chest, I turned to Nyktos as he grabbed the back collar of his shirt, then pulled it up and over his head. My eyes nearly fell out of my face as the lean muscles running down the length of his spine appeared, along with the swirling drops of blood inked into his skin—drops that represented all the lost lives Nyktos believed he was responsible for.

Proof that he cared deeply for more than one.

Muscles bunched along his broad shoulders and biceps as he tossed the shirt aside and pulled out a gray tunic from a lower cabinet in the credenza. His body was a masterpiece, proof of years spent fighting with heavy swords instead of using the eather inside him.

I knew I shouldn't stare as he tugged the tunic on. It didn't feel like I had a right to do that now, nor did it seem like something I should be doing at the moment. But he was...well, really nice to look at. And I really liked looking at him.

"I clearly remember someone saying that it was inappropriate to stare," Nyktos's low voice interrupted. "Especially when it's clearly *intentional.*"

My gaze flew to his as warmth blossomed in my chest. The wisps of eather were churning again. "It wasn't intentional."

He smirked. "You lie so prettily."

I had totally lied. The apples of my cheeks burned as he donned the tunic with an iron-hued brocade around the raised collar and across the chest in a diagonal line. But the warmth cooled rapidly. I was sure there was a coded dig there, except all I could think about was when he'd said that to me before. He'd been teasing then.

Rhahar cleared his throat, reminding me that we weren't alone.

"Saion, escort Sera to her chambers," Nyktos said, and the god looked less than pleased with the orders as Nyktos's cool gray eyes met mine. "We'll finish this conversation when I return."

"Looking forward to it," I muttered.

"I'm sure you are." Nyktos started for the doors, then stopped. A heartbeat passed. "Try to get some rest." Then he left, disappearing into the hall with Rhahar.

Saion gestured at the doors. "Let's go."

Resisting the urge to plant my ass on the floor for no reason other than the fact that I hated being told what to do, I went to the settee and grabbed my dagger.

"Should I be worried right now?" Saion asked, falling into step beside me as we walked out and down the hall. He eyed the dagger clenched tightly in my hand.

"Not unless you give me a reason to use it against you."

A smile softened the handsome lines of his face, bringing warmth to his deep black skin. "I have no plans to do such a thing."

"Really?" I pushed open the door. "You don't want revenge for what I planned to do to Nyktos?"

"What I want doesn't matter." His dark eyes met mine as he caught the door. "What does is the fact that if I thought you were a real threat to

Nyktos, I'd snap your neck myself. As would any of us loyal to him."

My skin chilled as I climbed the dark, dimly lit steps. No part of me doubted what he claimed.

"And, yeah, I know he'd kill me for it. That wouldn't stop me. That wouldn't stop any of us." Saion stayed a step behind me. "But you're not a real threat to him, are you? He may be attracted to you, but that's about as deep as that shit can ever go."

I flinched, grateful that he couldn't see how much the truth stung. Because even if Nyktos could love, he would never love me. *Breathe in.* I rounded the landing of the third floor. *Hold.* I shut off the flood of guilt, regret, and, more importantly, the bitter want—the almost keen desperation for *that shit* to run deeper. I searched for the veil of emptiness, and it took longer than it should have for it to seep into me. But when it did, I welcomed the hollowness. I became nothing, and only then did I exhale as I reached the final landing. "You're wrong, though."

"About what?"

I started to open the door. "About me not being a threat to him."

Saion's hand slapped down on the door, closing it. "Is that so?"

I inched back, creating some space between us as my hand tightened around the hilt of my dagger. Saion had gone still in the way only gods and Primals did, right before an explosive display of violence. It would've been wise of me to show some fear.

Unfortunately, I wasn't wise often enough.

"The dakkais attacked the Black Bay because of what I did. Kolis doesn't strike me as a one-and-done type. He's not going to stop searching for that source of power. I'm a danger to everyone here, including Nyktos, whether that shit runs deep or not."

The glow of eather pulsed in the center of Saion's eyes. "So should I just go ahead and snap your neck then?"

"If you want to try, then all I ask is that you not be a coward about it and wait until my back is turned." I widened my stance in case he did attack. "Just know that I won't make it easy."

"I wouldn't expect you to."

I gave him a close-lipped smile. "So, what's it going to be? You want to do this or not?"

Something akin to respect flickered across Saion's features. "As I said, *Consort*, I have no intention of signing my death note."

"I'm not the Consort."

"In a matter of days, you will be."

"But will I really be *your* Consort?" I asked.

Saion didn't respond. He didn't need to. We both knew the answer. He opened the door. "After you."

Brushing past him, I stepped out into the hall and came to a complete stop. A tall woman with long, dark hair was stationed outside the door to my bedchamber, her head bowed as she read from a book. I'd never seen the pale-skinned female before. "Who is that?"

Saion closed the door behind me. "Orphine."

I attempted to reconcile this very mortal-looking woman with the rather large, midnight-scaled draken I'd seen battle in the sky over the Black Bay. She'd been injured in the fight but appeared fine now.

Then I realized why she was here. "She's here to make sure I stay in my bedchamber?"

The corners of Saion's lips turned down. "She is here to make sure *you* are *safe* in your rooms."

"I don't think those things are mutually exclusive," I muttered, wondering exactly how Nyktos had managed to send her to my bedchamber on such short notice.

"You're right." Saion shrugged. "Did you expect it to be different?"

"No," I admitted.

"But I don't think those two things are weighed equally," Saion continued after a moment. "Protection more than punishment."

"Really?"

"Really," Orphine repeated from down the hall. My gaze snapped back to her. She turned a page in her book. "I could hear your entire conversation."

"Oh," I murmured as we started down the hall. Orphine knew what I had done with the embers of life, but I didn't know if she was aware of what I had planned.

She looked up then. Now that I was closer, I saw her crimson eyes and the vertical slits of her pupils behind thick lashes. The draken appeared as a mortal in her second or so decade of life. "If Nyktos was more concerned about making sure you stayed put and out of relative trouble, he wouldn't have given me permission to burn to ash anyone who comes to your doors."

"Anyone?"

"Anyone who poses a threat." Orphine smiled tightly, and there was nothing warm about that smile. "To you. Not him, which is unfortunate."

Saion smirked.

Well, I supposed I didn't have to wonder any longer if Orphine knew what I'd planned. "You'd rather burn me to ash instead?"

"For even thinking about killing Nyktos? Yes." Orphine snapped the book shut with one hand and pushed off the wall. She took a step toward me, and Saion tensed, his hand going to the sword at his hip. I fought the instinct screaming at me to back up. The draken was about my height, and the sleeveless tunic she wore clung to rounded hips. She looked *soft.* But so did I. "Nyktos is…special to us."

Ice crept up the back of my neck as I held her stare.

"But so are you." A lock of hair fell against her arched cheek. "You are *life.*" Her voice lowered…and I swore faint wisps of smoke wafted from her nostrils. "And that is the only reason you still breathe."

I'd gone into my bedchamber without saying much, because how could I respond to what Orphine had said? *Thanks for recognizing the value of the embers and not burning me alive?*

I hadn't been left alone for long, though. Baines, a mortal or godling I'd met my first night here, brought in some hot water. Like all who worked in the House of Haides, he did so out of choice—because he wanted to be of service to Nyktos.

That was the kind of loyalty Nyktos inspired.

I sat on the chaise, uncomfortable with Baines' presence even after he'd left—not because of him, but because of what his arrival had meant. Nyktos had sent him. The act would likely be considered small by most and easily overlooked, but not by me. It had been…incredibly thoughtful of him. And I didn't want him to be thoughtful. Or kind. I also recognized how messed-up those thoughts were.

You are his weakness.

Swallowing, I glanced down at the dagger Nyktos had given me after destroying my old one. I totally understood his reaction. I *had*, sort of, accidentally plunged my dagger into his heart, but I'd been furious, nonetheless. That dagger had been *mine*, and so few things belonged to me.

But Nyktos had more than made up for it with this gift. The *first-ever* present that belonged only to me.

The dagger was truly a piece of art with its smooth, lightweight handle and the pommel of the hilt crafted into the shape of a crescent moon. The shadowstone blade itself was delicate yet fierce, shaped like a thin hourglass and deadly sharp on both sides. The bladesmith had carved a dragon into the dagger, its spiked tail following the curve of the blade and the scaled body and head carved into the hilt where it breathed fire.

Nyktos had taken it away once he learned of my betrayal. But what the god Taric had done—the feeding and the prying into my memories— had been so painful and *terrifying* that I hadn't been able to hide that from Nyktos, let alone myself. He'd sensed my terror and acted upon it.

You may feel fear, but you are never afraid, he'd said and then pressed the hilt of the dagger into the palm of the one who had once sworn to use such a weapon against him.

Could losing the ability to love increase one's capacity to be kind? I didn't know, but I wouldn't be surprised to learn that it could.

A knot swelled in my chest as I rose and walked to the doorway of the bathing chamber. I stopped. The space was far lovelier than the stifling chamber I used in Wayfair. Clean water had rarely been brought into that chamber—let alone hot—and I'd often preferred to bathe in the lake. A pang of yearning twisted my heart. Would I ever get to see my lake again? Feel its cool water running over my skin? I didn't think so.

Thoughts heavy, my gaze roamed over the tub. My hand went to my throat. Soaking in the steaming water would be divine, but I couldn't even if I had time. Not when I could practically feel the sash from my robe digging into my skin and cutting off my air.

I wasn't sure if I'd ever be able to relax in a tub again.

Forcing myself into the bathing chamber, I stripped off the ruined sweater and breeches, placing the top and my undergarments into a small basket. Using one of the washcloths, I bathed without using the tub, cleaning away the dried blood from my fight with the gods in the throne room. I glanced at the mirror, only looking at the bite mark on my throat. The two puncture wounds were still an angry shade of red. Taric had bitten in the same spot that Nyktos had. No two bites could be more different. One had brought pleasure, the other immense pain.

Swallowing, I glanced down at my breast. The bite Nyktos had left there, just above my nipple, was a calmer reddish pink. I brushed my fingers over the shallow indentations and gasped at the sharp pulse of desire that shot through the pit of my stomach. I jerked my hand away. Thinking of his mouth on my skin, the pierce of his fangs, would do me no good at the moment.

Pulling on a slip and a dressing robe made of crushed velvet dyed black, I went to the balcony and tugged the drapes aside. The sky was a muted shade of gray now, the stars dim.

You're his weakness.

"What am I doing?" I whispered, looking around the chamber. There was no answer. Or maybe there *was* one, but I just didn't want to acknowledge it because I knew what I had to do.

Only I didn't want to do it.

That knowledge did little to calm my racing heart. I started pacing and didn't stop until a honey-haired draken arrived with supper. Davina silently placed the covered dish and wine on the table. She didn't even look in my direction, and I had no idea if it was because she had learned of my betrayal or not. Davina had never been the friendliest draken.

"Has…Nyktos returned?" I asked.

She arched a brow at me, said nothing, and stalked out of the room. I was alone once more. The food was delicious, but I couldn't remember what it was as soon as I placed the lid over the dish, eyeing the door that connected my chamber to Nyktos's.

Was it still unlocked?

I stood, taking several steps toward the door before stopping myself. Pushing out a deep breath, I returned to the chaise and tucked my legs under me. I was *tired*, and a seed of concern took root, despite all the many valid reasons explaining why I would be worn down: the lack of sleep. Feeding Nyktos. Taric's bite. Learning the truth about the embers, and, well…the stress of everything else. That's what I told myself as I closed my eyes. It was the only way I could fall asleep—something I needed if I was going to figure out what to do. Because if I acknowledged the other reason, that it was the Culling, there would be no rest for sure. Because the Culling ended only one way.

With my death.

A deafening crack woke me, and it took more than a couple of moments for me to remember where I was.

Slowly sitting up, I looked around the chamber lit by a lone wall sconce by the doors. Had it been thunder? That didn't seem right. I didn't think it could storm in the Shadowlands.

I started to rise but stopped myself as a soft blanket slid to my waist. Frowning, I sank my fingers into the plush material and glanced at the basket it had been rolled up in—now empty. I didn't remember getting the blanket before sitting down.

A sudden intense light flashed from outside, lighting the entire space. I jumped to my feet, my heart thumping as I went to the balcony doors. That was way too bright for lightning, but the boom of thunder followed, just as the chamber doors swung wide.

Orphine rushed inside, her crimson eyes as luminous as polished rubies. "Do not go out there."

I took one look at the unsheathed sword she held at her side and spun around, throwing open the doors.

"Godsdamn it," Orphine growled.

The breath I took immediately choked me. Smoke filled the air and smothered the starlight, stinging my eyes and burning my throat. Shouts echoed from the courtyard and the massive Rise surrounding the House of Haides as I rushed to the railing.

Gripping the cool stone, I leaned out and gasped. What I saw shocked me. Deep within the Red Woods, silver flames rippled and lit the night sky, burning through the crimson sea of leaves. A tree popped, exploding in a shower of silver sparks.

A sudden gust of wind tore across the balcony, whipping away the smoke in a frenzy. My head jerked up as a tan draken nearly the size of Nektas flew over the courtyard, heading straight for the Red Woods.

"Fuck," Orphine snarled. "You're going to get your ass back inside right now."

The draken in the air released a funnel of silver fire, striking the woods just outside the Rise. Flames shot up high, stretching above the Rise itself, briefly highlighting the guards. The fire blew back—

I staggered into Orphine as the embers in my chest heated and throbbed, and screams of pain rippled through the night sky.

"Oh, my gods," I whispered, rooted to my spot by horror as...*things* fell. My burning eyes tracked their flaming descent to the ground below. The fall took mere seconds, but it felt like an eternity as my palms heated in response to the death.

The tan draken fired on the Red Woods again, hitting the same spot as before. A crack of fiery energy hit the ground, shaking my bones. *That* was the sound that had woken me.

"Inside," Orphine snarled, grabbing my arm. "Now."

Another draken swept over the courtyard at breakneck speed, flying so fast I could barely make out the reddish-brown scales as Orphine dragged me toward the door. The draken latched onto the tan one's back, digging talons into scales and flesh. The tan draken shrieked, twisting sharply as it tried to shake off the much smaller draken—

Orphine shoved me inside, slamming the door shut behind her. Heart thumping, I stumbled around, snared by shock and confusion. My stomach hollowed as I tried not to breathe in the bitter scent of smoke that had followed us into the bedchamber. I couldn't process what was occurring—what I'd just seen outside.

Another thunderclap of fiery eather hit the ground and rattled the entire palace, causing the glass chandelier above me to sway violently. The realm outside the palace turned silver once more and shattered the surreal numbness.

I faced Orphine. "Is that one of Kolis's draken?"

"I don't recognize it." Orphine turned halfway back to the balcony doors, her chest rising and falling sharply. "It could be his or another Primal's."

I turned to the adjoining door, knowing without a doubt that Nyktos was out there somewhere, in the smoke and fiery nightmare.

Where I should be.

"Do you know if it's just the draken, or are there dakkais?" I went and grabbed the shadowstone dagger from the arm of the chaise.

"I have no damn clue. The attack started less than ten minutes ago." Her nostrils flared with anger as I started for the chamber doors. "What do you think you're doing?"

"What we should both be doing." I glanced at the now-dark space beyond the balcony doors as an eerie wail echoed from outside. "I'm going to help."

Orphine's fingers opened and closed around the hilt of her sword. "Absolutely not."

"If there are dakkais out there, you know that Nyktos won't be able to use eather against them."

"Nektas and the other draken will—"

"I don't care what Nektas and the other draken do," I cut her off.

"You should. Because that damn bastard out there isn't burning the woods for the fun of it." Another boom shook us. I half-expected the chandelier to come crashing down from the ceiling. "You hear that? That's not trees exploding. That's the *ground* erupting. You know what's under that ground, right?"

My body flashed cold. "The entombed gods."

Orphine nodded. "That draken is burning straight through the soil, the chambers, and the damn chains entombing them. If he isn't stopped, the entire Shadowlands will be swamped by hundreds of starved, pissed-off fallen gods."

I didn't have to think hard to remember the ravenous gods clawing their way from the ground. That had only been a few. Hundreds? "Then we really need to help."

"You can help by staying inside the palace, where it's currently safe."

"I know we don't know each other at all, but I am not the type of person who stands back and hides when I can fight."

"I really don't care what type of person you are." She started toward me. "If you don't sit your ass down and behave, *I* will sit your ass down for you."

Frustration crashed into my fury, driven by the unnecessary deaths and the knowledge that my actions were likely the cause. I squared off with the draken. "No."

Orphine drew up short. "Excuse me?"

The embers in my chest suddenly hummed, but it was different than when Nyktos was near or when I summoned the eather to give life. The vibration was deeper and stronger and pumped through me, filling my veins until I felt as if my entire body was thrumming. "I said, no."

"I heard you, but I don't know why you think you're in a position to say that."

"I don't know why *you* think you're in a position to tell me what to do." The humming pressed against my chest, and Orphine's pupils suddenly stretched even thinner. "Why do you think we're under attack? Is some Primal just that bored and decided to really piss Nyktos off? Or is it because of what I've done? Because I'm here?"

Orphine let out a low growl of displeasure.

"I'm going out there," I told her. "If your duty is to protect me, then protect me *out there*. Or don't. I couldn't care less."

A tense moment passed. I knew if the draken wanted to stop me, she could easily do so. "Fuck me," she muttered. "Let's do this."

"Thank you." Exhaling roughly, I turned to the doors and threw them open before she changed her mind. Orphine was right behind me as I hurried down the hall, the halves of the robe fluttering around my legs.

"You know," she said as we entered the back staircase that led to the exit closest to the courtyard facing the Red Woods, "you're not wearing shoes."

"That is the least of my concerns."

"Yeah, getting yourself killed should be your number one concern, but I don't think it has even made your list of things to be worried about at this point." She shot me a red-eyed glare. "You need to be careful so you don't end up dead. If that happens, I'm going to kill you myself."

"Not only does that threat seem really counterproductive"—I raced down the last of the steps—"it's going to be really hard to do since I'd already be dead."

"But you get my point." Orphine slipped in front of me as we reached the main floor landing, the ridges of scales in her pale skin far more noticeable now. "Stay close to me."

"*You* stay close to me." I brushed past her.

The string of curses Orphine let out was rather impressive. "Nyktos warned me that you were hard-headed."

"Did he?" I shoved open the exterior door and stepped out into…

Chaos.

4

My palms warmed, and the embers really started pulsating. Pain and death were everywhere—in the smoldering heaps on the ground and in those who still stood. Beyond the Rise, fire spread from tree to tree as they continued exploding under the heat of the eather. Smoke whirled through the air in thick tendrils, carrying the nearly suffocating stench of burnt wood and charred flesh. Orphine shouted as another draken crashed into the courtyard, kicking up soil and loose rock as it slid across the ground.

Guards rushed from all sides of the courtyard and on the Rise, kneeling and taking aim at the tan draken as it circled back, raining shimmering blood in its wake. The blood showered the west side and the guards there—

They shrieked, falling to the ground and writhing as they pulled out of their armor and clothes. Their agony turned my insides frigid. I'd never heard shrieks like that before. It sounded as if they were screaming for the release of death.

"Dear gods," I whispered. "What is happening to them?"

"Our blood," Orphine growled. "It will burn most alive."

"Fuck." I looked for Nyktos, unable to make out most of those in the smoke. "Even Primals?"

"It'll burn them, too, but it won't kill them."

I supposed that was a relief—kind of. I sucked in a short, smoky breath as the tan draken released another burst of flames. The stream cut short. A large, black-and-gray draken swooped down from the sky, crashing into its side.

"Nektas," I rasped, awed by his size. I couldn't even see the other draken.

"They're coming!" a guard shouted, drawing our attention to the Rise. "Shut the gates! Shut the gates!"

A chill of dread shot down my spine as I took off for the gates, ignoring the rocky ground under my feet. I raced past those *heaps*. I couldn't look at them. The urge to stop and change what had happened was already pressing down on me. If I looked, I didn't know if I could stop myself.

"They're not going to make it!" Orphine shouted. "They're already there!"

I didn't see them at first. It was too smoky beyond the Rise, but then Nektas and the tan draken appeared just outside it. Nektas dug his talons in, his wings whipping through the air as he twisted, throwing the asshole draken into the burning trees. A shower of silver sparks lit the ground beyond the Rise.

Jerking to a stop, I swallowed a shout of surprise as *they* slammed into the partially closed gates, splintering the wood. They poured in through the opening, a mass of sunken, chalky flesh and hungry, wide mouths. There had to be dozens of them—maybe even *hundreds*.

They swallowed the guards at the gate, taking them down in a frenzy. Then they were inside the courtyard, running faster than I would've thought their frail, malnourished bodies were capable of.

But I guessed I wasn't the only one motivated by hunger.

"Don't die," Orphine warned, tossing me the sword she held. There was a flash of silvery-blue as she shifted into her draken form.

An onyx-hued wing swept over me as she came down on her forelegs and extended her long neck, firing on a group of fallen. They went up in a wail of shrieks, some falling to the ground and others still running.

Head or heart, I reminded myself as my breathing slowed and became even. I braced myself, the short sword in one hand and my dagger in the other.

The first entombed god made it past Orphine, its fangs bared and the grayish skin around its eyes smudged black. Two more were quick to join it as Orphine swiped out with her horned tail, knocking several burning fallen back. I waited until they reached for me.

Snapping forward, I slammed my dagger deep into one. Hot, shimmery blood that smelled of decay spurted from the god's chest as I kicked it back into the other. I spun, sweeping the sword out wide in an arc. The sharp blade cut through the god's neck far too easily. My lip curled, and I twisted, thrusting my dagger into the chest of the third as Orphine lit up the courtyard once more. The light was brief but lasted long enough for me to catch sight of Bele fighting near the gates. The snarls of the fallen gods quickly overshadowed the shock of seeing her after I'd last seen her dazed and drenched in blood.

I had no idea how many of Nyktos's close guards were here at night, but the fallen gods were everywhere, running or feeding on the ones they took down and those already wounded.

Nektas suddenly took flight, appearing in the sky above the Rise. He flew out toward the deeper, denser parts of the Red Woods, where I'd originally seen the flames. The burning had stopped, but smoke billowed into the air.

A pain-filled scream jerked my head to where a guard was slamming his dagger into the side of a god that had him on his back.

Disgust and anger throbbed within me as I stalked forward, sheathing the dagger. How could anyone, Primal or not, unleash something like this? Using both hands, I shoved the sword deep into the god's back. As I withdrew the blade, the god pitched forward, falling onto the guard.

Shoving the fallen aside, I jerked back. The guard's eyes were open and blinking rapidly as blood frothed from his mouth and his…throat. My hands heated, and the embers pulsed. I knew I shouldn't, even if healing someone couldn't be felt by the gods and Primals of other Courts. But it was like instinct; a reaction I couldn't control, just as Aios had said. I started to reach for him—

Orphine landed beside me, nudging me back with her wing as she let out a thin stream of fire toward a group of fallen gods clamoring toward us. I stepped out of the path of her wings and saw that the guard's eyes no longer blinked. Blood no longer flowed as freely. The embers stretched against my chest. Shuddering, I turned away and found a new horror.

Entombed gods had swarmed the fallen draken, who had shifted into its mortal form. There were so many fallen near the draken that I couldn't see who it was.

I took off, leaping off the guard's body. The draken was in a far more vulnerable position now. I plunged a dagger into a god's head and shoved another into Orphine's path. Her head snapped down, and the crunch of bones was something I wouldn't forget for a very long time. Shoving aside another god, I caught a glimpse of reddish-brown skin that was *too* red, and honey-brown hair—

Oh, gods.

I began to hack at the gods, losing all sense of skill in my panic to get them off the draken. I reached Davina's side, air lodged in my too-tight throat. Half of her was burnt and unrecognizable. The other half had been torn apart by sharpened nails and fangs. It was clear…

My stomach twisted as nausea rose. Davina was gone. Just like that. My entire body spasmed with the knowledge that I could fix it. The embers wanted that. That was what *I* wanted. Because that had been Davina, and now she was *gone.*

"Stop!"

My head jerked up, and my gaze clashed with Ector's deep amber eyes. The fair-haired god turned, lifting a hand. A bolt of eather erupted from his palm, slamming into a fallen god and throwing it back several feet.

"Don't do it." Ector swung his sword with his other hand, cleaving through a fallen god's neck. I jerked back from Davina. "It will only make things worse down the road."

Pushing past the tightness threatening to seal off my throat, I forced myself away from Davina. *Breathe in.* Ector was right. If I brought any of them back to life, the other gods and Primals would feel it. *Hold.* Part of me wondered if it mattered since they already knew an ember of life was here, but it wouldn't help matters at all. The pressure on my chest increased.

"Keep it together," I whispered hoarsely, making myself go where Bele fought as I exhaled, breathed in again, and held it.

Shoulder-length black hair snapped around her shoulders as the goddess spun, driving her sword through a fallen's *face.* She saw me then, and both brows rose, forming deep creases in light brown skin that no longer carried the pallor of death. She yanked her blade free. "Nyktos is going to lose his shit once he realizes you're out here."

That was highly likely. "Where is he?"

"With Rhahar and Saion." Her eyes, now silver, glowed with eather. "They were in the woods, trying to catch the freed gods." She dragged the back of her hand across her forehead. A smear of blood remained. "They must've gotten swamped."

My chest clenched as I turned, striking out at a nearby god. I pushed it off the sword. Was that where Nektas had flown? Worry threatened to seize me. "They have to be okay."

"I know." Bele dipped and picked up a long, slender spear. She tossed it to me. "They're lighter, double-edged, and more fun."

The spear was significantly lighter, and given how I'd already begun to feel the strain in my muscles, I knew it wouldn't be nearly as physically taxing. I dropped the sword and shifted the spear into my right hand. "How many gods do you think were freed?"

"Too many." Bele whistled as Orphine clubbed a god with her tail. "I think several of the chambers broke open."

"Is Lethe at risk, too?"

"Ehthawn and a few other draken are there in case any of them broke off from this mess and are making their way there." Bele lifted her sword, pointing at the destroyed gate. Her eyes, tapered at the corners, narrowed. "And someone just rang the damn dinner bell because more are coming. We need to end the buffet they're trying to make of our people."

Our people.

I looked up and saw the guards on the Rise now, firing at the ground outside the wall. Coughing as a gust of smoke moved over us, I shut myself down as I started forward. They weren't my people. They never would be. I found the veil of nothingness welcoming as it settled over me. Then, I felt absolutely numb. No intense urging of the embers. No pinching guilt that stung my skin with each new scream. No agony of seeing Davina. No dread of others being hurt or worse. No fear of Nyktos being wounded or curiosity why I was so worried about that and the concern *that* fostered. I fell into the controlled madness of battle and became what I'd always been.

A killer.

A monster.

I drove the spear into a god's heart and then tore it free. Several strands of hair whipped around my face as I spun, striking down another and then another. Twisting sharply, I used the spear's side to knock a fallen god away as I jerked the spear back, impaling the god behind me. Snarling, I kicked the fallen free as I turned, driving the point through the back of a head. Orphine followed, catching others between her powerful jaws or burning them with fire. She stayed close to me as I worked my way through the courtyard.

I didn't keep track of how many lives were lost—how many I was taking—as sweat dampened my brow. I'd ended seventeen lives before

I came to the Shadowlands—eighteen if I counted Tavius. My lip curled in disgust as I thrust once more. I didn't count my stepbrother, as he was below even a barrat, but I hadn't tallied since I'd entered the Shadowlands, and I couldn't start now.

Blood stained my robe as I spun, driving the spear through a back and then a head. My muscles ached, but adrenaline pumped hotly through me as I whirled, jabbing the shadowstone spear through the chest of a fallen god on fire. Bolts of eather ripped through the smoke, coming from Bele and Ector as well as several of the guards. I quickly noticed that the ones Ector and the other guards hit with eather were only wounded, but the ones that Bele struck went down for the count. Hadn't Saion been willing to bet that Bele was stronger now? That was a bet he'd win.

Spinning, I slammed the side of the spear into one of the fallen gods that Ector had hit with eather, knocking it to the ground. I lifted the weapon—

My world turned silver as a bolt of eather arced and crackled mere inches from my face. I wrenched back, my bare feet slipping on what could only be blood pooling beneath them. I hit the ground, ignoring the wetness drenching my robe and knees as another streak of essence burned through the spot where I'd been standing—

Orphine yelped, staggering back as the eather struck her. I cried out as the energy raced over her body, lighting up the veins and ridges of her scales. I popped to my feet as Orphine reared up on her hind legs, swinging her wings back. One slammed into my chest, and I was suddenly off my feet, flying backward.

I hit the ground hard. Air punched out of my lungs, but I somehow managed to hold onto the spear. "Ouch." I moaned, knowing I couldn't stay down long. I rolled and got to my feet, about to yell at whoever had the worst aim, but as I turned—

I came face-to-face with a god.

A completely well-fed and well-dressed god, fair of hair and skin and carrying a healthy glow that screamed that he hadn't spent a second of his life entombed. Breathing heavily, I didn't strike out. I had no idea if this was one of the Shadowlands gods that I hadn't met.

"Pale-haired." He looked me over, his eyes narrowing. "Freckled. You must be her." The god's head tilted to the side as he began to smile. "And here I thought I would have to go inside to find you. But you are…charmed."

"Fuck," I whispered. This was a powerful god.

"Maybe later." He winked as I lifted the spear. His gaze flicked behind me. "Or not."

A hand clamped down on my braid, jerking me back. The smell of soil and decay enveloped me. Years of training kicked in as the fallen god gripped my shoulder from behind and went for my throat. I twisted to the side—

Sudden, shocking pain blasted through me as fangs shredded the skin of my shoulder. The fallen god latched on, its nails slicing through the robe. It didn't seem to care that it had missed my throat. I reacted without thought, tearing myself free. Red-hot pain swamped me, and flesh ripped—maybe even muscle. Gritting my teeth, I faced the fallen.

She was…fresh. Her skin wasn't as chalky or sunken as the others. She even looked young, about my age. Blood streamed down her chin—my blood. Her eyes flashed with eather, intense and unnerving. She launched herself at me.

Agony radiated from my shoulder and shot down my arm as I thrust up. I took the impact of the spear piercing her chest badly, falling to a knee under the weight as the spear ended up wedged between her and the ground. Cursing, I rose, unsheathing my dagger as I turned.

The male god was still there, unmoving and untouched by the chaos of smoke and death. "Interesting. Your blood. It smells like…*life*." He sniffed the air, and the glow of essence pulsed behind his pupils as his eyes widened. "Blood. Ash. Blood and—"

A stream of fire interrupted him, swallowing the bastard as Orphine landed beside me. Relieved to see that she was okay enough to remain in her draken form and fight, I shoved the strange words aside as I gingerly touched my shoulder. Air hissed between my teeth. It was a bloody, ragged mess, but it could've been worse. I'd survive, but if she had gotten me at the throat, I'd be dead.

Breathing through the burning pain of the bite, I stiffened as a low snarl rumbled through the courtyard, whipping the smoke into a frenzy. What in the world? Goose bumps spread across my flesh, and several of the entombed gods turned to the Rise, their heads cocking—

I turned at the sound of pounding footsteps, gasping as a fallen god rushed me. I planted my hand against its chest, thrusting the dagger through its temple. A dizzying rush of pain left me nauseous, leaving me slow to pull the blade free. And it cost me. Another fallen slammed into me. I hit the ground, throwing up my arm and blocking the fallen as it came down on me. Wrong move. I knew that. I'd screwed up. *Never get laid out on your back.* I knew that.

The fallen's fangs sank into my forearm.

I screamed as I brought up my leg, wedging my knee against the god's sunken stomach. I felt each swallow the bastard took. Felt the moan rumbling through its body. I pushed with all my strength, getting nowhere. The sound of pounding boots, shouts, and screams echoed as the ground shook beneath me. A bit of panic seeped in because this…this might be it. This might be how I died. I would be torn apart by fallen gods, just as Nyktos had warned I would be the first time I'd come across them.

No.

I would not die like this.

Kicking my head back, I shouted as I thrust the dagger into the side of the fallen's head. It toppled, my heart stuttering at the raw agony—

The realm turned black.

Silent.

Still.

I thought I might've passed out for a heartbeat, but my shoulder and arm still throbbed, and I felt the sudden thrumming of the embers.

Strikes of eather suddenly pierced the churning darkness above me. They came from every direction, spreading out across the courtyard and slamming into the fallen gods, cutting off shrieks mid-scream as the essence poured over their bodies. They shattered, one after another, after another…

Then, through the mass of thick, throbbing shadows, I saw *him.*

Nyktos, in his Primal form.

He hovered in the air, his wings a mass of pulsating eather and shadows spread wide, his skin shiny and hard, a stunning, whirling kaleidoscope of shadowstone and moonlight. Silvery essence crackled from his all-white eyes and palms. The shirt he wore hung from his shoulders in tatters, rippling around his form.

Gods, he was…terrifying in this form. Beautiful. *Primal.*

Orphine's rough-scaled muzzle nudged my arm. "Hi," I croaked.

She crouched over me, aiming at an entombed god that remained standing as Nyktos lowered to the ground.

Fine shivers broke out all over me. I could feel his stare on me as he stalked forward, catching the god before the draken could.

Nyktos gripped the fallen by the head and ripped him in two. Straight down the middle. With his bare *hands.*

Good gods…

Dropping the still-twitching limbs and limp pieces on either side of him, his wings snapped back, shattering into faint shadows as he stalked forward. The eather-pierced darkness faded from his flesh, but the shadows were still gathered beneath, swirling violently.

I thought that maybe I should sit up or do something, especially as Orphine backed off, bowing her diamond-shaped head. Nyktos was so going to be angry with me, and I'd just seen him rip a god in two with his bare hands. But all I managed to do was rise onto one elbow and…that *hurt*, sending a bolt of pain through my shoulder and arm.

Nyktos crossed the remaining distance between us too fast for me to track. Shadowy wisps bled into the air around him as he knelt. Only a hint of his eyes was visible in the pools of silvery essence.

I drew in a shallow breath, but it did nothing to ease the faint trembling invading all my limbs. "I think…there's something wrong with me."

The shadows stilled under his flesh, deepening as the eather pulsed through his eyes, momentarily erasing his irises once more. His arm lifted.

My breath caught as his warm fingers touched my cheek, sending a faint energy shock through me. "Because you just tore apart a god with your hands, and I found that…kind of hot."

A ragged laugh came from someone, and I heard Ector mutter, "For fuck's sake…"

Some of the hardness went out of Nyktos's jaw. "You're hurt."

"No, I'm not."

"Liar." His fingers slipped from my cheek. He peeled the bloodied collar of the robe aside and cursed. The shadows went wild beneath his flesh, and I saw the faint outline of wings beginning to form behind him for a moment. But when he turned his head to the bloody boots nearing us and said, "Bury our dead and burn the rest," there was nothing there.

Nyktos moved astonishingly fast once more, folding an arm around my shoulders. I winced at the fresh wave of pain. He halted, his skin thinning and features sharpening. "Sorry."

"It's okay—" Shock flooded me as he worked his other arm under my knees and lifted me into his arms, cradling my unwounded shoulder against his chest. "Y-you don't have to carry me."

"I have to carry you." He started walking.

Heat crept into my face. "I'm fine."

"No, you're not, Seraphena."

"I'll be fine."

Nyktos stared straight ahead, a muscle ticking in his jaw.

"My legs work," I told him, starting to wiggle, but the burst of pain stilled me, making me dizzy.

He glanced down. "Tell me how fine you are again."

"I can walk," I muttered, closing my eyes because even being carried caused the torn muscles in my shoulder to throb to the point where it wasn't the dizziness that worried me but the nausea.

"I can *feel* your pain. Taste it."

"It's really...not that bad," I forced out, pressing my forehead against his chest as the shivers increased. I was so damn cold. "And there's...more important stuff to deal with."

"I'm dealing with the most important stuff right now."

I heard a door open, and then someone spoke in a hushed voice that faded out. Or did *I* fade out? I wasn't sure. But, for a brief second, nothing hurt, and my mind was blissfully empty. I wasn't thinking about what I'd seen out there. *Who* I'd seen.

"Davina," I said, "She's..."

"I know." His voice had quieted.

"I'm sorry," I whispered.

"As am I."

I breathed through the burn of sorrow. "What...what about Lethe?"

"Lethe is fine."

Relief rose. "But what of the wounded—?"

"I don't give a shit about any of that right now," he interrupted, his tone harshening. "You're shivering."

My eyes flew open as I tilted my head back. His gaze met mine. The essence had abated, leaving his eyes a sterling silver, and the shadows beneath his skin were now faint. "That's not true. You give a shit. And I'm just cold."

"You're *too* cold." A door slammed shut behind us as he strode into a chamber I thought was one of the many unused receiving areas of the main floor. "Just this once, can you stop arguing with me?"

"I'm not arguing." I clenched my jaw to stop my teeth from chattering.

A chair scraped across the stone floor as we neared the fireplace, following us like a loyal hound. I began to wonder if I was seeing things. "You are almost always arguing with me."

"No, I—" Flames roared to life, an intense silver before fading to a deep orange and red. "Was that you?"

"Yes. Impressed?"

"No," I lied.

Nyktos smirked as he lowered us into the chair that had moved itself closer to the fireplace. My head sort of fell back, resting in the crook of his arm. It took a moment for his features to piece themselves together. They were all hard, unforgiving lines. "I'm going to check your wounds."

He didn't exactly wait for me to answer, but I didn't stop him either. Soaking up the warmth of his body and the nearby fire, I forced myself to concentrate. "There was a god out there."

"There were a lot of gods out there, Sera."

"I know, but this one...wasn't an entombed god. I don't think he was from the Shadowlands. Or at least I hope not," I said, and his hand halted as he reached for the sash. "He was looking for me. He knew what I looked like. Said he...thought he'd have to go into the palace to find me. Orphine sort of burned him to nothing."

"Did this god say anything else?"

"Yeah. He smelled my blood and said it smelled like life," I told him, inhaling slowly as I struggled to ignore the pain. "And like blood and ash."

The eather in Nyktos's eyes went still.

"Does my blood smell like that?" I asked as I sniffed the air. All I smelled was iron—iron and fresh citrus. My blood and Nyktos's. "That sounds gross."

"No, your blood smells like a summer storm."

My brows pinched. How could blood smell like that? Better yet, what did that even smell like?

Nyktos undid the sash of my robe. The front loosened. His breath was sharp as he parted the folds. "Fuck. The bite is deep."

"I was hoping it was the lack of clothing you were cursing at," I murmured.

A short, rough laugh left him. "You are..."

My eyes fluttered shut. "What?"

"Open your eyes, Sera."

I obeyed, only because he'd asked so softly—almost like a plea. His head was bowed, only his profile to me as he carefully peeled the robe back from my shoulder, easing my left arm free of a sleeve and then my right. He cursed. "You were bit twice."

I glanced at my shoulder, seeing the jagged tears there and the wet streaks of blood that drenched the chest of my slip.

"Your muscles are torn in both your shoulder and arm." His skin thinned again. "You fought your way free."

"Yeah, I think I might need to spend some time with a Healer." I didn't want to think about what he saw—about what that meant for the future, no matter how short it was. Muscles didn't always heal right, and I needed those muscles. "I hope the coronation gown isn't sleeveless."

"You won't scar. My blood will make sure that doesn't happen."

I couldn't have heard him right. "*What?*"

"You're in the Culling. You can't afford to lose this much blood, nor can your body work to heal these wounds while you're under the stress of the Culling."

"The wounds aren't that bad. I...I'm not going to die."

"No, but you're in pain, and I cannot allow that to continue. I won't."

Air snagged around a sudden knot of foreign emotion. I couldn't believe that he was offering *his* blood. To *me*. I would survive waiting for a Healer. Stopping my pain wasn't necessary. None of this was. "You should be out there with your people—"

"I'm where I'm needed," he cut me off again. "Take my blood."

My gaze darted between his wrist and his arm. "Why are you...?" I trailed off. I knew why he was offering. Maybe it was that he didn't want to see me in pain. Nyktos was kind. But also, the embers were important. "I'll be—"

I sucked in a sharp breath as he brought his wrist to his mouth. My heart might've stopped a little as his lips parted, and his fangs pierced his skin. Nyktos didn't even flinch, but I did as blood welled from his vein, a bright red with shimmery blue undertones.

"Let me help you, Sera." His voice dropped to a whisper. "Please."

A shudder went through me. *Please.* Hearing him saying *please*...it was a weakness.

"You'll enjoy it," he said. "I promise."

I glanced at the shimmering blood beginning to run over his skin. Drinking blood didn't disgust me. It just wasn't something I'd really considered all that much. But I didn't think I would *enjoy* it. Though the tiny drop of blood I had stolen from him hadn't tasted like blood.

"Okay," I whispered.

His eyes closed briefly. "Thank you."

Those two words rattled me even more than him saying *please* as he lowered his wrist to my mouth. The scent of his blood reached me, overwhelming the smell of mine. His was…it was almost sweet but also smoky.

"Close your mouth over the bite," he coaxed softly. "And drink."

His eyes, now bright as the stars, never left mine as I closed my mouth over the wounds he'd created.

My entire body jerked.

The touch of his blood against my tongue was a much stronger shock to the senses than when I'd recklessly tasted just a drop and sealed my fate, breaking off the one thread Holland had pointed to. Immediately, my mouth tingled. His blood ran over my tongue and down my throat, thick and warm, and I didn't know how death could taste like honey—both sweet and smoky. Lush. Seductive. I swallowed.

Nyktos shuddered as he pressed his wrist more firmly against my mouth. "Keep drinking."

I drank, taking a deeper, longer draw as his stare remained fixed on mine. The tingling sensation moved down my throat as his blood hit my chest, warming me—warming the embers there. They *vibrated*. My stomach warmed next. His blood…gods, I'd never tasted anything like it before.

"Good," he said, his voice deeper and raspy. "You're doing good. Just a little bit more."

Only a bit more? I could imagine never stopping. My eyes drifted shut as I drank from the Primal of Death, taking his very essence into me. Starting in my lips, the warmth hit my veins and spread. I didn't realize how tightly my hands were clenched until my fingers relaxed. The throbbing in my arm and shoulder began to fade as I felt the touch of his fingers against my cheek and then higher. He brushed some hair back from my face as I drank and drank. The warmth continued sliding through me, the tingling sensation following. Then I felt…I felt like those brief moments when I allowed myself to slip under the surface of my lake, where my thoughts stilled, and I could just be me. Where I found peace.

Like the kind Nektas said that I brought to Nyktos. Peace that allowed him to sleep deeply when I was near. I wanted that to be true, maybe even more desperately than I wanted to stay where I was, but Nyktos eased his wrist from me. I watched the wounds close with heavy eyes, his skin smoothing until no sign of his bite remained.

"Wow," I whispered.

"Impressed now?"

"No."

He raised a brow.

"A little," I admitted, still tasting his blood—on my lips, my tongue, and inside me, making me all tingly and warm. I shivered as his hand left my hair and slid down my cheek, but I wasn't cold. His touch...it was *amplified*. I felt it everywhere.

"Much better," Nyktos murmured.

I followed his stare to my shoulder, where there'd been jagged, angry tears moments ago. The skin was pink and slightly raised, but that was all. "Good gods."

Nyktos's thumb drifted over my chin, turning my attention from my shoulder. "How are you feeling?"

I...I really didn't know. "My skin is humming."

"It's my—" Nyktos stiffened as I flicked my tongue over my lower lip, finding the lingering taste of his blood there. Wisps of eather spread out from behind his pupils. "It's my blood," he finished, his tone rugged. Coarse.

"I can feel it—your blood." My gaze fixed on that single strand of hair resting against his cheek. I knew we had important things to discuss, but I became solely focused on the heat of him, more concentrated where the wounds had been—and in other places. "Your blood is really...*hot*."

Thick lashes lowered. "Is it?"

"Mm-hmm," I murmured, lifting an arm that no longer hurt. I curled my fingers around the strand of hair. My thoughts glided from one thing to another. "You're not mad at me?"

"For what?"

"I didn't stay inside."

"Right now, I'm just glad you're not dead." His head tilted slightly. "Ask me if I'm mad later."

I laughed. "I think I'll pass on that."

Nyktos had gone still again, but inside, I was anything but. Everything thrummed: my blood, muscles, nerve endings. "I feel different."

"At the risk of sounding repetitive, it's my blood."

"I didn't feel like this the last time." I took the strand of hair and tucked it behind his ear.

"You only had a drop last time." His eyes closed as I drew my fingers along the curve of his cheek, feeling the texture of his skin. It was smooth, like his blood, giving way to the faint scratch of stubble. "Not nearly enough to feel any of these effects."

"The humming?" I kept exploring, tracing the outline of his jaw to the corner of his lips, knowing he would never allow me to touch him like this at any other time. I would never let myself. "The tingling?"

"The heat." The tips of his fangs appeared between his parted lips, and a heaviness settled in my chest at the sight of them. It wasn't the painful pressure of anxiety but a sinful weight that sent a razor-sharp pulse of desire through me. "The essence in a god's blood has many effects, but they come on far quicker and stronger when it's the blood of a Primal."

"Oh," I murmured, following the lush curve of his lower lip.

Nyktos was quiet for several moments. "You miss your lake, don't you?"

My gaze flew to his as my fingers halted. "I do."

"I could tell."

"How could...?" I trailed off as he leaned into my hand. The pads of my fingers slipped over his lower lip. Muscles low in my stomach loosened and then clenched as my blood—*his* blood—pumped through me. An ache blossomed in the very center of me, so sudden and potent that I drew in a ragged breath.

"What other...effects does your blood have?" I asked, surprised by the throatiness of my voice.

"It can cause a brief sensation of general wellness. A high. It can make you feel stronger. Lure you into believing you're invincible." Nyktos's lashes swept up, and the tendrils of eather swirled lazily. "It can also make you *want*."

Desire licked through me, leaving behind a pounding flood of arousal. "I want," I whispered. "Very badly."

His nostrils flared as his fingers skated over my jaw. "I know."

My chest rose with a deep breath, and I wasn't sure if that helped or worsened things as the tips of my breasts brushed his arm. I lifted my other hand, pressing it to my heart, where I felt it beating fast. My fingers spread out, grazing a hardened nipple. The ache intensified as he drew his hand down the side of my neck and across my shoulder. The slight touch echoed through my entire body. My back arched as I bit my lower lip, moaning as I tasted traces of his blood there.

"It will only last a couple of minutes." His fingers stopped at the thin strap of my slip.

"Only a couple of minutes?" I rasped, my throat drying even as I grew *wetter*.

Nyktos stretched his neck, the cords and tendons there standing out starkly. "They will be the longest minutes of my life."

"Yours?" I laughed shakily, a little—or a lot—breathless from the slick rush of desire flooding me. My hand fell to his tattered shirt. Behind my palm, I felt his heart racing. My hips shifted, brushing against the thick, hard ridge of his arousal.

"I can sense your need. Feel it. Taste it. You're drowning in it." His eyes slammed shut. "I'm fucking drowning in it."

A sharp dart of desire sliced through me. "Then drown with me."

5

Eather brightened, spreading into the veins of the skin beneath his eyes as tension bracketed the corners of his lips. "What you're feeling is my blood, Sera."

"I don't think so." I breathed in deeply, taking in his scent. "What I'm feeling is how I always feel when you touch me. Like there is a fire in my blood."

Nyktos's fingers curled around the strap of the slip. His eyes opened, but only into thin slits. "Sera…"

"Hot. Wet. Aching." I squeezed my thighs together, but that did nothing to ease the throbbing there. "*Wanted.*"

The strap of the slip moved an inch and then two, taking the bloodied neckline with it. His teeth dragged over his lower lip as I gripped his wrist. He didn't stop me as I pulled his hand and the strap farther down my arm. I gasped as the lacy hem scratched the sensitive tips of my breasts. "*Please.*"

Nyktos made a rough sound that rumbled through every inch of my body. "I know better." His churning eyes lifted to mine, and his hand moved on its own now, drawing the strap over my wrist. "And yet…"

My pulse pounded fast as his hand dropped to the side of my hip, mine following his. His gaze left mine and glided over the blood-streaked swells of my breasts. I felt the tendons beneath my fingers as his hand tightened on my hip and then relaxed, coasting over my thigh and then under the hem.

The arm around me tightened as he bent over me, lowering his head. His lips glanced over the side of my throat, and the memory of *his* bite went a long way to erase the pain of the one delivered by the entombed god. He lifted my upper body slightly as his mouth moved over the healed skin. The touch of his tongue against my flesh sent a shockwave of sensation through me. I watched his mouth follow the glistening trail of blood down and then up over the swell of my breast. His tongue licked the blood. "I...I don't think I can breathe."

"Yes, you can."

I gasped as his mouth closed over my nipple, drawing it and my spent blood into his mouth. My hips jerked, pushing against his arousal. He caught the turgid flesh between his lips as he lifted his mouth and then his head.

"Open for me." He issued the ragged demand as he lifted the slip to my waist, baring me to him.

My stomach twisted with anticipation as my legs parted without hesitation. His intense stare drifted past my hips to the fine dusting of hair as his fingers pressed into the flesh of my thigh. "Show me."

Oh, gods. A red-hot bolt of shameless desire rocked me. Breathing fast, I gripped his wrist as my fingers spread over the skin below my navel. Nyktos's stare was unblinking, all-consuming.

"Show me." His voice was a silky whisper of midnight. "I want to see your fingers slick with your desire."

I sucked in a soft moan. My fingers grazed the dampness between my thighs. The chamber felt as if it were holding its breath, waiting right along with me. With Nyktos. The wait wasn't long. Slipping my finger inside my damp heat, my hips jerked against my hand as I gasped. The curling twist of pleasure deep inside was downright scandalous.

"That's it," he said in that same coaxing, seductive voice from when I had been taking his blood. "Fuck your fingers."

The punch of raw desire left me dizzy as I moved my finger in and out—his gaze fixed on my movements. He knew the exact second I eased another finger inside myself, and his eyes feasted on what he saw. This was utterly *wicked*, and I loved it.

Nyktos shifted me in his lap, drawing me farther against the hard ridge of his arousal. I rode my hand, rocked against his cock—

"Ash?" Nektas called from the hall. "You in there?"

I stopped, my heart lurching as my wide eyes swung to the door.

"I'm busy." Nyktos's stare remained focused between my legs.

"With Sera?"

I choked on a breath. Exactly how good were a draken's senses?

"Yes," Nyktos said, folding his hand over mine. My attention snapped to my spread thighs. He eased my fingers back inside. My hips nearly jerked completely off his lap. Oh, gods. A sinful bolt of pleasure whipped through me. "Don't stop."

"What?" came Nektas's muffled response.

Stark hollows formed under Nyktos's cheeks. "Wasn't talking to you."

"Okay." There was a pause. "She all right?"

Nyktos was breathing heavily as he watched me, feeling my fingers moving beneath his. "Yeah, she...she will be."

"You two need anything?"

"*Nektas*," Nyktos snapped, and I turned my head against his chest, smothering a moan as my knees curled.

"All right. All right," the draken replied. "I'll check back in a bit."

"You do that." Nyktos's fingers moved over mine, controlling the rhythm as I rubbed against his cock.

My head fell back, eyes closing and breathing coming in quick, short pants as tension curled tighter and tighter. His breath coasted over my breast. I cried out as his mouth closed over the throbbing flesh, and he sucked on my skin, on the spilled blood. My fingers moved faster, harder. Pleasure trembled deep within me. He groaned, pulling me closer, holding my ass to his cock. The sounds I made...gods, I should be ashamed, but I wasn't. I wanted him to hear them. I wanted him to feel the wetness coating my fingers. I wanted him to know that the way my body responded to him had so very little to do with his blood and everything to do with him. I wanted nothing between us. I wanted to feel the hard length of him against my skin. I wanted him inside me. I wanted him to pierce me, take me into him. I wanted so much—

The graze of his fangs over my nipple was too much. I came hard, falling over the edge as he shuddered against me. My breast muffled his harsh groan. Pleasure continued unwinding and spinning throughout my body until I was left limp and utterly boneless in his arms.

I was still trembling as he eased my fingers from me. My eyes opened, and I watched him...watched him lift my hand to his lips. He closed his mouth over my glistening fingers and sucked deeply.

"Gods," I moaned, my breath catching.

There couldn't be a drop of me left on my fingers by the time he finished. Quicksilver eyes met mine, and then thick lashes lowered as he kept our joined hands near his lips. "How do you feel now?" he asked thickly.

I opened my mouth, at a loss for words as I became aware of dampness against the curve of my ass, where his semi-hard arousal rested. He…he had found release. "Better. Much better."

"Good," he said, and that was all he said for a time.

In the silence that followed, my heart slowed, but the heat of his touch remained, while that of his blood faded. I stared at his hand folded around my fingers, his skin several shades deeper than mine. I…I liked it when he held my hand, and a…

A *want* still remained.

One different than all those earlier desires. I didn't want to leave this moment of him holding me to him, against his chest with my hand in his. This moment of his lowered lashes fanning his cheeks and the line of his relaxed jaw. I didn't want to leave this moment of *peace*.

But we had to.

I had to.

Because these moments wouldn't last. I knew that when those lashes lifted and he looked down upon the one who had planned to seduce and murder him, there would be regret in those silver eyes, no matter if he claimed that he was only *annoyed* by my betrayal. I didn't want to see that.

I wanted to remember *these* moments because what happened tonight had revealed a painful truth that couldn't be denied. There would be no more of *this*.

Because I knew what I had to do.

I slipped my hand free. His head lifted, and I quickly looked away as I gathered the bloodied halves of my robe. "Nektas will be returning soon?"

"He will."

"Okay." I swallowed, still tasting the lingering honey of his blood. I started to move.

"Careful," Nyktos said, taking hold of the robe and closing the halves over me. "You may feel strong, but you could be a little dizzy."

"I feel fine." I sat up slowly. Nyktos's arm tightened around my waist. "I need to clean up."

A long moment passed, and then his arm loosened. "I'll send water to your chambers."

I nodded as I slid out of his lap. Holding the robe together, I hurried across the room. I grasped the door handle, feeling his stare on my back. My eyes closed briefly. "Thank you."

There was no answer.

I opened the door and left, leaving Nyktos and those peaceful moments behind.

An hour later, I sat in the war room, the closed-off chamber located behind the thrones, tracking the numerous daggers and swords lining the walls. The last time I'd been in here, it was after I'd learned the truth about the Rot.

And Nyktos had learned the truth about me.

The chamber gave me bad vibes.

I decided it needed windows. Softer chairs. A table not so carved up by the gods only knew how many weapons. Less bloodstained armor of those in attendance.

My slippered foot began tapping off the stone floor as I twisted my hair between my fingers. Cleaning all the blood from my skin and hair without using the tub had been difficult. I'd tried to get inside. I'd even made it as far as standing in it, but as soon as I began to lower myself, I started feeling the sash digging into my throat. I'd scrambled out, nearly slipping on the tile in my haste. I'd felt foolish as I resorted to dunking my head in the water to wash my hair. I still felt silly. Weak. But I didn't know how to get past it.

And it really didn't matter at this point.

"There were at least three gods involved in the attack," Theon was saying, drawing my attention to him and his twin sister. Their armor was stained with blood, and their deep brown faces looked somber and tired. It had to be getting close to morning. "Including the one Orphine killed. I didn't recognize the two I saw as being from Attes's Court."

The twins were originally from Vathi, where Attes and his brother Kyn's Court was located. Apparently, it was the closest Court to the Shadowlands, and it seemed fitting to me that War and Vengeance would be located near Death.

"I didn't recognize the one I saw talking to Sera," Bele said from where she sat, cross-legged *on* the table.

Lailah's tightly braided hair swayed above her shoulders as she leaned back, looking down at the table. "And I'm guessing you didn't recognize the draken?"

I followed her gaze to where Nektas sat. There was a whole lot of coppery skin on display since he wore only a pair of loose, black pants. I tried not to stare at him, but I was fascinated by the pattern of faint lines over his shoulders and chest.

"I know it may come as a shock to all, but I don't know every single draken," Nektas answered. He hadn't spoken much since we'd all gathered here. I imagined his thoughts were on Davina. Had he been close to her? Did she have family?

Lailah stared at him, her brows raised.

"All I know is that I got the sense the draken was young," Nektas added. "Too young to be up to that kind of shit."

That had been a young draken?

"They could've been from any Court," Nyktos said from behind two fingers that tapped his lower lip slowly. Fingers that had—

I cut those really inappropriate thoughts off as I peeked at Nyktos. I sat directly to his right, only because that was where he'd basically put me after retrieving me from my chambers. He'd swept his hair back in a knot at the nape of his neck and replaced the tattered shirt with a new one. Tension had returned to the set of his jaw and shoulders.

The moments of peace were truly gone.

I'd waited by the doors in my chambers, luckily catching the sound of his door closing. I'd figured he was leaving to speak with his guards about what had occurred, and I wanted to know what he would say. He'd appeared surprised by my request to join him but hadn't stopped me. Though, he hadn't said much and had barely looked at me. I...knew regret had found him, even though he had clearly been an active participant in what'd happened and had also found release. I shifted in the chair, the wool sweater suddenly too thick.

"They could be," Rhain agreed. He sat across from me, his reddish-gold hair redder in the light. He'd stared at my wrists as soon as he sat beside me. Just as Bele had when she entered. I had a feeling they were the only two who sensed the charm, but the rest had been told about it. "But how many Primals would be bold enough to pull a stunt like that?"

"Does it require bravery when it wasn't them who carried out the act?" Nyktos countered.

Rhain nodded slowly. "Good point."

"It was likely Hanan." Bele spat the Primal's name like a curse. "He has cause to be upset, and he is one Primal definitely not brave enough to come to the Shadowlands himself to see if I've truly Ascended." Bele slid off the table and began to walk. She was a pacer like me. "Those entombed gods were freed to create a distraction—enough time to grab my ass. People died because of it. I shouldn't be here. I need to leave."

"You're where you're needed," Nyktos told her.

"I told her that." Aios watched Bele, her deep red hair a shock of color against her pale cheeks. "She doesn't want to hear it."

"He wants me here because it's safer," Bele countered as she came to stand beside Nektas.

Aios sighed, shaking her head. "And as I also said, there's nothing wrong with safety."

"She's right, and it can mean both things." Nyktos brushed a strand of hair back from his face. "I need you here, where it happens to be safer for you."

Bele's chin lifted. "I can't stay hidden forever. I don't want to. I refuse to."

"I'm not suggesting that. But for the time being, you need to keep a low profile. Hanan and others may believe you've Ascended, but until they've seen you, they can't one hundred percent confirm that."

"You're not the one drawing them here." I spoke up, and the hair swung around Bele's chin as she jerked her head toward me. Several pairs of eather-filled eyes landed on me. Nyktos had shared with them what I knew, but like Nektas, I hadn't said much during the meeting. I cleared my throat. "It's what I did. You shouldn't feel responsible for any of this."

Her brow pinched. "And you should?"

"Obviously. I'm the one who did it."

"What you did saved my life—and thank you for that," she said, two pink splotches appearing on her cheeks. "I don't know if I said that yet."

I nodded, feeling my face warm, as well.

"I don't get how that god could be looking for you," Ector said from my other side. "Neither Hanan nor Kolis knows what you look like. None of the Primals have been here to see you."

"Except for Veses," Rhain said.

I immediately scowled. I'd only seen the Primal of Rites and Prosperity once, and she'd been overly touchy with Nyktos. So much so that I'd assumed they had some sort of relationship. But there had been…no one else before me. "Veses didn't see me when she was here." I looked at Nyktos. "Right?"

A muscle flexed in Nyktos's jaw as he stared at Rhain. He nodded.

"People have seen her—at Court, when it was held here," Theon pointed out. "And on the Rise the night the dakkais attacked. She's a new face. Doesn't take a leap of logic to put two and two together and end up with the Consort. It could've been Hanan, and he'd given orders to find both Bele and her."

Nyktos's eyes flashed to him. "Our people would never betray her identity to another Court."

"How can you be sure?" My foot stopped its tapping. I wasn't even sure what I was doing here. None of what would be discussed or possibly revealed would matter.

"Because I am."

I waited for him to elaborate. He didn't. "Need I remind you of Hamid?" The godling had lived in Lethe and had befriended the young Chosen that still resided in one of the chambers above. He had been the one to report Gemma missing, and by all accounts, was known to be generous and kind. He was also known to carry a deep-rooted hatred of Kolis because he'd killed his mother—a goddess—and destroyed her soul. He, like many others, was so afraid of the false Primal of Life that when Gemma had told him I had to be the one Kolis had been searching for, he'd seen me for what I already knew to be true. That I was a threat to the sanctuary the Shadowlands offered. I didn't fault her for what Hamid had attempted afterward. Part of me couldn't really even blame *him*.

I probably would've done the same.

Except I would've been successful, where he had failed.

"Not like I've forgotten that." Nyktos's fingers stilled. "But that was different."

"Not to be *argumentative*," I said, and his eyes narrowed, "but exactly how is that different?"

"Because Hamid thought he was protecting the Shadowlands," Rhain answered, his stare far colder than it had been when I'd first arrived. Except for Aios, none had been extremely friendly before, but Rhain had been warmer than he was now.

Lailah nodded. "And what was done here tonight threatened the safety of the Shadowlands. Those who seek shelter here wouldn't jeopardize that."

"It's possible that a god from another Court was here the night the dakkais attacked," Nektas added. "Saw you at the right moment and gave a good enough description to allow someone to grab you."

"Or let me die," I said. "That god wasn't there on orders that required me to survive the attack."

Nyktos slowly turned his head to me. "Come again?"

"He saw an entombed god creeping up on me and did nothing to stop it." I frowned. "I thought I told you that."

He lowered his hand to the table. "You didn't."

"Oh." I sat back, twisting my hair. "So, yeah, I don't think they wanted me alive. Maybe just out of the picture, which kind of makes me think it wasn't Kolis, if what Penellaphe said about the embers of life is true." *And considering that I carry Sotoria's soul,* but I didn't tack that on. As far as I knew, those in the room only knew that I carried an ember of life.

"Well, whoever was behind it almost got what they wanted…" Bele trailed off as the air in the war room chilled.

A tangible tension flooded the space. Swords and daggers rattled on the wall. My eyes lifted to the ceiling as the overhead lights flickered.

"Ash." Nektas called his name softly.

Slowly, I looked at Nyktos. Shadows had appeared under Nyktos's skin. The air *crackled.* "Almost," I reiterated quietly.

Whirling silver eyes met mine. The essence slowed, and the charge of energy gradually faded from the room. His gaze dropped to where my fingers rested on his arm.

I was *touching* him.

In front of others.

I hadn't even realized I'd done it. Feeling my cheeks warm, I jerked my hand away. I didn't think Nyktos appreciated it. Touching in those rare, intimate moments after he'd given me his blood didn't equate to him wanting my touch whenever. I stared at the scarred table, breathing through the sting of…disappointment. But in what? Him? Me? I glanced up, and Rhain's icy stare met mine.

Clasping my hands together in my lap so I kept them to myself, I cleared my throat again. "Anyway, I just don't think it makes sense that it was Hanan. Wouldn't he want me alive? Wouldn't any of the Primals who figure my arrival and Bele's Ascension are related want me alive so they could hand me over to Kolis?"

"A Primal had to be behind this," Nektas said. "No other could command a draken to attack. The question is which one? Who would know or suspect enough about you to be willing to anger both Nyktos and Kolis by allowing you to die?"

Nobody had an answer to Nektas's question, likely because no one knew which Primal would be willing to anger both the Primal of Death and potentially the false Primal of Life.

To be honest, I wasn't worried about that as much as I was the risk to all the others if this mystery Primal launched another attack. Or if Kolis grew tired of just being curious over the embers and decided to summon Nyktos to find out what happened. My stomach pitched as my skin chilled.

"You were injured?" Aios asked as she walked with me to my chambers.

I glanced at the goddess. The shadows smudging the skin under Aios's citrine eyes worried me. The hollows of her heart-shaped face were deeper than before, and her concern was clear in the press of her full lips.

"Not much."

"That wasn't the impression I got from Bele." Aios tucked a strand of hair behind her ear. "She said you were bitten."

"Barely," I lied, not even sure why I didn't want to share what Nyktos had done for me. Maybe because a part of me couldn't believe it. "Are you staying here tonight—or what's left of tonight?"

Aios nodded. "I've been staying close because of Gemma."

Gods, the Chosen must've been terrified during the attack. "Can I see her?"

Aios looked away. "Maybe later."

Tension settled into my shoulders as I trailed my fingers along the cool, smooth stone of the railing. There could be a ton of reasons why I couldn't see Gemma now, starting with the fact that she was probably asleep. But my mind immediately went to the worst one. What if Aios didn't want me around the once-Chosen?

Aios had acknowledged that I hadn't wanted to harm Nyktos, but acknowledgment didn't equate to forgiveness. She'd been forthcoming with information when I first arrived, when most—including Nyktos—

hadn't. Aios had been kind and welcoming, but I had disappointed her. I'd heard that in her voice and seen it in her expression. In the brief times we'd been together since she'd learned the truth, Aios hadn't been as friendly as before, and that stung. Because I liked her.

I swallowed a sigh as we rounded the third floor. "How is Gemma?"

"She's okay. Physically." Aios smoothed a hand over a cream panel of her gown, her features pinching. "But I think it will be a while before the mind catches up with her body."

I wished my touch could heal those kinds of wounds, the deeper ones that no one could see. Glancing at Aios, I zeroed in on the shadows under her eyes. The empathy she'd shown Gemma when we'd spoken with her had come from a place of experience. Aios shared that same haunted look with Penellaphe.

And I had a feeling if Nyktos hadn't taken me as his Consort when he did, and I'd been left to my stepbrother's cruel and depraved whims, I would've had those shadows in my eyes, too.

"I worry that the guilt she feels rivals her fear," she added after a moment.

"What Hamid did wasn't her fault." My grip tightened on the shadowstone railing. "And Bele shouldn't blame herself for what happened tonight either."

"Neither should you. You saved Bele's life. You did nothing wrong."

"I…" I looked away from Aios, my gaze traveling to the foyer below. "When I brought Bele back, I didn't know that it would Ascend her."

"If you had known what would happen, would that have changed things?" Aios stopped on the step above, her eyes meeting mine. "Does knowing what will happen change what you would do if presented with that choice again?"

I started to say yes but couldn't because I'd wanted to bring Davina back. I would have if Ector hadn't stopped me. If it happened again to another I knew? Someone Nyktos cared for, and no one was there to stop me?

A faint smile appeared, and then she turned, continuing up the stairs. "In a way, I'm not sure you have a choice. You have an ember of life in you," she said as we reached the fourth floor, not knowing that I actually had *embers* of life in me. "It may have been a part of Eythos when he lived, but now, it's a part of you. Creating life out of death is in your nature. It's instinct."

"Yeah," I said, sighing as we reached the fourth floor. "But it doesn't feel that way sometimes."

No one was outside my chamber, but I figured it wouldn't stay that way for long. Aios hadn't lingered as I entered the room, where the faint, acrid scent of smoke remained. It was for the best, but I wished she'd spent a little more time. I would've liked to learn what her home was like away from the palace. Or how she'd become so close with Bele.

But I wouldn't discover these things.

I glanced at the adjoining door. Just like I'd never know if Nyktos had a favorite book or food. If he could remember his dreams or if he dreamt at all. Who or what he would choose to be if he had a choice to be anyone but himself. There were so many things I wanted to learn about him. Did he remember much about his father? Did he read or allow his thoughts to wander when he had spare, quiet moments? Did he like to visit the mortal realm?

Did he regret having his *kardia* removed?

But what I already knew was enough to know that he didn't deserve what this kind of life had dealt him: the loss of his parents and so many more, a Consort he'd never asked for but still had sought to protect, and living under the constant threat of Kolis. Nyktos deserved better. So did everyone in the Shadowlands.

And now I posed an entirely different threat to him and all who sought sanctuary here.

I walked out onto the balcony and looked down at the courtyard. The area had already been cleared, and only faint dark marks remained on the ground. I couldn't let myself think about what those splotches represented. I needed a clear head as I watched the guards patrol the Rise.

The embers were important. I understood that—contrary to what Nyktos thought. The sooner I died, the less time the mortal realm would have. I didn't know why Eythos put the embers in my bloodline, along with Sotoria's soul. Especially since that soul made me the perfect weapon against Kolis.

Not a Consort-to-be, hidden and protected.

Not a vessel that would be able to keep the embers safe.

I had a purpose, and there was no delaying it—no matter how distasteful it was, and no matter how much I wanted it all to be different.

I waited until I couldn't do so any longer. There was no activity in the courtyard, and I imagined that anyone who had been beyond the Rise had left the woods by now. I had no idea where Nyktos was, but I didn't think he'd returned to his chambers yet. There had been talk of meeting with the families of those who had perished tonight. My heart clenched. He could be anywhere, and I had no way of knowing if the path I had to follow was clear, but they were all risks I had to take.

Turning, I went back inside and headed to the bathing chamber, where I tugged off my leggings as I had been told they were called. They were thicker than tights but nothing like the breeches. I pulled a pair of those on, ignoring the stiff patches of dried blood as I shoved the slip I wore beneath the sweater into the waistband of the pants. Tugging on my boots, I grabbed a cloak and began fastening the hooks at the throat as I walked under the stunning glass chandelier to the balcony doors. Grasping the handle, I looked over my shoulder to the door leading to the adjoining room. My hand trembled.

I hesitated, looking at Nyktos's chambers. I thought about the blanket I'd woken covered in. Had it been him who'd done that?

"I'm sorry," I whispered, breathing through the sting in my throat and eyes. I wished he could hear those words and that he believed them.

I wished for many things in those seconds before turning back to the balcony, blinking back dampness. My shoulders tightening, I lifted the hood and stepped out onto the balcony before quietly closing the door behind me, focused on only what lay ahead.

I glanced toward the Red Woods, where the damaged gate once stood. The still-standing crimson trees stood out starkly against the iron sky. Entering those woods again where the fallen gods lay entombed was the last thing I wanted to do, but at least I knew they'd been cleared of any fallen gods. As long as I didn't bleed in them, I'd be fine. From there, I had to cut through a small section of the Dying Woods, another place I wasn't even remotely looking forward to traveling through, but it was the only way to get to where I needed to be in Lethe.

Ships entered the city through the Black Bay, meaning they were coming from other places within Iliseeum. I was confident that I could get on a ship and then to Dalos, the City of the Gods, where Kolis held Court.

Because other than killing, there was one more thing I was extraordinarily good at—not being seen.

I caught sight of an armored figure in black and gray patrolling the Rise's battlement. Pressing against the wall, I kept to the shadows and waited until they were out of sight. Then I sprang forward and didn't give myself time to think about how *reckless* this was. There was no time left to wait. I only had a few hours until dawn when someone would eventually come to my chambers. Gripping the cool shadowstone railing, I climbed over it and looked over my shoulder into the empty space between me and the hard-packed ground below.

That was a significant, bone-breaking distance.

Kneeling, I lowered my right and then left leg out into the vast nothingness. Muscles straining and burning like the fiery pits of the Abyss, I drew in a shallow breath and then stretched out my right leg until it felt like my arms would pull out of their sockets. My fingers slipped a little against the shadowstone just as I managed to reach the closest arrow slit.

I didn't want to think about if those slits had been a necessary addition. Once I was certain my foot was stable in the narrow opening, I lifted a hand from the railing and reached for a groove to grip. My stomach tumbled, then I let go and swung to the arrow slit.

Wobbling a little, I pressed my forehead against the stone. "Good gods," I whispered. "This is idiotic."

Planting my feet against the wall, I began to lower myself once more. All those years spent alone, climbing trees, walls, and anything even remotely vertical out of pure boredom had actually paid off. Glancing at the spiral staircase's railing below, I went for it, swinging myself down.

I landed on the railing and nearly toppled backward. Catching myself, I hopped down onto the landing. A wide smile broke out across my face. Proud of myself and somewhat surprised that I hadn't fallen to a gruesome, painful death, I wheeled around and hurried down the steps...and right into a dead end.

"Oh, for fuck's sake." Of course, I'd chosen a staircase that, for some godsforsaken reason, didn't go to the actual ground.

Leaning over the railing, I gauged the drop to be about seven feet. Shifting so I could hang from the railing, I said a little prayer to myself and let go.

There was a brief second of weightlessness, nothing but the bright stars overhead, and the rush of air on my skin. It felt like *flying*, and for a heartbeat of time, I was free—

The impact rattled me from the tips of my toes to the top of my hooded head, knocking a low grunt out of me. I stumbled forward, catching myself with my palms before I kissed the ground. I remained there for a couple of seconds, dragging in deep breaths as surprisingly dull spikes of pain darted through my knees and hips. That should've hurt more.

But I did have Primal blood in me.

Straightening slowly, I then took off for the gate, knowing there wasn't that much time between patrols. Within minutes, the packed earth gave way to the crunch of gray grass, and then I was under the canopy of leaves the color of blood and no longer within view of the House of Haides.

And I was one obstacle closer to fulfilling my duty—my true destiny.

6

Killing Kolis wouldn't be easy.

Obviously.

Even if Kolis recognized Sotoria's soul—saw me as her—I doubted it would be as simple as me plunging a dagger into his chest. I would have to be sure that he loved me first, and I couldn't even let myself think about what that would involve as I ran under the canopy of crimson leaves. If I allowed myself to entertain those ideas, I would be vomiting all over myself. So, I filed that away.

I didn't even know what killing Kolis would do—what kind of impact it would have on Iliseeum and the mortal realm—but Holland wouldn't have told me what he had if it were something catastrophic. The fact that Nyktos was a Primal of Death must mean there would still be balance.

Until I died.

Which would likely be as soon as I succeeded in thrusting my shadowstone dagger into Kolis's chest. I imagined that he, too, had draken that would immediately retaliate.

But right now, luck was on my side for once. I entered the Dying Woods without any issues. Probably because I'd run the whole way. The hood of my cloak had slipped, but I left it down as I doubted I would run into anyone in an area occupied by Shades—souls who had entered the Shadowlands but refused to face judgment for deeds committed when they were alive by passing between the Pillars of Asphodel. I had yet to see a Shade, and I really hoped that didn't change, considering I'd heard they could be *bitey*.

The muscles in my legs and stomach were beginning to cramp, forcing me to slow as I continuously scanned the thick rows of bent and broken trees. Each breath I drew reminded me of the Rot—stale lilacs. At least there was no ache in my jaw and temples or dizziness. I had no idea how long I had before the mixture of herbs—chasteberry, peppermint, and a whole bunch I couldn't remember—wore off, and the effects of the Culling set in once more. But when it did, I would have to do what I always did.

Deal with it.

Just like I knew Ezra would if she learned there was nothing to be done about the Rot. We might not share even a drop of blood, but she was resilient. Like me, she wouldn't give up. Nor would she pretend as if the end weren't coming, or hope for a magical fix like I knew my mother would. Ezra would do everything in her power to ensure that as many people as possible survived for as long as they could.

According to Holland, she was already doing that. Even if I could never get word to her, she was taking necessary steps—

A rattle from above drew my gaze to the dead, gnarled, and leafless branches. I jerked to a complete stop as a hawk—an enormous silver one—glided through the twisted branches, its massive wings spread wide, slowing its descent. The bird of prey landed on one of the limbs, its sharp, dark talons digging into the dead bark.

It looked just like the hawk I'd unintentionally healed in the Red Woods. But then again, I imagined most did. I was still surprised to see any animals in the Shadowlands other than horses and whatever the hell the dakkais were.

While I was relieved that it wasn't a Shade perched above me, silver hawks were notoriously fierce predators. I hadn't believed my old nursemaid Odetta when she'd told me stories of how they could pick up small animals and even children. But now, seeing one up close twice, I totally believed the hawks could do just that—maybe even snatch a slender adult.

I'd never been more grateful for my love of bread and pastries than right then.

The silver hawk slowly lowered its wings as I took a tentative step forward, hoping it remained right where it was and didn't try to make a meal out of me. The last thing I wanted was to harm any animal—well, except barrats and serpents. Those, I'd gladly kill all day and night.

I'd taken no more than three steps when the hawk's head swiveled toward me, its sharply hooked beak tipping down. Eyes full of intelligence locked onto mine—eyes that weren't black like the bird I'd healed, but a vibrant, unnatural, intense shade of blue even brighter than the goddess Penellaphe's eyes. It was a color I'd never seen in a bird before.

The hawk let out a soft chirping sound, reminding me of a less powerful version of the staggering call the draken made, and then it suddenly launched from the branch. Wings spread wide, the hawk darted straight toward me. Heart lurching, I quickly crouched, reaching for the dagger in my boot. I jerked the weapon free just as the hawk veered suddenly, swooping over my head—

A shrill shriek of pain sent a chill crawling down my spine. Rising, I whirled, swallowing a scream as fear exploded in my chest.

A heavy gray mass convulsed a few feet from me, flailing as the silver hawk sank its blade-sharp talons into something shaped like a head. The thing rapidly became more *solid* as the hawk's heavy wings beat across shoulders and a chest. Arms became visible, and hands and fingers made of shadow reached for the hawk, but the bird tore at wispy fingers, ripping off tendrils of gray that floated toward the grayish-brown ground.

Icy air kissed the nape of my neck, sending a bolt of adrenaline through me. I reacted out of instinct, shutting down the fear. Spinning around, I swept up with the dagger. My eyes went wide as the blade met *resistance* within the churning, throbbing shadow. The thing screamed as it jerked back. Pieces of shadow broke off, spraying into the air like blood as the thing lifted off the ground, *flying* into the limbs, just as another darted through the trees, its tendrils of shadow billowing several feet above the ground.

I had a sinking suspicion that I knew exactly what I was dealing with.

Shades.

And, somehow, everyone had failed to mention that they could basically *fly*.

I leapt to the side as a smoky arm swept out, then turned to see that the Shade the hawk had attacked was now gone as the hawk flew down, dragging its talons through the new Shade. Was the hawk actually helping me? Or just reacting to the bigger threat?

A low moan traveled through the Dying Woods. I wheeled around, catching glimpses of deep gray slipping in and out between the crooked limbs as if coming from the dead ground and trees.

"Gods," I muttered. "I really don't have time for this."

I turned to the closest one, wondering exactly how in the hell they got *bitey* when they appeared to be smoke and shadows. I cursed as the Shade darted to my left. Another flew across the ground, slithering like a large, shadowy serpent—because, *of course*, it would. Shooting forward, I slammed the dagger into what I assumed was its back as it began to rise. The blade sank into something, causing the Shade to screech and hit the ground. My eyes went wide as the Shade suddenly shattered into thousands of tiny filaments. Okay. I'd definitely hit something vital. Lifting the dagger, I noticed black splatter, some kind of oily substance, along the curve of my hand. A stale scent hit me, turning my stomach.

A teeny-tiny part of me felt bad as I wheeled around, thrusting the dagger into the widest part of the Shade. These things had been mortals once. They may have committed terrible sins or were simply individuals whose fear of consequence was greater than whatever indiscretions they may have committed. I had a feeling that when they broke apart into nothing, as the one before me did while I turned to another, it meant the destruction of their soul. There was no coming back from that.

I plunged the dagger into the next creature's chest without hesitation because the guilt was fleeting. I didn't want to become some wayward soul's late-night snack.

A Shade swooped down, much as the hawk had earlier. I leapt sideways, and something snagged my cloak, tearing it.

Claws. Right. Apparently, Shades had claws you couldn't see. I twisted, throwing up my forearm to block the Shade in front of me. My elbow connected with bone-deep coldness and something hard within the mass of gray—something that felt a lot like a throat as the sound of snapping teeth echoed from the void.

"No biting," I grunted, pushing the creature back as I thrust out with the dagger.

Suddenly, something jerked my head back with such force that pain shot down my neck and back. My feet went out from under me as the hawk let out another staggering series of chirps. I hit the ground hard, knocking the air from my lungs.

The Shade came down over me, the thick wisps and tendrils of shadow flowing around it, clouding the entire realm. Icy shadow fingers encircled my wrist, pinning the hand that held the dagger to the ground. The touch—its hold—was almost mind-numbingly cold as I brought my knee up and shoved my left hand in the general vicinity of where I thought its shoulder might be. My fingers sank into the cold air within the mass of shadows, and my palm flattened against what didn't feel like skin but something hard and smooth. Like...*bone*. I pushed up with all my strength—

And several things happened all at once.

The hawk swooped down over us, dragging its talons across the Shade's back. The creature shrieked, spasming as the hawk flew up into the trees. My chest suddenly throbbed, heating and *humming*. Static erupted over my skin—my arms and hands. There was no will, no demand, but I felt the eather in my blood building and building. I tried to stop it, but a silvery glow spilled out from my palm, beating back the Shade's shadows, peeling back the layers of dull gray, stripping away the wispy shroud until I saw the white of actual bones. A rib cage and a spine and dry, withered organs—a wrinkled heart that was a flat, gray color.

A heart that suddenly *beat*.

The color deepened to a bright red as pinkish-white tendons and muscles rapidly formed around the ribs and bones. Veins appeared throughout where nothing but gray had once been. A skull took shape, tendons wrapping around a jawbone, straightening a mouth full of crooked, broken teeth.

Oh, gods. Oh, gods. I was never going to *unsee* this. This would haunt me for however long I lived.

Lips began to take shape, turning a pale pink as they moved, and a throat that was barely put together vibrated with sound. "*Meyaah,*" it rasped. "*Liessa...*"

"What in the actual *fuck*?" I gasped as a milky white substance filled the eye sockets. As—

My chest warmed once more and hummed, the eather inside me— the embers of life—vibrating in response to the wave of pure, unfettered power. A silver, crackling light suddenly filled the woods, so bright and iridescent that, for the briefest second, I saw the swirling, circling Shades above me. And then they were simply...*gone*.

That kind of power was unthinkable.

Spitting, hissing energy swept over the Shade above me, filling the newly formed veins with burning white light as it threw the Shade into the air, and it shattered into utterly nothing.

I lay there, hand still raised as the intense, silvery light receded and faded, and the world turned gray and *almost* lifeless once more.

Above and among the warped branches, the silver hawk called out softly and then lifted into the air. My heart thundering, I watched it spread its wings and disappear from view.

Not even the fierce predator wanted to hang around.

"*Seraphena.*"

My chest seized at the hard, cold voice that had to be conjured from the darkest hours of the night. What I'd done to the Shade fell to the wayside, replaced by the knowledge that I should've seen this coming. He had my blood in him—lots of it now. He would've felt the extreme burst of fear, even if it had been brief—just as he had in the courtyard earlier. Maybe it wasn't even the blood as much as the Primal ember inside me that had once belonged to him. Who knew? None of that mattered at the moment. What did was the fact that I couldn't just lay here, wishing I could sink into the ground. My heart still hammering away, I slowly rose to my feet. Pressure clamped down on my chest as I faced *him.*

Nyktos stood several feet from me, appearing every bit the Primal ruler of the Shadowlands he was. He cut a striking figure in a deep gray tunic, his hair swept back. The lines of his face were harder and colder than I'd ever seen them.

And his skin…it was *thin.*

The longer I stared, the more I saw the shadows gathering beneath his flesh. His eyes were swirling, silver orbs. I didn't need his talent to read emotions to know that he was beyond furious.

The reality hit me with the speed of an out-of-control wagon. I wasn't going anywhere. My true destiny wouldn't be fulfilled. Nyktos would never let me out of his sight now. I would be trapped here, with all the people who would likely die because of me. The pressure on my chest and in my throat ramped up. The tightening became unbearable, and I did something I had never done before.

I turned and *ran.* I ran as fast and as hard as I could, racing through the twisted and bent trees, ignoring the sharp slices of pain as bare, low-hanging branches reached toward me like bony fingers, snagging my cloak and hair and nicking my skin.

The pressure in my chest was cool and thick, leaving little room for control or rationale. Like when Tavius had pinned me down, and I couldn't breathe. I'd reacted like a wild animal then, and I was that animal again.

He would burn through the Shadowlands.

Damp, clammy sweat broke out across my forehead as the wound left behind by the Shade ached. The gray, bare limbs of the trees were a blurred maze of twisted, gnarled, bone-like branches. My boots pounded over rocks and uneven ground as I kept running, not even knowing where I was running to. But I knew why. Desperation. Foolish, idiotic desperation propelled me forward, each step putting distance between me and the nightmares that were sure to become a horrific reality. I would never have a chance to reach Kolis. I would be nothing more than a bull's-eye, guiding Kolis right to everyone—to Nyktos.

Kolis has done all manner of things to him.

I couldn't stop the Rot. I wouldn't be able to stop Kolis. I had no duty—no higher purpose. I would die. And, worse yet, I would be the cause of untold horror. I was nothing but—

A rush of citrus and fresh air was my only warning. Nyktos's weight suddenly crashed into me, hard and solid. The ground raced up to me as his arm folded across my waist. He twisted, and then all I could see was the twinkling of stars between a spiderweb of bare branches.

Nyktos hit the ground first, and...gods, *that* must have hurt. He absorbed the impact of my weight against the rocky surface with a grunt. The back of my head bounced off the wall of his chest, momentarily stunning me. There was nothing but our ragged breathing for a beat and then...

"Did you seriously just try to run?" Nyktos's breath stirred the hair on the top of my head. "*From me?* Why? Why would you do that?"

"Why not?" I shot back, cringing at how utterly childish that sounded.

"Are you *fucking* kidding me right now?" he snarled. A tremor ran through me as I strained against his hold. "You fled the safety of the palace and ran straight into the second place I warned you never to enter. Was my very short list of rules that confusing? Or are you just that incapable of following rules meant to save your life?"

"Fuck your rules," I spat, tremors skating through me.

"And my sanity right along with them," he bit out. "Do you even understand how close you were to death, Sera? Even if you killed the Shade above you, there were at least a dozen more waiting. If I hadn't felt you and intervened—*yet again,* if I might add—"

"No, you may not."

"You would be dead," he seethed. "They would've torn into you, and no amount of my blood would've saved you. There would've been nothing left of you to even *bury*. For me to even—" He cut himself off as the fury backing his words punched into the air around us in a wave of icy-hot energy. My eyes went wide as the ripple hit the trees above, shattering them into *ash*.

Holy shit. My throat dried as I watched what was left of the trees fall to the ground like snow.

"What were you thinking, Sera?" He shook me.

What had I been thinking? That I could actually escape the Shadowlands—escape *him*? Somehow make it to Kolis alive?

"Answer me." I realized he wasn't shaking me. It was *his* body. It shook under mine. "Why were you running from me?"

I tried to sit up, but his arm shifted, holding me flat against him. Even in the chaos of my mind, I realized that he'd trapped my left hand against my stomach. Not my right hand. Not the one that held the dagger. That was a purposeful choice. No accident. The dagger may not be able to kill him, but it had hurt him before. A skilled warrior such as he would've removed the threat of a dagger first and foremost. It was what I would do. But he'd chosen not to. "I wasn't running from you."

"Then what were you doing? Striving to be the most difficult person I've ever crossed paths with?"

"Yeah, that's exactly it. Not that I was actually trying to save you, you jackass!"

Nyktos went completely still and silent, and I realized my mistake right then. His chest rose sharply against my back. "You couldn't have—no, Sera. *No.*"

I felt the moment the shock hit him. His arm loosened around my waist, and I knew it was my chance—my last chance.

Digging the heels of my boots into the ground, I launched myself upward, breaking his hold. I was free for a heartbeat before Nyktos caught my left forearm. Cursing, I twisted as he moved to sit up, clamping my knees onto his hips. He caught the thick braid hanging over my shoulder as I thrust the dagger down.

Nyktos's eyes went wide as I pressed the edge of the blade under his chin. My hand didn't shake. No part of me on the outside did. The inside was a different story—everything in there trembled.

"Let me go," I ordered.

Moonlight-bright eyes locked onto mine. "No."

"You need to let me go, Nyktos."

"Or what?" One side of his lips curled up. "You're going to slit my throat?"

Frustration and hopelessness crashed into a bitter tide of desperation and anger. "If that's what it takes."

"Then do it. Slit my throat." He wrapped the braid around his hand, putting just enough pressure on my neck to force my head down toward his. "Just make sure you cut deep. To the spine. Otherwise, all you'll accomplish is getting us both bloody."

My heart lurched. He couldn't be serious.

"Do it," he growled, his lips peeling back over his fangs. "Severing my spine is the only opportunity you'll get to make a run for it."

A tremor hit my arm, and I swallowed a gasp as he lifted his head. A bead of shimmery, reddish-blue blood appeared on the side of his throat.

"But you'd better run fast. Because I won't be down long," he warned, those wildly churning eyes never leaving mine. "You'll have about a minute. If that. But just so you know, you won't make it out of the Shadowlands, *liessa*."

Liessa.

It didn't just mean Queen in old Primal language. It also meant something beautiful. Something *powerful*. Hearing him call me that rocked me.

Nyktos struck then.

Grasping the hand that held the dagger, he flipped me with such shocking ease that it was clear he could've done it at any moment.

"That wasn't fair," I cried out.

He came down over me within a heartbeat, trapping me. "What about me makes you think I'm fair?"

"*Everything.*" Panic was a strange thing, sucking away one's strength one moment and giving near godlike power the next. I lifted my hips and clamped my legs down on his waist. I rolled him and popped to my feet with a shout, then jumped back, turning.

A low rumble from the sky shook the bare branches of the remaining trees, rattling them like dry bones. I looked up, catching only a brief glimpse of blackish-gray wings through the slowly drifting ash. *Nektas*. My heart seized—

Nyktos rose to one knee, twisting as he swept out his leg, catching mine. My feet went out from under me, and I hit the ground on my ass. Nyktos was fast—so damn fast. He rolled onto me again, but this time, he was smarter. One broad thigh wedged between mine as he captured both of my wrists, pinning them to the dry, dead grass as the shadow of a draken glided above us, coasting over the circle of land Nyktos had cleared in his rage.

"Drop it." Eather spilled from Nyktos's eyes and seeped *under* his skin, illuminating his veins as a thin trickle of blood coursed down his throat. "Drop the dagger, Sera. I don't want to make you do it, but I will. Drop it."

He could do just that, using compulsion. Panting, I forced my grip to relax. The hilt of the dagger slipped from my palm. It was over. Even if I managed to get free and somehow incapacitated Nyktos, I wouldn't make it far. Not with Nektas in the air. "Happy?"

His eyes became pure silver with no discernible pupil—just glowing orbs. Those essence-lit veins continued spreading over his cheek and down his throat. In an instant, the minor wound there was gone. Only the faint trace of blood remained. "Tell me I'm wrong, Sera."

My muscles went weak and my neck limp.

The essence bled out around him in thick tendrils of black laced with silver. Shadows churned under his skin. "Tell me I'm wrong. Tell me!" he shouted, the shadows spreading until his flesh was the color of midnight streaked with starlight, and the fingers around my wrists became as hard as shadowstone. "Tell me you were not going after Kolis!"

"I had to."

"*Wrong*," he snarled, the flash of fangs a shocking white against his skin.

My lips parted as he took his true form. Twin sweeping arcs rose behind him—as wide as he was tall. Solid, teaming masses of power that blocked out everything beyond him. I hadn't been this close to him in the courtyard when he took this form, but I'd been close enough that I recognized the striking lines of his features beneath the churning, hard flesh: the height of his cheekbones, the lush, full lips, and thick, reddish-brown strands of hair that fell against the curve of his jaw.

"Whatever you think you need to do," he said, his voice soft as a breath—it tripped up my heart even more—"whatever you believe you can accomplish, you are wrong."

"How can you say that? I can stop him." I trembled, the words spilling out of me. "You have to know that."

"Turning yourself over to Kolis is not the answer."

"You know it is!" I shouted. "Why else would your father put her soul in me? Why else would I have been trained to kill a Primal?"

His head was mere inches from mine, and the brightness of his eyes caused mine to water.

Instinct screamed at me to go quiet. That he was on the edge of losing whatever restraint he had. But I couldn't. He had to understand that this was our only chance to stop Kolis. "I know what I'm facing." I forced my voice to go steady and level like when I spoke to the wild kiyou wolf I had brought back to life in the Dark Elms. "But whatever happens to me will be worth it if I—"

Those twin arcs swept down, slamming into the ground and shaking the entire woods. Eather sparked from the tips of his wings, hitting the patches of dead, gray grass and turning it to ash.

"You h-have to understand." I shuddered as frigid air blasted off him. "I'm *his* weakness. What I've been preparing for my whole life? It was for him. Not you." My breath formed a misty, puffy cloud. "I can still try. Just help me get there, or...or let me go. Either one. I *will* fulfill my real destiny."

Nyktos had gone silent.

I swallowed, hoping I was getting somewhere with him, praying to whatever Fates might be listening that he would understand. "You shouldn't have to worry about hiding who I am. You'll be free of me, and so will all those who seek shelter under your care. Everyone in the Shadowlands will be safer this way. *You* will be safer. No one else has to get hurt or die."

"But you would be dead." Nyktos spoke in a voice I barely recognized, his tone thicker and more guttural. "Kolis will destroy you."

"That doesn't matter—" I sucked in a breath when his wings lifted, whipping the strands of our hair across our faces as they spread out behind him.

"And you argue that you value your life." A deep growl rumbled from his chest. "What little regard you have for it has never been more apparent than right now."

"I'm going to die no matter what. The mortal realm will be lost. You can't stop that. No one can. But I can at least do something about Kolis. Then, he won't be able to hurt anyone again. He won't be able to hurt you."

He lowered his head even more, his mouth barely a breath away from mine. "I will gladly suffer anything Kolis dishes out as long as my blood is spilled instead of yours."

I pressed into the ground, stunned. "Why? Why would you do that for me?"

"The embers of life and you—"

"Fuck the embers of life!" I pushed against his hold, getting nowhere, but something deep in me, something that had been there, tightening and building for *fucking years,* began to crack.

A messy knot of emotion seeped out, full of fear, need, shame, loneliness, sorrow, and a thousand other things I'd never been allowed to feel. Slices carved from me by all the times I'd been excluded by my family, treated like an unwanted guest, and seen as nothing more than a curse. Wounds made by my mother's disappointment left to fester each time she looked at me as if she wished she never had to do so again. I was just a vessel full of deep scars left behind from the first life I'd taken and all the times after that, leaving the wrong kind of mark behind. I was nothing more than bruises on a blank canvas because I didn't feel it. I didn't mourn those losses. I didn't care because no one else cared beyond what I could do for them.

My skin felt too tight and prickly. My chest throbbed, and that messy knot unraveled into rage, turning into something else that couldn't be hidden or contained. I threw my head back, a scream of frustration and fury burning my throat. From inside the vast cavern that had shattered open, heat rose from within the emptiness. *Power.* It felt like it had always been there, bright and hot, ancient and unending. Power flowed through my veins. Silvery-white light crowded my vision—

I slammed my hands into his shoulders as that energy, that pure Primal essence erupted from my palms and flowed into—

Nyktos.

7

Pure silvery-white eather slammed into Nyktos, spreading over him as
he rose and something threw him backward. His wings spread, stopping
him in midair.

"Nyktos," I screamed. Real fear exploded in my gut as I jackknifed
up, scrambling onto my knees. Eather crackled, racing through his
wings and body, filling the network of veins.

My gods, what had I done?

Darkness spilled out around Nyktos, thick and churning. His
mouth opened, and the sound he made…it was *power*. A roar hit the
dried-out branches behind him, shattering them. The temperature
dropped so severely that it momentarily seemed to freeze what air I
could get into my lungs. I was chilled down to my bones as he drifted
forward—

A great shadow fell over me, blocking out the trees and the faint
glimmer of the stars. I tensed. Air whipped through the clearing as
Nektas came from above, a wing sweeping over my head as his front
talons slammed into the earth before me. The ground and the still-
standing trees shook as if they were nothing more than matchsticks.

Squeezing my eyes shut, I didn't dare move. I knew death was
coming—a painful, fiery death. There was no way it wasn't. I'd attacked
Nyktos. I'd hurt him. I knew this because what had come out of me
had been pure, unfettered power. It hadn't been intentional, but that

didn't matter. Nektas was not only bonded to Nyktos, he also saw the Primal as a member of his *family*.

Nektas would kill me.

Except the flash of intense silvery fire I knew I would see, even with my eyes closed, didn't come. Neither did the pain.

Trembling, I opened my eyes. I was inches from the thick, grayish-black scales of Nektas's side. I knew he was big, but even on the road into the Shadowlands when I first saw him, I hadn't been *this* close to him in this form. His body alone had to be at least twenty feet. He had one of his leathery wings above me and was...crouched. *Around* me.

Nektas's head swooped down, the row of spiked horns vibrating as his lips peeled back from massive, bone-crushing teeth. The low growl of warning sent chills down my spine.

"It's okay," Nyktos rasped.

My gaze flew to him. Dizzy with relief to hear him speak, I swayed unsteadily on my knees, slowly becoming aware that the air no longer felt as if it were freezing.

"Nektas isn't...a threat to you," Nyktos forced out between gritted teeth. Snapping, silvery light continued rippling through his body. "He's...protecting you."

"From what?"

"Me."

That didn't make sense, but the large draken *was* eyeing the Primal. Not me. "I-I hurt *you*."

"He's worried...that I will...retaliate out of reflex." Nyktos twisted his head side to side. "That I...will do more than...just hurt you."

"You wouldn't." I twisted toward Nektas. "He wouldn't hurt me."

"I almost did."

Not a single part of me believed that. Maybe that made me a fool, but if he'd wanted to harm me, he could've done so a thousand times over by now.

Nektas didn't budge, though. He had his attention fixed on the Primal, his rumble of warning lower.

Nyktos suddenly lowered, going down on one knee. The shadows around him receded as he pitched forward, planting a hand on the ground. He bowed his head, his broad shoulders shuddering as the waves of eather eased and faded. His wings turned to smoke and scattered. The midnight-stone skin receded. Strands of hair fell against his golden-bronze jaw. He didn't speak. Minutes ticked by, and only his shoulders moved, up and down with his short, rapid breaths.

Maybe he wasn't really okay. Concern ate away at the relief. Still on my knees, I started to inch forward. "Nyktos?"

Silence.

Nektas had finally stopped growling. He stretched forward, gently nudging Nyktos's shoulder.

"I'm fine," Nyktos said hoarsely, reaching up and flattening a hand against the side of Nektas's broad jaw. "I just need a minute."

Nektas withdrew but didn't take his eyes off him, and that minute felt like an hour.

Slowly, Nyktos lifted his head. Essence-filled eyes met mine. "That was…" He cleared his throat, and when he spoke again, his voice was steadier, stronger. "That was unexpected."

"I…" Tears pricked my eyes as I shook my head and looked down at my hands. "I didn't mean to do that. I swear. I don't even know how I did that."

"It has to be the Culling. I didn't think it would happen—figured it would be more like a godling with you. But those embers in you— they're strong. They're making *you* stronger…" He trailed off, that damn awe in his voice returning and lingering in the silence. "When a god enters the Culling, their essence increases and grows stronger. And as they get closer to completing the Culling, they can have…outbursts. It's usually tied to heightened emotion, but that doesn't happen with a godling. Not when they go through the Culling. Many of them can't even harness the essence like that, even if they Ascend. They simply don't have enough eather in them for that."

Curling my hands against my chest, I looked up at him.

Nyktos had gotten closer. I hadn't heard him move. He was still on his knees. Nektas hadn't made a sound, but Nyktos was now under the shelter of Nektas's wing, too. "You were definitely feeling heightened emotions when it happened."

A shaky, weak laugh rattled out of me as the backs of my eyes burned. I quickly looked away, closing my eyes. "I'm sorry. I didn't mean to do it. I really didn't."

"I know," he whispered, and I jerked at the touch of his fingers against my cheek. His fingers—

"Your skin is cold again."

"It's okay."

"How is this okay?" I tried to lean back, but his hand followed, curving around my cheek. His skin was cool like it had been before. "I did that without even meaning to. I hurt you."

"You didn't."

"I think I did." I reached up, touching the hand on my cheek. Had the eather somehow undone what my blood had done for him? I dropped my hand. "Do you need to feed—?"

"That's not something you need to worry about."

I didn't understand how he could even suggest that. Or why he wasn't more disturbed by what I'd done. "What if I do that again? And I hurt someone else who's not okay afterward?"

His eyes closed briefly, his features softening. "We'll make sure that doesn't happen, Sera."

That sounded easier said than done. "How—?" I jerked back, this time falling on my ass as I remembered what I'd done before Nyktos had found me. "I touched a Shade."

"You shouldn't have been anywhere near them."

"That's not the point."

The gentling of his demeanor vanished as his jaw hardened. "That's the actual entirety of the point."

"You're not listening. I touched it, and it started to come back to life."

"What?" His hand lowered then as Nektas turned his head toward us.

"I didn't mean to do it. I didn't try. But I saw its...its veins and its muscles form. Its heart. The heart started *beating*," I said. "Right before you killed it, its heart was beating, and it spoke to me."

Nyktos drew back, his eyes widening. "That's not possible." He twisted toward Nektas. "Is it? I didn't feel it."

The draken...

Nektas *shifted* forms, right there beside us. A dazzling explosion of a thousand tiny silver stars appeared all over his body and above us where his wing had been. My mouth dropped open as the shimmery spectacle faded, and fingers took the place of talons, wings sank in, and flesh replaced scales. Red and black hair slid over *lots* of hard, faintly ridged, coppery flesh.

"You're naked," I whispered.

"Does that bother you?" Nektas asked.

"Maybe?"

Nyktos turned his head to me. "Perhaps you shouldn't continue staring then."

"How can I not?" I mumbled.

Nektas smirked as he waved a hand. There was a brief, faint burst of light, and then only his upper body was exposed. Loose, linen pants covered the rest. "Better?"

"I guess…" I blinked. Was I hallucinating?

"I wasn't asking you." Nektas turned a pointed stare on Nyktos.

The Primal's eyes narrowed as the corners of his lips pointed downward.

"How did you do that?" I asked.

"Magic," Nektas answered. I frowned as he knelt beside Nyktos. "You sure the Shade spoke?"

I nodded, letting the whole magic-pants thing go for the time being. "It said *meyaah Liessa*."

"My Queen," Nyktos repeated.

"Fuck." A slow grin spread across Nektas's face. "It's the embers."

I was getting really sick of hearing about the embers, but that *did* confirm that Nektas knew there were two embers in me and not one. Nyktos had obviously confided in him, but had he told the draken the whole Sotoria part?

"Eythos could do it," Nektas continued. "He could raise the bones of the dead. It was rare. I can only remember him doing it once. It's not the same as restoring life to the recently dead. That's why nobody felt it." He tilted his head as he eyed me. "Those embers are really strong in you."

"So I've been told," I muttered.

Nyktos frowned. "I didn't know my father could do that."

"I don't think even Kolis knew." He brushed a stripe of red hair back over his shoulder. "You should probably avoid touching anything dead until you get a handle on those embers."

My hands fell into my lap. "I'll definitely try to avoid doing that. It'll be hard because I do like to touch dead things."

Nektas's smile spread, and then he looked over his shoulder. "You level?"

Nyktos nodded, his attention fixed on me.

"You two should head back to the palace. The Shades won't be scared off much longer." Nektas rose, clasping Nyktos's shoulder before walking off into the maze of dead trees. A few moments later, branches rattled violently, and Nektas rose into the sky in his draken form once more.

"So…draken can conjure clothing out of thin air?" I asked. "Can Primals do the same?"

"Only clothing we've worn. It becomes an extension of us."

"Oh. That makes sense, I guess." Slowly, I met his stare as bone-deep exhaustion set in. So many things went through my head. "You're not going to let me go, are you?"

"*Never*," he swore.

Disbelief and frustration clashed. "So, you're going to hold me captive here, then? Against my will?"

Eather flared in his eyes again. "How you remain here, as my Consort or my prisoner, will be *your* choice."

"That's not really a choice when it's the same thing."

"If you choose to see it that way, then so be it." He rose fluidly, showing no sign that I had injured him. "Your destiny is not to die at the hands of Kolis."

My chest rose and fell sharply as the finality of my failed attempt and what it meant settled over me. This had been my one chance. There would be no more, not when he now expected it from me. "Then what is my destiny?"

"To be my Consort," he said. "Whether you like it or not."

Anger rose as I stared up at the Primal of Death. I latched onto it because it was far better than desperation and hopelessness. "You mean it's my destiny to die as your Consort?"

A muscle ticked in his temple as he glared. "There may be another way to prevent your death."

"Really?" I laughed. "Like what?"

"If I had five seconds of peace and didn't have to worry about you getting yourself killed, I might be able to think of one."

I rolled my eyes. "Okay. Sure."

He made a noise that sounded like he was choking on a scream of frustration. I smirked, my gaze falling on the dagger. I reached for it.

"I sincerely hope that whatever you plan to do with the dagger doesn't involve me," Nyktos warned as I quickly slid it into my boot.

"Don't...don't take it from me," I ordered, but it sounded more like a plea, which brought heat to my cheeks.

"If I planned on taking it from you, I would've done so already."

I watched him warily. "You're not afraid I'm going to slit your throat to your spine like you instructed?"

"No."

My eyes narrowed. "You should be."

He smirked, brushing his fingers over the cuff on his biceps, drawing forth a thin tendril.

I stiffened as the smoke rapidly spread out in the space before him, quickly taking the form of his warhorse. Odin shook out his black mane as he pawed at the ash-covered ground. I'd forgotten all about the fact that his horse apparently *lived* in his cuff.

"How is…?" I quieted when Nyktos glanced at me.

"What?"

"Nothing," I muttered, attempting to quash my curiosity about how he could conjure Odin into existence from a silver cuff. I failed five seconds later. "Is that also magic?"

"Primal magic, yes."

I thought about the chair he'd moved earlier, and the fire he'd started without touching either of those things. "So, he's not…real?"

"He is flesh and blood." He was silent for a moment. "I hope you're not planning to spend what remains of the longest night ever in the Dying Woods."

"And if I was?"

"I would pick you up and put you on Odin myself."

"I'd like to see you try."

Nyktos faced me, and his expression told me he was willing to do just that.

"Whatever." I pushed to my feet and sidestepped him, trudging toward Odin. I halted when the horse whipped his head in my direction. He pawed at the ground once more.

"He's not that happy with you."

"What did I do to him?"

Nyktos came up behind me, dipping his head as he said, "You held a dagger to my throat, and you hit me with eather."

"Yeah, but I didn't do those things—" I cut myself off. Primal magic. "He's an extension of you. Got it." I sighed, eyeing the horse. "I'm sorry."

Odin huffed, turning his head from me.

"He'll get over it." Nyktos gripped my hips and lifted me into the air before I even had a chance to react. I grasped the pommel, seating myself before I was flung over the other side. Nyktos swung into the saddle behind me. "Eventually."

Odin shook his mane.

I wasn't sure about that.

Nyktos reached around me and picked up the reins. "The next time you put a dagger to anyone's throat," he said, his breath coasting over my cheek as he guided Odin toward the palace, "you'd better mean it."

I stiffened. "Even if it's yours?"

Nyktos's arm folded over my waist, tugging me against his chest. "Especially if it's mine."

Orphine was waiting just inside the stable-facing doors, in the narrow entryway that led to the hall opposite Nyktos's office. She wasn't the only one. Ector leaned against the wall as she stepped forward, lowering herself onto one knee. "It was my duty to watch over her," she said. "I failed. I'm sorry."

Guilt rose. "It's not your fault."

"For once, Sera's right," Nyktos replied, and I shot him a narrow-eyed glare. "You don't need to apologize for her recklessness—"

"*Recklessness?*" I hissed. He made it sound as if I'd been out for a jaunty stroll through the Dying Woods.

"Or her bravery," he continued, returning my glare. I snapped my mouth shut, surprised that he'd even thought that, let alone said it. "Foolish bravery," he tacked on.

I was starting to regret feeling bad for hurting him.

Ector pushed off the wall as Orphine rose, his curly hair even paler in the lamplight. "Bravery?"

"She was attempting to make her way to Dalos." Nyktos took hold of my arm. "To kill Kolis."

"Damn," Orphine muttered, stepping back from us.

The blood drained rapidly from Ector's face. "You can't be serious."

"I wish I wasn't." Nyktos steered me around them, starting for the back set of stairs.

Ector followed. "Why would you do something like that? Even think about doing that?"

I stopped. "Because—"

Nyktos was having none of it. He let go of my arm, pointing up the stairs. "Go—"

"Do not order me about as if I'm a child."

"I wouldn't if you didn't behave like one."

I saw red. "You sure as hell didn't think I was behaving like one when you had me in your bed and your fangs in my throat!"

"Whoa," Ector murmured.

Fiery, silver eyes locked with mine. "*Sera.*"

Choking on more words I really didn't need to speak, I *stomped* up the stairs like a full-grown-ass woman. I made it to the fourth-floor landing before Nyktos caught up to me.

"Whatever you were thinking about saying down there," he began, reaching around me and yanking open the door, "don't think it again."

"What?" I stalked into the hall. He'd been right. I had been about to tell Ector why I'd gone after Kolis. "You don't trust your guards with the truth of exactly what I carry inside me? Or are you afraid that if they know, they might actually agree with me?"

"None of them would agree with what you were attempting to do, nor would they aid you in such a thing."

I laughed. And, boy, did it sound scary. "You don't know them all that well if you think that."

"And you do?"

"I know them well enough to be aware of the obvious. None of them like me, and they'd be glad to see me gone—either walking out or being carried out dead."

"What makes you think that?"

"Is that a serious question? They haven't forgiven me for what I once planned—" I gasped, stumbling back as Nyktos appeared in front of me. "Stop doing that!"

"What have they said to you?" His voice was low, but it hummed with the promise of violence.

"Nothing."

He came toward me. "Tell me what they said and who said it."

"They don't need to say anything for me to know!" My hands closed into fists. "Look, the last thing I need to do is make them more unhappy with me. And I don't want to. They already have every reason to dislike me. They're loyal to you, and I'm just the Consort you never wanted—who planned to kill you. If they had their way, I wouldn't be here." I stepped around him and continued down the hall, the exhaustion from earlier returning. "It is what it is."

Thank the gods, Nyktos didn't stop me. I reached my bedchamber, relieved to find it unlocked. I went in, closing the door behind me without saying another word. I moved past the bed and unclasped the cloak. It fell to the floor. I needed quiet. Time to think and plot—

The door flew open behind me. I whirled around.

Nyktos swept in like a storm. "No."

I took a step back. "No, what?"

"No to *this*. I would like to get at least a few hours of rest tonight," he announced.

"You're the one in my chambers!" I threw up my hands. "No one's stopping you from sleeping."

"You have proven that you cannot be trusted to be in here alone, and I need to rest. So, if I'm sleeping, you're sleeping."

"You cannot be serious," I exclaimed.

"Do I look like I'm joking?"

He looked like he wanted to murder an entire kingdom. "I'm not going to try anything right after you caught me."

"I would like to believe that, but I know better. I cannot have guards stationed outside your door and in the courtyard, dedicated solely to making sure you don't do something reckless. At least, not until I have locks put on the balcony doors…" He swung his head in the direction of said doors and then snapped his attention back to me, his brows raised. "How *did* you get down from the balcony, by the way?"

I had a feeling he wouldn't like the answer. "Magic? You know, those embers are really strong."

Nyktos's growl raised tiny hairs all over my body. "Did you *climb* down the side of the palace?"

"Possibly?"

He stared at me. "Part of me is impressed by the fact that you managed that."

"Can we stop with that part?"

"You could've broken your neck."

"But I didn't."

"For fuck's sake, Sera. There is such a thing as being too bold. *Too* brave."

"Aren't you tired? Let's skip this conversation." I crossed my arms. "Especially since I'm sure we've already had it like five hundred times."

He let out another curse. "You're right. I can yell at you more in the morning."

"You sure about that? Or will you be conveniently gone all day?" I snapped.

"Did you miss me?"

"No," I huffed. "You can go to bed."

"That is what I'm trying to do, but as I said, if I'm sleeping, you're sleeping. And you will be doing so within arm's reach."

My jaw had to be on the floor. "In your chamber?"

Nyktos drew in a breath, clearly searching for patience. "Where else?"

"No."

His brows flew up. "No?"

"That's what I said. It should be a simple enough word for you to understand. You can leave now." I pointed at the door he'd come through. "Good night."

Nyktos stared at me. "I don't have time for this."

"Well, neither do—" My eyes went wide as he started toward me. "What are you doing?"

"I'm not going to stand here and argue with you."

That look had come over his face again, the one he'd had when he said that he would pick me up and put me on Odin. I took several steps back. "Don't."

He prowled forward.

My eyes went wide, and I held up my hands. "I'm feeling really emotional right now. I might lose control and hurt you again."

"I would love to see you use eather like that again. That too was impressive." One side of his lips curled up. "But now that I know it can happen, I'll be prepared."

I bumped into the column of the bed and then turned—

Nyktos caught my arm and spun me around. One arm went around my waist as he bent, shoving his shoulder against my stomach. I shrieked as he lifted me off the floor. Suddenly, I was hanging from his shoulder—*his actual shoulder*—and staring at his back.

I was stunned speechless.

Then Nyktos turned.

"Let me down!" I screamed, my braid slipping forward and smacking the side of my face.

"Nope."

"Put me down!" I went to kick my legs, but his other arm folded over the backs of my knees, trapping them. "Nyktos, I swear to the gods—"

"You shouldn't swear to the gods. It's blasphemous."

I screeched, swinging a fist back as he opened the door that adjoined our chambers. I froze, staring into the dark corridor of the short hall. The door...*had* it been unlocked? Or had he used his power to unlock it?

"I have a feeling you're about to punch me in a kidney," Nyktos said as he carried me down the passageway and into his bedchamber.

My fist opened as the scent of citrus—of him—increased. "No, I wasn't."

"I don't think I've met someone who lies as much as you do." Nyktos turned sharply, dumping me onto the bed.

"Asshole!" I bounced roughly as the scant items in his chambers came into view, lit by the glow of the wall sconces. A wardrobe. A few chests, and the long settee beside a table and lone chair. I was a little startled by being in his chamber again.

Nyktos caught my legs before I could even move, tucking one between his arm and chest as he grabbed the boot of the other. He slipped the dagger out, thrusting it into the wooden footboard of the bed, then tugged the boot off.

"What the fuck?"

"Your boots are as filthy as your mouth." He grabbed hold of the other boot, and that too hit the floor with a thump. "And while I enjoy that mouth in my bed, I won't enjoy the boots." He glanced down at my soiled, bloodied breeches. "They need to come off, too."

"Wow. I don't think I've ever had a man ask me to remove my clothing so romantically before."

His eyes flicked to mine. They were the shade of the sky outside the palace. My fingers pressed into the thick blanket beneath me as he stared down at me, and I knew I looked as much a mess as my mind was. More hair pulled free of the braid it was in. Skin nicked from branches. He was furious with me, and I wasn't exactly thrilled with him and his manhandling, but...but something shifted between us. A different kind of tension thickened the air, quickening my pulse and sending a bolt of awareness through me. Suddenly, I wondered if he was thinking of the last time I had been in his bedchamber and on his bed. Or of us in the receiving chamber. I was. Heat hit my blood, followed by a pulsing ache.

Nyktos's nostrils flared, and his chest rose sharply. "Take your pants off, Sera."

Those words hit me like a hot stroke, lashing the particularly impulsive side of my nature. "You want them off?" I leaned back on my elbows and raised my brows. "You're going to have to take them off."

Nyktos went completely still. Not even his chest moved, but thin wisps of eather slipped into his eyes. He wouldn't do it. I'd known that when I made the demand.

My lips formed a tight smile. "Then I guess I'll be sleeping in them."

He came forward then, planting one knee on the bed. Air lodged in my throat. I tightened all over as his hands moved under the hem of the sweater, and then I loosened as his fingers curled under the band.

His eyes never left mine. "Will you lift your ass, or will I need to do that for you, too?"

I bit my lip and lifted my ass.

The wisps of eather in his eyes grew brighter as he tugged the breeches over my hips and then down my thighs, not even bothering with the buttons. Muscles low in my stomach coiled as he drew them down my legs, the backs of his fingers grazing my skin like a cool kiss. I didn't even hear the breeches hit the floor. His stare remained locked on mine as his fingers snagged my wool socks. They too fell somewhere beyond the bed.

Slowly, those thick lashes lowered. *"Fuck."*

The sweater and slip had bunched up around my upper thighs, and from his vantage point and that one word, I knew he could see that I'd skipped undergarments in my haste to leave earlier.

My heart was thundering as his gaze rose to meet mine again. The essence churned lazily in his eyes. "The sweater is also dirty."

Hollows formed under his cheekbones, and the tips of his fangs appeared. "Lift your arms."

I rose so I rested on my knees, my breath catching as it brought our bodies within inches of touching. I lifted my arms. His hands sank into the thick material. My eyes closed as he tugged the sweater up and over my head. Tiny goose bumps broke out over the skin of my now-bare arms. The slip bordered on gossamer, cinched tightly to my breasts and falling looser over my waist and hips. It barely hid anything, and I was nearly as naked as I had been when he gave me his blood. I could feel his stare, as heavy as a caress, over my shoulders—without even a hint of a wound now—and the swell of my breasts. Then lower.

The tips of his fingers brushed my arm, drawing my eyes open. He was silent as he reached behind me, collecting my braid. I watched his fingers smooth down the thick length, stopping when they reached the band doing its best to contain the mass. He tugged it off, sliding it onto his wrist. He began to slowly and carefully unravel the braid. My gaze flew to his.

"The braid can't be comfortable to sleep on," he murmured, his voice thicker, richer.

I fell quiet, holding completely still as he meticulously separated the curls. I was inexplicably moved by the act.

He draped the length of hair over my shoulders and back when he was finished, but his fingers lingered in the strands, moving toward the ends that touched my waist. "Are you done fighting me?"

"For now."

The curl of his lips returned as he lifted his gaze to mine. "And yet it feels as if we're still locked in battle." He eased his fingers from my hair and raised his thumb to my cheek, touching the skin beneath the scratch and then my throat, just below the healing bite.

Nyktos stayed there for several moments and then pulled back. He watched me as he kicked off his boots, as if he expected me to bolt. But I hadn't lied when I'd said that I was done fighting for the night. The exhaustion had returned once more, but this time, it was warm instead of brittle. I stayed where he'd left me, watching *him* as he stepped back and turned to the side. My gaze dipped, and I saw the hard line of his arousal, clear against his breeches. A pleasant ache settled in my breasts and lower when he pulled his tunic off. The swirls of ink along his sides and back were a blur in the dim light as he walked around the side of the bed, to his wardrobe. He opened a door and then reached down to his breeches. My lips parted as he undid them, revealing the hard curve of his ass. I didn't look away as I'd done at the lake. I soaked in the golden-bronze flesh and the dusting of dark hair on his legs.

His body was...it was indecent.

Nyktos pulled on a pair of loose, black pants like the ones Nektas had manifested. He turned back to the bed and freed his hair from the knot at his neck. As the strands fell against his shoulders, I couldn't help but think how intimate this felt.

The lights in the wall went out as he approached the bed, plunging the room into darkness.

"That was me," he said upon my gasp.

It took my eyes a moment to adjust. He was at the side of his bed. "More magic?"

"Yes."

The bed dipped under his weight, and I...I was still where he'd left me. In the darkness, he came to me. He folded his arm over my waist, and I didn't resist—mainly out of shock—as he tugged me back and then down, bringing a blanket over my legs. My head hit a pillow, and then the bed shifted more as he settled behind me.

His arm was still draped over my waist, but no other parts of our bodies touched, even though there couldn't be more than an inch or so of space separating us. My eyes were wide and fixed on the darkness. Several moments passed. "I didn't think you meant *within arm's reach* in the literal sense."

"I did." His cool breath touched my shoulder, sending a faint shiver through me.

The weight of his arm was…it was too grounding. Too *everything*. "I don't think I can sleep like this."

"If I can, you can."

"I don't know about that."

"Just close your eyes and try, Sera."

Gods, when he said my name like that—like it was a solemn vow—it always left me rattled and thrown. I closed my eyes, hearing only the sound of my heart and his deep, steady breaths, and focused on those breaths until I… I did the impossible and fell asleep. I didn't know how much time passed before I was jarred awake.

Something…something had happened.

I stared into the darkness, quickly becoming aware of how tightly Nyktos held me. He had his arm clamped down on my waist, and the slip was an inconsequential barrier against the cold press of his flesh to my back. His chest rose and fell sharply, and his breath came in rapid, short bursts against the curve of my neck and shoulder.

Was he dreaming?

I tried to turn my head to look back at him, but his arm clenched, drawing me deeper against the curve of his body. "Nyktos?" I whispered.

There was no answer.

Concern rose. I reached down, touching the tense, corded muscle of his arm.

A tremor ran through his entire body. "Promise me," he rasped. "Promise me you'll never go after Kolis again."

My heart stuttered as I sucked in a shallow breath.

"Promise me, Sera. Never again."

I squeezed my eyes shut against the sudden dampness gathering in them and spoke two words I shouldn't. "I promise."

8

Nyktos was gone when I woke, but my last words to him lingered.

Promise me.

I shouldn't have made that promise. Rolling onto my back, I turned my head. My gaze flicked from the nightstand and the small wooden box on it to where my dagger lay on the pillow beside mine. Drawing in a deep breath, I exhaled slowly and picked up the dagger. I spotted my robe at the foot of the bed. Nyktos must've retrieved it.

That new crack in my chest throbbed as I rose.

The stone was cool under my feet as I walked through the dimly lit passageway and entered my chambers. I stood beneath the glass chandelier for several moments, trying to get my thoughts in order. I'd failed last night. So, what was I going to do now?

There was no answer. Only the arrival of Baines and fresh water, followed by Orphine. Her apology to Nyktos the night before still scalded my skin with shame.

"Once you're ready, I'm to escort you to Nyktos," Orphine announced as she moved to close the doors. "I'll be waiting in the hall." She paused. "Please don't attempt to make a run for it again."

"I won't." I expected some sort of caustic remark from her, but all she did was nod before stepping out into the hall.

I turned back to the bathing chamber. At least what I'd said to Orphine wasn't a lie. I wouldn't try to escape *right now*. But I would have to try again. And that made the new crack in my chest feel even more unsteady, as if it were at risk of deepening and spreading.

I rubbed at the center of my chest, stopping my thoughts before they revisited the mess of emotions that had caused the fissure. Nyktos was waiting, and I might as well get what would likely be an epic bitchfest over with.

Shoving my hair back from my face, I frowned at the gritty texture. I withdrew my fingers and glanced down. A thin layer of ash coated my hands that had only ever wielded power that healed and brought life. But I had hurt Nyktos.

That kind of power killed.

Could the embers really be that strong? Were they giving me godlike abilities even now? It wasn't implausible when I thought about it. After all, the embers had always given me powers.

I just didn't want to...hurt anyone. Not on purpose.

I swallowed thickly, forcing myself to get a move on. I went into the bathing chamber and grabbed a clean washcloth. I placed a towel beside the tub and knelt. I tugged off the slip and already missed the faint trace of citrus that clung to the material. Keeping an eye on the entryway, I quickly washed myself and then dunked my head in the tub, vigorously scrubbing at my hair. It had taken an ungodly amount of time to work out all the tangles after, but it was nearly dry by the time I went to the wardrobe.

There weren't many options left when it came to attire: a few sweaters, a pair of thick, black leggings, and three gowns. I chose a sweater and some leggings and then joined Orphine in the hall.

The draken was silent as she led me to the palace's first floor, a book once again tucked under her arm. The only sound was that of our boots rapping off the stone floors.

"I'm sorry about Davina," I said, not knowing if she had been close to the draken or not. When I got no response, I glanced over at her. "And I'm...I'm also sorry for making you feel like you failed at your duty. It wasn't your fault, and it's not like you expected me to climb down from the balcony."

Orphine arched a brow, but that was it. Pressing my lips together, I looked away as guilt settled heavily in my chest. I imagined that her dislike of me had grown to rampant hatred, and I couldn't exactly blame—

"You're right," she said. "I didn't expect you to scale the palace walls. I doubt many would, but I do appreciate the apology...and what you intended to do."

My head swung to her as we reached the stairs. "You do?"

"What you did would've ended in disaster," she said. "But your willingness to take such a risk speaks of your integrity. And that is to be respected. Honored."

Respected? Honored? I tried to think of a time when I had been on the receiving end of either of those things as we crossed under an archway. Before the night of my seventeenth birthday, I'd been honored, but not for anything I'd done. Only for what my family believed I could do for the kingdom. They respected that. Not *me*.

We reached the empty but brightly lit foyer and passed under the cascading glass candles powered by Primal energy. I half-expected an entire armed fleet of guards to be waiting for us. Forcing out a short breath, I glanced at the plain, white pedestal with nothing on it, wondering for the umpteenth time what, if anything, had once sat there. A nervous sort of energy buzzed through me as we passed the entryways to the halls, one of which held Nyktos's office. The palace was eerily silent as we passed that corridor.

My anxiousness ramped up. "Where are we going?"

"To Nyktos," she answered. That much was already apparent, but she didn't elaborate.

I folded an arm over my stomach as my gaze shifted to the throne room. My steps slowed. I couldn't remember seeing the doors closed before. If I had, then I was less observant than I realized because there was a beautiful design painted on them. The same kind of scrolling vines embroidered on the tunics Nyktos and his guards wore had been engraved in silver. White poplar leaves bloomed from the vines. In the center of each door were two crescent moons facing each other, and in the space between them, across the closed doors and painted behind the spiraling vines, was the shape of a wolf.

A white wolf.

I blinked, my brows pinching as I stared at the design—

The ember belonging to Nyktos hummed in my chest as the doors silently swung open upon our approach, revealing two unfamiliar guards. My pulse skittered. Why was I meeting him in here? Senses on high alert, I entered the throne room and jerked to a stop.

Under the glow of the star-strewn sky high above the open ceiling, and the thousands of lit candles lining the walls, stood...good gods, there had to be *hundreds* of men and women standing in the throne room, garbed in the dark gray of the Primal's guards and armed to within an inch of their lives.

It couldn't be all of them because I knew the Rise and Lethe wouldn't go unprotected, but the vast, circular chamber was nearly full. My wide gaze swung over the sea of faces. I caught sight of Saion standing with Rhahar across from Rhain and Ector. Another male stood with them, one with dark, wavy hair and the same pale, ivory skin as Orphine. Rhain looked away, his jaw tight as my gaze touched his.

My confusion only rose as I saw Lailah and Theon, joined by a purplish-black-scaled draken that reached the height of their knees. It was strange seeing Reaver in his draken form when he'd looked like a boy of ten with shaggy blond hair, an elfin face, and solemn, too-serious eyes the last time I'd seen him. Then I looked at the dais.

Nyktos stood before the empty thrones, dressed in a loose shirt and dark pants. Even from a distance, his eyes found and held mine. My heart started pounding as I stood there.

"Come." Orphine motioned for me to follow.

As if I'd fallen under a spell, my feet moved. Guards and gods parted as we walked forward, the room so quiet I feared they could hear the thundering of my heart as I reached the rounded steps. I truly had no idea what was going on, but I didn't think Nyktos had brought me before all of these people to yell at me. He had to know how poorly that would go for him, Primal or not. I stopped again because Orphine had, and…

Because Nyktos's intense stare was still locked on me and my hair, which I'd left down. That choice had had nothing to do with his fascination with it or that he'd once said it reminded him of moonlight. Not at all. The back of my neck tingled as I slowly climbed the short set of steps.

"It's okay," Nyktos said in a voice that was barely above a whisper. Candlelight glinted off his cuff as he extended his hand to me. "Take my hand."

Too confused to deny him, I did as he ordered. Nyktos gave a nod as I turned to face those below. The guards at the doors closed them as Reaver prowled out from the mass of people. Talons clicking softly as he crossed the shadowstone floors, he climbed the steps. I didn't see Nektas, but I saw Aios standing near Paxton, the young mortal boy that Nyktos had brought to the Shadowlands after he'd tried to pickpocket him. The confused pinch to her features mirrored what I felt.

Nyktos placed his other hand on my shoulder, the chill of his fingers bleeding through the sweater, serving once more as a reminder of what I'd done to him. "Those gathered here are some of my most trusted allies," he continued quietly. It struck me then how he never referred to his guards or the gods under him as servants. He only spoke of them as *equals*. "They have sworn to protect the Shadowlands and stand against Kolis and those who support the false Primal of Life."

My stomach gave another tumble as Reaver crouched by my legs.

"All of them have done so with the knowledge that their oath will likely end in death. And yet, they actively work to restore Iliseeum to what it once was—a realm of peace and fairness to all. They're all brave, almost to a fault," he said, his voice rising. "Just as you are."

Air whooshed out of my lungs.

Nyktos squeezed my hand as he lifted his gaze to the crowd. "Any of them would have done as you did the other night," he spoke, allowing his voice to carry through the throne room. "Any of them would sacrifice themselves if they thought that would protect the Shadowlands and those who seek shelter here." He lifted his head as Reaver leaned against my legs, stilling the faint tremor that had begun there. "Seraphena has taken no oath, sworn no loyalties, nor does she yet wear the crown of the Consort. She has not been here long, but she was still willing to risk her life to protect all of you—all of those within the Shadowlands and beyond. Believing that she was the cause of the recent attacks, she planned to turn herself over to Kolis. Though she is not the cause," he said, the slight lies rolling off his tongue smoothly. "Her bravery is unmatched, even among all of you."

There were no dismissive laughs as shock rippled through the faces of those I recognized and those I didn't. And I...I was just as surprised as I stood there. I didn't know if I should throttle Nyktos or hug him. Because no one—utterly *no one*—had ever recognized anything I'd ever done in such a public way. I heard a low murmur as my gaze swept over the crowd, stopping on Aios. The blood had drained from her face.

Nyktos's thumb brushed across the inside of my palm, causing me to jerk. "Seraphena will be a Consort more than worthy of the swords and shields each of you will wield to guard her. One the Shadowlands will be honored to have."

I felt dizzy as I stared at Aios, then movement caught my attention. Ector stepped out from the throng, withdrawing his sword. He crossed it over his chest as he lowered himself to one knee. "Then we will endeavor to be deserving of such an honor."

I jerked again, bumping into Nyktos as Reaver lifted his wings and stretched his neck, letting out a staggering, high-pitched call. Nyktos steadied me as Saion did the same as Ector, then Rhahar and the twins.

Then shouts echoed Ector's vow as swords were lifted, and gods and guards alike knelt.

"None of them will harbor any ill thoughts toward you now. They will see you as you are. Brave and daring." Nyktos had lowered his head, speaking so only I could hear him. His cool breath danced over the shell of my ear, sending a shiver over my skin. "And if they still harbor any ill thoughts, they will be the last ones they ever have. No matter how loyal they are to the Shadowlands, I will destroy them."

I stiffened.

There wasn't a single part of me that doubted the sincerity of his threat. It was in the shadows of his voice, and I...well, I was still torn between wanting to strangle Nyktos and maybe kiss him.

He obviously hadn't forgotten what I'd said about his guards. This speech accomplished two things. It gained favor with those displeased with me and, in the process, checkmated me in a rather impressive way.

Because Nyktos had just ensured that all in the room would be highly unlikely to aid me in any future attempts to go to Kolis. Something Nyktos may have never considered if I hadn't opened my big mouth and told him how his guards would've been happy to see me gone. Not only that, they'd be watching me even closer now that they knew what I was capable of attempting.

I looked over my shoulder at him, my eyes narrowing. "Clever bastard," I whispered.

One side of his lips curved up. "I know." The essence brightened in his eyes as he tipped his head down to mine, bringing our mouths so close I thought for a moment he might actually kiss me. "But I meant every word I said. You are brave and strong. You will be a Consort more than worthy of their swords and shields."

Dampness rushed to my eyes, and I quickly looked away. I had to. Ragged, raw emotion swelled. What he said meant the realm to me, because every word he'd spoken had been about *me* and *my* actions. Not what he believed about me. Not what I or the embers could do for him, but what *I* had chosen to do. And for the first time in my life, I felt like I was more than a destiny I'd never agreed to. More than the embers I carried within me.

I felt like...*more*.

9

Orphine had led me off the dais, through the war room, and into the narrow corridor that led to the east wing and Nyktos's office, then left me standing in the shadowy alcove, still dazed by Nyktos's actions. Doubting that I was being left alone, I opened the door and halted mid-step.

What I saw was not at all what I'd expected.

Nektas sat on the settee across from a small table with a covered dish and a pitcher of juice, his long legs stretched out in front of him and crossed at the ankles. His arms were folded across his chest, stretching the material of his black shirt. His eyes were closed and his head tipped back, exposing the coppery flesh of his throat. His long, dark hair streaked with red fell over one shoulder where…

In her draken form, his daughter lay on her back beside him, her hind legs pressed into the cushion of the settee as she batted at the strands of Nektas's hair with her front talons.

Jadis turned her oval, greenish-brown head toward me. Her crimson-hued eyes widened as she let out what I could only surmise was a squawk of surprise. A happy surprise?

"Morning," Nektas's deep voice rumbled.

Jadis made that sound again as she pulled her talons from her father's hair, jerking his head several times before freeing herself. He gave no reaction, his eyes remaining closed. The tiny draken rolled over onto her belly. Thin, nearly translucent wings unfurled as she jumped down from the settee, landing with a soft thud.

Scurrying across the floor on two legs and then four, Jadis ran straight into me. Clasping my leggings, she hopped as she yipped once and then twice, tugging on the material.

"She wants you to pick her up," Nektas commented. "If you don't submit to that, she's likely to throw a temper tantrum." One wine-red eye opened. "You do not want that to happen. Trust me."

Considering she was starting to cough up smoke and flame, I really didn't want that. I hesitated, though, glancing at my hands. I swallowed thickly. "Are you sure you want me to pick her up?"

"Why would I have a problem with that?"

"You saw what I did to Nyktos." I cut him a sharp look.

"What you did to Ash was an accident. One I don't fear you repeating with my daughter."

I really hoped his confidence wasn't misplaced as I bent at the waist, extending my arms like Nyktos had shown me. Jadis didn't hesitate. The touch of her scales was cool against my skin as she latched onto my arms without using her claws. I lifted her, and she immediately plastered herself to my chest, wrapping her arms around my neck.

"Watch out for her—"

A wing smacked me in the face.

"Her wings," Nektas finished with a sigh. "Sorry."

"It's okay." I leaned my head back as Jadis wiggled closer, her taloned fingers sinking into my hair. Her breath tickled the side of my neck as she made a soft, chattering noise. "Just don't breathe fire on me."

Wide, bright red eyes met mine. Jadis chirped.

"I hope that was an agreement," I told her.

"She likes you," Nektas said. "So, if she does happen to breathe or burp up a little bit of fire on you, it will be purely by accident."

"Good to know," I murmured, patting the center of her back. I glanced around the office. "You weren't in the throne room."

"I didn't need to hear what I already knew."

Because he already saw me as brave and daring? Warmth crept into my cheeks. Or because he was already prepared for me to attempt another escape? Probably the latter.

"Ash should be here in a few." Nektas gestured to the table. "He had food sent in for you."

Ash.

Nektas was the only other person who called him that. My appetite was nowhere to be found at the moment, but I went to the *one* chair placed at the table and sat while Jadis continued her low chattering. I glanced at Nektas. He watched me as he had after I'd been wounded in the Red Woods. Curious about what he seemed to see. I didn't allow myself to think about how I'd seen him naked or how he'd borne witness to my utter failure of an escape.

Giving my head a shake, I shifted Jadis slightly as I reached for the pitcher of juice, pouring myself a glass. "Are you now tasked with watching over me until Nyktos or someone else is available?"

"I'm here because I chose to be."

I arched a brow. "You don't have to lie."

Nektas cocked his head. He appeared relaxed as he spoke, but an undercurrent of energy brimmed beneath his flesh. "Why would I lie about something like that?"

I shrugged, wanting to believe that Nektas was here because he wanted to spend time with me instead of with everyone else.

"Orphine would've stayed with you if I were needed elsewhere, but I wanted to keep you company until Ash arrived." Nektas's head straightened. "Anyway, I figured I'd be better company than Orphine."

I snorted as I picked up my glass, narrowly avoiding having Jadis's wing knock it from my hand as she swung them down. "A carpet would be better company than Orphine."

His chuckle was deep and raspy as I lifted the lid from the dish. Jadis's little head immediately whipped around, her chattering growing louder at the sight of the bacon, the mountain of eggs sprinkled with sliced peppers, and the buttery bread. There was also a hunk of chocolate.

I glanced over at her father and thought of Davina. "Did…did Davina have family?"

"She had an older sister, but she died years ago," Nektas said after a moment. "But other than her, none that I know of."

"Will there be a burial rite? Or has it already taken place?"

"We do not hold ceremonies for the dead," he told me. "We believe that forcing those who cared for the deceased to see them in their death does nothing to honor the dead. We know they know the soul has already left the body to enter Arcadia. When possible, one who was not close to the deceased burns the dead within hours of their death, and each one mourns how they see fit—either together or alone."

Having not known that draken entered Arcadia instead of the Vale, I took a sip of my juice. "You know, I kind of like that. I wouldn't want those close to me watching my body burn." I thought about seeing my old nursemaid, Odetta, wrapped in linen and placed on the burial pyre. "Burial rites are more for the living than the dead anyway. And, sure, I imagine it brings some closure. But I imagine it also creates more pain in others."

Nektas nodded.

My hold on Jadis tightened as she reached for a crispy slice of bacon. "I don't think you can have any of that."

She tipped her hornless head up at me, her eyes woeful and bigger than before. "Sorry. I've been told you're not allowed to have bacon."

Nektas snorted. "Did Ash tell you that?"

I nodded as I picked up a fork.

"Does he think I don't know that he lets Jadis eat whatever she wants?"

Since that was basically true, I said nothing as I got a forkful of eggs. Jadis huffed loudly as I took a bite. "Can she have eggs?"

"If you can get her to eat anything off a fork instead of with her grubby little fingers, she can."

Grinning, I scooped up a tiny bit of eggs on the edge of the fork and lifted it to her mouth. "Open up," I said as she eyed the fork as if it were a serpent. "Just take the eggs. Don't bite the fork."

Her head cocked as her tail thumped off my hip. She stretched out her slender neck, sniffing the eggs. She jerked back from the fork, hissing as she bared...shockingly sharp teeth.

Yikes.

"Watch me." I lifted the fork to my mouth, taking a dramatically slow bite of food. "See? Yum." I added some more eggs to the fork. "Your turn."

It took several more displays of how to eat from a fork before Jadis eyed the utensil seriously and then snapped her head forward. She closed her mouth over the eggs, and there was only a slight tug on the fork as she retreated.

"Holy shit," Nektas murmured, surprised. "Do you know how many people have tried to get her to eat off a utensil? Even Reaver tried."

"Good job, Jadis." I glanced at her father as I added more eggs to the fork. "I guess I have the magic touch."

Jadis tugged on my arm and held on as I lifted the fork to her mouth again. It still took her a couple of moments before she took a bite.

"You just might." Nektas cleared his throat, glancing away. "But I think you remind her of her mother."

All I knew was that Jadis's mother had died two years ago. I knew nothing else. "What...what was her name?"

"Halayna." He straightened, his features tensing. "She had hair like yours. Not as pale, but close. I don't think Jadis remembers much about her. She's still too young, but how can we ever be sure what a child remembers and doesn't?"

I ate the entirety of the chocolate, then took a small bite of bacon, aware of Jadis's greedy little eyes tracking the crispy slice. "Were you married?"

"We were *mated*," he corrected. "It is the same as marriage in many ways. It is not something we draken enter into lightly. The bonds we forge together in a mating can only be broken by death."

Divorces were rare among most in Lasania, but it was far more common among the nobles than I suspected marriages built from love were. "You loved her, then?"

"With my entire being."

I briefly closed my eyes. He *still* loved her. I didn't need to read emotions to know that. "I'm sorry," I whispered, smiling faintly when Jadis glanced up at me as she chewed her eggs. I wanted to know how Halayna had died, but I wouldn't ask the question in front of Jadis. As Nektas had said, there was no way to know what a child remembered and didn't. "My mother loved my father—my birth father. He died the night I was born." I took another bite of bacon, deciding to leave out the circumstances of his death. "I wonder if they were mates of the heart, you know? Maybe the legends about such a thing are real. Because I think a part of my mother died that night, too."

"Two halves that make a whole. Heartmates," Nektas said, drawing my gaze. He watched closely. "That's what the Arae call it. It's rare but real, and I never heard of it occurring between mortals. But that doesn't mean it's impossible. The loss of one's other half can be...catastrophic. If your parents were heartmates, then I pity your mother."

I wouldn't go *that* far. Not after doing nothing to stop Tavius or making any real attempt beyond relying on me to better the lives of her subjects. Not anymore. She was lucky I hadn't told Nyktos to take her into the Abyss.

"But it would make sense that your parents were that," he said, leaning into the settee.

"Why is that?" I scratched Jadis under her chin, and she hummed, her eyes closing. My smile grew.

"Heartmates usually only occur between two people whose unions are linked to some great purpose."

"Like how a *viktor* is assigned to watch over someone?" I asked, speaking of those who lived numerous mortal lives to serve as protectors or guides to those the Fates determined would be harbingers of great change and purpose.

He nodded. "Perhaps fate brought your parents together to make sure the embers of life were born as Eythos intended."

"Perhaps." I took a drink and then offered the juice to Jadis. She turned her nose up at it. "How much do you know about what Eythos did?"

"Everything."

"Then you know I wasn't being foolish last night. If I can make it to Kolis, I could be successful."

"Maybe. But at what cost?"

"Does the price matter when we're talking about stopping Kolis?"

"The price should always matter when it comes at the cost of a life," he said.

The crack that had formed trembled deep in my chest. "But that's a price I will pay either way."

"You don't know that." Nektas glanced at the doors at the same moment I felt a warm buzz in my chest. "He comes."

I busied myself by shoving half a slice of buttery bread into my mouth as Nyktos entered the chamber. I didn't look up, but I felt his stare on the back of my head. Jadis had the absolute opposite reaction, whipping around in my arms and stretching up to look over my shoulder. She let out a loud, excited chirp right in my ear as she strained against me.

The Primal swooped her up out of my arms as he passed.

"Traitor," I muttered, peeking up to see Jadis wrapping herself around him like a little tree bear, her eyes closed and tiny claws digging into where he had his hair pulled back into a small bun at the nape of his neck.

The scene was so sweet I was surprised my teeth hadn't started to ache.

"Sera got her to eat off a fork," Nektas announced.

"Really? And here I thought Jadis would be eating with her..." Rubbing the little draken's back, he turned to us. He scowled as his gaze landed on the table. On me. "Is that all you've eaten?"

"It is." I picked up a napkin.

"You can't possibly be done," Nyktos muttered, placing Jadis on the chair by his desk. She popped up, only one crimson eye visible above the back of the chair.

"You can't possibly be monitoring my food intake," I retorted.

"You two are entertaining," Nektas murmured. His daughter jumped down and scampered across the floor. Nektas bent, picked her up, and placed her on the couch. She curled into a ball beside his thigh.

"If you find this entertaining," I said as Jadis let out a loud yawn, "you must be bored."

Nyktos huffed. "He is."

The draken smirked.

"The only reason I was commenting on the food was because of the Culling. You don't want to run the risk of weakening and falling into stasis." His eyes met mine as he came forward and picked up a slice of bacon. "If you would like something else to eat, I'm sure I can have it prepared for you."

"That's not necessary." I fiddled with the hem of the tablecloth. "Besides, I don't think there's enough food or sleep in either realm that will prevent what's coming."

"And what's that?" Nyktos asked.

"Death." I jerked my chin at the Primal. "And I'm not talking about you."

Nektas gave me a small grin at that. "Death is not a foregone conclusion."

"Is it not?" I started tapping my foot.

"No," he said.

Pressing my lips together, I shook my head. I had no idea what Nektas was thinking then. If he knew everything, he would know that only the love of the man I had planned to kill—someone actually incapable of love—could save me. He was aware of that.

"There is no reason to deny what's coming." I met Nyktos's stare as he returned to leaning against his desk. "No matter how strong the embers of life are."

A muscle ticked in Nyktos's jaw. "We will have to agree to disagree on that."

"You like to say that, don't you?"

"And you like to argue, don't you?"

I rolled my eyes. "Yeah, well, arguing over this is pointless." My foot beat a fast tempo now. "So, whatever makes you happy."

"Nothing about any of this makes me happy," Nyktos retorted, and I couldn't fault him for that. "Either way, what Holland said may not have been entirely correct. There could be another option."

Remembering what he'd said in the Dying Woods about needing five seconds of peace to come up with another way of saving my life, I smirked. "Like what?"

"Like what Kolis did to my father. Remove the embers."

My jaw practically hit the table. "Is that possible?"

"I don't see why not." Nyktos watched me. "Embers are eather, Sera. It's the essence of a Primal. Kolis found a way to take it from my father without harming him."

Hope sparked, but I squelched it before it could catch fire and spread. There were far too many what-ifs—too many questions. "But he wasn't able to take all of it."

"That's because Eythos was a Primal," Nektas interjected. "And you are a Primal born of mortal flesh. Those embers are not fully yours unless you Ascend into a Primal."

"That really explains nothing to me," I admitted. "Explain it to me as if I'm Jadis learning how to use a fork."

Nektas grinned at that.

"What he means is that those embers have fundamentally changed you." Nyktos clasped the edge of the desk as he stretched out his legs, crossing them loosely at the ankles. "You're in the Culling. There's no stopping that. But if we can remove the embers, you should be like any godling entering the Culling."

Should? "Correct me if I'm wrong, but not all godlings survive the Culling, right?"

"They don't, but my blood would make sure you survive," he said. "Ensure that you don't fail the Ascension."

Shock blasted through me. Giving me blood to heal wounds seemed vastly different than aiding in my Ascension. "How…how much blood will I need for the Ascension?"

"All but the last drop of your blood would need to be removed," Nyktos explained. "Then you'd have to replenish your blood with mine."

"All but the last drop?" I whispered. "That's a lot."

"It is." Nyktos's gaze held mine. "That is why the Ascension can be so dangerous. You either take too much or not enough, but the alternative is unacceptable."

Sitting back, I exhaled roughly as thoughts raced past the confusion of why he was still determined to do such a thing, even after the embers were removed. I would be of no real use to him at that point. The breath I took was thin. "What would I become if that worked?"

"You'd be like any godling who survives the Culling," he answered. "But possibly more. Those embers are powerful. You could Ascend into an actual god."

Godlings who Ascended weren't exactly mortal beyond that point. They aged slower—every three decades of mortal life equated to one year of a godling's. They were susceptible to very few illnesses, and while not as impervious to injury as a god or Primal, they could live for thousands of years—at least, according to Aios.

But a god?

I couldn't even process the possibility of either of those options, but the hope was now a small flame. "Is that even possible?"

"It's never happened before," Nektas said. "When Eythos was the true Primal of Life and Ascended the Chosen, they became the same as godlings because of the eather being stronger in thirdborns. None had ever Ascended into an actual god, not even in the hundreds of years of the Chosen being Ascended. But none had Primal embers in them either. Anything is possible with you."

That was a scary thought. "You said only Kolis and Eythos knew how it was done."

"Someone had to tell Kolis," Nektas pointed out. "He must have learned it from somewhere."

"Before Penellaphe left, she said something to me that struck me as odd," Nyktos said, and I remembered seeing them standing together in the throne room, speaking too quietly for me to hear. "And it kept nagging at me. She said that Delfai would welcome your presence."

"Who or what is a Delfai?" I asked.

A shadow of a smile appeared on Nyktos's lips. "A very old and powerful God of Divination."

I frowned. "I don't remember hearing about a specific God of Divination."

"He was able to see what was hidden to others—their truths, both past and future," Nyktos explained, and that sounded like a god I didn't want to be even remotely close to. "As Penellaphe said, the Gods of Divination called Mount Lotho home and served in Embris's Court. Most were destroyed when Kolis took my father's embers. I assumed Delfai had been, too, but I checked the old records. He never entered Arcadia. He's still alive."

I leaned forward. "Can we find him? With your special Primal powers?"

Nyktos's lips twitched. "Exactly what kind of powers do you think

I have?"

"Hopefully, the kind that can find missing gods," I suggested.

"Unfortunately, I do not." His fingers moved along the edge of his desk, seeming to follow the rhythm of my tapping foot. "But I do know of something that can."

"The Pools of Divanash," Nektas shared, and I blinked. "They are divining pools, once overseen by the Gods of Divination. The pools can show any object or person the seeker searches for. They've been relocated to the Vale."

"Where I cannot go," Nyktos tacked on. "Also where Kolis can no longer enter."

And I knew at once why they'd been relocated. If these pools could show someone's location, they could've revealed where Sotoria's soul was. "Your father moved them there?"

"My father had them guarded, but I moved them as soon as I was powerful enough to do so."

"Thank you" rose on the breath I took, but it seemed…silly somehow to thank him. Because I wasn't her. I focused on the draken. "But you can enter the Vale."

"Yes. However, the pools are…temperamental." Nektas gave a slight smile. "They will only provide answers after being given what no one else knows, by the one who seeks the answer. There can be no middle person—"

"Then I would have to go."

Nyktos nodded.

"I can go now." I started to rise.

"You cannot go now," Nyktos said. "Not until after the coronation."

"But—"

"It will not be safe for you to travel anywhere before then," he cut in.

"Will it be safe for me to do so even after?" I demanded.

His fingers stilled. "What protection it offers is better than none, Sera. Nothing may happen on the road to and from the Vale, but even I have trouble controlling some things in the Shadowlands. Creatures that would happily devour anything that crosses their paths that is not a Primal or claimed by one."

Figuring he spoke of the Shades, I held his stare as the mere idea that being *claimed* offered protection blew me away. It also ticked me off. That was some bullshit. "I'm not afraid of what I may come across."

"Of course, you wouldn't be. But I will not risk you or Nektas without taking every possible safety measure first. He will protect you, but he cannot do so against a Primal until you are my Consort. This is not up for argument."

"And if I want to argue anyway?"

He pinned me with a bland look. "If it makes you feel better to do so, then go ahead. I'm sure it will entertain Nektas."

"It will," the draken confirmed.

I blew out an exaggerated breath. "I guess I'll just sit around and—" Something occurred to me. "If we find Delfai, and he's able to tell us what to do to remove the embers, will the process cause what happened when Kolis stole the embers in the first place? The death of gods and Primals?"

Nyktos's eyes met mine. "And if it does?"

My stomach dropped. "I would be exchanging my life for the lives of others." I saw the guards falling from the Rise, swamped in flames. I thought of Davina. "I can't do that."

Nyktos's head tilted. "No, I didn't think you would."

"It's a good thing neither of us believes such an event will occur then," Nektas said, and my gaze whipped between the two. "That happened because Eythos was the true Primal of Life. You would not yet be a Primal. The act wouldn't have the same catastrophic consequences."

"Why didn't you just say that?" I demanded.

"I wanted to see if I was right about what you would choose," Nyktos said.

I resisted the urge to throw my glass at him. "So, what would happen to the embers? Would they go into someone else?" My eyes went wide, the hope now becoming a wildfire. "Could you take them? They belong to you, don't they? The Primal of Life was *your* destiny."

"It was my destiny." Nyktos's eyes glimmered faintly. "And if this works, it will be mine again."

IO

I watched Nektas carry a sleeping Jadis out of the office. The little draken was sprawled over one broad shoulder, limbs and wings limp but tangled in her father's hair. He was taking her to one of the bedchambers on the second floor that I'd learned had been converted into a nursery of sorts.

Apparently, while sleeping, Jadis had a habit of unconsciously slipping into her mortal form, and as Nektas had put it, no one needed to see her naked as a jaybird.

Though I wasn't sure what that even meant. As far as I knew, jaybirds didn't wear clothing.

"You really got her to eat with a fork?" Nyktos asked.

Slowly, I twisted around in my chair to face him. He still leaned against the desk. "I did."

Nyktos smiled. It was close-lipped and faint, but it still had a transformative effect, warming the cold beauty of his features. "I've tried to get her to do it on more than one occasion. Usually end up with her knocking the fork from my hands or throwing herself on the floor. Sometimes simultaneously."

I grinned at that. "Nektas said I might remind Jadis of her mother—the color of my hair or something like that—and thinks that helped."

"Possibly." His gaze met mine and then flickered away. "Halayna's hair was on the lighter side. Not as fair as yours, though."

Not like moonlight? Thank the gods and the Fates everywhere I didn't ask that. "How did...how did she die?"

Nyktos didn't answer for a long moment. "She was murdered." He dragged a hand over his chest. "She was summoned to Dalos, and Kolis murdered her."

I sucked in a shuddering breath. "Why?"

"Kolis loathes Nektas. He wanted to make him pay for being loyal to my father and then to me since he believes that Nektas should've been honored to serve *him* after he became the Primal of Life."

Heart aching, I shook my head. "So he killed Halayna to punish Nektas?"

"Kolis would've preferred to kill Nektas, but he knows better than to do that without a really good reason." Nyktos lowered his hand. "Unless Kolis killed Nektas in self-defense, many of the other draken throughout Iliseeum would have taken the act personally. They would have gone after Kolis and any who defended him."

My brows shot up. "And the other draken didn't take him killing Halayna personally? And why couldn't the draken just take Kolis on themselves?"

"A draken can gravely wound a Primal, but they cannot kill one," he reminded me. "And many of the draken did take what Kolis did personally. But with Nektas, it's...different. He's old."

"How old?"

His gaze drifted back to mine. "He was the first dragon given mortal form."

I nearly choked on my breath. "You mean...?"

That smile of his returned, a little broader and warmer, and even more startling in its impact. "My father befriended him when he was a dragon. Nektas was the first to become a draken. He was the draken who gave his fire to the flesh my father lent to create the first mortal."

"Good gods, he would have to be..." I couldn't even do the math in my head, especially when all I could think about was that I'd been in the presence of the draken who'd helped to create the mortal race. "How long can draken live?"

"As long as a Primal if they are not killed."

I sucked in a shallow breath. "So, they are immortal?"

"Not even a Primal is immortal, Sera. Nothing that can be killed truly is, no matter how long we live."

"Is anything immortal?"

"The Arae. And before you ask, I don't know how old your Holland is," he said. And I *had* been about to ask that. "The *viktors* are also immortal, but in a different way."

It made sense since the *viktors* died but didn't stay dead, instead returning to Mount Lotho to await being born again. Sort of like Sotoria—

Clearing my thoughts of *her*, I refocused. "Does anyone other than Nektas know about this plan?"

"Only a few I spoke to this morning," he said.

"And who are those few?" I asked. Nyktos rattled off names of those who either watched over me or were seen with him often. The usual suspects. "And how much do they know about what is inside me?"

"They know you have more than one ember and that you're in the Culling—something they didn't need to be told since they know what those embers mean, and they've already seen you experience the symptoms. They know what those embers will do if they remain inside you. They support the plan."

I doubted the desire to see me live was the reason they supported it. "All of it? Including you Ascending me?"

"They don't have a say in that." He studied me. "But none voiced any concerns."

I also doubted that, even with his speech. "And what about Sotoria's soul?"

"No one here but Nektas knows that," he said. "Having that knowledge could endanger them—and you—if they were to be captured and questioned."

My smile of relief was part grimace. I didn't think any of his trusted guards would betray Nyktos. His unwillingness to share that little piece of knowledge was likely due to the fact that it could change the way his trusted guards viewed how things should be handled. But I let that go, switching to other questions. "If this plan of yours works, and you become the true Primal of Life, could you Ascend the Chosen?"

Nyktos nodded.

"Would you continue with the Rite?" I asked, curious.

"You know, I'm not entirely sure." His brows pinched. "I think I would prefer for it to be more of a choice. Not a requirement."

I liked the sound of that. "But couldn't you just do away with the Rite altogether?"

"That could be done, but the Rite was started for a reason. The Chosen once had a real purpose. They were needed to replenish Iliseeum by bringing younger, newer gods into the fold—gods who knew what it was like to be mortal. It's a balance in a way, one designed to offset those who would live such long lives they'd forget just how fragile and precious mortal life is." Nyktos watched me. "You seem...conflicted about that."

I was. Which was why I wasn't all that irritated about him clearly reading my emotions. None of the Chosen given over to the Rite had Ascended in *centuries*. Most were killed within days of entering Dalos. Others became something else entirely. But my distaste for the tradition had started before I learned of their true fates. "I understand their purpose. It makes sense. But the Chosen...while they may have everything provided for them in the mortal realm, they don't really live, you know? Their faces can't be looked upon. They cannot be touched or spoken to by anyone other than another Chosen or the Priests."

"None of that is necessary." Nyktos frowned. "We didn't start that. The mortals did."

"Then why hasn't it been changed?"

"I would if I were in a position to demand such things, but..."

"Only the Primal of Life can." I sighed, understanding. "God, what if...what if all those Chosen who haven't been killed are being turned into Craven like Andreia?"

"It's hard to even comprehend," he replied. "Though it seems like the Revenants are not the same as the Craven."

I nodded, thinking over what Gemma had shared. "It sounded like Kolis has been tinkering with his creations. Changing them. Maybe *improving* on them." I shook my head, exhaling. "If this plan works, what happens to Kolis? And the Rot?"

"If it works, I imagine I would Ascend again. The impact may be as...volatile as when Kolis stole the embers. It might not be. There is no way of knowing. But other Primals and gods would feel it. They would sense that Kolis was no longer the Primal of Life."

"So, that doesn't sound like he dies then."

Nyktos laughed roughly at the clear disappointment in my voice. "Kolis is the oldest Primal alive. We may never be able to kill him. We may only ever be able to weaken him enough to entomb him."

"Like...like the gods beneath the Red Woods?"

He nodded.

"But you're wrong, though," I said. "The way to weaken *and* kill him is sitting right in front of you."

The eather intensified in his eyes. "You promised," he said softly.

I squirmed in the chair. "I did."

He watched me. "I'm trusting you to keep your word, Sera, and that trust is a very fragile thing."

"I know." I lifted my chin. "I'm just pointing out the truth."

"It's not the truth." A muscle ticked in his jaw. "It never will be."

Looking away, I tried not to dwell on that fragile trust that he spoke of. "And the Rot?"

"Once I have the embers inside me, the Rot should vanish from the mortal realm—from your kingdom."

The relief that swept through me would've taken my legs out from under me if I'd been standing. It was that potent. An end to the Rot wouldn't fix everything in Lasania, but with Ezra and Marisol's leadership, there was more than just hope for my kingdom. There was a future for the entirety of the mortal realm. I could almost cry.

"Your relief," Nyktos murmured, drawing my gaze to him. "It's...refreshing. Earthy."

I wasn't surprised to hear that I was projecting my emotions. Nodding, I pulled myself together as something occurred to me. "The people here? They have no want for food?"

"Much is imported from other areas of Iliseeum, as well as the grain used to feed the cattle and hogs, but there is just enough to keep everyone fed."

"Is it possible that food can be exported from these parts of Iliseeum to Lasania so the suffering can be eased until the Rot is fixed?"

"I wish that were something that could be done," he said softly as disappointment swept through me. "The effects the essence has on mortals who don't carry it in their veins—and even animals—also impacts other organic matter. The food grown in Iliseeum would begin to rapidly decay as it crossed through the Primal mists between the realms."

I exhaled slowly, telling myself there was still a chance to end the people's suffering. "And what about the Shadowlands? You said it didn't always look like this."

"The Shadowlands were always different from the rest of Iliseeum—the stars were visible, even during the day, and the nights were darker than any other place in Iliseeum. But, yes, it would recede from here." He looked at the ceiling, dragging the edge of his fangs over his lower lip. The act snagged my attention, creating a soft whirl in the pit of my stomach. "The change here was slow at first. Parts of it fell to what you call the Rot by the time I was born. But most of the Shadowlands was still alive. Thriving. I think you would've found it beautiful. It resembled the woods around your lake—wild and lush."

Hearing him refer to it as *my lake* did strange things to my chest that were best left alone lest I project my emotions down his throat again.

Thick lashes lowered. "Where land is barren and lifeless now, there were once lakes and fields of flowers as vibrant as the moon."

"Poppies," I whispered. The flowers that were nothing like those in the mortal realm had delicate petals the color of blood in the moonlight on the outside and were a shade of crimson on the inside. They only opened when someone approached them. *Poisonous*, beautiful flowers that were unpredictable and temperamental and reminded him of me.

"The poppies," he confirmed. A few days after my arrival in the Shadowlands, one had blossomed in the Red Woods. He'd believed it was my presence bringing life back to the Shadowlands. "There were also seasons here. Hot and steamy in the summer, snowy and blustery in the winter. As a child, I used to spend many of those warmer days in the lakes that once stretched along the road leading to the gates of the Rise. When I grew a little older and had trouble sleeping, I would swim. It's one of the things I miss most."

"Is that why you were in my lake that night?" I asked.

"I'd been to the lake many times before," he admitted after a moment.

I couldn't help but wonder how many times we'd narrowly missed each other.

"Even when my father died, the Rot didn't spread fast," he went on after a moment. "It continued slowly, year after year, taking little pieces at a time and turning the world gray as the sun grew weaker and the nights even longer. Then, seemingly overnight, all the trees in the Dying Woods dropped their leaves, and all the lakes dried up. That was the last of the seasons and sunlight here. But outside of the Shadowlands, it continues to spread slowly."

Tension settled in my shoulders. I suspected I knew the answer to the question I was about to ask, but I wanted to be wrong. "When did that happen?"

His lashes swept up. "In five months, it will have happened twenty-one years ago."

Gods.

Sitting back, I turned my attention to the bare bookshelves. "Aios was right in a way, you know? When she said that the embers of life were protected while in a mortal bloodline. But when I was born, that was no longer the case. They entered a vessel with an expiration date." Focusing on him, I swallowed. "I'm sorry."

"Why would you apologize? It's not your fault."

"I know." I lifted a shoulder. "But I'm still sorry."

Nyktos stared at me for several heartbeats. "I have a question for you."

"Ask away."

"What do you think of this plan?"

"What do I think?" I rubbed my knees. "I hope it works. It'll stop the Rot and hopefully weaken Kolis. And if it does work..." I trailed off, my throat constricting.

"What?" Nyktos asked quietly.

I didn't know how to put into words what I was thinking, let alone feeling, because it was something I'd never considered before. A future without an early, certain death. A possibly very long future, one that could possibly span hundreds of years. I felt...hope. For myself. It felt a little selfish since his plan carried the risk of more attacks between now and then, and the possibility of us not being able to locate the missing god—or the god being of no help to us. There was a lot of risk, but there was also *hope*.

And hope felt as fragile as the trust he'd spoken of.

Aware that Nyktos was watching me, I cleared my throat. "I think it's a good plan."

He nodded and didn't speak for a few moments. "We need to talk about the coronation."

Gods, that *was* in two days. My stomach tumbled even further because it felt as if I'd forgotten.

"I realized we hadn't discussed what occurs during the coronation in any real detail." He chewed his food as neatly as he carved it. "I figured you would have questions."

"Should I? You said I would be crowned before high-ranking gods and Primals." I squinted. "Actually, you said that the attendance of other Primals was only a possibility."

"I lied," he admitted without shame. "I figured learning that Primals would be there would make you nervous."

"It doesn't."

He raised an eyebrow.

"Okay. It makes me a little nervous, but it's not like that news is something I can't handle."

"When we first discussed the coronation, you'd just been brought into the Shadowlands and discovered that it was not I who had made the deal that forced you to become my Consort. Your entire life, whatever it may have been, had just been upended right after you were *whipped*," he stated, his eyes flashing to a steely gray. I quickly shifted my focus to the bare shelves. "Even one as strong as you can only take so much."

"You never know how much you can take until you can't take more," I said. "But I...I appreciate the motivation behind the lie."

Nyktos chuckled. "Sure, you do."

"So, there is more than just me being crowned and calling it a night?" I asked, looking up at him.

"Is that how Kings and Queens are crowned in the mortal realm?"

"Gods, no. There are days-long celebrations. Feasts and parties. Fireworks." I smiled. "I do enjoy fireworks."

"There will be no fireworks."

I pouted. "That's disappointing."

His fingers partially hid his smile as he scratched his chin. "Nor will there be days-long celebrations."

"I'm relieved to hear that."

"But there will be a feast after the coronation."

"Here?"

"No. The coronation will be in Lethe, at the Council Hall," he said. "And we won't see each other tomorrow. It's tradition—a belief that not seeing one another before the start of the coronation will ward off bad luck."

"You believe in that?" I asked, genuinely curious.

"You know, I'd rather not take any chances, so I will honor the tradition to the best of my ability." He tipped his head back. "I will meet you before the ceremony. We will ascend the dais together, and it will be I who crowns you and bestows a title upon you."

Realizing I hadn't seen him with a crown yet, I wondered exactly what it looked like and if I would be expected to wear it. Crowns looked absurdly heavy. "So, what is my title?"

A wry grin appeared. "Not sure yet."

I arched a brow, "Nice."

"I'll come up with something," he promised. "If the Fates find us worthy and everyone behaves with the decorum that is expected, the feasts will begin."

"And if they don't?"

"You will be heavily guarded throughout the entirety of the event," he shared. "I will not allow any harm to come to you."

"I don't need you to keep me safe."

Thick lashes lifted, and those wisps of eather fragmenting the silver in his eyes were brighter than I'd ever seen them. "But you do."

"I think I proved on more than one occasion that is not the case," I replied, tensing.

"You showed no fear with the dakkais and didn't hesitate when the entombed gods were freed," he said as my gaze dropped to my hands. "I know you're strong and can fight. That you're brave. Needing me or anyone to look out for you doesn't mean you're weak, that you can't defend yourself, or that you're afraid. We all need someone to watch over us."

Heat crawled up my throat. "Do you?"

"Desperately," he whispered.

My gaze flew to him. Nyktos might be the youngest of the Primals, but I'd seen him in his true form. He was a winged being of night and power, able to obliterate gods with a mere look. I'd seen him turn trees into ash in anger. But there was a truth in that one word, a vulnerability I found myself wanting to protect.

Nyktos pushed off the desk and walked to the credenza. He opened a drawer and pulled out a thick, bound tome. "We will also need to get a handle on what happened last night."

"The dumping me on your bed and taking my clothing off part of last night?" I suggested.

He sent me a dry look as he sat. "The eather you wielded. Right now, that may just be tied to your emotions. I don't know if removing those embers will stop you from doing it again until you complete the Culling. It may not. What I know is that the embers have already changed you. There is eather in your blood. That will not be removed, and you will still be able to harness eather once you complete the Culling."

"But not restore life."

"Not without those embers."

I glanced down at my hands. I wasn't sure if I would miss the ability to restore life. The ability to create life out of death didn't always feel like a part of me, but it *was* a part of me. The embers in my chest warmed at the thought, but they were also bound and determined to kill me.

"The ability could come to you more easily between now and then," he continued as he began unwinding the twine. "Like it would for a god-born destined to Ascend to Primalhood."

"Like you?"

He nodded. "There are ways we can try to draw it out of you again that won't run the risk of weakening you, as long as you're not using the eather in other ways and are taking care of yourself."

"Really?" I sat forward, my interest more than piqued. "Is that something we can try now?"

A faint grin appeared, but he froze. His gaze flicked over my shoulder. A moment later, I heard a knock. "Come in."

I twisted in my chair as the doors opened to reveal Saion.

"There is...a problem at the gates," he said, and a wicked sense of déjà vu swept through me.

"Elaborate," Nyktos ordered, closing the tome.

Saion sent me a quick glance. "The Cimmerian are here."

I tensed as Nyktos sat. I'd learned of the Cimmerian during my studies. They were lesser gods a couple of generations removed from Attes, the Primal of Accord and War, and Kyn, the Primal of Peace and Vengeance. Gods born fully formed as warriors. There were even legends about them being brought forth during mortal wars by Kings brave—or foolish—enough to summon either Attes or Kyn. "Why would Attes or Kyn send warriors here?"

"Not all Cimmerian serve Attes and Kyn. Some serve in other Courts. These have come from Hanan's," Saion shared, and my stomach dropped.

Nyktos glanced at Saion as he replaced the tome and opened another drawer. "Where's Bele?"

"With Aios," Saion answered. "Nektas is taking Jadis and Reaver to them."

"Good. Bele will not leave the younglings." Nyktos grabbed straps that went around his waist and chest, designed to hold swords and other sharp, pointy weapons. "How many are at the gates?"

"About a hundred," Saion said.

"Fuck," Nyktos growled.

"Most of the guards are on the Rise along Lethe as you requested, keeping an eye on the Black Bay." Lamplight from a nearby sconce glanced over the rich, black skin of Saion's cheek as he cocked his head. "There are only about a dozen here. So, if things go south..."

"And if they do go south?" I rose as Nyktos opened a cabinet door and slid out a long, wide shelf full of weapons. "I've seen what you're capable of—"

"Cimmerian are not your run-of-the-mill gods. Using eather around them feeds their abilities," Saion said.

"Like the dakkais?" I asked.

"The dakkais want to devour those with eather in them, but the Cimmerian pull strength from it. The essence amplifies their abilities. Makes them stronger." Nyktos withdrew a sword, strapping it to his back so the handle pointed down, and leaving me to wonder exactly how deep the credenza was. "And they don't fight like anyone you've ever seen."

Dread quickly blossomed. "How *do* they fight?"

"They can summon shrouds of night to blind their opponents," Saion told me. "The kind that not even Nyktos can see through."

My heart kicked against my ribs. That had *not* been in any of my studies. "And they would try to fight you?" When Nyktos didn't answer, I twisted to Saion. "Will they?"

Saion nodded. "Fighting is one of the few things that seem to bring those fuckers any joy. They're willing to fight with just about anyone, including Primals."

Nyktos slid a dagger into the strap across his chest and another into his boot. "I want you to stay here."

"I can help," I protested. "I can fight—"

"She really can fight," another voice chimed in from the hall. "And with most of the guards—"

"Ector?" Nyktos cut in.

There was a beat of silence, and then the fair-haired, sharp-featured god appeared in the doorway. "Yes?"

Nyktos pinned him with a cold stare. "This is one of those times I've discussed with you on *multiple* occasions."

I frowned.

"When I need to…" Ector cleared his throat. "Shut the fuck up?"

"Exactly." Nyktos stalked out from behind the desk, securing a short sword to his waist. "I know you can fight. This isn't about that. We could be wrong about why they are here, especially with the draken attack and the coronation taking place the day after tomorrow. If someone is attempting to take you, they know I will have little support in retaliation if you're not my Consort. They could be here for you, and I don't want to make that easier for them. Stay here, Seraphena."

I decided at that very moment, when he said my name like that, that I wanted to punch him. In the throat. Hard.

Nyktos stopped at the door once more, looking over his shoulder. "I'll check in with you later. Until then," he said, his eyes meeting mine, "behave."

"Yes, *Your Highness.*" I bowed. "I wouldn't want to be grounded."

Out in the hall, someone—likely Ector—choked loudly. The swirling in Nyktos's eyes slowed as he locked his gaze on me. "Don't push me on this." His head swiveled toward Saion. "Stay here and make sure she doesn't leave."

Saion looked at me with a heavy sigh. "Honored to obey such a command."

I clamped my mouth shut, not even daring to breathe until Nyktos was gone. Only then did I allow my head to fall back so I could let out a silent scream as I clenched my hands.

"Did that make you feel better?" Saion asked. "Whatever it was that you just did?"

"No," I bit out.

"Didn't think so." He arched a brow as he leaned against the door. "So, you're ready for nap time? Or would you like a snack? Maybe some diced apples?"

My eyes narrowed on the god.

His lips twitched.

Disgusted, I looked away. I fully understood why Nyktos didn't want me out there. Even if the Cimmerian weren't here for me, the last thing we needed was more gods from other Courts recognizing me. Understanding didn't translate into liking it. "Will Nyktos and the others be okay out there with the Cimmerian?"

Saion was quiet for a moment. "You're really worried?"

Inhaling sharply, I turned to the god. "I wouldn't ask if I wasn't."

"I suppose not," he murmured, eyeing me with a slightly perplexed pinch to his brow.

I crossed my arms. "What? Are you going to talk about snapping my neck again?"

"No." He continued staring as if I were a puzzle with missing pieces. "Did you really try to escape so you could kill Kolis on your own?" he asked.

I tensed. "Do you think Nyktos would lie about that?"

"I suppose not."

"Then you already know the answer to your question."

"You had to know that what you tried would've ended in your death, and yet that didn't stop you," he said. "As such, it would now be dishonorable to speak of snapping your neck."

"But completely honorable to do so before?"

"Probably not, considering you're technically the true Primal of Life," he said. "Which means I should be bowing before you."

"Please, don't."

Saion grinned. "I won't," he said. "It's wild, though. True Primal of Life embers alive in a mortal."

"Wild is one way of putting it." I began to pace.

"None of us was all that surprised to learn that. Not after what you did for Gemma and Bele," he continued. "But still, suspecting it and having it confirmed are two very different things."

I nodded, distracted by what could be occurring outside. I knew Nyktos would be fine, but he was out there, dealing with the Cimmerian because I had Ascended Bele. He might walk away if it turned violent, but what of Ector? Or Rhain, who had to be around here somewhere? Theon and Lailah? Rhahar? The guards or any of the draken who might become involved while I remained inside? How many would die today?

I couldn't just stand by.

"What are you doing?" Saion turned as I started across the room. "I really hope it involves napping, but I have a feeling it doesn't."

Grasping the handles, I yanked open the doors. "It doesn't."

"So, where are you going, then?"

I stalked out into the hall. "I'm going to go *push*."

II

As I climbed the stairs of the Rise, the stars sweeping across the deep gray sky twinkled like a sea of gems, signaling that night wasn't too far away.

"This is such a bad idea," Saion muttered from behind me for the hundredth time. "A terrible, horrible idea. If something happens to you—"

"Nothing will happen." I reached the top of the Rise and crossed the battlement, passing several shadowstone-tipped spears and arrows beside bows stacked against the wall as I made sure I stayed hidden behind the parapet's solid wall.

"And that just ups the whole terrible, horrible idea part," Saion commented as I picked up a bow and a full quiver.

"Just in case," I told him, leaning against the shadowstone wall. I peered out the opening, finding Nyktos first without even trying to look for him. I suspected it was the ember that'd once belonged to him. It knew exactly where he was.

Which meant it was highly likely that he was aware of my presence, as well. And it was also probable that he would be really angry.

Deciding I'd deal with that later, I quietly pulled an arrow from the quiver.

Nyktos stood in the front, arms crossed and looking every inch a Primal—a bored one, at that, based on the bland set of his features. A dozen or so guards stood behind him, and I had no idea if they were mortal, godling, or god, but I spotted Ector standing with Rhain.

The ones who stood a few yards from Nyktos wore black balaclavas, leaving only their eyes visible. Sheaths of armor covered their bodies from their chests to their knees.

I squinted. "Is their armor made of...shadowstone?"

"It is." Saion crouched behind the other parapet.

"A ripple of power was felt throughout all the Courts," one of the Cimmerian warriors said. He stood in the front, hand resting on the hilt of a sword.

"Shit," Saion growled. "That's Dorcan. He's really old," he added when I glanced at him. "And not someone most want to cross on a battlefield."

I didn't know if I should be relieved or not to hear that the Cimmerian weren't here for me.

"Hanan knows the dakkais followed an earlier trace of power to the Shadowlands," Dorcan said.

"Is that so?" Nyktos replied.

"Are you suggesting that you were somehow unaware of the surge of power?" Dorcan asked.

"I haven't suggested anything."

There was a rough, quick laugh from behind the balaclava. "Is the goddess Bele here?" he asked, and I caught the slight movement of a Cimmerian behind him. One of the warriors had slipped a glove to the dagger strapped to their waist.

"Hell." Saion had seen the movement, too. He quietly withdrew his sword. "If they start fighting, I will join them."

I nodded, keeping my attention on the Cimmerian. There were a hundred warriors to our significantly outnumbered fighters. We had Nyktos, but if he couldn't use eather—

Our fighters.

Our people.

My stomach twisted sharply, but my fingers remained steady on the arrow. "Why isn't Nektas out here?"

"None of the draken will come unless they sense it's necessary," Saion explained.

"This isn't necessary?"

"Not when their presence could escalate things."

"And if you're telling me that she's not here, Hanan will discover your lie," Dorcan continued from the road. "As will *the* King."

"Is there any single part of me that looks like I give a fuck?" Nyktos replied, and I blew out a low breath.

I hoped Nektas was really close.

"You should." Dorcan tilted his head back. "Especially since I've heard you've had a rough couple of days. Dakkais. Draken. And you're about to take on a Consort."

"Oh, shit," Saion muttered, tensing.

The change in the air was sudden and tangible, charging with static. Both Ector's and Rhain's hands went to their swords. I doubted Dorcan was unaware as he said, "A piece of advice, old friend. I don't think this is the time you want to further anger any of the Primals. All we want is to take Bele to Hanan's Court."

"Then shouldn't Hanan be here?" Nyktos replied. "However, he's likely too much of a coward to make such a request in person. That's why he had you act as his errand boy instead. Either way, I'll give *you* a piece of advice. It's time for you to find a new Court to serve," Nyktos said. "One where the rulers have the courage to make such demands themselves."

"You know I can't do that."

"If you made a blood oath to Hanan—swearing fidelity to him—then that was a very unwise choice," Nyktos replied.

"Perhaps." Dorcan tilted his head toward those standing behind Nyktos. "What I do know is that the bulk of your guards are too far down the Rise, and your armies are at the western border."

"Armies?" I sent Saion a quick glance. "Nyktos has an army?"

Saion frowned at me. "Of course, he does."

That was news to me.

"It would be *wise* of *you* to just give us Bele," Dorcan said. "And then we'll be on our way, without having caused any…disturbances."

"You've already caused a disturbance." The coldness in Nyktos's voice sent a chill down my spine. "So whatever you think you're going to do, get on with it. This whole scene is becoming a bore."

Dorcan laughed again. "So be it."

"How good are you with a bow?" Saion asked under his breath as the Cimmerian who had been getting handsy with the dagger at his waist twisted, angling his body toward Rhain. I didn't hesitate.

I released the arrow, striking the Cimmerian between the eyes before he could let go of the dagger. "*That* good," I murmured, ignoring the throbbing warmth of the embers of life in my chest as they responded to the god's death.

Dorcan's head swung in my direction, but I knew he couldn't see me. I leaned back as the clash of swords echoed from the road below. I quickly nocked another arrow and moved farther into the parapet, peering down. My chest tensed.

I could only see Nyktos, taller than all the others in the swarm of Cimmerian, going sword to sword with Dorcan.

"Stay unseen," Saion ordered, starting to rise. "If Nyktos is overpowered for some reason, get your ass inside and go to Bele and Aios. Charmed or not, you can still be killed."

Nyktos overpowered? My throat dried. I'd seen him fight with a sword against Gryms and dakkais. He'd ripped an entombed god in half with his bare hands. He couldn't be overwhelmed.

"Do you understand?" Saion demanded.

"Yes." I dropped to my knees behind the shorter wall, beside several shadowstone spears.

"You'd better. They don't know what's inside you. Who you really are. They'll take your head back to Hanan on a spike," Saion warned. Then, with that lovely imagery, he leapt off the Rise.

Assuming Saion had survived a jump that would've surely broken every bone in my body, I took aim at anyone wearing a balaclava. A head on a moving target was harder than a chest, so I waited even as my finger began to twitch, until one of the Cimmerian warriors turned toward a Shadowland guard, bracing himself. I fired, reaching for another arrow as warmth pulsed in my chest once more and stayed that way, responding to the deaths. Readying the arrow, I saw Rhain kick a Cimmerian back as he thrust his sword behind him.

Shadowstone was indestructible...

The shadowstone blade pierced the armor with a spark of stone against stone, embedding deep in the Cimmerian's chest.

Apparently, shadowstone wasn't impenetrable against itself. Good to know.

Rhain jerked the sword free and spun, arcing his blade across the neck of the one before him. The other had gone down, but he didn't die immediately. He rolled onto his side, attempting to stand—

And then I saw it.

A black mist of night seeping out from the wounded Cimmerian. I fired, striking him in the back of the head. A cry of pain echoed from somewhere else, and my chest scorched my insides as I nocked another arrow. Dark shadows had gathered across the road, opaquer than even the Shades, spilling out from several of the Cimmerian.

I quickly sought out Nyktos, my breath catching at the hard set of his striking features as he whirled, cleaving a Cimmerian's head from their body as he met Dorcan's blow with his broadsword. He twisted at the waist, shoving Dorcan back as he turned and threw a second, shorter sword. It whipped through the air, slicing through the head of a Cimmerian who had driven one of Nyktos's guards to a knee. Blood sprayed as the short sword circled back through the air, right into Nyktos's waiting hand. He whirled, meeting Dorcan's attack with both swords, and that was…well, that was impressive.

Night swirled higher and higher. Once it reached their heads, I would be of no aid to them. I could see that the wisps of the thick, cloak-like mist weren't seeping out of the arms of all the Cimmerian, so I focused only on them. Giving up on the head, I took aim at the chest of a Cimmerian and fired. I held my breath, watching to see if the arrow pierced the shadowstone.

It cut through the armor, and a ragged breath punched from my lungs, but there wasn't a lot of relief. The arrow didn't go as deep as Rhain's sword had, only managing to stop whatever the Cimmerian had been doing to call upon the night. The Shadowland guard quickly seized the opportunity as the Cimmerian ripped the arrow from his chest, turning to the Rise.

The embers of life flared inside me as I found another warrior conjuring the mist and loosed an arrow, catching the Cimmerian in the chest. The embers pulsed again and again as I quickly fired and snapped another arrow into place on the string. I shifted on my knee, finding another Cimmerian—

Gasping, I fell back against the wall as a dagger hissed through the air, passing inches from my face. Heart thumping, I returned to the parapet to see Nyktos sever the head of the Cimmerian who'd likely thrown the blade.

As the warrior fell forward, Nyktos's eyes snapped to the Rise, the bright silver of his irises lashed with luminous eather as I leveled the bow toward him. Our gazes locked for only a heartbeat.

Nyktos's head tilted as I pulled the string taut.

And fired.

He whipped around as the arrow struck the Cimmerian charging him from behind.

I smirked as he looked over his shoulder, his lips tipping up faintly. He turned back to Dorcan, leaving me to wonder if he had actually smiled—just a little—as a Cimmerian lifted his sword and pointed at the

Rise. I reached for another arrow, keeping low. I readied the arrow and rose. Maybe Nyktos wouldn't be that mad—

"*Gods*," I exhaled. A void of utter blackness had risen up the side of the Rise, quickly cresting the top and spilling across the battlement.

Lurching to my feet, I swung the bow into the darkness. There was a curse from within the mass, echoed by mine as I twisted. Nyktos and Saion had failed to mention that the Cimmerian could somehow use whatever they manifested to scale a Rise in basically seconds. I grabbed a spear, the cool-to-the-touch metal in a firm grip as I spun.

My eyes went wide as a sword came down, and the night spread out. I blocked the bone-rattling blow, holding my ground as the black mist rose above me. If I ran, I would likely go right off the Rise. I pushed back, and a rough laugh came from within the darkness.

And then, in an instant, it smothered the stars above me. There was no light. Nothing but darkness, my pounding heart, and the throbbing embers. It was like a blindfold had been placed over my eyes—a *blindfold*.

The exercise helps you hone your other senses. That was what Holland had said when I'd asked him why he had me practicing with one. I almost laughed, thinking Holland really did walk that fine line of interference.

I tightened my grip on the spear. I didn't think my other senses were up to par as I vainly searched the utter stillness of nothingness around me. The only thing I heard were shouts of pain, swords meeting swords—

A brush of air stirred in front of my face, and I ducked, feeling the blade cut through the air above me. I swiped out and up with the spear, hitting nothing. I froze, a fine sheen of sweat gathering on my brow. The stirring of air came again, and I darted to the left.

A flare of stinging pain lanced my side, nothing compared to the agony of a fallen god's fangs. I gritted my teeth as I swung out with the spear. The broad side of the shadowstone struck legs. The heavy thump of the Cimmerian landing on their back came from my right. On my knee, I pivoted and jabbed down. The grunt of pain told me I'd struck some part of the bastard. The night began to break apart, becoming grayer than—

Air stirred behind me, and I whirled, jabbing up and out with the spear. The blade hit the resistance of armor and then sank through. I jerked the spear free, rising as an arm clamped down on my throat. Years of training and instinct took over. I let myself go limp, catching the wounded Cimmerian off guard. He stumbled, and I twisted, breaking free of his hold. Enough of the night had cleared for me to see the head, and that was where I aimed, shoving the spear as hard as I could. The crunching sound turned my stomach. I pulled the spear free and turned.

A hand clasped my arm, stopping the blow. I was spun before I could even take a breath. An arm went around my waist, and my back hit the hard wall of a chest as the darkness on the Rise continued to scatter. I sucked in a startled breath—

Citrus. Fresh air. The foolish ember in my chest wiggled even more fiercely.

"Striking me with the spear would not be how you should repay me for ensuring you live to see a crown upon your head." Nyktos's smoky voice was in my ear.

My grip on the spear immediately loosened. "How should I repay you?"

His arm tightened. The awareness—the *feel* of him so close that I felt his deep breath—stirred more than the embers. He didn't answer, and for a moment, it was just us standing there, without so much as an inch between us as the stars began filling the sky once more.

Nyktos moved without warning, whirling us around. He trapped me between the parapet wall and his body as a rush of air swept up from inside the courtyard of the Rise. Large, powerful wings swept over our heads. My heart tripped over itself as a spiked tail grazed the top of the parapet wall that my cheek was now pressed against. A draken had just arrived, but I wasn't thinking about that. My mind—good gods, there was something wrong with my thoughts because they immediately went to a wholly inappropriate place, conjuring up the memories of Nyktos behind me, his large and powerful body caging mine just as it did now, leaving no space between us. No opportunity to even move my head. There had been no clothes between us then either, when he took me from behind, branding my skin, claiming me. The memory was fresh and acute, sending a bolt of dizzying lust through me.

"Fuck," Nyktos growled, his breath hot against my cheek. "You will be the death of me."

I must've projected, but this was a rare moment when I didn't care. "We both know that's not possible," I whispered as the draken landed on the other side of the Rise.

He made a rough sound as the hand at my wrist slid up my arm. I opened my eyes, able to see the row of pointed horns framing Nektas's head. His grayish-black wings swept back, pushing Ector and Rhain to his side. The world below turned silver as fiery eather poured from the draken.

"You've been injured," Nyktos growled low in my ear. "Again."

"Barely."

"I can smell your blood." His palm grazed the side of my breast. I jerked. He skimmed his hand down my side to where there *was* a burning ache. "It makes me want to taste you."

His words sent a wicked pulse of desire from my pounding heart to my core. "I wouldn't stop you."

"Of course, you wouldn't." The arm below my breasts flexed. "You don't value your life."

"It has nothing to do with that."

"It has everything to do with that." His breath was a caress against my throat. "If I tasted you again, I don't know if I could stop."

"Yes, you would," I whispered, believing that more than I did anything in my life.

Nyktos made that sound again, part growl and curse as he dropped his arm, angling his body as he turned to the road. Surprised to find that I still held the spear in my hand, I willed my heart to slow as I peeled myself away from the wall and followed Nyktos's gaze to the road—

Nektas snapped forward, catching a Cimmerian between his powerful jaws. He shook his head, severing the god in two.

"Ew," I uttered.

"I've seen him do worse."

"I'll have to take your word on that," I murmured.

"Try to listen for once and stay here," Nyktos said, and then he was gone, leaping over the side of the Rise.

I shot forward, grasping the stone edge. Nyktos was on the road, prowling past the bodies of his fallen men. Five had...five were gone. The warmth swelled in my chest as I stared at them. My palms heated—

Nektas's head swung toward me, his crimson eyes with their thin, vertical pupils locking onto me. His lips vibrated, pulling back with a warning growl. I swallowed hard as I rested the spear against the wall. It was as if he'd sensed the eather gathering inside me. I pressed both hands against the stone, pushing down the urge and burying it as deeply as I could as Nyktos stalked toward the only standing Cimmerian.

Dorcan's balaclava gathered at his throat, no longer shielding his face. The man appeared to be in his third decade of life, but as a god, that could mean he was hundreds of years old if not more. "I'm assuming you have a message you want me to deliver to Hanan."

The way he spoke as Nyktos approached him made it seem as if this were something that had happened between them before.

"Nyktos," Saion called out from where he knelt by one of the soldiers. "He's seen her."

I tensed.

"Then my generosity has come to an end," Nyktos said.

Dorcan showed no reaction. "I don't know what you're thinking by refusing Hanan, but whatever it is, it will end badly for you. He'll go to Kolis, and more will come."

"I'll be waiting." Nyktos unsheathed a sword, striking as fast as a pit viper and severing the Cimmerian's head from his shoulders.

12

Rhain eyed me as if he expected me to run out of Nyktos's office at any given second and into the middle of a firestorm. He hadn't taken his eyes off me longer than it took to blink. Ector, on the other hand, was sprawled across the settee, eyes closed and quite possibly napping.

"It would calm my nerves if you sat," Rhain advised with a tilt of his golden-red head. "Instead of pacing."

"Pacing calms my nerves." I made another pass in front of Nyktos's desk. "And trust me when I say you'd prefer me to have calm nerves versus the opposite."

"You're probably right." Rhain inclined his head. His eyes appeared more gold than brown as they tracked me in the glow of the wall sconces. "But trusting you…"

I muttered a curse. Bad word choice on my part. I kept pacing, even faster now, the skin on the back of my neck tight. Nyktos's speech obviously hadn't had that much of an impact on Rhain, and that left me a little sad. Rhain had been all smiles before, less guarded and friendly.

"You should trust her," Ector chimed in. His eyes were still closed, but apparently, he hadn't been sleeping. "Besides what she tried last night for us—for *all* of us—that Cimmerian was gunning for you. She saved your ass out there. If she hadn't hit him right between the eyes, you might be standing here with a couple of extra holes in you. Or not standing at all. The least you can do is thank her."

"I don't need his gratitude," I said before Rhain could say something that would likely irritate me further.

"Well, you have mine." Ector opened his deep amber eyes.

"And mine," Rhain grumbled. "Thank you."

I snorted.

"That sounded as if it pained you." Ector shot him a look I couldn't even begin to decipher.

"It did. A little." A muscle ticked along his jaw as he glanced at Ector. "What? Why are you looking at me like I'm being an ass?"

I arched a brow, for once keeping my mouth shut.

"Maybe because you're being an ass," Ector responded. "To the person who had your back out there. Who has had *all* our backs. Who also carries the embers—"

"I think he gets the point," I interrupted. Ector's defense surprised me, even with Nyktos's speech. I'd had no idea where I stood with him. Then again, I hadn't known before. Ector was an...odd one, joking one moment and somber the next. He was also far older than Nyktos, having known Eythos and Mycella fairly well, which I guessed played a role in why Nyktos had sent him to watch over me while I'd been in the mortal realm, along with the godling, Lathan.

"You're coming at me?" Rhain demanded, taken aback. "In her defense? She plans—"

"*Planned*," I interrupted. "Pretty sure we already covered this."

"Does your change of heart erase the intentions that came before that?" Rhain challenged. "Does running off to get yourself killed somehow change it?"

"I didn't say it did."

"It doesn't. No matter what you supposedly planned to do about Kolis or what embers you carry." Rhain unfolded his arms and stepped forward. Ector sat up, alert. "You're not the true Primal of Life. You're a foster to the embers, and none of that makes up for plotting against Nyktos, no matter your reasons," he said, and my face began to sting. "You have no idea what Nyktos has had to give up. What he's been through. What he's sacrificed for you, and then for you—"

"Rhain," Ector warned.

I stopped pacing. "What has he sacrificed for me?"

"Other than his sense of security in his own home?" Rhain spat.

"Other than that," I demanded.

"Nothing," Ector said, rising. "Rhain is just being overdramatic. He's prone to being so."

My eyes narrowed. "Really?"

"It comes from a good place," Ector reasoned, going to Rhain's side. He placed a hand on the god's shoulder. "She's not the enemy at the end of the day. You should know that. But if you don't, all you have to do is go back out onto the Rise and look at the lives lost."

Rhain looked away as the annoying embers suddenly came alive, wiggling like a puppy greeting its owner. They might be happy for Nyktos's eminent arrival. I, however, wasn't.

The doors flew open, stopping midway as if invisible servants had caught them before they slammed into the walls. A ripple of icy-hot energy tore into the office first, tickling my skin.

"Daddy Nyktos is not happy," Ector murmured.

No, he was not.

"At least it's not in response to something we did." Rhain looked pointedly in my direction with a raise of his brows.

"This time," Ector added.

Nervous energy buzzed through me as Nyktos blew into the office with the force of a storm. Swirling, silver orbs locked on me as he crossed the room, unsheathing his swords.

"Did I not tell you to remain inside?" Nyktos stopped in front of me, slamming the swords down on the desk behind me. "To not push me on that?"

"You did."

His chin dipped. "And yet you did exactly what I asked you *not* to do and went out onto the Rise, risking not only your life but also Saion's."

"You didn't ask that of me. You *demanded* that of me."

"Same thing."

"It absolutely is not the same thing, and how did I risk Saion's life? He chose to follow me—"

"He had no choice in the matter, as he was tasked with keeping *you* inside," he said. Over his shoulder, I saw Rhain and Ector steadily slinking toward the doors. "He's lucky I'm not in the habit of punishing another for someone else's misdeeds."

Frustration rose, joining the anxious hum. "The only one committing misdeeds at this moment is you."

Nyktos's brows flew up. "I cannot wait to hear your rationale on this. I'm sure it involves something along the lines of: *I do what I want because I can and fuck the consequences.*"

Right then, something shifted from deep within that *crack*. Something absolute. I didn't reach for the veil of nothingness as a raw, volatile mix of anger and determination pounded through me. "From the moment I learned that I no longer had to answer to a duty I never had a choice in accepting, I became my own person. Someone who gets to make their own choices. I will not be ordered about and told what I can and cannot do as if I have no power or control over my life, no matter what risks I may be taking. I am *done* living like that."

Nyktos withdrew, taking several steps back. The wisps of eather slowed in his eyes, evoking a small change in the cold set of his features. A tense silence followed until he said, "One of you please retrieve a bowl of clean water and a cloth for me. The other needs to leave."

"You know, I think I'll get that stuff for you and then make myself...scarce." Rhain backed up, grabbing Ector's arm. "Come, be scarce with me."

"That's probably a good idea." Ector pivoted. "He's got the scary face again."

He kind of did.

Nyktos waited until we were alone. "Someone has to worry about something happening to you since you don't. You never do." Nyktos took a measured step forward. "You want to make choices no matter the risks? The problem with that is you don't ever think about those risks. Or the consequences."

"That is not—" I sucked in a sharp breath. Nyktos was suddenly standing no more than a foot from me. "Can you not do that?"

"Why?" He stared down at me, the wisps of eather growing brighter in his eyes again. "Don't tell me it scares you."

"It doesn't scare me. It just *annoys* me."

His lips twisted into a tight smile. "Of course, not. You don't have the instinct that warns most when they're in grave danger."

"Not true." I started to cross my arms, but the tug on the wound along my waist stopped me. "My instincts work completely fine. Earlier they warned me that you'd be angry with my decision to go out onto the Rise."

His eyes narrowed into thin, glowing slits. "Have you ever tried, oh, I don't know? Listening to it? Valuing your life?"

"I've never really had the opportunity to do so, now, have I?" I snapped.

Nyktos went completely still, all except his eyes. A long moment passed, and I wished I had his ability to read emotions, to gain some sort of insight into what he was feeling or thinking. He turned then, walking stiffly to the credenza and picking up a crystal decanter full of amber liquid. "I know I said this before, but I mean no offense when I say you don't value your life," he said, pouring a glass, stopping, and then pouring a second. "It's truly not meant to be an insult."

I snorted. "Sure sounds like one when you say it."

"Then I apologize. I'm sorry."

My head jerked. "You're seriously apologizing to me?"

He came back to me, offering me a glass. "You don't think you deserve one?"

"Uh…" I thought about that as I took the drink, unsure if I did or not. I shrugged.

His lips curled faintly. "Well, you have it anyway." He downed the whiskey in one swallow. "I'm trying to understand."

"Understand what?" I took a little less-impressive gulp, but half of the whiskey was gone when I lowered my glass.

He sat his glass behind one of his swords, dragging the edge of his fangs over his lower lip. "How you've become who you are."

The whiskey hit my chest and then my stomach in a warm rush. "I'm not really following what you're asking."

"Most wouldn't attempt to seduce and kill the Primal of Death. Not even if it was a duty drilled into them from birth. Not even for their kingdom. Then turn around and plan to do the same thing to another Primal. I wouldn't even say it would be a lack of courage on their part."

"Just a lack of common sense on mine?" I retorted.

That damn eyebrow rose again. "You said it."

I took another drink before I threw the glass at his face. "My kingdom is dying. I believed—we all believed—it was due to the deal King Roderick made. What was I supposed to do?"

"Literally anything else."

My fingers tightened on the glass. "Like what, All-Knowing One? Ask you to stop the Rot? Why would that have even crossed my mind when we believed the Rot was due to the deal expiring, and not something you were doing? We didn't even know who Kolis truly was." Or even who and what *I* was. But gods knew I wasn't going there right now. "So, what should I have done? Summoned a god or Primal again and tried to make another deal? Kicked the can down the road for someone else to deal with? Live my kind of life?" I laughed harshly. "Or just do nothing and let my kingdom die?"

"And what kind of life did you really live?" he asked quietly.

The heat returned, sweeping through my chest, and it had very little to do with the whiskey. I set the glass on the desk. Rhain returned then with the items Nyktos had requested. Sending me a sharp look, he quietly placed the bowl and towel on the desk beside the swords. He quickly left, closing the doors behind him.

But what the god had said before Nyktos arrived remained with me. "What have you sacrificed for me?"

Nyktos's eyes lifted to mine. "What has one of my guards said?"

"Nothing."

"I don't believe that."

"That's not an answer." My heart thumped heavily.

"It's because I haven't sacrificed anything," he said, and I wasn't sure I believed him. "Lift your sweater."

I blinked, wondering if the whiskey had gotten to me that quickly. "Excuse me?"

"You were wounded. I want to see how bad it is."

"It's not—"

"Lift your sweater and allow me to check your injury, Sera." He took a deep breath. "Please."

I hesitated, only because he'd asked this time. And only because he'd said *please*, and that was still a weakness of mine.

Nyktos briefly closed his eyes. "I don't think you're wounded enough that you'll need blood, so you don't have to worry about me taking advantage of you."

The fact that I felt even the tiniest bit of disappointment at hearing that told me I needed a hefty dose of whatever Nyktos had just insinuated I lacked. Common sense.

Thick lashes lifted. Silver eyes lit softly from behind pierced mine. Knowing my luck, this was probably one of those moments where he was either intentionally or unintentionally reading my emotions. He would've felt the disappointment, and I didn't even want to know what he thought—if he saw me as someone so desperate for affection that I would seek it from someone who didn't even want friendship from me.

And that would be accurate on some level. My entire life lacked not only touch but also affection. I did crave it, but I wasn't desperate enough to take whatever meager scraps were offered to me by anyone.

I just wanted *his* affection because I thought I'd had a taste of it before he learned the truth. He'd wanted me then, to the point of distraction, but I thought he had also been fond of me. That he cared. Now, there was only a physical desire, one that he'd likely deny to his very last breath.

Then what he said struck me. "Wait. Do you think you took

advantage of me after you gave me your blood?"

"I knew what my blood would do to you. I should've been able to restrain myself or left you alone the moment you started feeling the effects."

I stared at him. "My reaction had very little to do with your blood."

"Sera."

"And everything to do with my attraction to you. I told you that then. It hasn't changed."

His jaw flexed. "Even so, I should've been able to control myself instead of becoming a man with no control over his body."

I laughed. "You are not only a man."

"Just because I'm a Primal doesn't mean my body responds differently."

"I didn't realize that Primals—or men in general—had such little control over their cocks," I snapped, annoyed that he would excuse his reaction, *his pleasure*, as something he had no control over.

"That's not what I—*never mind.*" His eyes flared bright briefly. "Let me see your wound."

"Whatever." I grabbed the hem and the slip underneath, lifting them to my ribs. "It's not bad. See?" I looked down, cringing slightly at the thin gash running along the left side of my waist. "Just a flesh wound."

"There's no such thing as a flesh wound."

I started to lower my sweater, but Nyktos palmed my hips. The contact startled me enough that I didn't protest as he lifted me onto the desk. His hands lingered there. The reminder of his strength was always a surprise. It made me feel incredibly dainty, and I was not even in the same realm as *dainty*. No part of me wasn't, as Tavius had once said, *plump.*

Fucking gross bastard.

Gods, I almost wished he was still alive so I could shove something harder than a whip down his throat.

Nyktos's eyes lifted to mine. "You're projecting again."

"Sorry," I muttered as he reached for the cloth. "You don't have to do this."

"I know. I'm doing it because I want to."

He'd said that before. And my reckless heart leapt, just like then. He pressed his fingers to the skin beneath the wound, the touch gentle and yet another shock. I jolted.

"Sorry." He withdrew his hand. "I didn't mean to cause pain."

"You didn't. It's just...I wish your touch was warm again," I said, which wasn't entirely untrue. "Did it warm because you fed?" I asked, knowing that Nyktos rarely fed. From what I could gather, Primals didn't need to feed often unless they were wounded and weakened. And I had weakened him, just a little, when I hit him with that blast of eather.

He shook his head. "My skin has never warmed to the touch after feeding. It has always been cold."

"Then why...?" I figured it out. "The embers?"

"I am Death," he reminded me. "And you carry the embers of life in you. *Your* blood is what warmed my skin."

"Will my blood have any other effects on you?"

There was a quick upward curl of his lips. "That is yet to be seen."

I was staring way too hard at his mouth, so I shifted my gaze to his...throat. Something about what he'd said didn't make sense. He wasn't the true Primal of Death, just *a* Primal of Death. So why would his skin be cold in the first place? Then again, maybe it was because he was a Primal of Death.

Now I was just confusing myself. "I wonder if Taric could taste it. I mean, he knew I had at least one ember in me when he went through my memories, but if he hadn't, would he still have known?"

Eather flashed brilliantly in Nyktos's eyes. "No other will feed from you, so that's not something you'll need to worry about."

My brows rose.

"But, yes," he said, his voice thin. "He would've tasted it."

"Does my blood taste like it smells?"

He was silent as he dipped the cloth into the water. "It tastes like a summer storm and the sun."

An unsteady laugh left me as my chest warmed. "What does that even taste like?"

"Heat. Power. *Life*," he said without hesitation. "Yet soft. Airy. Like sponge cake. Like..."

I was staring at his mouth again. "Like what?"

Nyktos cleared his throat, shaking his head. "By the way, when you think I'm moving too fast? I'm not actually moving—not in the way you think."

I frowned. He was clearly changing the subject. "Then in what way *are* you moving?"

"I use eather to will myself where I want to go," he said, gently pressing the cloth to the skin around the wound. "It's called shadowstepping."

I stared at him, my brows raised. "Isn't that normally called plain old walking?"

Nyktos chuckled. "It's a bit different than that. When I will myself to move like that, I'm becoming a part of the eather—the air around us. Mortal eyes simply cannot see us do it."

Curiosity rose. "What does it look like?"

"A glimmer of shadow, moving very rapidly," he answered. "And the more eather a god carries, the farther they can shadowstep, and the faster they move."

"Is that what you did when you took me from the Great Hall in Wayfair?"

"Yes. I summoned mist to hide us first. And because you're mostly mortal, it would have been a very painful experience for you if awake."

I'd take his word for that, but then I remembered what he had told me about not being able to will himself from my lake. "So you *can* will yourself wherever you want to go..." He smirked. "How far can you...shadowstep?"

He glanced up at me. "As far as I want."

I blinked slowly. "Then why do you use a horse? Or walk anywhere? If I could do that, I probably wouldn't walk a foot."

A faint grin appeared. "Just because I can do something doesn't mean I need to."

He'd said some variation of that before when we were at my lake. "I bet there are many things you can do that I have no idea about."

His grin kicked up farther on one side.

"Will I be able to do that if I Ascend?"

"You will Ascend," he corrected. "And it will all depend on how much eather you have in you. Based on what you're already able to do, I imagine you will be able to shadowstep in some capacity. Many gods can. Though they cannot travel the distance a Primal can or cross realms."

I tried to picture myself shadowstepping out of one space and into the next, and quickly decided that I probably wouldn't ever walk normally again.

"What were you thinking about?" Nyktos asked after a couple of moments. "Just a few minutes ago when you felt as if you...wanted to murder someone."

Caught off guard, I blurted out the truth. "Tavius."

A muscle ticked in his jaw as he continued carefully wiping at the blood around the wound. "Part of me doesn't want to know what made you think of him." A lock of hair slipped from the bun he'd tied his hair back in, falling across his cheek. He was quiet as he dipped the cloth into the bowl again. "Did he hurt you before that day?"

I stared at the top of his head as he bent once more, all thoughts of shadowstepping disappearing.

"He did, didn't he? That bruise I saw on you. It was several days old, nearly faded. You said you walked into something, and yet I've seen few people as sure-footed as you." He paused. "Except when around serpents."

The corner of my lips twitched and then flattened when I thought of the cause of the bruise Nyktos questioned. Tavius had thrown a bowl of dates at me.

"Did he harm you?" Nyktos persisted.

I started to lie but realized I was simply too tired to do so. "He wasn't kind."

"And what does that entail?" He dabbed at the wound gently, but I still jerked at the sting of pain. "Sorry."

"It's okay." My cheeks burned, either from the conversation or his apology. Maybe both. "He could be mean. Growing up, it was mostly verbal. When I wore the veil, he wouldn't dare. For the most part," I said, thinking of how he'd tried to touch me the night I'd first been brought to the Shadow Temple to honor the deal.

"And that changed?" Nyktos eyed the wound.

I lifted my right shoulder.

"He touched you?"

"Sometimes." My gaze lifted to the black doors trimmed in silver. "Most of the time, he didn't get a chance."

"You kicked his ass?"

My lips twisted into a smirk. "On more than one occasion. But others couldn't always fight back." I suddenly thought of Princess Kayleigh sobbing quietly in the woods. "Tavius was betrothed at one point, to a younger Princess from Irelone. I don't think he was...kind to her."

"I'm sorry to hear that." He fell quiet then, but not for long. "The day he whipped you..." he said, and my gaze flew to him. Nyktos dragged the cloth along the flesh above the waistband of my leggings, washing away the thin trails of blood. "Why did he do it?"

He'd asked that before. I hadn't told him then. Nyktos waited, quiet as he bent his head. He didn't look up at me, and maybe that was why I felt I could speak. "Tavius hated me. I don't even really know why. Honestly, I don't think it was personal. He wasn't nice to many. He was just that kind of person, you know? Someone who derives strength and pleasure from dominating others. And when they can't do that, it makes them all the more determined to do so."

"I know the type," he said.

I imagined he did. "His father—King Ernald—died the night before, and the King, he sort of...I don't know. Reprimanded Tavius for his behavior before. I think I was more shocked than Tavius was, but with his father gone and him about to become King, it was like whatever had been holding him back was no longer there. He blamed me for the Rot," I added after a few moments. "He thought I should be punished for failing."

"Failing?" Nyktos's shoulders tensed. "For me not taking you as my Consort?"

I looked away from him, focusing on the pinkish water in the bowl. "Among many other things, I'm sure. Anyway, he wanted to punish me."

Nyktos lowered the hand that held the cloth to the desk. "And your mother? She acted as she did that day? Did nothing? Because she, too, blamed you for the Rot? Believed you had failed?"

There was really no point in answering.

"What would have happened if I hadn't felt you that day?" Nyktos asked as my gaze shifted to his hand holding the bloodied cloth. His knuckles had bleached white. "What would he have done to you once he had his fun with the whip?"

I shook my head, my stomach churning as I recalled Tavius holding me down on that narrow, uncomfortable bed. Pressing me into the thin mattress until I felt like I was choking. I shifted, gripping the hem of my sweater until I felt the thread beginning to pop.

Nyktos had picked up my glass with his other hand. "Drink."

Knowing I'd likely hurled those stifling, choking emotions at him, I grabbed the glass and finished off the whiskey.

He took the empty glass, setting it aside once more and then returned to studying the wound. "What would've happened?"

"It doesn't matter."

"It matters."

"To who?" I laughed hoarsely, and then because I couldn't bear the silence that was sure to follow, spoke again. "He...he would've done something that would've ended with his favorite part of him being shoved down his throat. He would've *tried*, that is."

Nyktos twisted his head to the side. A sudden charge of energy hit the air, causing tiny goose bumps to spread along my skin. A burnt smell rose. I looked down to see nothing but ash remained of the cloth he'd held—and a charred mark on the desk.

"Others had to be aware. Your stepsister?" His tone was cold, flat. Thin. "Holland?"

I swallowed the sourness gathering in the back of my throat. "What could any of them do? Holland would've been sent away or killed for speaking out—or at least they would've tried. He intervened more than once, in ways that he could. And I don't think Ezra knew the full of extent of Tavius's behavior."

"You defend them?"

"Because they deserve to be defended. He was a Prince, and I was—" I cut myself off and squeezed my eyes shut, unsure why I had even told him any of this. It had to be the shock of everything, the adrenaline wearing off, and the exhaustion settling in. Maybe it was because it felt as if there was no reason to hide when he already knew other ugly truths. When I knew how all of this would end. It could've just been the damn whiskey.

"You were a Princess."

"I was never that."

Nyktos didn't speak, and I didn't open my eyes. Several moments passed before he said, "When I didn't take you as my Consort, I wasn't giving you your freedom."

A faint tremor ran through me. It wasn't a question. It needed no answer.

"I'm sorry, Sera."

My eyes flew open, every part of my being seizing as I let go of my sweater. He'd lifted his head, and with his eyes on me, seeing me—really *seeing* me—it made his apology all the more unbearable. My skin burned hotly. My chest seized. "I don't want your apology," I choked out. "I didn't tell you any of that to get it. I don't want your pity or your sympathy."

"I know." He touched my cheek, his fingers damp but warm. "Breathe, Sera."

I sucked in air.

"I could never pity someone as strong and brave as you," Nyktos said. "But you do have my sympathy and my apologies."

I leaned back, but his hand followed. "I don't want that. Or need it and—"

"I know," he repeated, his thumb coasted across my cheek. "But they are there in case you are in need of them one day."

Raw emotion swelled so quickly that I had to close my eyes again, because if I didn't, that mess of emotion would make itself painfully visible.

Nyktos's thumb stilled. "I will go right now and end your miserable excuse of a mother's life and take her soul into the Abyss, placing it beside Tavius's, where it belongs."

My eyes snapped open. "You can't mean that."

"I have never meant anything more in my entire life," he swore. "All you have to do is say yes, and it will be done."

I sucked in air as a terrible part of me lifted its wretched head. The part that existed beyond the veil of nothing, that hid beneath the blank canvas and was the fire that forged the vessel into place. The part of me that wanted to scream *yes* and revel in the knowledge that it was I who'd brought about her end. *Me.* The one who wasn't even worth looking in the eye half the time. The irony was too sweet. Wouldn't it be? For it was she who'd built that canvas and wielded that fire.

Nyktos waited, and in that moment, I knew he would do it. Not because he was fond of me or cared, but because he felt responsible. Guilty. Maybe even remorseful. Sympathetic.

I exhaled roughly and forced out, "No."

"You sure?"

"Yes. It wouldn't be...it wouldn't be worth it in the end." I didn't want her blood on my hands. I already had enough.

"If you ever change your mind, I know a guy who can get it done."

I shook with a wet-sounding laugh. "Was that a Primal of Death joke?"

"Perhaps." Several long moments passed. Neither of us moved. His hand was still on my cheek. Our eyes were locked, and the contact, the closeness...I soaked it in. Then he drew back and lowered his hand, and I missed his touch immediately. "You need to rest," he continued before I could say anything. "And I'm not ordering you about. If you choose not to, it's up to you. But your body needs it. Whether you want to admit it or not, the Culling causes everyone to weaken more easily, and you've already pushed past that once. The headaches will come back faster and worse than before, and you could go into another rest."

"I don't want that," I murmured.

"Good. Neither do I." His gaze tracked over my face. "The embers of life in you are very strong."

"Yeah, I figured. You know"—I lifted my hands, wiggling my fingers—"I can bring people back from the dead and, apparently, summon them when I'm really angry."

There was a slight warming in his eyes. "I wasn't talking about either of those things. You were cut with shadowstone. That would kill a mortal. It would also kill a godling. Your skin and veins would already bear the mark of it, and what blood of mine you have in you wouldn't have stopped it."

"Oh." My eyes went wide. He was right. I'd forgotten. Looking down, I yanked up my sweater. The cut was there, angry but no longer bleeding. "Wow."

"Yes. Wow," he repeated dryly.

A giggle crept up my throat, and that was totally the whiskey.

Nyktos smiled faintly. "Makes you wonder how else the Primal embers may be protecting you."

13

There was a padlock on the balcony doors when I returned to my chambers.

Obviously, that wasn't to stop someone from taking me. It wasn't necessary with the charm.

Part of me couldn't be all that mad about seeing it there. I smirked as I stared at it. Did he think I couldn't pick a lock? The lock wasn't the only new addition to the room, though. It took an ungodly amount of time for me to see the book lying on the table by the doors, and I thought it was the one Orphine had been reading.

I ate my supper, once more alone. Fresh water came quickly after that, and I cleaned up as I had before. The wound on my side hadn't reopened, and as I gently prodded the skin, I thought it looked like a cut that was several days old instead of merely hours.

Makes you wonder how else the Primal embers may be protecting you.

I was beginning to wonder that myself.

More tired than I wanted to acknowledge, I dragged on a heavy forest green robe that I hadn't worn yet, not even bothering with a nightgown. I went to the chaise and picked up the book. The writing was faint but legible, and yet the words still blurred as I stared at the page. I couldn't focus. As the hour grew late, Nyktos's plan occupied my thoughts. If and when Hanan would send more warriors, the questions I had about this army I didn't know existed, and the fact that I couldn't believe I'd spoken about Tavius or my life in Lasania. I didn't like to think about those last two things, let alone speak about them. It made me feel itchy in my skin.

Rising, I went to the table and picked up the bottle of wine brought in with supper. It was sweet, and I took one long swallow, then another as I tried to distract myself with the book. That was a failure because the wine sure hadn't helped the process. It had me staring at Nyktos's door more and more, considering really foolish things.

I shrugged off the robe, letting it lay where it fell. I didn't bother putting on a stitch of clothing, too warm from the crackling flames in the fireplace and the wine. I then put myself to bed before the wine goaded me into doing something reckless.

Like going to that damn door.

I smirked, imagining Nyktos's reaction if I walked into his chamber, naked as the day I was born. He would...

What would he do?

My smirk faded as I turned my head, looking at the door. My thoughts found their way in there. In my mind, I saw his massive bed. Was he there? Resting? Or was he unable to sleep, too? Was he thinking of dark events that had taken place over the last several days? Or was he thinking about us on his bed?

I closed my eyes at the sharp pulse of desire. Shifting onto my back, I searched for something else to dwell on, but my mind betrayed me. It took me right back into his bedchamber, showing us on the bed, me on my knees, and Nyktos's large body caging mine as he had on the Rise. There was nothing between our sweat-slick bodies, and every stroke of his was deep. It was a pleasure that had bordered on punishing. The fierceness of how he moved was far too easy to recall. It didn't even seem like a memory, not when I could feel him even now, between my thighs and inside me. I closed my eyes, biting down on my lip as the need returned.

I kicked at the blanket twisted around my legs in frustration. Gods, why was I doing this to myself?

Carefully rolling onto my side again, I stared at the door once more. For a reckless moment, I entertained the idea of going to that door, finding it unlocked and entering his bedchamber. There was no smirk on my face now as I wondered if I would find Nyktos sleeping in his bed. Would he welcome me? Want me? Without regret? The breath I took was reedy as I imagined him curving his body around mine, touching me. Eyes drifting shut, I squeezed my thighs together, pressing my balled hand to my chest. My skin felt hot as I forced my fingers wide. My fingertips grazed the now-barely-there indentations left behind from Nyktos's bite, sending an illicit thrill through me. The ache deep inside me throbbed as I drew a finger over a hardened nipple. My hips rocked—

There was a sound, quiet and too quick for me to make out. My eyes flew open, sweeping past the door to the drapes drawn across the balcony door. I saw nothing but shadows and night, but the chamber...it felt different. The darkness seemed charged. Had I turned off the lamp? Had it even been on when I lay down? I couldn't remember thanks to the whiskey and the wine. But the chamber was empty except for me and my need, which felt as if it had become its own entity, filling the space even beyond the bed. I closed my eyes again, willing myself to sleep, but in the quiet, all I could think about was Nyktos's mouth closing on my throat, my breast.

Open for me.

I shivered at the memory of his heated demand, easing onto my back. I kicked at the blanket again, welcoming the cooler air as it washed over my bare skin. It did nothing to ease the fire. The charged air only seemed to enflame it. My other hand fell to my stomach, pressing against my bare skin. The tips of my breasts tingled under my fingers as I moved restlessly, pressing my rear into the mattress. The dampness gathering between my thighs only increased.

My pulse thrummed as I slid my hand down as I had when I answered his demand. I hesitated, not from shame or inexperience—I'd pleasured myself before, obviously. But I didn't let my mind wander to how I'd learned to do so—those memories were not welcome here—I hesitated because there would be no faceless, nameless visage in my mind like the times before. The lines and planes would be clear, as would the name. If I touched myself, it would be Nyktos's fingers I imagined inside me. There would be no denying that.

Show me...

I let my thighs fall open to the cool air and the darkness of the room. I slid my hand farther down as I went back to the memory of *us*. I was in his bed, and Nyktos's mouth was on my breast. But it wasn't my fingers that I rode as I eased one through the slippery wetness. It was his cock. I moaned, kicking my head back against the pillow as I began working my finger in and out, pressing the heel of my palm against the ultra-sensitive piece of flesh. The feel of him, stretching and filling me, was branded on my skin, too easy to recall. I eased another finger inside—

My eyes flew open as my heart pounded. There was no sound. Nothing I could hear over my panting, but there was that...*shift* in the chamber again. An awareness.

A knowledge that I wasn't alone.

My heart lurched as I looked down, past the fingers on my breast and between my legs, past my bent knees. I scanned the space at the foot of the bed, the unlit fireplace by the balcony doors, the shadowy chaise before it—

The *unlit* fire?

Air stalling in my lungs, my gaze swung back to the chaise and the thick mass of shadows there. My heart continued to skip. That cluster of shadows didn't seem normal. They weren't as opaque as what the Cimmerian had conjured, and I could see the muted glow of flames *behind* them now, but the shadows seemed to churn. I dragged in a breath. The scent of citrus and fresh air surrounded me.

The scent of *Nyktos*.

My body flashed cold and then hot as my lips parted. It had to be my imagination or the wine. He couldn't be in here, but as I stared at the shadows, I was reminded of when I'd first seen him in the Shadow Temple and he'd been cloaked in endless night. The shadows seemed to have stilled.

Could he...could he be in here? Watching me?

The sharp twist of pleasure curling deep inside me was downright sinful. As was the flush of heat and wetness. My desire-laden thoughts raced. Nyktos...he could sense extreme emotion, and what I was feeling was pretty extreme. Could he even sense my need if he were in another chamber?

And had he come to me?

That wanton curl of pleasure coiled even deeper, tighter. If he was here, watching...

My breath caught. Eyes drifting halfway closed, I dragged my teeth over my lower lip as I moved my fingers at my breast and inside me. The answering swirl of pleasure was echoed in those shadows at the foot of the bed. My hips lifted, following the slow rhythm. Those shadows seemed to solidify. Thicken. Pulse. My blood did the same. The feeling of awareness increased. Tiny bumps spread across my exposed flesh.

I could feel *his* stare.

Like all the times before, when I knew he was looking at me. His stare was always a caress, and it was then, too, heavy against my breasts, my belly, and the fingers between my legs. And I knew...I *knew* he was there. Either that or I'd really drunk far too much wine. Both were equally possible, but I chose to believe the former.

That Nyktos had snuck into my chamber, cloaked in the shadows, and was even now watching me.

The shadows throbbed, appearing to expand and darken at the foot of the bed. My back arched as tension spun.

Air grazed the bottom of my foot, icy and yet burning, and it was *real.*

It...it wasn't my imagination.

Oh, gods, I jerked my hand away, my fingers glossy and damp against my belly. I went completely still as I watched a misty tendril of night slip over the bed. I didn't close my legs. I did nothing but wait...and *want.* And I knew I shouldn't want such a thing, but oh, gods, I did.

I gasped as that wisp of dark air kissed my calf, and another licked my inner thigh. I held my breath, my pulse pounding as my hands fell to the bed. I grasped the sheet beneath me, my chest rising and falling sharply. Seconds stretched out for an eternity, then I dragged my feet over the bed, responding to some unknown instinct and opening myself farther for *him.* The icy yet hot shadow brushed against my core.

I gasped, crying out. The heels of my feet dug into the bed as I began to shake. The sensation—the pressure, the fullness—was intense. Primitive. Otherworldly. I could barely see the tendrils of night, but I *felt* them. The cool burn was all I could feel. I moaned, twisting and grinding. My hips lifted off the bed, and the icy-hot air flowed over the curve of my rear. The tension unfurled with shocking force. I cried out, climaxing as my wide eyes fixed on the thick mass of throbbing shadows. Trembling, I collapsed into the soft mattress as the wisps of night slowly slipped away from the bed.

Small aftershocks rocked me as I rolled onto my side and then my belly, and...*waited.* A charge of energy went through the chamber. The breath I took caught at that touch again, an icy-hot kiss against the back of my thighs, the curve of my ass. My heart kicked against my ribs. The sensation faded, but the presence was still there. Closer than before.

"Nyktos?" I whispered.

There was no answer in the charged silence, but I waited until my eyes grew too tired to keep open, and as I drifted off, I felt the bed shift beside me.

I felt Nyktos.

"Did you sleep well?" Nektas asked.

I nearly choked on the juice I sipped, my gaze immediately darting to my bed. What had happened last night now felt like a sinful, fever dream, but no part of me doubted that Nyktos had been in my chamber. That he'd watched me. *Touched* me. Lay in bed beside me. Heat crept into my face as I dragged my gaze from the bed.

Nektas watched me curiously.

I cleared my throat, fiddling with the loose sleeve of my gown. It was a rose gold one. The gown was without much flourish, but the sleeves, which loosened at the elbow and fluttered to just above the wrist, gave it a delicate feel. The bodice would've been considered modest if that area actually fit. I feared that the seams would burst at any second, but I'd liked that the gown had been cut with two slits on each side of the skirt, ending just below the mid-thigh. It made for easy access to the dagger I sheathed there.

And I sort of felt...pretty in it. It wasn't all that often that I wore one that was so soft and not completely see-through like the godsforsaken wedding gown. If I didn't come up with a better plan, stopping the coronation was highly unlikely, so I really hoped the gown for that was somewhat...decent.

"I slept well," I managed.

"Good." Nektas sat on the couch. He'd brought my breakfast this morning, and unlike everyone else, he stayed. Though he hadn't said much until now, it was nice to have company. "I remember when Ash went through the Culling. He slept terribly—worse than he normally does."

"Is that common?"

"For some. But I think for those who already don't sleep all that well, the Culling worsens it."

So had he been awake, lying in his bed? Nibbling on the last of the bread, I eyed the door to his chambers, and my stomach gave another tumble. What would Nyktos say when he saw me?

Better yet, what would I say?

Because I knew what last night had meant. What hadn't changed.

Nyktos still *wanted* me. It wasn't just a bodily need he couldn't control. I already knew that.

But I didn't know what I would do with that information. I knew what I *should* do. Forget about it. Ignore it. Nyktos wanted me in a carnal sense. Sex wasn't affection or acceptance. It meant nothing but a complication to an already messy situation. But I wanted him—his touch, the feel of him against my skin and inside me, coming undone. *I* wanted that. Not because I had to. Not for any other reason than it was what *I* wanted.

But everything that only sex offered was temporary, and I wasn't sure if I wanted more. I wasn't even sure what *more* was. Companionship? Trust? Comfort? That all sounded like *more*, but I didn't know. And I didn't even know why I wanted more when my life could be whittled down to months instead of years if Nyktos's plans didn't work. It would make sense if I wanted *right now*. And why couldn't I want that? Have that?

"You finished eating?" Nektas asked.

Blinking, I glanced down at my nearly empty plate and nodded.

"And are you done deep-thinking while you stare at a door?"

My lips pursed. "Yes."

Nektas rose with a half-grin. "I need to go check on my daughter." He stopped, glancing over his shoulder at me. "You coming?"

I held myself still, even though I wanted to leap from the chair because I was...well, I didn't want to be an interloper. Feeling entirely unsure of what I was doing, I lifted a shoulder. "I guess?"

"Then let's go." Nektas opened the doors. "She's likely no longer napping and seconds away from crawling out of a window, like her new friend."

I sighed.

Nektas hadn't been entirely incorrect. Jadis had been awake, and she was trying to reach the handle on the door that led to the balcony. She rushed her father, chirping and yipping and then greeted me with the same enthusiasm. From there, she took her father's hand and led us out of the chamber. Once in the hall, she let out a series of excited chirps as she jumped higher, fluttering her wings until she was able to hover for a few seconds.

"That means she's happy that you're joining us on her adventure," Nektas exclaimed.

I smiled, relieved. "As am I."

Her adventure took us to the main floor and the hall opposite

Nyktos's offices, into some kind of receiving chamber outfitted with formal, stiff-backed chairs and a narrow table. I wondered if meetings or card games were held at that table as Jadis inspected each piece of furniture with an admirable sense of curiosity.

When Nektas left to retrieve a pitcher of water and glasses, I was petrified that something terrible would befall Jadis while he was gone. She kept trying to scale the legs of the desk for some unknown reason, and I'd never been more grateful to see him return.

He wasn't alone.

A purplish-black-scaled draken only a few feet tall was with Nektas.

Reaver chirped a greeting as he started toward me. He didn't make it very far. Jadis all but tackled him, wrapping her slender arms around his stomach, trapping one of his wings between them.

I watched them, awed. I didn't think I'd ever get used to seeing the draken in this form. And to think they could grow to the size of Jadis's father?

Nektas joined me at the table while his daughter became solely focused on playing with Reaver.

Which meant chasing him around the room like a little dirt devil.

"In case you're wondering," Nektas said, pouring water into one of the wide cups, "they are always like this."

I grinned, thinking that Reaver probably wasn't running as fast as he could.

"I didn't get a chance to ask what you thought of Ash's plan," Nektas said as the two made another wide, wild run around the table. "The whole removing the embers part."

"I'm…tentatively hopeful." Tucking a strand of hair back behind my ear, I glanced over at him. "Do you think it will work?"

"I cannot know that."

I frowned. "That's not exactly reassuring."

"It's not meant to be." Nektas caught his daughter's arm as they made yet another run around the table. He held her still until she took several hasty gulps of water, and then he let her go.

She immediately went back to chasing Reaver.

"Delfai will have answers for us." Nektas placed the glass back on the table. "But Ash seeks to do what has only been done once before. There's no telling what is or isn't possible."

I hated not knowing and having to wait to find out. "I wish we could go now. I mean, how dangerous can the Vale be?"

"It's not the Vale that's dangerous. It's the road to the Vale," he explained. "We will need to travel to the Pillars of Asphodel to enter the Vale. Anything can happen between here and the Pillars, and as you should know by now, gods can enter the Shadowlands at will. So can Primals. There are no rules preventing me from burning a god to a crispy stick if I see fit."

I wrinkled my nose at his choice of words.

"The same cannot be said for Primals. I cannot fight one. Neither can the gods who serve in Ash's Court unless they attack Ash." Nektas paused. "Or *his* Consort."

"Oh." I glanced out the lone window in the chamber. The gray sky beyond was a muted, lifeless color broken only by the faint twinkle of stars. Too bad the charm couldn't prevent others from attacking me. "If Nyktos had said that, it would've made more sense."

"He hadn't?"

I shot him a look. His expression was so bland, the sky had to be envious. "No."

He gave me a faint smile as his gaze flicked to the door. "One second."

I turned to see Rhain through the narrow gap. Nektas joined him in the hall, and I watched them, curious about what they could be discussing.

And I really should've been watching the young draken.

Jadis let out a shrill screech, stopping my heart. My head whipped to where...Reaver had apparently flown to the top of an empty cabinet and was perched there, safely out of Jadis's reach.

Something she wasn't remotely happy about.

She jumped and flapped her wings, only managing to get a couple of inches into the air for a few seconds. Her cries were pitiful.

"Reaver," I called, pushing away from the table. "Why don't you come down?"

He shook his diamond-shaped head. And, honestly, I couldn't really blame him.

"She just wants to play."

Reaver shook his head again, and Jadis gave up on flying, opting to *crawl* up the cabinet, causing the entire thing to wobble.

"Oh, my gods." I rushed over, grabbing her as she made it about a foot. "You can't do that."

The moment I put her down, she raced right back to the cabinet. We repeated this series of events several more times before a full-blown, baby draken temper tantrum happened.

With wide eyes and mouth hanging open, I watched her throw herself onto her belly, wailing as she pounded her little taloned fists and clawed feet against the floor, scratching the shadowstone. I froze, having no idea how to calm a mortal child, let alone a draken one.

I glanced desperately at the door, seeing that Rhain and Nektas had moved out of view. "Are you kidding me?" I whispered, turning back to Jadis.

She flopped onto her back, going so still that I feared she'd knocked herself out. I started toward her when Reaver made a rough, huffing noise that sounded very much like a laugh.

That didn't help matters.

The draken was back on her feet in a flash, crimson eyes narrowed as she bleated and yipped at Reaver. He made no move to come back down, and I had no idea what Nektas was doing in that damn hall. I turned to find out. Just a second—*one second* had passed—and I smelled *smoke*.

I whirled, gasping as flames crawled across the leg of one of the chairs Jadis was crouched in front of. "Oh, my gods!"

Jadis jumped excitedly, eyes alit by the flames. I quickly grabbed the pitcher, dousing the fire. Heart pounding, I stepped back—

Nektas walked into the chamber then, coming to an abrupt stop. "I leave the room for two minutes…"

"That was *not* two minutes," I panted. "That was two years."

Jadis tucked her wings back and close to her body then took off, scurrying under a different chair.

Nektas looked up at Reaver, who let out a disgruntled-sounding chirp before gliding down to the floor, where he eyed Jadis. I kind of felt bad for her while her father coaxed her out from under it.

"Someone obviously didn't spend nap time napping," Nektas stated. "Time to do just that."

I trotted after them, feeling as if I'd narrowly survived a war. The embers in my chest suddenly warmed as we neared Nyktos's offices. My stomach immediately started flipping and flopping around like Jadis had in the middle of her fit as Nektas slowed, stopping in the alcove.

"You need anything?" Nektas called as I hung back. Jadis immediately started to struggle to get down.

"No," came the response that shouldn't have made my face feel like it was on fire but did. "You can let her down."

"You spoil her," Nektas muttered, but he let his daughter go, and she took off, disappearing into the office. There was a rough laugh from inside, and Reaver followed at a much more sedate pace. Nektas halted at the entrance, glancing back at me. He raised his brows.

I peeled myself away from one of the shadowstone pillars and came forward, willing my heart to slow.

Nyktos was behind his desk, and the little draken was plastered to the loose, white shirt he wore. She was either hugging...or strangling him. I couldn't be exactly sure which.

"What have you two been up to?" Nyktos asked, glancing to where Reaver was already perched on the corner of his desk.

Reaver gave a couple of low grunts, but Jadis was chirping and yipping rapidly. She leaned back in Nyktos's arms, turning her head to Reaver. She hissed at him, and I couldn't help but grin.

"Maybe Reaver will play with you if you don't chase him so much," Nyktos responded.

My brows shot up. I'd forgotten that Nyktos could understand them.

"By the way, she set one of the chairs on fire," Nektas announced. His daughter immediately planted her head in Nyktos's chest. "So, it's time for a nap."

Nyktos's brows rose as Jadis gave a pitiful, muffled whimper. "It's okay. I'm not mad." He rubbed her back between her wings. "We have plenty of chairs."

"It is *not* okay." Nektas came around the desk, extricating Jadis from the Primal's arms. His daughter all but threw herself over his shoulder, hanging limply as Reaver eyed her warily. "No matter how many chairs there are."

Nyktos grinned, brushing a strand of hair back behind his ear as he *finally* looked past the draken to where I hovered near the empty bookcases.

All I could think about was that icy-hot feeling against my skin, inside me.

Nothing could be gained from Nyktos's expression. I had no idea what he was thinking as his gaze drifted over my features and then lower. The line of his jaw tightened. "Remind me," he said to Nektas, "to check in with Erlina to see when she will be done with her clothing."

Frowning, I glanced down and saw that the bodice had slipped a little, either because it wasn't fitted properly or from trying to keep Jadis from injuring herself and burning down the palace. Either way, it wasn't like my breasts had actually fallen out. Yet. My eyes narrowed. "What's wrong with the gown, *Your Highness?*"

"Everything."

I inhaled sharply, no longer feeling all that pretty in the gown.

Nektas's brow pinched with confusion as he glanced at me. "I see nothing wrong with it."

"Of course, you wouldn't," Nyktos muttered, leaning back in his chair.

"I find it to be many things," Nektas offered, "none of which are wrong. I could list them for you…"

"Not necessary," Nyktos bit out. He dropped his hand to the desk, and his fingers began tapping beside the tome I'd seen him with the day before.

The nape of my neck burned. "If I'd known you were going to insult the gown that doesn't even belong to me, I would've chosen to visit what's left of the entombed gods instead."

Nyktos's eyes flashed to me, narrowing.

"I believe she's saying she'd prefer their company over yours," Nektas added helpfully.

"Thank you for the unnecessary explanation," Nyktos drawled. The Primal sent him a look of warning before focusing on me. Some of the tension eased from his jaw. A moment passed. "I didn't mean to insult your gown. I…apologize if…" He drew in a breath as I stared at him. "If that was rude of me."

"If?" I questioned.

"Okay, it was rude," he amended. "There's nothing wrong with your gown," he muttered. "You look lovely in it."

My brows shot up as I saw Nektas rub at his mouth, attempting to hide his grin. My annoyance with both of them flared. Nyktos had sounded as if he were speaking of a barrat in a gown, and Nektas had definitely failed at hiding his smile.

"I need to get Jadis to sleep," Nektas said, and the Primal nodded. Reaver launched off Nyktos's desk as Nektas headed for the door.

I started to follow them but stopped. Nektas didn't need me being a distraction while he tried to get his daughter to sleep. I remained behind as they left the office, even though I suspected that Nyktos likely would have preferred I hadn't.

As the doors closed behind Nektas, I slowly turned to the Primal. He was still leaning back in his chair, fingers tapping slowly on his desk as he eyed me. "How are you feeling this morning?"

"Good." I felt that damn warmth hitting my face again. "You?"

He lifted the hand from the arm of his chair, resting those fingers against his jaw and chin. "Perfect."

Silence ticked by. "Did you sleep well last night?"

Nyktos went completely still. I don't think he even breathed. "Like a babe."

I stared at him. "You sure about that?"

"Yes." Wisps of eather appeared in his eyes as disbelief crept in.

Was he really going to act as if he hadn't been in my bedchamber the night before, watching me? Touching me?

"It appears you've had a rather eventful morning," he said.

He *was* totally going to act like last night hadn't happened. I tamped down my frustration. "That is one way of putting it."

"Hopefully, for the sake of furniture everywhere, Reaver no longer shelters in places Jadis cannot yet reach."

"I think that will be unlikely."

"Probably. We went through this when Reaver was her age. I'm quite confident we lost at least two chambers' worth of items to his temper tantrums."

I had a hard time picturing Reaver having a tantrum in either form. "What...what happened to Reaver's parents?" I asked, realizing that all I knew was that they were no longer alive.

"They died defending the Shadowlands. Before he was old enough to even shift into mortal form," he answered, and several beats of silence followed. "Kolis grew annoyed when I didn't answer his summons immediately. He sent several of his draken and, after that, I learned that I could only delay answering his summons for so long."

My chest squeezed. "My...my sister? Ezra? She believes you can't hate someone you've never met. She's wrong. I've never met Kolis, and I hate him."

Nyktos was quiet for a moment. "I don't think you have to know someone to feel a certain way toward them. I don't even think you have to truly know someone to miss them."

"Really?"

"I miss many I barely know. The experiences never shared. The history never made." His fingers stilled on the desk. "The memories never created."

"The past that's never mourned." I thought of the mother I'd never been close to. The father I hadn't met. The friends I'd never made. *His* heart. That thought was like a kick to the chest—both the realization that I wanted his affection, something I desperately couldn't acknowledge, and that it would never belong to me. "And the future that's never anticipated."

"Then you understand."

"I...I think so." I blinked back the sudden wetness in my eyes, thinking about the guards who had fallen yesterday. "I'm sorry about those who were lost yesterday. I don't think I said that."

Nyktos nodded. "As am I."

I curled my fingers around the edges of my sleeves. In the silence, I remembered what Saion had said on the Rise. "The Cimmerian? The one called Dorcan. He mentioned you had an army."

"I do," he said.

"Is that something all Primals have?"

He shook his head.

My mind started racing. "How many do you have?"

"The army is substantial." His gaze hadn't left me. Not once since Nektas had left with the younglings. "They're stationed at the Shadowlands' borders."

"Why didn't they give aid when the dakkais attacked?"

"They would have if needed."

The attack had been rather large. To me, that should've warranted the involvement of his army. And the only reason I could think that he wouldn't send for them would be because he'd rather not risk losing any soldiers. Perhaps because he believed he needed all of them.

Which could mean...

My heart turned over heavily. "What would you have done about Kolis if the embers of life hadn't been placed in my bloodline?" I asked. "Based on what you said in the throne room, it's clear you haven't simply accepted this way of life. To live under someone who slaughters without reason and commits the gods only know how many atrocities."

Nyktos was quiet.

I held his stare. "Are you planning to go to war with Kolis?"

14

Nyktos's fingers continued to tap, matching the tempo of my heart. I tried to keep the awakening frustration at bay. If he didn't answer, I wasn't sure what I would do, but it would probably be loud and a little violent.

"To openly speak of such a thing against the King of Gods," he finally said with a slight curl of his upper lip, "would earn one, even a Primal, a sentence in the darkest parts of the Abyss, where even a god of death would not willingly travel."

And to speak of actively working against Kolis wasn't? Like he'd done in the throne room? I smirked. "I doubt that has stopped you from planning just that."

"What do you think a war of Primals would entail?" he countered instead.

"Something unimaginable."

"That would be accurate." He pushed off the desk and walked to the credenza. "No Primal in their right mind would attempt to go to war against the King of Gods, false or not."

I watched him pull the tome I'd seen him with before the Cimmerian showed closer. I knew I was right, and he wasn't speaking the truth. He just didn't want to talk about whatever plans he may have made or still plotted.

He didn't trust me.

It wasn't like I expected him to. Not after everything, but it still...bothered me. Stung. And the sting made me think of that unfamiliar thing again—a future. If Nyktos's plans regarding the embers worked, I could be Nyktos's Consort for hundreds of years—if not more. That was if we all survived Kolis. But would we continue this way once I was crowned in a day's time? Would we still live like this? Separate beds? Separate lives? A Consort in title only, uninvolved in the politics of Court and possible battles sure to come? Would I be left behind as he ruled as the King of Gods? A knot lodged in my throat. Or cast aside, no longer the Consort at all?

"What are you thinking about?" Nyktos asked.

Jarred from my thoughts, I looked up. "Just your plan."

"I don't think that's true."

"Why?"

"Because you just projected...sadness."

I stiffened. "I did not."

"Tell me something, Sera?" His head tilted. "When is it that you speak the truth?"

"When I'm comfortable doing so," I retorted.

An eyebrow rose. "I think that was actually the truth." He eyed me for a span of a few heartbeats and then opened the tome. "There are things I need to attend to..."

In other words, I was being dismissed. Without him even making a single reference to what had occurred between us last night. And, yeah, his refusal to acknowledge what'd happened was a nonissue compared to everything else. But I'd rather be frustrated with him over that than dwell on a future that may or may not come.

So, I welcomed the rising frustration. "When I first arrived, you said I could go wherever I wanted inside these walls and the courtyard. Does that still stand?"

"It does." He turned to a blank page.

"You're not worried about me making a run for it?"

"Not when I've made it so every guard who patrols the Rise and the palace is sure to watch the gates."

My eyes narrowed on his bowed head. "So I can go anywhere?"

Nyktos nodded.

I moved quietly toward him. "Even here? Your office?"

"I'm sure there are more interesting places to be."

"I'm beginning to doubt you actually live here if you think that."

"I live here, Sera."

"Well, you said anywhere. And I choose here." I paused by the chair. "With you."

The breath he exhaled practically rattled the walls as he looked up at me.

Fighting a grin, I tilted my chin at the tome. "What's that?"

"One of the Books of the Dead."

My heartbeat tripped as I eyed the book as if it would leap from his desk and choke the life from me. "The book that lists those who will die the day it's opened?" I whispered. "I was never sure it was real."

"It's real."

"Is no one going to die today? The page is blank."

"For now. I have yet to write the names."

"Do you need something to write with?" I glanced at his otherwise bare desk. "I'm sure I can get you something. I wouldn't want to delay you from ripping people away from their loved ones."

"I'm not killing people when I write their names," he replied dryly. "They would die with or without me doing so."

"Then what's the purpose of writing their names?" I picked up several curls and began twisting the strands together as I edged around the chair.

"Their souls cannot cross through the Pillars until I write their names."

"You left that part out when you told me that bodies do not need to be burned for their souls to leave them."

"I didn't think it was something you needed to know." His attention dropped and lingered where my fingers toyed with my hair.

I drifted closer. "Do you need me..." His gaze flew to mine. "To retrieve something for you to write with?"

"I have what I need."

"Is it invisible?"

"No. I haven't summoned it yet." He lifted his hand. A slender, shimmering swirl of silver-white energy appeared, and a second later, a thin black stylus lay in his once-empty palm.

My lips parted. "Did you...just summon a stylus from thin air?"

"I did."

That was somehow more mystifying than watching him conjure Odin from his cuff. "What about ink?"

"The names of the dead are not written in ink. They're written in blood."

"Your blood?"

Nyktos nodded.

My lip curled as he lowered the stylus to the bound parchment, and crimson appeared as he began to write. "Does it hurt?"

Nyktos shook his head.

I came even closer, stopping at the edge of his desk. I watched him in silence. He wrote name after name in neat, flowing lines of red until he turned the page and began to fill that one, too. "Your penmanship is beautiful."

"Thank you."

He filled another page.

Then a third.

"How...how do you choose who dies?"

"I don't." Another name. "The names come to me as I write."

I leaned my hip against the desk, curling my leg just enough that the panels of the gown parted, revealing my leg from the calf to just above the knee. "What if you make a mistake?"

He stopped writing, his gaze slowly sliding up the length of my exposed leg.

"What if you're making names up and don't realize it?" I asked as I untwisted the strands of my hair. "Or what if you misspell a name?"

"I don't make mistakes."

"Ever?"

"Not with this. In other things?" he muttered, the edges of his fangs dragging over his lower lip as his gaze lingered on the curve of my hip. "Far too often."

"Really?"

"I can think of a few right now."

"Like what?" I asked, knowing I was being a brat and thoroughly enjoying myself.

"Like not having Nektas take you with him when he left." He returned to writing. "He could've put you down for a nap. I'm sure Jadis and Reaver would've enjoyed the company."

I pressed my lips together to stop from laughing. "That was rude."

"Was it?"

"Yes." I watched him write several more names. Seconds ticked into minutes. Good gods, how many would die today? "Perhaps I should've left with Nektas. I wonder if he would've...*enjoyed* putting me down for a nap. He did seem to like my gown."

That got his attention.

The stylus stopped moving. His chin lifted, and thundercloud eyes pierced with lightning met mine.

Very purposefully, I placed my hands on his desk and leaned forward. The slight bend of the waist was enough to test the limits of the gown.

Nyktos's eyes lowered. The stylus vanished from his palm. I hoped that meant he was finished.

"I'm sorry," I said. "Am I being distracting?"

"You don't sound sorry at all." The line of his jaw flexed as he slowly drew his gaze to mine. "And you know exactly what you're doing."

"What's that?"

"You're purposely being distracting."

"I would never."

"And seductive."

"Why would you think that?" I asked, blinking wide eyes.

"Your breasts are inches from my face, Sera." His gaze dropped and then returned to mine. "I don't think. I know. And it's not going to work."

"Your failure to keep your eyes from straying to inappropriate places is not a reflection on my actions," I told him, tipping my head and letting my hair fall forward onto his hand. "But if I were trying to seduce you, *Your Highness*, it would most definitely work."

"You think so?"

"I don't think." I smiled then, bright and wide. "*I know.*"

That muscle began to tick in his jaw. "Well, you would know how to be successful in that endeavor, wouldn't you?"

"Ouch." My fingers pressed into the smooth surface of the desk. I'd most definitely opened the door and walked right into that comment.

"Did that offend you?" Those wisps in his eyes swirled.

"Not really. It's true," I said, glancing down. "I know all the ways to…" My eyes narrowed on the book. I frowned. "Correct me if I'm wrong, but is it not odd that so many with the same exact name died today?"

Nyktos said nothing.

A grin tugged at my lips. "You were pretending to still be writing names, weren't you?"

"I thought you'd realize that I was busy and decide to be less distracting," he told me. "Obviously, that didn't work."

Losing the battle against a smile, I let out a throaty laugh. "Maybe I will find someone else to *distract*," I taunted, pushing off the desk.

I didn't make it far.

His hand snapped out, closing around the nape of my neck. My breath caught as my gaze locked with his. "I want to make one thing perfectly clear, Seraphena."

The pressure he used was slight, only enough to force me to place my hands on the desk as I bent until we were at eye level, our mouths inches apart. My pulse skittered recklessly. His hold wasn't painful. I could slip out of it if I wanted to, but I didn't. I'd wanted his attention, and now I had it.

"As long as you're my Consort," he said, his tone deceptively soft, "you will be very selective about how you spend your time with others."

"I assume when you reference *how* I spend time with someone, you're speaking of what typically comes after the act of seduction?"

The Book of the Dead slammed shut and slid across his desk. Neither of his hands had moved. "You know exactly what I'm speaking of."

"Then I'm confused," I said in the little space between us. "You said I was to be your Consort in title only."

His gaze dropped again, just for a brief second, but I knew where he looked. "I did."

The breath I inhaled was all him. My blood heated and my skin flushed. "Then what of my needs?"

"Your needs?" he repeated, his voice smoothing to a decadent drawl that I wasn't even sure he was aware of.

"Intimacies. Touching. Skin-to-skin contact. Sex. Fuc—"

"I think I get it."

"So, what of them?"

He curled his arm, and it stretched me even farther. There was a really good chance my breasts would exit the gown. His head tilted. It was only a slight move, but it lined up our mouths perfectly. If either of us leaned forward an inch or two, our lips would meet. "I'm sure you can resist those desires or handle them yourself."

"Because you watched me do it." I wet my lips. Nyktos said nothing, his gaze now on my mouth. "You watched me last night. You *touched* me," I whispered, feeling a faint tremor in the hand on the back of my neck. "I felt you. Inside me. That was highly inappropriate of you."

"More inappropriate than you fucking your fingers while you knew I was watching?"

The breath I took went nowhere as liquid heat flooded my veins. The way he said "*fucking*" conjured images of silk sheets and tangled limbs. "What would've been more inappropriate was if you hadn't taken care of it, and I had to do it myself."

His nostrils flared.

"Why did you come to my bedchamber last night?"

"Arm's reach," he murmured. "Remember?"

"I remember, but was it truly that? Or did you sense my need? My want? Of you." I inched forward, half-expecting him to retreat. He didn't. When I spoke, my lips brushed the corner of his, and I felt a faint zap of static. "I was thinking of you when I fucked my fingers. Imagining that it was your touch—before I even knew you were in the chamber."

"Sera," he warned—or begged. It sounded like both.

"Just thought you should know." I drew back, stilling when his molten silver eyes locked onto mine. "I can take care of my desires, but that only goes so far."

"You'd better make it stretch as far as it can go," he ordered softly.

"And if I don't?"

"What I did to those gods in the throne room will pale in comparison to what I do to whoever satisfies your needs."

A jolt of surprise shot through me, quickly followed by a really twisted dose of pleasure at his jealousy-fueled threat. Anger was right behind it, though. I had no intention of satisfying my needs with anyone. But what he demanded went beyond arrogant when he claimed to want no such thing from me. "Let me make one thing perfectly clear to *you*, Nyktos. If you want me as your Consort in title only, then you have no say over *what* I do or with *whom*, from this point until I take my last breath—whenever that may be."

"If? You speak as if there is another option."

My pulse skipped. "Because there is."

"And what is that?" His head moved, and his lips brushed the corner of mine.

"We satisfy each other's needs." I was a little surprised as I spoke the words, but they were the *right now* I'd been thinking about earlier. "You don't need *fragile* trust, nor do you really even have to like someone when you have attraction."

His fingers curled into my hair. "I don't dislike you, Sera."

An unwanted emotion swelled in my chest, leaving me off-kilter and making me nervous. I tried to put distance between us, but his hold prohibited it. "There is no reason to lie. I know where we stand with each other. I'm not offering myself for whatever meager affections you or anyone can give."

A muscle ticked in his jaw. "Then what *are* you offering yourself for?"

"Pleasure."

The wisps of eather went wild in his eyes. "That is all?"

"Why does it have to be anything else when it's what *I* want?" I said, and that was the truth. Maybe there was *more* behind it, but I knew better than to pry too deeply into that. "Either way, I will not play the I-don't-want-you-but-no-one-else-can-have-you game. With you or anyone."

"There is no one else, Sera." His hand landed on the center of my back, causing me to jump.

"Only if there is you," I said, fully aware that I had no plans of easing my needs with anyone else at the moment *or* in the foreseeable future. Not because of anything he'd said, but because it simply didn't appeal to me.

But he didn't need to know that.

"So, that's the deal. Between us. Not between your father and some ancestor of mine."

His eyes flashed, the eather seeping into the veins just beneath them as his mouth came within inches of mine once more. "Pleasure for the sake of pleasure?"

"Yes," I whispered as I felt a strange warming in my chest.

"You're so reckless." His hand slid from my back to my hip, leaving shivers in its wake. "You have your dagger on you?"

My brows pinched at the unexpected question. "Yes?"

"Make sure it stays hidden," Nyktos warned. "Because a Primal has arrived."

The heat in my blood immediately cooled. "Were you expecting one to visit?"

"Not at all." Without warning, Nyktos hauled me across his desk and onto his lap. His strength and the feel of his body against and beneath mine was a shock to the senses. "There's not enough time for you to leave, so there's no avoiding this. No matter what I say or do, you'll stay right where I have you. Do you understand?"

I nodded.

Nyktos brushed my hair over my shoulder. "I'm being serious, Sera."

"I know." I turned my head to him. "I know when to be reserved and not reckless."

"Good. Just don't forget how to be so exquisitely reckless later." His gaze flicked to the closed doors. "I apologize ahead of time for how I'm about to behave. I have a feeling you will not appreciate it, considering what we just discussed."

Before I could respond to any of what he'd said, a charge of energy swept through the chamber, dancing over my skin before I could even formulate a response. Tiny bumps broke out across my skin. The breath I exhaled formed a faint, misty cloud. Gripping the arm across my waist, I stiffened as every part of my being reacted to the power pouring into the air.

"Relax," Nyktos murmured in my ear as his hand settled against my hip, squeezing gently. "What you're feeling is me. I'm basically showing off."

I wasn't sure if that was supposed to make me feel better, but I forced the air out of my lungs and my fingers to relax.

The doors to his office swung open, and a tall figure filled the entryway. The sword at the hip was a wicked, curved one, the kind crafted for beheading. Light, blondish-brown hair framed high cheekbones and a chiseled jaw as hard as the thin layer of shadowstone armor worn over a broad chest and shoulders. A shallow scar ran from his hairline and across the bridge of his straight nose, then down his left cheek, the healed wound a shade of pale pink.

What in the world could leave that kind of scar on a Primal?

My fingers pressed into Nyktos's arm as the Primal came to an abrupt stop, armored boots in line with the breadth of his shoulders. The way he stood there—the frenetic, violent energy brimming just beneath his flesh and the glow of essence pulsing behind his pupils said one thing.

He was a *warrior.*

The Primal's silver gaze slowly drifted over us as the corners of his lips tipped up. A deep divot in his right cheek appeared first, and then an identical one in his left. "Am I interrupting?"

Nyktos's chin grazed the top of my head, startling me enough that I jumped a little. "What does it look like, Attes?"

Every muscle in my body locked as I realized who stood before us. I'd been right on the mark, but he wasn't just a warrior. He was *the* warrior—the Primal of Accord and War. The one people prayed to on the eve of any battle to not only grant armies his deadly skill but also the cleverness to outwit all who tried to outmaneuver them. A Primal who could incite agreement between warring kingdoms or all-out, bloody violence with his mere presence.

Nyktos's fingers suddenly moved along my hip, sliding out and into his palm, pulling me from the downward spiral of my thoughts.

"It sure looks like I am." Attes's gaze came back to me. His unblinking stare was nearly as intense as Nyktos's could be, drilling into me until I was sure he could rattle all my secrets out into the open.

It took everything in me to hold still and not squirm or react. Instinct told me that if I showed discomfort or fear, he would do what any predator would when they scented blood—attack.

"And yet you still stand here," Nyktos said. "Without invitation, I might add."

A faint curve of the lips appeared as Attes's gaze remained fixed on me. He glanced at my arms, sensing the charm. "So, this is her? The mortal who has so many of the Courts abuzz with gossip."

"I didn't realize you were the type to entertain gossip," Nyktos replied, his tone one of chilly indifference as he slowly slid his hand over my lower stomach. I tensed. His hand made its way to my thigh, leaving a path of tiny shivers in its wake. "But, yes, this is my Consort."

Nyktos's touch had thrown me. I had no idea what had gotten into him, and, for a moment, I wasn't sure what he expected of me. Was I to be quiet and meek? Or do the normal thing when introduced to someone? I decided on the latter and managed a steady, "Hello, Your—" My breath snagged as Nyktos's hand slipped under the panel of the skirt, his fingers spreading wide across the *bare* flesh of my upper thigh. There was no way Attes missed the possessive placement of Nyktos's hand. I cleared my throat. "Your Highness."

Attes inclined his head in greeting as he continued studying me, his smile returning. "*Soon-to-be* Consort," he corrected Nyktos softly.

"I also haven't missed that she's no mere mortal." His gaze dropped to the swell of my breasts above the too-tight bodice. "She carries a...mark. An aura."

My eyes narrowed slightly. I had no idea exactly what type of mark he thought he saw in the general vicinity of my breasts. I twitched as Nyktos's finger began moving along the skin of my leg, back and forth in a straight, slow line. And I didn't know what to think of his sudden affection—sudden *sensual* affection. I wasn't used to being touched so casually or so openly.

"She's a godling on the cusp of her Culling," Nyktos stated so smoothly that I was impressed. His finger stilled on my skin. "And if you keep looking at her like that, I'll cut your eyes from their sockets and feed them to Setti."

My eyes went wide.

Attes laughed deeply, and the sound was nice—not as nice as Nyktos's, but deep and throaty. "My steed prefers alfalfa and sugar cubes over eyes." He brushed his fingers across the silver band on his biceps. "But he appreciates the offer."

"I'm sure he does." Nyktos's finger returned to tracing that line.

Attes adjusted his sword as he helped himself to the seat in front of the desk. "Is she a godling who already called Lethe home?"

Irritation burned on my tongue. To sit and be spoken about as if I were not in the room was the height of infuriating.

"No," Nyktos said.

Attes raised an eyebrow. "Then where did you find her?"

I'd just told Nyktos that I knew when to be reserved. This was one of those moments. A Primal sat before us. That alone was a precarious position to be in. So, I kept reminding myself of that as I searched for the veil of emptiness inside me, the one that allowed me to feel nothing—not even anger—and to just *exist*. I'd worn it so often that it almost felt like it had truly become who I was. But I struggled to find it.

I had a feeling it had to do with the hand on my leg.

"I found her in a lake."

Attes's brows snapped together. "I'm really hoping you'll elaborate on that."

"In my lake." I spoke then, unable to stop myself. "He was—" I inhaled sharply as Nyktos shifted his legs, drawing my backside more fully against his lower stomach. Nyktos's finger began to move, drawing a short line along my *inner thigh* now.

"He was...?" Attes prodded, his gaze lowering to where Nyktos's hand had disappeared. Suddenly, I knew why Nyktos had felt the need to apologize ahead of time for his behavior. Everything he was doing was in plain sight of Attes. Nyktos was making it very clear that I was *his*.

The problem was, I didn't entirely mind it.

Which presented another problem since my lack of disgust over this meant there was truly something wrong with me, and I would really need to think long and hard about that later.

"He was trespassing while I was swimming," I managed.

A brow rose as Attes glanced between us. "I think I need to visit more lakes in the mortal realm."

"You should," Nyktos suggested. "Though I doubt you will find such unexpected treasure as I did."

Treasure? There was a silly jump in my chest that happened before I could remind myself that if I took away the embers, a *treasure* was the very last thing Nyktos thought I was.

"Sadly, I think you may be right," Attes said after a moment. "I doubt I shall find a treasure as…*unique*."

Nyktos's finger halted. There was something in Attes's tone and the slight, almost secretive smile that graced his lips—something that caused tiny balls of unease to form in the pit of my chest.

"What's your name?" Attes asked, his thumb tapping the arm of the chair.

Nyktos said nothing behind me, so I took that as permission to answer. "Sera."

"*Sera*," he repeated in a low voice. "No last name?"

It was doubtful that he could find many in the mortal realm who would recognize my first name. The last would be an entirely different story. I gave a coy shrug.

"Intriguing," he remarked. "I think the others will understand why you've taken a Consort once they see her." The Primal gave a slow grin, showing off that dimple in his right cheek. He winked at me. "I have a feeling many of them will find themselves wishing to adorn themselves with such an alluring accessory."

Anger gathered in my chest for a second before Nyktos's arms gave a warning squeeze. I'd likely projected that emotion right down his throat. Because…an *accessory*? There wasn't enough common sense in the entire realm of Iliseeum for me to keep my mouth shut. "I doubt you prefer the taste of eyes more than your steed, but refer to me as an *accessory* again, and it will be you who feeds on them."

The moment those words left my mouth, I almost regretted them. The Primal of Accord and War went impossibly still in the same way Nyktos often did. His glowing, silver eyes fixed on me. Icy, dark energy ramped up, brushing against my skin as it built from *behind* me. I was suddenly unsure which Primal I'd angered more.

Attes smiled, revealing straight teeth and fangs. "This one has bite."

"You have no idea," Nyktos murmured, and my head whipped toward him. His eyes briefly met mine as that damn hand slipped *deeper* between my thighs. His thumb gave a swipe, nearly brushing the thin undergarment there. "Behave."

I drew back, my restraint cracking again.

"Has Veses seen her yet?"

Veses. My attention snapped back to Attes as the memory of the Primal touching Nyktos filled my thoughts.

"No," Nyktos replied, his tone cool enough to chill my skin.

"Well, that will be a complication, will it not? One I would not envy."

I opened my mouth, but Attes continued. "And you've had a lot of complications of late, it seems. I heard you had quite a few entombed gods escape on you."

"I assume you had nothing to do with that."

Attes smirked. "You should know me better than that. If I had a problem with you, I wouldn't send one of my draken, nor would I unleash those entombed here."

"No, you're not the type to plunge the sword into someone's back."

"Neither are you."

"Glad we have that in common," Nyktos replied, but he didn't sound glad at all. "What is it that you want, Attes?"

"There are many things I want, and very few of those things are available to me." Attes stretched out a leg. His gaze dropped to where Nyktos's hand was. "I've never seen you quite so...engrossed with another before."

I almost laughed.

"You haven't." Nyktos's lips brushed my cheek, causing my pulse to skitter in surprise. "I prefer to have her within reach."

Only because he feared I would do something reckless, but not *exquisitely reckless.*

"I can easily see why."

"And I can see you're nowhere near getting to the point before I run out of patience," Nyktos warned. "And I'm almost there, just so you know."

Good gods, the way he spoke to the other Primal was shocking. I knew there was a hierarchy to the Primals, with the Primal of Death and Primal of Life being at the top, but still. This was the Primal of *War.*

Attes's stare sharpened, hardening the handsome angles of his face. "You killed my Cimmerian. Those who came to your Rise."

The swift change of subject threw me as Nyktos said, "They were not your Cimmerian. They served Hanan. And if you had such concern for them, you should have taught them better than to serve such a coward."

Tension poured into the chamber, even as Nyktos's finger continued drawing short, idle lines over the flesh of my thigh.

"As much as it pisses me off to admit this," Attes said after a long moment, "you have a point there. But you also killed Dorcan. I was under the impression that you two were fond of each other."

Dorcan...he had called Nyktos an old friend. I hadn't thought much of it, because Nyktos didn't consider any of those close to him friends.

But that didn't mean they weren't.

"I may have tolerated him. But whatever tolerance I may have for someone ends when they come to my Court, make demands, and attack my guards. None of the other Primals would've done anything less."

"You are usually more lenient than the rest of us."

"Perhaps you don't know me as well as you think you do," Nyktos said. "So, what have you come to do, Attes? Lecture me on my lack of leniency? If so, what did you do to your brother's guards when they stepped out of line?"

"Kyn's guards were pieces of shit."

"From what I heard, they were simply intoxicated and celebrating that night."

"Their inability to handle their spirits wasn't why I gutted them."

"It wasn't?"

"No." Attes tipped his chin toward me. "I assume your soon-to-be Consort is wise enough not to repeat what is discussed here?"

"His Consort is wise enough," I snapped, yet again failing to control my tongue.

"I do hope so," Attes replied. "I also hope you're more careful with your tone. I may find your boldness refreshing. Alluring, even. Others will not."

"Those who do not likely won't live long enough to wallow in their insult," Nyktos responded before I could.

"Because you'll make sure they're dead before they can?"

Nyktos laughed darkly. "Because my Consort will likely plunge a dagger into their hearts before I'm even aware of what has occurred."

His words shocked me and sent my heart thumping. He'd made it clear that I was no damsel to be protected, and I liked that—maybe too much.

"So, I should take the earlier threat to feed my eyes to me more seriously?"

I smiled at the Primal.

"I'll keep that in mind." Attes refocused on Nyktos. "You going to tell me how in the holy fuck a god Ascended here in the Shadowlands?"

My heart stuttered at the blatant callout, but Nyktos didn't react. Nothing except for the swipe of his finger coming shockingly close to my thin undergarment once more. I bit the inside of my lip as a rush of slick heat answered the indecent touch. Attes's gaze lowered again, and I knew from where he sat and from how Nyktos held me, he could see precisely what Nyktos's hand was up to. With the Primals' increased senses, it was also likely he could tell how much it affected me. Heat scalded my skin, but not from shame. It should've been. Or, at the very least, anger. And there was a little bit of that—just enough to clear some of the languid warmth invading my senses. Nyktos was putting on a show. Not for me, but for Attes.

"It had to be Kolis."

Attes snorted. "Come the fuck on, Nyktos."

"I don't know who else it could've been."

"If it was Kolis, why would he have finally chosen to Ascend a god? Here, in the Shadowlands."

"You'd have to ask him that."

"I guess I will have to."

I didn't think Attes planned to do that, because it didn't seem like he believed Kolis was capable of such a thing.

"I know it was a god from Hanan's Court," Attes said after a moment. "The only one I know who is often found in the Shadowlands is Bele."

"She is often here," Nyktos confirmed while I willed my heart to calm.

"Well, Hanan is having a godsdamn fit right now *at* Dalos, convinced that you, the Primal of Death, have somehow managed to Ascend a god. The other Primals are *worried*. That if one god can Ascend to challenge their position, then so can another."

"You don't look all that worried," Nyktos pointed out, and he didn't.

"That's because I don't fear someone taking my place." He sat back, dropping his hand to his knee. "None of us has forgotten who your father was." Attes held Nyktos's stare, and my stomach dipped at the insinuation. "Or who you were meant to be."

"You think there are embers of life in me?" Nyktos laughed, stirring the hair along the back of my neck. "That it was not Kolis but me who did it?"

Oh, gods, what if they did? What if Kolis believed that? Pressure clamped down on my chest, and I held my breath as my heart started to race. Nyktos gently squeezed my thigh.

"If it wasn't Kolis, then there would have to be embers of life here," Attes replied. "And you haven't denied that."

"Nor have I confirmed anything," Nyktos countered, and I heard the smoky smile in his words. "I'm beginning to wonder if you're here because of your curiosity or if you came on Kolis's behalf."

Attes went still once more. "Both would be true."

My insides went cold as Nyktos leaned into my back. That dark energy rose again. "Is that so?"

"It is. I am curious about what has been occurring here." The aura in Attes's eyes brightened. "And Kolis has tasked me with delivering a message to you."

"I didn't know that he was now using you for such things."

"I believe he chose me because I'm the closest." Attes paused. "And one of the few you'd be less likely to toss into the Abyss once you hear the message."

"I wouldn't put a lot of confidence behind that belief." Nyktos's voice had dropped. "What is the message?"

"Kolis is aware that you've taken a Consort." A muscle flexed in his jaw. "And His Majesty has decided to deny your right to a coronation."

15

The very air in the room seemed to stop. Kolis could…he could do that?

"Has he now?" Nyktos's voice was soft—too soft.

"He has," Attes confirmed. "Since there hasn't been a coronation in many years, he wants it to be more…traditional."

"What does that mean?" I asked, my mouth dry.

Attes inclined his chin. "It means that Nyktos must gain Kolis's permission to crown a Consort." His gaze flicked to Nyktos.

My lips parted. "Son of a bitch."

The wisps of eather swirled in Attes's eyes as his grin returned. He dipped his head, dropping his voice. "Did you just call the King of Gods a son of a bitch?"

"Uh…"

Attes laughed even as Nyktos's body went icy against mine.

"And when does he expect me to do this when the coronation is to be held *tomorrow*?" Nyktos demanded.

Attes's grin faded. "There will be no coronation tomorrow. Instead, Kolis will summon you—both of you."

It felt like the office disappeared around us. My heart started pounding. I attempted to rise, but Nyktos's arm remained firm around me.

"When?" Nyktos bit out.

"When he is ready." Attes smiled, but there was no warmth to the curve of his lips. No dimple. "That was all he said."

"So, it could be tomorrow or a week or month from now," Nyktos surmised.

"Basically." Attes sat forward, his shoulders tensing. "You know, I think he would've done this even if a god hadn't Ascended here. After all, you are his favorite."

His favorite? I had a feeling Attes meant the exact opposite by saying that.

"Yeah." Nyktos leaned back. "I think it's time for you to leave."

"As do I." The Primal of Accord and War rose. He looked at me. "It was a pleasure to meet you." Primal eyes lifted to mine. "If you find you'd rather spend your time in a warmer bed and climate…"

I stared up at him, somewhat dumbfounded. "Thank you for the offer, but not interested."

"Too bad." A dimple appeared in his right cheek. "But if you ever change your mind, all you have to do is call for me. I will answer."

"Leave." The promise of violence hummed in that one word. "Before you have to be carried out of here."

Attes bowed in our direction, then left. The doors closed behind him. Neither Nyktos nor I moved or spoke for several seconds, but the temperature in the room had dropped even further. The arm around my waist and the hand against my thigh hardened. Shadows had bled to the surface of his flesh, and the breath I exhaled formed a misty cloud once more. I thought I saw tiny bursts of silver light throughout the space.

Shivering as the frigid air seeped through the gown, I touched his arm. Like I had the night of the draken attack. "It's…it's cold," I whispered, my lips beginning to tingle.

Nyktos's hand slid out from between my thighs, but the arm around me tightened. "Argue with me."

"What?" I whispered.

"Argue with me," he repeated, his voice full of smoke and ice. "Distract me. Something to stop me from going after Attes and taking my anger out on him. That will not end well for the Shadowlands or Vathi, and that's the last thing we need."

I twisted toward him. His eyes were nearly pure silver orbs. His jaw was as hard as the shadowstone walls. Churning darkness had blossomed across his cheeks. Eather lit the veins beneath his eyes, and the hardness in the stare fixed on the doors beyond me told me that he wasn't exaggerating in the least. So, I did the first thing that came to mind.

Clasping his now-icy cheeks in my palms, I did what he'd asked of me when he held me in the sweetly scented tunnels of the Luxe.

I kissed him.

His lips—cooler than before—were still that strangely enticing juxtaposition of soft and firm as his entire body jerked. He didn't pull away, but he went completely rigid against me. He was as still as he'd been in the vine tunnel, and I did once more what I'd done then.

Catching his plump lower lip between my teeth, I bit him.

Not hard enough to draw his blood or hurt him, but, like before, he was no longer still.

I kissed him, but he *devoured*. His head tilted, and he parted my lips with a fierce stroke of his tongue. The sharp scrape of his fangs against my lips sent a tight shudder through me as his hand fisted the hair at the nape of my neck. He held me there, his kiss hard, demanding, and I loved his nearly immediate, raw response as I flicked my tongue over his. A rumble came from deep within his throat, his chest. He tasted as decadent as his blood, smoky and sweet, and I quickly lost myself in the kiss. In him.

My fingers slid back, sinking into the soft strands of his hair as I pressed against his chest, wanting to be closer. Needing it. Because he kissed me just like he had the first time. As if he wouldn't let a single inch of my mouth go unexplored. As if he'd been waiting his entire life to do this. The thought no longer felt silly or whimsical. It felt like sinking under the surface of my lake. It felt like a wild sort of peace. It felt *right*.

And that scared me.

I broke the kiss but couldn't retreat far. His hand was still on the back of my head, buried in my hair, and I was close enough to feel his cool breath coming fast and shallow against my tingling lips.

Only then did I realize that the temperature of the room had risen.

"I hope that worked," I whispered, swallowing.

His chest rose with a deep breath against mine as his hand eased from my hair. "I'm level."

"Good." I started to put some distance between us, but his arm around my waist remained as tight as before. "I'm still in your lap."

"I know."

"It's not exactly comfortable," I lied. I'd never felt more comfortable, which made me unsteady. Vulnerable.

"Neither are you."

My brows shot up. "That was—"

"My dick was hard the whole time you were sitting in my lap," he said. "The kissing didn't help."

"—rude," I finished, blinking.

The shadows under his skin had slowed and were fading. "And here I thought getting my dick hard was what you were aiming for before Attes arrived."

My mouth dropped open. "Not anymore."

Some of the intense brightness eased from his stare. "Liar," he whispered in the scant inches between our mouths.

I was such a liar.

His eyes met mine. "I had to behave that way."

I knew immediately that he was speaking about how he'd acted in front of Attes. There were far more important things to discuss, but I said, "Really?"

"Attes is driven by three needs—peace, war, and fucking."

"In that particular order?"

A trace of a smile appeared. "In any order. If he so much as had an *idea* there was little attraction between us, he would've been more interested in you than he already was."

"More interested? I don't see why you'd think he was interested at all."

"You threatened to make him eat his eyes."

"Exactly. If that gained his interest, it would be a little bizarre."

"You stabbed me in the chest." Nyktos inclined his head. "And threatened to claw out my eyes. That didn't deter my interest at the time. What does that say about me?"

"Good question," I muttered, not missing the at-the-time part of that statement. "But you started the whole removing the eyes thing."

"I didn't want Attes thinking that either of us would welcome him acting upon his interests."

My eyes narrowed on him. "I don't think you have to worry about me welcoming that."

"Really? Did you not suggest mere minutes before his arrival that you were willing to seek out others to satisfy your needs?"

I gaped at him. "That is not what I said!"

"Actually, I'm pretty sure that's exactly what you said."

"It was not—" I cut myself off. "Okay. Now, I'm annoyed. I hope you're in control of your anger issues because if you don't let me go, I'm likely to hit you."

"I'm going to have to risk that," he replied. "Because we need to talk about the shit Kolis just pulled, and there's a good chance I won't remain level."

"What does that have to do with me staying in your lap?"

"Because if he loses his cool, he could hurt you."

My head whipped toward the now-open doors. Nektas stood there, and he wasn't alone. Ector was beside him. I didn't even want to think about how long they'd been standing there.

"And with you so close to him," Nektas continued, "he won't risk it."

I opened my mouth, but I really didn't know how to respond to that. At all. So, I said nothing. No one said anything.

"We just ran into Attes," Ector said, breaking the awkward silence. "Guessing what he said is true. Kolis is demanding you ask for his permission?"

"It is," Nyktos confirmed, his forearm tensing under my fingers. Remembering his reaction in the war room, I pulled my hand back.

"Fuck," Ector uttered.

I seconded that emotion as I glanced over my shoulder at Nyktos. "Did you know he could do that?"

"Gaining the King of Gods' permission was a tradition back when my father ruled." Nyktos leaned back in the chair, putting a little more space between us. "Primals and gods sought his approval before a coronation, hoping he would give his *blessing*. But Kolis hasn't done it once. Nor has he ever shown any interest in such a thing." The muscle along Nyktos's jaw flexed. "But I should've expected this—that he'd pull this shit."

After all, you are his favorite.

"He'll use this as a chance to find out how the embers of life were felt here," Nektas said. "I bet he'll offer that in return for his permission."

Ector's amber gaze darted from me to Nyktos. "You can't let him know the truth."

"No shit," Nyktos replied.

"But what will you tell him if that's the case?" As soon as I finished asking the question, I understood. "Attes said that neither he nor the other Primals had forgotten who your father was or who you were meant to be. Kolis could think it was you."

"That's far better than him thinking it's you," he countered.

I gaped at him. "No, it's not."

"Kolis would know it's not Ash," Nektas interrupted. "He's already tested Ash enough to know that he has no embers of life in him."

"Tested…?" I trailed off, thinking of the ink swirling over Nyktos's skin. I knew as Ector looked away, rubbing his hand through his hair. I knew without even asking. Some of those drops represented those that Kolis had killed to see if Nyktos could bring them back to life.

Gods.

Nyktos had gone still behind me, and I hoped I wasn't projecting and that he wasn't reading me. I didn't think he'd appreciate the sorrow I felt for him.

Nyktos finally spoke. "I would lie. I would tell him that I felt it, searched for the source, but haven't found it."

"He'd believe that?" I asked, looking back at him.

"I've had to convince Kolis of many things," he told me. "I will convince him of this when he issues his summons—whenever he's damn good and ready. Which—"

"Presents many issues," Nektas finished.

That was an understatement.

"Believe it or not, Kolis's interference isn't the only issue we're now facing," Nyktos said. "Not after Attes met Sera."

I twisted back to him with a frown. "I doubt Attes thinks I'm anything more than a mouthy pair of breasts."

Ector snickered.

Nyktos's eyes flared with eather. "He was *provoking* you."

My scowl deepened. "When he called me an accessory?"

"Not then. Later. I could sense him using eather. He was feeding into your emotions, amplifying either calmness or violence."

There was a reason Primals didn't often enter the mortal realm. Their presence could change the moods and minds of mortals and impact the environment around them. The Primal Maia could evoke love and fertility. Embris could increase one's wisdom or guide them into making poor choices. Phanos could stir the oceans into a frenzy. Attes's brother, Kyn, could engender peace or vengeance.

"You really think he was trying to do that?" I asked, thinking of when the eather in Attes's eyes had grown brighter. "To me?"

"Without a doubt," Nyktos confirmed.

"But I didn't feel calmer or more violent...than normal," I said, and he huffed out a laugh. "I didn't feel anything."

"Exactly," Nyktos said.

"Oh, shit," Ector murmured. "Attes would've realized that his presence had no impact on you."

A sharp slice of unease lanced my chest. "But Nyktos told him I was a godling—"

"Neither godlings nor gods are immune to a Primal's abilities," Ector said. "We don't react to their presence as quickly or recklessly as a mortal might, but it would affect us if a Primal wanted it to. That's why the gods in Kyn's Court are a bunch of bastards, and the ones in Maia's are a horny lot."

My lips pursed.

"Besides the Arae and the draken," Ector continued, "only one other would be immune."

Nyktos's gaze caught mine. "Only a Primal is immune to another Primal's presence."

"Good gods, that could mean…" I squeezed my eyes closed. It could mean that Attes might suspect the truth. That it was *me* who carried the embers of life. The Consort-to-be, who was about to be summoned by Kolis. My breath scraped against my throat.

"Give us a minute," Nyktos said, and when I opened my eyes, both Ector and Nektas were gone, the doors closed once more. More than a few seconds passed in silence before Nyktos spoke again. "It'll be okay."

A strangled laugh left me. "Attes might now realize it is I who carries the embers of life. And Kolis is going to summon both of us. How in the world is that okay?"

"It could be worse."

"How?"

"Kolis could've outright denied the coronation. Forbidden that I take a Consort."

"He can do that?"

Nyktos nodded. "I could still take you as my Consort, but you would not be recognized as such by the other Courts."

Meaning whatever protection the position offered would have no longer existed. Neither the gods nor the draken could defend me against a Primal. If one of the other Primals or Kolis himself seized me, Nyktos would have no support if he retaliated—and I knew he would. "Will he do that?"

"If you asked me that yesterday, I would've said no. Now? Anything is possible."

Anything…

My heart started beating in a way that made breathing difficult. My thoughts raced. Muscles tensed. "What if I…what if I look like Sotoria?" I whispered.

"He will not touch you." Nyktos cupped my cheek, and my eyes closed at the faint trace of energy moving from his fingertips to my skin.

"I will not allow it."

The safety in his promise, the security of it, threatened to wrap around me. It was already beginning to calm my heart, and I didn't want to fight it. I wanted to rely on the promise. On him.

Nyktos's forehead touched my temple, and some of the rigidness eased from my muscles. I started to relax into him. "He will not have a chance to learn if you look like her."

Eyes flying open, I jerked back. "Nyktos—"

"You will not go anywhere near him."

My stomach lurched. "You just told me what happened when one delays in answering Kolis's summons. I will not be the reason for *more* death."

"You have never been the reason."

"Bullshit."

"Kolis has been the reason. Not you. Not your actions. It has been him. Always him." Wisps of eather stirred in his eyes. "You need to understand that, Sera. You are not at fault."

It was hard to accept that when Kolis had been reacting to *my* actions.

Unable to stay still, I pulled on his hold. Nyktos's arm fell away. I rose, backing away from him. "I will not hide from his summons, Nyktos."

His hand fell to the arm of his chair. "And I will not allow you to be in danger."

"I'm already in danger! I've lived my whole life that way." The crack in my chest threatened to spread and deepen as I stared at the empty bookshelves. "If my refusal to answer his summons caused something to happen—for people to be hurt or killed—I couldn't..." I shoved the hair back from my face as I turned away from him. "I couldn't deal with that."

"Is that really why you are determined to answer his summons?"

Slowly, I faced him. "What other reason could there be?"

"Isn't this what you wanted?" His grip on the arm of the chair tightened, bleaching his knuckles. "To get to Kolis?"

I opened my mouth, but it struck me that I should be celebrating this. Not once—not from the moment Attes had delivered his message until now—had it even occurred to me that Nyktos wouldn't be forced into taking me as his Consort tomorrow. I could come face-to-face with Kolis without the risks of escaping. And if I looked like Sotoria, my duty would be even easier to achieve. Not only lives would be saved. Entire *realms* would be. I should be thrilled.

But I wasn't.

I felt anything but that. A wild mix of emotion brimmed beneath the surface, causing the crack in my chest to weaken even further. I was scared. Horrified. Angry. Desperate. On the verge of losing control—

I sucked in deep gulps of air, shutting it all down. Silencing the storm much like I had when I donned the veil.

Nyktos hadn't taken his eyes off me. His stare was as hard as it had been earlier. "This way, you wouldn't have to try to escape, would you?"

The breath I took fell short as the back of my neck burned. "Fuck you."

A muscle flexed in his jaw. I thought he might have flinched, but I wasn't sure, and I didn't care. I turned stiffly, leaving his office before the crack in my chest exploded again.

Before I lost control.

Nektas was waiting in the hall when I stormed out of Nyktos's office. I didn't see Ector as I turned, walking past the draken. I swallowed a curse as Nektas fell into step beside me.

"Great. You're following me," I muttered.

"You're very astute, *meyaah Liessa*."

I sighed.

"You don't like being referred to as a Queen, do you?"

"You're very astute, *meyaah* draken."

Nektas's laugh was short and rough as I opened the door to the stairwell. "I didn't know I was your draken."

I started climbing the narrow steps far less grand than the main staircase. "Yeah, well, you're my draken as much as I'm your Queen."

"You are our Queen with or without a coronation."

"That makes little sense, but whatever," I muttered, reaching for the door on the fourth floor.

Nektas stretched his arm over my head, pulling it open before I could. "You carry the only true embers of life in you, Sera. You're *the* Queen."

I looked over my shoulder at him with a frown.

He eased past me, quiet as he led the way to my bedchamber. I watched as he entered the room and proceeded to go straight to the bathing chamber. He pushed open that door and inspected the space before going to the balcony doors while I stopped by the settee. There, he shoved the drapes aside and looked out.

"Do you want to check under the bed, too?" I suggested.

He turned, arching a dark brow. "Was Ash wrong? In doubting your motivations?"

"Gods," I snarled. "Is eavesdropping a talent draken are particularly skilled at, or is it just something *you're* really good at?"

Nektas stared blandly at me.

I held his gaze.

"You want to know what I think?"

"No," I said.

"I'm going to tell you anyway."

"Then why did you ask?"

"I was attempting to be polite," he replied, and I snorted. "He was wrong."

I said nothing.

"But he was also right."

"Well, your commentary was helpful, as always," I said, shaking my head in frustration. "You know, the thing is, I don't blame Nyktos for questioning that. Not really. But, honest to gods, seizing this as an opportunity to get to Kolis didn't even cross my mind."

"Then who are you more angry with? Ash or yourself?"

"Both?"

He smiled faintly. "You can't be angry at both."

I looked away. "Yeah, but being angry doesn't matter. What Nyktos believes doesn't matter. What I want doesn't matter. What does is the fact that Kolis one-upped us—probably without even realizing he did. Now, we will both be summoned, and how can Nyktos convince Kolis that he has no idea how a god Ascended or that he doesn't know it was Bele?"

"As Ash said, he's had to convince Kolis of many falsehoods in the past."

"Like what?" I asked, unable to stop myself.

"That Ash doesn't hate him with every fiber of his being and wants to see him chained beneath the ground. Kolis doesn't know that. He thinks that Ash is only testing his limits when he rebels against him or pushes back on something. Kolis believes that Ash is as loyal to him as any other Primal."

Disbelief rolled through me. "How can Kolis not know the truth when he killed Nyktos's parents? How can he even think for one second that Nyktos would be loyal after that?"

"Because Ash has convinced him that he feels nothing regarding his mother. That wasn't difficult for Kolis to believe since Ash never knew her," he explained. "And he's convinced Kolis that he hated his father—that he considered Eythos weak and selfish. If Ash hadn't been successful in hiding his true feelings toward him, Kolis would've done worse than what he did after he took the embers."

"I'm afraid to ask."

"Kolis killed every god and godling that served under Eythos, ensuring that none could Ascend to replace the Primal of Life."

"Good gods," I whispered. "All of them?"

"Those who were not at Court were hunted down across Iliseeum and the mortal realm. Even godlings several generations removed from the Court, those who never went through the Culling, were slaughtered."

I clamped my mouth shut against the rising bile. I didn't know what to say, but I suddenly thought of the murdered mortals. The siblings and the babe. Could their deaths have been a result of that? Had Nyktos believed wrong? Or was it that he'd felt he couldn't tell me at the time?

"If Kolis knew how Ash really felt about him, he would've killed every god here," Nektas continued quietly. "Every mortal and godling. Chained every draken in the Abyss. Kolis would've leveled the Shadowlands."

I sat on the edge of the bed.

"So, convincing him of this will be no different."

"How…?" I clasped the bed column I sat near. "How can he be that convincing?"

Nektas's crimson eyes met mine. "It's the same thing that drives you to be so convincing. That it is his duty to do whatever is necessary to protect as many people as he can."

I flinched. "I'm not pretending—"

"I'm not talking about Ash."

He was talking about Kolis—about the duty I knew was mine. One that would allow me to do whatever was necessary. I pressed my lips together. "But it's different. Kolis hasn't made any personal attacks against me. There isn't history between us like there is with him and Nyktos."

"There isn't?" Nektas asked quietly.

I stilled. "I'm not *her.*"

"No, but she is a part of you, Sera."

Tipping my head back, I stared at the glossy surface of the ceiling. "Yeah, well, if I do look like her, and he summons us before Nyktos gets the embers out of me, we're screwed. Everyone is screwed."

"Then we must make sure those embers are not vulnerable for long."

I lowered my gaze to him.

Nektas watched me. "Why don't you call him Ash anymore?"

The question caught me off guard. "I don't know."

"That's a lie."

"How would you know?" I demanded, crossing my arms.

Nektas came forward, his steps surprisingly quiet for someone so large. "Ash is what his father called him."

I hadn't known that, and I didn't think I wanted to know that now.

"For him to introduce himself as such to you meant something," Nektas added.

"Maybe it did before." Sighing, I leaned against the column. "But he's not Ash to me any longer."

His head tilted, the vertical slits of his pupils expanding until they were almost more commonly shaped. "He is how you wish him to be," he said. "As you are what you wish to be to those of the Shadowlands and beyond. That is up to you. No one else."

16

There were too many what-ifs circling through my head after Nektas left—too much restless, anxious energy burning its way through me for me to sit still.

I needed to work it off.

And I needed to silence those what-ifs, at least for a little while.

I quickly braided my hair and spent the remainder of the afternoon going through as much training as I could remember and could be done alone. I pictured an imaginary partner, which wasn't hard. My opponent alternated between Nyktos and me—because I was annoyed with us both for different reasons—while I went through shadowboxing and footwork. I dipped and lunged, working first with just my hands and then my dagger. None of it was as good as practicing with another person, but it was better than nothing. Fighting was part muscle memory, but long periods of inactivity could be the difference between living and dying.

Plus, it helped keep my mind empty. I wasn't thinking about the summons, Nyktos's plan, what he could've sacrificed in addition to everything he'd already had to do, or the soul that belonged in me. I was a different kind of blank canvas as I stabbed and kicked at the air, but exhaustion found me quicker than it should, and I chalked it up to the missed training sessions. At least, that's what I decided to believe, because the alternative was the Culling.

I cleaned up using the cool water from that morning. Since it was getting late, I slipped on a flimsy excuse for a nightgown and then tugged on the robe. It felt like hours, yet only minutes had passed when Orphine arrived with dinner. Afterward, I returned to the chaise, where I cracked open a book, but just like the night before, I couldn't concentrate. Those what-ifs came back.

When would Kolis summon us? Would Nyktos attempt to hide the summons from me? And if he didn't, what if I looked like Sotoria?

Why did I dread that when I should welcome the possibility? Welcome what Nyktos had accused me of that afternoon.

Because Nyktos had been right. It made it easier for me to do what I needed to.

Except nothing felt easier.

Because what would Nyktos do if we arrived at Kolis's Court, and the false King recognized me as Sotoria? Would he truly allow Kolis to take me? Or would he intervene? I knew the answer, and it terrified me. If I had been able to escape, I could have made it to Kolis without Nyktos being there. Not only being endangered, but also being put in a situation where he had to choose between the Shadowlands—

And me.

How could he continue convincing Kolis of his loyalty if he attempted to stop the false King from taking me? Hell, how was Nyktos successful this entire time? I knew Nektas said it was duty, but my gods…even I couldn't have done that.

My gaze drifted to the silver-adorned door that adjoined our bedchambers, and I thought about that *kiss.*

He is how you wish him to be.

"I don't even know him," I whispered as the embers in my chest warmed—

I yelped, jerking upright as the door suddenly swung open. The book flopped onto the floor with a heavy thump as Nyktos strode in as if he had every right to do so.

"Did you even think about knocking first?" I exclaimed.

"No."

"You should have." I pressed my palm to my thundering heart. "I could've been busy."

"Doing what?"

"Many things," I muttered. "Use your imagination."

Nyktos stopped, his jaw tightening. "Not sure if using my imagination would be wise."

"I suppose not." I bent, picking up the book. When I glanced over at him, I saw that he'd quietly moved closer and was checking out the plates. "I ate all my dinner like a good girl, in case you were wondering."

His cool, silver gaze flickered from the dining table to me.

"Did you need something?"

"I only need one thing at the moment. Sleep."

"Okay." I opened the book and pretended to read. "Thank you for sharing."

"Arm's reach, Sera."

Slowly, I looked up at him. "Seriously?"

"Does it look like I'm joking?"

"Even with the lock on the balcony door? It worked just fine last night."

"I'm sure, given enough time, you will have figured out how to pick that lock."

"*I'm* sure that if I wanted to pick that lock, I would've already done so," I snapped. "I'm not going to try to escape, Nyktos. What would be the point now?"

His features showed nothing, but his words...they said a lot. "You promised me you wouldn't go after Kolis again. I want to believe that, but what I want cannot be more important than what I know. If presented with an opportunity, you will still take it. Even now. I'm not going to let that fragile trust be broken so quickly."

My heart lurched as I stared up at him. A messy knot of emotion worked its way out from that crack. Words bubbled up. "I don't want to."

"I know." His eyes lightened to a softer shade of gray, even as his chest rose with a deep breath. "Come to bed, Sera."

I wasn't even sure why I was fighting him on this. I *liked* sleeping in his bed. With him. Even when he irritated me.

That should concern me.

And it did, but all I could do was add that to the absurdly long list of things that worried me.

Rising, I went into the bathing chamber first to prepare for bed. When I cleaned my teeth and spat paste into the basin, traces of pink swirled through the foam. My gums had bled a little. My stomach tumbled as I quickly wiped at my mouth and then left the bathing chamber, following Nyktos through the dark, narrow passageway. I stopped near the bed, my mind traveling to the deal I'd offered him before Attes arrived. Gods, I'd forgotten about that.

Nyktos brushed past me. "At least you don't have breeches and boots that need to be taken off tonight," he said.

"I think you would prefer that once you see what's under the robe." Inexplicably nervous, I reached for the sash.

He turned to me, the light of the sconces glancing off the slope of his cheekbones. "Please tell me you're not nude under there."

Well, I supposed that indicated he had no intention of making that deal with me. "Are you worried you'll be unable to control your body's reaction again?"

"I live in constant fear of that," he murmured, his gaze locking on me.

A tiny part of me actually believed that. "I'm not nude. Not really."

"Not really?"

I undid the robe, letting it slip down my arms. Nyktos was now the one to go utterly still at the sight of the thin, nearly transparent nightgown.

His lips parted, revealing a hint of fangs. "That's what you normally wear to bed?" he asked roughly.

"Believe it or not, this is the most demure of the nightgowns Aios brought me." My cheeks warmed as he watched me drape the robe over the foot of the bed.

"Good Fates," he muttered, stiff for a moment, and then he came toward me, each step slow and measured. A sweet thrill of anticipation darted through me as I tipped my head back to look up at him.

Only a thin slit of glowing silver was visible behind his thick lashes as he slipped his fingers under the satiny strap. The backs of his cool knuckles dragged along my skin as he drew the strap up my arm. He lingered for several moments, barely touching me, but I felt the featherlight press of his skin in every part of my body. He slipped his fingers out from under the strap. "May I?"

I didn't know at first what he was asking permission for, but I realized he was once more staring at my braid lying over my shoulder. "You...you can."

Nyktos moved his hand then. He didn't pick up the braid or tug on it. Just below my shoulder, he curled his forefinger and thumb around the braid. I held still as he drew his fingertip down its length, grazing the curve of my breast. I shivered.

"Did I tell you"—he continued running his thumb over the braid— "that your hair reminds me of spun moonlight?"

"Yes."

"It's beautiful," he said, nearing the tie holding the strands together.

He carefully tugged the band free as he had before. Slipping it onto his wrist, he gently unwound the braid, letting the mass of waves and curls fall over my shoulders. "I'll be right back."

I stood there, my heart thumping as he went into the bathing chamber, closing the door behind him. I didn't move as I heard water splash, my skin still tingling with the imprint of his touch. Finally, I forced myself to move. I went to the side of the bed I'd slept on the other night and climbed in, pulling the soft blanket up my legs as I eased onto my side, facing my bedchamber. A citrus and fresh-air scent immediately surrounded me.

I heard the door open, but I didn't turn as he went to the wardrobe. I wanted to because I knew that he was undressing, but I figured there was no point in torturing myself further.

The bed shifted as he joined me, and then darkness swallowed the chamber. "You know," I said, "you could've just waited for me to go to sleep and then snuck into my bed again."

"I could've," he agreed. "But then what would I have found upon entering your chamber once you went to bed?"

I rolled my eyes. "It's not like I do *that* every night."

"Well, I find that news slightly disappointing."

My brows lifted. I started to roll onto my back, but he spoke. He stopped me with two words. "I'm sorry."

I stilled. "For what?"

"For earlier today," he said after a moment. "When I suggested that your motivation for answering the summons was so you could get to Kolis. I should've known that wasn't what drove you—at least not the main reason. You said that you wouldn't go through with my plan if removing the embers resulted in others getting hurt."

I wasn't sure if he needed to apologize for that. If I were him, I would've assumed the same thing. But he had been wrong. Getting to Kolis hadn't been the main reason, even though it should've been. "Thank you," I murmured, returning my stare to the dark wall. "Does that mean you're not going to try to leave me behind when he summons us?"

"I won't. Not because it's what I want, but because it's what you want."

I exhaled raggedly, wanting to thank him again but knowing that thanking him for this wouldn't be appreciated.

Silence fell between us, and it went on for so long that I thought Nyktos had fallen asleep, but then he spoke again. "Why do you hold your breath so often?"

My eyes flew open. "What?"

"You hold your breath. Usually for a count, and then you exhale."

"Gods, it's really that noticeable?" I asked, thinking of when he'd seen me do it in the throne room while Holland and Penellaphe were there.

"Not really."

I frowned at the darkness. "But you noticed."

"Doesn't mean others have." Several beats of silence passed. "Why do you do it?"

I closed my eyes. "It's just something that Holland taught me to do."

He was quiet for a moment. "But why do you need to do it, Sera?"

"I don't know."

Nyktos didn't speak after that. There was nothing but silence for a long time, and then it was I who spoke. "Are you worried about the summons? What will happen?"

"No," he said, and it was a lie. The bed shifted again. His arm came over my waist, the heavy, cool weight was…pleasant. "Arm's reach."

I closed my eyes, trying to ignore how much I enjoyed the feel of his arm. It wasn't until that moment that I realized I'd done something I'd never done in my entire life.

I'd left the dagger in my bedchamber.

I was in a…*mood.*

A morose mood as Holland would call it. It had been with me upon waking on what should've been my coronation day, but for the second time in my life, I'd woken on the day I was supposed to be married, only for those plans to change.

It was early, the sky still a deep shade of gray, but Nyktos had already left, and I hadn't lingered in his bedchamber. I'd cleaned up with the fresh water someone had brought in and changed into the last gown I had, one cut quite similarly to the one I'd worn the day before but in all black. It was only after practically squeezing my breasts into the bodice and fastening the last of the buttons that I realized my clothing had finally been laundered and returned, placed in a neat stack on the bed. I sighed, having no plans of undressing.

Instead, I went to the chaise and plopped down. That's where I stayed, my mind restless, even though my body was still. Too still.

The moods had seemed to come and go with the changes in the wind while in the mortal realm, often striking me in the night when I couldn't sleep and had nothing to occupy my mind. Those were the nights that even the idea of occupying my body in one of the hedonistic dens littering the Luxe held no appeal.

Those were the nights I wondered if my father had been plagued by the moods. If they had played a role in his *fall* from the tower the night of my birth. If so, was that the only thing he'd left me, if such a thing could be passed down? I wasn't sure. But if so, I would've preferred something a little less *dark*.

Had Sotoria felt the same? Experienced these moods? Was she—?

I stopped myself as my heart began tripping too fast, and the feeling of having no control rose swiftly. I couldn't think about any of that, so I sat there, the day yawning before me, empty and irrelevant. Would tomorrow be the same? The day after next? There was no training to take part in. No food to take to the families affected by the Rot. No unexpected visits from Ezra or requests to aid the Ladies of Mercy. Just more waiting. No escaping from where my thoughts wanted to linger—a place that thrived on replaying all the worst moments.

The disappointments and failures.

The embarrassments and desperations.

Except now, there were new ones. The destiny that had never been true. My betrayal of Nyktos and the fact that none of us had questioned what we believed would end the Rot. It was hard to look back now and not feel as if I should've known that Nyktos wasn't the cause. It was hard to sit here, warm and well-fed, while those in my kingdom starved and would soon face unimaginable hardship and death if Nyktos's plan didn't work.

And it was hard to sit with myself. With the knowledge that I dreaded the summons when I should look forward to it.

My fingers worried the seam on the arm of the chaise as I stared at the neat pile of clothing that had been placed on the bed. I wasn't used to such idleness. Such lack of *purpose*. It made my skin feel too tight and thin. A knot lodged in my throat, my thoughts becoming as heavy as my body felt. I leaned into the chaise, feeling as if I could sink into the soft upholstery and become a part of it until I faded away. And wouldn't that be kind of lovely—?

"*No*." My heart started thumping as I sat up, my muscles going rigid. *Breathe in*. That was a—a *bad* thought. Uncomfortable. Suffocating. I smoothed suddenly damp hands over my bare knees. *Hold*. The chamber was too small as I sat there.

I was too small, shrinking with each passing second. *Breathe out*. I continued the slow, even breathing and squeezed my eyes shut until I saw white and the pressure in my chest loosened.

Why do you hold your breath?

My eyes opened as I rose. I couldn't spend one more moment in this chamber. Slipping my feet into thin-soled shoes, I left the room, surprised to find Saion in the hall instead of Orphine. He didn't put up a fight when I told him I wished to take my breakfast elsewhere, and the farther I made it from my chambers, the more the constriction in my chest and throat loosened.

We stopped in the kitchens, and then I took my breakfast in one of the many receiving chambers on the first floor with Reaver, who ended up following us and was currently napping on a narrow couch the color of the Dark Elms beyond Wayfair. Having breakfast outside my chamber was a marked improvement, but the silence was getting to me.

So was the way Saion quietly hovered near the doors, one hand resting on the hilt of a short sword, watching me as he had the day the Cimmerian came.

Placing my spoon aside, I glanced around the chamber. Just like all the ones I'd seen when Jadis had led us in and out of rooms, this one was well kept, even though it appeared as if no one had stepped foot in it in decades—maybe centuries. There wasn't even a speck of dust on the wood adornments of the arms and legs of the couch Reaver slept on. I scanned the bare shadowstone walls, reminded of Nyktos's personal spaces—empty like a void. I frowned, realizing that other than the paintings of Nyktos's parents in the library, I hadn't seen another.

"Are these spaces ever used?" I asked as I ran a finger down my glass of juice.

Saion inclined his head, glancing at the walls. "Every once in a while, Jadis or Reaver explores them, but other than that, not that I've seen."

"Who keeps them so clean?"

"Usually Ector."

"Is he that bored?"

Saion chuckled. "I've wondered that myself, but I think he does it for Eythos."

My fingers stilled on the glass. "Like in his memory or something?"

"I think so." He glanced over the space. "When Nyktos's father was alive, he kept all these chambers open and clean. There used to be guests. Not as many as I imagined there were when Eythos was the true Primal of Life, but there was..." He trailed off as if he were searching for the right word.

"There was *life* here once?" I suspected.

Saion nodded. "Yeah," he said, clearing his throat. "There was."

That was thoughtful of Ector, and it was only surprising because I knew so little about him—about any of them. I leaned back in the chair. "Where are you from?"

Saion raised a dark eyebrow. "That's a random question."

It was. "Just curious."

He said nothing, and I figured that whatever change of heart he'd had only went so far. "Never mind," I said. "I suppose we can resume the awkward watching-over-me-in-silence thing."

"I was born in the Triton Isles."

My gaze cut to him, a little surprised that he'd answered. "You belonged to Phanos's Court?"

"Stayed there until I was about five decades past my Culling and then both Rhahar and I left."

"Why did you leave?" I couldn't help but ask. As far as I knew, the gods born to Phanos's Court drew their power from the lakes, rivers, and seas, and, well, there were no such things in the Shadowlands.

"You really want to know?"

"I wouldn't have asked if I didn't."

His head tilted to the side, and he rested it against the doorframe. "Have you heard of the Kingdom of Phythe? It existed several hundred years ago—about a hundred years before Eythos made the deal with your ancestor. It was a beautiful kingdom, full of people who lived off the land and the sea. Peaceful people," he said, and it didn't pass me by that I now knew that Saion was older than Nyktos. "In the mortal realm, it once stretched along the southern foothills of the Skotos Mountain range, all the way to the sea."

"The name is vaguely familiar." I frowned, searching my memories. "Wasn't it an old kingdom once favored by Phanos until one of the King's sons did something to one of Phanos's daughters or something?"

"That's what has been written. But the only truth in that was that Phythe was once a favorite of Phanos's—until they fell out of favor."

I clutched the glass. "I have a terrible suspicion I know where this is going."

"Yeah, you probably do." His eyes narrowed thoughtfully. "There was an oil spill off the coast of Lasania, wasn't there? About a decade ago?"

"I saw it. Phanos came out of the water and destroyed all the ships in the port. Hundreds died," I said. "What really happened then?"

Saion shook his head. "They used to hold these games in honor of Phanos every year, but they were dangerous. People often died during them, including the King's *only* son. After that, the King ended the games, believing Phanos to be a benevolent Primal god who wouldn't want to see his most faithful harming themselves."

"They were wrong?"

"Fatally wrong," he confirmed. "Phanos was insulted. Saw the ending of the games as a lack of faith. It enraged him, and he flooded the kingdom."

"My gods," I whispered, horrified.

"Yeah." He let out a heavy breath. "We visited Phythe often. The people there were—they were good. Not all of them were perfect, you know? But none of them deserved that. Phanos just wiped away a kingdom. There was no warning. No one had a chance to escape the waves taller than the Rise that came from the sea and traveled miles inland. Everything and everyone within Phythe were taken into the sea." He rubbed at his chin, shaking his head. "When Rhahar and I learned what he'd done, we were shocked. Couldn't believe it. He did that over games that we knew damn well he hadn't even paid that much attention to. And even if the King's son had done something to one of his daughters, that doesn't justify taking the lives of an entire kingdom. We couldn't serve him after that. We weren't the only ones who left, but"— he exhaled heavily—"that was why we left."

"Gods, I don't know what to say. That's terrible." I shuddered, imagining the fear the people of Phythe must've felt when they saw the wave coming toward them, knowing there was no way they could escape it.

"It is."

I swallowed, glancing down at the peacefully unaware Reaver. "Were the Primals ever truly benevolent?"

"I don't think anyone is truly benevolent through the entirety of their life. Not even mortals," he said, and I looked up at him. "But we didn't expect that from Phanos, so it has to mean that he wasn't always like that."

"You think it's simply because he lived too long?"

"I don't think it's that—or at least it's not the sole reason. The Primals are old. Soon, they too will become Ancients. But Eythos, along with Kolis, was older than them all. And he never descended into that kind of heartless existence. A few other Primals haven't," he told me, and I thought of Attes. "If you ask Ector and other gods who were alive when Eythos was the true Primal of Life, they will tell you that there was a marked change in many of the Primals when Kolis stole his brother's essence."

I set the glass aside. "You think that act impacted their behavior? Caused them to become less benevolent?"

"That's what Ector thinks." Saion shrugged. "There's no way to know for sure, but I think he's onto something."

If that were the case, could it mean that we could be successful at swaying at least a few Primals? "So, you ended up here, where there are no lakes or rivers beyond the Black Bay and Red River?"

A wry smile appeared. "Not at first. It was quite some time before we found our way to the Shadowlands or even came face-to-face with Nyktos."

"How did that happen?"

He was quiet for several moments. "Gods cannot leave the Court they are born into without the permission of the Primal who oversees it. It's not often that permission is granted. And if a god abandons their Court anyway, it's considered an act of open rebellion, which is punishable by death—the final kind."

I stiffened. "It doesn't sound like you and Rhahar got permission."

"We didn't." The half-grin returned. "Phanos sent others after those who left his Court following the incident with Phythe. Shortly after Eythos was killed, they eventually found us and brought us to the Court of Dalos, where gods are sentenced and punished. As we were being held there, waiting for Phanos's arrival, Nyktos visited us. Asked why we'd left. We told him the truth, and then he left."

My brows shot up. "He just left?"

"Yeah. At the time, we thought that was an asshole thing to do." Saion chuckled. "We didn't know much about him, only that he was young for a Primal—really young. But he had already become known as one of the last Primals anyone wanted to cross. Anyway…" He continued before I could ask exactly how Nyktos had gained that reputation. "Nyktos came to Court the next day when Phanos arrived, and just before we were sentenced, Nyktos intervened. Said that Phanos didn't have the right to sentence us as we no longer served him but served the Primal of Death instead. I doubt anyone was more shocked than Rhahar and me at the announcement, but Nyktos, man, he is a tricky son of a bitch when he wants to be. You see, when he visited us the day before, he touched us both when he left. Reached through the bars and patted our shoulders. We didn't think anything of it. The only thing we both thought afterwards was that the cell was colder—that *we* were colder. That was it. But when he touched us, he took our souls."

17

My mouth dropped open. "What?"

"Yeah." Saion laughed again. "Fucking chaos erupted. We knew what that meant, especially Kolis. You see, Kolis supposedly pulled that shit all the time back when he was the true Primal of Death. Except he did it when someone pissed him off. But, either way, Nyktos had our souls. None of the other Primals could touch us. We belonged to him."

Stunned, I rocked back. I knew that Nyktos could do that, summon a soul with a touch, but somehow, I'd forgotten just how deadly and dangerous he could be. "Can Kolis still do that?"

"I don't believe so. If he could, I imagine he'd be doing it left and right."

Thank the gods the bastard couldn't. "What happened after he did that?"

"Well, Phanos was ticked off. Strangely, it amused Kolis. He saw it as Nyktos one-upping Phanos or something," he said, and I thought about what Nektas had said about how Kolis believed Nyktos was loyal to him. "Either way, there was nothing to be done. Phanos went back to his Court super pissed, and we were taken into the Shadowlands."

"He gave you back your souls, right?"

"If he did and Phanos ever found out, he could claim us once more."

That wasn't a direct answer, but I was willing to bet Nyktos returned them. Those who served the Shadowlands didn't do so because they had to or because Nyktos had something as valuable as their soul. He would've returned it, and Saion and Rhahar were wise enough to keep that to themselves.

"He saved your lives," I said, glancing up at him.

"We're not the only lives he's saved."

I knew that, but still… Nyktos's actions were a lot to comprehend. Even thinking what would have happened if I'd successfully killed him made my heart stop and my chest ache. I picked up the glass of juice, finishing it off, but it did nothing to ease the knot in my throat or fortify the sudden weakness around that crack in my chest. "I…I truly believed that my duty to kill Nyktos was the only way to save my kingdom." I cleared my throat, my voice barely above a whisper. "No one—and I mean, *no one*—can hate me more for that than I do."

"You know," Saion said, "I actually believe that."

The tips of my ears burning, I rose from my chair, suddenly needing the quiet I had fled not so long ago. "I think I will return to my chambers now." I glanced at the young draken, who still slept. "Should we wake Reaver?"

"He'll be fine."

"You sure?" It felt a little wrong to leave him while he slept.

Saion nodded as he stepped out into the hall, waiting for me. "If you wake him, he'll likely get a bit…snappy. With his teeth, not his words."

I raised an eyebrow. "Then I think I'll leave him be."

"Wise choice."

I walked to the back set of stairs similar to those at the end of the wing where Nyktos's office was located and pushed open the door. The faint sounds of metal clashing with metal echoed in the stairwell. Saion showed no reaction to the sound, but curiosity sank its claws into me. I went to the exterior door.

"Where are you going?"

"Nowhere."

"It definitely looks like you're going somewhere, and it's not your bedchamber," Saion muttered.

I cracked open the heavy door and peered outside. I immediately spotted Nyktos in the shadow of the Rise, lifting a broadsword. I told myself it was because he was taller than the dozen or so others with him as he met another's blow. Or that it was the warming in my chest, the faint humming of the ember that belonged to him. I convinced myself it had nothing to do with the anticipation, the *eagerness* that sprang to life upon seeing him.

Saion moved in behind me, looking out over my head at the guards squaring off in pairs. "They're training."

"I figured," I murmured, enraptured by how Nyktos moved. There was a predatory gracefulness in how he used his large body, springing forward and back as if he were light as air.

I watched, thinking of how he'd saved Saion and Rhahar through clever trickery. What price did he pay, though, once Kolis's amusement faded? Because even though Kolis believed Nyktos was loyal to him, he had still impaled gods on the Rise.

Nyktos brought his sword down on his opponent's with enough force to disarm the guard. He caught the other sword, then aimed both blades at the man's throat.

A restless yearning swirled through me as Nyktos clasped the man on the shoulder. I looked away, quickly finding Rhain and Ector paired off with unknown guards. There'd been days in Lasania when I'd had to drag myself into the east tower to train. Days I'd wanted to spend doing only what I chose to do. But training had kept me occupied and maybe even helped to keep those moods I experienced at bay.

I wasn't used to existing like this, with my only options to pass the time sleeping, reading, or roaming around while annoying others with my presence. I wasn't used to not having a *purpose*.

"Thought you were headed to your bedchamber," Saion reminded me.

"I was." I nibbled on my lower lip as Nyktos motioned another guard forward—one thickly muscled and fair-haired.

"*Was*." Saion sighed. "Past tense. Great."

I ignored that. "How often do they train?"

"Every day, usually for a few hours in the morning."

"I used to train every day."

"Congratulations," he replied dryly.

Training was *something*. And I should be training, keeping my reflexes honed. There was only so much I could do alone. I looked over my shoulder at Saion, my mind racing. "Would you rather stand outside my chambers staring at a blank wall or train?"

He glanced down at me. "Is that a trick question? Of course, I'd rather be training."

Determination seized me. "Then let's train."

His brows shot up. "Train. With you?"

"Yes."

Saion made a choked sound. "Sorry. Not going to happen."

I frowned. "Why not?"

"Because I'd prefer not to be gutted by Nyktos, which is exactly what would happen if I raised a sword against you, training or not."

"That's ridiculous."

"It is what it is."

I gaped at him. "You're serious, aren't you?"

"Yes."

"Did Nyktos give that order?"

"Not in so many words, but it's not one that needs to be spoken aloud to be known and understood." Saion sighed as I turned back to Nyktos and the guards. "Why do I have a feeling you're about to do something ill-advised?"

Maybe I was, but I didn't care. I wouldn't spend another day wasting away in my chambers. I *couldn't*. I would no longer just exist, becoming a lifeless spirit that roamed halls instead of the woods. Not when I was done living as if I had no say in my life. And hadn't I already decided that? Spoken it? It was time to act upon those words because things had to change. Pushing the doors open wide, I walked outside.

"Knew it," Saion muttered.

The halves of my gown fluttered around my legs as I stalked across the courtyard. Several of the guards immediately noticed me, halting as I drew closer.

Nyktos blocked a blow with the side of his sword as his head snapped in my direction. His features were all cold lines and angles.

"Hold." He barked out the demand, and all across the field, training stopped. Guards began to bow in my direction.

"Your Highness," I said, more politely than I had ever said two words in my entire life.

A flicker of eather appeared in his cool gray eyes, joining the wary gleam to his stare as he faced me fully. He briefly glanced at Saion and then snapped his attention back to me. "Are you taking a walk?"

Taking a walk? Like the fine Ladies of Lasania would stroll through the gardens of Wayfair? I almost laughed. "I would like to know if it's possible for Saion to train with me."

"Whoa." Saion's head whipped toward me. "I told her that wasn't possible."

"He's afraid you will gut him if he does," I continued, aware of Ector's and Rhain's slow approach. "Which I'm hoping is an exaggeration to hide the fact that he's simply nervous that I will be far better with a sword than he is."

"That is not the reason," Saion shot back. "What you said first was the truth. I'm *simply* nervous that my insides will end up on my outsides."

"Why would you be worried?" I challenged, clasping my hands together. "I doubt you will hurt me; therefore, Nyktos would have no reason to harm you." I looked at the Primal. "Correct?"

Nyktos said nothing, but the hue of his eyes deepened.

"I wouldn't hurt you intentionally," Saion started, "but I am a god."

"*Congratulations*," I cut in, mimicking his earlier tone.

Saion's eyes narrowed. "Therefore, I'm far stronger than you."

"Strength has very little to do with skill when it comes to a sword," I said.

"She's actually right," Ector chimed in.

"Ector." Saion turned. "Can you shut the—?"

I snapped forward, grasping the hilt of one of Saion's swords and pulling it free. Saion spun toward me, his eyes widening as Ector choked on a laugh. "I have a sword to use," I announced, facing Nyktos and smiling up at him. "There's a multitude of logical reasons for why I should continue my training. But since your guards are too nervous to train with me, then shouldn't it be you?"

"Hell," Rhain murmured.

I lifted the sword, leveling it at Nyktos's throat. "Or are you also...*nervous?*"

Silence descended in the courtyard as Nyktos stared down at me. Wisps of eather began churning in eyes that had heated to quicksilver. "Nervous is the last thing I'm feeling at the moment."

Ector cleared his throat as he eyed the packed dirt.

"Good." I didn't allow my mind to take what he said straight into the gutter. "Then you should lift your sword."

The only thing that lifted was one corner of his lip. "And if I don't?"

"You will find yourself in grave need of a feeding."

His eyes became a fire of Primal essence, ignited by either anger or something I chose not to think about at the moment. "You do realize that most men would take their soon-to-be Consort holding a sword to their throat in front of their guards as a great offense."

"Which is one of the reasons I find most men to be easily offended." The sword's hilt felt good against my palm, the weight welcome. "But you're not like most men, are you?"

"I suppose not since most would send their wives to their chambers for such an act."

"Soon-to-be wife," I corrected softly. "And if you order me to return to my chambers, my grip on this sword may slip an inch."

"Accidentally, of course."

Aware that we'd gained quite an audience, I smiled tightly. "*Intentionally.*"

Nyktos's short laugh was rough, throaty and...*warm.* "You want to train with me? What are you waiting for?"

"You haven't lifted your sword."

"I don't need to."

My head cocked to the side as I glanced down at his weapon. He held it, tip pointed at the ground, not at the ready. Which meant only one thing. He believed he didn't need to defend himself. Keeping my anger in check at the unintentional—or not—insult, I lowered the sword I held. Our gazes locked as I began circling him slowly. If he believed he needed no defense, so be it. That would be his mistake. I waited until the other side of his lip quirked up.

Then I attacked.

Nyktos was fast, deflecting the blow without even facing me. "You went for my back." He looked over his shoulder at me, smirking. "I should've known you'd fight dirty."

"And I should've known better than to overestimate your skill."

His brows lifted. "Is that so?"

"Even a novice knows to never turn their back on someone with a sword." I made a quick, clean swipe with the blade along the back of his neck, nicking a piece of hair that had fallen free of the knot.

He spun on me, his eyes narrowing. Someone let out a low whistle as the lock of hair fell to the hard, gray soil.

"Huh." I feigned wide eyes. "These shadowstone swords are sharp."

"Touché." He struck out, not nearly as fast as I knew he could, but the blow of his sword connecting with mine rattled my entire arm, proving he wasn't entirely holding back.

"If you want, I could use a trim." I thrust the sword at his chest.

He cut the blow with a swipe of his blade. "I would never dare even think of cutting one strand of hair on your head."

"Too bad." Secretly pleased, I tracked his movements as he circled me, keeping the sword partially lowered. It was far lighter than the one he carried, but I knew my muscles would grow tired, nonetheless. I also knew I had no hope of holding my own against him if he truly decided to stop holding back.

But this wasn't about winning.

"Now that I have your attention," I began, watching him carefully.

"You have my full, undivided attention now." He practically purred the words, chin dipped and eyes glowing from behind his lashes.

Muscles low in my stomach curled. "I understand that I need to be watched."

"That's good to hear since we've already discussed that to the point of it being repetitive." He thrust.

I parried, lifting my sword with both hands and blocking his strike. "I wasn't finished."

"My apologies." He started to bow—

Shooting forward, I spun and swung back with the hilt of the sword, slamming it into his stomach. Nyktos grunted out a harsh curse.

Muffled laughs and whistles echoed through the courtyard as I danced out of arm's reach when he snapped upright.

"*Ouch*," he coughed out with a laugh.

I faced him, smiling not so tightly. "As I was saying, I understand you feel it necessary, even though I'm sure Saion would rather babysit Jadis while Reaver avoids her than follow me from chamber to chamber."

"You know," Saion drawled from the boulder he now sat upon, "I would actually have to think long and hard about which one would be preferable."

"I'll watch over her," a guard offered, and I gave him a quick glance. All I had time to see was that he was the fair-haired guard I'd first seen Nyktos with. "Seems like it would be an entertaining duty."

"That won't be necessary, Kars," Nyktos growled, his fangs appearing.

Pleased by his reaction, it took a lot to stop my grin. "Nor will I be forced to remain in my bedchamber to read or knit or whatever."

"No one said you needed to stay in your bedchamber at all times." Nyktos stalked toward me, sword raised as he stopped. "Wait. You knit?"

"What do you think?"

"I don't know." He dragged his fangs over his lower lip. "But I have a feeling you'd do terrible things with a knitting needle."

"Give me a pair and you'll find out." I swung on him.

Nyktos shot forward, blocking my blow as he caught my sword arm with his other hand. He hauled me toward him. My breath snagged at the feel of his chest against mine. "As much as I enjoy your threats of violence, you should spend less time making them and more time getting to the point behind why you interrupted me."

"But I so enjoy threatening you," I said, driving my knee up. Several curses exploded from the onlookers.

Nyktos dropped my wrist, using his thigh to avoid a direct hit to a very sensitive place. "The gown you were in yesterday was a distraction," he whispered, his gaze dropping to where the swells of my breasts strained against the black lace of the bodice. "But this one is rather indecent."

"As I said before, your failings to keep your gaze from straying is no reflection upon me."

"I would have to be made of stone for my gaze not to stray." A strand of reddish-brown hair fell against his cheek as his chin tipped down. "But I'm only flesh and blood, and you are…"

"What am I?"

"You are flesh and fire."

"Then you should be careful," I taunted, "lest you become nothing more than ember and ash." Twisting sharply, I broke his grip and backed off, winking at him. "I need something to do."

"Other than being a distraction?"

"In addition to that."

Nyktos laughed, making his move then. He swung hard—hard enough that if he'd connected with my sword, he surely would've disarmed me. I darted to the left and spun, swinging my blade down. The impact echoed through the courtyard.

"Nice," someone shouted—possibly this Kars or Ector. I wasn't sure.

There was no fighting my smile as it spread across my face. "I need to be training."

Nyktos brushed the now-shorter strand of hair back from his face as he straightened. "You do realize that if you wanted to train, all you had to do was ask."

My eyes narrowed. "Really?"

"Really." He swung again.

I dipped under his arm and spun, kicking out. My slippered foot connected with his midsection as I arced the sword up and around. The guards shouted as Nyktos leaned back. My sword cut through the air where his chest had been. He backed off, his eyes glimmering in a way Holland's did whenever I surprised him in training, and he approved of whatever I'd done.

I was practically floating as I circled him. "I'm asking now."

"I'm sure there is more." His sword was at the ready. "Unless you plan to spend all day training. If not, tell me what you want."

"I want to attend Court," I said after a moment. "Now. I don't want to wait."

"Should I be taking notes?" Rhain asked from where he leaned against the boulder Saion sat on.

"No need." Those silver eyes were locked onto mine. "I won't forget a thing." He wiggled his sword at me. "What else, *Sera?*"

He spoke my name like a kiss. I barely suppressed a shiver. "I want to be involved in any plans regarding Kolis instead of being told about them after the fact," I said. "Or not told at all. I want the truth when it comes to your plans regarding him."

"Is there more?"

There was, and it came to me just then—something that should've been apparent the moment Attes left after delivering his message. I lowered my voice so only Saion and those by the boulder could hear. "I don't want to wait to go to the Vale. We need to act on that, sooner rather than later, no matter the risks involved."

A muscle flexed in Nyktos's jaw. "Anything else?"

"I want to see my stepsister."

"Sera—"

My sword clattered off Nyktos's. "I know the charm only works on me while I'm in the Shadowlands, and that going into the mortal realm is also a risk, but it is one I'm willing to take. That is my right."

That muscle in his jaw was ticking even faster.

"And I know you are trying to keep the embers safe—"

"Not just the embers." He deflected my blow. "You."

I stumbled, quickly regaining my footing. "I...I appreciate that, but it is my choice, and I have gone along with everything you've wanted..."—I saw the incredulous lift of his brows—"mostly. I need to let Ezra know that we are doing what we can to stop the Rot but that she should prepare just in case something goes wrong."

"Is there more?" Nyktos growled.

More?

"Suppers," I blurted out.

"What about them?"

I lifted the sword, blocking his blow. "I no longer want to take them alone," I said, keeping my voice low.

His sword lowered an inch. "Just your supper?"

I swung, driving his sword to the side. "Just my supper. And I...I want to help."

"In what way?"

A fine sheen of sweat dampened my forehead as we thrust and parried. "In whatever way I'm needed."

Nyktos's eyes brightened. "And who determines how you're needed?"

"I do," I said, starting to pant while Nyktos showed absolutely no signs of tiring. "As do you."

Nyktos halted.

I struck. My blade cut through the air, nicking Nyktos's arm. I spun, kicking out and aiming for his chest.

He caught my ankle and held on. The halves of the skirt parted. My skin, from my mid-thigh to where his hand circled my ankle, was exposed to the heated caress of his gaze. His callused palm was rough against my bare flesh, sending my blood pulsing through me in a dizzying rush.

"You're staring at my unmentionables again," I said breathlessly, and it had nothing to do with the fighting.

His stare flicked to mine. "I know."

"Pervert."

Nyktos smiled, then dropped my ankle and slammed his sword, tip down, into the ground. I turned, but he caught my arm, spinning me. I moved to twist out of his hold, but he was faster, hauling my back to his chest. His head dipped as he ran his hand down my arm. The heat of his body against my back, and his breath against the slope of my neck sent a sharp bolt of awareness through me. "You do realize I now need to tear my guards' eyes out?"

"Why?"

"Because they too have glimpsed your unmentionables."

"Worth it," someone called out.

Nyktos growled, and I felt the rumble of warning all along my rear and back, where I...I felt the hard length of him. An aching heaviness settled in my breasts and lower as my chest rose and fell rapidly.

"That's unnecessary," I said, each too-quick breath full of his fresh scent.

"Is it?" His fingers pressed into the tendons with just enough pressure that my hand opened. There was no fighting it. The short sword slipped from my grip and hit the ground.

"It also makes you seem quite...*possessive*." I turned my head to the side, my stomach clenching as his lips grazed my cheek. I dropped my voice to a whisper as I lowered my right hand to my thigh. "Of what you refuse to claim."

Nyktos stiffened behind me.

Jerking to the side, I shoved my elbow into his stomach hard enough to catch him off guard. He let go, reaching for the sword he'd put in the ground as I whirled, but I didn't go for it.

I didn't need to.

Nyktos froze as silence fell over the courtyard. His gaze dropped to the shadowstone dagger I held at his throat and then flicked to mine.

I smiled at him.

"Bravo," he murmured.

A round of applause and hoots broke out across the courtyard, and my smile grew wide. "Who will train with me?"

"I'm sure there is now an exceedingly long list of volunteers," Ector commented, his words met by several raucous affirmatives.

"I will," Nyktos said, his voice stirring thoughts of tangled limbs and balmy nights. "You going to lower that blade now?"

Laughing under my breath, I withdrew the dagger and sheathed it. "Better?"

"Not sure." He straightened, his eyes never leaving mine.

Warmth crept up my neck as I clasped my hands once more, fully aware of the avid stares. Clearing my throat, I pulled my gaze from his and looked at Saion. "I think I will return to my chamber now."

Saion stared and then tipped his head back, laughing deeply. "Fates," he murmured, sliding off the boulder.

"Until later," I said to Nyktos.

Nyktos watched me with intense silence as I picked up Saion's discarded sword and handed it, hilt first, to the god. I took a couple of steps toward the doors and then stopped, turning back to Nyktos and his guards and giving them the most elaborate curtsy I was capable of.

There were chuckles, even from the reluctantly amused Rhain, but it was Nyktos's deep, rough laughter that stayed with me.

18

A knock came about an hour after I returned to my chambers. Unsure who it could be, I cracked open the door first and then swung it wider when I saw the young mortal.

I stepped aside, allowing him entry. "Hello, Paxton."

He made his way into the chamber, favoring his right leg over his left. A curtain of blond hair fell forward as he bowed. "His Highness asked that I see if you were in need of fresh water for a bath."

"I have the water that was brought in this morning," I told him.

He investigated the bathing chamber, immediately spotting the full, unused tub. "The water has to be freezing by now."

Probably, but it wasn't like I planned to soak in it. "It'll be fine."

"It's no trouble." He'd already turned, making his way into the hall.

He was faster than I expected him to be. I hurried after him. "It really isn't—"

"I'll get His Highness." Paxton headed straight for the door next to mine. "He'll fix it right up for you."

"You really don't have to do that—"

"It's no problem."

"I understand, but—"

"He'll take care of it. You'll see."

Nyktos's door opened before Paxton could even knock on it. The

Primal stepped out into the hall, and all coherent thought sort of abandoned me.

His damp hair was free, brushing his shoulders, and that piece I'd cut with the sword kissed the curve of his right cheek. He wore no shirt. Beads of water lingered on the hard, lean lines of his chest and stomach. His soft leather pants clung indecently to his lean hips as if he barely allowed his body time enough to dry from the bath before pulling them on. He hadn't even fastened them.

"What's going on out here?" Nyktos asked.

"I was doing as you asked, Your Highness, seeing if she would like water to bathe, but she said she'd use what was brought in this morning."

Nyktos said something, but I wasn't exactly sure as I was really engrossed in the swirl of tattooed drops that traveled along the sides of his waist and inner hips, disappearing—"*Sera.*"

Blinking, I lifted my gaze to his. "I'm sorry. Did you say something?"

There was that warmth in his eyes again, turning them a molten silver. "Perhaps if you stopped ogling me for five seconds, you'd hear me."

"I'm not *ogling* you," I muttered, blinking.

Paxton frowned. "What does ogling mean?"

"To look at someone amorously," Nyktos answered. "And rather impertinently." He paused, his eyes meeting mine. "As if they have no control over where their eyes *stray.*"

The boy grinned before ducking his chin. "Yeah, that's totally what you were doing."

I turned to Paxton. "You don't know what ogling means, but you know what amorously and impertinently are?"

"Pax is well familiar with all the various phrasings of impertinent," Nyktos said, and the boy's skin crinkled at his eyes as his grin grew. "You didn't use the water brought in this morning?"

"Not really, but I—"

"The water has to be freezing by now."

Paxton threw up his arms. "That's what I said."

Walking forward, Nyktos dropped his hand to the top of Paxton's head as he passed, ruffling the boy's floppy strands of hair. The gesture was...it was kind of sweet. "I'll heat it up."

"That's not necessary," I repeated to no avail as Nyktos brushed past me and entered the bedchamber. Wait a second... "How are you going to heat the water?"

"Magic," he tossed out in a light tone that I hadn't heard from him in far too long.

"Really?" I replied dryly, ignoring whatever silliness my heart and mind were engaged in. "You can use eather to heat water?"

"He's a Primal god," Paxton said, sounding incredibly exasperated for someone his age. "There's nothing he *can't* do."

"That's not entirely true." Nyktos glanced at the bed, a slight frown pulling at his lips. "There are many things I can't do."

"Name one," Paxton challenged.

"Getting my soon-to-be Consort to follow instructions would be one of them."

Paxton giggled as my eyes narrowed on the center of the spiraling ink scrawled across his back. I crossed my arms over my chest. "That's going to get even harder for you now."

"As if it would have gotten easier." Nyktos stopped at the entrance to the bathing chamber.

I inched forward, followed by Paxton. I wouldn't admit it, but I was curious to see just how Nyktos would warm the water.

However, much like I did every time I entered the space, Nyktos just stood there. The breadth of his shoulders tightened. He looked over his shoulder, first at the made bed and then me.

"Are you heating the water with your mind?"

"He has to actually touch it." Paxton shook his head as if I'd suggested something ridiculous. "I don't know what he's doing."

"Well, then, that makes two of us," I said.

Nyktos closed the doors and faced us, drawing his lower lip between his teeth, showing just a hint of fang. "Pax, why don't you go see if Nektas has returned?"

"Will he have Jadis with him?" the boy asked, his chin jerking up and eyes aglow with excitement.

"He should. And I'm sure he could use your help keeping her entertained."

"Awesome." Pax wheeled around and shuffled toward the door. He stopped suddenly, hastily bowing at the waist. "Good day, Your Highnesses."

"Bye," I murmured, thoroughly confused by...well, just about everything.

"He's not really going to be of any help to Nektas," Nyktos said after Pax had disappeared into the hall. "He's just going to join Jadis in whatever trouble she gets herself into, and then together, they will likely terrorize Reaver."

I turned to Nyktos, discovering that he'd moved closer in that silent way of his. A long moment passed as he studied me. The silence and the intensity of his stare got to me. I cleared my throat. "Did you...finish training with your guards?" I asked, which was an asinine question since he was standing in front of me.

"I did." His gaze finally left mine. "Wait here. This will take a couple of minutes, but I will be back."

I nodded, and it was only when he walked out my doors that I wondered why he hadn't used the door that adjoined our chambers.

Then I remembered. The door was obviously locked from his side, remaining only unlocked when he saw fit. Then again, if he could truly heat water with his fingers and had a warhorse living in his cuff, he could probably unlock the door with a thought.

Sighing, I returned to the chaise and sat. A little achy from handling the sword, I closed my eyes. I had no idea how much time passed, but it was more than a few minutes when the adjoining door opened, startling me.

Nyktos stood there, all softness gone from his features. The now-familiar hardness had settled into the set of his jaw, and his eyes had cooled. He hadn't even looked that cold—that detached—when I'd cut his arm or held the dagger to his throat only an hour or so ago. "Come." He held the door open. "I have something for you."

"Uh..." I rose slowly, peering into the darkness of his private quarters. "You sure about that?"

"I wouldn't ask if I wasn't." He waited. "Are you coming?"

Too curious for my own good, I got my legs moving and quietly followed him into his chambers and past the unmade bed. He went to where I knew his bathing chamber was located and pushed open the door to the softly lit space.

"You want to show me your bathing chamber?" My steps slowed.

"Not exactly," he replied, looking back at me. "You can come closer."

The stone floors were cool against my bare feet as I crept forward, feeling out of sorts as I stopped beside him. I had only caught a glimpse of this space before, when he had been standing at the vanity cleaning up the blood from when the dakkais attacked. There was another door straight across, but I had no idea what it led to. The space was like everything else about him—bare except for a few bottles lined up neatly on a shelf above the vanity and the—

My eyes went wide. I'd only seen a hint of the tub before, but now I saw that it was at least three times the size of the one in my bathing chamber, with a wide enough ledge to sit upon. Big enough for several people. Maybe even a small draken. Made sense. Nyktos was a large man, but the tub was…

It was full of steaming water and frothy bubbles, and my chest constricted. It had nothing to do with breathing. This was what had taken him so long.

"Baines said that he didn't think you were making use of the bath in your chambers," he stated, and I felt my skin start to warm. "It should've occurred to me that bathing in the chamber where you were attacked would be less than appealing."

"I haven't—" Whatever lie I had been about to tell got caught on the knot forming in my throat. I stared at the wisps of steam rising from the tub, my eyes blurring.

"You will be safe here," Nyktos told me, his tone softening, and a faint shudder rolled through me. "I will make sure of it."

I couldn't speak. Not yet. My mouth was clamped shut so tightly that my jaw was beginning to ache. This was…this was an incredibly thoughtful gesture. I wiped my suddenly damp palms against my hips. It was too thoughtful.

"Sera?"

I inhaled deeply through my nose. "You didn't have to do this."

"Yes, I did."

"No." I shook my head. "I…I don't deserve this."

"Everyone deserves fresh water to bathe themselves in, and to do so in peace."

"I don't deserve this from *you*," I corrected.

Nyktos stiffened beside me. I didn't look at him. I couldn't. But I felt the tension coursing through his body. "What you didn't deserve was to be strangled in your bathing chamber."

"I agree with that, but—"

"You must be covered in a fine layer of dirt from being out there in the courtyard. I'm sure you want to bathe. It's simply a bath," he said, but it wasn't simply anything. "One you're more than welcome to use at your discretion."

My head swung toward him. "This wasn't something I asked for."

"I know." He didn't look at me as he said, "There are soaps on the stool that you can use. And the towels are here." He gestured to the rack against the wall. "The other door is locked. No one can enter from there. Take your time. I'll be waiting in the bedchamber."

Nyktos didn't linger. He stepped out of the bathing chamber, closed the door behind him, and left me there, hands trembling slightly. I turned back to the tub, unsure what to make of this—of anything.

This was an act of kindness. I shouldn't be surprised, because despite whatever issues we might have had with one another, Nyktos was a kind man. He was thoughtful. I knew that, but this unexpected act frayed me at the seams and made that crack in my chest feel even more unstable. I felt as if I were one breath from unraveling. And that was the last thing I needed.

Besides, I really did want a bath. There likely was a fine layer of dirt covering me, and the hasty cleanups had left me feeling a little gross.

Unsheathing the dagger, I placed it on the ledge and then shimmied out of the gown. My chest immediately appreciated the freedom. I winced as I shrugged off my undergarments, seeing pink indentations in the flesh of my breasts from where the seams of the bodice had been too tight. Leaving the clothing and undergarments in a somewhat neat ball, I touched the sudsy water. Hot. Perfect. I stepped into the water and then sank into it. There was only a faint sting from the cut on my waist as the heat seeped into my tense muscles and the knots all along my back. Strands of my hair spread out over the water as my shoulders slipped under the surface. I stretched my legs out and didn't even reach the other side.

This tub was deliciously obscene.

Letting myself slide under the surface, I stayed there. I just existed, neither here nor there. I floated, holding my breath until my lungs burned and tiny bursts of light appeared behind my closed lids. Then I resurfaced, dragging in deep breaths of air as I blinked the water from my lashes.

Glancing at the closed door, I scooted across the floor of the tub, sending the bubbles into a frenzy and stirring up the scent of peppermint. I refused to think about the fact that Nyktos had thought to add that to the water since he didn't strike me as the type to enjoy bubble baths.

Grabbing one of the bottles, I quickly scrubbed the soap through my hair while also ignoring the fact that he'd even thought to leave two pitchers of clean, warm water by the tub. I also didn't think about how he'd washed my hair upon my arrival in the Shadowlands. Nor did I think about how he'd *helped* dry me off afterwards.

Once my hair was free of soap, I had no reason to linger, but the water was still wonderfully warm, and the size of the tub reminded me a little of my lake. My heart twisted as I pushed myself into the corner of the tub, letting my head rest against the ledge as I stared at the small window and the gray sky beyond.

What allowed me to relax wasn't that the tub or room was different. I knew that. It was who waited just outside the door. I knew I was safe.

I didn't mean for my eyes to drift shut or to be lulled into sleep. Honestly, I wouldn't have thought it possible, but that was what I did.

The sound of my name and a featherlight touch to my brow woke me, much as it had the evening before. My eyes fluttered open.

Nyktos sat on the ledge of the tub, the hair I'd cut falling forward, grazing his cheek and the curve of his jaw. He'd donned a loose black shirt but had left it untucked and unbuttoned.

The dagger remained where I'd left it, now beside his thigh.

"I think..." I cleared my throat. "I think I fell asleep."

Nyktos said nothing for a long moment, and I glanced down to confirm what I already suspected. Most of the bubbles had evaporated, leaving only patches of weak foam scattered throughout the tub. I was acutely conscious that nearly all of me was visible to him. "The water must be cold by now."

"A little." I forced a swallow. "Can you really heat water with a touch?"

He nodded. "It's not really magic. It's eather responding to my will."

That sounded like magic to me. "I bet that comes in handy."

"It can." A moment passed, and then he dipped a hand into the water.

My pulse skittered as a faint glow appeared around his fingers, muted by the suds. The water swirled gently, forming tiny whirlpools. A strange sensation hit me, a tingling along my stomach, legs—and between them. My breath caught as the water warmed—as *I* warmed.

"Better?" Nyktos asked.

"Yes," I whispered as the tingling sensation eased. "That was...a unique experience."

"Very," he murmured, his bright-eyed gaze traveling over my face so intensely it felt like a physical touch. His stare lowered over the slope of my throat, lingering on the faint bruise left there, and then to where my shoulders broke the surface before moving lower still. The tips of my breasts tightened under his heavy stare, and the muscles low in my stomach followed suit. His gaze drifted farther, over my hand resting against my navel and then to the space between my parted thighs. Heat flooded my veins as a sharp, twisting pulse darted through me.

Nyktos's gaze shot up. The aura behind his eyes was bright as wisps of eather seeped out.

My heart kicked against my ribs. "I think you're the one doing the *ogling* now."

Thick lashes lowered, shielding his eyes, but I felt his gaze. It had returned to where the tips of my breasts were just below the surface of the water. "You do know you don't have to allow me to look upon such *unmentionable* places."

"I know."

One side of his lip curled up. "And yet you continue to allow it."

The spark of irritation further flamed the fire in my blood. "I do. What do you think that means? That I'm trying to seduce you, *Nyktos*?"

His eyes rose to mine again. The strands of essence churned slowly. "Is that a serious question? Everything you do is seductive."

"You are the one who said you would await me and then chose to enter the chamber where I was bathing," I reminded him. "And yet you think I'm trying to seduce *you*?"

The knuckles of the hand on the rim of the tub turned white.

"How long did you sit there and look upon me while I was unaware?" I pushed away from the corner of the tub, sitting up. Water dipped below the swell of my breasts. "Better yet, how was I trying to seduce you when you came into my bedchamber uninvited and watched me pleasure myself? Then touched me?"

Every part of him went still. His chest. His features. The eather in his eyes.

I smirked. "Oh, I'm sorry. Was I not supposed to bring that up again? Forget that you watched me, wishing it was your fingers instead of mine inside me? Or were you wishing it was your cock?"

The air became electrified, filling with power as his eyes locked onto mine. That should've been a warning, but I was angry—with him for behaving as if his response to me was my fault, and with myself because that ache was there, throbbing and wanting.

"The thing is, Nyktos." I rose, stirring what remained of the suds. Water coursed down my stomach, running over my hips and between my thighs. "My want of you isn't something I can't control. It's a *choice*. I have the courage to admit that, and you don't. Now, if you will excuse me—"

"No." Nyktos's hands landed on my hips, stopping me. He stared up at me, his eyes swirling, burning spheres. "You are not excused."

19

There was a hitch in my throat and a highly idiotic shiver below my belly in response to the blade-edged sharpness of his tone. The unmistakable heat in his stare. The branding feel of his cool hands on my skin. "I didn't ask if I was allowed," I told him.

"Actually, you did." His hands tightened, squeezing the flesh on my hips. "You asked, and I'm telling you no."

Wet hair fell over my shoulders and breasts as I tipped my chin down and grasped his wrists. "Do you want me to just stand here?" The anger and the want of him was a dangerous, heady mix. "You should hand me a towel then. I wouldn't want my nakedness and your inability to avert your gaze to be seen as another forced attempt at seduction."

Nyktos's laugh was smoke and fire, coasting over my stomach, and my earlier taunting haunted me now because it was like nothing would remain of me but ember and ash.

I pressed my fingers into his skin. "Let go—"

"You were right. I did look at you longer than I should have while you slept in this bath, thinking about that damn offer you made me when there are far more important things to be consumed with while I looked at your breasts. Those fucking nipples." His lashes swept down. "Your pussy. And I did sit here and think about how it tasted. How it felt around my cock. The little jewel there and how a single touch makes you even wetter than anything I could've ever imagined."

Air stalled in my lungs, and a dizzying heat swamped my senses.

"But I'm thinking about that when I'm not even looking at it," he said, and he was looking at it now. His lips parted, revealing the sharp tips of his fangs. "Thinking about it so fucking much that I'm dreaming about you on my cock, riding me."

I jerked as his lips brushed against the skin above my navel and his hands slid back, fingers pressing into the cheeks of my ass.

"I kept telling myself you didn't know I was there as you touched yourself. That was the only thing that stopped me from getting between your legs and fucking you until neither of us could walk."

My legs went weak, and I would've fallen if he hadn't been holding onto me.

"And I sat here, looking at you and all your loveliness—wanting you so fucking badly." His voice was the silk whisper of midnight as he lifted his head, bringing his mouth to the skin below my navel. "Trying to remind myself of all the reasons—and they are vast—why I cannot acknowledge what you do to me. Why I cannot afford for you to be anything more than a distraction."

My heart stuttered, and I started to pull back.

His fingers splayed across my ass, stopping me. "But instead, all I seem to be able to think about is how I actually look forward to you doing the exact opposite of what I've asked. Or how much I enjoy your teasing and your boldness. I think about how much that fucking mouth of yours amuses me." The edge of his fang skated over my skin, sending a shiver coiling around my spine. "I *fixate* on how you felt under me. Soft. Warm. How I felt inside you when you came."

A series of tingles, much like when he'd heated the water, swept over me in waves. He guided me so my knees were on the floor of the tub. His hands left my ass. One caught the strands of my hair as he rose, tugging my head back as my thighs pressed against the side of the tub. The sudden change in positions sent my pulse racing as he towered over me. The way he had my hair caused my back to arch and my breasts to jut out and brush against his thighs.

My gaze dropped, just for a second, and that was all it took to see the hard, thick ridge of what I'd felt pressed against my back in the courtyard.

My heart tripped slightly—a realization that he had likely been on the edge, and I'd goaded him right over it. And every single reckless part of my being delighted in it. Wanted it. Needed it. I looked up at him, and the lust in the brutal set of his features—the baring of his fangs—was potent and all-consuming. My hands landed on the cool ledge of the tub as I steadied myself.

"Is that brave enough for you?" Nyktos demanded. "Real enough?"

There were many things I could say or even do, but the impulsive part of my nature had joined with the recklessness. That part of me was in control. "Are you thinking about it now?" I asked, my voice throaty and thick. My skin flushed with arousal. "Or are you thinking about how it felt for your cock to be in my mouth? Is that what you want now?"

"*Fuck*," he groaned, his eyes slamming shut. "What do you think, *liessa?*"

Liessa.

Gods, that one word had so much power, and right now, it was an astonishing aphrodisiac. "Show me, then."

His eyes flew open. They were pure, glowing silver.

My fingers pressed into the porcelain of the tub. "Show me that's what you want. Or are you back to being nothing more than talk?"

Nyktos didn't move. His chest didn't rise or fall with a breath. Not for several seconds.

Then he did.

He reached down, grabbing the flap of his leathers. The tear of material and the popping of buttons sent a wicked thrill through me. He tore his pants open and wrapped his hand around the base of his rigid cock. A small bead of liquid had already formed on the tip.

My lips parted on a heady exhale as I lifted my eyes to his. "Prove it."

The sound that came from him was raw and primitive and nothing mortal. The hand in my hair tightened further and then he proved that was exactly what he wanted.

Nyktos tugged me to him, but it was I who took him into my mouth. He kept pulling me closer, and I kept taking him, as far as I could—until my lips reached his hand. He pulled back slowly, but I only let him get so far, clasping his hips much like he had mine. His head fell back as he groaned.

This wasn't a seduction. There were no teasing licks or tastes. No easing into it. I sucked hard and deep, moving my head and my mouth in rhythm with his hand. His ragged breaths and groans filled the chamber. The earthy taste of his skin and how he thrust into my mouth heightened my arousal.

His hips began to lose any sense of rhythm. When I felt him stiffen, he didn't pull away as he'd tried to the time before. He held me to him, my name ground out between clenched teeth as he emptied himself.

I stayed with him as the spasms eased. His muscles were slow to loosen, as was his grip. Then I pulled back, and I...I did what I had done the first time. I leaned in to kiss one of the drops inked on his inner hip.

His hand fell away from me, and I sank a little into the tub, my breathing shallow. Seconds passed, and I began to lift my head, bracing myself for—well, whatever came next.

Nyktos came over the side of the tub, forcing me back. Water sloshed over his leathers. My eyes went wide. "What are you—?" My words ended in a sharp inhale as he grabbed my arms and lifted me.

Cool air swirled over my skin as he turned us, sitting me down on the ledge of the tub. His hands left me again, and then he went down on his knees, the water rising to his thighs.

"What are you doing?" I gasped.

A lock of hair fell across his face as his hands landed on my knees. "I'm assuming your offer wasn't a one-sided deal, was it?"

"No, but you're getting your clothing soaked—"

"Really don't care." His palms skated up, pressing my thighs apart, open and wide—to him. "You told me to prove it. My cock in your mouth wasn't the only thing I was thinking about."

"Nyktos." I gasped as his shoulders replaced his hands.

"Tasting you was one of them," he told me.

And he proved that, too.

His mouth was on me, his tongue delving deep. His lips closed over the bundle of nerves. My hips jerked off the tub, but he folded his arm around them, forcing me back.

He...devoured me. Licking. Tasting. Sucking. *Feasting.* For someone with little to no experience, he sure knew what to do.

Or maybe it was simply that he couldn't do it wrong.

That I was just that aroused by *him* because it was *his* mouth on me, *his* tongue inside me.

Either way, he was magnificent. We were. My head fell back as I gave in to him. His finger replaced his tongue, first just one and then another, thrusting deep as he sucked on that throbbing piece of flesh. My head pitched forward, eyes wide and fixed on his bent head, on the strands of hair splayed across my thighs. Tension tightened and curled as I rode his fingers, his mouth—

I cried out as he lifted his head. His glossy lips were parted, his fingers still buried inside me, moving slowly.

"When I was talking about tasting you," he said, "it wasn't just your pussy."

I jerked. "W-what?"

His head snapped down. The graze of his fangs was an icy-hot fire and then he struck, sinking into the skin just above the sensitive joining of nerves. The shock of the bite dragged a scream from me. Pain-tinged waves of pleasure swept over me. My legs stiffened. My hips tried to lift, but he held me there, his fingers plunging in and out of me, his mouth moving over my clit, sucking on the nub of flesh—sucking on the blood running from the punctures above. The sensation...

"It's too much," I gasped, my hands slipping on the ledge. I squirmed desperately, pressing my knees into his shoulders, wanting to move away. Needing to be closer. "I—I can't take it. Please, *Ash*—"

His growl rumbled through me, in me. He sucked harder, deeper, and the coils spun and spun. A quake hit me. I gripped a fistful of hair. I was coming apart.

Pleasure took me, and I fell into it without hesitation, shamelessly. I broke, shattering into silk-adorned shards of bliss. My entire body shook, the release leaving me limp as my hand slipped from his hair. If it had not been for Nyktos's hold on me, I surely would've fallen.

I moaned as he tugged on my skin one last time—one last pull of my blood as he eased his fingers from me. The warm, wet slide of his tongue along the very center of me and then over his bite was bliss. I shuddered, nearly going limp.

He lifted his head, gently easing my legs into the water. Stunning wisps of essence swirled in his eyes. Neither of us spoke for several moments, and I closed my eyes before I saw any hint of the regret that was sure to form in his features. That might make me a coward, but what I'd just experienced had been wonderful. And at no point during any of that did I think about anything other than how I felt and how I was making Nyktos feel. I had just been myself. Not the Consort. Not an assassin or a weapon. Not a monster.

And I didn't want anything to ruin that.

Not when his hands were still on me, the feel of his skin a little less cool and welcome against my hips.

"Stay here," Nyktos said roughly, the water splashing as he rose. "Please."

I nodded, palms braced against the ledge of the tub. He stepped out of the water. There were sounds of him undressing, of wet, heavy clothing hitting the floor. I still couldn't believe that he'd climbed into the tub fully dressed. A tired smile tugged at my lips.

"Beautiful," Nyktos murmured.

"What?" My eyes opened as I lifted my head. He stood by the tub, a towel knotted around his waist.

"You. Your smile," he said. "You're beautiful, Sera."

Cheeks warming, I opened my mouth but couldn't find words as he turned, reaching for another towel. It was then that I realized I'd called him *Ash*.

Oh, gods.

He returned to the side of the tub, his lashes lowered, but I could feel his gaze on me—on my face. Was he counting the freckles to see if they'd changed? Then his stare moved to the swells of my breasts, the curve of my hips. "Stand?"

Hoping my legs wouldn't fail me, I did as he asked, facing the small window across from the tub. From behind, he wrapped me in the fluffy, soft towel, arms and all. Before I could thank him, he lifted me from the tub into his arms and against his chest.

Shock hit me in waves, nearly as powerful as the release had been. The show of strength was quickly lost in the act itself. I was stunned into complete silence as he carried me from the bathing chamber and to his bed. He laid me down in the center, my hair no longer soaked but still thoroughly wet. He shucked off the towel at his waist, and I caught a glimpse of the ink along the inside of his lean hips and his semi-hard arousal before he too climbed into the bed beside me.

I lay there in my towel cocoon, covered from my shoulders to my thighs, utterly confused. It wasn't nighttime when he kept me within arm's reach. This was different. Yes, we had enjoyed each other. Sure, frustration and maybe a little anger had spawned it, but there had been no pretense. What we had shared wasn't a consequence of desire-fueled feeding, but I wasn't naïve enough to think it meant that the past or the future had suddenly changed. Nyktos wanted me then and now, that much was clear.

But what wasn't clear was *this*.

Just like it hadn't been clear when we'd had sex before and he'd wanted me to stay in his bed. Did he think it had to be this way after? Nyktos was a...a quick learner, naturally following what his body liked and paying attention to how I responded to what he did, but he had been a virgin. His experience was limited here. Hell, *my* experience was limited to getting off and getting going, but I knew enough to know that when he brought me to his bed at night, it was different than *this*.

"You're quiet," Nyktos said. I peeked over at him. He lay on his back, nude as the day he was born, an arm thrust behind his head and the other on his chest as he stared at the ceiling. "You're never quiet."

A short laugh left me as my gaze shifted to the ceiling. "I know an entire kingdom that would disagree with that."

"Really?"

I nodded.

"Why?"

I wasn't sure how to answer that, so it took a couple of moments. "As your Consort, I was not to be known by most."

There was a beat of silence. "What does that mean?"

"It's like with the Chosen, but even more. I…I don't know how to explain it other than to say that I…I didn't exist."

"You existed."

"I didn't, though," I told him, not able to blame this bit of honesty on whiskey like I had when I'd spoken about Tavius. Maybe this time, it was the orgasm. "I was shrouded like the Chosen, and that was what most assumed I was, but I was sure people questioned it because I wasn't at the Temples like the other Chosen. Either way, the same rules applied to me when I was veiled. But even after you didn't take me, and I no longer wore the veil, it remained the same. The people of Lasania didn't even know that I was the true heir to the throne. They didn't know that *Princess* Seraphena even existed. And the few who did, like the older servants who worked in Wayfair and had to suspect who I was? They never acknowledged it. Or me. I was a ghost."

Nyktos said nothing, but I felt his gaze on me.

Like before, I didn't look at him. But I couldn't deal with the silence that fell between us, which was highly ironic given the topic. I cleared my throat. "Anyway, I'm actually used to being quiet."

"But not with me."

"That's because you usually annoy me," I stated dryly, and his answering chuckle warmed my skin. There was that strange, pleasant sensation in my chest again, and that was…well, it could be concerning. "And because seducing you required me to actually speak, unless that's not what you liked. Then I would've been silent." The moment those words left my mouth, I cringed. "I probably shouldn't have said that."

Several moments passed. "You would've become whatever you believed I wanted?"

Closing my eyes, I pictured punching myself in the face. Hard. Repeatedly. I didn't even know why I'd brought that up when I wanted nothing more than to forget it.

"Sera?"

I swallowed. "I would have."

He shifted, drawing up a leg. "You talked before you realized I was the Primal of Death. You were never quiet then."

"Like I told you, you annoyed me," I said instead of what had immediately popped into my head. That it was because of how I'd felt heard and seen when I was with him. Respected. Counted. Opening my eyes, I finally turned my head to him. There was an ease about him and the lines of his features. Our eyes met. Words swelled in my throat. Ones best not given life. "I should get going. I'm sure you have—"

"Don't," he said softly, and I froze. "I have a few hours before anything needs to be done. I'm tired. You must be tired. So, here we are."

"Arm's reach?" I whispered.

"Yeah," Nyktos said after a moment.

I nodded, but he and I both knew that keeping me in his bed wasn't necessary during the day, when the palace and courtyard were teaming with gods. Honestly, it wasn't really necessary at night.

It suddenly struck me as I stared at him that maybe he...he had to be just as lonely as I was, but for far longer than I. And right now, we didn't have to be. I closed my eyes and just let myself be here, in the moment and nothing more.

"Sera." I thought I heard Nyktos whisper my name as I began to doze off. "You were never a ghost to me."

I woke sometime later, half-sprawled on my belly, toasty and covered in something far thicker and softer than a towel. A fur blanket.

Nyktos.

He wasn't there. The warmth was gone from my chest, and as I lay there, I thought that maybe falling asleep together was entirely different than waking up together.

That was an intimacy I knew neither of us had ever experienced. One that seemed to go deeper than what we'd shared in the tub and the words spoken afterward.

You were never a ghost to me.

My chest tightened and then loosened. Had he really said that? The words sounded like something one would conjure in a dream, but if he had spoken them, they were…they were kind and far more beautiful than he probably knew, and I would cherish them for what they were.

Words.

I started to roll onto my side but stopped. Something was lying across my feet. My eyes cracked open.

Jadis lay on her belly much like I was, her limp arms and legs widespread. She made a soft, snoring sound as her nearly translucent, greenish-brown wings twitched before stilling. I had no idea how long I stared at her before I realized that she wasn't the only one in the chamber.

I lifted my gaze, my breath stalling in my lungs as I saw Nektas sitting with his feet resting on the foot of the bed. A wicked sense of déjà vu hit me. But this time, there was an odd half-grin on his handsome face.

"Are you watching me sleep?" I asked, my voice a little hoarse. "Again?"

He shifted slightly, resting his elbows on the arms of the chair and loosely clasping his hands together on his lap. "Possibly."

Frowning, I snuggled deeper into the blanket as I eyed him. "That's…creepy."

"Is it?"

"Yes."

He shrugged a shoulder, drawing my attention to the single black-and-crimson braid lying there. "Jadis wanted to see you."

I glanced at the softly snoring draken. "You mean she wanted to nap on my feet?"

"Well, she wanted to wake you, but Ash told her you needed the rest," he shared, and my heart give a little wiggle. "It quickly became obvious that he spoke the truth since you slept through her jumping up and down on the bed."

My brows rose.

"Anyway, she likes to nap like that," he continued, sending his sleeping daughter a fond look. "I think it's her way of making sure you don't get up and leave her."

"Makes sense," I mumbled.

"And since she decided to sleep, I figured I'd wait for one of you to wake." He uncrossed his ankles, letting one knee bend.

"Oh." I zeroed in on his grin. There was something…satisfied about it. I became highly aware of the fact that Nektas had to suspect what'd led to me being in Nyktos's bed in the middle of the day. Naked. "This isn't what it looks like."

"What does it look like?"

"Like I'm in his bed—"

"Because he wanted you there," he cut in. "As did you?"

I snapped my mouth shut.

"Unless that's not what you wanted, and he somehow trapped you here." A pause. "Completely nude."

My eyes narrowed. "He didn't trap me here," I muttered. "He let me use his bathing chamber, and I was tired afterward."

"You don't need to explain any of this to me."

"I wasn't."

Nektas stared at me blandly.

"Whatever." I tugged the edge of the fur up to my eyes, feeling my cheeks warm. "I think I'm just going to go back to sleep."

His chuckle was rough and low. "Before you do that, I thought you would like to know that Erlina was here earlier while you were sleeping."

I popped my head up. "Why didn't anyone wake—?" I cut myself off. "Nyktos thought I needed the rest."

"You would be correct."

My head fell back onto the pillow as I let out a long sigh.

"He was only trying to be considerate," Nektas began.

"I know." I stared at the shadowstone ceiling.

"And that bothers you?"

"Maybe," I muttered. "I don't know."

"Irrational emotions can be a symptom of the Culling."

My head snapped up again as my eyes narrowed on the draken. "I am not being irrational."

"Just thought you should know." He grinned. "Erlina left what clothing she finished. She will return when the coronation is held to make any last-minute alterations."

Whenever the coronation was held. My stomach took a tumble, and I decided that I couldn't think about that right now. Doing so made me too antsy to remain still, and considering that I had a baby draken sprawled across my feet and was naked, pacing was out of the question. "Where...where is Nyktos?"

"At Court."

The next breath I took could've ignited a wildfire, and it took everything in me not to launch myself from the bed and set something on fire.

Nektas arched a brow. "Your current expression reminds me of Jadis in the moments before she throws herself onto the floor and starts screaming."

"I'm likely to do way worse than that. I told him…" I trailed off, realizing that Nyktos actually hadn't agreed to any of the demands I'd made in the courtyard, not even the part about the Vale or going to see Ezra. Damn it. I flopped back, groaning softly as I closed my eyes.

"You told him that you wanted to attend Court with him," Nektas finished for me.

I frowned. "How do you know? You weren't there."

"Ector and Rhain gave me a minute-by-minute breakdown of what happened."

"Great." I glanced at him. "I told him I didn't want to wait on going to the Vale."

"I haven't spoken to him about that, but I'm sure he'll address it soon enough," he said. I wasn't so sure. "Ash was supposed to hold Court this afternoon, but he was otherwise *occupied*. It had to be rescheduled for this evening."

Nyktos *had* said he had a few hours before he was needed. He'd missed Court to be here with me? Or had he simply slept longer than he'd planned? And why was I even thinking about it? None of that changed the fact that he hadn't done as I asked, whether or not he believed I needed my rest. "I'm assuming he's still at Court?"

"He is, but it's not being held here. With you and the newly Ascended Bele lurking the halls, he is holding Court in Lethe at the City Hall. He figured it would be safer that way until the coronation and whenever someone figures out what to do with Bele."

"I didn't even know he held Court anyplace other than here," I muttered. Hell, I hadn't even seen the building the coronation would've taken place in. I'd only seen the city at night and from a distance. A City Hall wouldn't likely have been visible from the places I had been, if they were anything like the old ones in Lasania. They were usually open-air, consisting of amphitheater-type seating surrounding a dais.

"He usually prefers to have them there," Nektas said. "Ash likes to be seen in Lethe. His presence is welcome, and it's also a reminder to those who travel in and out of Lethe that he is no absentee ruler."

And, of course, I didn't know any of that. "Gods, there's so much I don't know about Lethe or even the Shadowlands."

"Have you asked him about Lethe?" Nektas asked. "Have you

shown any interest in learning these things?"

I opened my mouth, but I...I hadn't asked.

Nektas eyed me. "When Ash decided to honor the deal his father made, he didn't want to force any of the responsibilities of being a Consort—something he knew you never agreed to—onto you. If he'd learned you were interested, I'm sure he would've volunteered whatever information you wanted to know. Instead, he learned that you never had any intention of fulfilling that deal either. That you had *other* plans."

My jaw snapped shut.

"Even though he understands what drove you and accepts it, why would he think you wanted to know these things when it was just recently that you told him you wanted to be of use?"

"Okay, you have made a lot of valid points," I admitted, my cheeks warming at the truth in most of what he'd said. "But there is no way he has truly forgiven me."

"I never said he has. I said he understands, and I'll tell you the same thing I told him when he was much younger. Forgiveness benefits the forgiver, and it's easy. Understanding is acceptance, and that is far harder." His gaze held mine as Jadis gave a little wiggle. "And if Ash didn't understand and accept your past actions, you would not be where you are right now. You would not carry his scent on your body, and I would've never sensed what I did when I found him with you."

"What did you sense?" I whispered, my heart stomping in my chest.

"What I sensed before." That odd little half-grin returned. "Peace."

20

Wrapped in the fur I'd left Nyktos's chambers in, I ran a hand over the soft blouses and sweaters hanging in the wardrobe, the leggings as thick as breeches, pants like the ones Nyktos and the others often wore made of soft leather, and vests, tunics, and gowns as silky as the array of undergarments I'd discovered in one of the drawers. There were so many colors, both pastels and vivid shades, and they were all mine. If the clothing Erlina had finished was any indication of her talent and taste, the coronation gown would be stunning.

Peace.

My heart started that wild staccato again as I dropped the fur and picked up an undergarment that seemed to be designed to cover as little of my private bits as possible. I started to pull on the scrap of lace, freezing when I laid eyes on said private bits.

Through the dusting of pale, fine hair, I saw that the skin Nyktos's fangs had sunk into was red, but there were no puncture wounds. I pressed my fingers to the flesh, feeling the two shallow indentations. Frowning, I lifted my hand to the side of my neck, where the bite had already faded. It had taken a couple of days for the marks on my neck and breast to fade, but hours for this one? That didn't make sense. Had something been different?

Making a note to ask him about it later, I tugged the new dressing robe from the hanger and pulled on the plush material dyed a dark blue-gray. Fastening the buttons along the side of my waist, I went over to the balcony doors. The sky above the crimson woods was a darker shade of iron, the stars brighter and plentiful but not as vivid as when night had fallen. However, it could not be much longer until it was night—a few hours, if that.

More tired than I should've been after napping, I retreated to the chaise and snuggled deep into the soft material of the robe after taming my hair into a braid. What Nektas had said entered my thoughts. Not the stuff that had to do with peace, but the part that I knew Nektas had been right about.

I hadn't given Nyktos any real indication that I was interested in anything beyond what he planned to do with Kolis and, well...me. Before the courtyard, I'd never mentioned attending Court or being of use. I'd asked about his army and his plans, but that was it.

And, gods, now I felt like an ass because before Nyktos had learned the truth, he'd given me space because he hadn't wanted me to feel overwhelmed. It was very likely that he'd been doing the same now, waiting for me to give some sort of indication that I wanted to be an actual Consort...outside of the bedchamber.

In my defense, there hadn't been any reason to think of a future until recently. But still, I cringed all the way to the tips of my toes. And I closed my eyes as I tried to figure out exactly how to make it very clear to Nyktos that I was interested in learning more about Lethe and the Shadowlands. Asking seemed simple enough, but I'd spent more time learning how to kill someone than understanding the basics of open, honest communication. Or how to overcome this...feeling of vulnerability that came with being open. I wasn't even sure if it was *normal* to worry about asking or saying the wrong thing like I often did. Or that I couldn't get my thoughts, which sounded so right in my head, to come out of my mouth the same way. Would it sound silly? Would whatever I said come back to haunt me? To hurt?

Talking things out always sounded easy, but the anxiety that the mere idea of it drummed up also seemed insurmountable.

But did I want to be...more? Not just his Consort but a real Consort to the Shadowlands?

As I lay there, asking myself that over and over, I must've drifted off. The next thing I knew, I felt a warmth buzzing in my chest. I opened my eyes, startled to find Nyktos crouched by the chaise.

"I was beginning to think you were never going to wake," he said. "I knocked a couple of times and called your name when I entered."

"Sorry." I cleared my throat, sitting up as I glanced down to where his hand rested between his knees. My cheek still tingled from the touch. "I can't believe I fell asleep again."

Concern pinched his features as his gaze swept over mine. "How are you feeling?"

"Fine." I rubbed at the back of my neck, working at the kink there.

"No signs of a headache or any jaw pain?"

I shook my head, dropping my hand to the chaise. "I guess I'm just tired."

That worry seemed to increase in his stare. "I shouldn't have…"

"What?" I asked when he didn't finish.

"I shouldn't have taken from you earlier," he said, his eyes meeting mine. "I should've known better—"

"I didn't mind," I cut in.

"I know you didn't." The eather pulsed behind his pupils as his voice roughened, sending a shiver over my skin. "But that's beside the point. I didn't take a lot from you, but the Culling already takes enough of a toll on your body. If you do start to have a headache, I want you to tell me. We can stop it from getting as bad as before."

"I will." I didn't want to feel that kind of pain again. "So, I wasn't imagining the whole biting me part then?"

His head cocked. "No."

"I have questions about that."

Two deep splotches appeared in the center of his cheeks as his shoulders tightened. "You do?"

I nodded as I watched the blush spread across his face, thinking how cute it was. "There was no bite mark left behind…"

The tension eased from him. "That's because I closed the wounds."

My brows shot up. "Come again?"

"I closed the wounds," he repeated. "With my tongue."

I vividly recalled the hot, slick slide of his tongue as he'd eased his fingers from me. Now, my cheeks warmed. "How is that possible?"

"I nicked my lip and drew my blood," he explained, the color of his eyes deepening. "Just a drop was on my tongue when I ran it over the wounds. So, in reality, my blood healed them."

"Oh," I whispered, suddenly finding the soft robe far too thick and heavy. "Why didn't you do that before?"

"My blood will only heal the bite I created. I couldn't remove traces of Taric's bite without you drinking from me, and that would've required more than just a drop." His jaw hardened. "But before that? After I bit you?" He frowned. "I don't know why I didn't."

"Interesting," I murmured, and he raised a brow. "Anyway, I'm okay. I thoroughly enjoyed that bath. It was a surprise—a very nice one. As were other things."

"Other things?"

Like what came after. The talking. What he'd said as I fell asleep. I couldn't make myself say any of that, though, no matter how hard I tried—or how much I wanted to push past the feelings of vulnerability. "You were very good at what you did with that tongue."

Nyktos stared at me. There was no flash of smug, male pride. Just a faint flush and a look of surprise as if he couldn't believe I thought that. He cleared his throat. "I fear the food will grow cold if we linger any longer."

My gaze swung to the table by the balcony doors, where only one covered dish usually sat.

Tonight, there were two.

My breath snagged at the sudden thumping of my heart. Two covered dishes. Two glasses. A bottle of wine.

"You said you didn't want to eat your suppers alone," Nyktos began as I stared at the two plates, a knot lodging in my throat. "It's late, so I thought you might not want to go to the dining hall," he added in the silence. "But if you changed your mind or would prefer other company, I can—"

"No. Don't leave." I lurched to my feet so fast my face turned the shade of the Red Woods. "I mean, I haven't changed my mind."

"Glad to hear." A faint grin appeared. "Otherwise, I was starting to feel rather awkward."

I didn't think it was possible for him to feel as awkward as I did just then. I hurried to the table like I was afraid he'd be the one to change his mind. And I was. I busied myself with getting seated. "How was Court?" I asked, praying to the Fates that this wasn't one of those moments where I was projecting my emotions all over.

Nyktos followed far more sedately, taking the seat across from me. "Nothing too eventful." He leaned over, lifting the lid from my dish and then his. "A handful of minor complaints between neighbors."

"I'm kind of surprised that such things are brought before a Primal." I unfolded my napkin, placing it on my lap.

That grin of his returned, deepening as he picked up the bottle, showing a hint of fang. My stomach twisted in the most distracting way as he pulled the cork, and an aromatic, sweet scent hit the air. "I'm actually glad they bring these issues to me."

"You are?" I watched him pour the deep red wine into our glasses.

"Yes." He picked up a carving knife as he relaxed into his chair. "It means they're comfortable enough to do so. That they don't fear me, and they feel safe enough to come to me."

"I didn't even think about that."

"Were the people of Lasania not comfortable enough to bring such concerns to the King and Queen?"

"They used to be. They'd hold town halls where things could be voiced or asked for." I eyed the fine tendons of his hands and fingers as he finished carving the thick breast, pushing the slices into a neat pile beside the glistening mound of vegetables. "But as the Rot grew worse, the complaints got louder, and more things were requested. They stopped the town halls. The protests began shortly after."

"And how was that received?"

"Not well," I admitted. "The Crown dealt with the protestors quite severely. And instead of stockpiling food or moving farms to lands untouched by the Rot, they did nothing." Old anger returned. "They waited for me to..."

"Stop the Rot?" He set his knife aside.

I nodded. "So, they did very little to prepare in case I failed."

"You didn't fail, Sera," he said, drawing my gaze to his. "Becoming my Consort wouldn't have stopped the Rot."

What he said wasn't new. I knew that the moment I learned that the Rot had nothing to do with the deal. But what that meant, what Eythos had done, didn't fully set in until now. I sucked in a sharp breath. "I haven't failed."

His brow rose. "That's what I said."

"No. I mean, you know how Holland talked about the different threads—about my duty?"

Nyktos's eyes narrowed. "If you're talking about going after Kolis—"

"Not that." At least, not now. "I can still save Lasania simply by staying alive long enough to transfer the embers to you. That will stop the Rot."

He eyed me. "I believe we already discussed that, Sera."

"I know. It's just—I don't know. It didn't really hit me until now," I said. "I guess I'm just used to..."

"Blaming yourself?" he said, and I shrugged. "Because your family blamed you?"

"Ezra never did," I whispered.

"And this Ezra, she will rule better than the ones before her?"

"Yes. She already is. Ezra is the Queen they deserve." I smiled as he lifted his plate and stretched across the table.

"I expect you to live longer than the time it takes to transfer the embers to me, by the way," he said. "And I suppose I will discover for myself just how deserving this stepsister of yours is."

"I can visit her?"

"That's what you want, is it not?"

"Yes, but..."

His gaze flicked to mine. "We will go tomorrow, but we cannot linger long. I've been lucky at times in the past, but others can feel my presence in the mortal realm. It's a risk."

I thought of the creepy Gryms that had found their way to my lake, but they had been looking for me and not him. "I know."

"And you must be selective in what you share with her," he continued. "I know you may want to tell her the truth about Kolis, but that kind of knowledge will be a death sentence for her if discovered. You can speak to her about the Rot, but not the cause."

"I understand," I said. "I don't want to endanger her."

"Good." He switched out our plates. "Eat."

I glanced down at my plate and then to the one he'd taken, befuddled. "You didn't need to do that."

"I know." He began carving the untouched piece of chicken. "And before you point this out, I know you're more than capable of cutting your own food, but there was far more meat to that breast than this one, and you'll need all the protein you can get."

My brows pinched as I glanced between my neatly carved pile and the one he worked on. They looked nearly identical in size and quality, but the intent behind his actions was...it felt thoughtful, not infantilizing. So, I stopped myself from making a caustic retort.

"You may not feel it, but your body is using a lot of energy as it ramps up for the Ascension."

I thought about how I'd dozed off after waking up and picked up my fork, shoveling several chunks of meat onto the thin tines. I was definitely feeling it. "Thank you," I murmured.

"You don't need to thank me."

"Well, I did." I ate the forkful of chicken as I peeked at Nyktos. His head was bowed, the hair I'd cut in the courtyard brushing his jaw.

The grin was there again. *Peace.* I squirmed in my seat. "And what of the Pools of Divanash? Have you given any thought to that?"

"I have." He chewed his food as neatly as he carved it.

Trying not to get my hopes up, I took a sip of the sweet port wine. "And?"

"And it's also a risk," he said. "That hasn't changed."

"Just because it's a risk doesn't mean something will happen."

He raised one eyebrow as he looked over at me. "True, but I've learned to be cautious—overly so."

I bet he had.

"But," he continued with a deep breath, "we have no idea when Kolis will summon us. It could be tomorrow. It could be a week from now or even longer. Time isn't a luxury."

I nodded in agreement. "But maybe Kolis delaying the coronation is a blessing. It will give us some time to remove the embers before Kolis summons us."

"I've considered that, even before this afternoon."

I speared a carrot. "But you were being *overly cautious?*"

His glass partially hid his smile. "I talked to Nektas after returning from Court," he continued, and I really hoped the draken hadn't mentioned what he'd said to me. "He's on board."

Excitement hummed through me, but I was still cautious. "Are you on board?"

"I don't like the idea of you being out there without the protection of the title, whether that is here or in the mortal realm." He set his glass down while I tried not to attach any deeper meaning to what he'd said. "And it's not because I'm trying to control you—"

"I know," I cut in, and I did.

"I'm relieved to hear that. I've feared…"

"What?" I asked when he didn't finish.

"I've feared that this situation we're in could make you feel that way." Nyktos stared at his glass. "That I've made you feel that way because I've used my authority to stop you from doing what you want, and I…" His brows furrowed as he shook his head. "I don't like it."

I stared at him for what felt like a small eternity, unsure what to say. He had used his authority to stop me from doing a pretty long list of things—stuff that would have likely resulted in me being injured or ending up dead. "There is a difference between someone trying to control you and someone trying to protect you. I know I may not behave like there's a difference, but I do know there is one."

Nyktos's softly lit eyes lifted to mine.

"There just needs to be a balance, you know? When the need to protect what's valuable doesn't get in the way of what needs to be done."

He nodded slowly. "I'm discovering that balance is not easy to find. But I'm on board. We have plans for tomorrow, it appears, and Nektas will be unavailable the day after that, but in two days, you will go to the Pools of Divanash with Nektas."

I tried to fight the smile, but there was no stopping it from spreading across my face. There was no hiding it from him either. His eyes had lightened even more, and I wondered if he was aware of how they'd changed.

Nyktos's gaze flickered away as he took a long drink of his wine. "Anyway," he said, clearing his throat, "I heard Erlina brought by the clothing she made. Were you pleased?"

"They are all beautiful."

"Hopefully, they're less distracting."

"They are."

"Thank the Fates."

I leaned back in my chair, eyeing him over the rim of my glass. In the loose, untucked black shirt he wore and with his hair free, he reminded me of how he'd been when I'd been with him beside my lake. A powerful, otherworldly being, but not one that existed outside my reach.

He is how you wish him to be.

It was hard not to see him as Ash in these quiet moments.

"I have a question for you," I said.

"Ask away."

"I'm not sure I should. I feel like manners dictate that I not."

"You have never struck me as the type to give much thought to manners."

"I have been known to pay heed to manners a time or two."

His eyes warmed as they settled on me. "What is your question?"

I took another drink of what I hoped served as a wee bit of liquid courage. "I'm surprised that you're here."

"That doesn't sound like a question, Sera."

The way he said my name... Muscles low in my stomach coiled even tighter. "You're right. It really wasn't a question. More of a statement. I just didn't think you'd have dinners with me."

"I was under the impression that you didn't believe I would meet any of the demands you made today," he said.

"Am I that transparent?"

"Usually, you are not. But in this, you are as transparent as a window," he remarked.

I rolled my eyes.

"Joining you for supper is a small thing," he added. "And an easy one to accommodate."

"That has to be the first thing you've done with me that you've found easy."

His eyes met mine. "It's not the first thing."

Silence stretched between us, and it felt like time slowed to an infinite crawl as I took in the softening of his gaze and the harsh lines of his features. He started to tilt forward and then caught himself. Clearing his throat, he looked away, breaking whatever strange spell seemed to have fallen over us.

In the quiet, I searched for something to say. Luckily, I remembered something Attes had said yesterday. "Were you friends with the Cimmerian? Dorcan?"

His attention shifted back to me. "I told you before. I have no friends."

He had said that, but I thought of his guards and Nektas, who considered him family. "Did he consider you a friend?"

"I cannot answer that."

"But you knew him," I persisted.

Nyktos shifted in his chair, his attention dropping to his glass. "I've known him for a while. He wasn't always a part of Hanan's Court."

That was more of an answer than I expected. "You said that he could've chosen another's Court to serve. But he said that wasn't possible. Why was he serving under Hanan if he was part of Attes's lineage?"

"Attes is not just the Primal of War. He's also the Primal of Accord. He prefers agreement over discord, so Vathi is mostly peaceful. At least, his half is," he explained. "The Cimmerian can get a bit...antsy if there's no blood to spill, so many leave Vathi to serve in other Courts. Hanan has a lot of them."

"Because Hanan is a coward and needs others to fight for him?"

Nyktos chuckled roughly. "Hanan loves the hunt if he is not equally matched. So, yes, that was a rather on-point observation."

I cracked a small grin as I tugged the edge of the napkin to my chin. "It's strange to me that a Primal can be a coward."

"Strength and power only go so far, and it rarely changes a person for the better." Nyktos dropped his hand to his chest as his words caused a shiver to curl down my spine. "Anyway, Dorcan likely pledged a blood oath to Hanan—one that can only be broken by death. That would be the only reason he couldn't leave Court. Stupid move on his part. I would've expected him to be smarter than that."

"That's a strange thing to expect from someone you don't consider a friend," I murmured.

Nyktos snorted.

I nibbled on my lip, telling myself to stay quiet, but I had to know. "You have friends."

"Sera—"

"Denying that you do doesn't change the fact that people care about you. Nor does it change that you care for them. It's okay to have friends." I could practically feel his gaze drilling into me. "But I'm sorry that you had to kill another."

Nyktos was quiet.

"You wouldn't have had to do it if he hadn't seen me," I admitted.

"It would've inevitably happened."

Was that the true, foregone conclusion? That there would be more death? If it came to war among the Primals, it would be.

"And you're wrong," he said. "It's not okay to care for others when it gets them tortured or killed."

My fingers tightened around the stem of my glass as I thought of what he'd said in the bathing chamber that afternoon. All of those *vast reasons* behind why he couldn't afford for me to be a distraction. "Kolis?"

Nyktos didn't answer. He didn't need to.

"I'm sorry," I whispered.

He stared at me, and after a moment, he nodded again.

"Nektas said…he said that you've been able to convince Kolis that you are loyal to him."

"I have."

"Then why does he treat you like this?" I asked, unable to believe that Kolis was simply punishing Nyktos for actions he believed were nothing more than Nyktos testing limits. "Is it because of your father?"

"Probably. But it's not that much different than how he is with other Primals who actually are loyal to him. One way or another, they fall in and out of favor with him as quickly as you go through clean clothing."

I huffed out a laugh, but I wished he'd told the truth. Instinct told me that while Kolis was likely cruel to others, it was different with Nyktos. That while his treatment of Nyktos may have originally stemmed from his father, it had to be more than that. That it connected with how Attes claimed that Nyktos was Kolis's favorite.

He was quiet for several moments. "The other night? When I came into your bedchamber?"

"Yes?" I somehow resisted the urge to taunt him with what he'd done, and I was, in fact, rather proud of myself for doing so.

"I...I would've come earlier," he said. "But there was an issue at the Pillars."

"That's why you left with Rhahar?" I asked, not letting myself focus on what had come before that. He nodded. "Was it souls that needed your judgment?"

"Not this time. It was souls who refused to cross."

"Does that happen often?"

"Far more than you'd think." He sighed. "More and more souls are refusing to cross and are entering the Dying Woods instead. It gets the ones already there stirred up."

"The Shades can't be fun to deal with."

"As you know, they're not." His fingers quietly tapped the side of his glass. "The moment the souls refuse to cross and enter the woods, they become Shades. Nektas believes that's it for them. They're lost and should be destroyed. Immediately. And I know I should. None has ever come back from that. But I think...what if one does? What if? There should still be a chance for them to either face justice or receive redemption. But once they're destroyed, that's it. There are no more chances."

Wetness gathered in my eyes as I blew out a shaky breath. Knowing he didn't like to kill the Shades twisted my heart, especially since my actions had led him to do just that. Him wanting to give them another chance was yet another sign of how *good* he was. And, gods, he deserved better than this life. One that wouldn't allow him to be close or affectionate with another because he feared those emotions would bring harm to them. In reality, it wasn't even a life. I knew that more than anyone. He simply existed, and that wasn't fair.

"I hope your plan works."

A dark eyebrow rose. "Is it because you're finally thinking of a future that doesn't involve your death?"

"No."

"Of course, not," he muttered.

"It's clear that you should be the true Primal of Life," I explained. "Not because it was your destiny, but because you're good."

A faint smile appeared, but it didn't warm his features like the ones before had. "That's where you're wrong. I told you before. I have one kind, decent bone in my body, Sera. But I am not good, and you would do well to remember that."

21

My heart turned over heavily, but I believed in what I'd said. "What makes you think you're not good?"

"I have...done things, Sera."

"Like killing out of necessity or by force?"

Nyktos said nothing as his unflinching stare settled on me.

"Or is it because you started to enjoy killing those who'd summoned you out of a desire to harm another?" I continued. "None of that changes that you're inherently good, Nyktos."

The line of his jaw tensed. "And how would you know? What life experiences could give you that sort of insight when you're a mostly mortal who is only on the cusp of living twenty-one years?"

I arched a brow. "I know because I'm sitting here alive when many, including everyone from your guards to gods and mortals alike, would've killed me when they learned of what I'd planned."

His gaze sharpened on me.

"And, yes, those embers in me are important enough to keep me alive, but those embers don't mean you have to be kind. You could've thrown me in a dungeon."

"That's still an option," he remarked, pouring wine into his glass and then mine.

"If you were going to do that, you would've by now instead of fearing you're trying to control me. All you've proven is what I'm saying." I picked up the refilled glass, toasting him.

He put the bottle aside. "All you've proven is what I've told you before. That one decent and kind bone I have in me belongs to you."

A worrying degree of satisfaction rushed through me, as did the urge to demand that he prove that. That the decent and kind bone really belonged to me and only me.

"But do not mistake my handling of you as a reflection of who and what I am," he added, taking a drink.

"Your...*handling* of me isn't the only reason I know you're good," I countered. "You didn't want to enjoy those killings, and you stepped away before it could change you. I know because you feel the marks those deaths left behind, and you carry them on your skin. I know because despite not having the ability to love, you are still kind and care deeply—more than most."

He smirked, looking away. "You don't know what you think you do."

"I *know* because I'm not good."

Nyktos's gaze shot to mine. "You think you're not good because of what you planned?"

I let out a dry laugh. "Yeah, that is just a drop in a very deep, messed-up bucket full of many more drops."

The eather brightened in his eyes. "And what are those other drops?"

"You'll find out if your plan doesn't work. You'll get to see my soul upon my death. It's not black. It's red, drenched in the blood of those I've killed. Lives I've taken that haven't left behind the marks you speak of." The embers in my chest vibrated. "I don't feel them. Not like you do. Sure, I may experience some remorse, but it never lasts. I felt the same as I did when I shoved that whip down Tavius's throat—"

"And you shouldn't have a second of remorse," Nyktos snarled, flashing his fangs.

"But I felt the same when I carved the Lords of Vodina Isles' hearts from their chests, and their only real crime was angering my mother." I lifted my brows at him. "Nor did I really feel anything when I killed the man in Croft's Cross who was likely pimping his children. Not that anyone should feel bad for killing that bastard, but I didn't make it clean and quick. The rest of them—and there are maybe...eighteen the last I counted?" I said, thinking of the guards Tavius had likely sent. It had been fourteen before that. "All I felt for them was pity and annoyance. And my stepfather? It may not have been my hand that took his life, but it was my actions, and I have barely thought about it. To be honest, I think the only reason I felt anything is because of the embers of life. If they weren't there, I probably wouldn't have felt anything." Shame scalded the back of my throat as I raised the glass to myself then and proceeded to finish off the wine. "So, I know what good is because I know what the opposite is in a real, up-close-and-personal kind of way."

Nyktos was silent as he eyed me, and it slowly dawned on me that, perhaps, I could've kept all of that to myself. But what did it matter? I had no reason to pretend to be anything but what I was. Still, I almost wished I'd kept my mouth shut because he was the one person who hadn't made me feel like the monster I'd just revealed myself to be.

"And yet," he said finally, in that soft, midnight way of his, "you were willing to endanger yourself to protect many you've never met. More than once. You were willing to sacrifice yourself for the Shadowlands."

I sucked in a sharp breath. "That's not the same thing."

"It's not?"

"No." I rose then, no longer able to sit. "I'm tired. I think I'm ready for bed—"

"There is no such thing as a good Primal."

"What?"

"The essence that courses through our veins is what made the realms, creating the air that is breathed, the land that is sowed, and the rain that falls from the skies to fill the oceans. It's powerful and ancient. Unbiased. It's absolute. And in the beginning, when there were just the Ancient Primals, the Fates, and the dragons, Primals were neither good nor bad. They just were. Purely impartial. A perfect balance because they felt nothing, neither love nor hate."

Nyktos stared up at me. "Eons passed that way, seeing the birth of many new Primals, including my father. And during that time, Primals didn't die. They simply entered Arcadia when they were ready. The idea of fighting one another hadn't even occurred to them, let alone killing each other. Procreation occurred for the sake of creation. And, eventually, gods were born. Then mortals. And for a time, there were no wars and no unnecessary deaths in either realm. There were disagreements in the mortal realm, skirmishes and the like, but the Primals always intervened, calming hot tempers and easing the pain of whatever loss had occurred. Then the first Primal fell, and that changed everything."

"Fell?"

"In love," he said, a wry grin appearing. "You see, each time the Primals and gods interacted with the mortals, they became more curious, until they were enthralled with the wide range of emotions that the mortals experienced—something that neither my father nor Nektas created. Mortals were the first to *feel*, from the moment they took their first breath—and until their last. And that was something that just occurred in them naturally. But Primals were meant to be beyond such…mortal needs and wants."

I slowly sat back down. "Why?"

"Because emotions can sway one's decisions, no matter how unbiased anyone believes they are. If they can feel, they can be coerced by emotion." He met my eyes.

"Then a Primal fell in love, and it troubled the Fates. They worried that love, held within a Primal's heart, could become a weapon. They intervened, hoping to dissuade other Primals from doing the same by making what they loved the ultimate weapon to be used against them."

"By becoming their weakness," I whispered. "I never knew why love could weaken Primals." I shook my head. "How are the Arae that powerful to create something like that?"

"Because they are the essence—the eather—that created the very first Primals," he explained. "My father once told me that they didn't even have mortal form for the longest time. They were simply in everything, everywhere."

I blinked slowly, unable to even understand how Holland, who was very much flesh and blood, could be something that existed in the wind and the rain. "Well, what the Arae did doesn't seem to have been all that effective."

Nyktos chuckled. "No, it wasn't. One Primal falling was like a domino effect. Other Primals fell in love and, eventually, even some of the Arae began to feel emotion," he told me, and I thought of Holland and the goddess Penellaphe. "But falling in love meant the Primals also began to experience other emotions. Pleasure. Displeasure. Want. Jealousy. Envy. Hatred. And what the Arae feared became a reality because they knew that what had once only belonged to the mortals couldn't exist within the kind of power a Primal held. Emotions began to guide the Primals' actions, and that once-unbiased balance of power became as unpredictable as it was absolute and bled into the mortal realm. The very natures of the Primals changed. Now, goodness does not exist in Primals—not the kind weighed upon a mortal's death."

He set his glass aside. "From the moment a Primal is born or is

Ascended, the new nature of the Primal essence starts to change us. And the older we grow, and the more powerful that essence becomes, the harder it is to remember what the source of those emotions was and to be anything other than the very mortal flesh that contains power," he said. "And that essence—the Primal essence that allows us to influence mortals to flourish or decay, love or hate, create life and cause death—is never just good or bad. It's only absolute. Unpredictable. Raw." His eyes lifted from his glass to me. "You've carried those embers from birth, Sera, and they are a part of you. Because of them, you are neither good nor bad, not by the mortal standards you understand."

I drew in a shaky breath. "Are you saying that how I...I feel is because of those embers?"

"Yes," he told me. "But you are still mortal, Sera, and that part of you *is* good."

"It—"

"It is," Nyktos cut in. "You wouldn't feel the sourness of shame if it wasn't. Or the bitterness of agony when you spoke of killing. You wouldn't even care if you were deserving. You would just take. You wouldn't be brave. You would only be strong."

"I—" I choked on my words. Could there be truth in what he said? I blinked back sudden dampness as I focused on the empty plate in front of me. I did feel shame and agony—even confusion over the coldness of my actions. I squeezed my eyes shut and took several moments before I trusted myself to speak. "But you are good by mortal standards."

"Only because I try to be."

"That's all mortals do—well, most of them anyway," I said, opening my eyes. "They try to be good, and you try harder than most mortals do."

"Maybe," he murmured.

As I sat there, letting his words sink in, I thought of something. "Why didn't the Arae make the Primals do what you did? Have the *kardia* removed?"

"The Arae believe in free will. And, yes, being that they are Fates, that is as ironic as it could possibly be," he said. "But they should've done it."

If they had, it would have saved a lot of lives and stopped a lot of heartache, but... "Do you really think they should have?"

"Depends on the day. Right now, no." He leaned forward. "You're finished with your supper?"

I nodded.

"Will you join me in my chambers, then?"

My heart immediately sped up at what awaited in the next several minutes. *Something* did. I knew this because it felt as if something shifted between us. That there had been a change. There had to be because I didn't argue with him or myself. I rose and went into the bathing chamber to take care of my personal needs and brush my teeth. I was inexplicably nervous as I walked out and saw him waiting by the adjoining door, the bottle of wine from supper in his hand.

My heart started tripping all over the place for some silly reason as he closed the door behind me and followed me into his chamber. It was only then that I remembered I wore nothing but the tiny piece of undergarment under the robe.

Oh, dear.

Nyktos offered me the bottle of wine as he eased past. I shook my head, deciding that I'd had more than enough. I sat on the edge of the bed, fingers fiddling with the tiny buttons on the robe as he excused himself and disappeared into the bathing chamber. All I managed to do while he was gone was scoot back a foot or so and tuck my legs under the hem of the robe. Then Nyktos returned.

Shirtless. The buttons of his leathers undone.

Neither of those two things helped with the nervousness I felt as I watched him walk toward me, the hair against his cheek and the bronze flesh of his neck and upper chest damp.

He sat before me. "May I?"

Stomach joining the flipping and flopping of my heart, I nodded.

Like the night before, he tucked the braid between his thumb and pointer finger and slowly, almost methodically, ran his fingers down it. I bit the inside of my lip as the back of his hand grazed the swell of my breast. I could barely feel his touch through the thicker robe, but a shiver still skated through me.

Nyktos unwound the hair band, slipping it onto his wrist. Then he set about undoing the braid and didn't speak until he'd finished. "I've been thinking," he said, thick lashes lowering as he drew the length of my hair over my shoulder. "About the demands you made."

"I wouldn't say they were demands." I watched him draw his fingers through my hair.

"What would you call them?"

"Gentle requests."

Nyktos laughed roughly. "Which part was gentle, Sera? The kicking me, or the holding your dagger to my throat?"

"The part where I didn't hurt you."

One side of his lips curved up. "There was one demand you didn't make."

"Which one was that?"

He spun one of my curls around his finger. "The offer you made in my office."

My heart immediately began its rapid beating.

"That wasn't part of your demands."

"But it was." I took a breath.

"Really?" He unwound the curl, letting it lay against my chest. "I'm positive I wouldn't have forgotten you bringing that up."

I dragged my teeth over my lower lip as he picked up another piece of hair. "The offer was a part of my request to be of help."

Lashes lifted, and quicksilver eyes locked onto mine.

"In whatever way I'm *needed*," I reminded him, my blood warming.

His lips parted, revealing a hint of his fangs. "That's good to know." His voice was rougher, harder. "So, that offer you made? Pleasure for the sake of pleasure? It still stands?"

A mix of emotions swirled through me as my hands fell to the bed. Sweet anticipation and blade-sharp desire crashed into a wild sort of anticipation that carried just the faintest twinge of something I couldn't name or place, but I said, "Yes."

Wisps of eather bled out from behind his pupils, lashing his irises. "Are you sure?"

"I am." And I was.

A ragged exhale left Nyktos. He lifted his hand, placing just the tips of his fingers against my face. I barely felt the faint energy shock as he sat there, still except for his fingers. He drew them down my cheek. His skin was a little warmer. Not as much as it had been before I'd hit him with eather, but what little blood he'd taken from me this afternoon had impacted him.

"Thirty-six," he murmured, trailing his fingers along my jawline. His thumb coasted over my bottom lip. "Still thirty-six freckles."

I started to grin.

"I wanted to make sure I'd counted them correctly." His fingers spread across my other cheek and then down the side of my throat to the panel of the robe folded across my chest. "You have two more." His hand slipped over my right breast. He cupped the weight through the robe, drawing a breathy exhale from me. "Right here." He ran his thumb across the area above my nipple. "Two little freckles right there. I think there's another on the side."

My trembling fingers dug into the blanket beneath me. "Do you want to check?"

"I do."

I leaned back a little, giving him access to the short row of buttons. Allowing him to take the lead. Wanting him to. Needing that.

And he did.

His fingers danced over the buttons, quickly undoing them. The material loosened at my shoulders. He said nothing as he slid his hand under one panel of the robe. The eather brightened in his eyes as his skin came into contact with my bare flesh. "Sera…" My name was a growl as he pushed the panels apart. The callused pads of his fingers and his palms elicited a sharp spike of pleasure, and I felt the intensity of his gaze as he bared more and more of me to him. The robe slid down my back, catching at my wrists. The tips of my breasts tingled, hardening under his gaze.

"Fuck," he breathed, his throat working on a swallow. His head tilted. The tips of his fingers grazed the side of my breast. "I was right. There's another freckle here."

My skin felt as if it were on fire. "Do you think there are more?"

"I know there are."

"Where?"

His hand skimmed my waist and then skipped to my bent knees. He gently pushed them down, straightening them. Spreading them. His lips parted even more as he saw the scrap of black lace. "I approve."

My cheeks warmed. "You have Erlina to thank."

"That, I do." He ran his hand up my inner thigh, stopping midway. "Three little freckles right here, clustered together." Both of his hands ran up my thighs to the thin strip of silky lace. "Your freckles are like a constellation."

I lifted my hips as he drew the lace down over my legs and then pulled the undergarment off. His hands returned to my hips, and I let out a startled gasp as he tugged me to the edge of the bed. He lowered himself to his knees on the floor. A pulse of pleasure darted through me as his gaze fixed on the throbbing space between my legs.

"That's another name I'll need to come up with. What I'll call this constellation," he said, threading an arm under my hips as he hooked one of my legs over his shoulder. The position forced me back onto my elbows. "I'm always more creative when I have something sweet on my tongue."

Air lodged in my throat as Nyktos lowered his head. His breath on the sensitive flesh there caused my hips to jump. My fingers dug into the blanket as he turned his head, dragging his lips along the inside of my thigh. Then over the very center of me.

My head fell back as his tongue traced the plump flesh there, unerringly finding his way to the ultra-sensitive joining of nerves. When his mouth closed over me, I cried out, shaking. He sucked softly, then harder, and the sound he made at the rush of damp arousal vibrated all the way through me. His head shifted, then his tongue was inside me, and he gave another throaty growl. I moved, rocking my hips against the wickedness of his tongue. He tasted me. Licked. Drank from me without drawing my blood, and the throbbing deep inside me intensified. His head turned, and the edge of his fang skated across the turgid flesh. I came apart. Hard. Fast.

I was still coming as his mouth left mine and he rose, his lips glossy and swollen as he shucked off his breeches. I was still shaking, muscles coiling and spinning at the sight of him, thick and hard, jutting out. I was still trembling as he lifted me, hauling me farther back on the bed. And I could barely breathe as his eyes locked on mine and he came toward me, the strands of his hair falling against his cheeks. The shortness of breath wasn't bad. It wasn't sparked by panic as he eased me onto my back. I lay there, skin tingling all over as he braced his weight on his strong arms. The catching in my breath and chest felt different.

All of this felt different.

It was that change from earlier. That intangible shift between us. What was occurring was fundamentally different than before. This wasn't a desire fueled by the need for blood, feeding, or anger. This was pleasure for the sake of pleasure. And it was…

It was a first for us.

And it felt like a first for me altogether. Any experience I had, fled. Nothing I knew before this moment seemed to count. I couldn't explain it.

Neither of us moved, even though I was trembling again. I didn't think he even breathed as he stared down at me, his eyes a storm of whirling eather. Then I moved, clasping his cheeks and bringing his mouth to mine. I kissed him because this *was* different.

He kissed me back, and I tasted myself on his lips and on his tongue. I was greedy. *We* were greedy, kissing and kissing until he moved, reaching between us to grip himself. The feel of his cock dragging through my wetness was a tantalizing promise of what was to come, and I didn't have to wait long. He eased into me, and the feel of him—the pressure and fullness—dragged a ragged cry from me. Nyktos stopped.

"It's okay," I said against his lips. "Don't stop. Please."

"You never have to beg," he promised. "Never."

Then he thrust into me to the hilt, and my cry was lost in his groan. He stilled again, chest to chest with me, his forehead resting against mine. I felt every breath he took and every beat of his heart in those moments. Then he began to move again, slow and steady retreats and even more decadent plunges. I curled my arms around his neck, my legs around his hips. He shuddered as he rocked gently, and I found his mouth again as the crescendo of sensations began to build once more.

We moved together. Our lips. Our tongues. Hands. Hips. Slow, teasing, shorter and shallow thrusts gave way to longer, deeper ones. My legs and arms tightened around him. He moved faster. Harder. The friction of his chest against mine enflamed the fire in my blood and my core, and those embers…they hummed inside me as Nyktos's skin began to harden against mine. Shadows gathered under his flesh, and as he lifted his head, streaks of eather filled the veins beneath his eyes. His features turned stark as he pounded into me, moving us up the bed as that tension tightened and tightened.

"Oh, gods," I whispered, clutching the back of his neck. I called his name as the tension broke again, this time far more intense and all-consuming.

Because I heard the word he whispered against my lips in that harsh, raw voice as he shuddered, his hips churning against mine. The one word that caused the pleasure to roll on endlessly.

"*Liessa.*"

22

Nyktos was gone when I woke but returned before I rose, almost as if he'd sensed that I'd awakened. He'd had a bath drawn for me and had breakfast ready when I finished. He'd been mostly silent throughout the meal—not distant or cold, just quiet, and I didn't let myself dwell on the reasons for why he had little to say. Instead, as I got ready, I allowed myself to enjoy last night, focusing on what he'd shared about the Primals' morality and the pleasure that had come afterward. I had so many more clothing options this morning and settled on a pair of laced leggings, a white blouse, and a black vest that had been tailored just for *me*. And I let myself enjoy that, too. Other than the wedding gown I loathed, everything else had been hand-me-downs. But not these. The clothing lining the wardrobe now belonged only to me, and that was a strangely empowering feeling that stayed with me as Nyktos and I left the palace to enter the mortal realm.

Despite what Nyktos had claimed that morning as he summoned Odin from his silver cuff, the steed was *not* over me holding a dagger to Nyktos's throat.

Odin eyed me as if he were debating biting me as I approached him. That disposition hadn't changed as we traveled the road I'd arrived in the Shadowlands on, but it hadn't diminished my excitement as the Primal mist enveloped us.

I was going to see Ezra.

nd I was about to see my lake.

wo things I'd feared never seeing again.

he white haze blotted out the realm as I tensed. I knew it would be temporary, but the inability to see still filled me with unease.

Nyktos's arm tightened around me. "Just a few more seconds," he , his voice soft against my temple.

I nodded, grasping the pommel of Odin's saddle. *Seconds*, I reminded myself, and seconds was all it took for the haze to scatter, and for a stream of faint light to pierce the brief void of darkness that came afterward.

Sunlight.

My lips parted as the mist eased off, revealing the lake's shadowstone floor and the still waters on either side of us. Seeing the lake split in two as if held back by invisible walls was an unsettling sight.

And an impressive one.

I tipped my head back as Odin took us across the lake. Only a faint, fractured sunlight pierced the clouds overhead. The heavy scent of rain hung in the air, and I hoped that meant some much-needed rain had already fallen—or would—and not the drizzle that did nothing but increase the humidity—something I was already beginning to feel under the cloak…the thinner of the two new ones Erlina had made for me. The soft material would soon become nearly unbearable, but it was wise for us to keep our faces hidden.

Nyktos lifted his hand once we were on the bank. The water immediately fell back into place, and he glanced down at me. "Impressed?"

"No."

He chuckled roughly, urging Odin into the Dark Elms. I cracked a grin as I scanned the ripples from the waterfall cascading off the Elysium Peaks and spreading across my lake, my chest feeling looser than it had in weeks. I kept my eyes on it until I could no longer see even a hint of the water, then faced forward, pushing down the keen yearning to feel the water on my skin and slip beneath the surface.

"I wish we could linger," Nyktos said after traveling a few moments in silence, his hand shifting on my hip. "So you could enjoy your lake." His thumb began moving in idle circles just above the waistband of my breeches. "Once it's safe, I promise we will return to your lake. You can come back as often as you like."

I pressed my lips together as the back of my throat suddenly burned with emotion. I'd likely projected something in that moment, and that wasn't surprising to discover. The lake felt like a part of me, and I wasn't sure if the fact that it was a gateway to the Shadowlands had anything to do with it. But what brought the faint sting to my eyes was his response.

His promise.

"I'd like that," I whispered.

We said nothing more as Odin navigated the thick clusters of trees. The Dark Elms were quiet, not even the faint moan or wail of a lost spirit could be heard. The breeze didn't even penetrate the woods. When we neared the edges, and the walls of Wayfair Castle came into view, a strange sense of nervousness filled me.

"We should walk the remaining distance," I suggested. "Any guards who spot us will already be suspicious of two people coming out of the Dark Elms. Odin will draw even more attention."

Odin huffed.

"It's because you're rather large," I said to the top of Odin's head. "And very beautiful."

He gave another huff.

I sighed.

Nyktos drew the horse to a halt. "He appreciates the compliments."

"Doubtful."

"He does." Nyktos swung himself off the horse with ease. "He just likes being dramatic."

Odin turned his head to Nyktos as he puffed out another aggravated-sounding breath. I gripped Nyktos's arms, accepting his aid as he lifted me by the waist. He was close, and as he lowered me to the ground, I was treated to a full-body slide that sent a rush of pleasure through me.

His hands lingered on my hips, the weight and feel of them igniting a pleasant hum in my blood and chest, where the embers wiggled. I lifted my gaze to his. The eather in his eyes had faded to a faint pulse behind his pupils.

"Ready?" he asked.

I nodded.

Nyktos didn't move. Neither did I, and the hue of his eyes heated to quicksilver. I thought he might kiss me just to kiss me, even though we didn't have time for that. Something about seeing him in the mortal realm made him seem more reckless, impulsive. More like…

Ash.

His jaw tightened as his hands left my hips and found the hood of my cloak. I didn't understand the small burst of disappointment. Kissing simply for the sake of kissing felt like something…more.

And while what we were now felt like something different than before, and definitely not like those hasty bids for pleasure I'd experienced in the Luxe, we were not *more*.

Nyktos lifted the hood of my cloak and then his. Pulling myself out of the somewhat-troubling direction my mind had gone, I turned to the wall and got myself moving.

"The guards who normally patrol this section of the wall aren't the most…astute," I told him, enjoying the feel and sound of the crunch of fallen branches under my boots. "They will likely assume that we're a part of the staff since the Dark Elms—"

"Are private property?" He grinned as I shot him a look from beneath the cowl of my hood.

"Nice of you to acknowledge that now."

Nyktos chuckled.

"But I was going to say since everyone avoids the Dark Elms, and they can't be accessed from outside the Wayfair grounds," I continued, "they'll probably think we didn't actually enter them…" I trailed off as we cleared the last of the heavily branched elms.

My mouth dropped open at what I saw.

Nyktos stopped. "Is something amiss?"

"The gates to Wayfair are open." I stared. "And there are…people."

There were people everywhere. Not nobles but *the* people of Lasania. They milled about the wall, their faces glistening with a sheen of sweat as some carried baskets and others armfuls of sacks.

"I'm guessing that's not normal?"

"No." I shook my head in confusion. "This isn't normal at all."

I started walking, half-afraid there had been some sort of uprising. If so, I couldn't blame the people for fighting back, but that likely wouldn't have ended well for any ruling party.

A fine drizzle began to fall, and many of those in the courtyard lifted the cowls sewn into their shirts and vests. I picked up my pace as we crossed the uneven, rocky soil and passed through the gates. Guards were stationed inside the easternmost part of the courtyard, but none in the ridiculous plum-puffed waistcoats and pantaloons of the Royal Guard. I squinted, searching the many entrances of Wayfair's east wing for them.

The doors there were open, unguarded.

I almost tripped over myself when I saw a young mother and her two red-haired children sitting beneath one of the purplish-pink jacaranda trees. Their plain linen shirts and gowns made it clear that they weren't nobles.

Shocked by what I was seeing, it wasn't until we were close to the entrances near the kitchens that I noticed those around us had become aware of our presence.

Steps slowed. Some stopped completely. A guard rubbed at the nape of his neck, frowning as he glanced around. A father holding the hand of a young girl toddling beside him pulled her closer as he carried a sack in his other arm. Others looked up at the sky as if searching for an explanation for the sudden drop in temperature.

The air *had* cooled.

Not by a lot, but enough that people noticed as nervous gazes bounced over us and then darted back.

"They feel me," Nyktos explained under his breath. "They don't know what they feel, but they know *something* is among them."

I frowned. "Does this happen every time you visit the mortal realm?"

"No, but I normally avoid large crowds for this reason," he said. "A handful of mortals has little impact. But this many? It gets the essence pumping, and it becomes almost like a tangible entity—not seen but felt. And what they feel unsettles them."

Because what they felt was death.

I glanced up at Nyktos as we entered the hall, but his features were hidden beneath the hood. "Does it bother you?" I asked quietly. "Their reaction?"

"What they feel is natural," he replied. "It does not bother me."

I stepped to the side to make way for a maid hurrying into the kitchens, her arms full of dishes. Her face blanched as she crossed before us, but she didn't look at us as she disappeared into the castle. "Honestly?"

"Honestly." Nyktos's fingers brushed mine, creating a faint zap of energy. "What they're feeling is instinct, and that instinct is telling them not to loiter near me. And they shouldn't."

Because all Primals impacted mortals simply by being in their company. The length of time before a mortal felt a Primal's effect varied. Some mortals would be more susceptible to violence or lust, and some Primals would likely *ensure* their presence was felt, but Nyktos was a Primal of Death. His presence could kill if he wasn't careful.

"How can I be bothered by their sense of self-perseveration?" Nyktos finished.

But Kolis had been.

It was part of what had driven his jealousy toward his brother—the fear that even I could sense in those who passed as we walked the hall mostly used by servants.

I nibbled on my lip as my steps slowed. Unease grew, having much to do with the fact that no one had stopped to question us. It caused my fear regarding some sort of uprising to grow, but it was also because the last time I'd walked this hall was the last day I'd spent in the mortal realm.

My instinct guided me to the one place I did not want to revisit.

The Great Hall.

Nyktos's hand brushed mine once more. "You okay?"

Stomach churning like the fans overhead, I nodded. "Yeah. Yes." I cleared my throat. "I'm just concerned about Ezra."

I could feel Nyktos's gaze on me as I forced myself through the marble pillars carved with golden scrollwork. *Breathe in*, I reminded myself as my chest tightened.

The Great Hall was as I remembered. Mostly.

Mauve banners hung from the dome-shaped glass ceiling, bearing the golden Royal Crest, that of a crown of leaves with a sword striking through the center. It still reminded me of someone being stabbed in the head. *Hold*. Far fewer people milled about the Hall. My gaze traveled down the marble and limestone and over the gold veining. The crack in the floor was new, caused by Nyktos's arrival when he saw what Tavius had been doing to me. *Breathe out*. I started to look at the statue of Kolis—

Nyktos's hand curled around mine, sending a jolt of surprise through me. My gaze flew to him.

His head was tilted forward. "I believe I've found your stepsister." He then gently squeezed my hand before releasing it.

Swallowing, I made myself look past the statue I'd been forced on my knees before as my stepbrother split my back open with a whip.

Two diamond and citrine thrones sat on the raised dais at the end of the Hall. Neither was draped in white or scattered with black roses to mourn their lost King.

The King I'd ultimately killed.

I winced, reminding myself that how I felt about that had more to do with the embers than with me.

The thrones were empty, but I saw Ezra. Suddenly, it was easier to breathe.

Ezra sat in a much less elaborate chair at the foot of the dais, her light brown hair swept up in a neat bun. There was no crown upon her head as she listened to a man across the table from her speak, one who leaned over a stack of parchment. The man's clothing and posture screamed *noble*, and the angry flush to his olive skin warned that he was unhappy. Guards stood behind Ezra, two to her left and two to her right. They were dressed as those on the wall were: tunics, breeches, armor.

The corners of my lips turned up as I saw that Ezra, despite the humidity, wore a neatly tailored waistcoat minus any frills. My smile spread when I spotted the familiar tilt of her stubborn jaw as she responded to whatever the man was saying. I was sure it was keen, clever, and deliciously cutting.

"I believe she is hosting a town hall," Nyktos commented.

Heart slowing, I nodded. That was exactly what Ezra was doing, and just as I'd imagined, she did not hold one from a throne or a balcony, far away from the people. She sat with them.

And she'd also opened the gates of Wayfair to them.

Nyktos's head turned sharply. A guard slowly approached us, his hand on the hilt of his sword.

He stopped several feet from us, his throat bobbing. "The Queen is currently seeing the last of those who wish to speak with her today," he said, and it pleased me to hear her referred to as Queen. "You may make an appointment to do so tomorrow by visiting the record keeper at the gatehouse."

It also pleased me that what Ezra was doing appeared to be more than just holding a weekly or biweekly town hall.

"We cannot return tomorrow," Nyktos spoke, and I swore the air chilled a bit. "We need to speak with the Queen today, and as soon as possible."

The guard visibly paled as he stared into the shadowy recesses of Nyktos's hood.

I cut the Primal a look and then stepped forward. "We do need to speak with her today," I said, gentling my tone. "And I believe she will make time for us if you tell her that Sera is here to speak with her."

The guard didn't budge as his wide-eyed gaze bounced between Nyktos and me. I could sense that he was about to hold his ground.

"Go," Nyktos urged, moving a foot closer in that quiet, unnatural way of his. He tilted his head back, letting the hood slip a few inches. "And speak with your Queen. *Now.*"

Whatever the guard heard or saw got him moving. He pivoted,

hurrying off.

I turned to Nyktos. "Did you use compulsion?"

"No." He laughed softly. "I think I just scared him."

"Rude," I murmured as I walked the secondary wall of pillars encircling the main floor and entered the private alcove furnished with settees and chairs.

He laughed again. "Perhaps."

I snorted, scanning those in the Hall, telling myself that I wasn't looking for one person in particular, but I didn't see her, nonetheless. We neared the dais just in time to see the guard work up his nerve to interrupt his Queen. I saw the moment he spoke my name.

Ezra went rigid for a heartbeat and then shot to her feet, pressing a hand to her slender waist. The noble across from her hastily followed as she searched the floor. I waited, knowing Ezra would remember that I'd favored the alcove the few times I was in the Great Hall.

She took a step forward before turning sharply. When she spotted us, she stilled once more, likely in disbelief. But Ezra was not one prone to panic. She was logical and calm in all things, and she was then, as well.

Turning to the man, she excused herself. The noble wasn't thrilled, but she turned her back on him anyway. She spoke to her guards, who scattered, quickly clearing the Great Hall, taking the noble with them.

Nyktos was quiet as Ezra approached us. The doors to the Hall closed, and only two guards remained, stationed in front of them.

Ezra halted at the top of the short set of steps. "Seraphena?" Her voice was barely a whisper as she glanced beside me. I saw her visibly swallow.

I stepped forward and lowered the hood of my cloak. "Ezra."

She jerked, her eyes widening.

"Or should I say, Queen Ezmeria?" I added, bowing.

"Don't you dare do that." Ezra snapped forward, reaching for me but stopping short. "I'm Ezra. Just Ezra to you."

A twinge of disappointment rose at the knowledge that she was still uncomfortable touching me, but as I straightened and saw that Nyktos had moved in closer, I realized her reaction might have had more to do with that.

"My gods, I thought the guard had misheard," she said, glancing at Nyktos with wide brown eyes. "I didn't think I'd ever…"

"See me again," I finished, and she nodded. "Because I was supposed to kill this one?" I added, jerking my thumb at Nyktos.

"Nice," Nyktos remarked dryly under his breath.

Blood drained rapidly from Ezra's face, and I wasn't sure if it was because of what I'd said or because Nyktos had lowered his hood.

Ezra clearly hadn't forgotten what he looked like when she'd seen him last. "I think I need to sit down—" She caught herself before doing so, beginning to kneel. "I'm sorry, Your Highness. I—"

"That is unnecessary," he interrupted. "Please, sit. We do not have long, and I fear you may pass out if you continue standing."

Ezra blinked slowly. "I have never fainted."

The Primal smiled, revealing just a hint of fang. "There is always a first time."

"Please, sit," I jumped in. "He's right. We don't have long, and there's something I need to talk to you about."

Ezra sat in the chair. "Is it the supposed-to-kill-him part?"

I choked on a laugh as I sat on the settee next to her chair. Nyktos crossed his arms, remaining standing. "It kind of is," I said, glancing around the now-empty floor of the Great Hall. My gaze got caught on the statue of Kolis for a brief second. I swallowed. "I'm sure you have many questions."

"Loads," she murmured.

"As do I," I went on. "But as I said, we cannot stay long, so I must get right to it." I took a shallow breath, remembering what Nyktos had advised could and couldn't be shared. "What we thought ended the Rot was wrong. The deal my ancestor made didn't cause the Rot upon my birth."

Ezra gripped the arm of the chair as she looked between us. "I don't know much about deals, so please forgive my ignorance on the subject, but the deal expired once fulfilled?"

"Or believed to be ended in favor of the summoner if the Primal is killed," Nyktos tacked on, his voice deceptively level.

"And that," Ezra said. "That, too."

I turned to Nyktos, my eyes narrowed.

His brows lifted. "What?"

"Just so you know, I was never a fan of the deal," Ezra continued.

"Because it wouldn't be wise to attempt to kill a Primal?" Nyktos surmised.

"Yes, but mainly because it was unfair to Sera."

That wasn't news to me, but it was still good to hear that.

Nyktos said nothing, but he eyed Ezra a tad less intensely than before.

Taking another breath, I faced Ezra again. Her brows were furrowed into thin slashes as she looked between us. "There would've been changes when the deal was fulfilled. The climate would return to what it was before, less temperate, as I believe it already has." That explained the hotter, longer summers full of drought and the vicious storms. "The ground wouldn't be as fertile as it once was, thanks to the deal, but Lasania would've returned to how it was meant to be, which didn't include the Rot."

Ezra leaned back, and I could practically see her turning the information over in her head. "Then what *is* the Rot?" she asked.

"You believe her? That easily?" Nyktos demanded before I could answer. "Didn't you and your families—her ancestors—believe the deal was the cause of the Rot?"

"I believe her," Ezra said, her chin lifting.

"Because I am here?"

"Well, your presence may have a little to do with it."

His head cocked. "A little."

"Just a bit," she said. "But I know how important saving Lasania was for Sera. She would not lie about something, knowing what it meant for her kingdom."

Her kingdom.

I briefly closed my eyes. "Lasania was never mine."

"That's not true. You should've been Queen, Sera. Not me. If I can acknowledge that, you should be able to."

Curling my fingers around my knees, I said, "But you are Queen, and that's what matters now. You'll be able to handle what I'm about to tell you, unlike my—" I cut myself off, took a moment, then continued. "The Rot was caused by something else entirely. Something much more complicated than a deal."

Ezra was quiet for a moment. "And whatever it is, you cannot tell me?"

"No," I said quietly.

"Then…" Her shoulders stiffened. "Then there is no stopping the Rot?"

"We're going to do our damnedest to stop it. I swear," I promised. "But nothing is guaranteed. There is a chance—"

"Barely," Nyktos growled.

"A small chance," I amended, "that we could fail. That's why I came today. I wanted to warn you so you could prepare." I thought about what Holland had told me and the people outside with their baskets and bushels. "But I think you've already begun to do that."

"Yes. I have," she said, her grip easing on the arm of the chair. "You know how I've felt about how the Rot was handled. I felt that we should be doing everything we could to build the pantries of the people, not just our own."

"The people we saw on the way in?" Nyktos said, asking his first non-antagonistic question.

"We've started a bit of a food bank where people can come on certain days, at certain times, if they have need," she explained. "I've also been in talks with the King and Queen of Terra, in hopes of strengthening their faith in Lasania. I believe I am being successful in such talks." A small smile appeared. "I believe we simply needed to prove that an alliance with us is beneficial. Something my father, gods rest his soul, was never that great in relaying."

I managed to fight back a cringe. Ezra loved her father, and I... My stare shifted to what would've been his throne.

"And how are you succeeding at that?" Nyktos asked.

I sucked in a soft breath, blinking. I didn't think Nyktos was all that curious about what Ezra was doing. He might have simply been preventing me from blurting out what I'd caused.

Which I likely would have.

And Ezra didn't need to know that.

"They have many fertile fields primed for crops, unlike us," she said. "But we have one thing in abundance that Terra does not. Labor. Paid labor, involving those who wish to relocate to Terra—at least for part of the year. Our talks are going well."

That was very smart.

"But if the Rot continues to spread..." She trailed off.

I nodded. "Has it spread?"

"A bit more. We've lost a few more farms, but it hasn't sped up or anything like that," she confirmed. I thought of the Masseys, knowing that their farm had to be one of those lost. "It is good to know this— what you've shared. It gives me, well, I don't know how else to say it, but it gives me hope."

My brows rose. "You didn't think I'd succeed at killing him?"

"I wasn't quite sure you'd succeed at the whole making-him-fall-in-love part," she corrected.

"Wow," I muttered.

"You are a bit...temperamental. And those around you do have a tendency to end up stabbed," she began with a sheepish grin. "I figured you'd probably get yourself killed by growing impatient and just stabbing him."

Nyktos barked out a short laugh. "Now, *that* was incredibly astute."

I narrowed my eyes at him.

Ezra opened her mouth, closed it, and then appeared to try again. "I am very…confused by you."

Nyktos stared down at her. "You are?"

She nodded. "You are Death."

"I am."

"You are not very Death-like."

His head tilted. "And how is one…Death-like?"

"We cannot stay much longer," I cut in, half-afraid of whatever Ezra might say.

"Must you leave?" Ezra asked. "Mari is currently with her father, but she should be arriving soon."

"I really would love to see her, but we cannot." I glanced at the doors. "Where is—?" I stopped myself from asking. I didn't need to know where my mother was. I didn't care. "How is your Consort?"

"Perfect." A bright smile appeared, lighting up her entire face. That was what *more* looked like. "She is utterly perfect."

"Good. I'm happy to hear that."

Her eyes searched mine, and I could tell she had much she wanted to ask. Wanted to say. "I…after everything happened here, I sent a missive to the Vodina Isles to check on Sir Holland, but I have not heard anything in return."

"Oh." I smiled. "I believe he's fine."

"You do?" Her gaze sharpened.

"It's time." Nyktos swooped in, nipping the string of questions Ezra surely had in the bud.

It was hard, but I stood in agreement.

"Will I see you again?" Ezra asked, the same as I had asked of Holland.

I gave her a far more hopeful answer. "I believe so."

"I hope so, too. I really do." Her voice thickened. "I miss you."

The breath I exhaled was ragged. "I miss you, too." I turned, hurrying to join Nyktos at the steps as the burn in my throat increased.

"Sera?" Ezra rose, stopping me. "Remember what you said about the lands tainted by the Rot? And why couldn't they be used to build homes for those in Croft's Cross living in the most cramped conditions?"

My brows knitted. "Yes?"

"That's where Mari and her father are. At the ruined lands. They're going to build homes. Nothing extravagant, but I discovered stores of lumber—at least enough to start with," she told me. "It was your idea. I thought you should know."

I left the Great Hall feeling far better than when I'd arrived. My chest was looser, even though sadness lingered.

I hoped I got to see Ezra again. And Marisol.

I glanced at the silent figure beside me. Nyktos was quiet as we traveled the hall. He'd lifted his hood already, and I would, too, once we stepped outside. "I'm glad—" We rounded the bend.

And came face-to-face with…her.

My mother.

I halted.

She stopped.

Neither of us said anything as we stared at each other. The low growl of displeasure radiating from Nyktos caused me to realize I'd taken a step back.

"You look well," I said, snapping out of my stupor. And she did. Her hair, only a shade or two darker than mine, was perfectly coiffed in an elaborate updo. An amber stone glittered from her neck, and the lavender gown draping her trim figure was perfect for her. There were shadows beneath her eyes, though. Perhaps a few more wrinkles than I remembered.

She clasped her hands—hands absent of jewelry. "As do you." Shock was etched into each of her features—features I shared with her, except everything about her was more refined.

I bit back the caustic retort that rose to the tip of my tongue.

"A guard said that someone with your name had arrived," she went on, sending the figure beside me a quick, uncertain glance. With his face hidden, she had no idea who stood there. "I didn't think it was true."

"It was." I fixed a tight smile on my lips. She would have questions, too, but where Ezra's would've been driven by curiosity, hers would've stemmed from the belief that I'd failed.

And I didn't want to see that fill her expression once the surprise faded. I didn't want to hear it in her voice.

I'd heard it enough throughout my life. I truly didn't need to see her. Hear her. Look upon her again. And I realized that was a blessed relief. "I came to speak with Ezra, and I have. Now, I must leave. Excuse me." I sidestepped, giving her a wide berth as I put one foot in front of the other.

"Seraphena."

I stopped, my eyes lifting to Nyktos. I saw nothing of his face, but his displeasure was becoming what he'd spoken of outside: a tangible entity, unseen but felt. Slowly, I faced her.

"I..." She cast a nervous glance in Nyktos's direction. "I didn't know Tavius was planning to do what he did—"

"That does not matter." Nyktos spoke, lowering his hood.

My mother gasped as she stumbled back, her hand fluttering to her chest. She dropped to her knees, the lavender gown pooling on the floor as she placed a shaking hand on the marble. "Your Highness."

His lip curled with distaste. "You had to know that your stepson was capable of harming your daughter, and yet...you did nothing to prevent it." Eather crackled from his eyes. "His death was not the only one owed that day. The fact that you still breathe is due to a grace you do not deserve."

She paled to the shade of my hair. "T-thank you," she said, trembling.

"Do not thank me. It was not I who saved your life. I wanted to take it. To put you where you belong, beside that bastard of a mortal you would've crowned King," Nyktos said, essence rippling over his skin. "It was your *daughter*. For reasons unbeknownst to me, she told me no. That is who you should spend the rest of your undeserved life thanking."

23

Hours after returning from the mortal realm and spending the better part of the afternoon training with Bele, who had been more than happy to knock me on my ass repeatedly, I was utterly, gloriously exhausted.

The edges of Nyktos's hair tickled my cheek as his lips grazed my brow, his heart pounding as fast as mine. Biting down on my lip, my nails skated over the coiled muscles along his spine, my back arching as he shuddered above me and deep inside me.

His raw, heated groan as he joined me in finding release sent a burst of rippling delight through me, nearly as potent as the waves of pleasure I'd experienced only moments before.

And that was a...a new discovery for me—the ecstasy that came from the knowledge that he was just as satisfied as I was. It wasn't like I hadn't cared if my previous partners found pleasure or not. It was that I, well, I never thought about it.

So maybe I *hadn't* cared?

But I did when it came to Nyktos.

His cool fingers smoothed my damp hair back as he dropped a sweet kiss onto my forehead. My heart gave a silly little leap.

He eased away from me onto his side, and I immediately missed the feel of him.

Nyktos was quiet as his hand drifted over the curve of my shoulder, along my collarbone, and then lower, over the peak of my breast. I, too, was quiet as I lay still, allowing him to explore. Reveling in it.

The rough pads of his fingers danced over one puckered nipple, drawing a quick breath from me before he moved on, tracing the swells and dips of my body. Finding it somewhat odd that his touch could heighten my senses, driving me to the brink while also providing such soothing calm, my eyes fluttered closed, and my thoughts drifted in the silence.

Our trip to Lasania was at the forefront of my mind. Knowing that Ezra more than had things together was such a relief. I turned my head toward Nyktos slightly. "I know you probably think the trip today was unnecessary."

"I don't think that."

"Really?" My eyes opened. Soft, buttery light from the nearby lamp cast a warm glow over half his face. "Because I...I think I knew—no, I *did* know that Ezra would be preparing no matter what, even if Holland hadn't said anything. But I had to make sure."

"I understand." Thick lashes shielded his eyes as his gaze avidly followed his fingers. "And I also understand that maybe you just needed to see her."

My chest warmed and swelled. That *was* likely what had driven my motivations. Because some part of me, a deeply rooted dread, feared that I wouldn't get a chance to see her again.

Nyktos's plans will work. I repeated that over and over until that dread retreated. I cleared my throat, focusing on the fact that Nyktos wasn't irritated by the risky trip. He could've been, and, at the very least, he could've pointed out that it had been unnecessary.

Gods knew I probably would have.

Which made me feel like I had more of my mother in me than I wanted to acknowledge. I squirmed a little.

"What are you thinking about?" Nyktos asked, his fingers stopping at my hip.

I turned my gaze to the ceiling. "Did I project?"

"You did." He paused. "I tasted tartness and...something sour."

My brows rose. "Not sure what that translates into."

"Confusion," he answered. "And shame."

"Nice," I muttered, feeling my cheeks heat. "You must often find yourself with bad tastes in your mouth."

"Sometimes." His hand curled around my hip. "You going to tell me what you were thinking about?"

"Do I have to?"

He chuckled. "No."

My lips pursed. "Do you want me to?"

"I wouldn't have asked if I didn't, but I'm sure you already know that."

I did.

"I was...thinking about my mother."

Nyktos shifted closer so his chest touched my arm and one of his legs brushed mine. "I wish you wouldn't."

"Same." I sighed.

His fingers left my hip, going to where several curls were tangled together on my arm. He set about unraveling them. "Was it what I said to her?"

"Good gods, no." My gaze shot to his. "I wish I could relive that moment over and over: her just staring at you, open-mouthed as we walked away."

A faint grin appeared. "But I probably should've kept my mouth shut. She's your mother. Yours to deal with."

"But I...I don't want to deal with her. I realized that today. That's why I didn't, you know, engage with her. Mainly because I just knew she would piss me off. But also because I..." My brows snapped together. "Because I just don't care. My confusion or shame or whatever you were picking up on had to do with thinking that parts of me are like her. And I...I don't like that."

"I think all of us have parts of us that are like our parents, but that doesn't mean we *are* them."

"True," I murmured, wondering what my father was like for the millionth time.

"And the not-caring part? It's not necessarily a bad thing." He curled one finger around a strand of hair. "Just because someone shares the same bloodline as you doesn't mean they deserve your time or thoughts."

"You're right." My gaze swept over his features. "You, more than anyone, would understand that."

Nyktos's fingers stilled around the curl. "Yeah. I would," he said, the sudden flatness of the sentence alarming me. "And that's why neither of us is going to spend another moment thinking about those we're unfortunately related to."

He rolled his large body onto mine then, and within seconds, I wasn't thinking about anything but him and the way he kissed. And how he used his mouth and tongue. His fingers and his cock. He chased away those other thoughts.

Even the dread that clung like a shadow and haunted like a ghost.

Hair still damp, I threaded the strands into a braid as I walked with Ector to Nyktos's office the following morning. According to what Orphine had shared as I ate my breakfast, I was to meet the Primal there when ready. Since the trip to the Vale wasn't scheduled until tomorrow, I hoped that Nyktos was fulfilling another of my demands.

Training.

But I wasn't sure, and it wasn't like I'd had a chance to ask Nyktos this morning. He had been gone when I woke.

Using one of the final bands I could find in the bathing chamber, I made a mental note to ask about the ones Nyktos had been taking after undoing my braids. He'd put them around his wrist, but they were nowhere to be seen after that. What was he doing with them? Using them in his hair? I focused on that instead of the blood I had seen again earlier when I cleaned my teeth. I refused to think about that.

"You're smiling," Ector commented, glancing down at me. "I feel like I should be worried when you're smiling."

I snorted. "There's nothing to be worried about."

"Uh-huh."

I felt my smile grow as we descended the stairs and I thought about last night. Every moment had felt like some sort of wild dream. Nyktos had shared dinner with me again, and then we'd shared each other. As his large body trembled in release, he'd whispered that word against my lips once more.

Liessa.

Something beautiful.

Something powerful.

Queen.

I caught sight of Lailah heading down the hall to our right as we crossed the foyer, Reaver flying near her shoulder as we turned toward Nyktos's office. The embers in my chest warmed and wiggled, and there was a swift, swelling motion that made me feel a little silly, then a little *reckless* when we entered the office and I saw Nyktos at his desk, writing in the Book of the Dead. He had his hair swept back from the sharp, stunning angles of his face.

My heart leapt as he lifted his head. Luminous, silver eyes connected with mine, and my skin immediately felt warmer than it should. Were hot flashes a symptom of the Culling? I'd ask Aios the next time I saw her. Definitely not Nektas.

"Perfect timing." Nyktos closed the Book of the Dead and rose, twisting the twine around the book. He was dressed as he'd been in his chambers—no embellished tunic, only a loose, black shirt with the sleeves rolled to his elbows and leathers. He turned to the credenza. "I just finished."

"Is there anything else you need?" Ector asked.

"No, but I won't be available this morning." Nyktos put the tome away as anticipation stirred. "Unless there is an emergency."

"Understood." Ector slid a sly look in my direction.

"Thank you," Nyktos said, coming around his desk.

Ector bowed and, with one quick look in my direction, exited the office, leaving me alone with the Primal.

Things still felt inexplicably *different*.

And I needed to get control of my wildly beating heart. "How many souls oddly shared the same name today?"

He sent me a faint grin as he crossed the office, and it did little to calm my heart. "None this morning."

"I suppose it's because you weren't so distracted." I clasped my hands together.

"Considering how quiet it was," he said, stopping before me, his gaze dipping to the swell of my chest pushed up by the vest, "and that there were no breasts inches from my face, I was quite focused."

I bit back a grin. "Well, you should be pleased to see that there is no threat of my breasts being such a distraction today."

"They are always a distraction," he murmured, picking up my braid.

"Which is more of a failing on your part than my breasts' fault."

He ran his thumb down the length. "So I've been told."

"So you should know," I told him, enjoying the lighthearted banter. It reminded me of before my betrayal became known.

The quick grin returned as he drew the braid over my shoulder, letting it fall down my back. "Come," he said, stepping back and starting for the office doors.

Arching a brow, I followed him into the hall and then down it toward the back stairwell. He opened a heavy door to our right, the last at the end of the hall. I peered around him. There was nothing but a black abyss. "What is this?"

He glanced over his shoulder. Torches along the wall flared to life in a shower of sparks. One after another, they lit, casting a rippling orangey glow over narrow, steep, winding stairs. "A stairwell."

I shot him a bland look. "You're so helpful."

"I don't think you mean that as a compliment." He started down the steps. "But I'll take it as one."

"You do you," I murmured, trailing my hands along the damp walls as I descended behind him. The musty, stale scent that gathered in the cramped space reminded me of the maze of chambers beneath Wayfair Castle that led to tunnels, which stretched throughout the entire city.

"You'll be happy to know that when you Ascend, you'll be able to use the essence in the same way I just did," he said, nodding at the flickering torches.

I stared at the width of his broad shoulders, my hands still on the walls. I liked how confident he was concerning the outcome of his plan. It was reassuring. "So, I'll be able to light fires with my mind, cast light, and move super fast with little effort?"

"You won't be able to power electricity. That is something only a Primal can do, but lighting fires and moving fast? Yes. And that is not done with your mind. It is done by your *will*." He followed the sharp turns of the stairwell with the ease that said this was a well-traveled space for him.

"Sounds like the same thing to me, but whatever."

"But it's not. Your mind takes thought. Time. Your will just is. It's immediate."

I made a face at his back. "Either way, I'm going to be so lazy."

Nyktos chuckled. "Careful," he warned as he turned, taking one of my hands from the wall. "The last step here is rather steep. About a foot."

The embers gave a happy little wiggle in response to his grasp. Or maybe it was my heart. I wasn't sure anymore. Holding his hand, I went down the last step and into the mouth of a wide, torch-lit hall.

My chest tightened as I took in the damp, shadowstone walls and the bars. The *rows* of bars the color of bleached bones on either side of the hall. Cells. "Should I be worried?"

It was Nyktos's turn to send me a bland look. "I really hope that's not a serious question."

I said nothing as I eyed the bars lining the cells. They weren't entirely smooth or straight. Some were twisted, and inside the cells, I saw chains that resembled the bars. I started toward them, noticing there were things etched into them. Symbols.

"Putting you in a cell now after everything," he said, stopping me with the hold he still had on my hand, "and especially after striking what is likely an ill-advised but very enjoyable deal with you wouldn't make very much sense, would it?"

I slowly looked over my shoulder at him. "Ill-advised?"

His eyes glimmered in the firelight. "I also said very enjoyable."

I started to point out that one thing didn't erase what'd come before it, but I remembered what he'd also said. That his attraction to me, and the subsequent pleasure-for-the-sake-of-pleasure deal we'd made, was something he considered a distraction. But I was beginning to think that *distraction* was a code word for *caring*.

And I knew what Nyktos believed would happen to those he allowed himself to care for.

Part of me was also beginning to believe that was why he'd had his *kardia* removed. Not to protect himself but to protect others.

Turning back to the cells, I stopped the rise of sorrow before he could pick up on it. "The bars? Is it just me, or do they look like actual bones? As do the chains."

"They are." Nyktos started walking, taking me with him. "Bones that once belonged to gods or the children of the gods."

My lip curled. "Like the kind that entombed those in the Red Woods?"

He nodded.

"What's carved into them?"

"Primal wards that make them very difficult to break," he said as we continued down the seemingly endless hall of cells. There had to be dozens of them. "The bones will even hold a Primal once weakened. The only thing they have no effect on is a being of two worlds."

"Dual life. The draken," I murmured, remembering him saying that before. "You said your father created more like the draken?"

"He did create more of dual life," Nyktos said as we came to the end of the hall, where it split into two more. He took me to the left, where a door was held open by a shadowstone sword speared through the wood and embedded into the stone behind it. I frowned at the blade, shaking my head. "But the draken are like the Arae. The dragons they came from are of ancient creation. What my father created after the draken are gods, and if there were ever others given dual life, they too would be godlike."

"What are the ones he gave dual life to?"

"There are only two. Ones that can shift into forms of large felines.

They're called wivern and can usually be found in Sirta. They are fierce fighters in both forms, and most gods know better than to get cornered by a pissed-off wivern."

It didn't surprise me that the gods who could take the form of such predators would be found in Hanan's Court.

"And then there are the ceeren," he continued, and I couldn't help but wonder if he was aware that he still held my hand. "They are usually found in the Triton Isles."

I sucked in a sharp breath. "Do they live in the water?"

"They can." He arched a brow. "You've heard of them?"

"I've heard stories of them—old ones. Legends of sailors being lured from their ships by beautiful creatures in the sea that were half mortal, half…fish." I wrinkled my nose. "Not quite sure how one is half fish."

He grinned as we passed several rough-hewn chambers that I figured were meant to be more cells. Only a handful had doors, and I tried not to think about how far underground we must be. "Yeah, they are unique to look upon when they take that form. I'm sure you will see them eventually."

I really wanted to see a ceeren. "And they're the only ones who can shift forms?"

A faint grin appeared. "Some Primals and even fewer gods can." Nyktos stopped then at the end of the hall, then pushed open a door. Letting go of my hand, he stepped inside. "Here we are."

Flames from dozens of sconces cast a soft glow over the wide chamber, which appeared to have been carved out of shadowstone, the walls not nearly as smooth as they were on the floors above. Some sort of stone table had been built from the wall, standing a little bit higher than my waist, but what rested in the middle of the chamber caught and held my attention as I slowly walked forward. It was a…a large body of water. Like a lake—but not.

The door closed behind me as Nyktos joined me. "It's a pool," he explained.

"A pool?" I repeated, clasping my hands under my chin.

"Yes, like a very large bathing tub. The end here," he said, gesturing to where water rippled over some steps, "is pretty shallow, but it gradually becomes deeper. Small mills at the end, where it is even above my head, keep the water moving, and the minerals that run off the shadowstone help to keep the water clean and cool." He tipped his head back to look at the low ceiling. "The kitchens are above us, and the fires there help keep this chamber heated. It's the closest thing I could get to a lake."

My gaze cut to him. "Did you create this? With eather?"

"Using that kind of energy to create something like this could've destabilized the whole palace. This was done by hand," he said, and my eyes went wide. "I didn't do this alone. Rhain and Ector helped carve out the stone. Even Saion and Rhahar pitched in over the years. So did Nektas." Another grin appeared. "Bele mostly just stood by and supervised."

I snickered at that. "How long did this take?"

"A very long time, but it was worth it." Pride crept into his tone. "Especially when sleep is hard to attain, or the mind is in need of a quiet place."

I stared up at him as he turned his gaze to the dark, glistening waters that reminded me so much of my lake. I wondered how often he disappeared to this space—somewhere I knew was special, based on his tone and how he looked upon it. It might even be a little bit sacred to him. I also wondered why he'd decided to show it to me.

You miss your lake, don't you?

That sweeping, fluttering motion returned to my chest as my gaze shifted back to the pool.

"Why did you visit my lake if you had this?"

Nyktos was quiet for so long that I looked at him. He was still staring at the pool. "Because it was your lake."

24

Out of everything I'd expected him to say, that wasn't even on the list. "What do you mean?" I angled my body toward his. "Because when I saw you at my lake, you acted surprised to see me there."

"I *was* surprised to see you there." He looked down at me. "Out of the many times that I had been there, you never came."

"But you knew it was my lake before that night?"

"I did."

My brows raised. "I'm going to need a little bit more explanation here."

He was quiet for a moment. "Before my father died, he told me about the deal he made with your ancestor. He didn't tell me why, but I think I would've known even if he hadn't told me."

"Because of how the Shadowlands changed?"

Nyktos shook his head. "That's what I thought it was until I learned about the embers. I felt you—or at least the ember that belonged to me." He tilted his head as he dragged his fangs over his lower lip. "I had Lathan and Ector watching over you after your seventeenth birthday, and as you grew older, but I...I checked in on you before that. I was curious about you." His eyes met mine. "I'd seen you go through the woods. Saw you sit by the lake. I never lingered too long, so I didn't ever see you do more than put your feet in the water, but I knew you went there."

"I had no idea," I murmured, surprised. "I really need to be more observant."

Nyktos shot me a wry grin.

"Why didn't you talk to me?" I asked.

"Why?" He laughed roughly, running a hand over his head. "Because even though I may be the youngest Primal—younger than even most gods—you were a child, and I was a fully grown man by mortal standards. You have to know that you would've likely been disturbed by a random male approaching you in the woods."

I thought about that. "Actually, yeah, that would've been really creepy."

"Exactly."

"But watching me walk through the woods is somehow *not* creepy?" I crossed my arms.

His attention shifted back to the pool. "I think it was borderline creepy."

A quiet laugh left me. "I'm messing with you. If I were you, I would've been curious, too. Except I probably would've been creepy and spoken to you."

Nyktos smiled at that.

"But that doesn't really answer why it being my lake mattered when you had this." I nodded at the pool. "Coming here has to be far easier than entering the mortal realm, even if you can do the shadowstepping thing."

"I don't know. The lake is different, and I…" He frowned, scratching his jaw. "I just felt drawn to it. Drawn to you."

"Because of the ember?"

"Maybe." He cleared his throat. "Anyway, I'd been meaning to show you this because I know you like water, but if I'd shown you this earlier, then I would have had to…"

He'd have had to explain why he'd created such a thing. His visits to my lake. Seeing me. And he hadn't been ready. I glanced back at the pool. Plus, I had a feeling that this place was a sanctuary for him, even if others used it. Just as my lake had been for me. Sharing this was something else he hadn't been ready to do.

Until now.

I inhaled deeply, awed and…*moved*.

Nyktos faced me. "Showing you this pool wasn't the only reason I brought you here. Remember when I said there were ways we could draw the eather out of you again?"

Every part of me zeroed in on that as I filed what he'd shared away to think about later. "Yes."

"I figured we could try that this morning. And this is a place very few other than I will venture. So, there should be no risk of anyone else seeing exactly what you're capable of or inadvertently getting caught in the crossfire."

Excitement buzzed through me, as did a small bit of trepidation. "Are you sure I can't hurt you?"

He nodded. "It takes a bit more than a blast of eather to hurt a Primal."

"But I did."

"It was just a sting."

"It turned your skin cold again."

"It was an icy sting," he amended. "You're not going to hurt me, Sera. We don't even know if you will have such an outburst again." His eyes glimmered. "But if you behave yourself, then maybe you can go for a swim."

"If I behave myself?" My brows shot up as I ignored the happy thrill I felt at the prospect. "Like some sort of child you've creepily watched walking through the woods?"

"Yes." His lips twitched. "Did that make you feel like you could call on the essence?"

"No, but it made me feel like I should punch you." My eyes narrowed on him. "Did you just try to goad me into using the eather?"

"I did."

I laughed. "Oh, you're going to have to do better than that. It takes a lot to anger me."

"I want you to repeat what you just said and ask yourself if that's the truth," he replied.

My lips pursed. "Let me rephrase. It takes a lot to make me *that* angry. I have way more control than you realize."

I'd expected some kind of—rightfully—sarcastic response, but there was none. Nyktos eyed me for a few moments. "Let me see your dagger."

"How do you know I have it?"

"You always have it, Sera. Hand it over." He paused, extending his hand. "Please."

"I hate it when you say please," I grumbled, bending over and reaching inside the shaft of my boot. I slid the dagger out, straightening.

"What a strange thing to hate."

I placed it, hilt first, onto his palm. "Yeah, you'd think."

"Thank you." Nyktos turned sharply, throwing the dagger.

My mouth dropped open as it flew through the air, striking the wall above the table with such force that the handle vibrated. "What the hell?" My head whipped toward him. "Now, you're just annoying me."

Nyktos smiled, and that, too, was annoying. "Right now, the essence is tied to extreme emotions. It'll be different once you Ascend, but before then, it can manifest when you're very angry or frustrated. Extreme grief. Pain." He began to circle me as he'd done in the courtyard. "I have a feeling if I best you in fighting, you'll get pretty frustrated."

"And that's why you threw my dagger into a wall?"

"I threw the dagger into the wall because I don't want to get stabbed again, nor do I want you cutting off more of my hair."

I opened my mouth.

"And don't even tell me you wouldn't stab me," he said. "You would."

"You're such a know-it-all," I muttered, tracking him.

Nyktos smirked. "If we're able to draw it out of you again, then we can move on to more controlled uses."

"So, what are we going to do?" I crept closer to him. "Fight hand-to-hand until I get frustrated and use the embers?"

"I have a feeling we're just going to tire you out before then, but that's the plan."

I lifted my right hand and extended my middle finger even as adrenaline surged through me. He was probably right, but I missed training. Fighting. "In case you don't know what that means, go fuck yourself."

Nyktos chuckled. "If you behave, maybe I'll fuck you instead."

A wholly inappropriate flush of heat went through me as I saw red. I went at him, swinging my arm—

Into nothing.

I stumbled into the empty space where he'd once stood, catching myself. I looked up.

He was several feet away. "You're going to need to be quicker than that."

Blowing out an already aggravated breath, I launched myself at him, kicking, but I hit nothing but air. I started to turn when I felt a faint brush across the center of my back. I spun, jabbing my elbow back. He'd shadowstepped several feet from me again.

"One day, I'm going to shadowstep my fist into your face," I warned.

Nyktos laughed. "Does that mean you don't actually plan to throw your life away then?"

Gritting my jaw, I stalked forward. I knew he was taunting me on purpose. He wanted me mad, and it was beginning to work. "You know what I think?"

"Hmm?" Nyktos glanced down at his shirt, flicking a piece of lint from it.

"I think you keep shadowstepping because you know I will land a hit if you stop doing it."

"I know." He winked. "But this is more fun."

Nyktos blinked out of existence just as I swung, reappearing behind me. He continued that way for quite some time, and I started to sweat. I didn't move when I felt him behind me, knowing he would shadowstep before I could respond.

"Tiring out already?" Nyktos asked.

"A little," I whispered.

There was a beat of silence. "It could be the Culling—"

I twisted, kicking out. I made contact this time, landing my boot in his stomach. Nyktos grunted as he staggered back. Bright eyes met mine. "Pure trickery."

Grinning, I started for him, and this time when he disappeared, I knew where he was headed. I swung around, bringing my knee up. Nyktos blocked me.

He tsked under his breath. "You'll never be fast enough." He moved, ending up behind me. An arm came around my waist, spinning me out. "No matter how much you try."

I caught myself, pushing the braid over my shoulder as my heart rate started to pick up. He shadowstepped in front of me instead of behind me as I'd expected—and caught my chin. The grip wasn't painful at all. "I'm a Primal."

"Congratulations," I spat, the words sparking a memory that made the embers in my chest hum as I reached for him, but this time, he was near the pool's edge.

This was what Taric had been doing, I realized. When I fought him in the throne room. Being reminded of that *did* piss me off. Because I'd been utterly helpless then. Fighting him had been pointless. I hadn't been fast enough. Just like I wasn't here. The crack in my chest hummed, the feeling becoming stronger and stronger as we continued, Nyktos taunting, and me being too slow. It happened over and over until my chest and skin felt like a fire.

Nyktos shadowstepped once more. Then he was behind me, his arms trapping mine before I could even take a breath.

"Godsdamn it," I growled.

His chuckle was rough as he hauled me back against his hard chest. "Now, how would you get free from me? You can't reach that dagger or any other weapon, even if you had them. What would you do?"

I strained against his hold, only succeeding in having him draw me closer. "Scream loudly?"

"No."

"Beg?" I suggested, tensing as I felt his breath on the side of my neck.

"There are very few things I would be interested in hearing you beg for, and your life is not one of them," he said. "I can feel the essence in you ramping up. It's there. Charging the air. You can summon the eather. Will it to manifest into energy that can break my hold. You won't hurt me."

I had been able to feel it, too. Keyword being *had*. "I'm not worried about hurting you."

His cool breath grazed the shell of my ear. "Then what's stopping you?"

"Those few things you're interested in hearing me beg for."

Nyktos went still behind me.

I grinned as I pressed my head back against his chest. I knew I should be focusing, but I couldn't draw upon those embers even if I did feel their power. And now I was feeling impulsive.

And more than a little reckless.

"I bet I can guess at least one of those things," I said.

There was a beat of silence. "And what would that be?"

"I don't know if I should speak it." I turned my head toward his. "It may be too bold."

"There is not a single part of me that believes you're worried about being too bold."

"But you may find me speaking it to be…distracting."

Nyktos's hold on me shifted. He drew me onto the tips of my toes and over, just a few inches, and I felt hardness against my lower back. "I'm already distracted."

I bit down on my lower lip as heat flooded my blood. "You may be *more* distracted."

"Tell me what you think I'd like to hear you beg for," he ordered, his voice full of silk and shadows. "Or is it you who has become nothing more than talk?"

I laughed, the sound deep and throaty as I stretched as far as I could, bringing my mouth close to his. "Your *cock*," I whispered, then I brought my foot down on his. Hard.

Nyktos grunted, likely more from surprise than pain, but his grip on me loosened. I broke free, twisting out of his embrace. Facing him, I backed across the packed soil and stone. "That's how I'll get free."

Eather seeped into his eyes as that lush, full mouth tilted up at the corners. "Is that your grand battle plan when you have no access to weapons? Speak of cocks?"

"If it works, why not?" I eyed the thick ridge clearly visible in his leathers. "And it most definitely worked."

"Perhaps a little too well."

"Is that so?"

Nyktos said nothing as he stalked toward me. The thrill of anticipation pumped hotly through me, mingling with the adrenaline. I waited until he was no more than a foot from me, and then I darted to my left, dipping under his arm. He spun, catching me, no longer shadowstepping.

He hauled me against him once more, my back to his front, one arm folded over my upper chest. "That was far too easy, Sera." His other hand landed on my lower stomach, causing me to jump. "I don't think you're seriously trying to evade me."

My breath caught as his hand slid down, over the laces running along the front of the leggings. "What do you think?"

I couldn't think.

"I'd say it's obvious." His hand continued its downward path, slipping between my thighs. A sharp pulse of desire whipped through me. "You wanted to be caught."

A ragged gasp left me as his fingers pressed against my center. "I don't like being caught." My hips twitched as his fingers began to move in tight circles. "Ever."

He chuckled. "Liar."

I was totally lying. I was also beginning to pant, and that had nothing to do with training. Shuddering, I gripped the forearm across my upper chest as his fingers continued rubbing me through my leggings. "Though being caught this way isn't all that bad." I swallowed a moan as his fingers pressed against the sensitive bundle of nerves. "Do all Primals fight this way?"

The sound Nyktos made against my back shouldn't have excited me, but it did, and I grinned. I yanked on his forearm as I threw my leg back, curling it around his. I twisted hard, attempting to throw him off.

"Wrong move," he growled, lifting me clear off my feet. He turned us toward the old stone table. "But I don't think you tried very hard then, either."

I gasped as he pressed me down until my stomach was flush with the table. My feet barely scraped the floor as I started to flip over, but he was suddenly on me, his chest against my back, and his legs twined with mine. He lodged his right forearm between my cheek and the stone, and all I could see was his bleached-white knuckles and my dagger, where it was still embedded in the wall above me.

I was trapped.

My fingers curled against the rough stone as I waited for the panic to hit me and for my chest to tighten. But when I dragged in a breath, all I could taste was citrus. All I could feel was Nyktos behind me, his chest rising and falling against my back, his breath teasing my cheek, and his hips pushed against my ass. Panic didn't find me at all. A hot, shocking flood of desire did.

Nyktos's chest rose sharply against my back. "You like it," he said, sounding a bit awed—maybe shocked. But he also sounded very *interested* as he drew a hand to my hip. "You like it like *this*."

I was trapped. Dominated. Vulnerable to his whims. And I...I more than just *liked* it. I felt damp desire hitting me, because it was *his* whims I was *open* to. It was *he* who was taking control.

"I can *taste* your desire." Nyktos's lips brushed my cheek. "Spicy. Smoky." He growled as he pushed in with his hips. I shuddered at the feel of him. "I don't even have to try to read you."

My fingers trembled against the stone as that damn hand of his found its way between my thighs once more. I closed my eyes, jerking against his fingers. "I...I do."

"Why?" There was curiosity in his tone, momentarily softening the granite-hard edge of lust in his voice. "Tell me."

The breath I took was hard to get into my lungs, and it had everything to do with the way he touched me. "I..." I moaned as he teased. "I don't know."

"I think you do know." His hand went to the laces of my leggings, finding the knot. There were a few short tugs, then the waist loosened—as did all of my muscles. "Or maybe I'm wrong, and you don't know." He slid his hand between the flaps of the leggings and beneath the undergarment. Then his fingers were pressing through the dampness, pressing into me. "But I am not wrong about you liking it like this."

He most definitely wasn't.

I whimpered as he eased his finger in. Then another. The way his legs were nestled between mine, I was open to him, and there was very little I could do with the weight of him holding me down. Another pulse of desire rolled through me.

"I like…" I moaned as his weight settled more fully against my back. My legs squeezed his as I grasped the fisted hand resting on the table.

"Like what?" His voice was a heated whisper against my ear. "Being dominated?"

I gave a full-body shudder as tension curled wickedly in the pit of my stomach. "I like…*submitting* to *you*."

"*Fuck*." His body jerked with a ragged exhale. "You never submit to me."

Turning my cheek, I opened my eyes, and his gaze immediately captured mine. "I'm submitting now."

Eather bled into the veins in his cheeks as his fingers stilled inside me. "Is that what you want? Now? Like this?"

My cheeks warmed. "I think you can feel that it is."

His fingers curled slightly inside me, dragging a sharp cry of pleasure from me. "I can."

I swallowed. "I know I can let this happen," I whispered, and I wasn't even sure if he understood what I was saying. What I meant.

Nyktos stilled, then he thrust once, twice with his fingers, and then slipped them from me. "I think I understand."

Did he? Did he understand that I wanted—no, that I *needed* control in my life? In the decisions I made, no matter how big or small? That I wouldn't be dominated in conversation, nor would I submit to authority or in battle. But with *him*, with *this*? I could. I could let go and be taken if I wanted because I knew I was safe with him. Because I…I trusted him.

His gaze held mine as he shoved the leggings and undergarment down to my knees, as far as they would go. He didn't look away as he undid his leathers, pushing them down just far enough that he now held his cock in his hand. I didn't even blink as I felt the head against my ass and then pushing into me.

I knew then, without a doubt, that he understood.

He leaned over me, his chest kissing my back as his cock spread me, filled me.

And this was nothing like the last time.

Or the times before that.

Nyktos took me from behind, his large body caging me as each stroke went deeper, almost punishing in its pleasure. Pinned as I was between him and the stone, I couldn't move. And I did like the utter control he had, the raw dominance of his hold and his thrusts that made the pleasure sharpen and pulse wildly. His breaths came out in short grunts against my cheek as my nails dug into his hand.

Maybe it was the building pleasure that loosened my tongue. Or the isolation of the chamber so far underground with the soft rush of water from the pool and the freedom of not needing control. Whatever it was had me whispering scandalous demands in our shared breaths. Words I'd never spoken to another before.

Harder.

Take me.

Fuck me.

And he did. He took me harder and faster, fucked me. The hand beneath mine unfurled, and his fingers threaded through mine. He held my hand as his hips plunged and churned against mine, and his breath left my cheek. The only warning I had was the brush of his nose, and then I felt a scrape on the side of my throat. He didn't pierce the skin or draw my blood, but the feel of his fangs, sharp and ready at my vein, sent me over the edge. The release was almost too much. I shattered in a way that bordered on pain, and he followed, pressing his body so tightly against mine that there was no space between us. Nothing.

Nyktos's body continued to shudder as he slowed behind me, the pressure of his fangs against my unbroken skin lessening as he whispered, "You are always safe with me, *liessa*."

25

I must've been really well-behaved, because sometime later, we made it to the pool.

The midnight water was warmer than my lake, but it was still refreshing as I made my way across the slippery pool under Nyktos's watchful gaze. He stayed close as if he feared I'd venture too far and drown. I wondered if the minerals he'd spoken of eased my sore muscles as I let myself slip under the surface, loving the feeling of water rushing across my face and over my head. Or maybe it was the orgasm. I smiled underwater. Could've been both. I stayed submerged, eyes closed, and arms outstretched, floating—

A cool chest touched mine, startling me. Nyktos's arms folded around my waist, lifting me. My eyes opened as my head broke the surface. Clutching his shoulders, I dragged in a mouthful of air as I looked up at him.

He scooped the wet hair plastered to my cheeks back from my face. "You were starting to worry me."

"Sorry." My face heated. I hadn't thought about how holding myself underwater must look to someone else. "I didn't think I was under that long."

His eyes searched mine. "It was close to two minutes."

My brows shot up. "You were keeping track of the time?"

He nodded, lowering his arm from my waist as he drew his hand along my jaw. "Why do you do that?"

"I…I really don't know." I bit my lip as I drifted back. The water was chest-deep here on me, but on Nyktos, it barely reached his navel, and he was utterly too distracting when water slicked his hair back and coursed down his chest. "It's just something I've done since I was a kid," I said, resting my arms on the ledge of the cool stone wall. "Maybe I started doing it because instead of feeling like I couldn't breathe, I was actually controlling it, and it wasn't controlling me? I don't know. But it made me feel in control. Not weak or something." I shrugged as Nyktos remained quiet. "Then again, I'm not even sure that makes sense. It's just a weird habit of mine." I cleared my throat. "So, anyway, I guess today was a failure."

"Not really." The water stirred as he drew closer. "Like I told you, I felt the essence in you. Honestly, I probably felt it in the woods that night, but I was…"

I glanced back to see him dip under the water and then resurface a few seconds later, rising like the Primal god he was. I got a little caught up in watching the muscles along his chest and biceps do all sorts of interesting things as he lifted his arms to run his hands over his face and push his hair back.

"I think we can draw it out," he said, joining me at the wall. He looked over. "You've got to remember it's not often that gods can use their eather in such a manner while in the Culling. You're already way ahead of the game."

Nodding, I rested my chin on my arm. "But I'm not supposed to even be *in* the game."

"There is that." Nyktos was quiet for a few moments. "Did I ever tell you about Lathan when he was younger?"

He hadn't. I shook my head.

"He would have these…strange sensations. They always came at night, right as he was about to drift off to sleep," he told me, resting his chin on his arm like I was. "And without warning, he would feel this sudden pressure in his chest and throat. Like he couldn't breathe."

I stilled.

"It was always swift and sudden, causing him to gulp for air. He said the attacks would come in spells, several nights in a row, and then he'd have nothing for weeks. He used to fear that a *sekya* was visiting him."

"A what?"

He glanced at me. "It's a creature that can be found in the Abyss and engages in a particular form of torture. They sit on your chest and steal your eather through your breath."

"What the fuck?" I muttered, shuddering.

Nyktos chuckled. "My father would never allow the *sekya* to leave the Abyss. Lathan knew that, but it was the only thing that made sense. It happened for years, but I never noticed until the one night I saw him do it—jerk as if he were waking up suddenly, gasping for air. Nektas was with us. Saw it, too. He taught Lathan similar breathing techniques to what I've seen you do."

"Did he...did he know what caused the attacks?"

"Lathan was never sure, but Nektas said he thought it was anxiety. That even if Lathan weren't thinking about anything when he was falling asleep, it was the things he thought about during the waking hours catching up to him when his mind was—"

"Quiet?" I whispered.

His gaze flickered to me again. "Yes."

I faced the walls of the chamber, doubt beginning to creep in on me. "Are you trying to tell me that a godling had issues with anxiety? Or are you trying to make me feel better about freaking out for no good reason?"

"First off, I don't think you freak out. Secondly, what causes you to feel as if you can't breathe is neither a good nor a bad reason. It just is," he said, and I arched a brow. "And, finally, you make it sound like it's impossible for Lathan to have had anxiety."

"Because a godling is powerful. Strong. Whatever."

"You have embers of life in you. Primal embers." His leg brushed mine underwater as he angled his body toward me. "You're strong. Lathan was just as recklessly brave as you are. None of that has anything to do with the mind."

Brave.

Strong.

I opened my mouth but fell silent for a couple of moments. "Did...did it ever stop before he...before he died?"

"There were years where he didn't experience them. At some point, they came back." He plucked up several strands of my hair that were stuck to my arm and draped them down my back. "But he managed them once he accepted that it wasn't a *sekya* coming for him."

I buried my chin between my arms. "When I was younger, I would hold my breath whenever I felt that way, not just when underwater." My face felt hot again. "That was before Holland picked up on it. You'd think that would have made the feeling of not being able to breathe worse, but I kind of had the opposite reaction. I don't know why."

"Even I don't know why the body and mind do what they do half the time," he said. And for some reason, that made me smile a little. "I don't think any of the Primals do. But if it helps you to do that and doesn't hurt you, do what you need to do." He lowered his head toward mine. "Either way, you're not weak, Sera. Not physically, but more importantly, not mentally. You are one of the strongest people I've ever met, mortal or not." The tips of his fingers grazed the curve of my arm. "With or without the embers."

The crack in my chest throbbed. A knot of emotion swelled so quickly in my throat that even if I had known how to respond to that, I wouldn't have been able to. The back of my throat burned as I rapidly blinked away dampness I knew had nothing to do with being in the water. I knew I was likely projecting whatever messy feelings popped up, but he'd said *I* was strong. Not the embers. Me. And that mattered.

Because it reminded me that *I* mattered.

Pushing off the wall, I turned away from Nyktos and let myself slip underwater before the knot of emotion decided to make an appearance in the form of hot, fat tears. I didn't know how long I stayed under, but Nyktos didn't come for me this time. He was waiting when I resurfaced, though. Watching. Our eyes met.

"I'm beginning to think you may have a bit of ceeren blood in your family line," he said with a faint grin.

"Shut up." I shoved a hand through the water, sending a small wave cresting over his chest.

He raised his brows. "Did you just…splash me?"

I shrugged. "Maybe."

Nyktos stared at me for several seconds and then placed his palm over the water. He didn't run his hand through it like I had. There was a charge to the air, and then the water began to rise beneath his palm, spinning into a small cyclone. My mouth dropped open as the water continued to spin, the funnel growing wider and taller until I could no longer see him behind it.

"I know you're impressed into silence," he drawled from behind the funnel, "but I'd close that mouth if I were you."

I snapped my mouth shut. That was all I could do as the cyclone of water arced and tipped over. A sound that was half-shriek, half-laugh left me as the funnel came down, pelting me as if I had been caught in a heavy rainstorm. I staggered back, shoving the hair from my face. "Okay, that's not fair."

"I know."

Grinning, I drifted closer to him. "Do it again."

Nyktos laughed. "So demanding."

But he did it again. And again. Drawing the water into multiple little funnels and larger ones that changed shapes from a winged creature to a large, racing wolf that whipped the water of the pool into a frothing frenzy. I was equally awed, amused, and completely enthralled by Nyktos as he eventually joined me in the center of the pool, keeping one arm securely around my waist as the water whipped back and forth around us. Not because he could create such things from water, but because he, a Primal of Death, *played*.

As our time alone slowly but too quickly came to an end, I felt that noticeable change again. That intangible shift between us as he retrieved towels from a shelf along the back of the chamber. In me as I dressed, finding it difficult to keep my eyes off him and the smile from my face. In him, in the relaxed lines of his features that made him seem so young as he took the time to blot the water from my hair. And I couldn't help but think this felt like...*more*.

That *we* felt like more.

I spent the rest of the day with the young draken and Aios, and even if I hadn't spent the morning training and then playing in the pool, the hours spent trying to keep Jadis from attempting to fly or set something on fire every other minute would've sufficiently exhausted me.

A moment to simply breathe without fear of something going epically wrong only came when Jadis scampered over to where I sat on the couch, lifting her thin, scaled arms to me. I bent to pick her up, but in a sparkling silver shimmer, she shifted into her mortal form, right then and there, naked as the day she was born.

Which caused Reaver to squawk and dart from the chamber faster than I'd ever seen him fly. I sort of wanted to follow him as Ector popped his head into the chamber, saw what had happened, and immediately returned to the hall, obviously wanting nothing to do with what was going on.

Luckily, Aios was prepared for the impromptu nakedness, whipping out a tiny light blue nightgown and managing to drag it over Jadis's dark-haired head as she all but crawled into my arms and buried her face in my hair. She was out in seconds.

"I wish I could fall asleep that easily." Aios lowered herself to the floor next to the plates of leftover food. I'd managed to get Jadis to eat from a fork again, but if I took my eyes off her for longer than a second, I likely would've lost a finger. "And don't worry about waking her. The palace could come down on our heads, and she'd sleep through it."

"Must be nice." I leaned back against the couch's arm as I glanced down at the wispy dark waves of her hair. "I wonder why she shifted. I've seen her sleep in her draken form."

"None of the draken sleep in their mortal form unless they feel safe." Aios brushed a wine-red lock of hair back from her face as she crossed her legs. I noticed the shadows had faded a little from her eyes. "Especially as younglings. So, it just means she feels comfortable with you."

"Oh," I murmured, glancing down at Jadis again. She'd turned her head slightly, baring one rosy cheek as she kept her hands clenched around my hair. Her lashes were unbelievably thick. "I think it's my hair. Nektas thought the color might remind her of her mother."

"Makes sense." Aios's smile was faint as she eyed the sleeping draken. "It's kind of sad but also a bit sweet if that's the case." She lifted her gaze to me. "I haven't gotten a chance to ask how you're dealing with the delay of the coronation and the news of the summons."

Keeping my arms folded around Jadis, I tipped my head back. "I really haven't been letting myself think too much about it," I admitted with a wry grin. "Probably not the best method, but it can't be changed."

"No, it cannot."

I nodded, even though we might be able to change things if we could find Delfai before Kolis summoned us. However, if we didn't, and I looked like Sotoria... I said none of that. Aios wasn't aware of that part, and if she knew that I was Kolis's *graeca*, I was sure those shadows would return. But I wasn't allowing myself to dwell on it. Any of it. If I did, I would be a wreck.

The sound of approaching footsteps drew our attention to the doors. I managed to keep any surprise from my expression. Reaver had returned, now in his mortal form. He wore loose, dark pants and a plain undershirt and carried a roll of something white in his hands.

Blond hair hid most of his angular features as he came to where we sat, kneeling by the couch. "She'll want her blanket," he said in that oddly serious voice of his. A tone that seemed far too mature for a child who looked no older than ten years of age.

"That is very thoughtful of you, Reaver," Aios said.

He shrugged a small shoulder as he draped the soft blanket over Jadis's shoulders with my help. Once he was sure she was covered, he sat on the floor near us.

I glanced at Aios.

She grinned.

Reaver looked up at me with expectant ruby-hued eyes as if waiting. For what, I truly had no idea, and I was quickly reminded of exactly how terrible I was with children.

"Would you like something to eat?" Aios picked up a bowl of mixed fruit. "I'm confident that Jadis didn't have her hands in this."

I snorted softly as Reaver hesitated and then nodded. The fruit was probably the only food Jadis hadn't had her fingers on—sticky fingers that were now wrapped tightly around my hair. "Do you know when Nektas is returning?"

"Later," Reaver answered as he nibbled on a piece of strawberry. "I think he went to Vathi to visit Aurelia."

"Aurelia?" I murmured, holding back a yawn.

"She's a draken in Attes's Court," Aios answered, glancing at me. "I've met her a couple of times. She's pretty nice." She poured Reaver a glass of water, something he hadn't been able to drink with Jadis chasing him around. Her eyes briefly met mine again. "I wonder if he's checking to see if she's heard anything about that draken who came here."

That would make sense.

"Don't know." Reaver took the napkin Aios handed him, dropping it onto a bent knee. "But I think Nek is sweet on her."

My brows shot up, at the nickname and the idea of Nektas being sweet on anyone when it was clear that he was still in love with his wife.

Aios grinned at the young boy. "And why would you think that?"

Reaver shrugged as he finished off a slice of melon. "He always smiles whenever her name is mentioned."

"That doesn't mean he's sweet on her," Aios said.

He pinned her with a very serious look. "Then why does Bele smile when someone says your name?"

I grinned as Aios's face flushed about a dozen shades of pink, thinking of how I'd seen the two of them interact with each other. I had thought there might be something between them.

"That's because Bele is silly." Aios cleared her throat. "Did Nyktos go with him?"

My heart immediately skipped, and *my* face felt like it was probably a dozen or so shades of red. I focused on rubbing the center of Jadis's back. While Reaver told Aios that he'd seen the Primal outside, working with the guards, and then proceeded to ask her why some melons were sweet and others sour, I stared at the glossy, black ceiling.

Nyktos.

I repeated his name over and over in my mind, and no matter how many times I said it, the name didn't sit right. I knew why, and it was all *Nek's* fault.

Because at some point, I'd started seeing Nyktos as I wanted to.

And that seemed like a problem because thinking of him as Nyktos felt wise. Less. Not *more*. Nyktos was *right now*, pleasure for the sake of pleasure, and that was the safest way to navigate this union with him. There was no guarantee that whatever this Delfai knew about removing the embers would work. Even so, there was still no promise of a future, not until we dealt with Kolis and restored some kind of order to Iliseeum.

And thinking of him as Ash felt too much like endless possibilities. Ash felt like *more*, and there could never be more with him.

Jadis wiggled a little as my chest tightened. I asked myself for the hundredth time what exactly I was doing here, going through a questionable plan when I had a duty, a destiny. When people were dying because I was here. And if Kolis ever discovered the whole soul thing? He would do just as Penellaphe had warned.

Pressure built because I…I knew why I hadn't made another attempt to escape. It wasn't because I feared being caught again. It wasn't because of the plan. It was the why behind wanting his plan to work. There were all the obvious reasons—stopping Kolis, ending the Rot, and restoring Nyktos to *his* rightful destiny as the King of Gods. But I had other reasons, purely selfish ones.

I didn't want to do what I'd have to do to weaken Kolis.

Instead, I wanted a future of my own, one where I could try to keep that part of me good—just like Nyktos did. A future that had more moments like the ones I'd spent with him earlier. Moments of *peace*. I wanted years like his friend Lathan had, where he didn't struggle to find his breath when things became overwhelming. Maybe even moments like this, where I held a sleeping child in my arms, one that was mine. I wanted a future where I was—

I tried to stop the thought from finishing, but it was too late. The *why* behind what I wanted was already fully formed, and the strangest, most terrifying thing occurred to me as I held Jadis closer.

Nyktos…he was all that I already knew—a Primal of Death who wanted to give the Shades the chance to face justice or redemption instead of the nothingness of the final death. He cared and thought of others, even at great risk to himself. What he'd done for Saion and Rhahar and countless others was evidence of not only that but also that he was succeeding at trying to be good. *Breathe in.*

Nyktos was a protector with far more than *one decent bone*, but some of that did belong to me and only me.

I didn't need him to prove that because he already had, three years ago when he refused to take me as his Consort. I just hadn't realized it then, and gods knew it hadn't turned out how he'd expected, but he'd wanted to give me freedom. *Hold.* And he'd proven it over and over again since then, when he prevented me from getting myself killed in the Luxe and didn't touch a single hair on my head when I stabbed him in the heart. He'd stopped Tavius when no one else would or could. He'd saved my life again by giving me a rare antidote to a deadly toxin, and he did so before he even knew about the embers. He'd taken my mother down by several notches and then some. Then there was what Rhain had claimed after the Cimmerian came to the gates of the Rise. The unknown sacrifice Nyktos denied. *Breathe out.*

Even after he'd learned what I'd planned, he had proven it. No one, not even me, would've blamed Nyktos if he had locked me away in one of those many cells I'd seen earlier. But he hadn't. He'd been angry, rightfully so, but the anger hadn't lasted.

I knew this. After all, he'd given me his blood because he didn't want to see me in pain.

Nektas had been right.

Nyktos did *understand* my actions. He *accepted* them. Two things even I knew were far more important than forgiveness. Nyktos knew *me*. Heard *me*. And he made sure I understood that a part of me *was* good. That he didn't see me as a ghost. Or a monster. He saw *me*, as someone strong and brave with or without the embers, and I now knew he'd been telling the truth when he claimed to be angrier about what he believed to be my lack of regard for my life. That he cared despite his resolve not to see me as anything more than a Consort in title only. Despite his very real inability to love. And because of that, all of that…

I wanted more.

I wanted to be his wife.

His partner.

His Queen.

I wanted to be Nyktos's Consort.

Afraid Jadis was falling, my arms tightened around her out of instinct as I became aware of her weight easing from my chest.

"It's okay. I have her now."

My eyes fluttered open in confusion at the sound of Nektas's voice. He was seated at my hip, carefully untangling his daughter's fingers from my hair. It was clear she still slept, her legs limp, even though her hold on my hair was stubborn.

"She doesn't want to let go," Nektas noted with a faint grin.

Realizing I must've fallen asleep, I glanced at the floor. Aios and the dishes were gone. My gaze flicked up to where Reaver was curled in the chair next to the couch, eyes open but sleepy.

"I've never seen her sleep this long." Reaver rubbed at his cheeks with his fist. "Ever."

Exactly how long had we been napping? I wasn't sure, and it didn't matter because I also realized my chest was humming faintly, meaning only one thing. My gaze swung back to Nektas's hands. Nyktos was here. In this chamber.

Everything that I had been thinking about before I fell asleep came back to me in a rush. What I knew. What I wanted. Oh, gods. My heart was pounding all over the place, and I was a second away from tearing my hair free and running from the room as if I'd woken up and found a *sekya* sitting on my chest. It might be a bit of an extreme reaction, but I didn't know what to think about any of this. What to do or how to act. The wanting of something I could have was foreign to me. Because just like Nyktos, I'd spent a life of just existing, and wanting felt like living.

And that scared me even more since there was a really good chance I'd screw up a possible future—if there turned out to be one—with Nyktos. One that could be real. I wasn't just a messy person. I was *the* mess. I *was* temperamental. Violent. Stubborn. Prone to moodiness, anxious one second and overly confident the next. I could barely deal with myself on most days, but I wanted Nyktos to be able to handle me.

My breath wheezed as Nektas worked all but one last tangle from Jadis's fingers.

"This is all your fault," I muttered under my breath.

Nektas's hands halted. "What is?"

"Everything," I grumbled. "Except the current situation with Jadis and my hair."

"It's been a long time since someone blamed me for nearly everything while I had no idea what I'd done." A quizzical smile appeared. "Strangely, I think I missed that." Nektas's eyes lifted to mine—

I stiffened.

His eyes flashed a shade of blue so bright and intense that they briefly resembled polished sapphires before they returned to the deep red hue I knew.

"Your eyes," I whispered as he finally got his daughter's hand free of my hair, tucking her and her blanket against his broad chest. "Not sure if you're aware of this, but they just changed color for a couple of seconds."

Everything about Nektas changed in an instant. The smile was gone. His features sharpened as the faint ridges of scales became more prominent. "What color did they turn?"

"Blue." I glanced at Reaver, who looked as if he was still half-asleep. "A really bright, intense blue." I thought his skin lost a little of the rich, coppery hue it usually had, but I wasn't sure. "Is that normal?"

"Sometimes," he murmured, then leaned forward. He pressed a quick kiss to my forehead, stunning me into silence. "Thank you for watching over the younglings."

I watched Nektas rise, not quite sure how I'd watched over them unless falling asleep counted. Reaver clamored from his chair as Nektas stepped to the side, and then I finally saw him.

Nyktos leaned against the bare wall, arms crossed over the dark gray tunic he must've changed into. His head was tilted to the side, and I was no longer thinking of changing eye colors because the expression on his face was *soft* and warm.

Nektas stopped by the Primal, speaking too low for me to hear. Whatever Nektas said to him caused Nyktos to push off the wall. His arms unfolded as he glanced at me.

I resisted the urge to wiggle myself between the cushions.

Nektas nodded at something Nyktos said, then turned to Reaver. The young boy gave me a little wave, and then the trio disappeared into the hall. We were alone, and Nyktos was walking toward me. I was a mess, only managing to sit up as he came to me, taking the seat Nektas had occupied as I busied myself with straightening the hem of my vest.

"I see someone likes your hair as much as I do."

"Yeah," I whispered, and that was all I said.

There was a beat of silence. "You okay?"

"I...I think my hair is sticky." Closing my eyes, I ordered myself to get it together. There was no reason for me to behave so strangely. My big, unnecessary epiphany didn't change Nyktos, and I needed to treat this the same way I treated the looming summons or the matter of who the soul inside me belonged to: deal with it by...not dealing with it.

Sounded like a plan.

I peeked up at him. Tension had gathered in the lines of his mouth and brow. Concern blossomed.

His gaze swept over my face so intensely I wondered if he was counting my freckles again. Or if I'd been projecting the wild mix of emotions earlier, and he was trying to figure out what had caused them. I really hoped it was the former.

It was neither.

"You've been sleeping a lot more lately," he said.

A little bit of relief swept through me, but it was brief. "I know. I feel fine," I quickly added. "No headaches or anything, but I didn't sleep this much before. I guess it's the Culling," I finally admitted aloud—and to myself.

Nyktos nodded. "It could've been the training this morning—"

"I don't want to stop."

He pulled back as I swung my legs off the couch and scooted to the edge. "I'm not suggesting we do."

"I feel like there is a *but* coming."

Nyktos was still watching me closely. Too closely. "You saw Nektas's eyes change color."

I frowned. "To blue. Is there something wrong with them?"

"No," he answered, brushing a few tangled curls back from my shoulder. "I've never seen them that color, but all of the draken used to have blue eyes."

"Really?" Surprise flickered through me. "Why are they now red?"

"They turned that way after Kolis took the embers of life from my father," he said. "It's a sort of *notam*—a Primal bond between the draken and the true Primal of Life. It was severed when the embers were taken, and their eye color has stayed that way since there has been no true

Primal of Life—no true Primal of Life who Ascended."

"Then why did they just—?" I sucked in a sharp breath, rising to my feet. "Did they momentarily change because of me? But I haven't Ascended. Obviously."

"The embers could be growing stronger in you, and that innate, Primal bond between the draken and the true Primal of Life was temporarily responding to them."

I crossed my arms. "Okay. I mean, that's not a big deal. Right?"

"Normally, the increase in the strength of Primal embers isn't a big deal," he agreed...or didn't, because the concern was clear in his deep silver eyes.

"What *is* the big deal then?"

Nyktos didn't answer for a long moment. "It could mean that you're closer to Ascension than we realized."

26

Being closer to my Ascension was a big deal.

Because being closer to it with these embers still inside me also meant being closer to my death. Not even Nyktos's blood could save me, because it required more than just his blood.

It required his love.

Something Nyktos had prevented himself from feeling with the removal of the *kardia*.

So, we needed to get the embers out of me, and today was the first major step in that direction.

The sky was only beginning to lighten as Nyktos and I left the palace the following morning, headed for the stables as my new iron-hued cloak trimmed in silver fluttered around my boots. The material was soft and warm, and I really hoped things didn't get messy where I'd end up ruining my new clothing.

Nibbling on my lower lip, I glanced up at Nyktos. At some point yesterday, I'd decided that he didn't need to know how I felt. That I...I *cared* for him. It didn't seem fair to put that on him, even though I knew he cared for me, too—and even though I thought what I felt might be more.

He had his hair swept back in a neat bun at the nape of his neck, all but that shorter piece I'd cut that rested against the height of his cheekbone. He'd continued to honor the deal—*both* deals—that he'd struck with me, joining me for supper and then, later, proving that he was an exceptionally fast learner when it came to using his tongue. My face warmed as memories rose of his head between my thighs and his mouth on me, doing all sorts of wicked, wonderful things for what felt like a small eternity.

Nyktos looked down at me as we neared the stables. "What are you thinking about?"

My eyes widened slightly and then narrowed on him. "Stop reading my emotions."

"I'm not."

"Sure doesn't sound—" I gasped as Nyktos shadowstepped without warning, grasping my arms. Within the blink of an eye, he had me against the wall of the stables, the entire front of his body pressed to mine. My breath snagged as I looked up at him. Iridescent wisps of eather bled into his irises.

Then his mouth was on mine.

Nyktos kissed me, and he—*gods*—he kissed like his very life depended on it, and this was one of those moments. There was no checked or banked passion. He went for it. Lips. Tongue. Fangs scraping, teasing. When his mouth left mine, my knees actually felt weak.

"You were projecting," he whispered against my throbbing lips. "Desire." His tongue flicked over my lower lip, drawing a gasp from me. "Smoky and thick. If you keep thinking about whatever you have in your mind, we'll never make it to the Vale."

Clasping the front of his cloak, I fought the urge to pull his mouth back to mine. "That wouldn't be…responsible of us."

"Absolutely not," he agreed, dragging his hands down my cloaked arms. "So, behave."

"You're the one manhandling and kissing me," I pointed out.

"I'd say you're the one driving me to do so." His lips grazed mine. "But I've been looking for a reason to kiss you since you licked that drop of juice from your lip at breakfast."

"You don't need a reason," I told him. "All you need is want."

"I'll keep that in mind." His forehead touched mine. Neither of us moved for the span of several heartbeats, and I almost wished we could stay this way. But that was a silly thought. Finally, he stepped back.

I peeled myself off the wall, noticing that a handful of guards were grouped together not too far away. Nyktos must have been aware of them long before I was, but that hadn't stopped him. Which confounded me a little as we returned to being responsible and got moving. His act—

his kiss—had been rather public. And, well, I wasn't exactly used to anyone even acknowledging my existence in public.

The scent of straw and hay reached me as we entered the stables. I quickly saw that they were empty except for the horses. "Where's Nektas?"

Nyktos led me toward the back row of stalls, his hand on my back a steady, grounding presence. "He'll join us on the road."

"In his draken form?"

"No, he'll be on horseback. It will be quicker and easier to travel that way once inside the Vale."

Meaning it was quicker and easier for *me* to travel that way. Not Nektas, who could take to the sky. But I bet Nyktos had wanted the draken in his mortal form beside me.

He stopped, the dim light of the stables glinting off his cuff as he slid open a stable door. "Meet Gala."

Peering around him, my lips parted as I saw a gorgeous mare standing in the center of the stall, already saddled as she nibbled on some hay. She was almost as large as Odin, quite a bit bigger than most horses in the mortal realm. Her coat had a unique roan pattern with white hairs on top of a black base, giving her a faint blue coloring.

Straw crunched under my boots as I walked to her. Gala lifted her head, twitching her ears at my approach. "She's beautiful," I said, slowly lifting my hand to her. She stilled, letting me run my hand down her smooth, broad muzzle.

"I'm glad you like her." Nyktos had entered behind me without making a single sound. "She's yours, after all."

My head whipped around. "Come again?"

"I planned on giving her to you for the coronation." Nyktos brushed past me, checking the straps on the saddle. "But I saw no reason to wait."

Gala nudged my hand since I'd stopped stroking her in my shock.

"You're surprised." He glanced over at me, the tendrils of eather faint in his silvery gaze. "And, no, I'm not reading your emotions. I can see it on your face."

I blinked. "I just...I wasn't expecting a gift." I cleared my throat. "Thank you."

"Is it not customary to bestow a gift on a wedding day in the mortal realm?" Nyktos turned to the wall behind the horse, where several short swords were sheathed and affixed to the wall. I would've thought that was a strange place to keep weapons, but then again, there seemed to be stashes in every other chamber.

"It is." I focused on Gala's beautiful doe eyes as mine burned. "I don't have a gift for you, though."

"I don't believe it's customary for the bride to give the groom a gift, is it?" Nyktos walked to Gala's side, thick lashes shielding his eyes, but I still felt his gaze. "And besides, you are giving me a gift. The embers."

"More like your father is giving you that gift." I scratched Gala behind an ear. "I've never had a horse."

Nyktos drew closer. "I imagine that wasn't for a lack of readily available horses. A Crown's stables are usually filled."

I shrugged.

"Did your mother believe that the promised Consort of a Primal didn't deserve her own horse?"

My chest tightened. "I don't think my mother believed it was necessary for me to have one. I wasn't allowed to leave the grounds of Wayfair until I was seventeen. All I needed to know was how to ride one, and Holland taught me that." I patted Gala's side, forcing my breath out, slow and easy. "Will you be riding Odin then?"

"I will when I head back." Nyktos lifted the reins. "You'll have to share Gala with me for now."

"Not a hardship." I gripped the pommel, hoisting myself into the saddle.

Wisps of eather brightened in his eyes as he grinned faintly. "I have a feeling I'll need to remind you that you said that at some point in the near future."

"Probably."

Nyktos chuckled as he easily swung himself up behind me. All of my senses immediately became hyperaware of the proximity of his body, the press of his thighs to mine, the arm around my waist, and the feel of his chest against my back. I'd fallen asleep in his arms last night, and it had felt different than him keeping me within arm's reach. Our limbs had been tangled. Both of his arms had been wrapped around me. One of his knees had been tucked between mine. He hadn't been in bed when I woke but had been in the quarters beyond the bathing chamber. I lay in bed, listening to him speak quietly to who I believed was Rhain.

"You said you weren't allowed to leave Wayfair until after I refused you as Consort," he said, and I guessed me trying to be polite about the timeframe had been unnecessary. "You left, though, to travel into the Dark Elms."

I frowned as he reached around me and picked up the reins. I knew that Nyktos had had his guards, Lathan and Ector, keep an eye on me, but that was after he'd rejected me. "The Dark Elms are technically part of Wayfair," I told him. "Was that one of the times you were watching me?"

He guided Gala out of the stall. "You don't need to make it sound like I was stalking you."

"You weren't?"

"No," he muttered.

My lips twitched, but then I thought of something else. "Exactly how much did Lathan and Ector see of my...travels in the mortal realm?"

"Enough."

I widened my eyes as we exited the stables, figuring that he must have known about my trips into the Luxe and possibly even what I'd been doing there. But I felt no shame. There was no reason to. He'd rejected me then. Or set me free. Whatever.

Movement at the Rise caught my attention. The guards there bowed as we rode past. I didn't recognize any of them, but my cheeks heated, nonetheless, remembering what they'd seen. Even if they were simply bowing for Nyktos, I wasn't used to such a show of respect.

Nyktos's hand left my hip. He lifted the hood on my cloak as my gaze swept over the terrain. The road to the palace split into two, one heading northwest and the other northeast toward Lethe. Gala followed the narrower road to the left. Buttoning the top clasp on the cloak that held the hood in place, I peeked at the walls of the Rise, glad to see them bare.

"Where do your guards think we're going?" I asked.

"They likely think I'm taking you to see the Pillars." Nyktos's hand returned to my hip. "But I'm sure some will be curious. Kars had questions."

Remembering the guard from the courtyard, I asked, "And what did you tell him?"

"That it was none of his business."

I snorted at that. "But I imagine all know what your prior plans regarding Kolis were, don't they?"

His chin grazed the top of my head. "I think you know the answer to that, Sera."

I did. His guards knew. I almost pointed out that it was just me that he'd kept in the dark, but I managed to stop myself. I eyed the crimson-leafed branches of the nearby woods, remembering what Nektas had said about my seeming lack of interest in the world here. In Nyktos's life.

I glanced up at the star-speckled, gray skies. No one else traveled the road. There was no wind. No scents other than Nyktos's fresh citrus one. The only sound was the clap of Gala's hooves against the packed ground as I worked up the nerve to ask again. I didn't know why it made me nervous to do so. Him being evasive or flat-out refusing to answer was the worst that could happen.

I took a shallow breath. "I...I would like to know what your prior plans were."

Nyktos remained silent.

Clamping my jaw shut until I thought my molars might actually crack, I ignored the sting of disappointment I felt.

"You were right, you know?" he said, breaking the silence. I had no idea what I was right about. "The day you asked me if I'd accepted this way of life. I haven't. From the moment I Ascended, I've searched for a way to destroy Kolis. To weaken him enough that he could be entombed. As you already know, I couldn't find anything."

It could've been the surprise flickering through me that prevented me from making the same mistake I did before by pointing out that he had. "Is that why you have an army?"

"It is why I began to build one." He was quiet again for several moments. "Are you at all familiar with war, Sera?"

"Lasania has been on the verge of war more than a few times, usually with the Vodina Isles, but there were other kingdoms that thought to exploit us as the Rot started to spread," I said. "Even if I wasn't party to the conversations between my mother and the King, I always knew when we were on the precipice again. The armies would intensify their training, there were drafts of those of age, and all was done to ensure the soldiers were as well-fed as the nobles."

"But your kingdom never went to war."

"Not during my lifetime, thankfully." A rattle of dry branches drew my attention to the woods. I stiffened at the sight of a large, onyx-hued draken gliding over the dead trees.

"Ehthawn," Nyktos observed. "He must've been near and saw us leave. He's just keeping an eye on us."

I nodded, relaxing.

"There have been times when Primals have fought over one offense or another," Nyktos continued. "In the end, they are left standing while thousands fall. And all because one felt insulted. But those skirmishes were never wars. If I were to go to war with Kolis, it would be a war of

Primals, and it would spill into the mortal realm. *Hundreds* of thousands would die, if not more."

My skin chilled.

"But then I found you."

I tilted my head back to look at him. "You didn't find me. Your father basically…gave me to you."

"That's one way to look at it." He shifted, his arm tightening around my waist, drawing my back flush to his chest. I faced forward, unsure if he was even aware of the act. "Up until the moment I learned that you carried the embers in you, I had no hope of avoiding such a war. It seemed inevitable. Not only because of what Kolis has wrought upon the Shadowlands, but because, eventually, he will turn his sights on the mortal realm. He's already started."

The back of my neck tingled as we finally passed the length of the Rise and a sea of untouched, crimson trees rose along the road.

"Kolis believes all mortals should be in service to the Primals and gods. That their lives should be dedicated to appeasing the whims of those more evolved than they are," he continued, and my stomach tightened. "That those who do not worship the Primals with dedication and respect should be punished. He has already ordered the Primals and gods to punish mortals more harshly, even for the simplest indiscretions. You may not have seen this play out in your kingdom yet, or were simply unaware, but failure to even bow before a statue of a Primal could result in death in other places."

I jerked in shock.

"While I do not relish the idea of wreaking the kind of havoc a war among Primals would cause, war seemed, as I said, inevitable."

"Until me?" Weight settled on my chest, and I forced myself to take a deep, even breath. "Your plan. You think it will avoid a war if it works?"

"My plan *will* work," he corrected. "Once I have the embers, Kolis will be stripped of his glory as the King of Gods. That alone will weaken him, but it might not be enough to entomb him. He won't go down easily. He will fight."

"And the other Primals?" I could now see the damage the draken had left behind in the Red Woods. Empty areas where trees once rose to the sky. "What will they do?"

"Some may opt to remain neutral."

My lips peeled back. "That's bullshit."

Nyktos chuckled at my curse. "It is, but Kolis will have his loyalists.

Not just his gods but Courts that have been able to rule with little to no order, able to do whatever they want to whomever they want, with their only concern being that of avoiding Kolis's ire. Primals who enjoy the way it is now and would not like to return to how it was when my father ruled."

"And how did your father rule?"

"That was before my time. But from what I know, it was with fairness. He wasn't without flaw, but he would not allow what happens in Dalos."

Honestly, did it matter how his father ruled, as long as it wasn't like Kolis did? "But there will be Primals who would fight against him? Who would help?"

"I have my supporters. None that have armies such as mine or Kolis's, but stripping Kolis of his title as King of Gods and rising as the true Primal of Life may be enough to sway others to abandon Kolis," he said. "How much destruction is caused will depend on how many Primals are swayed."

My grip on the pommel tightened. "There are a lot of possibilities there. No guarantees that the plan will weaken Kolis enough or cause other Primals to abandon him."

"There are never any guarantees," he said quietly.

He was right, and that made me think of the strange prophecy. "What Penellaphe saw in her vision? She made it seem like Kolis had gone to sleep."

"Or was entombed."

I nodded. "But it also sounded like he woke up again."

"Prophecies are only possibilities," Nyktos replied. "Parts of them may or may not come to pass. They, too, are no guarantee."

But I wanted guarantees when the lives of hundreds of thousands were at stake. And there was only one I could think of.

Me.

I could prevent a war among the Primals, but Nyktos's plan could go wrong. There could be enough Primals swayed that Kolis could be defeated without war, and I could fulfill my destiny, but not in the way Holland had inferred.

I noticed that Gala had slowed, and we were steadily creeping closer to where the Red Woods and Dying Woods converged. A few moments later, we left the road.

"Are the Pillars within the Red Woods?" I asked.

"No." Nyktos led the mare through the trees. "I want to show you something."

Curious, I fell quiet as we traveled on, under Ehthawn's large shadow. I couldn't help but wonder what the woods would look like in the sun. How rich would the leaves appear? How stunning? Once the Rot was vanquished, the sun would return to the Shadowlands, and I decided in that moment, without hesitation, that I would be here to see that.

Excitement built, but there was more to what I felt. The breath I took was unrestricted, deep and lifting. No threat of panic making it feel brittle or like it wasn't enough, but there was a shivering sensation along the back of my skull and a whipping motion in my stomach and chest. It reminded me of removing a too-tight bodice. A *release* even more tantalizing than what I felt in Nyktos's arms accompanied the excitement over deciding something as simple as wanting to see the leaves of a tree under the sun. But it was my decision.

My choice.

No one else's. Not my mother's or an ancestor's. Not Nyktos's. Not even Fate's. All mine.

"Here," Nyktos said quietly, drawing me from my thoughts.

I started to look back at him, but he caught my chin. The charge of energy caused the embers in my chest to warm. He directed my gaze down, past the glistening gray bark to the dry, gray grass—

I gasped.

A vine had sprouted from the dead soil at the base of a blood tree. Deep green and fragile, it wound its way up the bottom of the trunk. Tiny buds were scattered along the length of the vine, but one had blossomed.

It was half the size of my hand, petals the color of moonlight, folded up and closed in, revealing only a thin strip of crimson. It was what I'd seen Nyktos going into the Red Woods to check on before.

"The poppies," I whispered. "The poisonous, temperamental poppies that remind you of me."

"The powerful, beautiful poppies that also remind me of hope," Nyktos replied, his thumb smoothing under my lower lip before returning to my hip. "Those poppies are the hope of life. The power of those embers. Proof that life cannot be defeated, not even in death."

Nektas was waiting on the road just outside the Rise, cloaked and seated astride a chestnut steed. He greeted us with a nod, and then we continued on. I didn't know if I should feel relieved that the journey had been eventless or worried because it had been too calm. Eventually, as the three of us rode under Ehthawn's shadow, the woods on either side of the road gave way to flat, barren land.

"What used to be here?" I asked.

"Lakes," Nyktos said. "Just like on the road into the Shadowlands. There were lakes on both sides."

"Far deeper ones, though," Nektas added. "And they were the color of polished sapphires."

"Sounds beautiful," I murmured as Nyktos's thumb moved on my hip again. Even through the cloak and pants, I could feel him tracing the same slow, straight lines that he'd drawn on my thigh in his office as he spoke to Attes. It was utterly distracting in the most pleasant way, and it also felt...intimate. I liked it.

"Will they return once the Rot is gone?" I asked.

"I really don't know," Nyktos said, shifting the reins to his other hand. "The rivers that used to feed the lakes and streams here stopped flowing into the Shadowlands. It's possible that once the Rot is gone, they will once again feed these areas."

I started to ask exactly how the rivers had stopped flowing into the Shadowlands, but I noticed that the sky ahead had started to change color—a gradual shift to iron-gray brushed with faint traces of pink.

"We're nearing the Pillars," Nyktos explained, noting where my attention had gone. "And the Abyss. What you see is smoke from the fires darkening the sky and changing the color."

Realizing what the fires could be, I stiffened. "The pits?"

Nektas glanced over at us, a wry twist to his lips. "They never stop burning."

The Pits of Endless Flames were where souls that had committed the most atrocious crime were sentenced—some for an eternity.

And that's where Tavius was.

A rather twisted smile tugged at my lips. And maybe I should've felt disturbed by that, but I didn't.

We rode on, seeing no other signs of life. Then the land began a gentle climb, and the stars slowly dimmed until they could no longer be seen, now hidden behind...*clouds*—something I hadn't seen in the Shadowlands. But these clouds were entirely too low to the ground, reminding me of when storms festered and grew out over the Stroud Sea. I sat straighter, squinting as Gala neighed softly. The embers in my chest vibrated, causing my skin to tingle.

What I was seeing wasn't clouds.

It was mist, thick and heavy, obscuring the land and the sky, leaving only the road visible. I looked down, seeing tendrils of it seeping onto the road, but I knew this wasn't normal. It was the essence of the Primals, and the longer I stared into it, the more I could make out darker clumps within. Forms. There were shapes inside it—*bodies*—drifting slowly. My head snapped to the side as I looked past Nektas to the other side of the road. There were shapes there, too.

I drew back against Nyktos's chest. "What's in the mist?"

"The souls of the recently deceased." His arm tightened around me. "They're waiting to enter the Pillars."

Staring into the mist, I lifted my hand to the center of my chest where the embers continued to hum and spread warmth through my midsection. There had to be hundreds inside the mist.

"You okay?" Nyktos asked quietly, dipping his head to mine.

I nodded as I squeezed my hand into a fist. My palms were beginning to warm. "The embers are kind of vibrating like they do right before I use them."

"The embers of life are responding to the souls." Nektas drew his horse closer to ours as the mist steadily crept closer, narrowing the road. "When Eythos was the Primal of Life, he always found it difficult to be near the Pillars—close to death in such high numbers. It...wore on him."

Realizing that Nyktos was listening as closely as I was, I lowered my fist to my lap.

"He once told me it was hard to ignore the pull—the instinct to intervene." Nektas turned his gaze to the sky. "He knew death was a way of life. A part of the cycle that must continue uninterrupted. But it saddened him, especially here. He couldn't see their souls like his brother could—like Nyktos now can—but he knew each of their names. Knew their lives, no matter how short or long. The ones who lived the briefest troubled him the most."

My gaze drifted back to the souls shrouded in mist. I figured that Eythos's ability to know the lives of those who had died was like the names of those who'd died coming to his son to be written in the Book of the Dead. He simply knew, and I was grateful that I didn't know anything about the souls in the mist. That the embers weren't *that* strong in me. Ignoring the urge to use them was hard enough.

"Can they see us?" I asked.

"No. They cannot see or hear us. They cannot see each other," Nyktos told me.

My chest became heavy. "That sounds...lonely."

"It's for only a brief time, one they will not remember once they pass through the Pillars." Nyktos reached down, placing his hand over mine. The contact startled me, and I looked up at him. "Does it wear on you?" His voice was low. "The need to use the embers?"

"No." I looked ahead.

"Liar," he whispered, and I swore the arm around me tightened even further.

"Eythos couldn't be near the Pillars longer than a few minutes. If that," Nektas continued after a minute. "He would have to leave, knowing it was the only way to stop himself from using the embers. And yet, you are able to remain within their presence."

I glanced at the draken. "I only have two embers. He was the Primal of Life. It probably doesn't affect me as much as it did him."

Nektas's crimson gaze settled on me. "You carry two Primal embers in you. That is more than enough to feel the same impact as he did."

"He speaks the truth," Nyktos confirmed.

"How can that be possible when I don't know anything about the souls in the mist?"

"Have you tried?"

My brows furrowed. I hadn't, but I also hadn't tried to use the embers. They just sort of did their thing whenever someone was dying or injured.

"You're stronger than you realize, *meyaah Liessa*." Nektas smirked as I shot him a glare.

"The embers, you mean," I corrected him.

"He didn't misspeak." Nyktos's thumb swept back and forth. "He speaks of you. Not the embers."

I fell quiet as we continued the climb, a little relieved to know that the urge I felt to use the embers wasn't due to my inability to control myself. And also a bit disorientated to think that I would somehow have a better handle on them than Eythos. Both Nyktos and Nektas had to be mistaken, but Nektas's question echoed, and I found myself staring into the mist, focusing on one of the shapes. Seconds ticked by, and I...I thought the form became clearer. A head and shoulders became unmistakable. The shroud seemed to fade around the soul as the embers pulsed—

Sucking in a short breath, I quickly faced forward. Heart thumping unsteadily, I decided that I didn't need to know if I was capable of naming the dead or seeing their lives. There was no point when the embers would soon be in Nyktos.

But the embers continued to throb.

The mist had pulled back from the road and sky, widening and spilling out over the land. Even more souls were here, but I didn't dare look too closely into the mist.

Nektas's chin jerked up, and I followed his gaze to see Ehthawn veer off to our left, his long wings cutting through the faint tendrils of mist.

I watched until I could no longer see him. "Where's he going?"

"He must be checking something out," Nyktos answered as Nektas sent him a quick glance. We crested the hill just then, the stars returned, and the Pillars came into view.

They, like everything in the Shadowlands, were made of shadowstone. Two deep black columns rose from the mist, positioned several yards apart, and they stretched so high into the now-violet-laced iron sky, I couldn't see where they ended or if they even did. There appeared to be markings on them, similar to the ones I'd seen in the Shadow Temple. A circle with a vertical line through it. As we began to descend the hill, my attention shifted below.

The road ahead split, becoming a crossroads. The crossroads weren't empty. Three waited on horseback. All were cloaked and hooded, wearing white. Each horse was also shrouded in the same pale color. Their cloaks and shrouds rippled gently around them, but there was no breeze.

And the horses weren't exactly normal either.

What I could see of them beneath their shrouds reminded me of the Shades—little more than skeleton and tendon.

"That's really unsettling," I whispered.

Nyktos gave a rough chuckle. "That they are."

"What are they?"

"They are Polemus, Peinea, and Loimus," Nektas answered.

I frowned. "Those're their names?"

"Well, they're more of an embodiment of who they are than actual names," Nyktos shared. "It's Primal language."

"And they are..." Nektas said, shrugging as he glanced at Nyktos. "Well, I suppose you could call them riders."

My brows inched up as Nyktos snorted. "Of what?" I asked, definitely creeped out. Other than their shrouds, none of them had moved. Not even an inch.

"Of *the* end," Nyktos said, and I stiffened. "Their names mean war, pestilence, and hunger. And when they ride, they bring about the end to wherever they travel because death always follows them."

"What the fuck?" I whispered, my eyes widening as we neared the three riders.

Nyktos laughed again, the sound rumbling against my back, and I was so glad that he found this amusing. "Luckily, they can only be summoned by the true Primal of Life."

"Yeah." I cleared my throat. "Luckily."

The three riders lifted their heads as we slowed and then stopped before them. I couldn't see anything within their hooded cloaks, and I didn't want to. I didn't need to be haunted by whatever nightmare surely existed inside.

Then the horses moved, lowering their shrouded heads as each bent one front leg. They and the riders *bowed*.

"Huh," Nektas murmured, his head cocked. "Haven't seen that happen in a while."

I glanced back at Nyktos. He stared at the riders, his eyes slightly wide and luminous. Taut, pale lines bracketed his mouth. "I've never seen them do that." He blinked several times, and some of the brightness faded as he looked down at me, clearing his throat. "The entrance to the Vale is only a few feet to our right."

I saw absolutely nothing but swirling, silvery-white mist.

"I cannot go farther in that direction," he said as his hand left my hip and his arm loosened around me.

I turned as Nektas rode in front of the riders, who had returned to their eerily still positions. Nyktos swung off Gala's back. He unstrapped the two short swords he'd brought with him and secured them to Gala's side. "Just in case." Then he passed the reins to me, but his hand remained folded over mine.

Dark silver eyes locked onto mine, and I felt that same sweeping motion in my chest and stomach as he said, "She's very important to me, Nektas."

"I know," the draken responded.

I thought that was a strange thing for Nyktos to say, but he'd said that *I* was very important. To him. Not the embers. Me. And maybe that was why I blurted out what I did.

"I want to be your Consort, Nyktos."

The moment those words left my mouth, I was this close to diving headfirst beneath the riders' shrouds. My lips parted, but no air was getting into my lungs. My heart had stopped. The entire *realm* had stopped as I stared down at Nyktos.

What in the hell was wrong with me? Had I not decided to keep my big mouth shut?

Nyktos was completely still as he looked up at me. Seconds passed, and in that time, I felt the blood draining rapidly from my face before flooding back. My chest started to squeeze and ache.

He moved, lifting his other hand to my cheek. "Breathe," he whispered.

I sucked in air, shaking.

His thumb drew that line over my chin, just below my lip, and my heart was beating too fast for someone who was sitting. Because the way he stared at me, the wisps of eather beginning to spread out from behind his pupils, it felt like...*more*. Which I knew was impossible, yet...

He lifted the hand he held to his mouth and pressed a kiss against my knuckles. Then, slowly, he turned it over and pressed another kiss to my palm. He never took those now-heated, quicksilver eyes off me. "I'll be waiting for you, *liessa*."

27

Sunlight.

That was the first thing I noticed when the thick, swirling mist slowly scattered as we traveled down what sounded like a stone road. It had been so long since I'd seen the sun. Felt its warmth on my skin. I looked up, eyes stinging from the brightness as I lowered my hood. The sky was painted in shades of vivid blue and soft white, but there was no sun, and as the Primal mist continued to drift and fade, lush, rolling, green hills full of trees with purple and pink blossoms trailing down to the ground became visible. The landscape looked like a painting. There were no people. No homes or any other signs of life. My grip firm on Gala's reins, I glanced down. My brows shot up at the sight of the sparkling road.

"Are those…diamonds?" I asked.

"Crushed diamonds. The Vale was formed by the joyous tears of the most ancient Primals and gods," he said. "You'll find them just about everywhere here."

I looked over at him. He was grinning at me, and I didn't think he'd stopped since we'd left Nyktos at the crossroads. When I thought that Nyktos had possibly wanted to kiss me goodbye, and somehow felt that was almost as good as him doing so.

Nektas was still grinning.

"Shut up," I muttered.

"I didn't say anything."

"You didn't need to." More of the mist cleared. The diamond road appeared endless, snaking through the grassy hills and the heavily blossomed weeping trees, their hanging branches nearly reaching the ground.

"I didn't know you could read thoughts."

I shot him an arch glare.

His grin didn't fade, not for a second as he drew his steed closer. He was only quiet for a few moments. "Is it true? What you told him at the crossroads?"

My face warmed, and it had nothing to do with the sun. I still couldn't believe that I'd blurted that out. But I had, and I couldn't exactly say I regretted it. Maybe I'd been wrong to think it was better if Nyktos didn't know. "I did," I said finally. "I meant it."

We rode on for a few paces. "You care for him."

It wasn't a question but a statement of fact. Truth. I opened my mouth as I glanced over at him, my stomach tumbling as if I'd slipped from Gala—from the horse Nyktos had gifted me. "I do," I whispered.

That grin remained as he arched a brow. "I know."

"Well, glad that's established." I cleared my throat, facing the road.

"I knew that before you were ready to admit it to yourself."

"Congratulations," I muttered.

"Why do you think I told you to go to him when he needed to feed?" he continued as if I hadn't spoken. "I knew you needed to help him. Not wanted. Not because you felt like you had to. But because you *needed* to."

"Did you smell that on me, too?" I asked with a sigh.

Nektas snorted. "I saw it when you couldn't answer if you would've followed through on your plan if you had learned it wouldn't save your people."

The breath I took was thin. That question had left me as uncomfortable then as it did now. "I still can't answer that," I admitted hoarsely. "Part of me says yes because I would do anything to save Lasania. Anything. But the other part says no. But if I had, there would've been no need to kill me. I think that…that would've done the job for you."

I could feel Nektas's stare on me. "If that is the case, then I'm more right than I even realized."

I shot him a quick look, but he was now staring ahead, his brows a dark slash across his forehead.

"You know," he began after a couple of moments of silence, "I also took you to him that night because I knew he wouldn't hurt you."

My stomach gave another tumble. "But you thought he would hurt me the night in the Dying Woods."

"That was different. When the Primal takes their true form in anger, they are not themselves. They *become* anger and power and can lash out. And while I knew he wouldn't harm you in anger as he is usually, I didn't know what he'd do in that form." His gaze touched mine. "But now I do. He stopped himself. Not because I was there. He could've fucked me up. He stopped himself. Now, I know."

"Know what?"

"That what he feels for you goes beyond fondness. He cares for you."

"I...I know that, too."

He was quiet for a bit. "You know what he did to himself? And why?"

Swallowing hard, I nodded. "He had his *kardia* removed because he didn't want love to become a weakness or to be weaponized."

"You'd think it's because Ash doesn't want to become his father," he said after a moment. "Eythos changed after he lost Mycella. He was still good, but he lost most of his joy when Mycella died. If it hadn't been for Ash, I think he would've wasted away until he slipped into stasis."

I wondered if that was the same for Nektas. If it weren't for Jadis, would he too waste away?

"Ash grew up seeing that loss and sadness every time he looked in his father's eyes. He felt that himself, never knowing his mother's touch or hearing her voice," Nektas said. "But Ash doesn't fear becoming his father. He fears becoming his uncle."

I jerked. "He could never become Kolis."

"I don't think so, either, but even I never expected Kolis to go to such extremes." There was a pause. "He was never like Eythos. A bit more reserved. Colder. Preferred solitude. Part of that was because of what Primal essence coursed through his veins. He *is* Death, and Death does not want for company. And as Ash grows older, I see a bit of that in him already," he said, and my heart seized. "Life and death are not very different. Both are natural, a necessary cycle, for there cannot be life without death, but where Eythos was celebrated and welcomed, Kolis was feared and dreaded. That would foster jealousy in the best of us, and he was jealous of his brother. Still is, even now."

Nektas laughed without mirth, shaking his head. "But it wasn't until

Kolis experienced love and loss that he changed. That he began to become what he is today. Love can breathe life and inspiration into one, and the loss of it can rot and taint the mind of another. That is what Ash fears most." His gaze found mine again. "Loving someone. Losing them. Then becoming something even worse than Kolis."

I swallowed, finding those reasons even sadder. "But we're talking about caring for another. Not loving. Those are two different things. And I know it's impossible for him to feel such a thing."

"Are they that different?" Nektas questioned. "Because we're talking about the kind of caring that allows you to put yourself in harm's way for the one you care for. That doesn't stop you from feeling, even if you believe those emotions won't be returned. Even if you know the risks. Yet, you can still find peace."

"He *cannot* love me."

"I'm not talking about him."

I jerked again. "I-I don't love him," I denied, but the words rang a little hollow. "I don't even know what that feels like."

"Then how do you know?"

I snapped my mouth shut. A strange, heady mix of emotions swept through me, and I felt like I was falling and flying at the same time. "I can't think about this."

"Why? Because you fear that you love him, and he can't feel the same?"

"No. It's not even that. I don't want to think about it because it terrifies me," I admitted without shame.

"As it should."

I cut him a sharp look. "That's reassuring."

Nektas laughed, and I kind of wanted to hit him as I looked away. I didn't want to even think about the idea of love. It was easier to acknowledge that I cared for Nyktos. Cared deeply. But that wasn't love. And this was a conversation I didn't want to continue.

I glanced over the hills and the pendulous branches full of flowers dancing just inches from the ground. "Does the entirety of the Vale look like this?"

"Some common areas resemble this," he answered. "But for the most part, the Vale is ever-changing, accommodating a soul's ideal paradise and becoming whatever they desire."

"Wow," I murmured.

"All aspects of a soul's needs and wants are met in the Vale, even what they see. Arcadia is much the same." He shifted on his saddle.

"Look to your right and up, toward the skies. Do you see it?"

I followed his instructions, squinting until I saw shimmering mist gathering along the hills. "The mist?"

"It's called the Shroud," he said. "It's made of Primal mist and hides the Vale from those who do not enter through more traditional means."

As in, by dying.

The farther we traveled along the diamond road, the more I began to notice the mist gathering, clumping together to obscure all that lay beyond. Just like on the way to the Pillars, the Shroud steadily crept closer to the road, and in the silence, I couldn't help but wonder if I would enter the Vale upon my death if Nyktos's plan didn't work. Or would I find eternal peace in Arcadia if his plan did succeed? Did the Primal embers truly make up for the not-so-mortal morality? Or would it simply come down to Nyktos intervening upon my death and ensuring I found peace instead of punishment?

I shivered at what now felt like morbid thoughts, which was odd. I'd thought of death a lot in the past, having accepted that it was an inevitable outcome, sooner rather than later. But now, thinking about death even felt different. A too-soon end that I no longer accepted because there was hope. A possible future that offered a—

A soft hum drew me from my thoughts. My brow pinching, I looked to my right. The sound wasn't a hum. It was a voice. *Voices.* Singing. My grip on Gala's reins loosened and then firmed as I strained to hear the words. They were in a different language, one that felt ancient, and the embers buzzed in response to it. But the sound—the voices and the melody… They were a prayer. A celebration. Haunting as the voices rose and fell, beckoning. Tears filled my eyes. It was the most beautiful sound I'd ever heard.

Nektas suddenly grabbed my reins, halting Gala. "Stop."

"What?" I whispered hoarsely.

"You're getting too close," he warned, features drawn. "You can't go there."

"Go where…?" I sucked in a startled breath, realizing I was mere feet from the Shroud, closer to the soft harmony. Blinking back the tears, I looked at Nektas. "I didn't mean to."

"I know." He tugged gently on the reins, steering Gala to the center of the road. "You hear their songs?"

I nodded, heart thumping. "It's beautiful."

"It's the sirens singing."

"Sirens?"

"They are the guards of the Vale, and they've sensed us."

My attention slowly shifted back to the mist. "Why are they singing?"

"Only the draken and those who've Ascended can travel into the Vale," he said. "Whenever they sense something that shouldn't be this close, they sing to lure the trespassers into the Shroud. Not even you with Primal embers would survive that."

Skin chilled, I looked down at my white-knuckle grip on the reins and then Nektas's hand as the sirens kept singing. His fingers remained curled firmly around the reins and stayed there.

Hours later, the sirens finally stopped singing. Nektas had released his hold on my reins, and the rigid tension eased from my muscles. I ached all over from holding myself back. I'd come close to leaping from the saddle and entering the Shroud one too many times. Not even snacking on the jerky Nektas had brought with him had helped, and food was normally the ultimate distraction.

And I would have to experience that again on the way out.

I wasn't looking forward to that at all as we crested a hill, but all thoughts of the sirens and their call slipped away as a rocky horizon rose ahead. It was a mountain with sheer, vertical cliffs made of pure shadowstone and something else—something that glittered crimson under the sun, reminding me of Nektas's hair.

"Good gods, I really hope we don't have to climb that thing," I said. "If so, I think I'll take my chances with the sirens."

Nektas chuckled. "Luckily, the Pools of Divanash are beneath."

"Beneath all of that?" The mountain was a fortress of stone, an imposing sight amidst all the beauty.

He glanced at me. "You claustrophobic?"

"I don't think so."

"Well, I guess we're about to find out, aren't we?"

This will be fun, I thought as we entered the foothills and eventually stopped when Nektas spotted the slit of an entrance I wasn't sure how I was supposed to fit through, let alone Nektas. We left the horses tied beneath a weeping tree, where they nibbled on the grass and could rest.

With one final scratch behind Gala's ears, I followed Nektas. We were barely able to slide through the opening sideways, and then emerged into utter darkness.

I gasped, seeing nothing as I came to a standstill. I reached out blindly, feeling the cool, smooth wall behind me but nothing to my left. I searched the darkness, not even able to see the draken. *Breathe in.* My throat tightened as I croaked, "Nektas?"

"I'm here." His hand folded over mine, warm and firm. *Breathe out.* "Can you see?"

"I can." He started to lead the way.

"Draken must have really good eyesight," I said, my voice seeming to carry in the sweetly scented air. *Breathe in.*

"We have amazing senses."

I clung to his hand as I desperately tried not to think about the fact that I could see nothing, and anything could be within inches of me. *Hold.* Dakkais. Barrats. Giant spiders. Gods, that wasn't helping. *Breathe out.* "You said you smelled death on me before."

"I did. I still do," he answered, his voice seeming disembodied even though I held his hand like a frightened child. "I smell Ash on you."

I made a face.

"And I also smell death," he added. "Your body. It's dying."

"What the fuck?" I gasped, pulling on my hand.

Nektas held on. "You're actively dying, Sera. The Culling is killing you. You know that."

"I do." I took an even deeper breath. "But having you say that when I'm under a mountain and can't see shit puts it in a whole different perspective."

"I don't see how."

"Probably because you can see, and you aren't actively dying."

"Good point." He paused. "My apologies."

"Gods," I muttered. A moment passed with only the sound of our steps. "Do I smell bad to you?"

Nektas laughed.

My eyes narrowed. "There's nothing funny about my question."

"Yes, there is," he said. "Death does not smell bad. It carries the same scent as life but weaker. Lilacs."

Lilacs.

I'd smelled that before. Stale lilacs. I wondered if Nyktos could smell that on me. I stopped myself from asking that. I'd rather him think I smelled like a summer storm—whatever that smelled like.

We continued on in the tunnel for some time, and I didn't think we walked straight. I was about to ask if Nektas was lost when I heard the sound of water and then saw a pinprick of light that steadily grew larger. Sunlight, thank the gods. Soon, I could see Nektas in front of me.

His steps slowed. "Stay right there."

"I don't know where you expect me to go," I replied as he let go of my hand.

"Who knows with you?" He hopped down. "Someone turns their back on you for a few seconds and you run off."

"I do not."

He turned from below, offering his hands. I took them instead of kicking him. He helped me down, the drop several feet. The air was significantly warmer here and humid. Much sweeter. I took a step and immediately saw why. Thick branches smothered with lilacs snaked along the floor, climbed the walls of the cavern, and spread across the ceiling, nearly choking out the light coming through the opening above.

"That's a whole lot of lilacs." I looked around. "Is that why death smells like lilacs?"

"I don't know why death smells like that, but lilacs are special. They represent renewal, and both life and death are that—a renewal." Nektas roamed forward. "If you ever see lilacs like this near water in the mortal realm, you can be assured that you're near a gateway to Iliseeum—to Dalos, in particular."

I thought of my lake. "And if there are none?"

"Then the gateway likely leads to the Shadowlands," he said. "There it is."

Sidestepping Nektas, I saw a rocky outcropping that rose to about the height of my waist, forming a jagged circle that was roughly the size of Nektas in his draken form. The waters of the Pools of Divanash were still and clear as we approached them.

"So, what do I do?" I pressed my hands against the basin. "Just ask where he is?"

"Sort of. It will require a drop of your blood."

"Just a drop?" I reached down between the halves of my cloak and unsheathed the dagger from my thigh.

"Only a drop," he advised. "But you also have to give it something not known to others."

Gods. I'd forgotten about that part. I frowned as I stared at the Pools.

"Once you do that, the Pools should let you know it's okay to proceed. Ask who or what you're searching for, and the Pools will answer." He cocked his head. "Hopefully."

I hesitated, my hand and the dagger suspended above the water. "Hopefully?"

Nektas shrugged. "I've never seen them work."

"Great," I muttered, shaking my head. Something that wasn't known to others. "So, I basically have to admit a secret or something?"

"That's the gist of it. It's an exchange of sorts. An answer for a truth, one not known to others—likely not even to oneself."

"Not known to oneself?" I repeated quietly, my frown increasing. I started to ask what the hell that even meant, but I thought I understood what kind of truth it was looking for. One that made you uncomfortable to admit.

Gods, there were a lot of uncomfortable truths. And there wasn't enough time in the day for me to list them, starting with how I felt about my mother and ending with what I might feel for Nyktos. There were a whole lot of itchy, suffocating truths between those two things as I went through them.

But there was one that made me the most uncomfortable. One that left me feeling exposed and raw. Vulnerable.

Feeling my skin begin to crawl, I pricked a finger with the slightest bit of pressure. The wickedly sharp dagger stung, and blood immediately welled. Stretching my arm over the Pools, I watched the blood seep from my finger as I whispered words that scalded my throat, "The day I took too much sleeping draft wasn't an accident or a spur-of-the-moment decision." My hand trembled. "I didn't want to wake up."

The cavern was quiet except for the buzzing in my ears as the drop of blood slipped from my fingertip and splashed off the surface.

A hiss hit the air of the cave as I drew my hand back. The water burst to life, bubbling and roiling. Steam poured into the space above the Pools. Gasping, I took a step back as the mist swirled wildly before collapsing back into the Pools.

"I think that means it accepted your answer, *meyaah Liessa*," Nektas said quietly.

I didn't look at him. I pretended that he hadn't heard what I'd admitted. "Show me Delfai, a God of Divination," I said. "Please."

The blood sank, pulling apart as the waters rippled and swirled, swallowing the blood. Nektas moved closer as clouds formed deep under the surface, first white and then darker. It reminded me of the souls in the mist as the clouds took shape, but this was no washed-out image.

Color seeped into the pool, and a pastel blue rolled over the surface. A sky. Deep green pines rose behind a large, sweeping manor made of ivory stone, each needle on the trees glistening.

I gasped as another ripple scattered the sky and pines, erasing the manor. "I really hope that wasn't it because that told me absolutely nothing."

Nektas peered over my head. "I don't think so," he said. "Look."

The water was changing color again as shapes became visible. I tensed. A head and shoulders appeared. A body. Then another. One was taller, with skin that reminded me of amber jewels, and hair as black as night-blooming roses. It was a man, his oval-shaped face tipped to the side. He looked about the age I'd believed Holland to be, in his third or fourth decade of life. There was something in his hands. He was grinding something in a ceramic bowl as his lips moved silently. He seemed to be speaking to someone—

"That's Delfai," Nektas said, leaning around me to place a hand on the stone ledge of the pool. "Looking quite alive and well."

Whomever he spoke to was beginning to come alive in the waters. Long, thick, brownish-blond hair and straight shoulders. Pink, sun-kissed skin. A heart-shaped face. My breath caught in surprise. A face I recognized, one far fuller and with green eyes brighter and more alive than I remembered.

"I know her," I whispered, dumbfounded as I watched her smile in response to whatever Delfai was showing her in the bowl. "That's Kayleigh Balfour. The Princess of Irelone. Delfai is in Irelone—at Cauldra Manor."

28

"It has to be fate," Nektas said as we traveled back through the Vale. "That Delfai would be with someone you know at this exact moment."

"Maybe." Arms and legs already tense in preparation for the sirens, I kept my eyes trained straight ahead. "Or could it have been something this Delfai knew? Gods of Divination could see the past, present, and future, right? Maybe he knew to befriend Kayleigh?"

Nektas nodded. "They don't know all innately. It must have been something Delfai had either chosen to look into or had been asked to do. But if so, that means he would be expecting you."

I thought that over. "It was Penellaphe who told Nyktos to find Delfai. I don't know how old she is, but could it have been she who said something to Delfai?"

"Penellaphe was young when Kolis stole Eythos's embers, but old enough to remember the Gods of Divination," he said. "It would make sense that she would seek a God of Divination to learn more about her vision."

And Holland could have also walked that fine line of interfering again. Either way, it was no coincidence. "You know, Princess Kayleigh was betrothed to my stepbrother," I said, not having told Nektas how I knew her. "She came to visit Lasania with her parents, King Saegar and Queen Geneva. To meet Tavius. My stepbrother was an...unrepentant ass."

"I figured as much." Nektas leaned over, straightening my hood that must've slipped. "Considering the enjoyment Ash finds in *visiting* him in the Abyss."

"He does that often?"

"More than he has with any other soul in a long time."

I pressed my lips together to stop my smile because even I could acknowledge that was a twisted thing to find pleasure in. I cleared my throat. "Anyway, he was on his best behavior with her. At first. It didn't last long. I saw her crying one evening after taking an unsupervised walk with him in the gardens. I don't know what happened, but I know it was something terrible because when I warned her about him, she wasn't at all surprised to hear what I had to say."

"But she didn't marry him?" he asked, and when I shook my head, he inclined his. "She could walk away from such an engagement? I was under the impression that wasn't common in the mortal realm among nobles."

"It's not." My lips twitched into a small grin. "So, we concocted a plan to make her...unavailable for such an engagement."

His brows rose beneath his hood. "And how did you accomplish that?"

"I gained a potion from a Healer I knew, one that could make her appear sick—ill enough that the engagement would have to be postponed." I laughed at his smile. "It worked. Kayleigh convinced her parents it had to be the warmer, more humid climate of Lasania, and they took her home. I don't know if they believed it was some climate-related issue, Irelone is much cooler, but they...they love her. That much was clear when they didn't force her to remain in Lasania, nor made her return."

"Very clever of both of you," he said. "Though it's a shame that anyone would have to resort to such tactics."

"Agreed," I murmured. "Tavius, my mother, and King Ernald never knew for sure that I interfered, but I think they suspected something." I shrugged. "But if I hadn't? Would that have altered Delfai's decision? And would we not have been able to locate him in the mortal realm? I mean, it all has to be connected." I laughed again. "I guess every aspect of one's life is somehow connected—every choice to do or not do something creates a chain reaction. You can't help but wonder exactly how much is preordained."

"You'll drive yourself mad thinking about that," Nektas replied. "But none of your choices are preordained. Fate is not absolute. Fate is only a series of possibilities."

"How can you be sure of that?" I asked.

"Because I was there when mortals were created. I lent my fire to breathe life into their flesh," he reminded me. "Mortals were created in the image of the Primals, but they were also given more."

"The ability to feel emotion."

"And free will," he said. "Fate doesn't usurp that, no matter how much the Arae probably wish they did in some situations. Fate just sees all the possible outcomes of free will."

I felt some relief in hearing that, knowing that the decisions made, whether good or bad, were choices actively made and not a result of haplessly following a set of events already decided. I glanced at Nektas as the Shroud protecting the Vale crept steadily closer to the road, and I began to hear the sirens singing once more. "Do Primals have free will?"

"They didn't in the beginning."

I remembered what Nyktos had told me. "Their ability to begin to feel emotion changed that?"

He nodded. "Nothing is more powerful, more life and realm-altering than the ability to feel. To experience emotion. Love. Hate. Desire. To care for oneself. To care for another."

Nyktos wasn't waiting for us at the crossroads as we left the Vale like I'd expected him to be. The creepy riders were, though, and they bowed once more as we passed. I figured Nyktos had gotten caught up with something, either at the Pillars themselves or in Lethe. Nektas didn't appear concerned, so I didn't think anything too serious had occurred.

I didn't look at the souls waiting to cross through the Pillars, even though the embers throbbed, and my muscles were already tense and achy from fighting the sirens' call. But the Primal mist finally abated, and I could see crimson in the distance, glittering under the bright starlight. I nibbled on a piece of cheese that Nektas had handed over as my thoughts bounced from one thing to another and I ignored the faint ache building in my temples. I wouldn't once I returned to the palace. It may not be the Culling, but I wouldn't risk it if so.

"Sera?"

Finishing off the piece of cheese, I glanced over at Nektas. "Yeah?"

"You okay?" he asked, looking at me and then returning his gaze to the road ahead.

It took me a moment to realize what he was asking, and when I did, a flush swept through me. My hands tightened on Gala's reins. It felt like my tongue thickened, becoming heavy and useless as my heart began to pound.

You okay?

Such a simple question. One easily answered by many, I imagined. One I could've answered that morning without hesitation or much thought. *You okay?* Now, the question was loaded with meaning because not only the Pools of Divanash knew a secret not known to others. Nektas did, too.

"I…I think so," I said finally, beating back the prickly, uncomfortable wave. "I will be," I added with a shrug. "I always am."

"Not everyone can always be okay," he said quietly. "And if you happen to find that you're not, you can talk to me. We'll make sure you're okay. Agreed?"

Throat and eyes stinging, my head whipped toward him. His gaze was still fixed on the road, and I didn't know if he did that on purpose or not. Maybe he knew that it was easier this way. "Agreed," I whispered.

"Good," he replied, and for a time, that was all that was said. A silence fell between us as a knot lodged itself deep in my chest, where that crack had formed.

I was moved by his offer, a little shaken and caught off guard. It was an unexpected…kindness, and it made me want to dive face-first into the road at the same time I wanted to hug the draken.

"Halt," Nektas ordered sharply.

Jerked from my thoughts, I drew Gala to a stop. Concern blossomed. "What is it?"

He tipped his head back, sniffing the air. "We're about to have company." His chin dipped as his gaze swept over the land, barren except for the large boulders and scattered, dead trees that must've grown from the lakes that had once flowed here. "And it will not be of a friendly nature."

"Great." I reached along Gala's side and unstrapped one of the short swords Nyktos had placed there. "I knew this trip felt too uneventful." I followed his gaze, not seeing anything at first. Then movement by one of the frail, hollow trees close to the road snagged my attention. I squinted as my grip firmed around the hilt of the sword.

"Do not strike first," Nektas warned quietly. Thin, long fingers folded around the edge of the trunk, the color a muddy grayish-brown. The fingers curled, digging into the bark. Claws. I stiffened. A thin arm became visible, the skin appearing hard and craggy, like…bark. "They may allow us to pass without incident. Ride slowly. Stay alert."

I watched that hand on the tree as I nudged Gala forward. "What are they?"

Nektas brought his horse closer to mine. "They're nymphs, and they're ancient. They were normally kind, benevolent creatures that lived in the forests and lakes throughout Iliseeum, tending to the land that fed them. Friends of the dragons and then the Primals and gods," he said, and I zeroed in on the *normally* part of that statement and the past tense of the rest. "But they are now yet another repercussion of Kolis's actions. When he stole Eythos's embers, it corrupted them. Turned them into creatures of nightmares that now feed off pain and torture."

"Oh," I whispered. "They sound lovely."

"They used to be one of the loveliest creatures you'd ever see in Iliseeum," he returned.

I didn't let myself feel the twinge of sadness that accompanied the knowledge that Kolis had tainted them. It would do me no favors if I did and they decided that they wouldn't let us pass. "Were they here when we traveled to the Pillars?"

"They are always here."

I thought about how both Nyktos and he had been eyeing the land. "Are they what drew Ehthawn away?"

"Probably." Nektas's hand rested on the sword strapped to his horse. "They don't usually attack a Primal or their Consort. Anything and everything else is fair game. Neither draken fire nor eather does anything to them. The only way to stop them is to remove their heads."

"Great," I murmured as we passed the tree the one lurked behind. I caught sight of another behind a boulder. "How many do you think are here?"

"There could be hundreds," he said, and my heart seized. "But I have seen only about a dozen near the road."

"Must be that good draken eyesight because I've only seen two."

"It is. I also know what to look for."

We traveled several minutes in tense silence. I saw one more. This time, a little bit more of the nymph. A spindly leg. A foot latched into the bark.

The Rise came more into view, and I was just starting to be a little hopeful that they'd let us pass when Nektas muttered, "Shit."

Then I saw it.

A nymph crouched in the center of the road, shoulders hunched and so small it had blended into the road itself.

It rose slowly, and I, honest to gods, really wanted to see one of these things before they changed because this creature truly was a thing of nightmares. Skin like bark, twisted and knobbed. Talons for fingers and toes. Facial features cracked and distorted. Skull hairless with a crown of jagged, exposed bone.

"I want to hear you scream," the nymph hissed in a guttural, wet voice. "I want to see you bleed like a stream." It lurched into motion, racing toward us.

Nektas withdrew a blade from the sleeve of his cloak. He threw the dagger, striking the creature between the eyes. Thrown back, the nymph howled, thrashing as it grabbed for the blade embedded in its head.

The air filled with hisses from both sides of the road. I cursed, swinging myself down as Nektas did the same. They were a blur, seeming to bleed out from the uneven basin, the trees, and the rocks.

"I'll get this side," Nektas advised, striding forward, swinging the shadowstone blade across the throat of the nymph on the road, removing its head. The creature shattered into glittering silver dust. "You got the other?"

I braced myself. "I was considering letting them do whatever, but I suppose so."

He smirked from within the shadows of his hood as he turned to the right side of the road.

The nymphs converged on us. One was ahead of the others. "Need. Greed. Bleed," it seethed, leaping.

Stepping forward, I swung the sword straight across as it landed, sweeping the blade through the nymph's neck. As the creature broke apart, I spun, catching a second nymph. It too exploded.

Two crossed the road at once. "Hate," one rasped.

"Fate," another gurgled.

I twisted, kicking the first nymph in the knee. The creature's leg cracked, splitting up the center. "Ew," I whispered, driving the sword through the other's neck and then the first's as it hobbled toward me.

Glancing at the other side of the road, I saw Nektas methodically cutting through the nymphs. My head whipped as I darted to the side, narrowly avoiding a nymph's claws.

"Dead. Bled. Red." The nymph whirled.

"Do they always talk like this?" I yelled as I drew the blade across its neck. There appeared only to be a few left.

Nektas tossed a nymph as he slammed his sword through another. "If you consider rhyming nonsense to be talking, yes."

The hum of embers in my chest was a whisper in my blood as I swung. A dry hand clawed at the air, inches from my face as I spun. Cursing, I jerked back and turned, thrusting the sword back. The blade struck the nymph's chest. Dust puffed out, shimmery and thick. I drew the sword up, across its neck—

A horse neighed nervously, causing my heart to plummet. A nymph rushed the horses. "Fear is my spear," it hissed. "Pain is your gain."

"That doesn't even make sense." I shot after the nymph. "Oh, no, you don't. You are not going to touch them."

I clasped the nymph's shoulder, the skin rough and dry beneath mine, just as it swiped out at Gala. I knew I wouldn't be fast enough with the sword. The nymph would get its claws in the horse. Fury entrenched itself deep, stirring up the embers. Several things happened at once.

The embers vibrated wildly in my chest, heat flooded my veins, and silvery-white light crowded the corners of my vision as power built, ramping up inside me and charging the air. I gasped as eather sparked across my hand. I jerked back, but it was too late. The essence flowed over the nymph and seeped through the husk of its flesh. Light filled all the hundreds of tiny cracks all over its body, lighting it up from the inside and then from the outside. Eather poured from its open mouth and eyes.

The nymph exploded.

A wave of power blew back, so intense the burst of eather knocked me on my ass when it rolled into me.

"Holy shit," I whispered, lifting the sword as a shadow fell over me. Nektas stared down at me. "I thought you said eather didn't do anything to them?"

"It shouldn't," he said. "Only the Primal of Life can wield the kind of eather that can kill a nymph." Nektas jerked his hood back. "It's the same kind of power that can kill another Primal."

Nektas said very little the remainder of the journey back to the palace, and that left me a bit uneasy.

I wasn't a Primal, so I couldn't understand how I could have the kind of eather in me that could kill another Primal. Or how the embers could be *that* strong.

And I had hit Nyktos with that eather. I could've…

Gods, I couldn't even let myself finish that line of thought—a sure indicator of how much I'd changed. What I needed to do was work on controlling the embers until Nyktos removed them.

After giving Gala a quick brush down and some alfalfa, I parted ways with Nektas as I entered the palace, promising to go straight to Nyktos. Nektas left to return to Jadis, who was in the mountains I'd yet to see.

Figuring Nyktos must be in his office, I headed there and entered the hall. Within a few seconds, I grinned at the sensation of the embers wiggling in my chest. I stepped into the alcove, noting that the door was ajar as I pushed one side open—

I stopped, his name shriveling and dying on my lips before it could even become a whisper. I couldn't understand what I saw. It was as if my mind couldn't process what my eyes were telling me.

That it was Nyktos seated on the settee, one hand lax on the cushion beside him, the other clenching the arm in a white-knuckled grip. His body taut, head thrust back, and eyes closed, the striking lines of his face tense, and his skin paler than it should be.

Or that he wasn't alone.

Nowhere close to that.

Someone was in his *lap*. A female—a thin, willowy female wearing a shimmery, violet gown was in *his* lap. Straddling him. Golden-blond ringlets fell against *his* chest and shielded her face as she clutched *his* shoulders, pale fingers digging into the dark shirt—as she moved against *him*. I couldn't see her face, but I knew who it was.

Veses.

The Primal of Rites and Prosperity was in Nyktos's lap. Touching him. Riding him. *Feeding* from his throat.

29

My heart sped up and then slowed as my body flashed hot before turning icy. I felt utterly nothing as I stood there, staring at Nyktos. At Veses. At *them*. I tried to make sense of what I was seeing—why he was with anyone, let alone *her*, the one he'd called the worst sort.

It didn't make sense.

It couldn't.

Maybe I'd hit my head fighting the nymphs and was hallucinating because that seemed more plausible than this. Than her feeding from Nyktos. Than them *together*.

Because I'd told him that I wanted to be his Consort.

He'd called me *liessa*—someone he found beautiful. Someone he found powerful.

Someone who would become his Queen.

Then she moaned, the sound husky and sensual. The arm of the settee creaked under Nyktos's tightening grasp, and the noise—the *sounds*—knocked me out of the shocked numbness.

My mind. My body. Every part of me processed what I was seeing. Emotions came in a rising tide, swamping me, and they were intense and sudden as Nyktos's head jerked sluggishly. I shuddered under the hot, stifling weight of...of *hurt*. Raw, tangy agony drenched every pore. Suffocating, crushing *hurt* carved through muscles and bone. The crack in my chest shook as my skin prickled with heat.

With something else.

Veses' golden head lifted at the sound of air wheezing from my parted lips. Two deep, angry puncture wounds marred the side of Nyktos's throat. Thick, shiny hair slid back over one slender shoulder as the Primal looked at me. The pouty, blood-red mouth stood out grotesquely against the delicateness of her beauty. Surprise flickered over her features, then luminous silver eyes widened and then locked with mine as her pink tongue darted over her lower lip. She licked at the blood there. *Nyktos's* blood.

Bitter bile crowded my throat. I choked on it, still rooted in place, unable to move as Veses looked me over. Sized me up. The twist of her lip told me she found what she saw lacking, and, gods, I *felt* that all the way to the bone as I stared at her. At them. Two beautiful, powerful Primals. Together.

Veses' eyebrow rose. That scathing curl transformed into a painfully beautiful smile. "So, this is her?" she asked, speaking in that throaty voice I remembered before she giggled.

Nyktos's head turned slowly. His eyes fluttered open, and that—that was all I could take.

There was no thought behind my actions. It was instinct. I stumbled back a step, bumping into the door. Heart thumping once more, I spun around.

Veses laughed.

And that blade-sharp laugh followed me as I walked from the office. It clung to my skin because I'd never felt so naïve, so foolish. That laugh stayed with me as the crack in my chest shuddered violently. But it was Nyktos's words that haunted me as I broke into a run.

She's very important to me.

I ran blindly, my throat constricting.

You are one of the strongest people I've ever met.

I threw open the door as the embers in my chest pulsated, joining the throbbing agony.

You were never a ghost to me.

Some unknown need drove me down the narrow, musty stairwell.

Liessa.

My boots slipped on the steps. I went down on my ass, the flare of dull pain nothing compared to the sorrow crushing me from the inside. I'd never felt anything like it before as I scrambled to my feet and kept going. Not even when my family left for the country estates, and I had been too young to understand why they'd left me behind. Not even the stinging slap my mother delivered the night of my seventeenth birthday had hurt this badly. Wasn't as deep. Didn't steal every too-short breath.

I hit the gap between the last step and the floor with a grunt, but I didn't slow. I raced past the cells, trying to outrun what I saw. Outpace Nyktos's words.

You are brave and strong.

The bars lining the cells were a blur as I passed them, reaching the end of the first hall. I went left as pressure clamped down on my chest.

You will be a Consort more than worthy of their swords and shields.

The shadowstone walls crowded me as I tried to escape myself.

My stupid heart.

My foolish ideas of him—of Nyktos. Of what I could mean to him. Of what he meant to me. There was no running away from them as I fell against the door at the end of the hall. Each breath I took hurt as I pressed my forehead against the wood, squeezing my eyes shut against the welling dampness. But it was too late. My cheeks were damp, even though I didn't cry. I didn't allow myself that.

I clamped my jaw shut as I slammed my palm against the door, searching for anger. For fury. But all I found was grief. Hurt. Disappointment. In him. In me.

I shouldn't have made that deal with him. It was never pleasure for the sake of pleasure. I'd been lying to myself then. I could see that now. I wouldn't have been so torn up over what my betrayal had done to him if it was only about that. I wouldn't have wanted him and only him.

And for him to demand that I seek pleasure from no one else? How *dare* he?

Hands shaking, chest aching, I found the handle and yanked it open. I staggered into the dimly lit cavern of a chamber, closing the door behind me. I backed up, shoving my hands over my face as the pool trickled softly behind me. My fingers were wet, and I...I shouldn't have allowed this.

"Oh, gods," I whispered hoarsely, trembling.

I shouldn't have let myself feel anything. I should've known better. I had been trained better than this. I was smart. Fierce. Empty. Cunning—

The image of Veses curled around Nyktos assaulted me, and I

saw her moving against him. Feeding from him. And I remembered what his bite did to me. I couldn't forget how shocking that pleasure had been. Had she made her bite hurt like Taric had with me? Or did she give him the same kind of pleasure Nyktos gave me? I saw his white-knuckled grip on the arm of the chair. She had his blood in her. Did she have anything else inside her? With her gown, I couldn't—

Gagging, I spun around and bent, clasping my knees as the crack in my chest shook and shook. I straightened suddenly, staring straight ahead but seeing nothing of the pool's dark beauty. His pool.

He'd told me there had been no one before me. And his supposed lack of experience? How I believed him to be a fast learner? I closed my eyes, but it didn't stop me from seeing Veses again, so comfortable with touching him. I once more saw her in his lap, and I flinched.

I should've *fucking* known.

Nyktos couldn't love. Maybe he could care, but whatever stopped someone from doing that had to come from the same place that love did. The same place attachments were held. Bonds that ran deeper than blood. I should've expected there would be no such loyalty to me.

I laughed, the sound shocking and strange. My eyes peeled open as I grew hot. Reaching for the clasp on my cloak, I tore it free, letting it float to the ground, where it trembled. I wouldn't have given a damn if he'd slept with half the mortal realm and Iliseeum before me. But he had lied, and none of my lies made his sting any less. Because what I saw was *today*. Not *before*. He had her in his office, in his lap, and she had been feeding from him, doing the gods only knew what else. After me.

After he'd told me how brave and strong I was. How worthy I was. After he'd told me I had never been a ghost to him. After I'd felt safe with him. Slowly, I turned to the stone table and...I could *see* us there.

The anger finally came, pouring into me, filling my veins, and seeping through my bones. Rage flooded the crack in my chest, swallowing the vibrating embers, and what came rushing back felt as rotten and decayed as the nymphs. Fire swept through me, seizing my lungs as I stared at the stone table. Safe. I'd felt safe here with him. *Safe* enough to let myself *want more*. To feel. To live. To hope. Pressure built and built. Air charged around me and then stilled. The water stopped whispering. I trembled as I took a step forward, my mouth opening. The sound that came from me hurt my ears, and with it came a tidal wave of pain and fury and power—ancient, infinite power. *Unleashed.*

The stone table shattered into ashes.

Faint, flickering light and shadows danced against the now-bare wall. I looked down at my hands—at the widespread fingers lit from *within*. Silvery light pressed against the sleeves of my blouse as I shook, as dust drifted down, falling onto my wet cheeks. My blood and my lungs continued to burn. I kept shaking—no, it wasn't me shaking. It was the walls and the high, sweeping ceiling.

Heart tripping, I turned to the pool. The water tossed and tumbled violently but made no sound. Dust fell in thicker sheets like snow. Panic blossomed as the cloak appeared to vibrate along the floor. Pain lit up my chest. Real pain. I wasn't breathing. I was holding my breath.

I forced my mouth open to inhale, but my throat felt bumpy and scaled now. Only thin wisps of air got through as I desperately went through Holland's technique, struggling to control myself.

A fissure cracked along the wall, startling me. Another formed in the floor, sounding like thunder.

Oh, gods. I was doing this.

I needed to breathe, but I needed to calm first. I frantically searched for the veil in my mind as I sank to my hands and knees. In the distant part of my brain, I knew I was breathing too fast. That was the problem, but I couldn't find the emptiness, the blank canvas I hated so much. I couldn't find myself in the calm because I wasn't sure I would even recognize myself if I did. That I would even know who or what I was.

A series of shivers ran up my neck and along the back of my skull. My fingers curled against the shadowstone floor as thin cracks spread out beneath me like a fine spiderweb. The embers in my chest vibrated as the fractures in the floor deepened. The corners of my eyes turned white. Stars began bursting all across my vision.

Something…something was inside the cracks in the floor, growing and spreading—

Roots snaked out of the split stone and soil, unfurling over my hands like vines, wrapping my wrists, arms. My stomach seized. What…what was happening?

I could see the ashy roots, but I couldn't feel their weight against my skin. I couldn't feel my legs or my face. Oh, gods, was this it? Was

I dying now, and the ground was rising up to claim my corpse? It felt like that—felt like the realm was disappearing beneath me, and I could no longer feel myself. I was detached. Floating. Falling away—

Arms swept around mine, hauling my back against a chest, breaking the roots on my arms. They shattered into ash upon hitting the ground. *Sera.* I heard my name. I heard it spoken over and over until it broke through.

"Sera," Nyktos shouted, hauling us backward as roots reached out from new cracks beneath me, falling over my legs—over Nyktos's. He cursed, letting go of me long enough to grab one of the roots, snapping it off. "You need to slow your breathing. Listen to me," he said, his voice softening. "Put your tongue behind your upper front teeth."

The order caught me so off guard that I did as he ordered.

"Keep your tongue there and your mouth closed." He leaned back, keeping me close as he straightened my posture even as the roots crawled up our bodies, crossing my chest. I jerked, whimpering as the vines encircled our waists. He grabbed at the roots again, wrenching them away. "Ignore them. Close your eyes and listen to me. Focus only on me. I want you to exhale to the count of four. Don't breathe in. Just exhale. One. Two. Three. Four. Now inhale for the same count." His hand went to the side of my neck and his thumb moved in short swipes against my pulse, to his counting. "Now breathe out for the same count. Don't stop."

I followed his instructions, not too different from what Holland had taught me. I breathed in for four counts and then exhaled for the same length. Nyktos quietly repeated the instructions, his chest rising and falling against my back in time with mine. Inhale. Exhale. Rise. Fall. Over and over as the roots wound their way around us, slapping over the hand at my neck, our shoulders—

"It's not working," a voice scratched from the shadows, sounding so very far away. I opened my eyes then, finding Rhain crouched before me. His eyes were wide as he broke off pieces of root. "You've got to stop this, Nyktos." Black dust fell against his cheeks and into his reddish-gold hair. "Before it's too late."

Nyktos cursed behind me. The hand at my throat turned my head. Nyktos stared down at me, his skin too pale and too thin, but there were no shadows beneath his flesh. No eather filling his veins. Red marked his throat. Puncture wounds.

I jerked, pulling against his hold.

"Do it." Rhain tore another root free. "Do it now, or she's not only going to get herself killed but bring this whole damn palace down on our heads."

"Fuck," the Primal snarled, clasping the back of my head. "I'm sorry. I'm so sorry." His forehead touched mine briefly, and then he pulled back. "Listen to me, Seraphena." Eather swirled through his eyes, and his voice…it was deeper, slower. "*Stop fighting me and listen.*"

I stopped struggling.

I listened.

Waited.

Once more an empty vessel.

A blank canvas.

And when Nyktos spoke again, it was just one word, both a whisper and a yell that reached deep inside me, seizing me. Taking control.

Sleep.

30

I dreamt of my lake.

I was swimming. That was how I knew I was dreaming. I'd never learned how to swim, but I glided seamlessly through the cool, midnight water. I wasn't alone. A lone figure sat on the bank, watching.

A white wolf.

The wolf waited in the shadows of the elms, its thick fur a lush silver in the fractured beams of moonlight.

I didn't know how long I dreamed, but I swam and swam, full of *peace*. Surrounded by it.

The wolf waited.

My arms and legs didn't grow tired. My skin didn't wrinkle and prune. Neither hunger nor thirst found me. I swam above the water and then below.

And the beast waited.

"Sera."

I slowly blinked open eyes that felt as if they'd been stitched closed. It took a moment for my vision to clear and for me to piece together the rounded cheeks and chin, the onyx-hued hair and eyes that tapered at the corners—irises a luminous silver.

"Bele?" I croaked, wincing at the scratchiness of my throat.

"My name is Nell."

I inhaled sharply, surrounded by the scent of citrus and fresh air. "W-what?"

A quick grin pulled at her full lips. "I'm kidding." The goddess looked over her shoulder and yelled, "She's finally awake."

I winced, my ears strangely sensitive. *Finally awake?* Bele disappeared from view, and I saw smooth, black walls and a long, deep couch. My head turned, and my heart stopped as my gaze landed on the small wooden box on the nightstand by the bed.

I was in the Primal's bedchamber.

Memories surged through me—images of *him* and *her* in his office, the bite marks on his throat, and the crushing agony of my mad flight to the pool beneath the palace. The disappointment. The heartbreak—

No.

I wouldn't go there. Wouldn't feel that again—any of it. I started to sit up—

"Let's not do that yet." Rhain entered the chambers, the straps designed to hold his weapons hanging loosely across his chest.

I halted, remembering him being beneath the palace, breaking off...roots that had grown from the cracks I'd created in the foundation, witnessing my utter loss of control. My face warmed.

Rhain approached the bed I had no idea how I'd gotten into. "How are you feeling?" he asked, the line of his brows furrowed as he sat on the edge of the bed. He sounded concerned but also...relieved, and I didn't understand why he would feel either of those two things.

Or why he would be in these chambers.

"Okay," I whispered hoarsely, glancing around and seeing only Bele lingering by the couch, swathed in the gray of the guard. "Thirsty."

"Bele," Rhain called out. "Will you do me a favor and get us some water and juice, please?"

"Do I look like I want to do you a favor?" Bele countered.

The answer would be no.

Rhain shot a sharp glare at her over his shoulder. She sighed heavily, rolling her eyes. "Whatever," she muttered. "I'll be *happy* to."

The god's lips twitched as he watched her stomp toward the doors. "Thank you."

Bele flipped him off.

Rhain's soft laugh faded as his attention returned to me. "Do you have a headache? Any jaw pain?"

"No." Trepidation mounted, joining the rising confusion. "Should I?"

"Not sure." He shrugged, and none of that was exactly reassuring. "You want to try to sit up and see what happens?"

"I don't know." I stared at him, even more confused. "Do I?"

A grin appeared, one I hadn't seen since he'd learned of my betrayal. It quickly faded. "Let's try it."

I had a lot of questions, starting with what had exactly happened to me under the palace and ending with the one I didn't want to ask. Where was Nyktos? But I didn't want to know where he was. Planting my hands on the soft mattress, I pushed up.

"Slowly." Rhain leaned forward to help, his hand brushing my arm—my bare arm. A flicker of energy buzzed from my skin to his, drawing a hiss from him as he jerked back.

"Sorry," I gasped. "Did I hurt you?"

"No." He blinked rapidly. "Just wasn't expecting the charge of energy to be that strong."

It was similar to what I felt when my skin came into contact with…with Nyktos's, but this hadn't felt *that* strong to me. The blanket slipped as I sat up, falling to my waist and revealing that I was completely nude. I hastily yanked the soft fur to my chin as my eyes flew to Rhain's. "Why am I naked? And please tell me it wasn't you who undressed me."

Rhain smirked. "Don't worry. I'm not even remotely interested in what you just flashed me. Now, if you were Saion or Ector, I would've been all into the peepshow."

"I didn't flash you," I grumbled, clenching the blanket. "On purpose."

He watched me lean against the tufted headboard. "By the way, it was either Aios or Bele who did that. You were coated in dust and dirt, and Nyktos didn't want you to wake up covered in filth."

My heart gave a too-sharp twist. "How thoughtful of him."

Rhain's head cocked once more, his eyes narrowing.

I glanced at the doors again, then to the one leading to the bathing chamber. Both were closed. I refocused on Rhain. "What in the hell happened?"

"I was hoping you could answer that for me."

"I just woke up, so how am I supposed to know?"

"I was talking about what came before you lost your shit and nearly collapsed the entire palace," he replied, and I tensed. "Never seen anything like that—not even from a Primal in their Culling." His chin lifted slightly. "You're powerful, Sera."

"Thanks," I murmured.

"Not sure if it's a compliment," he replied. "What's the last thing you remember?"

It took a couple of moments to put the panicked, disjointed memories into order. "I...I shattered a table, and the whole palace was shaking. There were these roots coming out of the ground." I shook my head. "Then...Nyktos was there. So were you. I was..."

"Losing your shit?"

I arched a brow. "That's one way of putting it," I muttered. "I didn't mean to lose control and do whatever I was doing. It just happened, and I..." My face warmed further. "I panicked." There was more, faded memories of Rhain telling Nyktos something. "That's the last thing I remember."

Bele swept back into the chamber then, carrying a glass in one hand and a pitcher in the other. The daggers strapped to her hips and thighs glittered darkly under the nearby sconces as she came closer.

"I feel like I missed something," I said, eyeing the cup Bele held, wanting to snatch it from her hands.

Bele snorted.

Rhain sent her another disgruntled look I wasn't sure she even noticed—or cared about if she did. He took the cup from her and handed it to me, careful not to let his hands contact mine.

Which made me even more concerned. But Rhain's behavior left me all the more unnerved. "Why are you being nice to me?" I blurted out.

Bele let out a loud laugh as Rhain leaned back a good foot. "I don't know what you mean," he said.

"You don't like me. We both know that," I pointed out, watching the slopes of Rhain's cheeks turn pink. "But you're here, and you're being sort of nice. So, did I almost die or something?"

"Well." Bele drew out the word.

My unease grew as I lifted the cup to my parched lips. The first swallow of water was bliss. I drank greedily, my eyes closing as I gulped down the cool liquid.

"Slow it down," Rhain advised softly. "It's been a while since you ate, and I don't want you to get sick from drinking too fast."

A while since I ate? I'd had a rather large breakfast, and that couldn't have been that long ago. I glanced between the two. Unless it had been longer than I realized. I *sipped* the water. "Exactly how long have I been sleeping?"

"For three days," Bele answered.

I choked, spitting water all over my chin and onto Rhain's arms.

"Could you have waited until she finished swallowing?" he asked the goddess.

Bele shrugged. "Considering how much she is drinking, that would have been an hour from now."

"I'm sorry." I dragged my arm across my chin. "I've been asleep for *three days?* How is that possible?"

"The Culling." Rhain took my cup, placing it on the nightstand. "And it's not really a sleep. It's stasis. It can happen when the body is overworked. Basically, your system shuts down to give itself time to rebuild the depleted energy required for when you're in the Culling. It doesn't always happen," he said, and I remembered Nyktos mentioning it before. "It all depends on how much energy you've been using, and what you've been doing to replenish that energy."

"I slept once for four days." Bele crossed her arms. "It was like hibernating. I kind of wish I could do that now, to be honest."

Rhain sighed as I dragged my gaze from her and reached for my water. He grabbed the cup, handing it over. I finished the contents, wishing it was whiskey. "Anyway, you exhausted yourself, so your body gave you time to recover."

"You're lucky it was only three days." Bele went back to the table to grab the pitcher of what I hoped was juice. "You could've been knocked out for weeks."

"Weeks? That can happen?" I mumbled.

Rhain nodded. "It's happened to gods who haven't been feeding. But most in their Culling don't survive that kind of energy depletion."

I frowned. "The roots that came out of the ground? Is that what happens normally?"

Rhain scoffed. "Hell, no, it's not. That only happens when Primals go into stasis. The roots—they're meant to protect a Primal as they rest. They were protecting you."

"They were *choking* me."

"They were trying to cover you, to keep you safe. Okay, let me explain it this way," Rhain said when he saw my look of disbelief. "Primals are a part of the very fabric of the realms. The roots keep them connected to the realms while they rest. Understand?"

"Yeah," I whispered.

Rhain squinted. "You don't understand."

"No." I turned to Bele. "But either way, I'm not a Primal."

"But you have *Primal* embers in you. So, yeah, you're basically a Primal in their Culling." Bele refilled the cup. "You're a little ball of specialness."

Rhain looked a little less than impressed by that statement.

"You just need to make sure that doesn't happen again," Rhain said as I took the cup from Bele. "Because the next time you go to sleep, you may not wake up."

"Like…at all," Bele added as I took a drink of the sweet fruit juice. It did so much more to ease the scratchiness of my throat. "It's common enough that you kind of prepare to die during the Culling."

"Bele," Rhain groaned.

"What? It's true. I told my mother I wanted a ceremony if I died," she went on. "A large, obnoxious one full of endless prayers to the Primals and a countless stream of mourners to speak only of how great I was. I want loud, heartfelt sobbing—not just a few tears. I'm talking full-on, ugly crying. Snot running down the face kind of sobbing." The skin above her brows creased as her lips pursed. "And at least one good fight as my body burns. Like a full-on fight that even knocks over the pyre."

I stared at Bele. "Wow."

"That about sums it up," Rhain remarked.

I looked at him and then remembered what he'd been saying to Nyktos. *You've got to stop this. Do it.* And I remembered becoming empty. Blank. My grip on the cup tightened. "I didn't go to sleep."

"No, not on your own," Rhain confirmed.

"Nyktos…he used *compulsion* on me."

"He didn't want to," Rhain said, and I remembered that, too—remembered Nyktos trying to get me to calm my breathing. His near-palpable reluctance. "But if he hadn't, you wouldn't be here. If you didn't bring the palace down on us, you could've gone into your Ascension. And that would've killed you. Do you understand? Because that was likely what was happening. You were forcing yourself into Ascension."

I wasn't forcing myself into shit, but I got what he was saying. "I...I understand," I said, and that was hard. "I get why he had to do it, but that doesn't mean I have to like it."

Rhain's nostrils flared. "Yet again, I don't think you understand."

Anger sparked as I held his stare. "I spent my whole life without free will, but I was aware that I had no control. With compulsion, I have no awareness. That may not seem like a difference to you or one that should matter, but it does to me. But like I said, I understand why he did it. The alternative would've been death."

Something flickered over his face, but it was gone before I could understand what it was. "Just don't hold it against him." He looked away. "He'll do that for you."

Something else Rhain had said suddenly struck me. That I had no idea what Nyktos had sacrificed for me—

Juice sloshed as Bele plopped down on the side of the bed, weapons and all. Rhain sent her an exasperated look.

Clearing my thoughts, I took a careful drink as I refocused on what was important. "How do we keep this from happening again?" I asked. "The going into stasis—"

"And likely dying?" Bele finished for me.

"Yeah," I muttered. "That."

"Eating. Lots of protein." Bele propped herself against the headboard. "Chocolate, too, if I remember correctly."

Chocolate. Now I understood why that often accompanied the food brought to me and why Nyktos was always so focused on my meals.

"Physical activity," Rhain tacked on. "That helps."

"And, yeah, that sounds counterproductive," Bele said. "But there's science behind it that I never cared to learn. Sleeping. Like not that sleep-of-the-dead thing you were just doing, but normal, good old eight hours of sleep."

"I don't think I've ever slept eight hours multiple nights," I said. "The chocolate I can deal with, though."

"Blood also helps." Bele lifted an eyebrow as I glanced at her. "Blood of the gods, that is. Or a Primal's." She winked at me. "You'd drink it just like you're chugging that juice," she said, and I glanced down at my cup. "It can be a little weird that way if you don't keep it warm. Gets kind of thick and congealed."

"Fates," Rhain muttered, running his hand down his face.

My stomach churned as I leaned into the headboard. I should've paid way more attention to Nyktos when he warned me about the Culling instead of getting annoyed with his comments about making sure I was eating and resting enough. I lowered the cup, glancing past Bele to the chamber doors. "Has anyone else been here while I rested?"

"Not that I know of," Bele said.

I glanced at Rhain. He was staring at the pitcher. Did neither of them know about Veses' visit? Rhain must have been close by to find me by the pool with Nyktos, but that didn't mean he knew she'd been here. As far as I knew, gods couldn't sense a Primal's arrival like another Primal could.

"Where is he?" I couldn't stop myself from asking.

"At the Pillars, dealing with some nervous souls." Bele stretched out her long legs, dropping her crossed ankles in Rhain's lap. "He's probably going to be super disappointed to learn that you decided to finally wake up when he wasn't here."

I doubted that.

"You know, he's been here nearly the whole time you've slept," Bele said as Rhain knocked her booted feet from his lap. "Sleeping beside you. Not straying farther than his office unless he had to. Clucking over you like a mother hen of death."

My fingers pressed into the cup as that sliced straight through my chest. "He was worried about the embers. If I die, they go with me."

"Yeah, I don't think that was it." Bele plopped her feet back in Rhain's lap. "He was worried, wasn't he, Rhain?"

"Yeah," Rhain grumbled, not bothering to remove her feet this time. "I honestly thought he was going to kill Ector at least five times in the last three days."

Bele grinned at that.

And I...I didn't know what to do about any of it as Rhain and Bele started to argue over whether Ector had deserved the many threats of death he'd received. I understood enough about emotions in general to know that one could care for another and still do things that could...hurt them—intentionally or not. I'd seen that enough in the mortal realm, and I doubted Primals were any different since they got their emotions from mortals. And now, a little removed from what I'd seen in his office, I could admit to myself that Nyktos cared for me. He'd proven that. But what I'd seen showed how shallow those feelings ran. Not only that, he'd clearly lied to me about his relationship with Veses—how he felt about her. Who knew what else he hadn't been truthful about. But I also...

I cared too much.

I wouldn't have reacted the way I did otherwise. I would've been more angry than hurt. My heart wouldn't have felt as if it were breaking. I had feelings for him, and that was never a part of the deal I'd struck with him. That was never in the cards for me. But I'd opened the door to him, letting myself feel safe with him and want more than I should. And that was on me. But what was on him? The mistake he'd made? He'd walked through that open door.

And that felt like an unforgivable mistake.

On both our parts.

Because we could've had what I'd offered in that deal. Pleasure for the sake of pleasure. Fucking and nothing more. No long conversations about anxiety or my fears about what kind of person I was. He didn't need to ask about my life in Lasania. I didn't need to wonder about his.

I stared at the dark, ruby-red juice, my eyes burning. If I were being honest with myself, it never could've stayed purely physical. I had started to care for him when I'd been determined to kill him. I'd started to want *more* even then.

Closing my eyes, I willed the stinging away and forced my thoughts to what would come next. What I saw between him and Veses didn't change that there were far bigger issues to deal with. There was finding Delfai in Irelone. Removing the embers. Dealing with Kolis. All things that required Nyktos and me to work together. But most importantly, I couldn't lose control again. Doing so was too dangerous. For others. For me.

And contrary to what Nyktos believed, I didn't want to die. Not when there was the possibility of a future that wouldn't be dictated by a destiny I'd never agreed to. A life that I and no one else owned. I needed to survive to live that.

Because I wanted that.

Deserved it.

Which meant I needed to become Nyktos's Consort. Until we dealt with Kolis, I needed the protection the title offered. But it couldn't be anything more than that. I was mature enough to acknowledge that, no matter how much I enjoyed being in Nyktos's arms. No matter how much I wanted that. Because the physical stuff led to wanting more. To feelings. And that wasn't safe. Not for me. Not for others. My chest ached even now, a sure sign that I wanted too much.

But once we handled Kolis? I could want to my heart's content—and what I wanted was freedom.

I knew what I had to do.

Resolve formed as I opened my eyes. Bele and Rhain still argued. Over what, I had no idea. But Rhain watched me. I reached over Bele, placing the cup on the nightstand.

"What are you doing?" she asked.

"Getting out of this bed." I tugged on the fur, but half of it was stuck under both her and Rhain. "Could you all move? If not, I'm going to have to get out of this bed completely naked."

"I don't necessarily have a problem with that," Bele remarked. "But Nyktos might."

"That's his problem, not mine," I said. "And the last time I checked, I am more than capable of deciding how long I want to stay in bed."

"It's not about being capable or controlling you," Rhain argued. "It's about making sure you are ready to be up and moving about. You weren't napping, Sera. You were in *stasis*—something that you shouldn't have been able to survive. Mentally, you may think you're all good, but physically, you may not be."

He had a point, I'd give him that. But I didn't want to be in Nyktos's bed when he returned. I couldn't. "I need to use the bathing chamber."

"Why didn't you just say that?" Bele sighed as she rolled herself off the bed.

Rhain hesitated, the look on his face saying he didn't quite believe me, but he rose, too. I gathered the fur around myself and scooted to the other side of the bed. I stood, thankful to discover that my legs didn't collapse on me. They felt a little weird as I took a step, though—a bit tingly from the lack of movement. Holding the fur close, I headed straight for the narrow corridor between the two chambers.

"Where are you going?" Bele demanded.

"To my bathing chambers. And that is where I'm staying," I announced with as much authority as I could while draped in a blanket.

Neither stopped me. They followed, though. My bedchambers

were as I'd left them. The drapes on the balcony doors were pulled back, revealing the dark gray sky. It was night. One of them turned on the lights in the walls as I padded into the bathing chamber, grabbing the dressing robe on the way. I closed the door, not allowing myself to think about what had happened in this space. I needed to get over that because I would not be making use of Nyktos's bathing chambers again.

I ignored the twinge of disappointment I felt as I took care of personal needs and then asked through the door, "Can I have hot water brought up?"

There was a muffled affirmative, and then I waited, taking the time in the silence of the bathing chamber to find calm. I searched for the veil, and this time it wasn't a failure. I found that nothingness, the thing that let me shut off the disappointment, the pain, and the anger. Sealed off the desire—no, the need—to know exactly what Nyktos had been doing with Veses down to the last disgusting detail. I took all those messy emotions and, in my mind, locked them away in an indestructible box made of shadowstone.

A knock came. I exhaled, long and slow, letting the emptiness invade every part of my being as I cracked open the door. It wasn't Baines with water but Rhain. I stood back as he filled the tub and then thanked him when he finished.

"I'll make sure some food is sent up," Rhain said and then left, closing the door behind him.

I took the fastest bath of my entire life, but I got my ass in the actual tub. I faced the door this time, though, and my heart pounded through the whole thing.

It was a success—a minor one, but still. I quickly combed out the tangles in my wet hair and braided it because my stomach had decided to wake up at some point during the bath. I was starving.

Only Bele remained in my chambers when I stepped out. I didn't see her at first as my eyes were glued to the covered dish on the table.

"It's soup," Bele said, and my gaze darted to the couch. She had planted herself there, legs outstretched and ankles crossed on the arm of the sofa. "Easily digestible."

"Thanks," I murmured, hurrying to the table. A rather large bowl of soup waited, along with two slices of bread and a hunk of chocolate. I devoured it all in silence.

"Still hungry?" Bele asked.

Leaning back in the chair, I briefly considered asking for more, but my stomach was already feeling stretched too tight, and I deserved the bottle of wine that sat nearby. "I'm good." I glanced over at the couch. All I could see was the back of her dark head and the pointed tips of her boots. I grabbed the bottle of wine and the glass and rose, moving to the bed so I could see her. I sat on the edge. "Are you watching over me until Nyktos's return?"

"Nope. Orphine is nearby." She rocked her feet back and forth. "I'm here because I'm nosy."

My brows shot up.

"I was here, you know, when the whole damn palace started shaking the other day," she continued after a moment. "At first, I thought it was another attack and got kind of excited. That's how bored I've been. But when I looked outside and saw nothing, I figured Nyktos was in a pissy mood. That was the only logical explanation since not even the oldest, most powerful gods could make the entire palace rattle."

I poured myself half a glass of wine and then, on second thought, filled the entire thing, figuring I'd need it for whenever Nyktos made an appearance.

"But it was you doing it." Bele craned her neck, looking back at me. "A mortal with Primal embers in their Culling."

I took a long drink at the unnecessary recap.

"Like what the fuck? How is that possible? I get you're super special, but…good Fates," Bele said, and I nodded in silent agreement at the disbelief in her tone. "Anyway, what pissed you off?"

I took another gulp of wine.

"And I know something had to because that's about the only thing that gets the eather going during the Culling." She sat up. "When I was in my Culling and near the Ascension, I shattered windows if I even got slightly upset about something. Lots of them. By the time I finished the Culling, there were no windows left in the home."

"Has anyone ever suggested that you may have anger issues?" I asked.

Bele snorted. "Says possibly the most argumentative, combative person I've ever met."

I frowned. "I am not combative."

She raised her brows.

"I'm…assertive."

"Aggressively assertive," she countered. "As you should be—as all of us need to be. So, no shame there."

"Okay," I murmured, taking another drink. The sweet wine warmed my blood. "Why are you really here, Bele?"

"That was a rude question."

I stared at her.

Bele hadn't done anything wrong, but when I found that veil of nothingness, it wasn't easy to put it on and take it off at will. The more I allowed myself to feel anything, the harder it was to find that calm emptiness. And that was why it had been so difficult for me to find it within myself to shut down my emotions. I'd left myself open for too long.

So, this was how it would be.

Then Bele said, "I know Veses was here."

31

My hand tightened on the stem of the glass as Bele spoke. "Ector and Saion were heading off to Lethe, and I was waiting for Aios to come. I was on my way to the kitchens, minding my own business, when I saw her entering Nyktos's office," she told me. "And I was like…great, that bitch is here."

I started to lift the glass to my lips but saw that it was empty. I thought about refilling it but decided there came a point between the first and second glasses where liquid courage turned into liquid ridiculousness.

"I thought things would change," she said, and my gaze flew to her. Bele rose, crossing her arms. "That Veses wouldn't be…visiting now that Nyktos was taking a Consort."

"Well, apparently, they haven't," I said, wiping my hands on the soft dressing robe.

Bele opened her mouth and closed it. Several seconds ticked by. "I don't know what's going on there—between Veses and Nyktos," she said, and the wine immediately soured in my stomach. "Hell, I don't even really know what's going on with you and Nyktos. None of us do."

"Please tell me his guards don't sit around and discuss Nyktos and me," I said.

"We don't sit around and talk about you. We're usually standing while doing it," she replied, and I sighed. "None of us really gets it. You two. Nyktos didn't want a Consort. Didn't need one. And you wanted to kill him—or thought you needed to. Whatever. But I've seen the way you look at him," she said, and my cheeks warmed. "I've seen how comfortable you are touching him. Very few would even dare think of doing such a thing."

Veses had.

And did.

My veneer of emptiness cracked a little. I got up and moved to the table, needing to pace a bit.

"And I've never seen him so involved with another as he is with you. So annoyingly concerned."

Annoyingly concerned? I almost laughed. "It's the embers, Bele. It's important that I stay alive."

Her nose wrinkled. "If it were just the embers, he wouldn't have verbally slain us the morning he gave his speech in the throne room about how brave you were."

"What?"

"Yep. After you left with Orphine and most of the other guards went back to their stations, he laid into the rest of us." She grinned. "Honestly, Nyktos can come up with some impressive and creative threats, and he delivers them with a level of coldness where no one doubts his sincerity."

"I didn't know he'd said anything to you all," I murmured, having figured that had been what his speech was about. He could've made a point to speak to his most trusted guards directly because he feared they would be more likely to aid me in escape. Or he could've just wanted to make sure they were simply more welcoming toward me. I shook my head. It didn't matter either way. Nyktos cared about how I was treated. What he was doing with Veses didn't change that.

"Anyway, I'm guessing you saw something," Bele said, drawing my attention back to her. "Because that's the only thing I can think of that would cause you to get that angry."

"Why would you think that?" I sat and rocked the chair back, propping the toes of my feet on the edge of the table.

"Because I've seen them together before."

I stopped breathing, just for a few seconds as I stared at her, and then I dragged in a deep breath, holding it as the realization that what I'd seen hadn't been a one-off thing sank in. Not that I had really believed it to be, but I supposed I had wanted it to be that.

"What...?" I swallowed, telling myself I didn't need to know any more. I let the chair settle on all four legs and dropped my feet to the floor. The movement didn't stop me from asking, "What did you see? Them fucking?"

"Good Fates, no. I would be traumatized. It would be like walking in on your brother having sex." She shuddered as she turned, walking back to the couch. "I saw her feeding from him. That doesn't always lead to or include sex."

I guessed it didn't, but the way Veses had been moving... Biting down on the side of my lip, I stopped those thoughts. I didn't need to replay what I had seen. "When did you see them?"

Bele flung herself onto her back once more, propping her feet up on the arm of the couch again. "About a year ago. I was getting back from doing some scouting in the Court in Dalos and had some news to give him. I walked in on them. Never in my life have I *nope-d* out of a chamber as quickly as I did then." She looked away, dragging her sharp teeth across her lower lip as it sank in that this thing with Veses had been occurring for a year. A whole year. "I shouldn't even be talking about this."

I went to the bed and sat on the edge again. "Because Nyktos would be angry with you?"

"I don't give a fuck if he is. Don't get me wrong, I love Nyktos as if he were my blooded brother. Just as Aios does. But if he doesn't want people talking about what he's been doing, he should make sure that no one finds out about it," she said. "I shouldn't be talking about this because I don't know what the hell I saw the day I walked in on them. I mean, I know what I saw, but I don't get it."

Neither did I.

"Aios claims that Veses was decent once, but after some of the shit I've seen her do in Dalos, I find that hard to believe." Bele's eyes flashed with an intense burst of eather and then calmed. "Nyktos knows what kind of Primal she is. Not only that, she supports Kolis. Nyktos doesn't trust her. He doesn't like her."

A conflicting mix of emotions budded, but I crushed them before I could make sense of them. Instead, I kept them locked away in that box. "If that's the case, then why would he allow her to feed from him—for at least the last year?"

"As I said, that's what I don't get." Bele stared at the ceiling. "Why would he allow her to do that? There has to be a reason."

I stared at my hands—at the nails that had cracked and chipped from clawing at the ground. I couldn't think of a single reason that not only explained but made sense for why Nyktos would allow Veses to feed from him. I curled my fingers inward, hiding my nails. And I didn't want to think about those reasons—about any of this.

The embers suddenly shimmied to life inside me, stretching as if waking up. I tensed as my gaze flew to the doors, my heart thumping.

She followed my gaze. "What?"

"He comes," I said.

"Fucking special Primal embers," she muttered. "Like why don't I feel that since I've technically Ascended?" she went on. "It's total bullshit."

The door swung open, but not the main one. Nyktos walked in through the adjoining door and came to a halt as his gaze landed on me.

Time felt as if it stopped as we looked at each other, and an urge to rise and go to him came out of nowhere. I even pitched forward as if to stand before I caught myself.

Then Nyktos moved and approached the bed. The steel-gray of his tunic and the silver brocading across the neck and over his chest and stomach reminded me of the color of his eyes and the wisps of eather in them. He halted again, seeming to suddenly become aware of Bele's presence.

She kicked her head back and grinned up at him. "Hi."

"Can you give us a moment?" he said.

"But I was just getting comfortable," Bele protested.

Nyktos stared at her, and whatever she saw got her moving. "Fine." She popped up. "I'll give you two *several* moments," she said, and I almost reached out and stopped her.

I knew what was coming, and I wasn't ready.

But I wasn't a coward. That was what I told myself as I watched her slowly leave the room and close the door behind her. I may have been foolish and naïve—too *reckless* this time around, in a way I'd never experienced before—but I wouldn't run again.

Feeling Nyktos's stare, I pulled my attention from the door. Our gazes locked. Only faint traces of eather were visible in his eyes. "How are you feeling?" he asked.

"Perfect for someone who has been in stasis for three days," I said, proud of how steady my voice was and how unbothered I sounded.

Something I didn't recognize rippled in his eyes. He glanced at the bathing chamber, and then his gaze settled on me. He didn't speak. Silence fell between us.

It was me who ended it. "I found where Delfai is."

"I know. Nektas told me. He's in Irelone."

"Then I need to go there—"

"I don't want to talk about that right now," he interrupted, taking a deep breath. "I mean, that's not what I'm here for."

The impenetrable emptiness felt more like a veneer in that moment. "What is it that you want to talk about?"

He came forward about a foot before stopping. "I'm sorry."

Every muscle in my body locked up. "For the compulsion?" I waved my hand. "I didn't like it, but I understand why you did it. I doubt anyone wants to rebuild this palace."

His brows pinched as his gaze swept over my features. "I do need to apologize for that. I don't like to use it, even when it's necessary."

"I know."

Eather stilled in his eyes as he stared at me. "But I'm apologizing for what you thought you saw."

Disbelief rocked the emptiness, threatening to shake it up. "I know what I saw."

"You don't."

Anger sparked, but I refused to let it ignite. I knew it wouldn't stop there because a far more dangerous emotion loomed behind it. One that hurt. One that could hurt others. "I saw you with the Primal you called the worst sort in your lap. She was riding you as she drank from you. Is that not what I saw?"

"She wasn't—" Tension bracketed his mouth.

"Wasn't what? Tell me how what I saw wasn't what it looked like," I demanded. "That it wasn't the first time it's happened."

His gaze sharpened. "What was said to you?"

"Does it matter?" I thought of Bele's confusion over why he would allow this. Of my own. "So, this *wasn't* the first time?"

He stared in silence for several moments. "No."

I already knew that. I didn't even know why I'd asked. Didn't know why I continued to open my mouth. "Why were you with her?"

The glow dimmed in his eyes. "Because I was."

"*Because I was,*" I heard myself repeat as I stared at him. A shocked laugh left me as my stomach pitched. "That's all you have to say?"

He turned his head away. Silence.

Of course, he would go silent now. I felt another spark of fury, stronger than before. "When I made that deal with you—pleasure for the sake of pleasure—I should've made the same demand you made of me. That such intimacies remained only between us. My mistake." The embers in my chest hummed as I forced a deep, slow breath in and out of my lungs. But the anger let some of the bitterness seep from the box and rise to the surface. "Or, at the very least, discussed who else you would be sharing such intimacies with so I could be prepared in case I happened to walk in on something hours after telling you that I wanted to be your Consort."

He flinched.

The Primal actually *flinched*. I should've celebrated the blow I'd intended to land, but I couldn't. It didn't feel good. I rose and walked to the fireplace. "We don't need to discuss this."

"I think we do."

"We don't. Because I don't care."

"That's not true," he argued, and I turned, not even surprised to see that he had followed in that annoyingly quiet shadowstep way of his. "What happened by the pool was because you care, and I—" He looked away, his chest rising sharply. "What matters is that I caused you to lose control. I hurt you." His eyes met mine again, now full of whirling wisps of eather. "I didn't want that. I never wanted that. And I hate that I hurt you. I am sorry, Sera."

I stepped back, a physical reaction I couldn't stop because he sounded genuine. Like he really *did* know that he'd hurt me. That I had a reason to be hurt. Somehow, him acknowledging that was so much worse than I could've imagined. I felt the veneer becoming even more fragile. "Don't apologize," I said, finding my voice as I folded my arms over my chest. "What you hurt was my ego. That is all."

Nyktos shook his head. "Sera—"

"It is I who is sorry."

He jerked, his eyes widening. "For what?"

"For what you think you know," I parroted his words. "I was foolish and naïve to believe you when you said there had been no one before me. I should've seen right through that the first time we were together. That is how you hurt my ego."

His nostrils flared. "That wasn't a lie."

"I think it's time for *you* to stop lying."

"I've wanted no one but you, Sera."

I laughed, the sound cold as I refused to let his words sink in. Because I couldn't trust him, and I couldn't trust what I would do with those words.

"I know what you think you saw, Sera, but we were not having sex," he said, his eyes flashing an intense silver as my gaze snapped to his. "If you think you saw that, you are wrong. I have absolutely nothing to gain by lying."

I backed up but then stopped. I wasn't sure what he had to gain by lying, nor was I sure what *I* had to gain by the smidgen of relief I felt. "Then what did I see?" I asked again because, as I'd already proven, I was a fool.

A muscle ticked along the curve of his jaw, and I let myself glance at his throat. There was no bite mark, but I could still see it in my mind. "What you saw is…it's complicated."

I inhaled deeply, confused and rapidly losing control of my hold on my anger. "Again, that's all you have to say? Don't even bother answering. I don't care that you were with her. That's not—" I stopped myself with another laugh. *Stop lying.* I stiffened, realizing there was no face to save. When I lost control under the palace, I'd laid myself bare. "You know what? Seeing you with her did hurt my feelings. I don't know why. It shouldn't have. You have made no promises to me. And I have asked none from you. This union between us was never something that either of us desired. We don't need to discuss what you were or weren't doing any further. I know what I saw. You've apologized. It is what it is."

"What's that supposed to mean?"

"It means the deal we made? It's over. The only thing between us now are these stupid embers. I want them gone, and then *I* want to be gone."

He took a measured step toward me. "Gone from *what* exactly?"

"From here," I said. "From you."

Hollows formed beneath his cheekbones. "You can't be gone from me."

I stiffened. "If you say that because I must become your Consort, I understand all the reasons why. But I will be that in name only. And once you remove the embers and Kolis is defeated, I want out of this. I want my freedom. That's the deal I should've made with you."

Eather churned in his eyes. "Is that the deal you're asking for now?"

I lifted my chin, holding my arms tight against me to stop them from trembling. I had to, or that shaking would move into my chest. And I had to say what I did next because I couldn't feel that hurt again. I couldn't lose control. "Yes."

Nyktos went completely still. "Then so be it," he said, and the words felt like an oath.

A bond.

Unbreakable.

32

"Are you sure you're well?" Orphine asked, glancing at me as we walked toward the stairs the following morning.

This was the second time she'd asked, and both times she posed the question, I had been surprised. "I'm fine."

Orphine said nothing to my response, but doubt settled into her features. She didn't believe me.

I was tired and not in the greatest mood. I'd barely slept the night before, and I wasn't sure if that had to do with being unconscious for three days or my conversation with Nyktos.

Or how I kept looking at the adjoining door, wondering why Nyktos suddenly no longer believed he needed to keep me within arm's reach.

And hating myself a little for even wondering that.

But I was fine.

Empty. Blank.

Which was perfect. I had plans. Something I'd decided in the midst of my marathon pacing session during the night. I needed to discuss traveling to Irelone, and I would do so with the utmost maturity and detachment.

If I could handle my mother, I could handle Nyktos.

The embers in my chest vibrated as we reached the first-floor hall, but I hesitated in the shadowy alcove. The doors were ajar. Before, I wouldn't have thought twice about walking straight in. Aware that

Orphine was watching me, I raised a hand to knock. Something Bele had said intruded in that moment. If Nyktos didn't want people to talk, then he would make sure no one found anything to discuss, right? But I really—

"You can come in," Nyktos's voice rang out from within the office.

I froze, my hand suspended in the air.

"Whenever you're ready," Nyktos added after a moment.

Lowering my hand, I ignored the way Orphine stared at me and briefly closed my eyes, silently mouthing a string of curses. Then I opened the door.

Rhain stood to Nyktos's right, and *he* sat behind his desk, closing one of the Books of the Dead. His hair was swept back, and I thought…he looked paler around the corners of his eyes and his mouth. There were also shadows beneath his eyes as his muted gaze swept over my thick braid, vest, and tailored leggings like thick tights. That was all I let myself notice as I walked forward, but something I shouldn't be feeling blossomed at the sight of the paleness and those shadows. Concern.

"I've never known you to knock." Nyktos's gaze rose to mine, and the glow of eather pulsed faintly behind his pupils.

"I didn't want to interrupt," I explained.

Rhain stared at me.

"That is also not something I've seen you worry about in the past." Nyktos leaned back in his chair. He wore a dark gray tunic, though one without the silver brocade.

"Well, I've learned to knock," I replied.

The corners of his mouth tightened.

I clasped my hands together, reminding myself to breathe deeply, slowly, and not to, as Rhain had so succinctly put it, lose my shit. "I hoped I could have a moment of your time." I peeked at Rhain. He continued staring at me as if he'd never seen me before. "If not, I can come back."

"Are you feeling unwell?" Rhain blurted out.

"I feel quite fine," I told him. "And I don't know why everyone keeps asking me that."

"Keeps?" Nyktos questioned.

"Orphine asked if I was fine about two dozen times," I said, exaggerating.

"Probably because you're being…" Rhain frowned. "Polite."

My expression mirrored his. "I don't know why that would make anyone think I'm unwell."

"Have you met yourself?" Rhain countered.

Nyktos glanced at him, and the god sighed. "I'm heading out to the Rise." He bowed, and then with one last curious look in my direction, he left us.

Alone.

Nyktos watched me as he remained reclined in his chair, one hand lifting to curl around his chin.

I sat on the edge of the seat before his desk. "I won't take up much of your time—"

"You can have all the time you want, Seraphena."

Seraphena.

Gods, I wanted to hate how he curled his tongue around my name, making it sound like both a wicked whisper and a reverent prayer.

I kept my hands clasped. "Thank you, but I don't think I will need that much. I'm sure you're busy."

He drew his thumb across his lower lip, his gaze still fastened to mine. I didn't think he'd blinked once. "What is it that you want that won't take much time?"

Something about his tone left me a little unsteady. A...softness. "I want to discuss Irelone. I would like to go there as soon as possible. I figured Nektas could travel with me."

"I'm going with you," he said, the eather brightening behind his pupils. "I need to hear exactly what Delfai says about the embers to ensure that I can carry out the process of removing them."

Irritation hummed from deep within. Traveling with Nyktos anywhere was...well, not opportune. And I was confident that Nektas could relay any pertinent details effectively. Still, I squashed my irritation. "Okay."

He arched a brow. "Okay?"

I nodded.

Nyktos's eyes narrowed slightly as he drew his thumb along his lip once more. "I'm assuming you would like to leave right now."

"I would."

"I would like to wait until tomorrow."

I gritted my teeth. "And why would you like to do that?"

"Because one of Kyn's draken was spotted this morn over the Black Bay," he shared, and I tensed. "The draken hasn't made any move against us. He's just been circling at the edges of our territory."

Us. Our.

I squeezed my hands. "What do you think he's doing?"

"Scouting. Likely seeing how many guards we have on the Rise," he said, and I tensed even further as he dragged the edge of his fangs across his lip. "And probably trying to get a good look at the armies, which he will not be able to."

"Do the other Primals not know the size?"

"They only know that I have one, and that it's sizable. But not even Dorcan knew the exact size," he answered. "I want to be here just in case my suspicions are wrong."

"Understandable," I said. "If the draken attacks, I want to be of aid."

"Of course."

Now it was my turn to stare in confusion. "Of course? As in you will not demand that I remain back?"

"I have learned not to ask that of you," he replied. "Or to expect you to stand down when you need to help—when you *want* to."

"You're not worried that I'll get myself and the embers killed?"

"I worry about that every waking second," he said. "But I've also learned that it's something I will need to deal with." He shifted, straightening in his chair. "Besides, the other deal you made, the one in the courtyard, was that you wanted to be of aid. I agreed. That has not changed."

I blinked rapidly, having figured that all our agreements had been voided. "Then we leave in the morning."

Nyktos nodded. A moment passed. "Nektas said you knew the woman Delfai was with? Was she the one you spoke about before?"

"It's Princess Kayleigh—Tavius's once-betrothed," I said with a nod. "She should be at Cauldra Manor, in Massene—a village in Irelone, near the capital. I remember her saying it was the Balfour ancestry home. I'm hoping there's a gateway near."

He smiled then, a little wider, warmer. "We lucked out with one being so close to Wayfair, but there are none within Irelone that I would trust using. However, we don't need a gateway. We will shadowstep."

I started to ask how that would be possible, but then I remembered how he'd taken me from the Great Hall in Wayfair. "So, you're going to have to knock me out."

"I will do my best to make sure you feel no pain and that it's quick," he assured me. "The only alternative is that we enter through Spessa's End or Pompay, where the closest gateways to Irelone are, which would be rather time-consuming."

"It's fine," I told him. "I can deal with it."

"I know you can." A pause. "You can deal with anything."

I stilled, once again struck off-kilter by his too-soft tone as he continued to eye me closely, enough to make my skin prickle with awareness. I was grateful we had nothing else to discuss. I unclasped my hands, beginning to rise—

"Nektas told me you ran into the nymphs on your return from the Vale."

"We did." I remained tense in the chair, like a bird perched on a cliff, prepared to take flight. "I'd forgotten about them."

"You killed one," he said. "With eather."

I nodded.

"You shouldn't be able to do that."

"That's what Nektas said. The embers...I guess they really are that powerful. But that will soon be something I won't need to worry about." I cleared my throat. "I don't want to keep you—"

"I don't want you to do this."

Confusion rose once more. "Do what?"

"This."

I waited for more of an explanation. There was none. "I'm going to need you to elaborate."

One side of his lips curled up. "You don't need to become someone you're not."

The muscles along my spine clenched. "I'm not."

"You're being amicable. Understanding. Reserved. Even polite." He fired off what most would consider admirable traits.

"It's not an act."

"I didn't suggest that it was."

I frowned. "Then what exactly are you suggesting, Your Highness? Because I'm confused as to why you would now demand that I be...what? More argumentative? Irrational?"

"As I told you before, I quite enjoyed the more...reckless side of your nature."

I was still on the outside. Inside, however, I trembled.

"But this?" He lowered his hand to the surface of his desk. "This was how you were raised to be, wasn't it?"

I sucked in a breath.

"Pliable. Submissive. Quiet." He paused. "Empty."

A sharp swirl of tingles swept along the nape of my neck as my eyes locked with his—with a gaze that continued to be intense and...and searching. I gripped the arms of the chair. "You're trying to read my emotions."

"Yes," he confirmed without any hint of shame. "And I feel nothing."

My mouth dried. "So?"

"There hasn't been one time that I've been in your presence for more than a handful of minutes where I haven't felt you project an emotion, be it joy, desire, or anger," he said. "Not from the first moment I saw you in the Dark Elms till I tried to slow your breathing beneath the palace."

I shook, my calm cracking.

"This isn't you. You have never been like this with me." His palm flattened against the desk. "Whether it's because I've annoyed you or something else, you have always been yourself. You have more than earned the right to be yourself. To think what you want, feel what you want. That shouldn't change."

"It shouldn't?" I whispered.

"No." A muscle ticked in his jaw. "No matter what I've done to you."

What he had...? I stopped myself from finishing that thought. "The problem with that is that my feelings could've killed me and destroyed the palace."

"Not your feelings," he corrected quietly. "What I did to them. What happened is my fault, Sera. Not yours." His gaze never wavered. "You do not need to change. And as...as selfish as this is, I don't want you to."

"I don't want to be like this," I whispered before I could stop myself.

Nyktos jerked—actually recoiled—and shadows became visible beneath his skin for a brief second.

My broken nails scraped the chair's wooden arms, and I focused on my breathing until the abyss that pained whisper had come from was sealed off once more. "But I can't feel like that ever again. So, we can't always get what we want." I rose. "Not even Primals."

"Sera." He stood, both hands flat on his desk. "I didn't—" He winced, air hissing between his clenched teeth as he lifted his right hand from the desk and looked at it. His nostrils flared. "Fuck."

"What?" My eyes searched his face when he didn't respond. "What is it?"

Nyktos turned his hand over so his palm faced me. My lips parted at the reddish-black slash cutting through a circle seemingly inked into the center of his hand. "Kolis," he growled, his eyes filling with vivid streaks of eather. "He's summoned us."

I'd never seen so many people in Nyktos's office at once.

Every single one of his most trusted guards were present, including Aios and Nektas, who'd arrived with the two young draken. Jadis was in her mortal form, nestled against her father's chest and fast asleep with what appeared to be half her hand in her mouth.

I glanced down at my lap. Somehow, I had ended up seated on the settee with Reaver, who was awake but currently had his diamond-shaped head resting on my knee. I think he'd done it to stop me from repeatedly tapping my foot on the floor.

Part of me also thought maybe he'd sensed my nervousness and was responding to it, which didn't seem like a normal thing.

My gaze shifted to my bare wrists. The charm was there, invisible to me, but it wouldn't work outside the Shadowlands. I could be *kept* in Dalos.

"He summoned you before I thought he would," Nektas said, gently rocking Jadis from where he stood behind Nyktos's desk. "I figured he'd take his sweet-ass time."

"That's what I'd hoped," Nyktos said, leaning against the front of his desk, his arms crossed over his chest. Like the last time I'd looked at him, he watched me. Only me.

"Wait. I'm confused," Ector said.

Theon snorted. "No one is surprised."

Ector ignored him. "Being summoned to Dalos isn't going to be fun, but getting his permission means crowning her as the Consort sooner rather than later, giving her the protection you've been wanting."

"It does," Nyktos said. "But it would've been preferable to get the embers out of Sera first."

Aios frowned as she exchanged a look with Bele. "Are you worried that Kolis will be able to sense them in her now that they've grown stronger?"

My head cut toward Nyktos then. I hadn't even thought about that. "Will he?"

"He may be able to sense something that alludes to you being no ordinary godling." Only a faint glow of eather pulsed behind his pupils. "But if so, that can be explained away."

"How?"

"Blood," Nektas answered, rubbing Jadis's back. One of her tiny feet peeked out from the edge of her blanket. "His blood. If anyone drinks enough of a Primal's blood, they will give off some Primal vibes until the blood is completely absorbed into their system."

"Oh." I wanted to relax at hearing that, but we had a far bigger issue with me coming face-to-face with Kolis.

"So, as long as you play nice with Kolis, he'll give his permission," Saion said. "Really nice, Nyktos."

"Yeah, good luck," muttered Lailah. I looked to where she stood on the other side of a silent Rhain, her hand resting on the hilt of one of the swords strapped to her hip.

"It isn't him I'm worried about." Ector looked pointedly in my direction, and Rhahar gave a low cough.

I thought of what Nektas had shared about Nyktos convincing Kolis that he was loyal. "Exactly how nice will we have to play?"

"You will do whatever Kolis demands of you," Rhain stated, speaking for the first time. "No matter how distasteful or vile you find it to be. There will only be a few things that Nyktos can refuse on your behalf."

Pressure settled in my chest. I started to ask what sort of things, but I fell silent at the way Nyktos's features turned stark. Reaver nudged my hand, drawing my attention. He bumped his nose against my palm once more. Swallowing, I ran my fingers over his forehead, mindful of the small bumps that had sprouted along the crown of his diamond-shaped head. One day, they would grow into horns larger than my hand, if not half my arm.

"That means no threatening to cut his eyes out and feed them to him when he inevitably angers you," warned Rhahar, the smooth, rich brown skin of his cheek gleaming under the sconce he stood by.

"How did you hear about that?" I exclaimed.

"Everyone has heard about you threatening Attes." Nyktos smirked.

"He actually told Theon and me on his way out that day," Lailah said. "He was rather amused by it."

Theon frowned. "And kind of turned on by it," he said. A low rumble radiated from Nyktos as the air charged. Theon held up his hands. "Sorry. Forget I mentioned that."

I stared at Nyktos, using every ounce of willpower I had not to say anything. The utter *audacity* of him being angered over another person being attracted to me—no matter how bizarre that attraction was—when I wanted to set the settee I sat upon on fire because of what he had been doing with Veses on it…

Nyktos's gaze flickered to mine, the pulse of eather brighter. I held his stare for a moment and then looked away. My attention collided with Rhain's. He watched us, his lips drawn in a tight, thin line.

"When are you all leaving then?" Saion asked, rocking back on his chair as he planted his boot on the edge of the desk.

Nyktos knocked his foot off the table. "After we return from Irelone and have removed the embers."

I stiffened, my hand stilling.

"Got it." Saion lifted his chin. "We'll hold it down here."

"Wait," I said. Reaver turned his head toward Nyktos. "We don't know how long that will take."

"We know where to start looking for Delfai," Nyktos responded. "And we will take however long is necessary."

I glanced at Nektas. The draken said nothing as he tried to tuck Jadis's foot under the blanket. "How long did it take before Kolis grew angry when you last delayed in answering a summons from him?"

Nyktos said nothing.

Irritation rose as I glanced around the room, my hand sliding along Reaver's back. "How long?"

Everyone studiously studied the floor, the ceiling, or one another. Everyone except Rhain. "Less than a day."

"Fuck," Nyktos growled, pushing off the desk as he turned to the god. "Normally, I expect that shit from this *one*." He jerked his chin.

"Hey," Ector grumbled. "I kept my mouth shut this time."

Rhain didn't back down, but he did take a step back. "She should know what the delay will cost."

"Pretty sure he wanted the exact opposite," Bele murmured. "Either way, we've got it covered."

Theon nodded. "That we do."

"No," I said.

Every head turned to me—even Nektas's and Reaver's. But it was only Nyktos who spoke. "Sera—"

"No," I repeated, and Reaver rose onto his haunches, eyeing the Primal. "I don't want to be a part of whatever Kolis will do in retaliation for us not answering his summons in a timely manner."

Eather seeped into the skin of Nyktos's cheeks. "You are more important than—"

"Don't say it," I warned as he took a step forward. "The—"

Reaver expanded his wings, startling me. I leaned back as he stretched out his thin neck and lifted his head.

Nyktos drew up short as a low rumble radiated from Reaver's chest, and smoke wafted from his nostrils.

Stunned, I stared at the small draken. My gaze flew to Nyktos, then to Nektas, who had started grinning. "Ha!" I exclaimed, reaching down to pat the top of Reaver's head. "That's a good Reaver-Butt."

Reaver hummed as he eyed Nyktos. He made a low, chattering sound.

"Man," Theon drawled, his mouth twitching as if he fought and then lost the battle to hold back a laugh. "That's kind of wrong."

"It's the embers," I guessed. "He's probably responding to that."

"No, it's you." Nyktos looked at me. "He's protecting *you*."

I frowned at the back of Reaver's head. "You're not going to do anything to me."

Nyktos sighed. "He knows that, but he's just letting me know that he doesn't appreciate me upsetting you."

I snorted. "Well, he's going to be busy letting you know that, then."

Someone, and it sounded like Aios this time, laughed under their breath. Reaver settled beside me, draping his head over my knee again. This time, he didn't need to nudge my hand. I got to petting him.

"You can stop grinning anytime now," Nyktos said without looking at Nektas.

"I know," the draken replied, still smiling.

"We answer his summons," I said, looking up at Nyktos. "We don't wait. We take care of that first."

A muscle ticked in Nyktos's jaw. "Then we leave within the hour."

Aios had followed me to my chambers, offering to help pick out the appropriate attire.

"Is what I'm wearing not appropriate?"

"It is." Her back was to me as she flipped through the garments in the wardrobe.

"But?"

"But Kolis will think you too casual," she said, and that was the last thing I was worried about him thinking. "And he would see it as disrespectful."

I crossed my arms over my chest. "It seems like he sees many things as disrespectful."

"He does." Aios pulled out a deep crimson gown that Erlina had made. I had glanced past it when going through the clothes. Not because it wasn't beautiful but because I wasn't sure where or why I would wear something so elegant. "This will do."

Seizing on irritation instead of focusing on the rapidly building dread, I took the gown and, with Aios's help, changed into it.

"It's beautiful on you," the goddess murmured, toying with the chain around her neck as she stepped back.

"Thank you." I ran my hands over the velvet and lace. The gown was tailored perfectly, hugging my breasts, loose at the waist, and tight at the hips. There was no fear of falling out of it with the neckline that swept around the back of my neck and draped over one shoulder. A fine layer of lace had been stitched over the bodice and hips, and there were slits on both sides of the skirt, something that had to be the style in Iliseeum and was of benefit to me as I strapped the sheath to my upper thigh.

"You're so much like Bele," she remarked. "Stashing weapons here and there."

"I wish I had more than this."

"As do I." She smiled tightly as she glanced at the closed chamber doors. Nyktos had said he'd come for me when it was time. Currently, he remained with the others, going over things for when he was gone. "Hopefully, you won't be there long enough to worry about any other attire."

My heart skipped, and I didn't want to consider the possibility that this wouldn't be an in-and-out journey. Or the oath Nyktos had made.

Or what terrible things Rhain had spoken of.

"Can I...can I ask you something?"

"Of course." I smoothed the skirt of the gown as I straightened.

"Will you attempt to go after Kolis while you're there?" Aios asked.

Her blunt question caught me off guard. I shook my head.

She pressed her lips together as she looked away. "I hope you speak the truth. I don't understand why you would've tried something like that before, and I worry that you will do so again."

"It was different then. I didn't think there was any other option," I said, feeling the uncomfortable weight of my words. The guilt. "Now, there is."

Aios was quiet for a moment. "Why would you think that was an option in the first place?" Her eyes met mine. "You're brave. Strong. You have embers in you—powerful ones—but why would you even think you could somehow harm a Primal?"

"I have reasons to believe that I can."

"Whatever reasons you have, you're wrong."

The slippered heels I wore barely made a sound as I took a step toward her. "There is something you don't—" I let out an exasperated breath, not finding it in me to lie. "I'm Kolis's *graeca*."

Aios's chest rose with a sharp breath. "That's impossible."

"I have Sotoria's soul," I said, giving her a brief explanation of how I knew. "Eythos placed her soul in my bloodline, along with the embers," I said, my voice low even though no one was around us to hear. "Eythos knew what he was doing when he put her soul in with the embers. He was creating a...a weapon. I *am* Kolis's weakness. If I'd made it to him, I could've stopped him. That is why I left."

"But..." Creases formed above her brows as she shook her head. "You don't *have* Sotoria's soul. You *are* Sotoria."

I sucked in a sharp breath. "I'm Sera. I'm not her."

"I know. I'm sorry. You are you." Her fingers went to the thin chain again. "I...I just wasn't expecting you to say that."

I laughed hoarsely. "Yeah, well, I didn't expect to hear it when Holland told me either."

She exhaled heavily. "If Kolis were to discover..."

"That was my whole point in leaving before," I said. "I don't know if I look like her or not. I was hoping I did, and it wouldn't require me to...seduce him." My stomach soured. "So, that's why I left. It wasn't just what you said. It's my destiny. It's *been* my destiny. Becoming Nyktos's Consort isn't. It never has been."

"Couldn't your destiny be both?"

My gaze flew to hers, and my mind immediately went to how I had wanted to be Nyktos's Consort.

"Now, I understand," Aios said, her lips puckering. "That's why Nyktos wanted to delay this. He wouldn't have risked Kolis taking out his frustration on the Shadowlands for anything else." She brushed her braid back over her shoulder. "And you no longer hope that you look like Sotoria?"

My skin chilled with my reluctance to answer the question. To speak the truth. But I did. "No," I whispered. "And I shouldn't feel that way, even with Nyktos's plan. Because I could still do something. I could still try. That's what I've been preparing for—"

"I never told you what my time with Kolis was like, did I?"

I blinked, shaking my head.

"I, like Gemma, was one of his favorites." Aios laughed, but this one was like shards of glass. "He kept me in a cage."

My lips parted as horror seized me.

"Granted, it was a large cage of gilded bones."

"As if that makes it okay," I blurted out.

Her smile was tight. "It doesn't, but..." She swallowed. "As sick as this feels to say, and as hard as it will be to understand, the cage wasn't as bad as what happened once Kolis grew bored with his favorites. And that always happened. Sometimes, in days or weeks. Other times, months or even years."

Years? Spent in a cage? I would...

I would lose myself in days.

I sat on the edge of the couch, only because I thought I might fall down if I didn't.

"You see, his Court is lawless and yet full of unknown rules that, if broken, result in death. There is no other way to explain it. Only the cruelest, most manipulative survive in Dalos." Her fingers twisted the chain. "But his favorites were always protected—and, yes, he often had more than one at a time. Every need or want, except for freedom, was provided for. Decadent food. Jewels. Lush furs." Her fingers stilled. "No one was allowed to speak to us. Touch us. He routinely killed his own guards when he believed they looked too long in our direction. He never...he never forced himself on his favorites. Barely even touched them. Not even the ones who offered themselves to him as a means of escape."

I hadn't expected that.

"He just wanted us there, like pretty adornments that he could visit whenever he wanted to gaze upon them. Those who could do naught but listen to him prattle on endlessly for hours, about how Eythos was the real villain and how unfairly he'd been treated." She rolled her eyes. "Fates, there were times when I honestly would've preferred to take a dagger to my ears than listen to him. But Kolis...he could be deceptively charming when he wanted to be. Enough that you started to relax around him, maybe even let down your guard, even though you knew better. I think that is one of the worst things about him. His ability to cause someone to doubt what they know to be true. To somehow be surprised when that charming veneer vanishes. You see him for what you always knew him to be as he throws you to the serpents."

"What...what do you mean? About the serpents," I asked, half-afraid of the answer.

"Other gods. Primals. Godlings. Those who serve him. Honestly, I shouldn't even refer to them as serpents. That's an insult to the serpents."

"Actually, I don't think you can insult serpents. They're the worst."

Aios cracked a grin, but it faded quickly. "Everyone in his Court knows that Kolis eventually grows tired of his favorites. So, they wait while you're showered with things they want—while their friends or even family are killed for the crime of looking in your direction. They know they'll get their due. The moment a favorite got their freedom was often the last moment of their life. The things they did to people who had done nothing wrong—whose only crime was becoming the unwilling object of Kolis's fixation..." She inhaled sharply as my stomach continued to churn. "And Kolis, he did nothing. Not when they were beaten. Raped. Killed. That is what he took pleasure in. Watching those he'd chosen and cherished be stripped to nothing. If you survived the initial release, then the real fun began. You were watched by his most trusted—and they were allowed to do whatever they wanted. They could kill you if that pleased them. You had no rights. It was like a game. Seeing how long they survived. There were often bets. Once, one of his cast-off favorites became pregnant. It was not her choice. Nor was it when I saw Kolis take the babe from her arms and plunge a dagger through the poor child's heart."

I pressed the back of my hand against my mouth. Bile rose. "How...?" I cleared my throat. "How did you escape?"

"I survived," she said, and the horror of what her survival must've entailed haunted those moments of silence. "And when the opportunity presented itself for me to leave Dalos, I gutted one of his favored guards and made my escape."

My lips twisted in a smile of vindictive pleasure.

"I see you approve of that."

"I do. I hope it hurt."

The glow of eather shone brightly in her eyes. "It did."

"I'm...I'm so sorry," I whispered. "I can't even comprehend how someone could do or allow that. Any of that."

"Most cannot, and for that we should be grateful."

I nodded. "You are...you are very strong. I hope you know that. But I wish you didn't have to know."

"It doesn't feel like that some days, but thank you." Her chin lifted. "It was a long time ago. I've had time to process what was done to me. I'm lucky to have those around me such as Bele and Nyktos."

But that didn't mean the horrors didn't still find her, and she had to be revisiting them now.

Aios came forward, kneeling and clasping my hand. "I didn't tell you that so you'd feel sorry for me."

"I know." I squeezed her fingers.

"I told you because I knew no other way to tell you what I know to be true—just in case you decide to follow this destiny you believe to be yours. It doesn't matter what soul you carry inside you." Aios lifted our joined hands. "What does is whether or not Kolis is capable of loving again, even his *graeca*. And he's not. There's nothing but rot and decay where his *kardia* should be. Kolis has no weakness."

33

Aios left shortly after that, but the horror she and far too many others had experienced lingered in the chamber as I waited for Nyktos.

Truly sickened on a mental and physical level, I closed my eyes. I didn't need details on how she'd survived to know that Kolis and every single individual who'd taken part in her *survival* should be destroyed until nothing was left of them—not even ashes.

I normally wasn't in the business of stacking up and comparing losses to see whose were greater, but it was hard not to in this instance. Nothing I'd ever experienced in my life could compare to what Aios, Gemma, and countless others had suffered.

Dampness clung to my lashes as I forced myself to take a long and deep breath. I took what Aios had shared and tucked it away in the same place I'd hidden my emotions. I had to. It was the only way I could ignore the voice whispering in my thoughts.

You're his weakness.

Aios had to be wrong. No one was without weakness.

The embers in my chest vibrated, alerting me to Nyktos's presence. A knock sounded on the adjoining door as I hastily wiped at my cheeks. "Come in," I called out, clearing my throat.

Light glinted off the cuff around Nyktos's upper arm as he entered. He'd also changed, now wearing black leathers and a midnight-colored tunic tailored to his broad shoulders and lean waist. Silver brocade trimmed the collar and the chest. Something about seeing him in close to all black left me strangely uneasy.

Maybe it was because he looked different to me—more predatory than normal. Untouchable. Otherworldly.

Primal.

I rose, a little unsteady, and turned to him. He stopped, his gaze sweeping over the length of my hair brushing the curve of my hip. "Aios picked the gown," I said, lifting my arms at my sides. "She said Kolis would likely be offended by pants or something."

His throat worked on a swallow. "The gown is beautiful." His chest rose with a deep, shuddering breath. "You're beautiful."

I took a step back, even as my foolish heart gave a happy, idiotic leap. "Don't say that."

That shorter strand of hair slipped over his cheek as his head tilted, and his eyes lifted to mine. "I'm sorry. It's true." His head straightened. A moment passed. "I know things are…different between us now."

I almost laughed but managed to stop myself.

"But none of that can matter right now. We have to set all else aside," he continued. "Remember how I was when Attes was here?"

"Not like I'd forget," I muttered.

"It will be like that in Dalos," he said. "If we behave as if we cannot stand to be in each other's presence instead of appearing as if there is some sort of attraction between us, it will raise questions. I need to know if you're able to handle that."

My spine went rigid. "Do I really have a choice?"

"You were willing to pretend to be infatuated with me to seduce me, so I would *think* you would be willing to do the same to keep yourself alive," he replied.

I curled my hands into fists. "I wasn't pretending to be *infatuated* with you."

Nyktos eyed me. "You weren't pretending at all."

The back of my neck tingled. "That wasn't what I was saying."

"I know, but that doesn't change the truth of it. It was never an act. None of it."

I sucked in a shrill breath. "Congratulations on realizing that when it's too late," I snapped.

Eather pulsed faintly behind his eyes. "Too late for what?"

Crossing my arms over my chest, I said nothing.

"Wanting to be my Consort? In more than title?" Nyktos drifted closer in that silent way of his. "To the people of the Shadowlands and, eventually, Iliseeum? To me?"

The embers in my chest hummed as my skin prickled, heated. "Why would you speak of this now?"

"I don't know." A look of genuine dismay skittered across his normally stoic features. "Because why would you want that from me— want more— when you know I'm incapable of giving you what you deserve."

"And what is it that I deserve?"

"Someone who loves you, unconditionally and irrevocably. Someone who had the courage to allow themselves to feel that," he said. My arms slipped free of my hold as I stared at him. He looked away, shoulders straightening. "You were sad. Before I entered the room, I could taste your sorrow. Tangy and heavy." His gaze flicked back to mine. "When I could sense nothing from you before."

I wasn't surprised to hear that I had projected that strongly. "Aios told me about her time in Dalos."

"She did?" Surprise filled his tone.

I nodded. "She was worried that I would try something to stop Kolis."

"And does she have a reason to worry?"

She should, but... I shook my head. "I want a future—a life that I control. Not death. I want to survive this."

"So you can finally live? Be free?"

Chest heavy, I nodded once more as I turned from him. An unseen clock ticked over our heads, and I knew we couldn't delay this. But I also knew that if I allowed myself to feel more than what had broken through during my talk with Aios, I would also find that I was what Nyktos claimed I wasn't. Afraid.

I rubbed my hands over my arms. "What if...what if he recognizes me as Sotoria?"

"Then there will be a war," he said.

Heart lurching, I faced him. There had been no hesitation in his response. Not even a heartbeat. "Nyktos—"

"You do not belong to him. You do not belong to anyone," he bit out. "If he recognizes you as Sotoria, he will try to keep you. I will not allow that to happen."

A chill spider-walked down my spine.

Nyktos stepped toward me, his chin lowered. "He may be eons older than me, and he may have the entire Court and most—if not all— of the Primals behind him, but if he makes even one move toward you,

I *will* leave the entire City of the Gods in ruins."

Air snagged in my throat. No part of me in that moment doubted that Nyktos was capable of doing just that. "I don't want it to come to that."

"Neither do I," he said quietly. "My guards are aware that things can go south. They don't know all the reasons, but they will be prepared to defend the Shadowlands, as are the armies."

I forced breath into my lungs, breathing long and slow. As wrong as it was, I didn't want Kolis to recognize me. I didn't want to have to use what I'd spent my life training to do to end him. But I didn't want the kind of bloodshed Nyktos spoke of. That level of destruction would not only rip through Iliseeum; it was sure to spread to the mortal realm, as well. The only way either realm survived was if I lived—at least, long enough for Nyktos to take the embers. But if Kolis realized who I was...

Then all I could do was prevent a war. That wasn't much. The mortal realm would be lost and, eventually, at some point in the distant future, so would Iliseeum. But it was something.

"I have never asked anything of you," I said, meeting his gaze.

"You have asked seven things of me, to be exact."

"Okay. Forget those things. What I'm asking now—no, what I will beg of you is far more important."

Nyktos stiffened, the eather flaring brightly in his eyes as if he knew what I was about to say. And maybe he did.

"If Kolis recognizes me as Sotoria, I don't want you to intervene."

"Sera—"

"I cannot be the cause of a war that will destroy cities and end in countless deaths. I would never be free then. Whatever life I had wouldn't bring me any joy, knowing that," I said, my voice trembling. "I couldn't live with it. I would be as good as dead. I know the embers are important, but—"

"It is not only the fucking embers that are important, Sera. *You.*" He inhaled sharply as I jolted. "You are important. And what you ask of me is to walk away, leaving you to not only certain death but also with Kolis. If Aios told you all, then you know what that will entail. And you also have to know that it will be far worse for you because you won't be his favorite. You will be his in all the ways he believes he has a right to."

Nausea rose. "I know."

He was right in front of me now, his eyes full of swirling eather.

"Then you have to know that what you ask of me is to do exactly what you say you cannot do—what I've already *had* to do my entire life. To live while knowing I've left others behind to suffer and die in unimaginable ways. To live when I'm already dead inside."

I drew back. "You're not dead inside."

"You really think that?" He laughed, and it was icy. Smoky. "Even had I never had my *kardia* removed, I wouldn't be capable of love. Not after what I've had to do. What I've allowed. That alone would have left me unworthy of experiencing such an emotion. And that goodness you see in me? That part of me that you believe extends to all others, it's almost gone. Letting Kolis destroy yet another innocent—destroy *you*—will take what is left of that goodness. I will become something far worse than Kolis."

He fears becoming Kolis.

I hadn't thought that possible when Nektas had said it. I still didn't, but I knew that didn't matter if Nyktos believed it. If I demanded that others not tell me how to feel, it was not my place to then do one of those things I hated.

Which meant we were at a crossroads. In a stalemate and left with two options that neither of us could live with.

And neither realm would likely survive.

"Then I guess..." Exhaling roughly, I looked up at him. "Then I guess we're screwed."

He stared at me for a moment and then barked out a short, ragged laugh. "I suppose that is one way of saying it."

"Or maybe you two will get lucky and he won't recognize you." Nektas came through the open adjoining door with Jadis still sprawled over his shoulder and chest. Reaver followed in his draken form, gliding to the couch. "Jadis wanted to see you before you left," Nektas explained. "And I decided to eavesdrop."

"Not shocked to hear that," I murmured.

At the sound of my voice, Jadis lifted her ruddy cheeks. Blinking sleep-heavy, crimson eyes, she stretched two little arms in my direction as Nektas brought her to me. I didn't know what to do, but when I lifted my hands, she grasped fistfuls of my hair and bent over, pressing her lips to my forehead.

It was the messiest, wettest, and *sweetest* kiss I'd ever received.

"Night-night," she murmured, pulling back.

"That's her way of saying goodbye," Nektas explained.

"Night-night," I whispered, voice strangely thick as I carefully untangled her fingers from my hair.

Her rosy lips parted and spread in a beautiful smile. Then she turned to Nyktos and repeated the same. The strangest thing happened as the Primal moved closer to the little draken. It was like a flush of the muscles. They went loose and then tightened as I watched him bend his head to her and take her tiny arms in a gentle grasp. The wet smack against his forehead and his answering smile made my heart do all kinds of weird things.

I quickly looked away, swallowing the sudden thickness in my throat. There had been nothing fake about his smile. His entire face had warmed. And, gods, that expression, the gentle way he held the child's arms, said there was a lot more of him that was still alive than he realized.

"I want to go with you two," Nektas said quietly. "But only you and Ash can answer the summons."

Clearing my throat, I nodded. "You really think we'll be lucky?"

"I don't see why luck couldn't be on our side this time." Nektas clasped the back of my neck with his free hand. "I will see you again."

I believed him.

I just hoped it wasn't at the beginning of a war.

Nyktos and I stood on his balcony under the light gray skies. We wouldn't be traveling by horse. I was about to experience the oddity that was shadowstepping again.

"You ready?" Nyktos asked.

Not at all, but I didn't say that as I tipped back my head to look at the faint glimmer of stars. All that *hurt* I'd tucked away just a day ago seemed insignificant in the face of what awaited us. "You know," I said, heart pounding, "I've discovered that I'd rather not know when I'm about to pass out."

"Understandable." He was close, standing behind me. "Once you Ascend, you won't pass out or feel any pain from this. You'll be able to do it yourself."

As I touched the smooth railing, *once I Ascended* felt like a longshot instead of a possibility. "Before we go, can you tell me what to expect?

Like what are some of the things Kolis may demand of us?" I asked.

There was a gap of silence and then, "The possibilities are endless," he said, his tone flat. "Once he demanded that I rip out the heart of a godling who hadn't bowed as quickly as the others when I passed."

Embers of eather vibrated as I closed my eyes. "How many of the marks on your skin are because of what he has demanded?"

"One hundred and ten," he answered.

Bile clogged my throat. He'd known that without having to think about the number.

"I've lost count of the atrocities I've witnessed," he continued after a beat. "I used to have to force myself to watch if there was nothing I could do. I miss those days. Because now...now I don't believe I even bat an eyelash."

He might have no physical reaction to the horror, but I knew it still got to him. It was in the rasp of his tone. "Have you been there when he...when he gets tired of one of his favorites?"

"I have."

My stomach continued to churn. "And?"

"And I've had to look the other way until I could try to get them out. Sometimes, I was too late to do anything."

"But you have intervened." I gripped the railing, thinking of Saion and Rhahar and the Chosen he'd saved.

"When I could be sure my intervention didn't carry a price others would pay." He paused. "I wish you didn't even have to think about that or be in this position."

I nodded, forcing my grip to loosen on the railing. "I'll be able to do whatever is necessary."

"Because you've killed upon your mother's request?"

Unable to speak, I gave a curt nod as I opened my eyes.

"Just remember, no matter what happens, a part of you is good. That cannot be tainted by what may come. You are not a monster. And you will not be one when we return."

That damn knot swelled once more in my throat, replacing the sour taste of bile. "Maybe I'm not a monster, but I, like you, am capable of monstrous acts. And when I really think about that, I'm not sure there's really a difference between the two."

"Then all of us, those good and bad, are a little monstrous," he said.

Preparing myself, I turned to Nyktos. "I'm ready."

He took my hands in his, and the charge of energy danced up my arms. He fitted me to his chest, and the contact sent a startling rush of sensations through me that I ordered myself to ignore.

"Hold on," he said, his voice roughening.

Inhaling sharply, I placed my hands against the front of his tunic, breathing in the scent of citrus.

His cool breath skimmed my cheek. "A bit tighter than that, Sera."

"I don't remember being required to hold on tighter before."

"You held me as if your life depended on it before," he remarked.

"I don't recall doing that," I muttered.

Nyktos chuckled as he folded an arm over my lower back. His head dropped, and his breath touched the curve of my neck, eliciting an unwanted shiver.

The air charged, and Nyktos's body hummed against mine with power. The white mist I'd seen in the Great Hall in Wayfair didn't come from the floor this time. It came from Nyktos, heavy and thick. It swirled around us, laced with dark shadows. My chest tightened as the swirling mist reached my hips. I locked up.

"Breathe with me," he said, dragging his hand to the center of my back as his chest rose against mine and held for a count of four, then exhaled. I matched his next breath as the mist churned at my shoulders. "Breathe."

Nyktos's lips touched the same spot Jadis had kissed as the mist swallowed us. The Shadowlands fell away, taking me with it.

And I held on.

I blinked.

That was what it felt like this time.

I simply blinked, and when I opened my eyes, we were standing under a shimmery canopy of golden leaves. The branches above our heads were so heavy with them that the glow cast upon us didn't come from the patches of blue sky but from the sun reflecting off the leaves. I'd never seen anything like them.

Cool fingers touched my cheek as I heard the soft trill of birds calling to one another, a sound I hadn't heard since arriving in the Shadowlands. Nyktos drew my gaze to his wide, swirling eyes. "Sera?"

he whispered.

"Yeah?"

He was quiet as he stared down at me, and I began to grow concerned. "You barely went unconscious."

I hadn't realized I had gone unconscious at all. "Is that a bad thing?"

His jaw flexed. "We need to get those embers out of you," he said, still whispering. "Soon."

My heart tripped over itself as I stepped back, looking around. The trunks of the cluster of trees we stood in glittered with specks of gold. "They're beautiful."

Nyktos's hand fell away. "They're called trees of Aios."

I glanced at him. "I assume the name isn't a coincidence?"

A wry grin appeared as he looked up at them. "No. Aios grew them with her touch."

My mouth fell open. "She can do that?"

"She can create many beautiful things when she wants to," he said, and I wondered if Aios had grown these trees after she'd fled Dalos. "We're at the very gates of Dalos. Once we leave these trees, we must be very careful."

I nodded.

"Do not allow anyone to lure you away," he continued. "And trust no one."

"Wasn't planning on it."

"Good," he said. "They will already know we've arrived. It would've been felt."

My heart kicked against my ribs. "I'm ready," I told him, and I wasn't sure if that was a lie or not. Regardless, we began walking through the shining trees, our steps strangely making no sound.

I took the time to focus on making sure my emotions were locked away and that my heart and mind were calm. I breathed in the balmy breeze that reminded me of home, held my breath to the count of four, then exhaled. I did this as we reached the edge of the trees, and the Rise around the city of Dalos came into view. The wall was as tall as the one circling the House of Haides and Lethe but constructed of polished marble that glittered with chunks of glittering stone. Diamonds.

Fancy.

But what caught my attention was the thick mist above the Rise, a shroud much as I'd seen in the Vale that obscured all that lay beyond.

Warm sunlight bore down on us, and when I looked at the sky, I saw no sun, just like in the Vale. Nyktos was quiet as my gaze fell upon the gate of the Rise, which lay open to us. A dozen guards stood at the sides of the gate, and they immediately reminded me of the statue of Kolis in the Great Hall of Wayfair.

Golden chestplates engraved with the same symbol that had been carved into Nyktos's palm were worn over white, knee-length tunics. Greaves covered their calves. Swords with golden blades were sheathed at their waists. Their heads were bare, but some sort of thick golden paint adorned their faces like a mask—one shaped like wings.

Something about it struck a chord of familiarity in me, but I couldn't place it as a shadow fell upon us. I sent a quick look over my shoulder, and air lodged in my throat. Massive statues of men carved from marble rose beyond above the trees of Aios, standing with their arms at their sides, in a line that traveled east and west as far as I could see. They were taller than any building in Lasania, even the Temples, and cast an imposing shadow on us as the guards by the gate knelt.

We passed them in silence, crossing into the City of the Gods, and I saw what the Rise and mist hid. I knew my mouth was hanging open as I took in Dalos, awed by the size of the city. It was far greater than Carsodonia, the capital of Lasania.

Trees similar to those in the Vale lined a road shimmering with crushed diamonds, their low, sweeping branches falling in a canopy of white blossoms that stirred gently in the breeze. My gaze followed the road to an immense structure behind a glittering wall shorter than that of the Rise, not too far from the entrance. Its four staggered towers rose from the middle of the dome, seeming to drink in the beams of sunlight. I could see the tips of ivory and gold canopies rolling just beyond the inner Rise. Despite the warmth, my skin chilled. Instinct told me that was where *he*, the true Primal of Death, waited in the sprawling diamond and crystal fortress.

I dragged my gaze from the fortress and looked out over the sparkling city. Buildings large and small dotted the many hills and valleys as far as the eye could track, some flat and square and others round with sweeping colonnades, their sides diamond-bright. Throughout the city, crystalline towers rose upward in graceful, spinning arcs that disappeared into wispy, white clouds. Vines appeared to grow over many of the buildings, crawling their way up the spires.

"It's beautiful."

"From a distance, it is."

A bolt of unease skittered through me. I glanced at Nyktos as he led me down the center of the narrow road, the only sound that of the breeze playing with the trees' graceful, arching branches and the whisper of wind. A frown pulled at my lips as I glanced around, seeing no one and...and hearing no one. Not even the birds calling to one another in the trees of Aios could be heard here. Tiny goosebumps spread across my flesh with each step that brought us closer to the fortress.

"Where is everyone?" I asked, my voice low.

"Do you know what many have taken to calling Dalos?" Nyktos said, gaze alert as he continuously scanned the trees. "The City of the Dead."

That didn't bode well.

"Those who still live are likely at Court." He gestured with his chin at the fortress. "Held within the grounds of Cor Palace."

My mouth dried as we neared the pillars of the inner Rise. There were no guards at this gate, but there was a strange scent in the air—a sweetness mixed with something metallic. The trepidation amplified, and the embers in my chest hummed unsteadily as we walked between the pillars and entered the courtyard of Cor. Nyktos cursed under his breath as our steps slowed and my gaze swept over—

I jerked to a stop as horror gripped me. It hadn't been the wind I'd heard. Good gods, it was *moans*. The sound came from the trees inside the courtyard, from the gleaming coves of the fortress, and from the billowing white cloths that weren't canopies but veils, torn gowns, and tunics rippling in the wind.

Nothing—absolutely nothing—could've prepared me for this. My gaze darted from the nude body strung above the golden doors of Cor, stained with dried rivulets of crimson, to the swaying, limp forms beyond the white blossoms of the willows. Bile choked me. My heart pounded as my throat tightened and seized at the sound—the *moaning*—echoing from the branches and from the spaces between the pillars lining the colonnade, where hands and feet had been spiked to the stone.

I thought I heard Nyktos whisper my name, but I couldn't be sure because the moaning was a chorus far more brutal than that of the sirens'. I couldn't even count how many bodies there were—there were that many. My mouth moved without sound, and the embers...

A new horror dawned as the embers vibrated frantically in my chest, responding to not just the death but also to the dying. I tried to look away, desperately hoping that would stop the embers, but there was nowhere to look. Bodies hung like wind chimes from trees and balconies. My skin heated and hummed, and I could feel my weak control over the embers slipping away. The corners of my eyes started to turn white as my legs moved without will, drawing me to the colonnade, where a male's blue eyes screamed what his stitched mouth could not beg for.

Life.

Or death.

A release.

My arm started to lift. I couldn't stop it. The power of the embers was too strong, the shock of what I was seeing too much. The crack inside me began to crumble away as power seeped out, spreading.

The embers—the source of life—rose inside me, in the heart of Dalos, and there was nothing I could do to stop myself.

34

Nyktos spun me around, tugging me to his chest. I barely noticed the charge of energy coasting from his body to mine as he clasped my cheek.

"I didn't know it would be like this. I would've warned you. I swear," he said. "Take a breath, Sera. Just take one breath with me."

My wide, panicked gaze shot to his as the embers pressed against my skin, sparking eather into my veins. "I can't stop it," I whispered, chest rising and falling rapidly. Understanding flared in his eyes. "You need to stop me, because I'm—"

Nyktos's mouth closed over mine, stunning me. I gasped, and he took full advantage of the opening, delving in with his kiss. The press of his lips, the unexpected flick of his tongue along mine, and the minty taste of his mouth were like a streak of lightning through my senses, scattering the cloud of panic and then all thought. I never knew a kiss could have such power, but Nyktos…his did. His hand smoothed over my cheek and through my hair, cradling the back of my head as the kiss deepened.

His lips moved against mine, hard and wild as traces of midnight and smoke flowed out from him in thick, rising tendrils. They rose over our legs and curled across my lower back. The icy touch was another shock, reminding me of the night in my chambers when he'd watched and then touched.

I clutched at the front of his shirt, the edges of the brocade itching against my palms as the throbbing in my chest intensified. Silvery light sparked from my fingers and was snuffed out by his shadows.

Nyktos was stopping the embers, not in a way I had foreseen but in the same manner that I had distracted him after Attes had left his offices. I'd been about to beg him to use compulsion, and he must have known that. Instead, he'd kissed me.

And he *kept* kissing me.

We stood in the courtyard of the dead and dying, but we couldn't have been farther away from it as his mouth and tongue traced mine. I relaxed into him, shuddering as his fangs nicked my lower lip, drawing just a hint of blood that he licked away.

He didn't stop kissing me, not until the power invading my blood retreated and the embers calmed, still thrumming but manageable.

And still, he drew from my lips. His mouth danced over mine until a different kind of heat flushed my skin, coaxed forth not from the horror of the courtyard but from how I responded to him. No matter where we stood. No matter what I had seen him do. No matter how unwise this was.

A throat cleared.

I tensed.

Nyktos's lips slowed against mine. He took his time, gentling the sweep of his tongue and the press of his mouth. When he finally lifted his head, and my eyes opened, the shadows of eather he'd called forth had disappeared.

His gaze met and held mine. There was a question in his stare. Was I in control? I thought so now that I knew what surrounded us. I gave him a small nod.

"So strong. So brave," Nyktos murmured, sliding his fingers from my hair. He dragged his palm along my cheek as he said in a louder voice, "Is there a reason you're interrupting, Attes?"

Thank gods it was Attes and not someone else, but that relief was short-lived. Attes likely suspected that I was not as Nyktos had presented me, and none of us knew what he would do with that information.

Calling on the bravery Nyktos had spoken of, I looked over my shoulder and saw that the Primal wasn't alone. A dark-haired male stood beside him, face painted with golden wings.

I blinked as that painted mask stirred memories that I couldn't quite latch onto. The twist of the unknown male's lips was nothing like the amused smile on Attes's, but I kept my eyes on them, not allowing myself to look anywhere else because I knew what I would see.

"It wasn't me who interrupted," Attes replied, arms folded over his armorless chest. He jerked his chin to the one who stood beside him. "It was Dyses. I was enjoying the show."

The spark of energy radiating from Nyktos was as cold as my cheek was warm against his palm. "You really are bound and determined to lose those eyes of yours, aren't you?"

Attes chuckled. "Worth it."

I watched the Primal of Accord and War raise a dark blond brow as Dyses stepped forward and bowed. Pale blue eyes looked me over as he rose. The god lifted his chin. "His Majesty is currently holding Court and isn't yet ready to receive you," Dyses said, his voice carrying a heavy lilt that reminded me of the Lords of the Vodina Isles. "Others are in the atrium. I will escort you and..." He cleared his throat. "Your mistress there."

I blinked once, then twice.

Attes ducked his chin as he dragged his hand over his mouth, failing to hide his widening smile.

"And how long will His Majesty be occupied?" Nyktos asked as he dropped his hand from my cheek and moved so he was beside me.

"He will join you when ready," Dyses replied, his pale gaze flickering over me.

"I'm sure he will," Nyktos all but purred as frustration scratched at my skin. "And she is not my mistress. She is my Consort."

"Only if His Majesty grants such a title," Dyses corrected, his lip curling as he eyed me. "Until then, she should realize that she's in the presence of her betters and bow."

I stiffened, realizing I should've done that the moment I'd laid eyes on Attes. Though I had a feeling Dyses was more offended that I hadn't shown *him* respect. Swallowing my annoyance and proving that I did, indeed, have common sense, I started to bow.

"You will not," Nyktos said quietly, stopping me with a hand on my arm. His eyes briefly met mine, and then he turned to Dyses. "My soon-to-be Consort will bow when she's in the presence of those deserving of respect." His lazy smile set off warning bells. "But until then..."

Nyktos shadowstepped, appearing behind Dyses in the span of a heartbeat. There was no warning. Dyses' chest simply exploded in a spray of hot, shimmery red-blue blood.

I jerked back out of instinct, hand going to my thigh where the dagger was strapped, but then I saw Nyktos's hand.

My gods... Nyktos had punched his hand straight through the god's back—through bone and tissue.

Nyktos jerked his hand free, and he was…he was holding a fleshy, reddish-blue lump in his palm. Dyses looked down at his chest, his mouth gaping.

"*You* will bow before her." Nyktos's fingers closed over the heart, destroying it in a burst of silvery eather.

"Fuck," Dyses rasped, falling to his knees.

Then to his face.

I stared at the bloody, jagged hole in the center of Dyses' white tunic, then slowly lifted my gaze to Nyktos.

"Well," Attes drawled. "That's either going to annoy His Majesty or amuse him."

"Probably the latter." Nyktos knelt, using the god's tunic to clean the blood and gore from his hand as his gaze rose to mine. "I did *not* like his tone."

"Neither did I," I said hoarsely, finding my voice. "But that was, maybe, a little excessive."

There was nothing to discern in the hard, striking lines of Nyktos's face. "He was testing exactly what I would allow when it comes to you." He stood. "He failed, and others will know."

"I have a feeling there's going to be a lot of heartless, dead gods by the end of the day," Attes remarked, glancing at me. His smile returned. "Their blood will match your lovely gown."

"As will yours if you keep looking at her that way," Nyktos warned, stepping over the fallen god. "I assume you were waiting for our arrival?"

Attes appeared unfazed by the threat. "I was. Hoping you'd arrive soon, since you are, by far, better company."

"That's not saying much." Nyktos folded the hand that hadn't been inside another god around mine. "Was there a reason?"

I looked down as Nyktos led me around the fallen Dyses, hesitating as I stared at the god's hand.

"Sera?" Nyktos glanced back at me. "Someone will retrieve him."

"It's not that," I said, having sworn that Dyses' hand had twitched. But that was impossible. Gods, unlike Primals, couldn't survive without their hearts. However, I hadn't felt the embers responding to the god's death either. Knowing I couldn't share that at the moment, I shook my head and frowned. "It's nothing."

"He doesn't feel right, does he?" Attes said, drawing my attention. He lifted his gaze from the god to Nyktos. "Dyses always felt…off."

"Yeah," Nyktos murmured, the corners of his lips turning down.

"But none of Kolis's servants have felt right, have they? Not in a long time." He continued staring at the god, his head tilted. "I sense no...soul."

Attes's head swung sharply back toward the fallen god. "That's impossible."

"And I see none." Nyktos steered me farther away from the fallen god. He looked at the other Primal. "Either his soul hasn't left his body yet or he has none. I would know."

"Yeah, you would." Attes nudged the god's leg. There was no reaction. "Intriguing." He lifted his head, silver eyes flat. "We should be on our way."

As we started forward, I glanced back at Dyses. The god was dead, but could he have truly been...soulless? I swallowed, thinking of what Gemma had said about some of the Chosen who'd disappeared and returned as something she'd never seen before.

Unnerved, I faced forward as Attes led the way, careful to avoid walking beneath the body left to rot above. I shuddered, focusing on the feel of Nyktos's cool hand and the rough calluses of his palm. There was something grounding about his touch that I didn't want to think too deeply about as we made our way along a diamond and granite pathway.

"I see His Majesty has been doing some *redecorating,*" Nyktos commented as we walked into another courtyard that I was too afraid to check out.

"So it appears." A muscle flexed along Attes's jaw, a small reaction that seemed to speak volumes. "I'm not sure what sealed their fate, but I believe some were Chosen taken from a recent Rite."

The breath I took scorched my lungs as I briefly closed my eyes.

Nyktos squeezed my hand, saying nothing as Attes led us under a heavily flowered breezeway, the sweet floral scent and pale pink-and-purple beauty of the blooms completely at odds with what I'd witnessed.

"Were you summoned here?" Nyktos asked as we passed the smooth sandstone walls of several bungalows.

"Kyn was." Attes glanced at Nyktos. "So, I decided to join him."

Something passed between the two Primals as Attes refocused on the winding pathway. "Hanan is also here. Whether he was summoned or not, I do not know."

Unease stirred even stronger, but Nyktos only smirked. "And why is it that you decided to join us?"

Attes stepped in front of one of the bungalows. "I was hoping to see Sera."

Nyktos slowly turned his head to the other Primal as eather crackled in the air around his eyes.

I sighed. "I think you find some perverse pleasure in irritating Nyktos."

"I have many perverse pleasures," Attes admitted. "But I wanted to make sure you remembered what I told you when we first met." His steps slowed. "That while I found your sharp tongue to be refreshing, and even alluring," he said, his cool silver eyes meeting mine, "others will not. Especially those you will find here at Cor Palace."

Within the shadowy alcoves lining the gold-adorned halls leading to the atrium, *individuals*, partly clothed and fully nude, engaged in every sexual act imaginable—and some I hadn't even considered—both alone and in groups. I didn't look close enough to tell if they were all gods or not, because…good gods, there was a lot happening everywhere if the moans and gasps echoing around us were anything to go by.

Neither Nyktos nor Attes appeared all that bothered or even aware of the flashes of bare limbs and glistening skin beneath gilded ceilings, leaving me to wonder exactly how common this was.

"When did you arrive?" Nyktos asked as I worked to keep my gaze away from the plated columns lining the entrances of the alcoves and only on the golden, brocaded curtains at the end of the hall.

"Only a few hours ago," Attes answered, his eyes slightly squinted. "You likely won't be surprised to hear this, but Kyn is already deep in his cups."

Nyktos smirked. "Not even remotely."

"Is anyone else here?" I asked. I didn't say her name, but I felt Nyktos's gaze on me.

"No other Primal that I'm aware of. My presence alone more than makes up for their absence." He sent me a quick, teasing grin.

I rolled my eyes, relieved to learn that Veses was absent, but worried that Nyktos might just remove at least one vital organ or piece of Attes by the time we were finished here.

The embers thrummed faintly as the golden curtains parted ahead. My heart kicked around in my chest. The space beyond was a large, circular chamber, but not one I would necessarily call an atrium. Deep couches and settees sat at the foot of thick swaths of material which appeared to cover the windows lining the walls, and the ceiling above looked to have been painted over by…gold.

My gaze immediately went across the chamber to the raised, columned dais between two closed archways. Gold curtains were tied back to the columns, revealing a throne trimmed in what appeared to be diamonds and…gold.

I was beginning to see a theme—a rather gaudy one—in the Cor Palace as we crossed the marble floor with gold veining throughout.

I noticed the atrium was not empty. A tall, dark-haired male stood to the right of the dais with his back to us as he spoke to someone I couldn't see. He was dressed like Attes and Nyktos—dark leathers and a sleeveless tunic. A silver cuff adorned his upper biceps. He had a cup in his hand, half-full of a dark, amber liquid.

"Hanan," Nyktos advised under his breath, dipping his head toward mine.

My stomach felt like it was full of serpents as I gave a short nod. There were others in the atrium, spaced throughout, resembling the guards we'd passed—fully armored and faces painted gold.

Nyktos guided us to a settee to the left, as far as possible from the guards. He sat, pulling me into the space between his legs. I went stiff for half a second before I remembered why he'd positioned me so. I relaxed against his chest, keeping my expression blank.

Attes arched a brow. "I must locate my brother," he said, glancing back to the very…active hall we'd traveled through. "Before he gets himself into some sort of predicament I'm likely to find displeasing."

"Attes?" Nyktos stopped the other Primal as he folded his arm across my waist. "Why did you kill Kyn's guards?" he asked, keeping his voice low.

Attes's shoulders went rigid as I remembered them speaking about Kyn's guards when Attes had come to tell us that the coronation would need to be delayed. "They were taking young ones years out from entering their Culling to their encampments," he said, and a rumble of disapproval radiated from Nyktos and against my back. "It wasn't to keep them safe, so I gutted them and then ended them."

The Primal then bowed before pivoting on his heel. I watched him leave the atrium, the curtains settling back into place behind him.

"Were you not expecting that answer?" I asked.

"I wouldn't have a few months ago," he said, stretching out one leg as I kept mine tucked between his.

I turned my head toward his, speaking as quietly as he had. "Did it seem like Attes was...looking out for me?"

He nodded as he glanced over the atrium. The eather had subdued in his eyes, but his gaze remained alert. "It did—does."

"So maybe you can stop threatening to rip out his eyes?" I suggested. "He could be a...*friend*."

"Then he should stop looking at you like he wants to taste you."

My brows shot up on my forehead. "First off, he was not looking at me like that."

"That is the only way he looks at you."

"And even if he was, you have no right to be jealous," I reminded him.

"Agreed. But that doesn't change the fact that I am, and that Attes will inevitably find himself having to regenerate his eyes." He turned his head to our left.

A door near the dais opened, and a woman walked out carrying a tray of glasses. She had her tightly curled hair swept back from her face, and her painted mask shimmered against the cool, black tones of her complexion. My attention shifted to the body-length garment—a loosely fitted peplos gown made of a nearly transparent material. Golden bangles were stacked on her slender arms from her wrists to her elbows.

"Is everyone required to wear gold here?" I asked as the woman approached us.

Nyktos snorted. "His Majesty does favor the color—the symbolism."

The woman stopped before us, keeping the tray level as she bowed deeply. "Would you care for refreshments, Your Highnesses?"

My gaze lifted to hers. The woman's eyes were a dark brown, and there was no hint of an aura behind the pupils. Was it possible that she was a godling who hadn't Ascended? Or a mortal? A Chosen. My chest squeezed as I looked over the glasses, my gaze settling on one with dark, purplish liquid inside. Curious, I reached for it.

"That would be an unwise choice," Nyktos murmured, reaching around me to pluck a slender glass of amber liquid from the tray. He handed it over to me and then took another. "Thank you," he said to the woman.

Surprise flickered across the woman's face, gone in a blink as she ducked her chin and bowed once more. Rising, she turned to make her way to where Hanan stood, still not having taken notice of us.

Which was okay by me.

"What was in the other glass?"

"Radek wine, made from grapes found in Kithreia," he said, taking a sip.

"That's...Maia's Court, isn't it?"

"It is. The wine is a fairly potent aphrodisiac."

"Oh." I glanced quickly at Nyktos and then back to where the woman offered the tray to Hanan. "Exactly how potent?"

"I've never partaken of it, but I've heard it will leave one wanting for three full days."

Eyes widening, I took a drink of what turned out to be whiskey. "Kind of hard to imagine one would have the stamina for that."

"I can," he murmured, irises bright behind half-open eyes.

I stared at him. "I bet you can."

One side of his lips curved up. I looked away, slowly sipping the whiskey as I tracked the veining in the marble, following the lines and curves to the atrium's center. I squinted, lowering the glass as I leaned back just an inch or so. Nyktos's arm tightened as I followed those lines in the floor again. They weren't natural marks, but in the design of a...

A wolf.

A large, prowling, snarling wolf.

Nyktos tilted his head to mine. "Did you feel something outside? With Dyses?"

Blinking, I drew my gaze from the floor. "I...I felt *nothing*."

He nodded, his jaw hardening. A sign that he understood what I wasn't saying.

"Is it just me, or is there a design in the floor?"

"It's not you," he confirmed. "That is if you see a wolf."

"I do. It reminds me of the crest on your throne doors."

"It should because it's nearly identical. It's the crest of my father's bloodline. Both his and Kolis's." He paused. "And mine."

The smoky whiskey scorched my throat. I wanted to ask how he felt about sharing the same crest as his uncle, but I knew that this wasn't the place for it. My gaze drifted back to the wolf, and I thought of the kiyou wolf I'd brought back to life—how fierce and brave it had been, even on the edge of death. "Why is the wolf the crest?"

"My family has always been...partial to wolves," he explained after a moment. "My father once told me that there was no other creature as loyal or protective as a wolf. Or spiritual. He saw them as he saw himself. As a guardian."

"Do you see yourself as such?" I murmured. His chest rose against my back, but he didn't answer. So, I did. "You should."

His hand firmed on my hip as his chin grazed the side of my head. "You think that? Even now? After everything?"

I knew what he was talking about. Veses. "Even now," I admitted. "You being a complete jackass doesn't change that."

Nyktos said nothing.

Taking another drink, I looked at a guard's stoic, painted face. Those faint memories stirred once more. "There's something about those masks," I said, clearing my throat. "I can't put my finger on it."

"They're another symbol that once belonged to my father," Nyktos said after a moment, the fingers at my hip beginning to move idly. "Hawks represent intelligence, strength, and courage. A reminder to be careful, but to also be brave." His whisper grazed my temple. "The wings are those of a hawk, but when my father ruled as King, they were always silver."

I stiffened. "Silver? Like a silver hawk?"

"Like the great silver hawk," he confirmed. "My father was always fascinated with the creatures. He thought they were…" Nyktos trailed off as his hand tightened on my hip. "You tensed. What is it?"

"I don't know." I turned my head to his, swallowing a gasp as my lips brushed his. My grip on the glass trembled as I swallowed. "I keep seeing silver hawks. Like the night in the Dying Woods. There was one then."

"That's impossible." Nyktos's fingers began to move once more, trailing in idle circles along my hip and waist. "You were lucky to see one in the Red Woods, but not even a hawk would enter the Dying Woods."

"But I did—" I went quiet as a door behind the dais opened, and a broad-shouldered male entered, bare-chested with two-toned hair like Nektas—crimson and black. I didn't need to be any closer to see his eyes or whether his tan flesh carried the faint ridges of scales to know this man was a draken.

"Davon," Nyktos shared quietly, having followed my gaze. "He's a distant relative of Nektas."

"Oh."

"Not distant enough, according to Nektas."

"*Oh*," I repeated, watching the draken hop down from the dais.

Brushing the long hair over his shoulder, he looked over at us as he stalked across the atrium. Then he smirked.

I stiffened.

"Ignore him." Nyktos swept his thumb over my hip.

It was kind of hard to do that as he continued eying us as he went to the curtained doorways. How in the world would a relative of Nektas's remain in Kolis's Court after what he'd done to Nektas's wife? But hadn't Nektas said that some of the draken who served Kolis had been forced into it? Therefore, corrupting them? Either way, it took no leap of imagination to figure out why Nektas wished this Davon was a far more distant relative.

An arm parted the curtains as Davon approached them. I could only see a bit of the man who waited in the hall since his back was to us. Golden skin. Fair, shoulder-length hair.

"We've got something to take care of," the man spoke.

I frowned as Davon replied, "Of course, we do."

There was something familiar about that voice—the soft lilt of his speech. I was almost positive I'd heard it before.

Nyktos turned his head again, catching my attention with a slide of his lips over mine. "Hanan comes."

All thoughts of the hidden man and the draken fell to the wayside as Nyktos sat his glass of barely touched whiskey on the side table.

He pressed a kiss to the corner of my lip, one that sent a shiver of mixed reactions through me before I could remind myself that this was an act. A show. Slowly, he lifted his mouth from mine. "Hanan."

"Nyktos," came the deep, gruff reply.

With my heart thrumming unsteadily, I turned my head and looked up at the Primal of the Hunt and Divine Justice. He looked to be about Attes's age, in his third or so decade of life, with pale and sharp, angular features—beautiful in a predatory, cunning sort of way that left me cold.

"I was wondering when you would show me the respect of acknowledgment," Nyktos said, and I heard the icy, smoky smile in his voice. "But I figured you were waiting for a small army of Cimmerian to accompany you before doing so."

Good gods…

I watched Hanan's lips thin. I still wasn't quite used to the swift change in demeanor when another Primal was present—how quickly Nyktos could go from dangerous to deadly.

"Well, since you killed those I sent to your Court," Hanan began, "you should not be surprised to see that I have none with me."

"And what a shame that was." Nyktos's fingers continued their slow traces along my hip. "To have wasted so many Cimmerian lives on your boldness and cowardice."

Hanan stiffened. "That mouth of yours will get you into trouble one day."

"I believe it already has, but here I am."

"And here..." Hanan's gaze settled on me. "She is."

Ice pressed against my spine. I placed my whiskey on the side table just in case I needed both hands. The smirk settling onto Hanan's lips concerned me, as did the frigid power ramping up behind me.

"She is not what I expected," Hanan said.

Nyktos trailed his fingers up my waist to the band of my bodice. "And what did you expect?"

The Primal of the Hunt and Divine Justice raised a brow. "Anything but a diamond that will inevitably be shattered into tiny pieces."

I sucked in a sharp breath, surprised by what might actually be a compliment...and a veiled threat. "I am not the type of diamond easily broken," I said before I could remind myself of Attes's warning. "After all, diamonds do not crack."

Hanan tilted his head. "But they do break."

"Careful, Hanan," Nyktos warned softly as Hanan knelt at our feet, bringing himself to eye level with me.

The other Primal ignored Nyktos as he inhaled deeply, sniffing at...at the air much like a predator would upon scenting its prey. "You are but...what? A godling? Or so I'm told. On the cusp of her Ascension," he said, and I couldn't have been more grateful for his apparent lack of senses. "But as of now, you are just a mortal." He smiled, revealing two sharp fangs. The embers hummed in my chest, threatening to loose violent anger. "And there is nothing more breakable than that."

"You know what else is breakable?" Nyktos asked, his thumb swiping beneath the swell of my breast. "Your bones."

Hanan's lips parted, but before he could respond, he was scooting backward over the marble. His eyes flared wide, bright with essence as he smacked a hand on the floor, stopping himself. If I could taste anger like Nyktos, I imagined I'd be drowning in it.

"I warned you once, purely out of amusement," Nyktos drawled, tone soft and at complete odds with the words he spoke. "I will not warn you again. Speak to her one more time? Look at her? And I will shatter every bone in your cowardly body and then drag you into the Abyss to bury you so deep in the pits that it will take you a hundred years to claw your way out. Do you understand me?"

It was now my lips that parted. A hot, heady flush swept through me, pooling low in my stomach. No part of me should've been anything but terrified or disturbed by Nyktos's words, especially since I didn't doubt them for one second. But a whole lot of me was…aroused. And I didn't think any of those parts were the Primal embers, even though they seemed to throb in agreement with Nyktos's words.

Hanan rose, tension bracketing his mouth. "You think it wise to threaten me?"

"I think it's fucking unwise of you to even *dare* to speak to me after you sent your guards to my Rise to make demands," Nyktos replied. "And baseless accusations."

"Baseless?" Hanan laughed as streaks of eather whipped through his eyes. "A god from my Court Ascended into Primalhood within *your* Court. All you had to do was turn her over to me, and we could've possibly avoided what is surely to come."

"Her?" Nyktos said, and that was all he said.

"Bele."

I kept my face blank even as my heart sped up. I hated even hearing her name on the Primal's lips.

"I haven't seen Bele in many moons. Nor would I know where she is, as she is not a member of my Court." Nyktos lied so smoothly I almost believed him. "You should keep a closer eye on your vassals."

"You're really going to go this route? Pretend you have no knowledge of a god Ascending in your Court? Or whom it was?"

Nyktos's thumb swept back and forth, creating the only warmth in the entire atrium. "And are you really insinuating that it couldn't have been Kolis to have done it? Maybe you've fallen out of favor with him and he's setting you up. Or perhaps you don't believe he's able to do such a thing? Is that it?" Nyktos laughed. "Then I would be really careful. Because I don't think you want Kolis to know you have such little faith in his…strength."

Hanan blanched. "That is not what I'm saying."

"It's not?"

"No. But I do believe we will see just how quickly this one breaks," Hanan spat, the eather pulling back from his eyes even as the embers hummed in my chest. "Sooner rather than later, I imagine, since His Majesty is about to arrive. And I have a feeling he will have more questions about how exactly a god Ascended than he will about your would-be Consort. I will have what I want before the day is over, and you will…well, likely return to rule over your Court of the Dead with nothing, per usual."

Nyktos's fingers stilled as he leaned forward, then stopped. The air left the atrium with the breath I took. Goose bumps spread over my flesh, and my chest tightened.

Smirking, Hanan backed up as a flurry of painted guards filled the atrium, doors leading to the dais opened, and...

Kolis, the false King and true Primal of Death, entered.

35

An enormous presence poured into the atrium, settling upon my skin as the scent of stale lilacs choked me. My eyes stung as golden-laced eather churned along the floor and spilled over the edge of the dais, sparking off the marble and licking over the pillars of the dais, stirring the curtains. My bones felt as if they would crumble under the power flooding the chamber. The eather spread like whirling fog kissed by sunlight, but there was something in that light.

Something...wrong.

Nyktos's chest pressed against my back. I barely heard him whisper "*breathe*," but I obeyed as the mass of swirling, throbbing power began to recede. A roar of rushing blood filled my head as the essence collapsed to the floor at his bare feet, where it coiled like a pit viper against his white linen pants, waiting to strike.

I became aware of Nyktos standing—of *me* standing. His hands were on my hips, guiding me to my knee. It felt wrong, in every part of me, to kneel, but I placed one trembling hand on the floor and the other over my heart as I bowed.

Because if Nyktos could, I sure as fuck could.

The back of my neck prickled. Awareness rose. I could feel Kolis's stare, and the embers inside me throbbed. Panic threatened to take root as I bowed to the monster who had ruled my life before I was born.

Ruled all the lives I couldn't remember.

Calling on that veil of nothingness, I slipped it on, snuffing out my fear and anger as I counted the seconds between each breath. I would not crack here. I would not break. *I would not. I would not. I would not.* Not today. My hands steadied. My chest loosened. My heart beat. I breathed.

I was nothing once more.

"Rise" came the voice drenched in warmth and sunlight. A voice that, if listened to closely enough, carried a blade-sharp, bitter edge to it.

The crimson gown slid across the floor like a puddle of blood racing toward me as I rose. Nyktos had positioned himself so he stood partially in front of me, and only then did I realize that Attes had returned with his brother, who had slightly darker hair but was of the same height and breadth of shoulder.

He wavered slightly on his feet and was half-undressed.

"And sit," Kolis ordered. "Before this jackass falls on his face."

At any other time, I would've laughed because Kyn did appear as if he were seconds from doing just that.

Nyktos turned, his iron-hued eyes meeting mine as Attes all but shoved his brother into a nearby chair. He took my hand with a small nod, guiding me back to where we'd been seated.

"Not her."

I went stiff.

The skin tightened at the corners of Nyktos's mouth as his nostrils flared. Wisps of eather spread out from behind his pupils.

"I want to see her," Kolis added. "Get a good look at who has captured my *nephew's*...attention."

The hollows of Nyktos's cheeks deepened as the veins beneath his eyes began to fill with a faint glow of eather, and I knew something bad was about to happen. My senses tingled with the knowledge. And I didn't think I was the only one who felt the violent storm brewing within Nyktos. Attes had turned from his slouched brother, angling his body toward Nyktos's.

I didn't give myself time to think. I quickly stepped to the side, revealing myself fully. Nyktos's swift inhale fell like ice against my skin, but I didn't tremble as I stood there, hands at my sides. I didn't panic as I watched that churning mass of golden light swirl around Kolis's legs. I breathed.

"There she is," Kolis drawled, and then he was right in front of me, having shadowstepped.

Muscles tensed all along my spine as I fought the urge to recoil from the eather that drifted over the hem of my skirt. I stared at his chest—his bare chest, keeping my gaze lowered as one would in the presence of such a Primal. There were...shimmers of gold in his bronze flesh, a pattern of sweeps and swirls.

"Lift your eyes to mine," he whispered. Coaxed. Urged.

Muscles obeyed even as my stomach and chest hollowed. A compulsion. It was a *compulsion*—an unnecessary one that was nothing more than a show of power. Of force, to remind everyone in the room exactly who he was. I lifted my eyes just as he'd compelled.

The breath I took snagged in my throat as I saw Kolis. Not from a distance. Not how he was depicted in paintings or stone. There was no mistaking the similarities between him and Nyktos. Yet, somehow, even with their shared features, the differences were striking.

Nyktos's beauty was harsh and icy, a silvery sculpture of hard angles and unyielding lines come *alive* in an almost terrifying manner. His beauty *demanded* that you look upon him and be filled with the urge to try to capture his features with charcoal or clay.

But those features, the strong curve of his jaw, the high, arched cheekbones, and the lush, wide mouth...things that were so wild and unfettered on Nyktos, were utter perfection on Kolis—golden and *warm*. His beauty beguiled you. Welcomed you to look closer, to stare and be comforted. Coaxed you to come near.

They were the same yet opposites, one whose beauty had been designed to be infinite in its finality, to strike fear in your heart. And the other whose beauty was nothing more than a pretense. A façade. A trap.

Silvery eyes flecked with wisps of gold tracked over my features slowly, intensely. My skin began to prickle and crawl, but I showed nothing because I *felt* nothing as I stood before the beast that had started all of this.

The one I had spent my life training to kill.

"I've been told your name is Sera?" Kolis asked as I glanced up, taking note of his crown—a series of swords made of diamonds and gold, the center ending in the shape of a sun and its rays. "Is it short for anything?"

Uncertainty rose. I didn't know if I should tell the truth, but I thought that fewer lies meant less possibilities of being caught in one. Even a small lie could cause closer inspection. "Seraphena, Your

Majesty."

"*Seraphena*," he repeated, curling his lips inward. "A name that burns. Interesting. I've also been told you're a godling." The shimmery swirls moved up his throat and over his jaw, bleeding through his flesh until they formed a crackling, winged mask like those painted on the others' faces. "She does not feel like one."

"She is a godling," Nyktos answered. "Father is a god. Mother is mortal."

Gold hair brushed his cheek and shoulder as he tilted his head. The crown remained straight. "There is too much eather in her for that to be the case."

"Perhaps you're sensing my blood. She has quite a bit of that in her," Nyktos said. Normally, that smug tone would've grated on each and every one of my nerves.

But I understood the mission here.

"I see. I also see you've been charmed. Clever, Nephew," Kolis noted, an amused look playing across his lips as he continued staring at me. "Your hair is...captivating," the false King murmured, and I remembered what Gemma and Aios had said about his favorites. They were all either fair or red-haired. He lifted his hand—

Nyktos was like a strike of lightning, capturing Kolis's wrist before even a single finger could touch a strand of my hair.

My heart lurched.

Kolis slowly turned his head to Nyktos. None of the guards moved as the false King looked down to where Nyktos's hand clasped his wrist and then back to Nyktos's eyes.

"I do not wish for her to be touched." Nyktos's voice deepened. "She is mine."

I bit the inside of my cheek.

"And if I wish to touch her?" Kolis asked, so quietly I barely heard him.

Nyktos smiled, and my stomach tumbled at the mockery of such a gesture. "I will do to you what you have done to those who dare to touch those who belong to you."

My jaw began to ache from how hard I kept my mouth clamped shut. Those who belonged to him. His favorites. The ones Aios had said were caged.

"He's quite possessive of this one," Attes added from where he sat, half-reclined, half-sprawled. "Threatened to rip out my eyes at least three times."

I wasn't sure that helped.

Nyktos's smile increased, revealing a hint of his fangs, and I definitely didn't think *that* helped. "That threat is more of a promise," he replied as he still held Kolis's stare. "She is not to be touched. By anyone but me."

A long, tense moment passed, then one side of Kolis's lips tipped up. I felt no relief, only more tension. "Nephew," Kolis purred, the gold swirling through his irises. "You…please me."

What?

"But you should release me," Kolis went on, "before I become *dis*pleased."

Nyktos lifted one finger at a time, dropping the false King's wrist.

The smile on Kolis's face grew as he eyed his nephew. "This side of you…" His chin lifted as he inhaled deeply. "I always enjoy it when I see it come out." He flicked a too-lingering gaze toward me. "This should be, at the very least, entertaining."

I was beginning to think that the word *pleased* didn't mean what Kolis thought it did. Or maybe it was I who had it wrong.

Nyktos smirked, though, turning his back on the false King. He took my hand, folding his arm around my waist. His gaze didn't touch mine as he said, "May we both sit?"

"You may do as you like."

Nyktos guided me to the settee, returning us to the same position as before with me placed in the vee of his legs. I turned my head, but Kolis watched. Stared. At us. At me. And it was only then that I allowed myself to feel any sort of relief.

I didn't look like Sotoria. Because Kolis didn't recognize me.

A faint tremor went through me as Kolis returned to his throne upon the dais, tendrils of golden eather trailing behind him. Nyktos gently squeezed my side as I exhaled heavily, resting a hand on his knee. Nektas had been right. Luck was, for once, on our side. At least, with this. Everything else? I wasn't so sure.

Kolis was still watching me, staring, his head tilted, yet the crown not slipping an inch as his fingers rapped on the gilded arms of his throne. "My feelings are hurt, Nyktos," he began. "I would've thought you would have sought my approval for such a…joyous event—your union with the fiery Seraphena."

"I didn't think you'd have much interest in such an event," Nyktos replied as he dragged his thumb back and forth on the side of my waist. "I figured you were far too busy for such a request."

"You figured wrong." Kolis gave a close-lipped smile. "It is a show of respect that you, of all people, should've known was due me."

"Then I apologize," Nyktos said.

He didn't sound even remotely genuine.

Kolis's tight smile said he sensed the same. "We shall see how sorry you are, I'm sure."

Ice coated my insides, but there wasn't even a minor hitch in the slide of Nyktos's thumb.

"But there is something else we must discuss," Kolis added.

"If you're speaking of the vassal I encountered upon my arrival…" Nyktos's tone was lazy, partly amused, and it reminded me of how he'd spoken when we'd been at my lake. "I didn't like his tone."

Kolis snorted. "It is not Dyses I'm speaking of. He'll be fine."

"Unfortunately, I don't think he will be," Nyktos said. "Considering I removed his heart."

The false King's smile grew then, flashing teeth, and my unease ramped up. "Yes, well, we will see about that, too." He leaned back as Nyktos's fingers halted for a brief moment in their path on my waist. "I'm sure you're aware of why else I summoned you, Nephew."

My fingers pressed into Nyktos's knee. I decided right then that I hated how Kolis made a point of reminding Nyktos of the blood they shared.

Nyktos's thumb resumed its idle movements. "Is it because Hanan believes I have knowledge of how a god was Ascended or who it was?"

Primal Hanan's head turned in our direction. "It is not what I believe. It is what I *know*."

"I didn't give you permission to speak," Kolis said, his gaze remaining on us. "Did I, Hanan?"

Hanan stiffened where he sat. "No, you didn't. I apologize, Your Majesty."

"Do not force me to make an unfortunate impression on the lovely Seraphena by angering me," Kolis warned.

"That wasn't my intention," Hanan quickly said, bowing his head. "I just don't appreciate that he would attempt to speak falsely to you about something so serious."

"I'm *so* sure that's what motivates you to speak so freely," Nyktos purred, the words rumbling against my back.

Eather sparked from Hanan's eyes as he glared at Nyktos, but

Kolis raised a hand, silencing Hanan. "The power to Ascend a god is one felt by all. It is a power that should not exist beyond this Court," he said, knowing damn well that likely everyone in the chamber— besides me—knew the power no longer existed in Dalos. "But it does?"

"It does," Nyktos confirmed.

The tendrils swirled at the base of the throne as Kolis's head cocked once more. "And that is all you have to say?"

"It is all that I *can* say, Uncle," he said, and I tensed upon hearing him refer to Kolis as such. Still, he kept moving his thumb in those slow, comforting swipes. "I felt it myself. Felt it before in the mortal realm, though less powerful. I, too, have searched for it. I have found none in the Shadowlands who could've been responsible for such a burst of power."

Hanan practically vibrated with his need to speak, but he waited until Kolis nodded. "And how would that be possible?"

"Is that a serious question?" Nyktos countered as Attes dragged his fangs over his lower lip, barely concealing his smirk. "Whoever was responsible is clearly no longer in the Shadowlands. I assumed that it was our King."

I almost laughed, but I was far too impressed by how calm Nyktos was, how convincing. And was also too dumbfounded by all of this. Kolis had sent his dakkais as a warning that he was aware of the embers of life. He could've possibly sent his draken, despite Nektas not recognizing the one that attacked. He had to know that Nyktos didn't, not for one second, believe it was him. Something wasn't right here.

"You're suggesting that Kolis Ascended a god in the Shadowlands for no reason and then left?" Hanan demanded.

"Who else could it have been? Only the Primal of Life can Ascend a god," Nyktos said.

My breath snagged in my throat as the air in the atrium became hot, thick, and humid.

The gold in Kolis's eyes brightened. "What *are* you suggesting, Nyktos?"

"I believe that he's suggesting that only one person could've been capable of such a miraculous event," Attes said. "You."

Then, and only then, did Kolis look away from us. The essence along the floor throbbed as he looked down upon the Primal of War and Accord. "Yes," he murmured, clearly not as annoyed with Attes speaking out of turn as he had been with Hanan. "Only I have the power to Ascend a god. To return life to what has passed on." Slowly, Kolis turned back to us as the tendrils of essence rose, coiling. I saw it again, a shadow in that essence as Kolis raised his hand once more.

The doors behind him opened, and—

Dyses walked onto the dais, the front of his tunic smeared with dry, rusty-colored blood.

My lips parted on a sharp inhale as Nyktos went stiff behind me. Attes sat up straighter, pitching forward as the god stopped beside Kolis and bowed—the god I'd seen Nyktos punch his hand through. A god who shouldn't be standing because Nyktos had destroyed his heart.

It was impossible, but...but hadn't I thought I'd seen his fingers twitch? I hadn't felt his death as I did when other gods perished. Both Attes and Nyktos had said something had felt off about Dyses.

"He was dead the last time I saw him," Nyktos remarked coolly.

Kyn gave a short, muffled laugh.

"I was, Your Highness." Dyses bowed once more. "But the Primal of Life saw fit to restore me."

But that...that didn't make sense. When I restored Bele, I Ascended her. This god's eyes were still that incredible, pale shade of blue. Had I simply done it wrong because I hadn't known what I was doing? Or was this different?

My heart started pounding. Was this what Gemma had spoken of? The Chosen who disappeared, only to return as something cold, lifeless, and hungry? Dyses was nothing like Andreia had been. He wasn't a Craven. So he had to be one of what Kolis had called his Revenants.

But Dyses had been out in the sun, and Gemma had said that those things only moved about at night. And that Kolis needed his *graeca* to perfect them.

Kolis smiled as he looked up at Dyses, but the expression faded as his gaze settled on Hanan. "Just because I chose not to restore life or to Ascend a god does not mean I will not, when one is deserving. It is not my fault that most lack such blessings," he said, lifting his chin. "Do you think I'm unaware that my vassals have sworn their loyalty to me but question my strength? That I do not know that you and a few of your brethren doubt I am as strong as I was the moment I Ascended to rule as your King?"

"I... I..." Hanan stuttered, his skin paling several shades. "I didn't mean to imply that you were incapable. You didn't say it was you—"

"Why would I need to tell you that?" Kolis countered.

Hanan went silent.

There was nothing he *could* say.

Because Kolis had him in a corner. If Hanan admitted that he believed it was someone else who'd Ascended a god, something that *should* be impossible, then it *could* mean that he believed Kolis wasn't capable of doing so. Thinking something was completely different than saying it.

"I would advise you to be more thoughtful in voicing your concerns, Hanan, lest you find yourself falling out of my favor." Kolis echoed Nyktos's earlier words. "And it would be considerably unwise to do so when there is another who could take your place."

"Yes, Your Majesty," Hanan said, clearly shaken.

"Leave my sight." The tendrils spun along the dais. "And do not return until I summon you."

The Primal of the Hunt and Divine Justice rose, bowing stiffly before turning and leaving the atrium without acknowledging those left in the space.

Silence fell, and then Kolis said, "I apologize that you had to bear witness to such absurdity, Seraphena."

I jolted, my gaze flying to his. His words. His behavior. None of it fit with what I knew of Kolis. "It's...it's okay."

The false King smiled. "You have a kind, forgiving nature."

Nyktos's fingers halted, and seconds ticked by—moments filled with the knowledge that we knew he hadn't Ascended Bele. And that whatever stood beside him wasn't quite right. Out of the corner of my eye, I saw Attes glance at the guards, and I wondered if he was thinking what I—and likely Nyktos—was.

How many of these guards were ones reborn under Kolis—a Primal who shouldn't be able to restore life?

"Both of you seemed surprised to see Dyses alive and well." Kolis glanced between Attes and Nyktos. "Have you two shared the same concerns as Hanan?"

"I have not seen you bestow the honor in a long time, Your Majesty." Attes shrugged. "It's just a surprise to see you do such a thing."

Kolis nodded, then his attention shifted to Nyktos. That smile of his deepened, tightened. "And you?"

"It is unlikely that Hanan and I share any concerns," he replied smoothly. "I, too, am surprised for the same reasons as Attes. And for the dakkais you sent to my lands shortly after the energy was felt."

A shiver tiptoed down my spine as I braced myself.

Kolis leaned forward, letting a hand drop over the arm of the throne. The crown glimmered as brightly as the sun. "Why would you think those two things are related?"

"They're not?"

"No."

"Bad timing, then?"

"Yes, bad timing." Kolis's head tilted in a...a serpentine manner. "I was displeased with your failure to announce your intentions to take a Consort. I am still not pleased that you sought to hold a coronation without my approval."

I stilled.

So did Nyktos.

That was bullshit, and I doubted that Nyktos believed him. I wasn't even sure Kolis thought we believed him. Unease ratcheted up. This felt like a game where the rules were kept hidden.

"You know what happens when I'm displeased, especially with you." Kolis's voice slipped and slithered across the atrium, coating my skin in oil. "And yet it seems you take great joy in doing so. I have been so very tolerant, but you disrespected me, and that cannot go unpunished."

"I know," Nyktos said, and that was *all* he said. Fear, cold and hard, bolted through me.

"It was my fault," I blurted, heart seizing as Attes's head swung in my direction.

"Sera," Nyktos hissed, straightening as he grasped my hips like he fully planned to lift me and run from the room—or throw me from it. "That is—"

"No." Kolis rose. "I want to hear what she has to say." Those golden, churning eyes fixed on me. "How is it your fault?"

"I..." I swallowed, my heart thumping as my thoughts raced. "He didn't seek your permission because I asked him not to."

"That is not true," Nyktos growled.

"Yes, it is," I argued, scooting forward as far as I could go as Kolis's gaze flicked between us. "You see, I feared—"

"Me?"

"No," I quickly denied, willing my heart to slow. "I have no reason to fear you."

Kolis came to the edge of the dais, *glided* to it, and those tendrils of eather spilled onto the marble.

"I feared that you'd find me unworthy. I am just a godling. And Nyktos, your nephew"—I choked on the word, widening my eyes—"he is the Primal of Death. Surely, many gods are far more worthy than I."

Kolis said nothing as he stared down at us.

"We truly didn't think it would be a cause for concern because Nyktos did believe you to be too busy for such things. But it was I who was the cause, and I am deeply regretful." Icy anger pressed against my back, and I knew I would never hear the end of this—that was if Kolis didn't strike me down right here. But I couldn't allow him to punish Nyktos. I wouldn't. "I hope that I can be forgiven and am able to prove that I can be worthy of such honor and graciousness."

Kolis remained silent for long enough that I began to feel pressure creeping into my chest. But then a slick smile appeared. "You are…brave, Seraphena, to admit such a thing to me, *the* King. That alone would make you most worthy. But I will have you prove yourself to me."

Nyktos suddenly had me on my feet, then was standing before me. "If anyone needs to prove their worthiness, it is I."

"I am sure there will be other ways for you to do so in the future. But if you want my permission to take her as your Consort"—the mask faded from around his eyes and churned down his cheeks—"she must earn it in the same manner I would ask of you."

"I can do that," I said, not letting myself think about what manner that could be as Nyktos's wild, swirling eyes clashed with mine. I drew in a shallow breath. "I want to prove myself worthy, Your Majesty."

Kolis looked at Kyn. "Did you bring what I asked?"

My gaze swung to the Primal of Peace and Vengeance. Kyn leaned over, half-sitting up as Attes frowned. "Yeah," the Primal replied gruffly. "In the hall."

Kolis snapped his fingers, and two guards peeled away from the walls, disappearing behind the curtain.

"Fuck," Attes uttered under his breath, turning to face the dais. His eyes closed, and my stomach…dropped.

"It should be—" Nyktos started.

"I command silence," Kolis interrupted. "Do not disobey me,

Nyktos. It will not be you who suffers."

Nyktos's hands clenched at his sides as he held himself still, and my stomach kept pitching, falling.

The guards returned with a…a young male. One a few years younger than me. He was fair-haired like Reaver and pale of skin, soft in the face. My heart pounded fast as he lifted his chin, and I saw…

Crimson eyes.

A draken.

A draken, who would still be considered a youngling.

"How do you pay the price of disrespect, Nyktos?" Kolis asked.

The Primal stared at me, his chest rising and falling in short, shallow bursts. And my heart…it wasn't slowing down. "With a life."

Oh, gods.

My hands started to tremble as I stared at the young draken. He couldn't mean…

No. *No.*

Kolis couldn't have summoned Kyn to bring one of his younger draken with him just to be slaughtered. This couldn't be happening. This couldn't be the price Kolis demanded.

But wasn't that what he'd done so many times that Nyktos's flesh was riddled with those reminders, those warnings?

Still, I heard myself whisper, "I don't understand."

Kolis inclined his head. "A life is owed to me to pay for the dishonor."

"But he…" I gestured at the draken, swallowing. "What has he done?"

"Nothing," Kyn bit out.

My wide gaze swung to the young draken. He stared straight ahead, his lips pressed firmly together, ruby eyes clear. He did not speak. He did not blink. He did not cry.

"Pay the price," Kolis said as Kyn withdrew a slender dagger. The dark blade trembled in the Primal's hand. "And both you and Nyktos will be forgiven. You will have my permission."

I shook my head as I stared at the shadowstone, horror clawing and scraping its way through me. "And if I…if I don't?" I asked. Nyktos turned to me, his face bloodless. "You will refuse the coronation?"

"He will kill me instead," the draken spoke then as he looked up at the false King. "And then he'll kill you. But not before he summons a draken from the Shadowlands to also be killed."

Kolis chuckled softly. "I detect no lies."

I choked on my gasp. "There has to be another option—"

"He spoke the only other option," Kolis snapped, appearing on the floor within the blink of an eye. The eather around him spun. "Refuse me, Seraphena, and I will do exactly as he warned."

I shouldn't have been surprised. Not a single part of me. Not when I'd been warned there were things that Kolis could make us do. Things that would haunt us. But no matter what had been said or what Aios had told me, nothing could've prepared me for this. This was something I couldn't even comprehend.

"Why? Why this?" I whispered hoarsely, my heart thumping. "What do you gain from this?"

Where was the *balance* in this?

Something akin to confusion rippled over Kolis's features, almost as if no one had asked this of him before. Then his face cleared. "Everything," he said. "It will tell me everything I need to know."

That made no sense to me.

Nyktos stepped forward, his hands raised. "Allow me to do this. It is I who has angered you—"

"I will only warn you one more time." Gold and silver eather sparked from Kolis's eyes. "Silence. Or it will be her heart I hold in my hand."

Nyktos inhaled sharply as his skin thinned. Shadows blossomed beneath his flesh.

"Control yourself, Nephew," advised Kolis. "You would do well to keep that temper in check."

Nyktos's restraint was impressive. He reined it in, his chest and body incredibly still as he did so.

"He is young enough that either the head or the heart will do," Kolis said, and there was no emotion behind his words. It sounded like he was instructing me on how to stitch a seam in clothing. This was...

This was the Kolis I'd expected.

I shuddered.

Attes wrenched the blade from his brother's hand and rose, his features hard and remote as he turned to us.

"And if anyone but Seraphena pays the price, I will demand that she pay *the* price with her blood," Kolis warned. "Not that either of you would be silly enough to dare such disrespect."

Attes passed Nyktos, the scar on his face standing out starkly as he stopped in front of me, handing me the blade. Opening my mouth, I glanced at Kyn. I wanted to apologize. He had a hand folded limply over his eyes. I couldn't find the words as I made myself look at the draken.

His eyes met mine. Resigned. "Do it," he said quietly. "I am prepared to enter Arcadia where my family awaits me."

The horror clamped my throat shut. He truly expected this, and that…that made it worse. "What is your name?"

"It does not matter," the young draken said.

"It does," I whispered, my eyes blurring.

"No," he said quietly. "It is not a name you need to remember."

Another shudder took me.

Nyktos turned to me, his features stark and etched with deep lines of sorrow, the wisps of eather in his eyes frenzied and full of barely leashed anger.

"Do it," the draken said. "Please."

The seconds that passed felt like an eternity. I had no choice. I didn't care about gaining Kolis's permission for the coronation. I didn't even care if refusing meant forfeiting my life. It was the knowledge that if I *didn't* do this, the young male would still die. It was the other lives that would be lost if I refused. I had no choice.

At least, not now.

"I'm sorry," I said.

The draken gave a curt nod and then closed his eyes.

I shut it down. All of it. Just as I had when my mother had ordered me to send a message to the Lords of the Vodina Isles. I felt nothing as I lifted my gaze to Kolis. That slippery smile was on his beautiful face as the eather spun, coiling at his sides, and the crown burned brightly.

There *was* something in his essence.

In that power of his.

I hadn't seen it before at the Sun Temple when he'd come for the Rite. But it was there now.

Something tainted.

Twisted.

Defiled.

It dulled the arcing, golden light. Smudged bits and pieces sparked a flat, lifeless gray that reminded me of the *Rot*. What was in the essence surrounding the false King, what was inside him, caused the embers in my chest to hum violently—caused the crack inside me that had opened the night in the Dying Woods to widen. And just like then, an ancient sense of knowing awakened and stretched, rearing its head. Suddenly, I was there but not.

This *entity* fused itself with my bones, wore my flesh, and saw through my eyes.

Rage, pure and *primal*, set fire to my blood as my chin dipped, and a voice among my thoughts whispered: *mine*, becoming a chorus of many screaming, "*Mine!*" His stolen power. It was *mine*. His pain. It would be *mine*. Vengeance. Retribution. Blood. *Mine*. All of it would be *mine*.

And I knew *what* that voice was as my grip on the blade steadied. *Who* it was. It was not the source of the embers. It was a spirit. Ghosts of many lives. A soul.

I met Kolis's stare, and while it was my lips that curved, it was Sotoria who smiled as I paid the price.

36

Everything that came next happened in a daze as if I were watching from high above. Kolis laughed as the embers of life hummed violently in my chest.

He laughed as I dropped the blade, and it clattered off the marble floor.

He gave his permission as I watched Attes lift the fallen draken, the Primal's jaw tensing as the male's blood singed his flesh—as Kyn locked eyes with mine—eyes now clear of the liquor haze but full of burning hatred.

He deemed me *worthy* as Nyktos took my hand that had frozen in midair.

He dismissed us as the voices calmed, and that entity inside me settled to wait for what *she* was owed.

He left a *mark* that remained as I exited the atrium.

I didn't remember walking the hall or the courtyard. I didn't see Attes or Kyn, and if Nyktos spoke, I didn't hear him. We'd accomplished what we'd come for. We entered the trees of Aios with the knowledge that Kolis didn't recognize me as Sotoria and left knowing that Gemma had been right: Kolis had figured out how to create life.

But I left a piece of myself behind in that atrium—a small sliver of that goodness that Nyktos had spoken of. It had been carved out and now lay beside that blade on the marble scorched by the draken's blood.

As Nyktos folded his arms around me, preparing for us to shadowstep back to the balcony of his private quarters, I knew I would never get that piece back.

An image of the draken flashed before me. "Take me to Attes and Kyn's Court," I rasped, feeling those tight, shallow breaths as he held me to his chest. "Take me to Vathi. I can bring him back."

"Sera," he whispered—pleaded, really. "You can't do that."

"Bringing him back won't cause another's death, right? The draken must be like a god."

"Yes, but—"

I grasped the front of his tunic, keeping my voice low. "I can try. It hasn't been that long, and we don't know if Kolis will feel it, right? How can we be sure? I never brought a draken back. It's not like I'll Ascend him. I've brought animals back before and no one—"

"A draken is not the same thing as an animal, Sera," Nyktos cut me off, his eyes flat as a balmy breeze stirred the golden leaves above us. "And when you did, it *was* felt. It was faint. Different. We didn't know what we were feeling then, but we do now."

"Okay. Then maybe he will feel something, but I have to do this. Please." My hands shook as I tugged on his tunic. "What is the point of any of this if innocents are allowed to die? What is the point of sacrificing the few to save the many when the few become so numerous? Why is there even a balance if evil is allowed to continually upset it?" How does anyone stay *good* living like that?

Shadows bled beneath Nyktos's flesh as he stared down at me. "We don't. We survive instead. That is how we honor the sacrifice the draken never should've had to make."

But that wasn't enough.

Not for me.

Not for *her*.

"That's not enough," I told him. "It will never be enough."

Nyktos's eyes closed as he cursed. Then the shadowy eather rose around us. My heart lurched as I tried to pull away, but Nyktos held me tight to his chest. Only seconds passed, and then cooler air that smelled of the *sea* replaced the warm air.

My eyes flew open as I jerked back. I didn't get far. Nyktos had a hold of me, but I twisted in his embrace, realizing that we were on some sort of white stone balcony. Stunned, I saw *green*—the tips of lush, dark pines sweeping over rolling hills that swept up and up to snow-capped mountains. I turned, looking past an ivory-hued Rise as tall as what surrounded the House of Haides and then out to the pale blue waters of a sea.

"Where are we?" I whispered.

"In a place of bad life choices," Nyktos muttered.

Wind suddenly roared across the balcony, whipping my hair as something large and black swept up. Wings. Large, leathery *draken* wings. Nyktos hauled me against his chest as a horned tail glided a hairsbreadth from where I'd stood.

"What the hell are you two doing here?" Attes demanded. "Without invitation or warning, I may add."

Vathi.

Nyktos had brought me to Vathi.

I almost collapsed with relief as we turned to the open doors. Attes was striding toward us, patches of his tunic burned straight through to exposed, raw flesh.

"The draken," I said in a hurry. "Where is he?"

Attes drew up short. "Kyn took him to burn—"

"Stop him! You need to stop him right now." I lurched forward, panic blossoming. "Please. Go get him and bring him to me. Please."

A deep frown appeared as he glanced at Nyktos. "What the hell?"

"Go!" I shouted, causing Attes to blink.

"Do it," Nyktos ordered. "Quickly."

Attes hesitated for just a moment, then a silvery mist whirled around him. A heartbeat later, he was gone. Slowly, I turned to Nyktos. We weren't exactly alone. Across the courtyard, a black draken perched on the Rise, eyeing us warily.

"Thank you," I uttered.

"Don't thank me." Nyktos stepped away, scrubbing a hand over his head.

"I'm sorry. I have to do this." Heart twisting as Nyktos looked away, I rubbed my bloodless palms over the bodice of my gown, jerking them away when I felt tiny holes there. The draken's blood had burned through my gown but hadn't reached my skin. Memories of his pale, resigned face appeared once more, and bile choked me.

Nyktos made a rough sound as he turned, reaching for me.

"No! Don't—" Unable to bear the contact, I stepped to the side. A gods-awful sourness settled in my chest, curdling my stomach. "I need to bring him back because he didn't deserve that—I mean, he was basically a kid. And I don't understand why Kolis would do that to one of Kyn's draken. Simply because he can?"

"He did it because he knew the draken are one of the few things Kyn cares about. Kolis obviously planned to demand that price, and summoned him for that very reason," he said, and I wondered if that was why Kyn had been so intoxicated. "Kolis knew what he was doing. He was making Kyn our enemy."

I'd seen the hatred in Kyn's eyes. There was no doubt in my mind that Kolis had succeeded. "But that draken did nothing wrong—"

"You're right. He didn't." Tension bracketed his mouth. "But that doesn't matter to Kolis. I doubt it ever has."

I inhaled, but the breath barely went anywhere. "Do you think we can trust Attes?"

"It's a little late to ask that question now," he said. "But I fucking hope so."

I shoved a mass of tangled curls back from my face as that oily, insidious weight slithered through my veins again.

What if we were too late? What if this didn't work? I'd never brought back someone with a dual life.

Pressure began to build, and I turned, grasping the railing. I felt…sick in my own skin. As if I couldn't scrape off the ugliness even if I took a wire brush to it.

"He returns," Nyktos stated as I felt a faint tremor in my chest.

I turned back to the room, almost crying out when I saw Attes laying the slender, fair-haired draken on a table inside. I rushed in, nearly knocking over a potted snake plant in my haste.

"Kyn left to find himself some whiskey before he got started," Attes said, his brows pinched as he drew a hand over the draken's bloodless cheek. He looked at us. "I really don't know what either of you think you're going to do."

"Yeah, well, you're about to find out." Nyktos stalked in behind me as I reached the draken's side. "No one comes here."

The blow I had delivered had been clean, but not all that quick. It would've taken several minutes for him to bleed out, and I hated thinking about those minutes, but I needed that extra time. The draken's soul could've already entered Arcadia, and I couldn't let myself think on what it meant to pull his soul back. And maybe I should. Because who was I to make this choice?

But nothing about this draken's death had been natural. It hadn't been his time. It hadn't been my choice.

This was.

And right or wrong, I was willing to live with this one.

I placed my hands on his chest, mindful of the dried blood.

"No one ever comes into my private chambers," Attes said in response to Nyktos's order. "Until today, that is."

"And you will not speak of what you're about to see," Nyktos continued, coming closer to the table as I closed my eyes, summoning the embers of life. "If you do, I will level your Court, Attes. And I will hunt you down. And it will not be your eyes I remove when I find you."

The embers responded with a rush of heat and energy, flooding my veins. I saw silver, even behind my closed lids. I felt the power rushing through me, running down my arms and across my fingers. My palms warmed as eather sparked, tingling and absolute.

"You know, I'm getting really tired of your threats, Nyktos. You could actually *think* to—" Attes cut himself off with a gasp as the scent of freshly bloomed lilacs filled the space. "Holy fuck."

I opened my eyes, sucking in air as a silvery glow rippled over the draken, washing over the puncture wound in his chest and then seeping inside. A staggering, high-pitched sound came from outside, something I recognized as a draken's call. It was answered in a chorus that must have echoed through the entirety of the Court.

"Holy fuck," Attes repeated, stumbling back from the table.

All the draken's veins lit up, first at the chest and then along his neck and cheeks. For a brief second, the draken was luminous, bright as a star. Then the eather faded.

Heart pounding, I lifted my hands. "I…I don't know if it will work."

Nyktos leaned in. "If it doesn't, it will—"

"It won't be okay," I whispered. "Maybe I need to try again. I might need to try harder." I went to place my hands on the draken's chest.

"Sera." Nyktos reached over, catching my hand. I started to pull free—

The draken's chest rose in a deep, ragged breath as his eyes fluttered open—eyes that were an intense, cobalt blue. Just as Nektas's had briefly been. The staggered call came again from outside.

"Thank gods," I whispered, falling against the table as I smiled. "It worked."

Nyktos squeezed my hand. He smiled, but it didn't reach his whirling eyes. "It did."

"I…" The young draken cleared his throat, blinking eyes that deepened into their normal polished, ruby hue. He looked down at his chest, placing a shaking hand against the now-healed skin. His gaze flew to mine. "*Meyaah Liessa*," he rasped.

"No. Just Sera," I told him, voice thick and trembling. "How do you feel?"

"I feel...okay," he answered, glancing at Attes as the Primal inched closer to the table. "Just tired. Really tired."

"I think that's normal," I said, lightly touching his arm. "You'll likely need rest for a while. I hope you're—" I cut myself off. "You will just need rest."

"Yeah." He looked at Attes again.

"He'll need to shift forms," the Primal explained, glancing at me before focusing on the draken. "You'll be safe here to rest."

He nodded, eyes closing. "Thad."

"Excuse me?" I questioned.

"Thad," he repeated sleepily. "My name is Thad."

"You're going to have to keep him hidden," Nyktos said as I stood by the open doors. The mountains of Vathi were beautiful, but it was hard to see them with the dozen or so draken now lining the Rise. "Kolis likely felt that."

Attes snorted. "Yeah, he did. We *all* felt that."

"He may even need to be hidden from Kyn."

"That could be a problem."

I glanced over my shoulder, first checking the brown-and-black-scaled draken now curled up on his side on the table. His tail, still without its spikes, hung off the edge.

"Kyn cares for the draken." Attes was pacing by the table. "He may think that one of the others took care of Thad, but he spends a lot of time in the mountains."

"Then, when he wakes, you can bring him to the Shadowlands," Nyktos offered. "Nektas will keep him safe and hidden."

Attes nodded. "That he will."

"We cannot linger."

"No." Attes cocked his head toward me. "That charm she bears will not work here."

"No," I said. "It will not."

"Kolis may send the dakkais here," Nyktos warned. Nothing had happened yet, but I knew that didn't mean anything. "To search for the embers."

"We'll be ready if he does."

"And?" Nyktos insisted.

Attes stopped in front of him. "And they will not learn of what happened here. I swear." He turned toward me. "To you."

I watched the Primal lower himself to one knee, placing one hand over his heart as he flattened his other palm against the floor. "I swear I will not betray what you've done today, *meyaah Liessa*."

"That's really not necessary," I said. "The my-Queen part. I'm not your Queen."

Attes lifted his head. "But you are—"

"No, I'm not anything," I cut him off.

The Primal of War and Accord frowned as he rose, turning to Nyktos.

Nyktos shook his head.

Attes glanced back at me. "I knew something was…different about you. You didn't feel like a godling." He then said to Nyktos, "But I thought it was what you told Kolis. That you'd given her a lot of your blood."

"You had to know when you left that wasn't the case. You're clever. You may have thought I was the source of power when you arrived, but you must have had your suspicions upon leaving."

"I did," Attes confirmed, his gaze sweeping over me. "I had a lot of suspicions when you didn't respond to my presence like you should have."

I tensed. "It was rude of you to even try."

"There are far *ruder* things I could try," he replied, but when Nyktos's eyes narrowed, he added, "But I prefer not to be threatened for the sixteenth time today."

"It hasn't been sixteen times, but I'm sure we'll get to that number soon enough," Nyktos growled, the eather in his eyes stilling. "Why not say something to Kolis, Attes? You could've gone to him with your suspicions before. You could now. You'd be favored like Hanan once was, and you know what that means. You don't have to worry about your draken or vassals being dragged to Court to be slaughtered."

"I know. And I could've." Attes faced Nyktos. "But as I said before, I remember who your father was. I remember who you were meant to be."

Shadowy tendrils of eather settled around us as we returned to the Shadowlands. The stars were still faint, but the sky was beginning to darken as I stepped out of Nyktos's embrace and turned to his balcony railing.

There were no snow-kissed mountains or deep green pines to look upon here, but there was a unique, eerie beauty to the crimson sea of leaves and the iron skies.

"What do you think will happen now?" I asked, folding my fingers over the cool stone railing. "With Attes? Kolis?"

"There's really no way to know. Kolis may do nothing at the moment, or he may send a warning just as he did with us." Nyktos joined me, placing his hand beside mine. "But I trust Attes. At least, with this. He was shaken, and I've never seen him shaken. He'll keep quiet—at least long enough for us to hold the coronation and transfer the embers."

I nodded as the embers pulsed in my chest, pressing against my skin. I ignored the feeling. "I know that we could be wrong and that what I just did could come back to bite us. But I had to...fix that."

"I know," he said. "Just because the rest of us have lived that way, it shouldn't be...it shouldn't be how it is."

I glanced at him, but he said no more for several moments.

Then he did.

"Why?" he asked. "Why did you speak out? You shouldn't have done that, Sera. I could have handled whatever he would've dealt."

I closed my eyes.

"I knew that he would demand a price. I knew it would be sick. Twisted. And I was prepared to do it. To carry the mark it would leave behind." He was closer now, his voice low. "You didn't have to speak up. You didn't need to feel this way. And I know you still feel guilt. Fixing it only lessened a little of that. You don't deserve this."

"And you do?" Opening my eyes, I looked over at him. "You deserve to carry those marks?"

Wisps of eather appeared in his eyes. "I'm used to it."

The cool railing pressed into my palms. "That's all the more reason it shouldn't have been you."

"That is *exactly* why it should have been me."

"That's bullshit," I snapped, latching on to the anger because that was a far better feeling than this. "I'm sorry that I took that draken's life, but I am not sorry that I prevented you from being forced to kill. And I hate myself for doing it, but I hate Kolis far more for demanding that it be done. So, yeah, even though I was able to bring Thad back, I still feel like shit over it. I'll deal with it. And if you're mad at me for stepping up, you're going to deal with *that* and get the fuck over it."

"I'm not mad at you, Sera." His eyes flashed with intense bolts of essence. "I'm horrified that you put yourself in that position, and that you now have to live with that because of me."

I sucked in a rattled breath. "I didn't do it because of you. Kolis gets that honor. I did it *for* you. There's a world of difference."

Nyktos drew back as if I'd slapped him. "Again, I ask…why would you do that for me? I don't deserve that. Not after I've hurt you. Not even before then."

That was a good question.

One I knew the answer to.

I wanted to protect Nyktos, even now, and that desire led to another question I didn't want to think about right now. I couldn't.

I turned my gaze to the crimson leaves, refocusing on far more important things. My voice trembled slightly as I said, "Do you think Dyses is what Gemma spoke of? Kolis's reborn? These…Revenants?"

Nyktos didn't answer for a long moment, but I felt his stare on me. "She said she never saw them during the day, but it has to be, right? Only a Primal could survive the destruction of their heart. Not a god."

"But she also said that Kolis needed his *graeca* to perfect them." My lips twisted. "Not sure how to *perfect* beyond being able to survive one's heart being destroyed."

"Neither do I. I can't even be sure that Dyses was a god. He felt like one but…off in a way that was hard to process." He exhaled heavily. "All I can hope is that Kolis doesn't have many of them. That could prove problematic."

A short, hoarse laugh left me. "I think that's an understatement," I said, swallowing. "How in the hell did he bring him back to life? He doesn't have the embers of life in him anymore. Or could we be wrong about that?"

"We're not wrong. And I have no idea how the hell he did that because Dyses isn't a demis."

It took me a moment to remember what Aios had told me about them. They were mortals Ascended by a god; those who didn't have enough essence in them like the third sons and daughters to be Ascended. It was an act forbidden because it rarely succeeded and often changed the mortal in unpleasant ways. "How would you know?"

"I would feel that. They have a certain presence that a Primal can sense. A...wrongness," he said, watching the distant figures of the guards patrolling the Rise. "Gemma said that the Revenants were Kolis's work in progress. It's possible that she's seen them at different stages of creation." His shoulders tensed. "Either way, he found a way to create life without the embers, something that could convince the other Courts that he does have that power within him. But who knows what kind of life he's conjured? Or what they truly are."

A shiver went through me. "Do you think he believed you? That you thought he had been the one who Ascended a god in the Shadowlands?"

"Fuck, no." Nyktos laughed under his breath. "It's possible that he believes I may not be aware of who it was and that I searched for the source, but there is no way he thinks that I believe it was him. He was saving face in front of Hanan and the Primals of Vathi."

That made more sense than Kolis actually believing that Nyktos thought it was him. "But then that also means he knows that you realize another has the embers of life. Why would he let that slide?"

"It's the same reason there was no immediate attack on Vathi. It's because of what your Holland said. There is only so much he can do to me before he risks exposing exactly how much of a fraud he is," he reminded me. "His control over the other Primals would weaken if they truly believed he no longer had embers of life in him. It's possible that he believes he can find the source before anyone else. But now I wish we'd had time to ask Attes what he thought about Dyses."

I nodded, rubbing my palms back and forth over the railing. So did I, but lingering in Vathi wouldn't have been wise, and I'd already engaged in enough unwise behavior for the day. Several moments of silence passed. "Kolis wasn't what I expected," I said, clearing my throat. "I mean, what he demanded as a price was what I expected, but before that? He was..."

"Measured? Calm?" he said with another short, dry laugh. "Kolis can be incredibly charming when he wants to be, and that is when he is the most dangerous."

I remembered then what Aios had said. That Kolis had a way of making someone forget who and what they were. I looked down at my hands, seeing blood that had never touched my skin. "We have his permission."

"It's not the only thing we have, even though I don't really trust that he gave his permission," Nyktos said, and I had to agree with that sentiment. "We also know he didn't recognize you."

I nodded again.

"Something happened there. With you." Nyktos angled his body toward mine. "I felt it."

Throat constricting, I looked up at him. "Felt what?"

"Rage." His eyes searched mine. "A rage I don't think was yours. It felt different. Tasted different."

"It wasn't just mine," I admitted quietly. "I don't know how or why, but I know. I felt it." I placed a hand on my chest. "Her anger. I could feel her looking through my eyes. Sotoria."

Nyktos inhaled sharply. "I think Holland was wrong. I think a lot of us were wrong, and you were right." His gaze swept over me. "You're not Sotoria. You have two souls. Yours. And hers."

37

The idea that I had two souls inside me felt more right than thinking that I was Sotoria.

Nyktos wouldn't be able to confirm such a thing until my death—whether I had two souls or not—and that was something I hoped didn't come for a while. But could an Arae be wrong about that? I didn't know, and it really wasn't the most pressing issue as Nyktos met with the *usual suspects*, filling them in on what had occurred in Dalos. Dyses. Kolis behaving as if he had Ascended Bele. The permission we had been granted. He told them everything.

Everything except the price Kolis had demanded and who paid it.

I was glad that he hadn't said anything because I hadn't paid shit. The young draken had, and I'd been lucky that I was able to reach him in time to fix it.

But I knew he would tell Nektas about what had gone down. The others might learn of it eventually, but right now, it wasn't something they needed to know.

I didn't linger as they began discussing how Dyses could've been created. I couldn't sit. I needed movement. Space. We'd already decided that the coronation would be held the following day, and then we'd leave for Irelone. I didn't need to be present for anything else. No one followed me, not at first, but I swore I still felt Nyktos's gaze on me long after I'd left the office.

I walked the halls and then the courtyard. Eventually, Reaver joined me. He glided in the air beside me as I followed the length of the Rise around the entirety of the palace, his quiet presence as welcome as it was painful.

Because I thought about the other draken.

I didn't want to. I wished I could find that place inside that had allowed me to forget the lives I'd taken. The part that was able to move on from the things I'd done. I wondered if I'd left that on the floor of Cor Palace, as well.

Because that horror and ugliness still lived inside me, even though Thad breathed again. As did the what-ifs—and they were vast. Could I have done something to prevent what went down? I didn't think so because it would require me to undo many things that I'd done in the past. But even then, we still could've landed here. And what if Thad hadn't wanted to come back? I'd taken that choice from him, just as Kolis had taken the choice from us. I could live with that, but it was still a part of the ugliness that sat heavily inside me.

Growing tired, I sat on the boulder Jadis had once attempted to jump off. Reaver landed beside me, placing his head in my lap as he tucked his wings against his sides. My fingers shook as I ran them over the bumpy ridges of scales down his back. My vision began to blur.

"I'm sorry," I whispered.

Reaver made a soft chattering sound as he lifted his head, placing it on my shoulder. I squeezed my eyes shut as emotion—sorrow and anger and so much guilt—burned the back of my throat.

I cried.

I didn't stop the tears from falling. I wasn't even sure I could have if I'd tried. They came from deep within, silent and heavy and a little bit broken.

I didn't know how long we sat there, but when I opened still-damp eyes, the stars were much brighter, and the sky a darker iron hue. Reaver drew back, stretching his wings.

"Hungry?" I asked, wiping my palm over my cheek.

Reaver yipped as he drew in a deep breath, rising. I took one step before noticing something on my hand.

Red.

Faint traces of watery red.

My tears.

Just like the legends said happened to Primals when struck by deep sorrow. I'd cried tears of *blood*.

It was late when I returned to my chambers, Aios and Bele catching me when I returned to the palace.

That evening held a different kind of first for me.

I took my supper with Bele and Aios in one of the receiving chambers, along with Reaver. I'd been so surprised by their invitation, and my head hadn't been in the right place, so I didn't think I'd said more than a handful of words as I learned that Nyktos had gone into Lethe to make sure everything was ready for the coronation. I might've drunk a wee bit too much wine, reluctant to leave the warmth of the chamber they occupied as Aios had spoken about a godling in Lethe they expected to Ascend at any moment, and a couple who was marrying. The normalcy had only been broken by the quick glances they sent each other. They started out concerned but became something else when their brief touches began to linger. Sensing they likely wanted some alone time, I left with Reaver in tow, joining Ector, who waited in the hall to escort me to my chambers.

"Where is Orphine?" I asked.

"With Nyktos," he answered as he jerked his head to the side, narrowly avoiding one of Reaver's wings as the draken flew ahead of us. "Fates. One of these days, I'm going to lose an eye."

Reaver gave a disgruntled yelp as he flew up the stairs.

I glanced at Ector. "They're still in Lethe?"

"Sort of. Some adventurous Shades traveled to the edge of the Dying Woods and are too close to the city," he said. "They and a few others are dealing with them."

Irritation sparked. I could've helped deal with the Shades, but that would've meant Nyktos returning to the palace to get me. And, well, even I could admit that made no sense. "How often does that happen, the Shades causing trouble?"

"Used to be pretty infrequent, but it seems to be happening more often." Ector's brows pinched. "They've been gathering in pretty sizable groups, which means they're a bit more than just a nuisance to deal with."

Concern loomed, but I reminded myself that Nyktos was a Primal. He'd be okay, even though the Shades had injured him before. He'd make sure that all the others with him would be okay, too. Plus, they had a draken with them.

Something about the Shades nagged at me as I entered my chambers, but I couldn't quite put a finger on what it was as I held the door open for Reaver. "Want to hang out?"

The draken flew in.

Ector remained in the hall, looking at me as if I were inviting him to an evening of debauchery in the Luxe. "No, thanks."

"I wasn't talking to you," I retorted. Reaver made a soft huffing sound behind me.

The god smirked. "Uh-huh."

Rolling my eyes, I closed the door and turned. Reaver was slinking around the chamber, inspecting every corner of the space much like Nektas had done. I shook my head and made my way to the bathing chamber to ready myself for bed. It wasn't until I picked up the nightgown I'd grabbed that I saw it was little more than silver gauze that barely reached my thighs. I sighed, thankful that I'd also picked up the robe.

I was fastening the line of buttons on the robe when my chest suddenly hummed. My breath caught as I opened the bedchamber door, and my gaze swung to the other doors. They remained closed.

The feeling reminded me of when Nyktos was near, but it was fainter as I stood in the doorway of the bathing chamber.

Reaver eyed me curiously from where he'd planted himself on the chaise.

"Do you feel anything?" I asked, rubbing the center of my chest.

He gave a little chirp that could've been a yes or a no, so I waited, unsure which I dreaded more—the doors remaining closed or opening. Seconds ticked by. Neither door opened, and the strange sensation faded.

Nibbling on my lip, I retrieved the brush from the bathing chamber, wondering if I simply had indigestion.

Perhaps that was yet another symptom of the Culling.

Sitting on the edge of the bed, I worked at the tangles in my hair. While I was more than a little tired, I was grateful for Reaver's presence because I thought he sensed that maybe I needed the company.

And I did.

"Is Jadis with Nektas in the mountains?"

Reaver nodded.

"So, are you staying at the palace to hide from Jadis?"

He huffed again, ducking his chin.

I laughed as I dragged the brush through several knots. Reaver winced. "It sounds worse than it feels, I promise. I should probably cut it," I said, picking up several still-tangled curls. "At this point, I'm going to end up sitting on—"

The embers vibrated again. I dropped my hair as my head snapped to the doors. Reaver did the same, drawing back. His wings spread out.

A shout came from the hall, startling me. Dropping the paddle brush, I grabbed the dagger from the bed as I rose, the stone cool under my feet as I stalked forward.

"Stay there, okay?" I said as Reaver moved to jump down. He halted, blowing out a puff of air as I rounded the bed. "Ector—?"

The chamber doors suddenly blew open in a flash of intense, silvery light. I jerked back, momentarily stunned as Ector *flew* through the chamber, arms and legs spread. I only knew it was him because he'd been in the hall, but I couldn't see him under the crackling, spitting wave of eather sparking over his body. Ector crashed into the dining table, collapsing the legs as he hit the floor hard. The vase that had been on the table shattered, scattering stones.

He was alive.

I told myself that as I swung forward, grabbing Reaver's arm before he launched himself into the air. I pulled him down, keeping him between me and the chaise. Ector was alive because the embers in my chest only pulsed. They didn't throb with the intensity of death.

Instead, they hummed with something else.

An awareness of...of *another.*

"Sorry," a silky voice said from the doorway. "He knew better than to refuse me entrance."

Heart strangely calm, I turned to the doors and came face-to-face with Veses. Suddenly, and for no reason, something Attes had said when he first was here came to me. He'd referred to the situation of the Primal God of Rites and Prosperity and me as a complication he didn't envy.

And she was definitely that.

"Hello." Veses smiled, and...gods, she was so damn beautiful.

So much so, I imagined it wasn't hard to overlook whatever unsavory or cruel things she was involved in when she looked like some delicate painting come to life.

She glided into the chamber, the hem of her lilac gown fluttering silently around her feet. I was surprised to see that for someone as thin as she was, she was shockingly endowed. And I only knew that because her dress was as transparent as the nightgown I wore beneath my robe.

"I said"—she cocked her head—"*hello?*"

Alarm swept through me, keeping the anger threatening to lead me to another unwise choice in check. No matter what she'd done with Nyktos or how she was involved with him, she was a Primal, and not someone I wanted to anger. I kept the dagger hidden beneath the sleeve of my robe as I quickly glanced at Ector. He hadn't moved. Not once. "I heard you."

Veses' head tilted as her mouth, wide and the color of lush, red berries, curved up at the corners. The smile would've been lovely if not for the cold, calculating edge.

It hit me then, what had nagged at me as I'd returned to my chambers. Ector had said that the Shades finding their way to Lethe had once been infrequent. But when Taric and the other two gods had come to the palace, they had led the Shades into Lethe first as a means to pull Nyktos's presence away from the palace. As a distraction. I couldn't remember if I had told Nyktos that or not, but it was mighty convenient that Veses was creeping around the palace now, throwing gods through doors, while Nyktos was otherwise occupied.

Footsteps pounded down the hall and then came to a halt. Rhain appeared in the open doors. "*Fuck.*" That one word said everything. "I'm sorry, Your Highness. I was unaware that you were here." Rhain bowed stiffly, glancing at Ector's prone body. "These are not Nyktos's chambers. I will send word to him and let him know of your arrival. Come," he called to me, his eyes holding mine.

"That's not necessary." Veses glanced down at the small draken trying to peek around me. I moved, shielding Reaver. He was far too young to see all that Veses had going on. "I'm not here to see Nyktos."

Fear. Rhain's eyes widened, and I thought I saw fear in them. "But—"

Veses flicked a finger.

Rhain went skidding backward, out of the chambers and into the hall. That was all it took—a move of her finger. "You can take him with you," she said, and Ector's unconscious body went sliding across the floor and out into the hall, as well. "He should wake up… I think."

Rhain pushed off—

The doors slammed shut, one of them hanging crookedly from the frame. They'd broken when she threw Ector through them, but I doubted anything but another Primal was getting through them now.

"What do you hear?" Veses asked. "It's silence, isn't it?"

Utter silence. No one banged on the doors. There were no more pounding footsteps.

"At least Rhain remembers his place. Perhaps he'll remind Ector of his when he wakes," she continued. "And maybe I will forgive him for his grave overstep and for standing between me and..." That smile returned, but it was mocking. "You." She shook her head.

"Do you know he actually drew his sword on me?" Veses laughed as my eyes widened. "What was he thinking? Striking out against me when you're not Nyktos's Consort."

Shit.

What *was* Ector thinking?

Feeling that Reaver was still behind me, I swallowed. "Maybe his sword slipped and fell into his hand."

Veses laughed again, a full-body laugh that shook parts of her I shouldn't be able to see. "I'm not sure. But perhaps Nyktos will be able to convince me of such."

I didn't let myself respond. I didn't even bat an eyelash.

"You know, I couldn't believe it when he told me the rumors were true." Kohl-lined eyes drifted over me in a way that made me painfully aware of how I must appear in the robe with my hair looking like I'd been caught in a windstorm. "What little he did say about you left me confused." Laughing softly, she began to prowl. And that was exactly how she moved. Like the large, striped tigers that roamed the drylands of Irelone. She sat on the couch, draping her arms along the back as she crossed one leg over the other. "Sera? That's your name, is it not?"

"It is."

"Well, it's Seraphena, to be exact," she said, and unease blossomed. Had she been to Dalos? And had Kolis spoken of me? Or Hanan? "I thought we should have a little chat, Seraphena."

I flicked a glance at the doors. "About?"

"Many things." Her smile remained. "Don't worry. I doubt we will be interrupted. Rhain will find it a bit difficult to make his way to Nyktos. At least, for a little while."

I couldn't let myself think about exactly how Veses had ensured that.

"How did *you* become his Consort?"

"He didn't tell you?"

"As I said, he spoke very little of you." Her eyes glittered as if made of gray diamonds. "Of course, I'm dying with anticipation to learn how."

Too bad that wasn't a literal statement. "We met in the mortal realm. I was swimming in a lake when he stumbled upon me."

Pale, pink-tipped fingers splayed across the back cushions. "And?"

"And we spoke."

"That can't be all."

"It wasn't."

Veses went so still, I wasn't sure her chest moved for one breath—and I thought I'd know, since I could see straight through her gown. "Do tell."

"I think you must already know since I'm here," I said, angling my body so Reaver stayed behind me.

"Actually, I do." Veses shifted, drawing her elbows to her thighs and resting her chin in her cupped hands. The fact that she actually looked even more stunning was highly displeasing. "Which is how I know you are...lying."

"I'm not lying." I held her stare.

She laughed. "But so was Nyktos." Eyes glowing faintly with essence narrowed slightly. "I suppose it makes sense."

"What does?" I reached down, blocking Reaver as he started to inch around my legs.

Her smile returned, a tight slash of berry. "That he would take a freckled and fat Consort."

My brows shot up so far on my forehead I wouldn't have been surprised if they hit the ceiling. The insult was so pathetic, I couldn't feel anything but disappointment. I'd expected better from a Primal.

"Your hair is lovely, though, I'll give you that. And"—she rolled her eyes—"your face is pleasant enough, I suppose, even with the freckles."

"Thanks." I drew out the word.

Veses smirked. "But then again, you are his Consort in title only, correct?"

Prickly heat scalded my skin, causing my throat and face to flush. It was the truth. But he had told her that? There was no other way for her to know. That shook the box inside me free enough that I felt a quick jab of pain... It stung like it had upon seeing them together in his office.

"Oh." Her eyes widened as she pressed slender fingers to the base of her throat. "I'm sorry—"

"What are you apologizing for?" I cut in, sealing myself off. "You didn't say it."

"True, it wasn't me. It was your soon-to-be *husband*. That's gracious of you to acknowledge," she said, and I almost laughed. Not for one second did I believe she thought that. Thick, dark lashes lowered. "Did he tell you about me? About us?"

I stiffened. "He did."

Eather-filled eyes lifted to mine. The essence wasn't the only thing brimming in them. So was eagerness. The cruel kind that I'd often seen in Tavius's stares. "What did he say?"

"He didn't say much, to be honest," I said, even as I told myself to be quiet. To not needle this Primal. To not taunt her with her own words. That voice went largely ignored. "It was my turn to be confused. You see, I saw you when you were here last. I saw how beautiful you are. But all he has said about you is that you're the worst sort."

"Did he say that?" Gravel replaced the velvet in her voice.

"He did." And he had at one time, so it wasn't a lie.

Her lips thinned. "Nyktos does have a poetic way of speaking of the women in his life, doesn't he?"

A short, dry laugh escaped me. "That he does."

"And that doesn't bother you?"

"Does it bother *you*?" I asked in return.

Golden ringlets slid over her chest as she tipped her head. "I'm not the one who will become his Consort."

"So, is that what bothers you? That it's me, freckled and fat, who will? And not you?"

"Come now." She rose with fluid grace. "I am a Primal. I can be no Consort."

"But you could still be his *wife*. You want him," I said. "Obviously."

"Want him?" Veses moved closer, stirring Reaver. I reached behind me, grasping his hand. His talons pressed lightly into my skin. "My dear, I already have him."

The sharp twist in my stomach and chest sickened me. "Is this what you wanted to talk to me about?"

She shrugged. "Well, since your future with Nyktos includes me, I figured we could get to know each other better."

Acid pooled in the back of my throat. "My future with Nyktos has nothing to do with you."

"Is that what you think?" Veses' laugh was as brittle as dry bones this time.

"That's what I know."

"Then what you think you know is a joke."

"The only joke I know is the one standing before me," I spat, my restraint snapping. "And it's a pathetic one."

A soft huffing sound came from Reaver. It sounded an awful lot like a laugh.

Veses drew back, her brows rising. "What did you just say?"

"Do I need to repeat myself?"

Shock rippled across her face. "How dare you speak to me with such disrespect—?"

"It's kind of hard to speak to you with respect when you have earned no such thing, Your Highness."

Two pink splotches appeared on her cheeks as she stepped toward me—

Reaver shot out from behind my legs, wings spread, growling. Real fear exploded in my gut. I grabbed a slender, scaled arm. He fought me. And the little cuss was strong, pulling away as he stretched his neck and opened his mouth, emitting sparks. They hit the skirt of Veses' lilac gown, charring the gossamer fabric.

Veses reacted as fast as a Primal could. Reaver yelped as she kicked him, knocking him free of my grip. He flew back, hitting the wall next to the fireplace. Falling to the floor, he crumpled into a ball several feet from where he had stood.

"Stupid draken," Veses sneered. "You're lucky I didn't kill you."

A veil of red slipped over me. There was no time to think. It was just like when I spied the gods in the Luxe, and they'd tossed that poor babe to the ground as if it were nothing more than trash to be discarded. I reacted out of pure, vengeful fury.

And this time, Nyktos wasn't around to stop me.

Closing the distance between us, I stretched up and plunged the dagger deep into her eye, straight through it and into her brain.

And I didn't feel even an ounce of guilt.

Veses shrieked, jerking back so fast I didn't have a chance to pull the dagger free. She bumped into the corner of the bed but caught herself. She didn't fall. She didn't go down at all, not even for one second.

Damn.

Her head lifted. Blue-tinted blood poured down her cheek as she wrapped her fingers around the dagger's hilt and pulled it free. Thick, gelatinous tissue clung to the shadowstone, turning my stomach. Eather seeped from her one good eye and into the air, spitting and crackling as she threw the dagger aside. It clanged off the floor, and orbs of shimmery energy pulsed over her hands.

"Oh, shit," I whispered.

I didn't see her move, but I felt the blow as it hit me in the chest. It was like a punch—if being punched by *lightning* was possible. A wave of pain swept over me as I flew backward, smacking into the wardrobe. My muscles were so rigid I barely felt the impact as I fell forward onto my knees. Lightning coursed through my veins and nerves. Dimly, I realized that she hadn't actually laid a hand on me. That had been *eather*. Tiny starbursts danced across my vision.

"You stupid bitch." Veses grabbed hold of my hair and threw me like I was nothing more than a pillow.

I hit the floor hard, knocking whatever air was left in my lungs out of me. I rolled until I hit the column of the bed with a grunt.

"What did you think that would accomplish?" Veses demanded. "I am a *Primal*."

The floor came into focus as the waves of shocking pain eased. Something didn't feel right inside me. Several somethings. I felt a little…loose inside as I lifted my head. Reaver…he lay where he'd landed, still curled tightly but in his mortal form. Panic rose as the embers in my chest throbbed. I rolled onto my back, wheezing as something dug into my back. A hilt. The dagger.

Veses knelt beside me. Her left eye was a bloody mess, but it was already beginning to heal. She grabbed hold of my hair again, lifting my head from the floor. Her lips twisted into a sneer. "Perhaps you and Nyktos are well suited for one another since he has a habit of doing the most illogical things. After all, he took you as his Consort. I tried to stop him. Sent my favorite draken and guard to retrieve you. And, well, we all know how that turned out—rather pointless considering you're charmed."

Surprise rolled through me. "It was you who sent the draken to unleash the entombed gods."

"I had to do something before he got himself into any more trouble. Like, does he think no one realizes Taric and the others weren't here before they disappeared?" She rolled one full and one half-formed eye. "And how convenient was that? They were looking for something in the mortal realm, and do you know what that was? I do. Life. They were looking for *life*. And they followed it right to Death's home. Where *you* are. Does he really think no one will figure that out?" She raised her brows. "I thought I'd get lucky, and Kolis would deny the coronation before Nyktos realized it was me. But…males. You can always count on them to do one thing. Make the wrong choices. So, here I am. Trying to help Nyktos, and him being pissed at me for it. But you know what they say, no good deed goes unpunished."

"Good deed?" I sputtered. "People *died*—"

"People always die." She yanked me away from the bed. The grip sent a fiery sting across my scalp as she wiped at the blood on her face.

"And now look at what's going to happen. He's going to know it was me. And have you seen him when he's mad?" One eye lit with bright eather. "He's quite destructive." Her voice lowered as she licked the blood from her fingers. "It's kind of hot. He's so deliciously unpredictable then."

"You...you're twisted."

Veses laughed. "Oh, you have no idea."

"I think I'm getting a good idea."

"So am I." Veses stopped, kneeling once more. She dropped my hair, but the relief was brief. She gripped my chin instead. "I knew there was more to all of this, no matter what Nyktos claimed. There had to be a reason he'd be willing to do anything for you." Her fingers pressed into my chin, and I gasped as pain skated along my jawbone. "I felt you when you were first brought here. I thought I was imagining things, but when you showed up the other day and interrupted what had been a rather lovely evening, I felt you again. So, that means one of two things. Either he's given you so much of his blood that I can feel him in you, or..."

My eyes locked with Veses'. The *sensation* I'd felt in my chest. The *hum* of energy. It had reminded me of when Nyktos was near because another Primal was close. I had felt something similar when Attes arrived. I just hadn't recognized it, and...

"Or Nyktos didn't find himself a Consort." Veses brought her mouth to within inches of mine. "He found himself a Primal in their Culling. And not just any Primal. Because you know what else I felt today, coming out of Vathi? *Life.*" She nipped at my lower lip. "Which, as impossible as that sounds, is still more believable than him sharing what is mine. His blood."

"Oh, I've had his blood." I smiled at her. "I've had *all* of him."

Her one eye widened.

I struck, slamming the side of my hand into her throat as hard as I could.

Veses let go of my chin, staggering as she choked, clasping her hand over her throat. I scrambled forward on my hands and knees to Reaver. The embers in my chest continued throbbing as the energy ramped up in me. Heat swirled down my arm. Eather sparked.

Grabbing the back of my robe, Veses threw me backward. I slid, smacking into the foot of the couch. That box that I stored all those volatile emotions in shuddered, shaking and cracking—

The doors to the bedchamber burst open. Veses wheeled around, but it wasn't Nyktos who stalked in.

It was *Bele.*

38

"Your eyes," Veses uttered in a hoarse but awed voice.

"Yeah?" Bele glanced to where Reaver lay unmoving in his mortal form and then to me. "What about them?"

"Don't play coy, Bele. It was you who Ascended." She gave Bele a bloody smile. "It must be my lucky day. There's a bounty on your head."

"By the look of your face, I would definitely say it's *not* your lucky day." Bele smirked. "And that bad day is going to continue when Nyktos returns."

Taking shallow, too-short breaths, I pushed onto my knees. That was as far as I got for a moment. Pain radiated across my ribs and pelvis. Blinking until my blurred vision cleared, I saw my dagger lying between Reaver and me.

Veses lifted one shoulder. "Not as bad as the day you're going to have when Kolis rips your heart from your chest and devours it."

"There are far tastier parts of me, but whatever." Bele inched farther into the chambers, watching the Primal closely as I forced myself toward Reaver. Each inch I half-crawled, half-slid across the floor felt as if daggers were jabbing my ribs. "If you're here for me, you've found me."

"I wasn't here for you," Veses said as I snatched the dagger from the floor. "You're just a boon."

Bele frowned. "Well, if you're here for her, that sounds like a problem."

"You think?" Veses snapped.

"For you," Bele added as I reached Reaver's side. "You do realize who she is, right?" Bele jerked her chin at me. "That's Nyktos's Consort. You have to know that. And that's one of his draken—one of *Nektas's* draken."

"Do I look like I care about either of those things?"

Bele laughed softly as she circled the Primal. "You will."

"What do you think you're going to do with that sword?" Veses demanded, turning her back on me completely.

A deep, angry-red bruise had formed on Reaver's chest. I ran a hand across his too-pale forehead, smoothing his hair back. His eyes were closed, and the embers...they throbbed, nearly as acutely as they had in the aftermath of paying the price Kolis had demanded. He wasn't just injured.

"Reaver's hurt." I glanced over my shoulder, wiping the blood off my chin with the back of my tingling hand.

Bele's gaze briefly met mine as she managed to get between Veses and us. "How bad?"

A knot of emotion lodged in my throat. "Bad."

"He'll be fine." Veses rolled her eyes, but her voice wavered. "He's a draken."

"He's a child!" I spat.

"So?" Veses lifted her chin. "He shouldn't have come at me."

"Veses." Bele tsked softly. "Are you that weak that you saw a youngling as a threat?"

"Not a threat. A disrespect." Veses sneered. "And you didn't answer my question about the sword. You can't attack me."

"I can't?" Bele continued edging toward Veses, forcing her farther away from me—and Reaver.

"You know the rules," Veses said. "She's not his Consort yet, and the draken, youngling or not, has no right to defend her against me. I've done nothing wrong."

"Ah, yes, the rules. But as you said, there's already a bounty on my head," Bele said. "One I'm sure involves bringing me to Dalos, dead or alive. So what if I break a rule?"

"Reaver?" I touched his cheek. His skin was clammy. Wincing, I grabbed the soft blanket from the chaise and draped it over him. His chest barely moved. Concern grew rapidly. He hadn't woken up, and he seemed to have unconsciously shifted forms. I'd seen draken do that when gravely injured.

My throat dried as I sent Bele and Veses a quick glance, knowing I was about to take another huge risk. Veses might only suspect that I was the source of the power she'd felt, but I had to do something. I couldn't let Reaver die, and I feared the throbbing embers were warning me of that. They sensed that death was imminent.

I sensed that.

And whatever risk I was taking by confirming what embers were inside me was worth it. Reaver's young life was worth it. Just as Thad's had been.

The embers continued to buzz, pressing against my skin. My senses opened and stretched as I laid the dagger beside Reaver and placed my palm flat on his chest. It was almost like when I'd done it earlier with Thad, but that had been faster, even more instinctive, as if using the embers made them stronger and more responsive. As if the embers were truly mine as I called upon the eather, and it responded to *my* will.

Pure, ancient power poured out of my chest, flooding my veins for the second time that day. A hot, heady thrill flowed with my blood. The rush of energy felt different this time, like a reckoning. A...*homecoming*.

There was a gasp as I inhaled deeply, catching the scent of lilacs—freshly bloomed lilacs. *Life*. Eather hummed through me, sparking from my fingertips and off Reaver's chest. The shimmering light swept over Reaver's small frame in one rippling wave and then seeped through his skin, filling the veins beneath the pale, slightly ridged skin and bruised flesh.

The eather flared and pulsed, then receded slowly into a faint glow that lingered for only a few more moments. The bruise on his chest faded, and then the most beautiful thing happened.

Reaver's chest swelled with a deep breath, and his eyes opened—eyes a shining, cobalt blue before returning to crimson. "*Liessa*," he whispered. Tears filled his eyes, clinging to his lashes.

I shuddered, brushing his hair back from his cheek. "It's okay."

"The fuck it is," Veses exploded as Reaver's eyes closed. My head snapped toward her as I placed my hand on the hilt of the dagger. "I was actually right. It's been you." She took a step back, her eyes—the one I'd stabbed now healed—widening and filling with *horror*. "What has Nyktos done?"

"He hasn't done anything," I said.

Veses shook her head. "You're what—?"

Bele lifted the sword.

The Primal struck like a pit viper, moving faster than I could even track. She caught Bele's sword. The blade shattered in a flare of silver light. Veses slammed her hand into Bele's chest, throwing her back several feet.

Bele hit the wall by the balcony and fell forward onto her knees. She lifted her head, shoving the dark strands of her hair back from her face. "Ouch."

Veses brushed the shadowstone dust from her hands as she started toward Bele. I moved, sucking in a sharp breath of pain as I lifted my arm and threw the dagger at the back of Veses' head. The Primal spun. Her head tilted. "Really?"

The dagger stopped in midair and then flung back toward me.

Gasping, I ducked. The blade whizzed over my head, embedding deeply into the wall behind me. "Shit."

Bele rose, rushing Veses—

The Primal held up her hand, and Bele went flying. I didn't take my eyes off Veses, but I heard Bele's fall. It was *hard*. "If you were smart, Bele, you would stay down. If you do, you may live to see another day," the Primal warned, turning her attention to me. "But you? You're definitely going to die. Because you"—she inhaled sharply—"you're an *abomination*."

"That's rude," I wheezed.

Eather sparked along her flesh, charging the air as I positioned myself over Reaver, tensing.

"What if I don't stay down?" Bele asked, rising to her knees.

Veses' eyes turned into silver orbs. "Then you can die, too."

Bele spun on her knee, rising as silvery-white light spiraled down her arms and erupted between her palms. Eather arced, rapidly forming the shape of a bow and arrow. Smirking, she pulled the string of eather taut. "Bitch, I hope you try."

My mouth dropped open. Taric had summoned a sword of pure eather, but I'd never seen Bele do that before.

"You let go of that arrow, and all you'll do is piss me off," Veses warned. "And I mean, really piss me off."

"Oops." Bele released the arrow.

Veses spun. The projectile grazed her cheek, splitting it open. She shrieked, lifting into the air as eather sparked from her eyes and fingertips—

The ember belonging to Nyktos suddenly vibrated frantically. A faint tremor moved under the shadowstone floor as Veses' head whipped to the open doors, to where night had gathered, thick and dark. Another charge of energy swept through the chamber, dancing across my skin. Tiny hairs rose all over my body. The breath I exhaled formed a faint, misty cloud. Every part of my being recognized the source of power pouring into the space.

Thick tendrils of midnight and moonlight spilled into the room, reminding me of what I had seen in my bedchamber that night. Coils of churning mist rolled along the floor and climbed the walls. Whatever air was in my lungs left me as Nyktos stalked forward, his eyes locking on mine. I tried to regain that breath, but the temperature of the air continued dropping, becoming so frigid that my lips started to tingle. I couldn't take my eyes off him.

His skin had thinned to the point where he was more shadow and moonlight than flesh. The power radiating off him drenched the air. Wisps of eather had gathered around him, swirling around his legs and licking over his shoulders. Through them, I saw the faint outline of his wings.

Nyktos was a storm of whirling fury. Shadows laced with thin strips of silver lashed out from him and blossomed beneath his skin. He'd never looked colder, harsher, or more like a Primal of Death than in that moment.

"She knows." Bele rose, the crackling bow of eather still trained on Veses, another arrow of pure energy at the ready. "About Sera."

Golden ringlets whipped around Veses' head like snapping serpents as she lowered herself to the floor. "Nyktos—"

"Shut up," he snarled, his gaze remaining fixed on me as he lifted his hand. A bolt of eather exploded from his palm and arced across the chamber like lightning. I flinched against the blinding light, gathering Reaver close to me out of instinct.

Veses wasn't faster this time.

The blast of energy hit her in the chest, throwing her back. I gasped as her entire body lit up. For a moment, she was suspended in the air, her veins glowing as light flooded her mouth, nostrils, and eyes. Then she flew backward more, slamming into the wall, and I didn't think I'd ever been more thrilled to hear the fleshy sound of a body smacking into an unyielding surface.

Veses slid down the stone, twitching and shaking as she came to a stop, slumped over. The crackling energy faded, leaving behind the scent of charred flesh. Blood dripped from her nose, mouth, and trickled from her ears. The skin above her elbows and wrists was dark and burnt.

Veses was out, but I didn't know for how long.

"Take her," Nyktos ordered as he crossed the chamber, the faint outline of his smoky wings briefly visible once more before they faded. "Lock her in one of the cells."

I blinked as Orphine came forward, along with who I guessed was her brother, Ehthawn.

"I wish we could just toss her ass in the Abyss," Ehthawn muttered, gripping the arm of the unconscious Primal and hoisting her over his shoulder like a sack of lumpy grain. I thought I might be smiling.

"Sera."

I jerked at the sound of my name.

Nyktos knelt in front of me, and I saw no one else. Blood smeared his left temple, and I didn't know if it was his or someone else's.

"Reaver was hurt," I rasped, glancing down at him. "She *hurt* him."

He touched the young draken's cheek as I felt his gaze on me. "But he's not hurt any longer."

"He's just sleeping right now." I trembled as I stared down at Reaver, his skin having returned to its usual dusty, golden hue. "I had to do something. He was *really* hurt, and I couldn't—"

"It's okay." Nyktos's hand rose, and just his fingertips touched *my* cheek. "You saved him. That's all that matters."

"But she *knows*," I warned him. "And she's not like Attes. She won't keep this secret. No matter what is going on—"

"She won't get a chance to tell Kolis," Nyktos interrupted, carefully dragging his fingers along the curve of my jaw where the skin ached. "She won't be able to get out of the cell."

"She didn't want to tell Kolis. She wanted to kill me once she realized what I could do." My back throbbed as I leaned forward. I winced. "That doesn't make sense, right? But she...she was afraid once she realized what I could do."

Eather flared in his eyes as his gaze swept over me. His jaw tightened. "Bele? You okay?"

"Yeah." The goddess drew close. "Sera is right. Veses looked freaked the hell out."

"She felt what happened earlier today," I told him.

"What the hell happened earlier today?" Bele asked.

Nyktos held up a hand, silencing her.

I drew in a shallow, pained breath. "But she came here because she said she'd felt something different about me when I saw—when she was here last," I said, not looking at him then. It was important that I tell him this. "And that's why she came back. The Shades—"

"It was her," Nyktos interrupted. "I didn't realize that until Rhain found us. He would've gotten to me sooner, but there were a lot of Shades. So many they were overwhelming Orphine and Ehthawn."

I winced, knowing that meant he'd had to kill the Shades, and I knew that would get to him. "I'm sorry."

Nyktos jerked so forcibly that I looked up at him. His eyes were wide and fixed on me.

Figuring he was confused by what I was apologizing for, I said, "I know you don't like to kill the Shades. I'm sorry you had to do that."

He continued staring at me as if I'd sprouted two heads.

"It was her." I pushed past the growing pain. "One of her draken freed the entombed gods. She sent them and one of her guards to take me. She said it was because she knew there was more to why you'd take a Consort," I said, and the eather lashed through his eyes. "She was behaving as if she were helping you."

"That is the *last* thing she was doing." He looked at Bele. "Take Reaver to my quarters. Stay with him. He'll likely be confused when he wakes."

"Will do." Bele bent, but I held onto Reaver's small body, reluctant to let him go. She looked up at me. "I've got him."

I knew he was okay, but for some reason, I held on.

"You can let him go, Sera." Nyktos carefully turned my head to his. Pressure clamped down on my chest. "He's okay. You're not. Let Bele take care of him so I can take care of you."

My heart tripped up as my grip on Reaver loosened enough for Bele to gently work an arm under Reaver's shoulders. Nyktos drew the blanket up, keeping him covered. "Thank you," I whispered, feeling a little out of it. "Thank you for coming when you did."

"No need to thank me." Bele lifted the slumbering youngling in her arms. "I've been waiting for ages to get my hands on that bitch."

I laughed, and it hurt in my jaw, chest, and other places too numerous to count.

A muscle ticked in Nyktos's jaw as he looked over his shoulder. I saw Saion and Theon. "Keep watch over Veses."

The gods nodded. Both looked a little ragged around the edges, as if they'd been through battle, and I wondered exactly how many Shades Veses had managed to work into a frenzy.

"Ector?" I called out, sucking in a breath as a sharp ache skated across my ribs. "Is Ector okay?"

Saion nodded. "He will be."

Relieved, I closed my eyes and leaned back against the chaise. "Ector tried to stop Veses from coming in here," I shared, vaguely aware of the others leaving. "Why would he do that? He knew better."

"So did Bele." Nyktos brushed my hair over my shoulder. "They were willing to take that risk to protect you."

I opened my eyes. "They could've died."

"They know that."

"They could still be punished if Kolis or anyone else finds out they went up against a Primal."

"They know that, too."

He was on his knees, leaning over my legs. "You're injured, Sera."

"Yeah," I breathed. There was no denying it. "I think a couple of my ribs might be broken."

Shadows gathered in his cheeks. "I don't think that's all," he said, running his thumb along the corner of my lip. Red smeared the tip when he withdrew his hand. "You're in a lot of pain."

"True, but I stabbed her in the eye. It was gross." I gave him a grimace of a smile. "But worth it."

His laugh was soft and a little strained. "You're going to need my blood."

My heart gave a sluggish lurch, even though I wasn't surprised to hear that. Because there was a good chance that I was hurt in a far worse way than when the draken had attacked. I didn't feel *right* inside. Like important parts of me weren't exactly connected right.

"We can't risk you going into another stasis, Sera. You may not wake up," he said, sensing my hesitation. "I will leave immediately afterward. You don't have to worry about how my blood will affect you."

"It's not that."

A look of doubt crept into Nyktos's features as I lifted a strangely weak arm and touched the hand that rested on the floor beside my hip. The charge of energy was faint. "Your skin is icy. As cold as it was before." The why suddenly occurred to me, and my chest twisted. "It was...her feeding from you, wasn't it? That's why your skin is so cold."

His features tensed. "I told you why my skin is cold. I'm Death."

He *had* told me that, but that hadn't really made that much sense to me.

Nyktos stared at me for a moment. "It doesn't matter," he said, and I thought it did. "I'll be okay. You, however, may not be."

I sighed, knowing it wasn't wise to argue over this. I didn't want to slip into another several-days-long sleep that I might not wake up from.

"Okay," I said. "Let's get this over with."

Nyktos raised a brow but wisely didn't respond to that. He shifted closer, sitting on the floor beside me. I couldn't stop myself from watching him as he lifted his wrist to his mouth. I caught only a brief glimpse of his fangs before they sank deep into his flesh. I winced, just like I had before. He lifted his mouth, revealing the seeping puncture wounds. Shimmery, bluish-red blood pooled in two perfect circles, and his scent, that citrus and fresh air, was more potent.

Neither of us spoke as he brought his wrist to my mouth, but I didn't hesitate like I had before. It almost felt natural as I lowered my head. And maybe that was the embers. But perhaps it was me.

Closing my mouth over the wound, I drew on his bite as my eyes drifted shut. The first taste of him was a shock to my senses. A jolt to my entire body that would likely never dull, no matter how many times I tasted him.

A tingling sensation swept over my tongue and the insides of my mouth, then moved to my throat as I swallowed. It struck me as odd that his blood could be so warm, yet his skin so cold, but the memories of how he'd tasted hadn't done him any justice. Sweet and smoky honey. Luscious. Captivating. I swallowed, more and more, marveling at the heady warmth coursing into my chest and stomach, easing the aches along the way.

"Just a bit more," Nyktos said, his voice lower, thicker.

I drank deeper, only vaguely aware that I was holding his arm and that my fingers were curling tightly around his. I thought that I probably shouldn't do that now, but that thought was just a flicker. An inconvenience. The hum of his blood coasted over that hollow part of me, snuffing out the pain in my ribs and my stomach, taking with it a deeper, more entrenched hurt that went beyond the physical.

Then I found it.

Felt it.

Peace.

It was like slipping beneath still waters, surrounded by silence and *peace*. But in that cool darkness were *colors*. They came alive with a spark of silver and black, and like the images that had formed in the Pools of Divanash, one rose in my mind. It was me. I was standing in the courtyard of the House of Haides in a black gown with the gray, starswept sky behind me. Cheeks flushed and eyes a feverish wild green, I held a short sword, the shadowstone blade glittering as a pale, silver curl danced across my cheek, touching the corner of my lip as I grinned up at—

This was a memory of me, but not my memory.

"I think that's enough," Nyktos grunted, shattering the memory as he gently pried his wrist from my grip.

My eyes fluttered open as my hands fell to my lap. Beside me, Nyktos sat, one leg bent as he lifted his wrist to his mouth, sealing the wound he'd created. There were no shadows beneath his flesh now, but his skin was even thinner, the hollows of his cheeks more prominent, and his flesh paler.

"How are you feeling?" Nyktos asked.

I took stock of myself, somewhat dazed. "Better," I exhaled, long and slow without even a hint of pain. Considering what I could do with my hands, the healing ability of a Primal's blood shouldn't shock me, but it did. "Thank you."

Nyktos nodded, and his lashes swept down, hiding his eyes as he started to rise. "I'll await you in my chambers—"

"Wait," I stopped him. His jaw flexed. "I saw myself standing in the courtyard when I held the sword to your throat," I told him, my skin beginning to thrum as the warmth of his blood continued working its way through my muscles. "Why would I think of that?"

"You weren't thinking of that day," he said gruffly. "I was."

"But how…?"

"That can happen when a god or a Primal feeds from another. They can sense—or see—what the other is thinking. Or find a memory. Some are skilled at dragging older memories out while they feed."

"Like Taric," I murmured. "But it didn't hurt you, right?"

Nyktos shook his head. "You weren't able to do it the last time you fed, but you're even closer to Ascension now."

"That's not good."

"No." Nyktos's lashes lifted then. "We need to get the embers out of you."

Dread began to build but then quickly evaporated. There was no warning before the pleasant warmth in my blood and muscles turned to molten heat. Even though I knew what his blood would do, the sharp and swift arousal was still brutal, stealing the breath I took. My fingers curled into the soft cloth of my robe as an ache blossomed, throbbed.

Oh, gods, I was hot. Too hot. My fingers went to the row of buttons on the robe, hastily undoing them. The material fell to the sides, and blissful cool air slipped over the gauzy nightgown and my heated flesh.

The reprieve lasted only a few seconds—if that.

My heart began to pound. I shuddered, gritting my teeth, but there was no stopping the intense wave of tingling sensation sweeping over me, or the gasp I let out at the slippery heat suddenly invading every part of my being and senses. A heaviness followed, settling in my breasts and then my core. My nipples grew tight, hardening.

I *wanted*.

It didn't matter how much I told myself I shouldn't.

I *needed*.

And, gods, I welcomed the feeling because it left no room for the dread, uncertainty, or the ugliness of the day.

"I should leave," Nyktos ground out, his voice sounding like smoke and gravel.

I looked at him and realized I shouldn't have done that either.

He shifted back from me, just enough that I saw the thick ridge of his cock straining against his leathers. I nearly moaned at *his* visceral reaction to *my* lust—to *me*. Gods. I pressed my thighs together, but I was empty, and it was all too easy to recall the feel of him inside me, stretching me—

I moved without thinking, grasping Nyktos's arm. The charge of energy, and the feel of his flesh under my hand sparked another rush of damp, hot desire.

"Sera," he hissed.

Pulse pounding, I lifted my gaze to his. His eyes were quicksilver, heated and whirling with so much power, so much *need*. My nails pressed into his skin.

Stay.

I didn't speak the word. I thought it. I prayed it, even though I knew I could bring an end to my torment. Give myself pleasure. But I wanted it. I wanted him despite the dangers of what that desire led to. In spite of what I'd seen with him and Veses and still didn't understand.

Stark lust carved into his features, hollowing his cheeks as he stared at me. "You know what will happen if I don't leave," he growled. Warned. "No matter how much you hate me now, you will hate yourself more later."

"I don't hate you," I whispered.

"My blood is making you think you don't."

He was wrong. I wished he was right. Everything would be so much easier if I did, but I didn't. "I think I proved earlier today that I don't hate you."

His arm trembled in my grip. "You should."

"I should." I ran my tongue across my teeth. "You could leave if you wanted to."

His eyes darted to mine. "I know."

"But you haven't."

Tension bracketed his mouth as his gaze dropped to my chest. The tips of my breasts were clearly visible beneath the nightgown. A predatory gleam pinched his lips and filled his eyes as he watched me shrug off the robe.

"Sera," he rasped, his lips parting and gaze sweeping down the translucent nightgown to the throbbing space between my thighs. "I don't know if I love these things you swear are gowns or fucking hate them."

My entire chest rose and fell sharply as our gazes locked. A second passed. Another.

"But there are a hundred reasons why one of us needs to leave," he said, his breath matching mine. "And only one reason neither of us is."

"Want."

He gave me a curt shake of his head. "*Need*."

Then I was in his arms.

I didn't know who moved. Wasn't sure if it was me who climbed into his embrace, him who'd grasped my arms, or if we'd both moved at once.

But it didn't matter.

His mouth was on mine, his kiss wild and desperate. Starved. I could feel his cool flesh beneath his torn tunic, soothing my overly sensitive skin and then igniting another maddening rush of desire. Both of our hands went to his pants. My fingers curled around his thickness, stroking him through the soft cloth. He tore at the buttons, and raw lust scorched the breath I took as he freed himself.

Nothing mattered then. Not Veses. Not the hurt. The pain. The ugliness. Not how close Reaver had come to death. Not what saving him would do, or how close I was to the Ascension. I didn't think about anything as Nyktos's hands went to my hips to steady me. He consumed my thoughts and my body. This did. Us. I gasped when I felt the broad head of his cock, easing through my wetness and pressing into me. I clutched his shoulders. Nyktos trembled, holding himself still as I lowered myself, moaning against his lips between kisses. The pressure, the burn was exquisite. His fingers pressed into the flesh of my hips as I took him, inch by decadent inch, to the hilt. I panted as I held myself still.

He felt…gods, my head fell back. He felt like we were made for each other.

Nyktos's arm encircled my waist as he buried his hand deep in my hair, clasping the nape of my neck. He drew my mouth to his. "Fuck me," he ordered.

This was one of those rare moments where I was more than happy to obey.

I lifted, slowly retreating before lowering myself once more. My ragged cry got lost in his harsh groan. The friction of our bodies moving, and the full impact of him, as deep as he could go, nearly undid me. I moved, slowly and steadily, my pace matching that of his tongue.

I moved faster, rocking and grinding against him, clamping down on him. There was no rhythm. No more kisses. Just our shared breaths and pleasure as my knees dug into the hard floor.

"Fates," he groaned harshly. "Nothing—*nothing*—feels like this." His hips punctuated his words with a deep thrust. "Nothing feels like you."

I shuddered because he was right. Nothing felt like *this*. I could spend an eternity searching for it, but I knew I would come up empty-handed. Because it was *him* that I rode. He who was inside me. And that made me even more desperate to capture this moment somehow.

My fingers tangled in his hair. The arm at my waist loosened. His hand slipped under the fluttering hem of my nightgown, splaying across the center of my ass. I rubbed my chest against his. Nipped at the skin of his throat, tasting the salt there. I moaned as he dragged my mouth back to his. We kissed, his fangs clashing with my teeth. Our lips swelled. Our bodies shook. His fingers dug into the flesh of my ass as he pulled me down on him, harder with each plunge. We feasted on each other. Devoured. All my tiny inner muscles began to quiver, clenching him. I was gasping with pleasure. He was snarling with it. And all of this…

All of this felt like *more*.

Nyktos pulled me tighter against him, holding me in place with him deep inside as he moved to his knees and then drove me onto the floor. His hand remained around the back of my head as he pounded into me, creating a shield between me and the hard surface. Wrapping my legs around his hips, I took all of him as he thrust deeper, harder, faster until the only sound was that of our bodies coming together.

I cried out as he pulled my head back, exposing my throat. His fangs grazed my pulse and then pressed in. Nyktos shook. He didn't break the skin, simply held his fangs there, and that was all it took. I exploded, shattering into silken shards of pleasure that dragged him over the edge and into the storm with me. Nyktos came with a roar against my throat, his body buckling as he spent himself.

His weight settled on me as spasms of pleasure rolled through both of us. I still held on to him, my fingers lost in his hair, my nails pressing into the skin of his arm, and my legs still wrapped around his, still slowly rocking my hips. Our breathing was ragged, slow to calm, and his fangs...

They were still at my throat.

My belly fluttered, and I tightened on him, drawing a hoarse groan from him. "If you need to feed," I whispered. "You can."

Nyktos's hips went still, but I felt him throb inside me. He just didn't need to. He wanted to. And I wanted to feel the pleasure-pain of his bite. The deep, languid draws. I wanted him at my throat, my breast, and between my thighs, sucking me, taking from me as I took from him. I bit my lip, moaning. His fangs scraped my skin, and every part of me trembled.

Nyktos shuddered and then eased back. "I can't. I won't," he panted, dropping his forehead to my shoulder. "I do not deserve this. And I sure as hell don't deserve that from you."

39

Nyktos's private quarters were a lot like his office and his bedchambers—a wide-open space outfitted with only the necessities. A large, oval table sat before doors leading to a balcony on a raised dais framed by two shadowstone pillars. Several chairs sat around the table, and I wondered how often he held meetings here. Two high-back chairs were seated by a credenza stocked with decanters of various sizes. I didn't spy any of that radek wine. The only other piece of furniture was the thickly cushioned couch I sat on.

The walls were bare. No personal mementos, paintings, or portraits—not even a spare piece of clothing left about.

I glanced down at Reaver, sleeping with his head resting in my lap, and wondered what his room looked like in his home. Before she left to check in on Ector and find Aios, Bele had shared that Reaver had awakened briefly to ask for me. His concern pulled at my heart as I combed my fingers through his hair. He'd tried to protect me. Had nearly died because of it, and that still sent my heart racing. He was too young to experience any of this, and I knew if Kolis wasn't stopped, the worst was yet to come.

As I watched Reaver's chest rise and fall under the too-long shirt Bele had found for him, my thoughts spun from one thing to the next. But there was one thought that I kept coming back to.

He'd be willing to do anything for you.

What Veses had said lingered in the back of my mind like a bad dream, making me think of something else I'd heard. What Rhain had claimed after the Cimmerian came to the Rise.

I thought about those I'd seen in the courtyard of Cor Palace. Attes had appeared disgusted, but had Hanan shared the same sentiments? Kyn? Those who had been in the shadowy alcoves? If they had not been bothered by the horrors in that courtyard, they were likely also capable of depraved acts. And Veses...

I brushed Reaver's hair back from his cheek as I counted his breaths.

Veses was likely capable of anything. And if Nyktos were truly willing to do anything for me?

Pressure settled on my chest as my thoughts traveled to terrible places. The kind that made the embers vibrate, but not with the urge to heal and restore life.

To end it.

I focused on breathing until I heard the soft click of the door. I lifted my gaze, my fingers stilling in Reaver's hair as Nyktos walked out of the bathing chamber, dragging a towel across his damp chest. He'd waited until I finished bathing to take care of himself, and we hadn't spoken much—and definitely not about what we'd shared.

I wasn't sure we needed to discuss it.

I had no regrets. It wasn't like I hadn't been in control of my actions. I'd wanted him despite what I did and didn't know. But that veneer of nothingness felt all the more fragile.

And I wasn't sure if that was because of what we'd shared or what I was beginning to suspect.

Nyktos draped the towel over the back of a chair. "Still sleeping?"

I glanced down at Reaver, nodding as concern picked away at me.

"A young draken could sleep through a war." He crouched before us, gently rearranging the blanket around Reaver's waist. "But I think the process of healing—*fully* healing—takes longer than the results we can immediately see. Both Gemma and Bele slept for some time, so you shouldn't worry."

I exhaled slowly, not even bothering to wonder if I had projected my concern or if Nyktos had simply read my emotions.

"And you?" he asked quietly. "How are you feeling?"

"Nothing hurts."

"I'm not talking about that."

My eyes lifted to his, and...gods, there was a lot we needed to talk about. But I knew what he was referencing. "I wanted you," I said, my voice barely above a whisper. "That was my choice. Mine. Not your blood." I leaned into the cushion, careful not to disturb Reaver. "What will you do with her?"

"She'll remain below." He brushed a damp strand of his hair back behind his ear. "I didn't hold back. The blast of eather put her in stasis. She'll probably be down for the count for a couple of days."

I was relieved to hear *one* part of that. "And then what? You can't keep her locked up forever."

"And I can't free her either."

"Because she will go to Kolis."

"Yeah, but besides that? I want to believe that once you become my Consort, she'll know it's a line she can't cross and that she no longer has control." Nyktos's jaw tightened. "But I can't be sure, especially knowing now that she's already tried to take you before." He looked at the table, his brows furrowing. "She never let on to the fact that she felt you."

"How was she able to feel the embers when not even Kolis could?" I asked, frowning.

"Veses is the Primal of the Rites—of *Ascensions.* And not just mortal ones. If any Primal could sense a godling or a god when they were near their Ascension, it would be the true Primal of Life and her," he explained. "But she hasn't been able to sense even a godling nearing the end of their Culling since Kolis took my father's embers—something she's been vocally annoyed about over the years."

"Let me guess," I said. "Kolis's act weakened her abilities?"

He nodded. "But none of us realized how powerful those embers in you are."

I thought that over. "So, she knew that Taric and the other two gods were searching for the source of the energy that was felt in the mortal realm, and they ended up here. She also sensed *something* in me— eventually realizing that what she felt were the Primal embers. She put two and two together and ended up at me, and then figured...what? That Kolis would be angry with you for hiding me, so decided to have me dealt with so it didn't blow back on you?"

"Seems to be that way," he murmured, scratching at his chin.

"She cares about you." The words soured my tongue, and I hated thinking them, let alone saying them, but if she was worried what might happen to Nyktos, she cared about him. Not only that, her actions could incite both Nyktos's and Kolis's anger.

Nyktos huffed out a humorless laugh. "In her own twisted way—or so she claims."

I liked that even less than I did the idea of her remaining below in the cells for all the many reasons I didn't want to think about. But also because I felt like I was missing a key piece of information.

A delicate charge of energy danced from his flesh to mine as he touched my arm. "You should try to get some rest. It's late. We can talk more about all of this later."

"I don't want to leave Reaver or risk waking him by moving," I said, and Nyktos smiled faintly before lowering himself to the floor, sitting just below me. "Are you going to stay here?"

Nyktos tipped his head back against the cushion and stared at the ceiling. "As long as you are, I will."

"You don't have to do that."

"I know."

"There has to be better seating."

"I'm fine just here." He glanced at me. "But you should still try to get some rest. Reaver will be fine."

I nodded.

"But you're not going to rest."

I half-shrugged.

"I could use compulsion, you know." His fingers rubbed a patch of taut skin above his heart. "And make you do the sensible thing and rest."

"But you won't."

"I won't." He sighed. "Morning will be here soon enough, and the day will be long."

The coronation. Finally. Tomorrow would be long, as would the day after when we left for Irelone, but my mind wasn't ready to relax. I couldn't shake the feeling that a whole lot about Veses—and him *and* Veses—didn't make sense. There was something I needed to know—had to understand. "You told her I was your Consort in title only."

A shadow of emotion danced over his features, gone before I could decipher it. "I did."

The breath I took hurt, and that should've served as a warning—one I didn't heed. "Why?" I whispered. "You wanted the other Primals to believe that we shared some sort of attraction to one another, but you didn't want her to think that?"

"She's different," he said, turning his head away as he dragged a hand over his face.

I tensed and then forced myself to relax as I glanced down at Reaver. "How so? Better yet, how did you even begin to explain why you'd take a Consort in title only?"

Nyktos didn't answer for several long moments as he stared at the bare stone walls. "It's complicated, Sera."

"I'm sure I can understand."

"But it's something that I cannot explain."

The veneer cracked even further. "You mean it's something you *will* not explain."

Nyktos's eyes closed as he dropped his hand to his bent knee.

I waited. When he said no more, it took a lot for me to keep the whirlwind of emotion rattling around inside me contained. "Do you care for her?"

"Fates." He laughed flatly, shaking his head. "I pity her. I loathe her. That's all I feel for her."

His answer left me even more confused. "And what do you feel for me?"

Nyktos was silent and then tipped his head back to look at me. Eather pulsed intensely behind his pupils. "I feel too many things. Curiosity and excitement that remind me of what I think yearning must feel like. Need. *Want,*" he said roughly, his voice low. "Amusement at times. Sometimes, even anger. But always *awe*. I am always in awe of you. I could keep going, but most of all, what I feel is the closest thing to peace I've ever experienced."

The messy knot of dark hair slid a little as the once-Chosen, now seamstress, tilted her head. "Don't move," Erlina ordered softly.

"Good luck with that," Bele commented.

Erlina laughed quietly.

I sent the goddess a narrow-eyed glare from where I stood on a stool in my bedchamber. Someone had cleaned up the mess Veses had left behind before I returned, but I swore I could still *feel* her here. Smell her. Roses. My lip curled.

"By the way," Bele added from where she was sprawled across the settee, her head resting on one arm and her legs propped on the other. She wasn't even looking at me as she flipped a dagger in her hand for the umpteenth time, something she'd been doing since Aios had finished styling my hair and left. "I heard Jadis threw a massive fit when Nektas was leaving her and Reaver in the mountains and she realized that she wouldn't be at the coronation."

My brows lifted. "Really?"

"Yep."

Hearing that made me a little sad. I would've loved to have the younger draken there. But even with Kolis's permission, that didn't mean things wouldn't go south. And after what'd happened to Reaver, no one wanted to risk the younglings.

"You're moving again," Bele said.

I glanced over at her. "No, I'm not."

"You're swaying," Erlina confirmed.

I was?

"Yeah, swaying like you had one too many glasses of wine," Bele tacked on.

"What are you even doing here?" I asked as Erlina snipped a thread near the curve of my hip. My tone bordered on my mother's whenever she'd seen me somewhere I wasn't supposed to be. My earlier happiness at seeing Bele when she arrived with Aios had faded about five hundred remarks ago.

"Making sure you stand still."

"You haven't done a good job of that," Erlina said around the needle she held between her teeth.

I rolled my eyes.

Bele snorted.

"I haven't moved that much," I defended.

Erlina's hands stilled as she looked up at me with dark brown eyes, her brows raised.

"Whatever," I muttered.

"I have never seen someone as antsy as you." The dagger flipped into the air once more. "It's like you have *sparanea* in your veins instead of blood."

I frowned. "*Sparanea?*"

"Yeah, they're everywhere in the mountains of Sirta, where it's snowing," she said, referencing Hanan's Court. "They're basically tiny spiders that are really fast and super venomous."

"What the fuck...?" I whispered, shuddering as my mind immediately began hurling images of tiny spiders crawling around inside me.

"That didn't help," Erlina said.

Bele giggled, the sound soft and airy. "Sorry. But, hey, at least I'm not talking about the spiders that are the size of a large dog."

"Spiders the size of a dog?" I whispered.

"Yeah. They love the wetlands. Freaking huge. Scare the shit out of you when you see them scurrying about. But they don't bite," she continued while I decided I no longer had any desire to see more of Iliseeum if those things lived in the rest of the realm. "They're more scared of you than you should be of them."

"It is impossible *not* to be afraid of a spider the size of a dog."

Bele snickered. "Then I probably shouldn't tell you about the snakes—"

"Please stop talking," I told her.

The goddess laughed.

Erlina snipped another thread. "It's okay," the seamstress said quietly. "You know…if you're nervous." She glanced up at me. "Anyone would be."

"True." Bele caught the dagger an inch before it plunged into her chest. "It's not every day that someone is crowned the Consort of the Primal God of Death before a massive crowd made up of gods and Primals."

I stared at her as she tossed the blade into the air once more. "I hope you drop that dagger, and it ends up in your eye."

Bele caught it. "And the entirety of Lethe," she went on. "When I saw Ector earlier, he said that much of the council house was already bursting with people. You know, I'm kind of glad I have to remain behind. That is way too many people."

My heart hammered. While I was relieved to know that Ector was up and moving about, I *was* more nervous than I'd thought I would be, and maybe even a little overwhelmed. Okay. A lot overwhelmed, which felt strange considering I had planned for this moment for most of my life. All of this felt surreal, and I doubted the lack of real sleep had anything to do with it.

"There." Erlina straightened and stepped back, eyeing me. "That should be it."

I blinked, slowly coming back to the moment. "What is?"

"The gown." The once-Chosen took my hand. "Here."

She guided me to turn around on the stool so that I faced the standing mirror she had brought in with her. I saw myself.

My hair hadn't been brushed to within an inch of its life but tamed by some serum Aios had rubbed between her palms after braiding the sides back. Pale curls and waves cascaded down my spine, glistening.

No veil covered my features, but I barely noticed the freckles. A shimmering gold powder highlighted the arch of my brow and cheekbones, and the mocha hue that Aios had lined my lids and lower lashes with somehow deepened the green of my irises. She'd stained my lips a color only a few shades darker than they normally were.

And the gown...

It wasn't white or transparent but a warm, silver shade close to the rare color of Nyktos's eyes when he was amused or relaxed. The sleeves were a delicate lace pattern that resembled the scrollwork I often saw on Nyktos's and his guards' tunics. That same scrolling design traveled over the rest of the gown, where it fit like a second skin from my breasts to my hips. From there, layers of soft gossamer and chiffon had been painstakingly stitched together so the skirt fell in wispy layers to the floor. Tiny diamonds twinkled from my arms, breasts, the waist, and the skirt. The gown was starlight.

"What do you think?" Erlina asked as she slid the small loop that was connected to the underside of the sleeve onto my forefinger on both hands.

"It's beautiful," I whispered.

"You're beautiful." Bele's face appeared above my shoulder. "Really."

I cleared my throat. "Thank you." I turned to Erlina. "Thank you."

Her golden-brown cheeks warmed. "It was a pleasure and an honor to make this gown."

"I don't know how you did all of this. It would've taken me years." I laughed shakily. "Actually, I couldn't even do this in a lifetime."

"Same," Bele murmured, and Erlina shrugged off the comments, but her smile spread.

With Bele's help, I carefully stepped down from the stool. "Will you be at the coronation?"

Erlina nodded. "Luckily, coronations are much like the Rites. All the mortals and godlings in attendance will be masked."

I was happy to hear that she would be there, but concern still blossomed as I stepped into heeled shoes. "And will that be safe?"

"Mortals and godlings will be far enough away from the rest that they won't be able to tell who is among them," Bele answered. "And most of the Chosen who were brought into the Shadowlands have been here long enough that if any of the gods or Primals fed from them while in Dalos, their blood would've weakened by now."

"Thank the Fates," Erlina murmured. She then clasped my hands. "I will see you there, Your Highness."

"Don't—" Catching Bele's pointed glare, I sighed. "I will see you there."

Erlina left then with her sewing bag, leaving the mirror to be retrieved later. Bele closed the door behind her as I went to where the shadowstone dagger and its sheath lay on the chest by the wardrobe.

I picked it up and gently hiked up the skirt.

"What are you...?" Bele chuckled as I strapped the sheath around my thigh. "Nice touch."

"Never leave without it," I remarked, securing the sheath and then lowering my foot. I watched the skirt sparkle its way back to the floor.

"Just remember that dagger won't do shit to a Primal," Bele offered. "You know, in case any of them decide to give tradition a giant Primal middle finger."

"Yeah, not like I'm going to forget that after shoving a dagger through Veses' eye, and her pretty much brushing it off."

"Fates, I wish I'd been there to see that."

"It was really gross." I glanced over at her. "She still sleeps?"

Bele nodded. "Hopefully, for the next hundred years, but I doubt we'll get that lucky."

"Yeah, but how long do we have before she's missed and someone comes looking for her?" I asked. Though, hopefully, Nyktos managed to transfer the embers, and Veses' whereabouts would be the least of anyone's concerns as he Ascended as the true Primal of Life.

She snorted. "You really think the crowd Veses runs with would care enough to realize she's missing? The answer would be no. To be honest, I bet most are grateful she's gone."

Well, that kind of...made me sad. And I didn't want to feel bad for her because I was petty and still didn't fully understand what the hell was going on between her and Nyktos. He claimed he couldn't stand her but let her feed from him and do who knew what else. And Veses did care about him, at least enough to not want to see him get in trouble with Kolis.

But I had a feeling someone knew what was going on between them.

"Do you know if Rhain is still here?" I asked.

"He is. He'll be one of your escorts to Lethe."

I glanced at the closed doors. Now probably wasn't the best time for this conversation, but... "I would like to see him really quick, if you know where he's at."

Curiosity marked her features. "He's nearby. I'll get him." She looked at the gown. "Remember. Less movement is better."

"I remember," I said, smiling, even though standing still while Bele retrieved Rhain was easier said than done. Thankfully, she returned within minutes with one very confused-looking god.

"You needed to see me?" Rhain asked, coming to stand with his hand on the hilt of a sword.

"Yes." I glanced at Bele. "Can you wait for us in the hall?"

Her brows shot up. "Do I have to?"

"I would like it if you did."

"But I'm nosy."

I stared at her while Rhain looked even more bewildered.

"Fine," Bele grumbled. "I'll wait in the hall."

Once the door was closed, I turned to Rhain. "There's something I need to ask you."

His head tilted toward the brighter light of the chandelier, turning his hair more red than gold. "And this isn't something you could ask in front of Bele?"

"I didn't think you'd answer if she or anyone else were present," I told him.

"I have a bad feeling about where this is going," he muttered, clearing his throat. "What is it you want to know?"

"In a few hours, I will be the Consort. I assume that means I have some level of authority when it comes to those here—even Nyktos's guards."

Rhain's golden-brown eyes narrowed. "It does."

"So, that means if I ask you something, you'd have to answer me *honestly*, correct?"

"Yeah." He drew out the word. "I guess so."

"Then I'm hoping you'll answer what I'm about to ask so that I don't have to order you to do it in a few hours," I said as wariness settled into his features. "I know this is likely a very inopportune time to ask this, but I want to know what Nyktos sacrificed for me."

Rhain blinked, and it took a few seconds for his expression to smooth out. "I didn't mean—"

"I don't think you were being dramatic, as Ector claimed. You know something."

He stared at me, his shoulders tensing. "Why do you want to know?"

"Because I do."

"Let me rephrase. Do you actually care if he did or didn't?"

I stiffened. "I wouldn't be asking you if I didn't. You can believe that or not. I know I won't be able to change your mind. And, to be honest, at this moment, I don't really care if you do. Just answer my question. *Please.*"

Rhain held my stare, but then his gaze cut away. He cursed. "I shouldn't have said a damn thing. He just might kill me if he finds out I did."

I doubted that Nyktos would kill Rhain. "I won't repeat what you tell me."

His eyes shot back to mine, the glow behind his pupils brighter. "And I'm supposed to trust that?"

"Contrary to what you may believe about me, and despite your dislike of me, I don't want to see you or anyone else here murdered," I replied dryly. "Especially by Nyktos."

"Yeah, well, I sure as fuck hope that's true." Rhain shifted from one foot to the other, cursing again as he lifted his gaze to the chandelier. "Eythos kept that damn deal he made with your ancestor quiet for a long time."

Surprise flickered through me. I hadn't expected *this* to come up.

"So did Nyktos. None of us even knew about it until…until another discovered it a few years back. How? The fuck if I know. The deals are only known to those who forged the deal and the Arae because those nosy bastards have to know just about everything," he said, his lips pursing. "She only learned of the deal—not everything Eythos did on the side. But learning about you was all she needed."

A chill of knowing swept up the back of my neck. "*She?*"

"Veses." He laughed, but it was dry and rough. "Yeah, she found out a couple of years back. Threatened to tell Kolis that Nyktos had a Consort in the mortal realm—something she knew Kolis would be very intrigued by. And by intrigued, I mean Kolis would've taken you from the mortal realm and used you to get to Nyktos."

Suddenly, I saw Veses in my mind, standing with Nyktos outside his office, touching him. *I heard that you have taken a Consort.* I'd assumed that question meant she hadn't known. But there had been a strange tone to her voice—one not of surprise but of…annoyance.

And it would make sense that Nyktos had told her that I was a Consort in title only because she knew about the deal—knew better. Still didn't sting any less, but it made sense.

"And, lucky for you, I guess, Veses' obsession with Nyktos is greater than her loyalty to Kolis," Rhain said, and unease exploded in my gut. "Nyktos was able to bargain with her. Got her to stay quiet." He stared at the floor, his lips twisting into a sneer. "For a price."

I went cold. Suddenly, I didn't want to know. Felt maybe *this* was best left unknown. But what Veses had said about Nyktos lying to her clicked into place. Rhain had confirmed what I already knew—she didn't know about the embers, but she suspected there was more. Something that he was hiding, even though he hadn't known about the embers *years* ago. Something that he would be...

He'd be willing to do anything for you...

I needed to know exactly what that was.

"What was the price?" I asked hoarsely.

"He agreed to...service her needs with his blood. To feed her whenever she desired."

My lips parted, and for a moment, I felt absolutely nothing.

"You would think that wouldn't be often. Primals don't need to feed that much unless they've been weakened, but Veses doesn't go long without paying a *visit*. And what could he do? He couldn't refuse her." His gaze lifted to mine. "Not when your ass was on the line."

Then I felt *everything*.

I jerked back a step, my entire body recoiling from what Rhain had said. I hadn't understood why Nyktos would allow her to touch him or feed from him. Until now. But I did understand why he wouldn't tell me. That he serviced Veses to keep the knowledge of the deal, of *me*, a secret.

Oh, gods. I thought I might be sick. "Why would he do that?"

Rhain stared at me. "You know why."

I slammed my eyes shut. He was right. I did know. The same reason he hadn't taken me as his Consort three years ago. To protect me from Kolis. "Dear gods, I..."

The box I'd closed all those emotions away in shattered, and I couldn't speak around the storm of them exploding through me. Disbelief and horror seized me, much like they had when Kolis had demanded his price, but this was *ugly* in an entirely different way. I took another step back as if I could distance myself, but I couldn't. There was no distancing to be done.

How could he agree to something like that to protect me, even before he really knew me? Why would he subject himself to *that*—her demand of a thing that wouldn't have been offered to her under any other circumstances?

He'd sacrificed the right to deny someone.

I suddenly thought about how shocked they had all been after learning that Nyktos didn't react when I touched him. How they'd said he didn't like to be touched—

And when he'd said he wanted no one but me. *Wanted.*

Oh, gods.

"Maybe Veses wanted to take you out because she figured out what you had in you and how that could blow back on Nyktos. But she also knew that the leverage she had over him was coming to an end," he said, and I heard what Nyktos had said the night before—*that she no longer has control.* "No one can tell me that doesn't have something to do with her coming at you. Because once you become his Consort, you will no longer be a secret to protect."

"He could've stopped—" I couldn't bring myself to say it. "Others found out about me weeks ago. He didn't know that she could still feel me nearing my Ascension..." I trailed off, falling silent.

Because the embers didn't matter.

Nyktos hadn't been protecting them. Not a week ago. Not months ago. Or even years ago.

He had been protecting *me.*

"None of us understood why he tolerated her presence when it was clear that he couldn't stand her." Dragging a hand through his hair, he clasped the back of his neck, and my chest felt too tight. "But he didn't tell us, you know? Only Ector and I found out because, after one of her visits, he was in bad shape. She had..."

It took no amount of imagination to fill in what he wouldn't say. If Nyktos were in bad shape, it could've been because Veses had taken too much blood.

"His cold skin," I rasped. "He told me it was because he was Death."

"But he's not the true Primal of Death," Rhain said. "His flesh shouldn't feel that way."

"It does because—" I sucked in a ragged breath. "It does because of her *feeding* from him."

Rhain didn't answer. He didn't need to because I knew. I'd been right about my suspicions.

Then my skin warmed, the embers in my chest vibrating as red-hot fury flooded my system, invading every cell of my body. A tremor hit me—

"Holy shit," Rhain whispered, light flickering over his face and the walls as he stared at the shuddering chandelier. "That's...that's you. You're doing that." He snapped forward, crossing the distance between us. He clasped my cheeks, forcing my eyes to his. "You need to calm.

Because I cannot stop you like Nyktos could without knocking your ass out in a far more painful way. That's not really an option because Nyktos would get really pissed at me for hurting you. But I also don't want to know what it feels like to have a palace come down on my head."

The embers hummed powerfully, but the rage...it was like what I'd felt when I stared at Kolis—when I'd felt *her* inside me. But this was all *me*. My fury was so great, so terrible that it calmed *me*. Not the embers. *Me*. The embers still hummed, but I willed the chandelier to still.

And it did.

I inhaled sharply. "I'm going to kill her."

Rhain's eyes widened in alarm. "You can't kill a Primal, Sera."

"Watch me try," I promised.

40

Rhain darted in front of me, blocking the doors I was stalking toward. "You cannot do what you're thinking."

My eyes narrowed on the god. "I can't?"

"Besides the fact that she's a Primal, and you cannot actually kill her?" he said. "You have a coronation to get to."

"I can try." I sidestepped him. "And still accomplish both. It's called multitasking."

Rhain let out a low growl and continued to block my progress. "I know you're angry—angrier than I thought you would be. But I cannot let you do this. Veses will be dealt with."

"How?" I demanded. "Exactly how will she be dealt with?"

Eather pulsed brightly in his eyes. "Do you really think Nyktos will let what she did to you and Reaver slide? He won't. That bitch's days are numbered. She's not long for this realm. The moment Nyktos has those embers in him and Ascends, that's it for her."

It took a moment for what Rhain said to penetrate the haze of rage. My gaze flew to the door over his shoulder, where Bele waited in the hall. When I brought Bele back to life, I'd Ascended her and, therefore, threatened Hanan's position as Primal of his Court. Once the embers were transferred, Nyktos would be able to Ascend another to replace a fallen Primal—namely that bitch.

I stared at the door, hands opening and closing at my sides. I prayed that Rhain was right. That her days truly were numbered, but I wanted nothing more than to rip her fangs from her horrid mouth and shove them down her throat.

Rhain stepped toward me. "Nyktos is waiting for you, Your Highness."

I blinked, startled. "Don't call me that."

"But you will be my Queen," he said, shoulders stiffening once more. This time, they nearly bunched all the way to his ears. "You already have been."

I stared at him, unsure how to process *him* saying that, but I didn't have the mental space for it.

Not when all I breathed was fury.

And sorrow.

Chest squeezing tightly, I closed my eyes. Acid pooled in my stomach. Nyktos...his blood was a part of him he likely never would've shared with her if she hadn't discovered who I was. It was coercion whether he'd offered it or agreed to it. Blackmail. I hated that he'd been in that situation. Loathed that it was because of me, and I hadn't even known.

Why would he do that for a Consort he'd never wanted?

That went beyond goodness and into a realm I couldn't even fathom, one I knew beyond a doubt that I didn't deserve. Hell, I could only think of a few people who *would* deserve that. Ezra was one. Marisol. My breath snagged. *Nyktos.* No one should ever have to do such a thing. But he deserved the same kind of *sacrifice.*

Guilt festered, and not because I felt responsible for what Veses had forced upon him. Because, like Bele had said, Nyktos and Veses hadn't made sense. I'd known that, but my hurt feelings had overshadowed what was right in front of my face.

But I never would've imagined that this was why. I wouldn't have wanted to.

"How many know?" I asked. "You and Ector?"

"And Nektas."

I wasn't surprised to hear that. There seemed to be very little Nektas didn't know. But he wouldn't have shared this with me.

"You level?" Rhain asked quietly.

"No," I whispered, opening my eyes. "I...I don't want him to have done that for me—for anyone."

"I know," he said, watching me. "Veses was here..." Understanding flickered across his features. "That's what set you off that day. You saw them." He cursed, shoving his hand through his hair. "I couldn't figure it out—what obviously had changed between you and Nyktos. It was her."

There was no point in lying. "I saw them."

"And he didn't tell you why he was with her."

I shook my head.

Rhain's jaw tightened. "He wouldn't want you to know his shame."

"That's not his shame." I stiffened until all the many tiny diamonds felt as if they were cutting into my skin. "It's hers."

His eyes shone more amber than brown. "You and I know that, but would either of us feel like that if we were in that position?"

"No." I didn't need to think about it. And, gods, that…that broke my heart. I could barely bring myself to talk about how Tavius had behaved toward me. I'd even downplayed his actions because it was too hard to speak of them. And what he'd done was nothing compared to what Veses had to Nyktos. I pressed my lips together as I blinked rapidly, trying to clear away the dampness there.

A knock on the door interrupted. "Everything okay in there?" Bele called out.

Rhain looked at me.

Dragging in a deep breath, I nodded as I exhaled slowly, forcing my hands to relax at my sides. "Nyktos is waiting for me."

He turned for the door, then faced me. "Do you love him?"

The floor felt as if it shifted under my feet. Love? Nyktos? My mouth opened, but I couldn't find any words to speak.

Rhain tilted his head back. "I…I think I was wrong about you."

"Did you all notice anything strange?" Lailah asked as we entered the foyer. Shoulder-length braids fell back from her face as she glanced up at the glass candles. "I swear the entire palace was shaking a couple of minutes ago."

"Odd," Rhain murmured, and that was all he said.

I couldn't even think about the fact that I hadn't actually lost control. That the rage I'd felt had somehow calmed me. There was no space for that, either. I was reeling from what Nyktos had done to keep me safe—what he'd put himself through before I even knew him.

Bile gathered in my throat, threatening to choke me as Saion and Rhahar turned from the doors. They were speaking, but they fell silent and stared, and it went on long enough to draw me from my thoughts.

Bele fluttered her hand in front of her face. "She's so pretty, isn't she?"

I shot her an arch glare.

"We already knew that," Saion said, his brows raised. "But the gown…"

"Looks like starlight," Rhahar finished.

Feeling my cheeks warm, I murmured, "Thank you."

Saion grinned as he reached for the heavy stone doors, pushing them open. I walked out, descending a short set of steps into the courtyard. The first thing I saw was Orphine and her twin Ehthawn. The two massive, midnight-scaled draken were perched on the Rise, and in the distance, I could see the faint shape of more draken circling over the Dying Woods. The turning of wheels drew my gaze.

A horse-drawn carriage rolled forward amidst a small army of mounted guards. There were nearly…a hundred. I blinked, focusing on the artwork scrawled across the side of the carriage. The vines. The white wolf. It was the same as the doors to the throne room.

One side of the carriage doors swung open, and Ector popped his head out. His eyes widened slightly, and then his expression smoothed out. He extended his hand. "Ready?"

Forcing a swallow, I nodded as Saion straight-up leapt into the driver's box. I started forward but halted as the other gods mounted horses. Only Bele lingered back by the doors. "Wait," I called out, my concern rising. Saion looked over his shoulder. "If all of you are here, who is with…Nyktos?"

"Nektas," Rhahar said as he tightened his grip on the reins. He faced forward again. "And I do believe the entirety of the Shadowland armies."

Oh.

"Sera?" Ector wiggled his fingers.

Taking a deep breath, I lifted the hem of the gown as I took his warm hand in mine and stepped into the dimly lit carriage. There were two benches, outfitted with thick, white cushions. I sat carefully on one.

"I'll be out here for most of the trip," Ector advised.

"Be careful," I murmured.

Ector hesitated and then shook his head. I watched him climb out of the carriage to stand on one of the rails along the side. Rhain drew his horse near Ector, and then the door closed. I heard a tap on the roof.

The windowless carriage jerked forward.

Do you love him?

My palms felt damp, so I placed them on the cushion beside me as I tracked the vines and poplar leaves etched along the interior walls and ceiling. The carriage was traveling at a fast clip, and I had no idea how much time passed before the reality of what Nyktos had sacrificed for me, what I felt for him, and why I had reacted so strongly to seeing him with Veses and then learning the truth, hit me.

Do you love him?

"Oh, gods," I whispered, sinking into the bench's cushion as I pressed a hand to the tiny diamonds adorning the bodice of my gown. I could feel my heart beating wildly, even through the layers of gossamer fabric. My chest felt warm and like it was swelling, and it wasn't the embers.

There was only one reason I'd react in such a way. I stared down at the hand pressed to my chest—to the space above my heart.

My heart.

I…I loved him.

I loved Nyktos?

Another tremor ran through my hands as I lifted my gaze to the empty bench across from me. I swallowed thickly. I had no idea what love even felt like, so I needed to remain calm. This could just be a byproduct of stress—of everything. Maybe only indigestion.

A strangled laugh left me, echoing through the empty carriage. *Indigestion?* Sure.

The carriage door opened, letting in a rush of air that carried the stale scent of lilacs as Ector closed the door. He slid onto the bench across from me. "We're almost to the entry house of Lethe. It feeds into the City Hall, where Nyktos is waiting for us."

I stared at him, my heart feeling as if it were the wheels of the carriage.

"There hasn't been any trouble. Just a few Shades, but nothing that wasn't quickly handled…" Creases formed between Ector's brows. "Are you okay? You look a little pale."

"I think I might vomit," I whispered.

He blinked twice. "Do we need to stop the carriage?"

"No. No. I don't think so." At least, I hoped not.

"Bele mentioned that you were nervous. I didn't believe her. I don't think I've ever seen you nervous." His head tilted. "But, yeah, you're definitely that." He leaned forward, resting his hands on his bent knees.

"You remind me of my sister."

That snapped me out of my panic spiral. "A sister?"

He nodded. "She looked as scared right before her wedding as you do now. Said her stomach felt like it was full of winged creatures."

My stomach felt just like that.

"Of course, that was an entirely different situation. Love match and all." He smiled faintly. "But I'm guessing the nervousness is the same no matter what."

"Love match?" Now those winged creatures had invaded my chest.

"Childhood sweethearts or something." He grinned, a distant but warm glint filling his gaze. "Look, I know you came into this whole thing with…other plans, and probably hadn't given much thought to a future. And I have no idea what is going on between the two of you half the time, but Nyktos will always be kind to you."

"I know. Gods, do I ever." Another laugh rattled out of me. The crease returned to the space between his brows. "It's not that."

"Then what is it? Are you worried something will happen? You shouldn't—"

"I want to be Nyktos's Consort," I blurted out. "I want it more than I think I've ever wanted anything…" Well, I likely wanted the Rot to end more, and for Kolis to be dealt with. And I also wanted to murder Veses, slowly and very painfully, so there *were* other things I wanted just as much, but… "I want this."

Ector's mouth remained half-open as the carriage ground to a halt. Neither of us moved. Not even when a knock sounded on the roof. "I wasn't expecting you to say that," he whispered, eather pulsing behind his pupils. "Any part of that."

"Neither was I," I admitted in an equally quiet voice.

"And that makes you nervous?"

I nodded.

The carriage doors opened, and this time I couldn't detect the scent of stale flowers. There were too many other smells—wood smoke, food, and burning oil. "Everything okay in here?" Rhahar asked.

"Yeah." Ector's smile was slow but wide. "I really think it is."

"Okay." Rhahar drew out the word, turning to me. "Nyktos is waiting for you inside."

My chest tightened until I feared I was on the verge of an attack, but then it loosened. I rose on what felt like toothpicks and took Rhahar's hand, seeing nothing but the lines of mounted guards beyond him and a section of the Rise. He helped me step out of the carriage as one of the draken flew low over us, its wings outspread. I followed the draken's descent to the top of a colonnade that had been built upon solid blocks that formed multiple archways which fed into the Hall. I stepped back, taking in the sprawling, pillared structure of shadowstone backdropped by the stone-gray sky and scattered starlight. The City Hall was as I expected, open to the air but at least several times larger than what I was familiar with in Lasania. Beyond the pillars, a soft, buttery glow of light and the hum of…of music and laughter drifted out.

My gaze fell to those stationed at the entrances to the Hall and surrounding the entry house. They were guards, but these wore helmets constructed of a thin layer of shadowstone that covered their faces and necks. The soldiers.

"This way." Rhahar's hand stayed firmly around mine, and as the lines of soldiers parted, I realized that it probably had a lot to do with how badly my hand was trembling.

Ector and Rhain fell into step behind me, along with Saion and the twins as Rhahar led me toward a tower that was like a smaller version of the Shadow Temple. The windowless structure, which must've been the entry house, was less grand, but it still reflected the light of the stars in such a way that it appeared as if thousands of candles lined the walls.

Rhahar walked fast through the rows of soldiers, and I wasn't sure if the speed was due to his eagerness to be rid of me or to have me safely within sight of Nyktos.

The winged creatures Ector had spoken about now felt as if they were attacking my heart. The doors of the tower opened, and I immediately recognized hair a shade of red wine under the darker sky. Aios stood next to who I believed was Kars, the muscular, fair-haired guard who'd offered to watch over me. Aios's gown was sleeveless and an emerald green.

She came forward, taking my hand from a likely relieved Rhahar. "You look beautiful," she said, smoothing her other hand over one of the plaited braids on the side of my head as Kars bowed. She then folded my arm under hers, walking at only a slightly more sedate pace as the guards surrounded us. "Do you have any questions before we enter?"

Maybe the winged creatures had finally made it to my head because my mind was empty except for… "Have you ever been in love?"

Surprise flickered over her face. "I have."

"What does it feel like?" I whispered.

Her pace slowed. "It's hard to explain, and I don't think it feels the same for everyone," she started. "But to me, it felt like…like being *home*, even in an unfamiliar place."

I felt that, but there was also the ember that recognized Nyktos. I knew the ember didn't drive what I felt for him, but I could have mistaken it for a more significant emotion.

"And it feels like you're being seen for the first time," she continued, a soft smile appearing on her lips while my stomach plummeted. "Like you're being heard. I know that probably doesn't make sense, but it's like being...*known* in a way you haven't felt before."

Gods, it *did* make sense. I felt heard and seen by Nyktos, but I also hadn't been known by many, so...

"I believe it's something you just know." Aios squeezed my hand. "Because you would do anything for them. Anything. And you can't fake or force that."

Anything.

I thought about when he'd asked me why I had volunteered to pay Kolis's price. Deep down, I'd known why I'd done it.

I...I'd loved him long before today. Before I learned about the deal he'd made with Veses. Before I acknowledged that I wanted to be his Consort.

And it was why sharing my body with him had felt like *more*. Because it was for me.

"Fuck me," I whispered as Rhain fell into step beside us.

Aios's brows pinched as she shot a look at Rhain over my head. A moment passed. "Are you all right?"

As several rows of guards passed through the doors of the entry house, I nodded, even though I really might hurl this time around. The embers began to hum and wiggle, and my throat shrank in size. I saw another set of doors, ones with the same artwork as the throne room and the carriage. They opened to reveal a brightly lit chamber, now full of armored and heavily weaponed soldiers among the guards.

But I found *him* immediately.

He stood at the other end of the chamber, near a rounded archway I thought might lead out to the Hall's main floor. His hair was free, brushing broad shoulders that stretched the iron-hued material of his sleeveless tunic. As the guards stepped aside, clearing a path to him as he slowly turned, my gaze locked onto...*Ash's.*

Nektas's words suddenly came back to me then. *He is how you wish him to be.*

And I knew right then, as I stood there trembling, who he was to me. He wasn't Nyktos. He never had been. He was *Ash*, and I...

I was in love with him.

Everything stopped. My heart. My lungs. My steps. The air in the chamber. The entire realm. The harsh cut of his jaw loosened, and those full, lush lips parted. His eyes became luminous, silver pools as he stared back, as motionless as I was. I had no idea how long we stood there. My pulse raced, and my chest swelled as a hundred different thoughts cycled through my mind. It could've been seconds. Minutes. I had no idea, but I felt like my feet no longer touched the floor.

And then…*Ash* was moving, prowling toward me in fluid steps with the grace of a predator. I was struck by the memory of watching the kiyou wolves roam the Dark Elms. He moved the same way, and not once had he taken his eyes from me.

I was only vaguely aware of Aios slipping her arm from mine as…*Ash* stopped in front of me. His touch replaced hers, sending a shock of awareness through my entire system. His fingers curled around mine as he leaned in, lowering his mouth to my ear to whisper, "Breathe, *liessa.*"

Something beautiful.

Something powerful.

I inhaled suddenly and deeply, sucking in air. His hold on my hand tightened as he stepped in closer, stopping the wild tremor in my fingers and arm. The scent of citrus and fresh air filled me.

"That's it," he whispered, his lips brushing the shell of my ear and sending a shiver through me. Several moments passed before I stopped gulping in air. He stood so close his thighs nearly touched mine, and…thick tendrils of shadow had spilled out around him—around *us*—blocking out the chamber and shielding us from those within. His hand shifted slightly in mine, and I felt his thumb run across the inside of my palm. "Better?"

"Yes," I whispered hoarsely.

Ash didn't move away. He stayed there, sweeping his thumb back and forth across my skin. "I want to tell you that you look beautiful," he said, his voice as soft as the shadows moving around us, warm against my cheek. "But beautiful doesn't adequately capture what I see. I don't know if there is a word that does. You have taken my breath with yours."

My heart skipped as he stepped back, and I lifted my gaze as the shadows dissipated around us. I saw that the brocade along the neck of his tunic, and the slanted, vertical line cutting across his chest and ending at the hem above his thighs were brighter than before. Sharper. Jeweled. The black breeches and boots he wore were spotless. He wasn't armed.

He wore only the cuff, but as I tipped my head farther back, I...I saw the *crown*—one that was the opposite of the crown Kolis wore.

Nyktos's sat low, just above his brow and was the color of midnight. The row of swords carved from smooth stone surrounded the middle spike that had been shaped into a crescent moon. The tip of each sword and the entirety of the moon glittered with diamonds.

It was a fearsome yet beautiful crown, made of shadowstone and starlight, just like its bearer.

Ash's hand still held mine. "Sera?"

"The crown looks heavy," I said, because that was the only thing I could say despite all the thoughts running through my head.

One side of his lips kicked up. "Wait until you see yours."

My brows lifted. "Is it heavy, too?"

He chuckled, lowering our joined hands. "Don't worry. You don't have to wear it after tonight."

I nodded, swallowing against the dryness in my mouth and throat.

"Saion?" His gaze flicked away from me but returned quickly, skipping over the lace and beaded diamonds along my waist and hips. "Update?"

The god stepped forward. "All the soldiers are stationed along the aisle and at the foot of the dais."

Turning my head, I saw that the chamber was mostly empty except for Aios and a handful of guards. She smiled at me, and I thought I returned the gesture. I hoped I did, but it felt a little weird. "Where...?" I cleared my throat. "Where is Nektas?"

"He's around." Ash's stare glided over my jaw and lips. "Can someone get me a glass of wine?"

"On it," came a response. A moment later, Kars appeared with a bronze chalice. He handed the wine to the Primal, only briefly glancing in my direction before stepping back.

"Here." Ash placed the chalice in my free hand.

"Thank you," I whispered, greedily but carefully taking a drink of the sweet and crisp wine.

He watched me, remaining quiet until I took another drink. "Are you all right?"

"Of course."

Ash stared at me, his head tilting just a bit. The crown didn't move even an inch. I saw that his eyes had narrowed.

My back stiffened, but I forced my voice to come out soft instead of blade-sharp. "Please, don't read my emotions."

Ash's brows snapped together. "I think that was possibly the nicest way you've ever made that demand." His eyes searched mine. "What's wrong?"

Heat crept up my throat. How could I answer when the only thing currently wrong with me was that I was...very likely in love with him. And because of that, I didn't know what to do or say.

Ash watched me closely. "Did something happen?"

"No," I said quickly—maybe too quickly. And perhaps I needed to pull myself together as quickly as I'd responded. Or maybe I could stop behaving this way if I just told him. Not what I'd learned about Veses, because this wasn't the place for that, but I could...I could be honest.

"Sera?" Ash touched my chin, tipping my head back.

I closed my eyes because even though I was less afraid, I still didn't feel very brave. "I just...I want you to know that I want this," I told him in a strangled whisper. "I mean, when I told you before that I wanted to be your Consort, that still holds true. I want this, Ash."

Silence.

Cracking open one eye and then the other, I saw that Ash stared down at me with eyes full of whipping, luminous strains of eather. He looked shocked. Dazed.

"I thought I would let you know." My face warmed as my *brain* seemed to cringe, but some of the pressure had left my chest. There was still a series of wiggles in my stomach, but I felt a little better as I stepped back. His fingers fell from my chin as my hand slipped free of his. I glanced at the opening. The music had stopped at some point. "Should we do this?"

Ash blinked, clearing his throat. "Yeah. Yes. We should," he said, sounding shaken.

Saion came forward then, and I hoped that no one else had heard my rather awkward declaration. Aios watched us with a perplexed expression, and I suddenly wished I'd asked who she loved. I started to, but Ash's hand found mine again, and then we were walking toward the entrance.

"Thirty-six," he murmured, stopping at the mouth of the City Hall.

My brows pinched. "What?"

"Thirty-six freckles," he told me, staring ahead. "I counted them again. It's become a habit. And I may have lied about not knowing how many were along your back. I do. Twelve."

My chest swelled, and the embers...they *buzzed*. There had been a feeling of rightness before, but this...*this* was different. A smile spread across my lips as I looked up at him. The rightness felt as if it were inked onto my skin, filling my veins, and carving itself into my bone and muscle. And it felt good. Not confusing. Still scary as hell, but *good*.

Drawing in a shallow breath, I turned my attention to the Hall, finding a draken perched on the columns. There were…dozens of them, but I didn't think I saw Nektas among them. Iron-gray banners hung from the tops of the columns, bearing the symbol of two crescent moons facing each other below what appeared to be the shape of a wolf's head. Strings of soft yellow crisscrossed over the entirety of the coliseum, casting a warm glow over the endless rows of tables and the seating under the banners. I'd never seen such light before, and I could only assume that Primal energy fueled them.

"Bow," Rhain's voice boomed from the end of the aisle, startling me. The dais was so far away, I could barely make out his form, but his words carried. "Bow for the Asher, *the* One who is Blessed."

The slide of slippers and boots over stone echoed, somehow drowning out the sudden pounding of my heart. Ash squeezed my hand, and I felt that. I felt him. Only him.

"The Guardian of Souls," Rhain continued, and I swore the stars above pulsed. "And *the* Primal God of Common Men and Endings, *the* ruler of the Shadowlands. The Primal of Death."

41

I didn't realize we'd started walking until I became aware of the utter silence and the weight of *thousands* of stares. The breath I took was weak. The embers in my chest vibrated as my gaze bounced off shields held by the soldiers lining the aisle, the splashes of color from the vivid gowns and tunics, and the blurred faces. No one spoke as we walked forward, but they watched. All of them. Behind us. Ahead of us. I felt their gazes on the strands of my hair, on the cut of the glittering, lacy gown, and on my face.

Never had so many people looked directly upon me. My gaze swung to the dais at the end of the seemingly never-ending aisle. The back of my neck tingled. My chest started to ache—

"Breathe," Ash murmured, his hand tightening around mine.

My racing heart slowed a little at the sound of his voice, and all I could manage from that point on was focusing on taking slow, measured breaths. I didn't realize we'd reached the dais until Ash stopped, giving me enough time to lift the hem of my gown so I didn't trip and land on my face. I knew I recognized the features of those who stood by the dais, but for the life of me, I couldn't figure out who stood there.

I gripped the gown tightly, the diamonds digging into my palm as we ascended the rounded shadowstone steps, and the thrones came into view. They were situated before the banners, identical to the ones in the House of Haides. A white podium stood in front of the thrones.

And a crown sat upon it.

My lips parted. The crown was...I'd never seen anything like it. Spires carved from shadowstone formed a halo of glittering crescent moons. Delicate chains of black stone hung between the peaks, dripping clusters of diamonds along tiers of chains, which also connected to the front of each spire.

I was supposed to wear *that*? On my head?

Ash led me across the dais, passing the podium and stopping so we stood between the thrones, exactly where the shadowstone wings touched between them. Ash angled his body toward mine and stopped so the podium and thrones were directly behind us. "Look at me," he said under his breath, and I did just that. "It's only us."

Throat dry, I held his gaze as if it were a lifeline in the silence of the coliseum. Wisps of eather swirled slowly through his irises as he smoothed his thumb over the top of my hand. Movement caught my attention out of the corner of my eye, but I didn't look away. It was Rhain, lifting the crown from the podium. Ash swept his thumb once more and then let go to take the crown, but his gaze never left mine as he...

Ash lowered himself to one knee, bowing *to* me.

A rush of shocked murmurs went through the crowd situated in the tiered levels of the City Hall as I stared down at him in confusion. He hadn't mentioned that any sort of kneeling was supposed to occur. Based on the response from those watching, I didn't get the impression that this was normal. I also didn't understand why *he*, a Primal, was the one bowing.

"Now that's a man who knows his place." A smooth voice I recognized cracked the stunned silence. My gaze snapped to the source near the dais and landed on the sandy-haired Primal as soft giggles and chuckles traveled throughout the coliseum.

I wasn't at all surprised to see Attes, dressed in black. Upon his head rested a helm of reddish-black stone. I hadn't expected Kyn to show after what had happened in Dalos, but he was there, too, kneeling beside Attes.

The Primal God of Accord and War winked as a dimple appeared in his right cheek.

I quickly returned my gaze to Ash.

A half-grin had appeared on his lips. "You will need to bend a little for this to work," he instructed quietly. "Keep your neck and head straight."

Blinking rapidly, I bent at the waist. Ash once more held my gaze as he lifted the crown of moons and placed it atop my head. The chains of diamonds kissed my forehead and brow as he ran his fingers along the bottom of the halo, shifting the crown ever so slightly back so the tiny teeth along the bottom caught on my hair. I didn't feel the weight, only because I was sure my entire body had gone numb.

Then Ash took my hand, and I straightened as he rose, his gaze flickering over my face and where the diamond chains rested against my forehead. "Exquisite," he murmured before turning so each of us stood before a throne and faced the crowd.

The crowd quieted.

"Rise," Ash's voice was deeper, louder. A powerful thunder. "Rise for the One who is born of Blood and Ash, *the* Light and the Fire, and *the* Brightest Moon," he said, and my eyes cut to him as my breath caught.

My title.

I had forgotten about that amidst everything.

What he said sounded almost part prophecy. Magical. And completely beautiful.

Flecks of essence swirled through his eyes as he lifted his chin. "Rise for the Consort of the Shadowlands."

All across the coliseum, Primals and gods, mortals and godlings rose as Ash lifted our joined hands high between us, applause lifting to where the draken were perched on the pillars—

I gasped at the sudden, intense series of tingles erupting along the palm pressed to Ash's. My gaze swung to our joined hands as silvery-white light swirled around our palms and down our arms as the embers in my chest hummed fiercely in response. The glow of the eather reflected off Ash's face as his eyes widened slightly. The crowd went silent.

"Is that you?" I whispered.

"No," he rasped, features sharpening, skin thinning until a hint of shadow was visible beneath his skin. Disbelief filled his eyes as his gaze met mine. "*Imprimen*," he said, clearing his throat. "*Suu opor va id Arae. Idi habe datu ida benada.*"

"W-what?" I only recognized one word spoken in the Primal language.

Ash swallowed thickly. "Imprint," he translated, staring at me in…awe as shocked murmurs eroded the silence. "It must be the Arae. They've given their blessing."

The Arae? Holland? I slowly looked out over the audience, catching only glimpses of slack jaws and wide-eyed Primals. My gaze connected with a Primal with smoky, reddish-brown skin and curly, russet-colored hair beneath a stunning, pale blue quartz crown of many branches and leaves.

The crowd erupted in cheers—feet and shields slamming into the floor as all the Primals but this one stood in open-mouthed silence. This Primal gave me a small smile and pressed a hand free of jewels to the center of her chest before nodding.

I sucked in a shallow breath as Ash stepped back, guiding me to the throne. Heart thumping, our hands remained joined as we sat—as a sudden rumble echoed through the Shadowlands. A burst of intense, silvery fire lit the sky beyond the pillars as the draken lining the columns lifted their heads, letting out a staggering, high-pitched call. With wide eyes, I watched them take flight, circling the coliseum as a larger, thicker shadow fell over the crowd, blotting out the starlight. A gust of wind stirred the strings of lights and lifted the tendrils of my hair as I looked up.

Massive black-and-gray wings spread out as Nektas descended from above, landing in front of the thrones. Sweeping his wings back over our heads, his front talons slammed down on the edge of the dais. The thick frills around his head vibrated as a sound like thunder rolled from him. Those near the dais took several steps back, exchanging wary glances as smoke wafted from Nektas's flared nostrils, and I looked at Ash…

My husband.

Ash's lips curved into a shadow of a smile as he squeezed my hand and then released it. I drew my hand back and slowly looked down at it.

A series of luminous golden swirls swept over the top of my hand and between my thumb and pointer finger, sweeping in several whirls along the lines of my palm. I looked at Ash's hand.

He bore the same mark as I did.

"It's an imprint," Ash explained quietly, his left hand—the newly inked one—closed and resting on the table that had been placed before the thrones. "It appears when a union is favored."

"By the Fates?" I traced the golden swirls on the inside of my palm. Unlike the charm that had been placed on me, this imprint didn't fade into my skin.

"I suppose they *could* do such a thing," he said in a low voice, leaning in so I could hear him. I imagine to those celebrating down below, it looked as if he were whispering sweet nothings.

"So, they didn't?" I stared at the golden marks.

"I don't think so."

"You lied?"

He brushed a curl back over my shoulder. "Just a little. I had to give some sort of explanation for what has been rather impossible. No one has been blessed upon their union in many centuries."

I arched a brow. "Then how did this happen?"

His fingers lingered around the curl as he said, "My father was known to do this when he favored a union and wanted it known to all others. He'd give his *blessing*."

I then remembered Ash mentioning that, but if this were something his father would do, it was something the *true* Primal of Life could do, meaning... My lips parted. "It was the embers."

Ash leaned back with a smile, turning his gaze to the crowd.

"And they will believe it was the Arae?"

"The Fates are capable of anything," he answered. "So, it's more than possible that they could do something of the sort."

And yet, Ash was pretty confident that it hadn't been them.

Looking down at my hand, I drew my finger along a shimmering whirl. Had it been the embers? Or had it been *me*? Either way, it seemed a little...self-indulgent to favor one's own union.

"It won't rub off," Ash commented under his breath.

My finger ceased moving as I glanced over at him. He was watching the Primal with the crown of ruby antlers. Hanan. He stood with Kyn. Both appeared as if they were one refill away from being highly intoxicated. It was likely that I, too, would end up that way if I continued drinking instead of eating. In my defense, it was quite difficult to stuff my face at a table that had been prepared on the dais, in plain view of the thousands of people in attendance.

Meanwhile, Aios sat with several masked guests behind the dais. I would've preferred that.

"I'm not trying to rub it off," I said, watching Kyn once more. What had Attes told him about the young draken, Thad? I'd learned that morning that he'd been brought to the Shadowlands and was currently in the mountains. "I just can't stop touching it."

"Hopefully, you'll get used to it," he told me. "The only way it fades is upon death, and I don't plan on that occurring."

I blinked as I closed my hand. "What if we decided to no longer continue this union?"

"Honestly?" He looked over at me, his brows pinched. A moment passed. "Not sure. None who've borne the imprint chose to separate."

I wondered if he was thinking about the deal I'd struck with him—the bid for my freedom. But that was before I realized that I was…in love with him. Now, I wasn't sure what to think about the deal we'd struck. Being done with him didn't feel like freedom. It felt like a different kind of prison. I shook my head, telling myself there would be time later to dwell on all of that. "Are others with the imprint still alive?"

Ash shook his head. "Those my father blessed no longer live."

A chill crawled down my spine. I didn't have to ask. I knew. Kolis. Killing those his brother had favored for whatever reason sounded like Kolis's particular brand of childish cruelty for the sake of cruelty.

But didn't that make the imprint feel like a bit of an omen? I slipped my inked hand beneath the table to my lap as I looked out over the revelers. Ash had already pointed out the Primals I hadn't recognized.

Maia. The Primal Goddess of Love, Beauty, and Fertility was just as she'd always been depicted. Full-figured and utterly stunning, her warm blond hair cascaded down her back in thick curls and framed yellowish-brown skin. Her pearl crown was one of roses and scalloped shells. She was fascinating to watch. Every move she made, every smile and flicker of her gaze, carried an air of softness and a hint of spice. I couldn't see her now, as she was almost constantly surrounded.

I'd recognized Phanos, but it would be hard to miss him in the crowd. He was taller than all other Primals, possibly even Ash, and bore a crown shaped like a trident. He stood at least half a foot above all others, his bald head a burnt umber under the glow of the string lights. I'd tensed when I saw him briefly speaking to Saion and

Rhahar, but no one else seemed that concerned, and he'd eventually walked off with the Primal of Wisdom, Loyalty, and Duty.

Embris reminded me of a hawk—a quiet, watchful man despite the mop of curly brown hair lending a boyish quality to his features. His bronze crown... disturbed me, having been molded into olive branches and what appeared to be *serpents*. Embris had left. Or at least I thought he had, as I hadn't seen him or Phanos in a while. Ash didn't seem surprised by their quick departure as, according to him, they had done what was expected of them by showing and had no reason to linger.

My heart skipped as my attention shifted to the Primal who had smiled at me. I hadn't seen the striking Primal in the crowd again until then. "Who is that?"

Ash followed my gaze. "Keella."

The Primal of Rebirth, who had helped Eythos. I watched her as she sat quietly while several attendees spoke with her, a welcoming—if reserved—smile on her face. Out of all the Primals here, she was the one I wanted to speak to.

But she hadn't approached the dais. None of the Primals or anyone other than those who worked closely with Ash had. I figured that had something to do with Nektas, who remained in his draken form and took up nearly all the space on the dais as he watched those below as if he wasn't above biting off an arm or two.

"Do you think she knows?" I murmured. Ash leaned in closer to me. "About me—about what your father eventually did with the soul?"

Ash didn't answer for a long moment. "Did you know that when a babe dies, their soul is reborn?"

I turned my head to him. "No."

He nodded, his gaze flicking to Keella. "They're the only souls that do not pass into the Shadowlands. Keella captures them and sends them back."

My stare drifted back to her. "So, they are reincarnated?"

"No." He shook his head as his fingers drummed the surface of the table. "Not in the sense of how reincarnation is understood. You see, a babe who dies as their first breath is taken hasn't truly lived. They have no past or present to relive. Keella gives them a *rebirth*. A chance to truly live."

"Oh," I whispered, my throat thickening at the *fairness* of the act.

"She can see the soul of all those she captures. My father once said she sees them as her children and then often follows them throughout their lives."

"Like a…" Air whooshed out of my lungs. "She captured *her* soul."

He nodded. "I do not know if she could still follow that soul since it wasn't a rebirth, but it is possible," he told me, and I thought of her smile. "Kolis thought it was, but she never told him who carried Sotoria's soul. If she had, Kolis wouldn't still be looking for it."

My chest ached. Holland had said Keella had paid dearly for intervening with Sotoria's soul. I stopped my imagination from filling in all the terrible ways that Kolis could've ensured that Keella was punished. "Why wouldn't she have?"

"Keella's not much younger than Kolis, but she is one of the few Primals who still believes in right and wrong and a balance that shouldn't be adjusted to fit one's wants or narratives." A warm smile appeared, faint but real, and my heart skipped for a totally different reason. "She tries to be good."

"Sounds like she *is* good."

Ash lifted a shoulder as I took another sip, recognizing the honey-haired goddess swathed in white approaching the empty seat next to Keella. It was Penellaphe. Her stare lifted to the dais as she sat. Penellaphe smiled as she bowed her head to Keella, speaking. I looked away from her, searching for a familiar, ageless face I knew I wouldn't find but was still disappointed when I didn't.

Penellaphe's appearance made me think of something else.

"The title."

I paused while Paxton refilled my chalice. "Thank you," I said to him.

The boy grinned and nodded, then hurried off, careful to avoid Nektas.

"What about the title?" Ash said, stare fixed on the crowd much like Nektas. His wine remained untouched.

"I like it," I shared, feeling a bit foolish as my cheeks warmed.

"You do?" Ash asked, turning to me. I nodded. "I'm glad."

Hoping my face didn't look as hot as it felt, I refocused on the crowd. I found Keella and Penellaphe once more, their heads tipped together as they continued chatting. "There was a little bit of Penellaphe's prophecy in there."

"Not enough that it should raise any alarms," he assured. "It was the only thing that kept coming to my mind. Your hair. Moonlight." The center of his cheeks were the ones that flushed now. He cleared his throat. "And you do look like the brightest moon tonight."

The buzzing warmth of happiness in my chest rivaled that of the embers, and the feeling was as exhilarating as it was terrifying. "And the blood and ash part?"

"It is something the draken like to say," he answered. "It has different meanings. Strength of the blood and bravery of the ash is one of them. Some believe it symbolizes balance and represents life and death." Starlight glinted off his crown as he tilted his head back. "It just all seemed fitting for you."

"It...it is a beautiful title," I said.

The smile he gave me was warm and real, and it wrapped its way around my heart and made me even more desperate to see Veses burn.

My gaze roamed over the faces of those below and beyond us as I shoved thoughts of her aside. There were more masked faces than bare ones. I saw many smiles, but not from most of the Primals. I imagined that if I could sense emotions as Ash could, I would likely be drowning in agitation.

I saw Saion and Rhahar step aside to allow Attes to ascend the dais stairs. I didn't think I could've been more grateful to see the Primal. "I think we're about to have company."

"Appears so." Ash's fingers stilled.

Attes nodded at Nektas as he passed the draken and then stopped before the table, bowing deeply. The crown covered half the scar slicing across his nose and left cheek, but the combination of the two made him appear all the more dangerous, even though he bore no weapons—none of the Primals did. He rose. "I thought I'd be the first to give my congratulations and well wishes as I will be taking my leave soon."

"Appreciated," Ash remarked coolly.

The less-than-friendly greeting didn't go unnoticed. A dimple appeared in Attes's right cheek as he turned luminous eyes on me. "The crown suits you, Consort."

I smiled. "Thank you."

"As does the imprint," he added. "That was an...unexpected development."

I kept my expression the same, even as trepidation skittered through me.

"I feel as if I now truly must make time to visit the lakes in the mortal realm," he said. "Maybe the Arae will bless me with a beauty such as you and an imprint."

"Now is a better time than ever to do so." Ash's fingers slid over the table, curling inwards against his palm as I fought my grin and lost.

That divot deepened as Attes's lips tipped up farther.

"I'm assuming there have been no...events in your Court since the last time we spoke," Ash said.

"Nothing but a few dakkais sniffing around. They left without causing much trouble," Attes confirmed, sending a bolt of relief through me. But also wariness. Kolis must have felt my use of the embers. Why hadn't he come at Attes harder? The Primal tipped his head in Ash's direction. "We need to make some time to speak," Attes reminded him. "The three of us."

An emotion I wasn't quite familiar with surged through me, leaving me a little confused as Ash said, "That can be arranged."

"I look forward to it." Attes bowed deeply. "May your union be a blessing upon the Shadowlands and beyond."

"Thank you," I murmured, reaching for my wine glass as I watched Attes walk toward Nektas. He stopped to speak to the draken.

"Reminds me of a cool iced drink." Ash leaned back, glancing at me. "Your surprise."

I arched a brow. "Was I projecting?"

"You were," he confirmed. "It wasn't the only thing you felt just now."

"Well, I'm hoping you can shine some light on that." I sipped the wine. "Because I have no idea *what* I was just feeling."

"Satisfaction."

My head cut to him.

"Care to share what that jackass said to make you feel that?" he asked, a teasing glint in his gray eyes. "Because that is something I've only felt from you on a few occasions. One of them not quite fit for public conversation."

I snorted. "I can assure you that is not the only time I've been satisfied."

"I know. You projected an indecent amount of satisfaction when you stabbed me in Stonehill."

A short laugh burst from me.

"As you do whenever you hold a weapon to me or manage to

nick my skin or hair," he went on. "I could continue."

"Not necessary," I said, my amusement fading as I tried to figure out why I had felt satisfaction. The answer was all too easy to discover. Acknowledging it was something else entirely. "I...I guess I'm not used to being included in discussions of importance, even ones that involve me, so I was surprised to be included."

"And then satisfied with knowing that you were?"

I shrugged, feeling a bit of warmth creep up my throat. "I know it sounds silly."

"It doesn't."

Peeking over at him, I saw that he watched me intently. I refocused on the crowd below, drawing in a deep breath. "I was never included in any type of conversation, whether it be about the weather or something of importance like the growing tensions between Lasania and other kingdoms. I suppose that doesn't bother many, but for me, it made me feel like anything I may have thought or had to say didn't matter. I...I didn't count. You know, like I wasn't a person, but a..."

"A ghost?"

I nodded, squinting. "Like I was there, but no one actually saw me—interacted with me. It's the only way I can describe it. And being included makes me feel seen. Accepted." Wondering how I allowed the conversation to wander to this point, I cleared my throat. "Anyway, do you know what Attes could want to speak to us about? I feel as if the possibilities are endless at this point."

When Ash didn't respond, I looked at him. He still watched me, his gaze intense, but his stare had softened. "What?" I whispered.

"I hate that you spent so long being made to feel that way. And I loathe that I likely added to that feeling. For that, I do not think I could apologize enough. You are seen and heard, *liessa*."

The embers wiggled and vibrated along with my heart as his comments struck me silent. *Liessa.*

"And you matter. Always." Ash bent, pressing his lips to my temple. The chaste, sweet kiss was as shocking as his words. I melted like butter left in the sun. He withdrew, glancing forward. "Keella approaches."

I blinked, rocked out of what had honestly begun to feel like a *swoon*. I followed his gaze to where Keella had paused to greet Nektas. The draken nudged her arm in response to whatever the Primal had said, and she placed her hand against his cheek, stroking the scaled flesh.

I couldn't recall *anyone* doing that to Nektas.

Eyes wide, I set my glass down before I dropped it. Awe battled with a nervous jolt of energy as the Primal of Rebirth approached us, her flowing gown the same pale blue of her quartz crown.

"Nyktos," Keella spoke, her voice reminding me of the winds in Stonehill. Silver eyes flicked to mine. Lingered. "Consort."

"Hello," I croaked, managing to stumble over the one word.

Ash greeted her with far more grace and confidence. "It is a pleasure and honor to see you, Keella. I hope you are well."

She inclined her head in a regal way that had nothing to do with the crown she wore. "I am." A faint smile appeared as she glanced down at his hand—his left hand. "It has been far too many years since I've seen a *benada*. An *imprimen*. It is truly a blessing. A beautiful one. May I?"

It took me a moment to realize that she was speaking to me. I lifted my right hand. Ash didn't blink as Keella took my hand between hers. A charge of energy skittered up my arm, but she didn't react as she drew a warm finger over the golden swirls on the center of my palm.

Russet curls bounced as she gave a slight shake of her head. "I honestly didn't believe I would see such a thing again."

"Neither did I," Ash stated smoothly, even as my heart tripped all over itself. If there were any two Primals in this entire coliseum who might not believe it was the Arae, it would be Embris—who'd left— and Keella.

"I am glad that I have." Her eyes, a whirlpool of silver, lifted to mine.

My throat tightened as so many questions rose—things I could not ask at the coronation and risk being overheard. But it took great effort for me not to ask if she knew it was I—the one who Eythos, with her aid, had placed Sotoria's soul in. Could she see Sotoria even now? Inside me? Could she tell if one soul existed or two?

"Truly." Keella patted my hand before releasing it. Her smile mirrored the earlier one she had given me...

And I...I begin to think that she *did* know. "As am I."

The Primal's attention shifted to Ash. "The title you bestowed on your Consort is also beautiful. Perhaps even...another *blessing*. May I ask what inspired such wording?"

The question was politely asked, but there was an edge to it—not one of anger but something different.

"You will likely be disappointed to learn that I was simply inspired by my Consort's hair."

I nearly choked on my breath at his honest answer.

"Not at all. More like...enthralled to learn that. Hopeful," she said, and my gaze flew to her. "I do not wish to take more of your time. May your union be a blessing." Her gaze met mine again, and then she turned.

Jolted out of my shock, I said, "Thank you."

The Primal of Rebirth faced us once more, and that smile returned. An old smile. Knowing. Clever. The embers in my chest hummed. She inclined her head and then looked at Ash. "Your father would be so proud of you."

42

There wasn't time to speak privately with Ash or to take more than a few moments to make use of the privy as celebrators descended upon the dais. The elaborate crowns of the Primals, their reserved, wry greetings blurred into masked faces and looser, warmer smiles as they flooded the shield-lined aisle to where Ash and I sat.

Shouts echoed above the music every couple of minutes, jarring me as one well-wisher replaced another.

"Should I be concerned?" I asked Ector, who had come to stand at my side.

"No." Ector smiled down at me. "They are cheers for their new Consort."

A little thrown by the declaration, I glanced at Ash. He smiled at what a masked male said, but at some point during the greetings, he'd lowered his hand to where mine rested on my thigh. No one, except possibly Ector and Rhahar, who stood at Ash's side, could see where his hand was, but it was a shock to me, nonetheless. The touch wasn't for display, and the weight of his hand against mine was grounding, comforting as I…as I was *seen* by so many.

Only Kyn and Hanan didn't approach, and I lost sight of them in the throng of people who continued forward in a wave. I'd been growing tired, my neck starting to ache from the weight of the crown, but the shouts—the cheers—had beaten back the exhaustion. It was...nice to be *welcomed*, and I couldn't help but wonder if my mother had ever been welcomed by her people. Or my father before he died. I couldn't remember. King Ernald and my mother had grown so distant from the people they were supposed to care for, but Ezra was different. She wasn't ruling from a tower behind a wall.

Plates of food had been replaced with cups that were kept full, the music more frenetic, heavier, and I didn't think any of the Primals remained in the Shadowlands by the time Ash leaned in, letting me know that it was time for us to take our leave. Deafening cheers reverberated off the star-strewn sky as we made our way back to the entry house.

The carriage I'd arrived in waited for us outside the coliseum, surrounded by guards and soldiers in gray. Saion stood at the open doors, bowing upon our approach. "*Your Highnesses*," he drawled.

Ash sighed. "You're really going to start with that?"

"It's not for your benefit," Saion remarked, winking at me.

"Of course," Ash murmured, a faint grin appearing as he climbed into the carriage, then turned, extending a hand toward me. "Consort."

The wild fluttering feeling was back as I took his hand, welcoming the zap of energy coursing from his palm to mine. He helped me into the carriage as several of the draken took flight from the pillars, lifting to the sky above us. I moved to the bench opposite Ash when Rhain appeared in the carriage's open door, holding two large shadowstone boxes. He placed them on the floor of the interior.

"Crowns," Ash explained, reaching up to remove his.

A little relieved that I could remove the heavy—albeit beautiful—crown, I carefully worked it free from my hair as Rhain opened the first box. My neck immediately thanked me.

Ash knelt between the benches, placing his crown in the ivory velvet interior. As Rhain closed one box and opened the other, Ash took my crown, his fingers brushing mine and sending a shiver of awareness through me.

"They will remain with you two," Rhain explained, sending me a quick glance as he slid the heavy boxes against the foot of the bench I sat on. "And then they will be moved to a small chamber off the throne room, where they are stored and can be retrieved whenever you like."

"Thank you," I said, and he nodded with one more skittering glance. I hoped he wasn't thinking of what he'd told me before the coronation.

It was something I couldn't allow myself to think about as my gaze found its way to where Ash lounged in the seat across from me.

"We will be on our way in a few moments," Rhain announced before closing the doors and leaving us alone in the soft, dim light of a sconce, either powered by fuel...or Ash.

"Some of my soldiers will ride ahead," Ash explained, his elbow resting on the ledge of the carriage wall. "To make sure the road is clear for us."

"Is that necessary?"

"Not really," he admitted with a shadowed grin. "But they're taking the safety of their Consort seriously."

I arched a brow. "But not their Primal?"

"I think they're more worried about you than me."

"Sounds a bit...sexist."

"Possibly." His grin deepened, revealing a hint of fang in the glow of the sconce. "But not all the guards nor the soldiers are aware of your ability to handle yourself. However, even if they were, they would still want to make sure the path you travel on is a safe one. That is their duty."

"One they chose?"

His fingers slid across his chin as he eyed me. "All those who serve as guards or soldiers do so out of choice, fully prepared to take on all the responsibilities of such a position. Is it not that way in Lasania?"

"Some say there is a choice for whether one joins the armies. But is it really a choice for those who weren't able to learn skills while growing up or cannot afford to attend universities to discover new ones?" I said. "For many, joining the armies is the only way to feed themselves or their families, so I don't see it as a choice."

"Neither do I," Ash agreed, and he was silent as the carriage remained still. He offered his hand to me once more. "Sit with me?"

I halted for a moment, mostly out of surprise, and then I rose, taking his hand. He didn't lead me to the seat beside him; instead, he adjusted himself so he sat with his back against the carriage wall and placed me on the bench between one bent leg and the other that he had propped on the floor. The shimmering gown spilled over the side of the bench and his right leg.

"I can taste your surprise," he murmured as he brushed the strands of hair from the nape of my neck.

I gave a little jerk at the touch of his cool fingers against my neck. "When you asked that I sit with you, I didn't think you meant that I was to basically sit in your lap."

"Do you mind?"

"No." I drew my thumb against the inside of my palm, following the swirl there.

"Good," he replied. "How is your neck?"

"A little achy."

"That's what I thought. The weight can take a bit to get used to." His fingers pressed into the tight muscles on either side of my spine, moving in slow circles. My lips parted on a heady sigh. "How does that feel?"

"It feels…" My eyes drifted shut. "Like magic."

His chuckle was rough as his thumbs pressed in, soothing and working out the knots gathered there. My back arched, my breasts straining against the bodice as he worked his way down. It really was like magic, how quickly he eased the tension that had gathered there.

And how quickly he built up a wholly different tension that gathered itself far from his touch. One relaxing. One exhilarating. I couldn't pick which was better, not even with a sword held to my throat.

Ash's palms slid over the diamonds to curl around my shoulders. "How does your neck feel now?"

"Perfect," I breathed, only then becoming aware that I'd reclined against his chest, and that the carriage had begun to move at a snail's pace. "Thank you, Ash."

He tensed against me.

My eyes opened as my stomach tumbled. "Do you…do you mind that I call you that?"

"No. Not at all," he stated roughly, trailing his hands up and down my arms. "I missed it when you didn't."

Now it was my heart that spun as I turned my head to the side. "Really?"

"Really." His breath danced over my cheek as his hands found their way to my waist. "I feel a need to admit something to you."

"What?"

"I know we could be discussing many things right now. Plans for Irelone. What provoked this change in what you wish from me—from us," he said, and my breath skipped as my eyes opened. "Your thoughts on the coronation."

I bit my lip as his hands coasted down my hips, relieved that he had moved on. "But?"

"But only one thing has occupied my thoughts from the moment I saw you in this dress and heard you call me Ash." His words were a silken caress in the carriage. "And it's not seeing you out of this dress, although that is a close second."

I trembled.

"Nor was it seeing you bare with nothing but the crown atop your head."

My pulse picked up as his left hand slid across my stomach. "Was that a close third?"

"A close fourth." His hand moved even lower on my abdomen, sending a wave of rippling pleasure. "Third was imagining you naked upon the throne."

"I'm beginning to see a trend here."

"More like an obsession," he countered, lips brushing the curve of my ear and sending a delicate series of shivers through me. "One I'm likely not worthy of exploring."

I stiffened. "You're worthy."

He made a rough sound against my neck, moving his left hand in slow circles that steadily made their way below my navel. "Am I? Doesn't really matter at the moment because I'm too greedy, too selfish to care," he said, and he was none of those things as he slid his other hand down my outer thigh.

I started to tell him he wasn't greedy or selfish, but before I could get my tongue around the words, his hand drifted lower and over my thigh.

"What is this?" Ash asked, tilting his head to the side as he hiked up the skirt of the gown, not at all mindful of the many tiny diamonds as he bared my leg all the way to the top of my thigh. "Your dagger." He made a deep, rumbling sound as his hand closed over the hilt. The touch of his cool fingers against my flesh caused me to jerk. "Fuck."

I felt the scrape of his fangs against my throat. I gasped, places all over my body tensing deliciously.

"I think seeing you with nothing but that dagger strapped to your thigh has taken second place. Not first, though," he told me. I jolted as his fingers coasted over my inner thigh. "Do you know what that is?"

My heart pounded as his fingers skated over the lacy edges of my undergarment, slipping over them. My hips nearly came clear off the bench as his fingers pressed against the center of the thin garment.

Heart thrumming, I couldn't answer his questions as his fingers drifted back and forth. The touch was featherlight until it wasn't. He rubbed me, drawing his fingers up my very center to the most sensitive part of me. There was no doubt in my mind that he could feel the dampness of that thin undergarment increasing with each drag of his fingers, or that he could taste the rising desire. And that there was no hiding my response to him. My want. My need.

And I *loved* that.

Eyes open and fixed on the carriage wall at the other end of the bench, I gripped his arm as he began moving his fingers over the undergarment, dragging them down and back up to where desire throbbed.

"Sera?" His lips brushed my temple.

"W-what?"

"Do you know what took first place in occupying my thoughts?"

"No," I rasped in a rush of liquid heat.

"Hearing you call me Ash," he murmured. "When you come."

I shuddered, a heaviness settling in my breasts. And lower, where his hand was between my thighs, sharp, aching desire pulsed.

"Will you appease my obsession?" he asked. "Will you call me Ash when you come?"

My chest rose sharply as I gripped his knee with my other hand, my hips beginning to move restlessly against his touch. "I'll call you whatever you like."

He nipped at the skin between my shoulder and neck. "That's all I want to hear."

"I can do that," I promised as the carriage rocked forward, traveling over the bumpy terrain.

He groaned, pulling me tighter into the vee of his legs. "I can't wait to hear it."

"Then don't wait," I whispered.

"Wasn't planning on it," he growled.

My hips jerked as he slid his fingers under the thin undergarment and through the dusting of fine curls.

Ash...he teased. He *played*. For seconds. Minutes. Longer. I was shaking, gasping by the time he delved a finger inside me. The shock of sensations between my heated flesh and his icy finger was maddening, and the feel of his second finger left me burning for more.

I tipped my head back. "I need you," I said. His chest was rising and falling as rapidly as mine against my back. "I need *you*." I reached down, gripping his wrist. "Inside me."

Ash's fingers stilled.

"I want *you* inside me," I whispered against the curve of his jaw. "When I come and call you Ash."

"Fuck," he growled, easing his fingers from me. He gripped the lace, tearing it with one sharp pull that sent a wicked thrill through me. "What's stopping you?"

Nothing.

Absolutely nothing. Not even the swaying motion of the carriage as I rose, and Ash straightened himself, dropping both feet to the floor. He undid his breeches, gripping himself as I climbed onto the bench. Grasping the bar near the ceiling with one hand to balance myself as I planted my knees on either side of his hips, I hoisted my skirt with the other. He pulled me to his chest, trapping the gown between us as he drew me down onto his rigid length.

I moaned at the icy-hot feel of him, stretching and filling me in one scorching slide. His hand fisted my hair, drawing my mouth to his. The kiss stole my breath in a clash of teeth and tongues as he rocked beneath me. My fingers slipped from the bar, falling to his shoulder as I rode him, as we panted into each other's mouths.

The sound of our bodies coming together got lost in the churning of the wheels outside, but inside the carriage, we were *lost* in our gasps, our moans, and in building, coiling tension. He shook, grunting as his hips thrust, and I ground against him, quivering.

The release came hot and cold, hard and quick as I spasmed on his cock. Intense waves of pleasure swept through me as I tore my mouth free from his and called him what he wanted as I came.

Ash.

My muscles still felt like liquid when Bele greeted us on our return to the palace. Nothing had happened in our absence. Veses remained in stasis. Bele was mostly bored.

Ash and I hadn't lingered, making our way upstairs as Rhain took the crowns to the chamber near the throne room. An inexplicable nervousness invaded my senses, causing my heart to feel like it was bouncing all over my chest by the time we neared the doors to our quarters.

Would we go our separate ways, only to reunite in the morning to leave for Irelone? Sleep in our own beds? What'd happened in the carriage—what I'd admitted to Ash—didn't change things.

But I wanted it to.

I wanted to spend tonight together. And every night going forward. But so much had been left unsaid between us, and too much had been spoken in haste. It was likely that we'd continue as—

I stopped.

Stopped walking. Stopped the anxious spiral of questions that I couldn't easily gain the answer to.

Ash halted a step ahead, turning to me. "Sera?"

Pressure threatened to squeeze my chest, cutting off my air, but I forced in a deep breath, holding it as I curled my fingers inward, against the imprint. All I had to do was *speak* and share what I wanted. And while I could easily make demands of every sort, this was different. This was *more*, and it left me feeling fragile. I wished I was privileged enough to even think that being honest about feelings or needs was nothing more than a simple conversation.

"I don't want to sleep alone tonight." Warmth slid across my cheeks. "I mean, I would like to stay with you. To sleep. Or talk. Or whatever. I...I just want to be with you."

The flecks of essence in his eyes spun to life, beginning to swirl wildly as Ash went completely still. I could've sworn the very air in the hall ceased to move right along with him, but then his chest rose sharply. Tension left his features, and for the briefest moment, he—a Primal of Death—looked as vulnerable as I felt. "I would like that, Sera. Very much."

My smile was immediate and so wide it felt like my face might crack. "Okay," I whispered, some of the nerves beginning to calm. "Your chambers, then?"

Ash didn't move, though. He stared as the eather continued whipping through his irises at dizzying speeds, as if something were occurring that he had no idea how to proceed with.

I shifted from one slippered foot to the next. "Are you all right?"

"Yeah. Yes." Ash blinked, giving a small shake of his head. "It's just that you're...you're beautiful."

A pleasant, heady thrill swept through me despite the tension returning to the corners of his mouth. "I'm not sure if you think that's necessarily a good thing. But thank you."

His eyes widened slightly. "It's a good thing. I think—I mean, it *is* a good thing. More than just good," he said. A faint pink splotched his cheeks as he rubbed his hand over his chest. "Your smile just then? I don't think I've ever seen you smile like that before."

"Was it a bad smile?"

"No." He came forward, taking my hand in his. A soft breath shuddered out from him. "It's not bad."

Ash then led me to his doors, the imprint on my hand tingling a bit against his. He was quiet as we entered his chambers, several of the wall sconces flickering to life.

"Are you sure I won't be able to do that after I Ascend?" I turned to him, breathing in the scent of him that pervaded the air.

"Likely not," he said, closing the door. "Other than the Primals, only the eldest of gods can turn their essence into power—electricity."

"That's really disappointing."

Chuckling under his breath, he strode toward the table near the balcony, where a decanter sat. "Care for a drink?"

"Yes, please."

He arched a brow at me as he picked up the decanter. "Since I became so distracted in the carriage," he said, and I grinned, hoping for more distractions like that in the future. Many more. "I didn't get a chance to ask what you thought of the coronation."

"It was beautiful—the lights and the people." I sat—carefully— on the edge of the couch, placing my hands over the diamond-adorned skirt of my gown. I was still surprised that none had fallen off during the return to the Shadowlands. A true testament to Erlina's skill. "And it was easier than I expected."

"You thought there'd be some sort of disturbance?" He twisted off the crystal stopper.

"I did. Or that Kolis would change his mind and show. Do you think it's odd that Kolis only sent a few dakkais to Vathi instead of an army of them?"

"I imagine the dakkais lost the scent since it wasn't as strong as when you Ascended Bele. If the trail had lingered, they likely would've done to Vathi what they tried to do to the Shadowlands."

Nodding, I watched him pour the amber liquor into two glasses, thinking of the Primal of Rebirth. "I think Keella knows it's me—that

I'm the one she helped place Sotoria's soul in. It's hard to explain, but it's the way...I don't know. How she smiled at me." Realizing that didn't exactly sound like legitimate evidence, I shrugged as I took a sip. The liquor was a bit sweeter than the whiskey I'd drunk before. "What is this?"

"It's whiskey but made differently. Caramel forward, or so they say," he said. "Do you like it? If not, I can get you something else."

"It's fine." I took another drink, liking it. "I could be wrong— about Keella."

"You may not be, Sera."

I blew out a low breath, unsure how to feel about any of that. "But she's to be trusted, right? If she does know that Kolis is searching for me, she has never told him."

He nodded. "She's one of the few Primals that I somewhat trust."

"Somewhat?"

"I trust no Primal one hundred percent." He glanced at me. "Especially not when it comes to you."

I didn't know what to say to that, so I took a longer drink. I knew better than to ask about Attes. His trust of that Primal was a rather reluctant one. I glanced at Ash, finding him watching me in that wholly intense way of his. Dragging my finger around the rim of the glass, I changed the subject. "Are you nervous about tomorrow?"

"I'm excited. We'll have the knowledge of how to transfer the embers." He paused. "Are you?"

"I think I'm a mixture of many things. Nervous that we won't be able to find Delfai or that he won't be able to help us. Excited about the prospect that he will have the knowledge," I admitted. "I know it won't change everything immediately even once the transfer happens. We'll still have Kolis to deal with. But you'll be the true Primal of Life soon, as you always should have been. And that's important."

"What's important is that your life will be saved. That's what matters."

My gaze cut to his. *You matter. Always.* Those three words were more powerful than the ones I hadn't been able to speak. One could easily argue that him seizing his true destiny was far more important than my life, but I...I believed he truly felt that my life was more important.

And that made what I felt for him root itself even deeper.

"I've been wanting to ask you something all night," he said. "What changed this?"

I bit down on the inside of my cheek. "Changed what?"

He gave me a knowing look with a raised brow. "You said that you only wanted to be my Consort in title."

"But I did say that I wanted to be more than that before," I pointed out. "Am I not entitled to change my mind?"

One side of his lips kicked up. "You're entitled to the realm, Sera, but that's a rather stark change in emotions when I would think that Veses' most recent actions would've fortified your wishes to remain distant."

My mouth dried, and I didn't think any amount of whiskey would alleviate that. I'd been doing my best not to think about what I'd learned—mostly succeeding in that endeavor. "It wasn't a change in emotions. What I feel for you didn't change," I said carefully. "My opinion on how I wanted to proceed changed."

"My apologies," he drawled, thick lashes shielding his eyes. "What provoked this change of opinion then?"

I squirmed a little. "Does it matter?"

"It does."

My grip on the glass tightened. I didn't want to betray what Rhain had shared with me. I also couldn't tell him that I loved him—that I'd been in love with him before I learned of the deal he'd struck with Veses to keep me safe. I glanced at him, and my silly heart swelled so fiercely that my breath snagged. A storm of emotions flooded me. I didn't feel fear or disbelief as I looked at him. I felt *wonder*. A wild fluttering in my chest and stomach. A need for him that went beyond the physical. A powerful empathy for him—the need to protect him even though he was more than capable of doing that himself. A feeling of rightness, or as Aios had said, the feeling of being at home. Of being *seen*. The knowledge that I'd do anything for him. Anything. The fear that I would never be worthy of what he had sacrificed for me. And the determination that I would do everything to be that. I was drowning in all those feelings until my heart began to pound with the intensity of what I felt—with the knowledge that it was he who held my heart—only him.

Those thick lashes of his lifted as his gaze roamed over my face. Seconds ticked by. "What are you thinking about?"

I stiffened. Oh, gods, I'd likely been projecting. "What do you feel?"

"I don't know." He sounded confounded, curious. "I...I taste sweetness." His brows pinched. "It reminds me of chocolate and strawberries."

"And you don't know what that is?"

"I don't," Ash said, frowning.

Gods.

My heart cracked a little as I quickly looked away. He didn't know what he tasted because he didn't know what love *tasted* like. Or felt like. Neither did I. Not until I realized what I'd been feeling, but Ash...it was different for him because his *kardia* had been removed. Love was never something welcomed or wanted.

I swallowed the knot, hoping I wasn't projecting anything and that he wasn't reading me. I didn't want him to feel that sorrow.

"You still haven't answered my question," he persisted softly. "Why am I now Ash to you? Why would you want to be more than a Consort in title only after I hurt you? After I—"

"I know," I cut in, briefly closing my eyes.

"Know what?"

"I know you didn't betray me." I sat the glass aside, choosing my words carefully. "And that you truly didn't want to hurt my feelings. That it...it wasn't like that."

Ash was quiet.

Squaring my shoulders, I pushed anything I might feel down so deep, he wouldn't be able to pick up on it. Other than my anger, I doubted he would want to taste anything else. I twisted toward him, hoping I didn't tear any of the diamonds free. "I know about Veses."

His features sharpened as he lowered the glass to his knee. That was the only change. The only sign that he knew what I was referencing. "Did she tell you?"

I opened my mouth but decided it was probably best that he believed that. I didn't want him to be upset with Rhain. "I..." I trailed off, having no idea what to say. The deal he made involved me, but he had been the one who sacrificed. Him that Veses' cruelty had impacted. This wasn't about how I felt about it. My horror or anger or agony. There was only one thing I could say. "Thank you."

The glass shattered in Ash's hand.

Gasping, I shot to my feet as liquor and glass fell across his knee and onto the floor. Streaks of red smeared his palm. "You cut yourself."

"I'm fine." He closed his fingers over the pieces of glass.

"You're cutting yourself even more!" I bent, grasping his hand as I brushed the shards of glass from his knee and the settee. The charge of energy was stronger. Blood welled between his fingers. "Good gods," I whispered, returning to sit beside him. "Open your hand."

"I told you, I'm fine."

"Open your hand, Ash!"

He made no move to do so.

Cursing, I pried his fingers loose. Pieces of glass were embedded deep into his palm, slicing through the golden swirl. The slices free of glass had already begun to heal. "I know you're a Primal," I said, straightening his hand out as I placed it against my knee. "And you'll heal just fine, but I'm also pretty sure you won't with glass in your hand."

"You're going to get blood on your dress," he stated.

"I don't care." I picked out a sliver of glass, dropping it onto the small table. "It's not like I'll wear it again."

"Why not?"

"I don't think one wears their wedding dress more than once." I dug out another larger piece. Ash hissed. "Sorry."

"Don't—" He drew in a deep breath. "Don't apologize. Don't thank me."

I briefly closed my eyes, cursing at myself. I wanted to apologize again because I'd obviously said the wrong thing.

"And you can wear the damn dress again whenever you feel like it."

Nodding, I swallowed as I plucked out another piece. The scent of his blood washed over me as I smoothed my thumb over the imprint, searching for specks of glass I couldn't see.

"Is that why you call me Ash now?"

"What?" I looked back at him.

His flesh had thinned, deepening with shadows. "Because you learned that I've been Veses' personal blood meal and suddenly realized you wanted to be my Consort?"

"No."

His beautiful mouth twisted into a cold, cruel smirk. "Really, *liessa?*"

"*No*," I repeated. "I told you I wanted to be your Consort before."

"But that changed."

"It did. Because I didn't know everything when it came to her, and I..." I turned back to his palm, seeing that several more places still seeped blood. "I don't want to say the wrong thing."

"You won't."

I scraped a tiny piece of glass out with my nail. "I just did."

"That has nothing to do with you," he bit out. "Speak."

His tone would've set me off at any other time, but not now. "My feelings were hurt when I saw you two together. That changed what I wanted. You know that. But now that I know why you two…were together, my thoughts on it have changed."

"We weren't *together*," he stated, and the temperature of the room dropped.

"I know. I…" Despite him demanding that I speak, he was the one that needed to, but only if he wanted to. Other than what I knew I needed to say, I had to shut the hell up. "What you did to protect me isn't why I feel that way. I wanted to be more to you than a Consort in title only before I learned about that. What it did was help me understand a bit of what I saw. We don't need to talk about it if you don't want to." I looked over my shoulder once more. "But know that if you don't kill her, I will find a way to do it myself."

He stared at me for a moment and then laughed. Deeply. Hard.

"I'm being serious," I told him.

"Not a single part of me doubts that."

I held his gaze. "The bitch is dead."

"Agreed."

"Good." I returned to his palm, carefully plucking out the remaining glass. I only knew I'd gotten them all when no fresh blood seeped. "All done."

"Thank you," he said roughly.

Pressing my lips together, I ran my finger across his palm—over the golden swirl. I reached the end near his thumb and then his fingers curled, threading through mine. His blood stained both our hands, but him holding mine was a…well, a beautiful sight. I brought our joined hands to my mouth and placed a kiss on the top of his.

His shudder flowed through to me.

Minutes ticked by.

"I didn't want you to know," he uttered. "I didn't want you to feel responsible."

I fought the urge to tell him that what I felt was the last thing he needed to be worried about.

"And I…I didn't want you—anyone—to know what kind of control she had. What kind of *complication* she is," he continued after a moment, speaking to the back of my bowed head. "Attes knows she feeds from me, but he doesn't know why. Only a few do. But we were never together. She fed from me. Sometimes, she made it pleasurable. Other times, it burned like the Abyss. And if I disagreed with where she wanted to feed from, it was almost always the latter in terms of how she did it. I actually preferred when it was that way. It was far better than the alternative. Gaining any sort of pleasure from her was—and is—the last thing I want. But the only thing of mine she has ever had in her is my blood."

Whatever relief I felt at learning that it hadn't gone further than her taking his blood was short-lived because forcing pleasure onto someone without their consent was still a violation, no matter what their history was. Blackmailing them into servicing any need was still a violation.

Closing my eyes, I kept my emotions in check because this wasn't about me or how I felt. I pressed another kiss to the top of his hand. The backs of my eyes stung as I beat back the building rage and sorrow. I couldn't allow any of that to take center stage. I stayed in control.

His hand tightened around mine, and a few moments passed. "Whatever skill you believe I have is pure luck because I honestly had no idea what I was doing." He exhaled, and...gods, I wished I hadn't said that to him. Why anyone, including me, assumed that someone without experience couldn't give pleasure. That was so incredibly childish of me to think. "Still don't, to be honest."

I kissed his hand a third time.

"But Veses...she didn't want me. She still doesn't want me. Not really. She wants Kolis. Always has," he said, and surprise bolted through me. "And since he's never wanted anything to do with her, I'm the next best thing. But I also didn't want her. It was the refusal that got her coming back. Probably the same thing with Kolis."

I still thought that perhaps her feelings toward Ash had changed. That she had come to care for him. But gods, how could you do what she did to him to someone you cared about?

Ash curled his arm, tugging me back. Another burst of surprise rippled through me as he pulled me between his legs and against him. His chest rose sharply but fell slowly. He relaxed into me. All but his hand. His fingers remained tightly joined with mine.

"She found a way in eventually," he finally said. "She followed me the night you were brought to the Shadow Temple. We cannot feel the presence of other Primals in the mortal realm as strongly as we can in

Iliseeum. I didn't even realize she was there until she came to the Shadowlands a few days later. She must've overheard enough to put two and two together, and when she was here last, she knew there would be no more times beyond that. So, she was really pushing the limits that night."

Three years.

He had been forced to feed her for three years.

I wondered if it was possible to make someone's *death* last for three years.

"I hadn't expected her to come so soon, and I know I locked that door because I didn't want anyone to see that. Especially you. She must've felt you..." He cleared his throat. "I don't know. I should've told you when you asked after waking up, but I couldn't get the words out. I just..."

"It's okay." I turned in his embrace, tucking my head against his shoulder. "I understand."

"I just...I couldn't let her do what I knew she would if I refused. That was my decision. Not yours."

I took a deep breath, swallowing all the questions of how and why he could have decided that at a time when he didn't know me or anything about the embers. "I wish she hadn't put you in a situation to make that decision."

"There are a lot of things I regret. But keeping you out of Kolis's hands is not one of them," he said. "And that doesn't erase or make anything all right." His chin brushed the top of my head. "But it's done now."

"It will be," I whispered. "When she's dead."

He laughed, the sound rough but warm. "Bloodthirsty."

I didn't even try to deny it.

Ash was quiet for some time. When he spoke again, his voice was barely above a whisper. "Thank you."

My eyes opened. "What are you thanking me for?"

"For just... Just for being you," he said.

"I'm sure many people would not thank me just for being myself, but you're welcome."

"Those people should die, too."

I laughed softly.

"Sera?"

"Yeah?"

"I wish..." His voice thick, he trailed off and then swallowed.

"What?"

Whatever Ash had been about to say was lost as he tipped my head back and brought his mouth to mine. He kissed me until the ugliness of Veses faded into the background, until any concerns or worries about what we would find in Irelone went away, and until there was no space for anything but the feel of his lips against mine. Then there was nothing more than his arms around me, holding me. Me holding him.

Nothing but this moment.

Us.

It was all that mattered.

43

I awoke sometime later to the feel of Ash's body through the linen shirt I'd borrowed after he'd patiently undone every single tiny button on the coronation gown.

The garment was no barrier against the hard, icy-hot press of his body, nor had it stayed in place as I slept, riding up to my hips. I knew this because absolutely nothing separated his rigid cock from the curve of my ass.

I blinked open sleepy eyes, unable to make out much in the darkened chamber. I had no idea how long we'd slept, but it didn't feel like that much time had passed after we'd left the couch and gone to bed. *Together.*

To sleep.

I'd thought both of us were exhausted—physically and emotionally—from the coronation, the carriage ride, and what we'd discussed upon our return.

And I figured he was still asleep, his body's response some sort of physical reaction and not necessarily a purposeful one. Which meant I also needed to go back to sleep and not dwell on the feel of him or think about that carriage ride. Which was easier said than done as I wiggled restlessly in his embrace—

The quick, deep rise of his chest against my back stilled me. Was he awake? I started to turn my head but stopped as his hips shifted behind mine. I bit my lip as his cock slipped over the curve of my ass, eliciting a sudden, sharp slice of pleasure.

My heart kicked up. "Ash?"

"You shouldn't call me that," he said, his voice rough in the darkness.

Confusion rose. "I thought you wanted me to."

"I do." A pause. "But that may have been an unwise choice."

"Why?"

"I would think it's obvious." His breath stirred the hair on the top of my head. "Hearing you call me that makes me think of the other things occupying my mind for most of the night."

Heat slipped through my veins as sleepiness vanished. "The one in first place?"

"Especially that."

"Do you want to hear me call your name when I come again?"

"What do you think?" His body hardened even more behind mine.

The flame of desire was shockingly quick to ignite. "You can have that," I whispered, and he groaned as I rocked my ass against his cock. "You can take me if you want."

"I want to, but I'm..."

"What?" I reached up, finding his cheek in the darkness. His skin was cooler...harder, almost like stone. My pulse skittered. "What's wrong?"

He didn't answer for a long moment. Then he finally did. "I'm hungry. And if I get inside you right now, I wouldn't be able to stop myself. I shouldn't even be in this bed right now. I was going to get up, but you feel... You're so warm."

I flashed cold and then hot. "Will taking my blood harm me? Because I'm so close to the Culling? Even if you took just enough to ease you?"

"It's not that." His voice had roughened. Thickened. "It wouldn't hurt you for me to take a little."

I forced a swallow. "Then feed."

He didn't move.

And in the quiet, I remembered how he'd wanted to feed when we'd been on the floor of my chamber but hadn't. I began to understand his reluctance. It went beyond what Kolis had made him do in the past. Feeding had become tied up with Veses, even if he hadn't fed from her. And I knew he didn't feel worthy of taking from me, no matter what I told him.

Only the gods knew what kind of emotions were associated with feeding, but I knew he needed to feed, and the only way I could help was to offer myself.

Drawing in a shallow breath, I arched my back, stretching my neck and exposing the length of my throat as my rear pressed against him.

His shudder rocked me.

I slid my palm down his cheek to his granite-hard jaw. Then I placed my hand on the bed before me. "I'm your Consort now, and I want to be of aid to you," I whispered, hopefully choosing the right words. "If you will allow it."

Ash went silent and still behind me. I didn't feel his chest move, and a deep sorrow rose. A pain that was not for me but for him—

Then he moved in that fast way of his. I was suddenly on my belly, my cheek on his forearm, and then he *struck*.

His fangs pierced my flesh with shocking speed. The burst of sharp, burning pain left me momentarily stunned, but it was brief. A heartbeat, maybe two passed as he closed his mouth over the wound and drew my blood into him. The pain became raw, nerve-stretching *pleasure*.

Ash drank.

He drank deep as his fingers dug into the flesh of my hip, and mine curled into the soft sheet beneath me. His mouth moved hungrily against my throat as the heat spread from his bite, flaming those earlier sparks into a wildfire. I wanted to move beneath him, to lift my hips to him, but I remembered what he'd told me. How she used to push the limits. So, I held myself still. I flamed. Burned. But I didn't move. I let him have complete control. He needed that more than I needed him to seize it.

And he did.

Ash swallowed as the weight of his body settled over mine, trapping me between the bed and him. A heady thrill joined the flush of desire as he lifted my ass and thrust into me. Hot, wet, and aching, I was more than ready to take him.

And I did.

He moved over me and in me, hard and fast. There was no chance of catching his rhythm or following it. He set the pace, and he didn't slow, not even when I came apart, calling out his name so he could hear it. Feel it. He still didn't stop, his hips pounding into me as he took and took, and I loved it—the wildness of him in control. The drag and pull of his cock, of his mouth. And when he came, I whispered his name over and over, and it was a brief forever before I felt the slide of his tongue against my throat and his hips slowed. I wasn't sure how long we stayed that way, with him inside me, and his cheek pressed to my shoulder. All I knew was that I wanted to stay there, and I immediately missed the feel of him as he eased onto his side, tugging me so I was once more nestled against his chest.

"You okay?" he asked.

"Yes." I cleared my throat as my heart rate finally began to slow. "You?"

His hand slid across my belly to my hip. His *warm* hand. "I wish…" Voice thickening, he trailed off into the darkness, never finishing what he'd been about to say.

Telling me what he wished for.

Ash and I shadowstepped into Massene, a village not too far from the capital of Irelone, the following afternoon.

We arrived in a forest on the outskirts of Cauldra Manor in a blink of an eye. Maybe two. It had felt like the last time, but a strange nervousness invaded my system, making me jittery.

"That was quick," I whispered.

"It was." His gaze searched mine.

"I'm guessing it wasn't supposed to feel *that* quick to me," I surmised.

Ash was still holding me tightly, my feet several inches off the ground, chest to chest, heart to heart. His was beating faster than mine. "We traveled even farther than the last time. And between realms. It should've knocked you out."

"The embers," I said, sighing. "I know. They're getting stronger."

Lowering me to the ground, he drew his hand up the length of my braid. "They'll be out of you soon."

Hopefully, I thought, but I didn't say that. I didn't want to give life to the possibility that we wouldn't find Delfai or that he wouldn't be able to help us. "So, what are we going to do? Walk straight up to the manor's entrance and demand to be taken to the Princess?"

"Sounds like a good enough plan to me."

I raised a brow. "Really?"

"Do you think they will refuse a Primal's request?" Ash gave my braid a gentle tug.

My forehead creased. "You're going to reveal who you are?"

"It makes things a hell of a lot easier, doesn't it?"

"It does."

A grin appeared, beating back the shadows that had gathered under his eyes, and I felt the curve of his lips tug at my heart. "Plus, there's some level of amusement to be had when mortals realize they're in the presence of a Primal."

Some of the anxiousness eased as I laughed. "I bet it will involve a lot of screaming and yelling."

"And praying."

"This should be entertaining." I stepped back.

Ash's hand slid to mine, stopping me. The feel of his skin being warm once more sent a pleasant thrill through me. "It's going to be okay, Sera."

My breath caught. "Am I projecting again?"

"You were." The eather had calmed in his eyes.

"What...what does anxiety taste like?" I asked.

"Like too-heavy cream." He swept his thumb over the top of my hand. "What does it feel like to you?"

Pressing my lips together, I thought about how to explain it. "Like it tastes to you. Like something...too thick to swallow. Suffocating." Uncomfortable, I looked down at our entwined fingers. The golden imprint along the top of his hand shimmered in the soft, dappled sunlight. I shook my head as we stood in silence. "It's this...constant feeling that something bad is about to go down, even when nothing is happening. And when there's a chance that things can go bad? It becomes the only thing that *can* happen." My throat thickened. "I know that probably makes no sense, but it's like a crushing weight on your chest, and it's always there, even when you get used to it and don't really feel it. It's still there, just waiting. And I...I don't know. That's how it feels."

"I get it," he said, his throat working on a swallow. "I don't know how it feels firsthand, but I understand what you're saying." His thumb kept moving over the top of my hand, tracing the lines of the imprint. "I wish I could do something to change how it feels for you."

The swift, swelling motion in my chest threatened to lift me to the needled branches. My cheeks warmed, and I wasn't sure if it was from what I'd shared or his words. His understanding. His desire to make it better. I wasn't entirely embarrassed by what I'd shared. I just wasn't used to talking about it. But it felt…good to do so. Almost like a chunk of the weight upon my chest had eased. I imagined that was a little like how he'd felt after speaking about Veses.

"I do think it will be okay," he continued quietly, his gaze catching and holding mine. "We'll find out how to remove the embers, and we'll be successful. I believe this."

I inhaled sharply, wanting to believe that, too, but the dread was there. It had been there when I awoke and was now nestled deep, along with the embers. For once, I didn't think it had anything to do with the anxiety, but I nodded. "I guess it's time to go scare some people."

He chuckled roughly. "I think so, too."

Fallen needles crunched under our feet as we started toward Cauldra Manor—it was the only sound to be heard. Tipping my head back, I searched the heavy branches for birds, but they remained quiet and hidden. There were no signs of life. No wind. The Pinelands were still, holding their breath. It was like nature recognized that a Primal of Death walked the realm and had gone quiet, wary, and watchful as we left the forest.

Sunlight bathed the rocky hill that Cauldra sat upon, reflecting off the bronze armor of the guards who patrolled the land around the manor. Unlike Wayfair, no inner walls separated the royal estate from the farmlands and those who tended the swaying cornstalks and other crops. As we climbed the hill, as yet unnoticed, I looked down at the sweeping valleys dotted with modest, stone homes and the fields full of those working at the end of harvest. Irelone was a part of a vital shipping chain with its capital serving as the port, but my mother and King Ernald had also sought a union with Irelone for the lands full of rich soil, untouched by the Rot.

Cauldra Manor came into view, the gently swaying ivy clinging to the ivory stone stilling as we crested the top of the hill. From the nearby stables, horses whinnied nervously.

"Halt!" a guard near an open set of doors shouted, striding forward, steel sword drawn. Several guards at the stables turned, and I imagined it wasn't often they came across people strolling out of the Pinelands. "Announce yourselves!"

I glanced at Ash.

One side of his lips curved up as he continued several more steps, something the guards coming from the stables didn't appreciate. They, too, drew their swords. "I am the Asher, *the* One who is Blessed. The Guardian of Souls," Ash said, and I swore even the clouds above stopped moving. "The Primal God of Common Men and Endings, *the* ruler of the Shadowlands. I am Nyktos, the Primal of Death, and this is my Consort."

Silence.

About half a dozen guards stared in utter silence.

Then the one who'd spoken first laughed. "And I'm the fucking King of Irelone," he scoffed, his declaration met with raucous laughter.

"Well," I said under my breath. The guards were too far away to notice anything *off* about his eyes. "That didn't go as expected."

Ash smirked as he turned his attention on the guards. The embers in my chest suddenly vibrated, responding to the charge of power hitting the air around us.

Behind us, a rush of birds took flight from the pines in a flurry of wings. They flew over in a wave of black, startling the guards. Tiny bumps spread across my skin as I glanced at the Primal. In the distance, from the valley below, dogs howled, and the horses' whinnying increased.

Ash's chin dipped as his skin thinned. Shadows blossomed beneath its surface, spreading and churning as eather-laced midnight poured out into the space around him, billowing above the grass.

The air near his shoulders thickened and sparked. A rush of wind tossed tendrils of hair across my face as the faint outline of wings arced high above us. "Then you must be the King of Irelone," Ash said, eyes filling with churning wisps of eather. "It's a pleasure to meet you."

The guard had gone slack-jawed and as pale as a corpse. I would've laughed, except he and the others looked close to passing out. Several of them stepped back. None ran, though. Or screamed.

They dropped to their knees like dominoes. Swords clattered off rock and earth as heads bowed, and they pressed shaking hands to the ground and against their chests.

"I'm sorry, Your Highness." One spoke above the murmurs of...*prayers*. "We didn't know. Please—"

"There is nothing to apologize for," Ash interrupted. The charge of energy faded from the air as the rippling shadows vanished around us. The howling stopped. Horses quieted. Ash's grin had spread to a smile. "Rise."

The guards clumsily stood, eyes wide with fear and bodies trembling. I couldn't blame those whose lips still moved in silent prayers, but it struck me—what had been said about how mortals felt when near Kolis, the true Primal of Death. How they reacted to him.

How *Sotoria* had reacted to him.

It was the same as those who stood before Ash now—those who would have likely wept with joyous tears if it had been Kolis who'd walked out of the Pinelands. They would have rushed to greet him and worship at his feet. They'd welcome a monster who presented himself as a savior, all because they believed him to be the Primal of Life.

A label. A title. A belief regarding what was good and what was bad changed everything. And it shouldn't be that way.

"We're here to speak with Princess Kayleigh." I spoke then, drawing the guards' stares. I had no idea what they thought when they looked upon me, if they believed me to be a god or not. "Is she in residence?"

"S-she is," a guard said. "She a-always is. Prefers t-the manor over Castle Redrock."

"Good." Ash smiled, and I wasn't sure if that put any of the guards at ease. "Will one of you take us to her?"

Ash displayed a new Primal power I hadn't known him to be capable of.

Coin didn't fall from trees as I'd once heard King Ernald tell Tavius, but coin *did* spring forth from the soil beneath Ash's boots as we followed a stunned guard into the manor. He left behind enough riches for the guards to feed themselves and their families for several years.

He said nothing as I glanced at him questioningly, but I knew he'd done it to make amends for the fright he'd given them.

Just as he had done for the guard who led us past the banners of green and yellow bearing the emblem of a ship that adorned the hall of Cauldra Manor. The pouch at the guard's hip had swollen with the quiet jingle of coins the man had remained unaware of. He stopped in front of a small receiving chamber.

Inside the sunlit-drenched space, the Princess sat on a couch, her legs tucked beneath the hem of a lilac day gown. She was reading from a book in her lap as she idly ran her hand down the back of a black and white cat curled up beside her, Kayleigh's mass of brown hair piled into a knot atop her bowed head.

The cat noticed us first, lifting its furry head to give us a sleepy-eyed glare. The look gave the distinct impression that it was annoyed by our interruption.

The guard cleared his throat, bowing deeply. "Princess Kayleigh, you have visitors."

Kayleigh gave a little jerk at the sound of his voice, her head snapping up. The vision I had seen of her in the Pools of Divanash had been accurate. She looked healthy. Happy. Nothing like the last time I'd seen her in person.

And she looked right at me. Surprise widened her eyes. "My gods, is that you, Seraphena?" she said, her chest rising sharply as she closed the book in her lap.

I nodded. "It is."

"How did you...?" She trailed off as she glanced at Ash. Blood drained rapidly from her heart-shaped face. "My gods, you're a..." She rose so quickly the book fell from her lap to flop against the thick carpet. The cat gave an irritated thump of his tail off the now-vacant cushion. She started to lower herself—

"That's unnecessary." Ash stopped her, much to my relief and her and the guard's surprise. "You do not need to bow."

Her forest green eyes were bright. "But—"

"It's all right," I jumped in. "He's not the bow-to-me type of Primal."

"Well, sometimes I am," he murmured.

I shot him a look as Kayleigh stared in confusion. "We need to speak with you." I flicked a glance at the guard. "In private."

She nodded, swallowing. "Thank you for bringing them here, Rolio."

The guard hesitated, but the Princess gave him a steady smile and a quick nod. Rolio backed out of the chamber, giving us a wide berth. He didn't wander far, though, instead moving only halfway down the hall. I liked that he was loyal despite his fear.

"Am I in trouble?" Kayleigh asked.

"What?" I focused on her. "No. Why would you think that?"

She didn't look all that confident as she glanced at Ash. "You're a...a Primal god. I can tell by your eyes." She swallowed. "Only the Primals that I've seen have silver eyes."

My brows lifted. "How many Primals have you seen?"

"Enough," she said, then briefly closed her eyes. I really hoped Ash kept what Primal he was to himself. "I'm sorry. I meant no offense."

"None taken, Princess," Ash replied, watching her intently. I knew he was reading her. "There is no reason to fear us. We are not here to harm you."

She nodded, but distrust settled in her features as unease blossomed in me. I thought about what Ash had warned was already beginning to happen in other kingdoms. "What has happened when Primals have come here?"

Her lips parted on a short breath as she looked at Ash. "I...I know they can take great offense when respect is not given to them."

"Respect is earned, even for a Primal. And I have not yet done anything to warrant honor or disrespect." His tone had gentled. "We've only come to speak with a man we believe you know. He could possibly be going by the name Delfai."

Kayleigh stiffened. "The scholar?"

"Perhaps," I said and gave her a quick description.

"Yes. That's Delfai. He's been here for a couple of years now. He's been teaching me how to read the old language." Kayleigh clasped her hands together as her gaze bounced between us. "Is he in trouble?"

"No," I whispered, my heart twisting. What had she seen the other Primals do? "We just want to speak with him."

She nodded. "I believe he's in the library just down the hall." A brief, fond smile appeared. "He likes to file the ledgers and journals the way he feels they should be found. Drives my father mad when he comes here." Kayleigh's laugh was nervous. "I'm sorry. I'm just so utterly confused. I haven't seen you in years, Seraphena, and now I'm standing before a Primal who wishes me not to grovel at his feet—" She cut herself off again. "I'm sorry—"

"Again, no need to apologize," Ash assured her. "Not when it is I who obviously needs to apologize for the behavior of those of my ilk."

Kayleigh's lips formed a perfect circle. "You are..." She cleared her throat. "May I ask which Court you rule?"

"Uhhh." I drew out the word.

Ash inclined his head. "I am Nyktos."

The Princess stared. I didn't think she took a breath in the several moments of awkward silence that followed. "You're the Primal of..."

"Death," he finished for her.

She nodded slowly, blinking rapidly as her head cut toward me. "How are you—?"

"With him?" I jerked my chin at Ash, and his brows furrowed. "It's a long story."

Interest sparked. "I like stories."

I grinned. "This may be one you'd be better off not knowing," I said, worrying that my true mortal identity and new title as the Primal of

Death's Consort could cause her or others problems. "Are you able to take us to Delfai?"

"Of course." She bent quickly, picking up the fallen book. The cat eyed her with impressive displeasure as she placed the book where she'd sat. She started forward, then stopped, staring up at me. "When I left Lasania, I never thought I would see you again."

"I thought so, too," I said.

She peeked at Ash. "I don't think I thanked you for your...*help*."

"You didn't need to."

Her mouth opened and then closed. "We received word some time ago that Princess Ezmeria had taken the throne of Lasania, but there was no word on Prince Tavius's fate."

"The former Prince of Lasania is most definitely no longer a concern—to you or anyone," Ash said, his voice dropping to a near growl. "He spends his eternity in the Abyss."

I tried to stop my smile and failed, wondering if I would ever feel bad about the twisted burst of pleasure that accompanied thoughts of Tavius's fate.

Probably not, especially when I saw the relief skate over Kayleigh's features, relaxing the tension around her mouth and eyes. "Oh, my gods. I...I was too afraid to believe that was the case, but..." She laughed, pressing her hand to her chest. "Gods, I shouldn't laugh. That makes me seem like a terrible person, but I haven't..." She squeezed her eyes shut. "Our betrothal had all but ended, but not in the eyes of many. As long as there was a chance that I was still promised to him, I have been, well..." Her eyes glimmered with tears. "Stuck in this waiting period of him becoming betrothed to another or..."

"You're not a terrible person. Tavius was a wretched excuse for a mortal," I told her, wishing I'd known that Kayleigh's life had been put on hold. I would've figured out a way to send word to her. "You should laugh and celebrate. You are no longer stuck."

Her smile was shaky but tremendous as she looked at me, her glistening gaze tracking over my features before dropping to my right hand—to the golden imprint. "You were never the Queen's handmaiden, were you?"

I sucked in a breath.

Princess Kayleigh glanced at Ash. "Was she?"

"No," the Primal answered, the lines and planes of his face softening. "She was the one who should've been destined to rule Lasania."

Ash's proclamation ignited a flurry of emotions inside me, ones I would have to dwell upon later.

The Princess led us down the hall to a set of heavy wooden doors. It was clear that she wished to join us, but I coaxed her back to the receiving chamber. I had no idea how Delfai would respond to us.

Or how *she* would respond to knowing that she had a god cataloging her father's library.

I nodded when Ash glanced at me. He then pushed open one of the doors, taking no more than a step before a voice spoke from the dimly lit cavern of a chamber in a rush of softly scented sandalwood.

"I've been waiting," a man spoke. "For three long years."

44

Tapestries blocked out any sources of light as the door closed behind me. My gaze swept over the portraits of those with emerald eyes and the heavily stacked shelves lining the wall, stopping on the source of the voice.

A man stood near the bookshelves, his dark hair brushing the shoulders of a brilliant blue tunic. His back was to us, arms cradling what appeared to be a stack of books.

Ash moved to the center of the library by a golden cushioned settee and chairs. "Is that so?"

"It is," the god replied, bending to slide a book between two others. "I was beginning to grow a little impatient. Thankfully, Cauldra Manor is a lovely place. As is the Balfour family. Their name will be honored long after the great kingdoms fall."

I sent Ash a questioning raise of brows as I joined him. "It's a name of honor now."

"But it will become an old, honored one, long after my bones turn to ash." Delfai looked over his shoulder. Onyx eyes deeply set in amber skin met mine. He barely looked older than me, but those eyes…they were as black and endless as Holland's. "It is a name, Fates willing, you may one day know."

A shiver coursed down my spine.

"But the Balfour name is an interesting one," he went on before Ash or I could respond. "As are their ancestors. One comes to mind. An oracle. The last one to be born." A faint smile appeared as he tilted his head to the side. "She was very kind, and I enjoyed conversing with her. The Princess here reminds me of her. Perhaps that is why I am comfortable here."

"We're not here to discuss the Balfour family," Ash interrupted.

"I know." Delfai turned to us. "You've come seeking knowledge of how to repeat what never should've happened."

"That would be it," Ash said, crossing his arms. "We want to know how the embers were transferred."

"You want to know more than that," Delfai corrected. "The Arae, even with all they can see, worried about what they couldn't predict. The unseen. Unknown. The possibilities. And nothing worried them more than an imbalance of Primal power. The Fates wanted something in case there ever came a time when a new Primal must rise, but there was no Primal of Life to Ascend them." Delfai's dark head bowed as he walked along the shelves. "Obviously, one of them foresaw some of what was to come, but none of them had enough foresight to see that what they created could be used to bring about what they sought to prevent: a false King." He chuckled, bending down. "Fate even fucks with *the* Fates."

I exchanged a look with Ash. "What was it they created?"

"A conduit powerful enough to briefly store and transfer embers both volatile and unpredictable in their raw, unsheltered state." Delfai ran his fingers over the books' spines, lips moving in a silent murmur until he found whatever he was looking for. He shoved several tomes aside and slid in the one he held. "They had to go deep within the Undying Hills to find such a thing."

"The Undying Hills are in the mortal realm," I said as I ran my thumb along the inside of my palm and over the imprint. "A stretch of mountains along the northern region of the kingdom of Terra."

"But they were once nameless, just another stretch of untouched land yet untainted by man or god." Delfai faced us. "Until the Arae conjured forth the heart of the mountains—a precious stone created by the flames of dragons that used to inhabit this realm eons ago before Primals could shed joyous tears. It was the first of its kind, known for not only its indestructible strength, but also its irregular, jagged beauty and silver sheen. They called the diamond the Star."

Ash frowned as my brows shot up. "I've heard of no such thing."

The god smirked. "You weren't meant to. No one but the Arae was supposed to know of its existence."

"Why did removing the diamond cause the mountains to be called the Undying Hills?" I cut in.

"Are there not more important questions to ask?" the god queried.

I stared at him. "I'm fully aware of the fact that there are, but I'm curious."

Delfai snorted. "Have you seen the Undying Hills?"

"No." Come to think of it, I hadn't even seen paintings of the land.

A wry grin tugged at Ash's lips. "They got their name because only the most tolerant of plants and creatures can survive the mountains, which have long, barren stretches of land, providing little food or shelter. No mortal would survive long in those conditions."

I crossed my arms. "But why did removing the diamond have that kind of effect?"

"The Arae had to erupt half the mountain to find the diamond," Delfai explained. "The heated rock and gas irrevocably changed the landscape."

"Oh," I murmured. "I suppose that would do it."

"So, the Arae got their conduit," Ash said, getting us back on track. "How is it used?"

"For many purposes. But for your intent?" Delfai sat on the settee with a sigh that matched a god of his age, where his appearance did not. "It's a rather simple process. Either a Primal or an Arae would be needed to use it—only they have the kind of essence needed to force such a transfer. Then contact. Between either the Primal the embers are currently in and the god they are to be transferred to…or in the case of how it was used, held by both Primals. The Star would transfer the embers."

"That's all?" Ash's tone rang with disbelief.

"As I said, it is a rather simple process." Delfai smiled up at us. "The Arae are known for their often-simplistic nature, are they not?"

I wasn't so sure about that, but I was glad this didn't involve some sort of complicated spell.

"Wait. If the diamond was not supposed to be known, then why in the hell did a Fate tell Kolis about the Star?"

I sucked in a sharp breath, realizing that Holland must've known this but lied. Or had he? Could sharing this information be seen as crossing a line? Then again, what this Arae had done had definitely crossed all the lines. "Aren't the Arae supposed to be…I don't know, neutral and not interfere in fate? Giving Kolis the Star sure sounds like interference to me."

His dark eyes flicked to mine. "The Arae often walk a fine line of guidance and interference, don't they?"

I stiffened, and Delfai's smile grew until a shiver of unease drifted down my spine. Then I remembered what Ash had told me about how the Primals fell. "When the Primals began to feel emotion, so did the Arae."

Ash nodded. "I imagine that most remained neutral, but the capability to feel emotion changed everything."

"And *everyone*," Delfai added, turning that eerie smile on Ash. "I have no knowledge of which one gave Kolis what he wanted, nor the true reason behind doing so. It could've been a nefarious act, or they simply fell prey to what they feared would happen to Primals if they could love. It is possible their emotions were exploited, forcing them into such an act to protect someone they loved."

"Love," I murmured, swallowed. "Maybe it is a weakness."

"I believe it to be the one thing more unpredictable than even a Primal ember. Therefore, stronger," Delfai countered, drawing my gaze to him. "Love makes *anything* possible. Makes *anyone* capable of the unexpected."

I shifted my weight from one foot to the other, uncomfortable as the god continued staring at me. "Where is this diamond now?"

His dark eyes glimmered. "Kolis has it," he said, and my stomach sank. "He knows what it's capable of. He wouldn't want anyone else to be able to access it."

"Great," Ash snarled with a flash of fangs.

"But you want to know how to remove the embers from *her*," Delfai said. "To do so, you wouldn't need the Star."

My head snapped up. "Can we get a little more detail on that?"

"At this time, you are simply the mortal vessel for the embers—"

"She is not simply a vessel," Ash growled as eather charged the air. "Not now. Not before this moment, and not going forward."

The catch in my breath and my heart left me a little dizzy as I stared at Ash. I wanted to hug him. Kiss him.

"My apologies." The god bowed his head. "What I meant to say is that she is the current holder of the embers, a living being allowing the embers to grow in power. Therefore, transferring them from her will not be the same as it would be to remove the embers from a Primal born and fully Ascended." His eerie, unflinching gaze settled on me. "They would just need to be taken from you. And doing so will mean only a rather minor impact on the realms."

I...I felt relief. Sharp and sweet. But there was also dread blossoming in my chest.

Delfai's gaze slid to Ash. "You will become what you were once meant to be after your father entered Arcadia. The true Primal of Life, and the King of Gods."

I thought that sounded right and just, but the embers...they hummed erratically. Almost as if they didn't like what they were hearing. But the embers weren't some kind of conscious entity. They were...they were responding to me. To my emotions. To what I was thinking.

To thoughts I might not even acknowledge.

Relief had eased the lines of Ash's face as he asked, "How exactly would I take them from her?"

"Another simple process. One that could've occurred at any point during her Culling and before her Ascension." Delfai was still staring at Ash in the same unsettling manner that he had looked upon me. "You must feed from her."

"That's it?" Frowning, I glanced at Ash. "But he has fed from me."

The odd little smile faded from Delfai's lips. "He must feed until the last drop of blood is taken. Until there is nothing but the embers left. Then, they will transfer to him. He will Ascend. But you..." He sighed. "You will not survive. You will die."

45

You will not survive.

I jerked as the god's words echoed over and over.

"No. *No*," Ash snarled as energy charged the air. Shadows blossomed beneath his flesh, churning rapidly. "You're wrong."

"You can successfully remove the embers. Any Primal could because she is, whether or not your father intended, a placeholder for them," Delfai said quietly enough, but it sounded as if he shouted the words. "The realms are lucky no one else has learned of their existence in her," he said, and I flinched. "But she cannot survive such an act."

Death always finds you. Holland's voice whispered through my thoughts. *By the hands of a god or a misinformed mortal. By Kolis himself, and even by Death.*

Ash.

I laughed.

As I stared at them, I *laughed.* I couldn't help it. The sound was strange, too loud yet too brittle.

Ash's head snapped to mine. His eyes were nearly pure orbs of eather. Shadows raced over his cheeks as faint tendrils spilled into the space around him. He was close to shifting, losing control, and I…

I was just *there.*

The floor didn't feel as if it moved beneath me as it had the last time I'd heard someone speak about my demise so bluntly. There was no surprise. No shock. And maybe it was because I knew this. Didn't I? I could allow myself to escape my fate for a time. But, deep down, I'd known that I wouldn't be able to run from it.

"No," Ash repeated as if the single word changed what Delfai had said. What an Arae had already told us. He shook his head, lines of tension bracketing his mouth as his eyes locked with mine. "There has to be something," he rasped, turning back to Delfai. "It cannot be an either-or situation. There has to be a way to remove the embers without causing her harm. My father survived—"

"Your father was born a god destined to Ascend into his Primalhood, just as you. The embers belonged to him. They were hidden in her bloodline, in her mortal body. They didn't belong to her," he said in that same quiet, flat tone. "All it took was one drop of Primal blood for them to grow stronger in her and make it impossible for anyone to remove the embers." He said what Holland had warned us about. "They have merged with her. Even if you had attempted to do this the moment you became aware of both embers being inside her, the end result would still be the same. It would be like cutting out her heart. There are only three options here. Either you become the true Primal of Life and restore balance to the realms. Someone else, another Primal, takes them—and I don't think any of us wants that. Or she completes her Ascension, and you already ensured that—"

"Don't." My eyes flew open as the embers in my chest vibrated, pushing a flood of heat and energy through my veins. It hit the air. Glass cracked. "Do not finish that sentence."

Delfai sat back. "I'm sorry, but you will die either way." He sighed, and the sound was something…accepting. *Resigned.* "Whether the realms are saved in the process is up to—"

Ash shadowstepped, grasping the god by the throat and slamming him into the bookshelf several feet *behind* the settee and *off* the floor, rattling the furniture. Books pitched forward, falling like rain and thumping off the floor.

"Stop!" I cried, racing forward.

"Her death will not come at my hands," Ash snarled in a guttural, barely recognizable voice. The hazy outline of wings made of eather appeared behind him. Essence sparked along his bare arms. "That is an unacceptable answer."

My stomach lurched as I reached them, seeing that only eather filled his eyes now, and blood…blood began to drip from Delfai's nose and the corner of his mouth. The god started to spasm, and the veins beneath his skin lit up.

Ash's lips peeled back, revealing his fangs—

"Don't!" I shouted. "This isn't his fault."

"Maybe not." Ash's voice dropped low, becoming nothing more than blood and shadows. "But perhaps he will become more creative in his answers once he spends some time in the Abyss."

"That isn't going to help. He told us what he knows. That answer isn't going to change." I grabbed Ash's arm. The shock of the essence blew the wisps of hair back from my face. His skin felt like ice and stone. "*Ash.*"

His head snapped toward mine, and my heart stuttered. The shadows had stilled, leaving his flesh a striking mosaic of golden bronze and midnight. He was more Primal than man.

"This isn't his fault, Ash." I swallowed, smoothing my thumb over the hard skin of his forearm. "You're hurting him, and he doesn't deserve this. *You* don't deserve another mark. Let him go. *Please.*"

A second passed. Just a heartbeat. But it felt like an eternity as he stared down at me, his body taut with power and violence, the striking lines of his features twisted in rage.

Then he released the god.

Well, dropped him.

Either way, Delfai was free.

He landed hard enough to shake a few more books free. They hit the floor around him as he leaned onto his side, hand at his throat, wheezing. Injured but alive.

I didn't let go of Ash's arm, and he didn't look away from me as I forced him back from Delfai. Slowly, the shadows faded from his flesh, and the eather receded from his eyes.

"I should be dead," Delfai rasped. "I've seen my death."

Frowning, I glanced at the god but didn't let go of Ash's arm.

"You were supposed to kill me." Delfai leaned back against the bookshelf, patches of skin along his arms and neck charred. My stomach churned. "That was how I died."

"Well, you're not dead, thanks to her." Ash's jaw worked as he glared at the god as if he were about to change his mind. "Congratulations."

Delfai's fingers stilled around his throat. "It may be cause for celebration." His hand dropped to his lap. "Perhaps there is a silver beast and a brightest moon. Two. Not one," he rambled. "Two then one."

"What in the hell are you talking about?" Ash demanded.

"Nothing." He smiled widely, revealing blood-streaked teeth. "Nothing but hope."

There was a good chance that Ash had done some damage to Delfai's mind because what he'd prattled on about made no sense. Silver beast? Brightest moon? It reminded me of the title Ash had given me, but I really didn't know why he'd be rambling about that—and it honestly didn't matter.

Neither of us spoke as we left Cauldra Manor, passing guards who hastily bowed but kept a healthy distance. I'd wanted to say goodbye to Kayleigh but knew it wouldn't be wise for us to linger.

Not when violent, frenetic eather still leaked into the air around Ash.

And I didn't think I had it in me to hold an appropriate conversation. My mind was too focused on what was to come.

What could no longer be denied.

It was the strangest damn thing as we made our way down the rocky hill, feeling the sun's warmth on my face. The devastation of all the what-ifs that would not happen. The knowledge that the end was truly coming this time. And the utter collapse of hope.

It was all rather...*freeing.*

A calmness settled over me.

The ever-present pressure on my chest was still there, but it didn't squeeze as tightly as it had. And maybe it was because I'd always expected to die. Maybe it was because the soul inside me had also lived through many deaths.

After all, death had been my constant companion, an old friend that I always knew, deep down, would visit one day.

I looked at Ash. He stared straight ahead, the muscle in his jaw ticking with each step. We'd just reached the pines when I said, "Stop."

"We need to return to the Shadowlands," he bit out.

"We need to talk."

"I need to think."

The breath I took was shaky as I followed him into the thick stand of pines. "You have to do it."

Ash halted. "There is nothing I *have* to do."

"That's bullshit, and you know it." I stopped a few feet from him, understanding dawning. "You...you knew how to remove the embers from me this whole time, didn't you?"

His shoulders went rigid.

"Gods," I whispered hoarsely. Because I knew—*I knew*—I was right.

"I didn't know for sure. It's not like there has ever been another like you—a mortal with Primal embers in them." His head bowed. "But I figured that draining you completely was a possibility."

He could've done that at any time. Taken the embers from me. He could've Ascended. Stopped Kolis. Stopped *Veses*. But he hadn't.

Because he knew that it would kill me.

I let my head fall back as I dragged in deep, stinging breaths.

"But I knew that wasn't how Kolis took the embers," Ash gritted out. "I knew there had been another way."

But there wasn't.

Blinking the dampness from my eyes, I lowered my head. "We came here to learn how to transfer the embers, and now we know."

He said nothing, but the air thinned and chilled. A few needles fell from the pines' branches, drifting to the ground.

My heart began to pound as my throat tightened. "There is no other option. We can't allow someone else to learn about the embers and take them."

Slowly, he faced me, his features stark. "There *has* to be another way. Maybe the Star—"

"How would we retrieve it? Do you know where Kolis keeps it? Know anyone who would be willing to share that little piece of information with us? No. And even if we could find the Star, you heard what Delfai said. It's too late. The embers have merged with me. Removing them will kill me either way, and I—I don't want to die."

"Glad to hear that you finally feel that way."

I ignored that. "I want a future. I want to *live*. I want to experience a life where I have control of my future. I want us," I whispered. "But I *need* a future where we defeat Kolis and the Rot goes away. Where those in Iliseeum and in the mortal realm are safe. That's what's important. The only thing that matters."

"No, it is not the only damn thing that matters, Sera." His eyes flashed. "You. Not the godsdamn embers. Not the fucking realms.

You matter."

My breath snagged as I closed my eyes against the wealth of emotion that rose. I...I did matter. Me. But this wasn't about only me. I knew that. So did he. "There's no other way." A tremor went through me as I opened my eyes. "I *understand* that. And it's not your fault."

He looked away, swallowing. "Stop—"

"It's *not*," I insisted. "This isn't right or fair, but you know what you have to do, Ash."

"Do not," he snarled, head snapping back to mine. He took a short, measured step toward me and then shadowstepped, appearing directly in front of me. "Do *not* call me that when you speak of me ending your life so casually."

Pressure seized my chest as a knot lodged in my throat—a mix of emotions too raw for me to fully understand. "I'm sorry."

"You're sorry?" A ragged laugh left him. "Fates, you *are* sorry. I can taste it. Vanilla but tangy." He shook his head in disbelief. "You feel sympathy—anguish—for *me*."

I sucked in a short breath, pressing my right palm to my heart. Sympathy. Anguish. That and bone-deep resolution were what I felt. "You've done nothing wrong."

"Neither have you."

"How the fuck can you even say that?" Ash roared, loud enough that even with the distance we'd traveled, it was still likely someone heard. I doubted anyone would dare to venture into the pines, though. "Because there *was* another option. I could've saved you."

"This isn't on you." Reaching up, I clasped his cool cheeks. He started to pull away, but I held on as the embers hummed. Essence shattered his eyes—anger and agony, too. I drew in a short breath and nearly choked on the scent of pine. "Even if you had your *kardia*, Ash, there was no guarantee you'd love me—"

"Yes, there is." His eyes were wide and wild as he caught my wrists. "I would've loved you if I could have. There would've been no stopping me."

A jolt ran through me. His declaration was as powerful as one of love, and it shook me. Rattled me until the embers began to hum and throb, until I tasted the eather gathering in the back of my throat. The corners of my eyes started to brighten.

"Kiss me," I whispered.

There was no hesitation.

Ash drew me to him, lifting me onto the tips of my toes as his mouth lowered to mine. We both shuddered at the touch of our lips. The kiss was gentle and tentative, full of reverence and sorrow. Tears rushed my tightly closed eyes. A soul-torn groan rumbled from Ash's chest and through mine.

The embers continued to hum.

My heart ached.

Ash's arms swept around me, hands fisting my braid, my hip. He pulled me even closer to him, our bodies flush. His head tilted, the kiss deepening with a sweep of his tongue against mine, a clash of teeth against fangs. And from all the anguish, desperation was born, one of need and want, and it was all-consuming.

There was no hesitation when our mouths parted and our gazes collided. There were no words as his lips returned to mine and we reached for each other, buttons being opened, pants and undergarments shoved down. Our lips didn't part as he lowered me to the pine-needled ground and took me with one deep stroke of his hips.

His mouth captured my cry of pleasure, and he answered with a heated growl. With my pants gathered just below my knees, I couldn't lift my legs or widen them. The restricted movement made every thrust tight and nerve-wrackingly intense as I gripped his arms.

That was all I could do—hold on as he moved in and out, going as deep as he could, rushing, driving me to the blade-thin edge of pleasure and pain.

He seated himself deeply within me, lifting his mouth from mine as he clasped my cheek, stilling. "I wish..." he whispered hoarsely, dragging his fingers across the freckles sweeping over my cheek. "I wish I'd never had my *kardia* removed."

My eyes fluttered open.

His eyes glinted with a...a sheen of red. Primal tears of grief. "I never wanted to love. Not until you, *liessa*."

Air lodged in my throat as my chest squeezed and swelled, a conflicting rise of emotion. "I know."

He shook, then lost all semblance of control. His hips plunged against mine, each thrust a promise of what his heart couldn't give. Each ragged breath between us raw and beautiful. The pleasure rose. Sorrow followed. And when release found us, it took us both, leaving us shaken and a little bit destroyed.

Neither of us moved for a long time. In the silence, I soaked up the feel of his heart beating against my chest, the cool weight of his body as I stared up at the needled pines above us. "Can you make me a promise?"

He lifted his head, and eyes full of silver moonlight met mine. "Anything, *liessa*."

"When it comes time," I whispered, "can you take me to my lake? I want it to be done there."

Ash's chest stilled against mine. His eyes slammed shut as the tendons of his throat stood out, and his features sharpened and thinned. "I promise."

46

Ash held me tightly to him as if he feared I might slip away. I could feel his heart pounding against my cheek as he prepared to bring us back to the Shadowlands.

Where we needed to prepare. Make plans. Try to figure out how long I had before…I died. It couldn't be too long. Not with how strong the embers were. It was possible I only had days left—weeks if I was lucky.

A shudder worked its way through me. Ash's chin grazed the top of my head as his fingers curled around my braid. Tendrils of moonlit darkness rose.

Would this be what death looked like? A rise of darkness? Nothing before I entered the mist before the Pillars, unable to hear or see anyone near me? A sharp swirl of raw panic darted through me, threatening to fracture the calm evoked by the failure of all those what-ifs. I closed my eyes, swallowing the knot gathered there.

I could deal with this.

I had to.

There was no other option.

As the whirling strands of eather settled around us, the normally stale, cool air of the Shadowlands reached us, carrying the strong scent of burning wood. The embers vibrated in my chest.

"Something's wrong. There is…*death* everywhere," Ash bit out as dread exploded throughout me. A shout echoed from the Rise. "Fuck."

Ash turned sharply as stinging heat roared over our heads. *Fire* slammed into the palace. I gasped as the entire structure shook under the blast of flames.

Everything we'd learned in Massene fell to the wayside. We were under attack.

"Hold on," Ash ordered.

I gripped the front of his tunic, expecting him to shadowstep once more, but he took a step forward instead, lifting me as he launched onto the railing of his balcony.

Ash *jumped*.

"Holy shit," I gasped, squeezing my eyes shut as acrid air rushed up. My stomach plummeted at the brief seconds of utter weightlessness, and then we were falling.

Ash slowed before landing hard in a crouch. I didn't feel the impact, and I wasn't sure if that was because he'd taken the hit or from the shock of him leaping off the balcony.

He lowered me to my feet as he rose, releasing me. With my heart thundering, I turned to see several guards on the Rise aiming at the ground outside, firing arrows.

The high-pitched yelps and guttural growls sent a cold shiver down my spine as Saion raced from the gates.

"Veses?" Ash clipped out.

"She's still in stasis, in her cell, but there are dakkais at the Rise— here and in Lethe. Bele and Rhahar are down there, but—" Saion skidded to a halt as a shadow fell over the courtyard.

Ash yanked me back as a reddish-black draken dove toward us, releasing a stream of fire. Heat blew back. The fire slammed into the ground, kicking up soil and rock. For a moment, I couldn't see Saion through the flames, and my heart stopped.

The fire receded, revealing Saion, picking himself up from several feet back. "And *that* fucker just showed up," he growled. "And is already starting to piss me off."

"Davon," Ash snarled, and it felt like we were leaping off the balcony once more. It was the draken I'd seen in Dalos—Nektas's distant relative. Ash prowled past the now-several-feet-deep gash in the charred, smoking ground, keeping a hold of my hand. "How many draken?"

"There is at least one more making a run at Lethe," Saion said, and my free hand curled into a fist. "Nektas and Orphine are fending him off, but Nyktos, my man, it..." Saion swallowed, shaking his head as he turned at the waist, he thrust a hand over his head as the archers along the Rise fired another volley of arrows. "*He's* here."

My skin chilled as Ash halted.

No.

He couldn't mean Kolis.

But the pale tightness at the corners of Saion's mouth, the pulsing eather in his too-wide, too-*bright* eyes... And the way he choked as he continued sent a deeper, stronger wave of dread through me.

Through Ash.

Shadows immediately blossomed under Ash's flesh. "Kolis?"

Saion gripped his sword. "Kyn."

Every part of me went still. "Kyn?" I uttered, glancing at the Rise as guards raced along it. If Kyn were here with Kolis's draken and his dakkais...

"He came before the dakkais, looking for you—for both of you," Saion said. "Surprised the guards—surprised all of us." He started turning from us but stopped. "There was nothing we could do. He's a Primal." He bent suddenly, clasping his side as he dragged in a deep breath. "The fucker just—" Saion choked and then said no more.

He couldn't as he gnashed his teeth together, dragging a hand—a bloodied hand—over his face.

Picking up on what Saion was feeling, Ash inhaled sharply, his skin thinning even further. Energy charged the air, and the embers in my chest hummed and shook.

Ash started walking toward the west courtyard. I followed, my unease amplifying and growing.

Saion caught my arm as I passed him. "Don't," he rasped. "You don't want to see this."

I stilled, my chest rising and falling in short, shallow breaths. A part of me wanted to listen to his warning because I knew that something had happened. Something bad. An act that Saion wished he hadn't seen.

But I couldn't.

Because Ash wouldn't.

I slipped my arm free. Saion's curse got lost in the order for another barrage of arrows. I hurried, catching up to Ash as I scanned the skies for the draken, seeing no sign of him.

The air smelled different here. It carried a...a hint of damp metal. A recognizable scent. Blood. *Death.*

Oh, gods.

Suddenly, I was in Saion's place, wanting to stop Ash from

discovering what awaited. "Ash," I called out.

He didn't stop.

Not until he rounded the corner of the palace. Then he did. He *jerked*, stumbling back a step. I'd never seen him *stumble*. Fear of what he'd seen seized me as I crossed the short distance between us, seeing dark red across the gray, cracked soil and discarded swords. Streams of red. Splatters of crimson. Puddles of blood.

Ash threw his arm out, blocking me, but it was too late.

I saw...

I saw *them*.

On pikes, drilled into the ground. Hands and arms bound. Their mangled skin and torn-open chests empty of hearts. Throats slashed to the bone. Others were cut so deeply that their heads were no longer on their shoulders but the ground.

The embers hummed in response to the death. To the utter lack of life as I dragged my gaze over faces I didn't recognize, lifeless eyes of those I'd passed in the courtyard or saw training with Ash. I looked down.

Fair hair. Sharp, bloodless features. Lifeless, dull amber eyes.

That was his...that was *his* head.

Ector.

I staggered, my throat sealing as I clapped a hand over my mouth, and a softer red snagged my attention.

The color of wine.

The flash of a silver chain around a throat, soaked in blood.

"No," I whispered, skin flashing hot and then going numb. "*No*."

"She came outside to help," Saion said raggedly from behind us. "I told her to get back, but Kyn saw her. And Ector—fucking Ector tried to stop him."

I swayed, chest throbbing as the embers responded to me—to the storm of emotions roaring through me. My blood heated, filling my veins with fire.

"Bele doesn't know," Saion rasped. "She was already on the way to Lethe. She doesn't know—*fuck*, you're starting to glow."

He wasn't talking about Ash, who had gone completely silent and still.

It was me.

A distant rumble echoed in the sky. Davon was near. That was a problem, one we needed to figure out how to handle, but I couldn't think beyond Aios and Ector and the dozens of lives lost on these pikes.

I couldn't understand why.

What had any of them done?

The embers throbbed as I started toward Aios—toward them—but I forced myself back. Using the embers had caused this. If I were to do it again, it would lead to more attacks.

My hands curled into fists as fury clashed with grief. I could do something. I could fix this, but who would pay for it?

Not the one who should.

Kolis.

"Is Kyn still here?" Ash demanded, his voice cold and flat as the temperature suddenly dropped several degrees.

"The last I saw him, he was outside the Rise," Saion answered. "Behind the line of dakkais. He had Cimmerian—" Saion turned to the sky. "That fucker is coming back."

Ash turned from the pikes, away from the carnage. "Summon the armies." Eather sparked from his whirling flesh as his lips peeled back over his fangs. Power poured into the air. Shadows spilled into the space around him, spinning and whirling, and when his eyes met mine, they were pure orbs of silver. The rumble of Davon's roar was closer as Ash tipped his head to the sky.

Then Ash rose.

Straight up like a launched arrow. Streaks of silver light radiated from him, hissing and snapping. The hazy outline of wings appeared as his hands splayed open. Outside the rise, the dakkais howled as Saion ran toward a guard on horseback, giving her orders. She took off for the gates facing the Undying Woods. I could only hope that she and the armies were quick.

"Fire! Fire!" I heard—thank the gods—Rhain shout from the Rise. "Now!"

The air around Ash crackled, flashing a lighter gray as the eather built inside him, turning his skin the shade of mottled shadowstone. His wings looked almost solid as clouds darkened the sky—actual dark *clouds* that gathered and thickened.

Ash became a storm.

Davon appeared over the palace, jaws open and scales vibrating. Flames sparked from inside his throat.

Ash *laughed*.

And the sky trembled with thunder. The draken spread his wings, slowing as he curled his body, but he wasn't stopping.

Ash was stopping the draken.

He'd lifted a hand, twisted his wrist.

The crack of Davon's wing was lost in the answering howl of pain.

"My gods," I whispered.

"Yeah," Saion breathed. "You haven't seen a really pissed-off Primal, have you?"

Eather erupted from Ash. Blinding streaks lit up the sky, slamming into Davon. The draken tumbled as eather raced through his scaled body.

"It ain't pretty," Saion finished.

Davon hit the courtyard on his forelegs and pushed up again with a roar, still crackling with eather. He flew back up, even with a broken wing.

No, it was not pretty.

Telling myself that Ash would be okay, I turned to the pikes. I needed to focus. I had a job to do. I started forward, unsheathing the dagger.

"What are you doing?"

"Help me." I hurried to Aios. I hated choosing, picking one life over another, but she was the closest, and she still...she still had her head. I didn't know what I could do for those who didn't. I didn't understand how the embers worked to reattach limbs and parts, but Aios...I could help her and then try with the rest. "Help me get her down."

"Fuck, Sera. You're sure about this? It'll be felt. You'll Ascend Aios, just like you did with Bele." Saion followed. "It will make things worse—"

"Worse?" I laughed, and the sound broke off. "Worse than this? Really?"

"It can always get worse."

Like it had for Aios, who had already experienced far more horror than anyone should ever have to live through.

"The risks," Saion began.

"I know what the risks are, but it won't matter." It wouldn't. Because as soon as we had the chance, Ash would take the embers from me. There would be no more waiting. No plans made to figure out what to do with whatever time I had left. He had to because, after this, he'd have to Ascend.

And he'd need to stop Kolis.

"They will not die today," I said. Ignoring the blood-stained edges of Aios's gown, I bent and cut through the ropes around her ankles as the sky overhead lit with silver flames. I tensed and then relaxed as Davon let out another pained screech.

I rose, freeing the wrists tied at Aios's back. Her skin…it was cold, clammy but not stiff. "Help me get her down," I said again before cutting the rope around her waist. I met Saion's stare. "As your Consort, I *demand* it."

Saion briefly closed his eyes, then nodded. He came to my side, folding his arms around Aios. "I've got her." His gaze met mine. "You're going to want to get your hand behind her head as quickly as possible or…"

Clamping my mouth shut, I nodded. I knew what could happen. "On the count of three," I said. "One, two, three." I cut through the rope and then moved, bracing the sides of her too-loose head as Saion took her weight. "Lay her down. Not in the blood." I looked for a nearby place free of gore. And looked…

"No place is clean." Saion began to lower her. "This will have to do."

Blinking back tears as Ash's lightning arced across the sky, catching Davon once more, I dropped to my knees and placed the dagger down as I tapped into the embers, willing them to respond. They throbbed and surged, the essence flooding my veins.

"Keep that dagger close," Saion advised, his eyes on the Rise as he moved to brace Aios's head. "Ash is getting the dakkais riled up." His gaze flicked over me. "As are you. The dakkais. Remember, they don't just trace the essence," he said, "they devour it."

I placed my hands over Aios's damaged chest as I snarled, "Fuck the dakkais."

Saion let out a short laugh. "I like you," he said, shaking his head as his gaze returned to the Rise. "You know that? I really do."

The essence flared from my palms. "I like you, too."

I looked down at Aios, not seeing or hearing Saion's response as I channeled everything I had into the goddess. The flow of power responded without hesitation, faster and hotter than before. I focused on her face, no place else. The eather rippled over her body and seeped into her skin. All her veins lit up, the light intensifying.

Shouts ramped up from the Rise, as did the howls and growls.

The glow beneath Aios's flesh expanded and rose, spreading beyond her body. Beneath my knees, the ground began to tremble.

"Here it comes," Saion warned.

The eather pulsed and then exploded in a blast of pure power, causing both Saion and me to scoot back on our knees. I lost my hold on Aios as the wave rippled out from the courtyard and moved beyond the

Rise—beyond the Shadowlands. A brighter, more distinct bolt of lightning streaked across the sky.

Then it stopped. The wind. The shaking.

I scrambled back to Aios's side, peeling back the torn collar of her gown. A thick pink line encircled her throat. The skin was bruised over her heart but healed.

Her chest rose with a deep, singular breath.

"Aios," Saion gasped.

Her eyes fluttered open— silver and bright. "Saion? I…" Her throat worked on a swallow, and her head jerked so quickly toward me that I winced. "*Sera.*"

Hands shaking, I smiled weakly. "Hi."

"Hi," she whispered.

Screams rippled through the air, sending a bolt of fear through me. We needed to get Aios out of here. The sleep that came after what I'd just done didn't seem like something anyone had any control over. Saion twisted toward the Rise, his jaw hardening.

Aios struggled to sit up as Davon fell from the sky like a sack of boulders, slamming into the ground but righting himself quickly. "W-what is…?"

I caught her by the shoulders. "You need to get inside. Hide."

"But—"

"*Now.*"

Saion twisted. "Kars?"

A guard stopped at the foot of the Rise and changed direction, heading for us. His steps slowed, eyes widening.

"Get Aios inside. Now."

Blinking, he shook his head. "On it."

I rose as the god helped Aios to her feet and then lifted her to his chest, turning to… "Help me get Ector down."

"Sera—"

"I can try." I went to Ector's ankles. "I have to try. Just like he did." My throat burned. "Just like he has."

"Yeah. Okay. We'll get him down, and I'll get his…"

I flinched, but we did it quickly, laying Ector out so that he almost appeared whole. Briefly meeting Saion's stricken gaze, I summoned the eather—

"They're coming over," Rhain shouted from the Rise. "Get back. Everyone get back!"

Screams shattered the air, and the embers flared and pulsed, over and over as I reached to place my palms on Ector's still chest.

"Fuck." Saion rocked back. "The dakkais are over the wall."

"Keep them back," I ordered, breathing in deeply.

The scraping of claws over stone overpowered the sound of my pounding heart. The essence flared, deep and powerful, and my vision turned white—pure white—for a second as the eather swelled—

"Stop. Stop!" yelled Saion as the eather rippled out from my palms, splashing against Ector's chest. "It's drawing them to you. Stop!"

All I needed was a few more seconds. That was all. I could bring Ector back—

Saion grabbed me by the waist, hauling me back.

"No!" My eyes went wide as the essence flickered over Ector and faded. "Let me go!"

"There's no time." Saion pulled me back as muscled bodies slick like midnight oil charged the courtyard, jaws snapping and claws digging into soil. Their snarls fell upon me like daggers.

I struggled against Saion. "I can bring him back. I just need—"

"No." Saion twisted, shoving me back several feet. His eyes flashed with essence as my boots slid on the blood. "You do that, and they'll swamp you. You'll die."

I was going to die anyway.

I started toward Ector as arrows pounded into the courtyard, striking the dakkais.

But I...I couldn't die yet. Because the embers were important. More so than Ector. Than me.

And I knew that.

Gods.

I knew that.

And I hated that I did.

Saion shouted, twisting as he drew the swords from the sheaths at his back and side. A dakkai launched at him, and another veered past him. I screamed in fury and anguish as I bent quickly, swiping up a fallen shadowstone sword instead of going for my dagger.

Spinning, I brought the sword down on the neck of the faceless beast, severing its head. I dipped, grabbing another sword. I thrust forward, shoving it deep into a dakkai's chest. Foul-smelling blood coated the blades as I spun, dragging the sword through the air. Lightning rippled across the sky.

A dakkai veered past Saion, past the guards now in the courtyard. Then another. And another. I whirled, horror knocking the wind out of me as they went for the power—the eather.

Ector.

"No!" I screamed, launching across the slippery ground and driving the sword into the dakkais, into any part of them I could as they swarmed Ector's body in a nightmare of claws and teeth. I lost all sense of skill. I simply hacked away at the beasts.

Saion was there. Then Rhain. Another guard—a god—used eather, firing at the dakkais, but it only drew more, and they kept coming, crowding the pikes. They kept coming, even as we struck them down, their mouths and claws coated with shimmery reddish-blue blood.

The embers inside me throbbed wildly. Pained-filled shouts filled the courtyard and the Rise as Rhain kicked a fallen dakkai aside, off to where Ector had been laid out—

The god staggered back from…from what was left behind. He turned, vomiting. The sword slipped from my fingers. A mess. That was all that remained of Ector. A *mess.* My hand shook. I shuddered, and deep within the cavern inside me, the essence of the Primal of Life *roared.* My skin hummed. A metallic taste coated the inside of my mouth as dull pain lanced my jaw. A whirling motion swept through me as my lips parted.

A scream of rage, of ruin tore from me as the corners of my vision turned white—pure white.

All across the courtyard, the dakkais reared, jerking their heads toward me. And the power inside me built and swelled until nothing could hold it back.

I didn't even try as the other sword shattered in my hand. A pulse of power rolled out from me, leaving me dizzy as it swept into a wave of dakkais, knocking them away from Saion and Rhain and into the air, where they simply vanished.

Were obliterated.

A bone-deep exhaustion sank in, the kind I'd never felt before as the wave of power retracted. I stumbled a step forward, panting. Something warm and wet dripped from my nose, hitting my arm. Blood. My blood. I looked down and saw the silvery sheen fade from my hands as a swarm of dakkais crested the wall.

I heard my name being called, heard calls for retreat, but the voices were dull as Rhain ran for me. He grabbed my arm, my waist, but I couldn't feel his touch. I didn't feel connected to my body at all. It was like I was floating. I blinked slowly, my vision going out…

And then coming back in.

"Sera!" Rhain shouted, his voice loud enough to cause me to wince.

"Are you all right?"

"I-I don't know." Sensation returned to my body as Rhain turned my head to his. Some strength filled me, but not a lot. I swallowed the blood that had gathered in my mouth. "I think so."

He didn't look like he believed me as he quickly wiped the blood from my nose.

"We need to get inside," Saion said, breathing heavily. A dakkai had clawed the front of his chest. I saw that Rhahar was with him.

We turned, but there was no path to the palace—to safety. No matter which direction we turned, there were snapping jaws and flat, flared nostrils, heads without features, and bloodied claws.

Dakkais surrounded us.

"Damn it," seethed Rhahar, dragging the back of his hand over his bleeding cheek. "Godsdamn it."

"Sounds about right," Saion remarked, lifting his sword as he glanced over his shoulder at me. "You think you can do that thing again? It'll draw more, but it may clear enough of a path."

"I..." I searched for the embers but felt no flare. No wiggle. Nothing. My gaze met Saion's as my throat started to close off. I couldn't feel them. I couldn't—

A draken suddenly crashed into the Rise, cracking it and taking out a large chunk. Shimmery light cascaded over Davon's body as he fell to the courtyard, shifting into his mortal form.

And then the air turned frigid. Our breaths puffed out in small clouds as tiny bumps rose all over my skin. Rhahar slowly turned to our right.

To where a Primal hovered, shadowy wings spread wide and body encased in wisps of crackling eather.

Mist poured from Ash, *out* of Ash. Primal mist. It spilled to the ground, full of churning streaks of essence.

The dakkais' heads swiveled and lifted, lips peeling back as they sniffed the air. Scented. Traced.

Tracked.

"Shit," Rhain breathed behind me. "*Shit.*"

Ash's silvery eyes locked on me for a moment, and I swore I heard his voice like a whisper among my thoughts.

The dakkais took off, one after the other, heading straight for Ash, just as he wanted. For a moment, those silvery eyes locked onto mine, and I swore I felt him—a cool brush of tendrils against my cheek like I had felt the night he'd been in my bedchamber. A shiver of awareness skated over the nape of my neck.

Run, liessa. Run.

I jerked into Rhain as I stared back at Ash. His voice. I'd heard his voice in my thoughts—

A dakkai cut in front of Ash. He caught the creature by the throat, throwing it back as he strode forward. Another raced at him as a silvery glow pulsed over his body.

Real, potent fear pounded through me, even as the mist snuffed out a line of dakkais. Dozens clamored over the fallen. Ash would be swamped. Primal or not, he would go down. What I'd seen left of Ector flashed in my mind.

"No!" I tore free of Rhain and grabbed a sword. "Help him!" I shouted, but Rhahar and Saion were already on it.

I ran, slower than before, slower than I'd ever been, but I pushed on. I'd crawl if needed. I lifted the now-heavy sword—

A funnel of fire slammed down on the ground between Ash and me. *Nektas.* He cut through the dakkais as he flew low. And he wasn't alone. Orphine was with him. She released a stream of flames behind Ash as she dove.

"She's too low!" Rhahar shouted.

A dakkai leapt as she veered, digging its claws into her side. She rolled, shaking the creature off, but another landed on her. And another—

Something blotted out the stars, darkening the ground. My gaze jerked to the Rise. Shadows gathered along the top and spilled over the wall—shadows thick and full of solid forms. Bodies.

"The Cimmerian," I panted.

They were still here.

Kyn was still here.

The wave of Cimmerian came fast and hard, feeding off the eather until a cloudy night descended upon us.

And then I couldn't see anything. Not Orphine or Nektas. Not Ash.

I froze, taking shallow, too-short breaths. *Breathe in.* Someone shouted. The clang of sword against sword echoed strangely in the thick darkness. *Hold.* The sound of flesh giving way to stone and metal and claws followed. Yells. Screams—

A tidal wave of bodies slammed into me, pushing and forcing me back. I didn't know if they were our people, the Cimmerian, or the dakkais. I could barely keep a hold of the sword, and then it was knocked from my grasp. Hands pushed into me. Elbows hit my sides, my back. I couldn't hold my ground. The rise and fall of bodies swept me up, the stench of fear, falling weapons, and darkness—darkness streaked with bursts of eather and gold—swallowed me. *Breathe in.* I caught glimpses of shimmery gold in the darkness. Gold clothing. Gold hair. I choked.

The wall stopped the flow of bodies without warning.

I hit the cold stone hard. Air punched out of my lungs as pain exploded down my back. My legs went out from under me, and I ended up on the ground—on gravel. I twisted to my side, curling in on myself as the bodies met the wall, too, some falling, some making it out. I tensed as knees connected with my shoulder and head as the sound of thunder shook the ground. Was it more dakkais? Horses? Our armies?

Our people?

Our people.

I lifted my head, staring into the mass of eather-lit shadows smothering the courtyard. Swords and bodies still clashed as I searched for Ash. *Breathe in.*

I needed to find him.

Then we needed to find a place that would be safe and secure for long enough that he could take the embers. It had to happen now before more died. Before this became the war he'd hoped to prevent.

The war it already felt it was.

Hold. I rose, pushing off the wall. The embers were still silent in my chest as I shuffled forward, tripping over bodies littering the ground. A dakkai growled nearby. I kept going, catching glimpses of those fighting. Flashes of gold that made my heart race. A roar rumbled in the sky I couldn't see, and I hoped it was one of our draken as I found a sword.

Ash would find me. I knew he would. He would sense me, just as he had all the other times. As long as the dakkais hadn't completely swamped him. As long as he was still conscious. We'd find each other.

Silvery flames cut through the darkness, catching those fallen and those not, scattering the thickest of shadows—

Gold.

A flash of golden hair and golden paint only feet from me.

I stumbled back, my stomach lurching as my grip tightened on the sword's hilt. Shadows reclaimed the space as I veered to my right, closer to what I thought was the palace. *Breathe in.* I kept going, one hand stretched out. We'd find one another. We would—

I halted.

The tiny hairs all along the nape of my neck rose. *Hold.* A wave of awareness tiptoed down my spine. My stomach hollowed as I firmed my grip on the sword. Tension settled in my shoulders as I heard Ash shouting my name, drawing closer and closer until the sound of hooves drowned him out. Our armies *had* arrived, but something…someone else was close. A hunter. I felt it in my bones. And I was the prey. Instinct seized me.

Spinning, I thrust out with the sword.

A hand clamped down on my wrist as a stream of fire overhead broke apart the shadows. The air cleared enough for me to see blondish-brown hair. High cheekbones. A scar across the left cheek.

Attes.

The rush of relief nearly took my legs out from under me. He'd come to our aid, even at the risk of not just angering Kolis but also to take up arms against his brother. Thank the gods he'd stopped what would've been a fairly painful blow, even with the shadowstone armor protecting his chest.

"Thank you," I scratched out.

Tension settled in the corners of his mouth. "You shouldn't thank me yet."

I stared up at him as the breath I drew in went…nowhere. Every part of my being rebelled against the instinct suddenly screaming at me.

"Why?" I cried.

His stare was expressionless. "Because this is the only way."

"No," I seethed, red-hot anger exploding. "No, it's not."

Attes pressed his fingers into my wrist, between the tendons. The flare of sharp pain was intense and shocking, forcing my hand to spasm. The sword fell as horror and fury pounded through me.

"Sorry," he grunted.

I twisted in a desperate bid for freedom. Attes sidestepped me, spinning me around. Before I could take another step, he hauled me back against him.

"Sera!" Ash thundered, and a flash of intense light followed.

Through the mass of bodies and dakkais, clashing swords and racing horses, I saw Ash several yards away, drenched in shimmery blood. Clothing ragged. Face clawed. Arm torn. Enraged. Beautiful. Fierce silver eyes locked on mine as he ripped a Cimmerian from the shadows, tearing the god apart. A dakkai came at him from behind. He caught it, shattering the creature with a touch.

Attes's hand curled around my chin, forcing my head back against his chest as smoke and shadow poured over us. "All we want is you. Remove the charm, and no more blood will be shed this day. No more lives will be lost."

Ash roared my name in the darkness as rage and desperation swirled through me.

"Refuse?" Attes continued softly. "And my brother will leave none but the Primal standing."

Ash appeared in the darkness, his body charging with eather as he shoved a dakkai aside, and I saw Rhain behind him, fighting back one more beast.

"Sera!" Ash roared, beginning to rise, but the dakkais, they kept coming at him, jumping on him as they had with Orphine, taking him down. I struggled against Attes's hold and attempted to get to Ash as he threw the dakkais off.

"It's your choice," Attes said. "And you should make it quickly."

My eyes locked onto Ash's, and they didn't leave him until the smoke and shadows whipped through the space between us.

"Promise me," I rasped. "Swear to me that no one else will be harmed."

"No one else will be harmed," pledged Attes. "I swear."

I shuddered, my insides going cold. "I will leave."

A sharp swirl of pinpricks swept over my wrists, just like when Vikter had placed the charm on me. The ancient words appeared briefly on my skin, a faint glow that faded quickly.

Attes turned sharply into a void of smoke-choked midnight. "You made the right choice."

He was wrong. Because there was no choice to be made.

There never had been.

47

I dreamt of my lake.

I was swimming, gliding effortlessly through the cool, dark waters. I knew I wasn't alone as I rose to the surface. A figure waited on the bank.

A wolf, more silver than white in the splintered streams of moonlight, watched.

And as I let myself sink back into the water, I thought I'd seen that wolf before. Not in a dream, but many years ago when I walked these woods as a child. But that thought floated away as I drifted through the water.

I wanted to stay here, where it was peaceful and calm and nothing terrible could disturb me. I swam and swam until I felt the faint wiggle of the embers in my chest. Pushing to the surface, I turned to the bank of my lake.

To where the white wolf once sat.

And Ash now stood.

My head thumped with dull pain that traveled down and along my jaw as I drew in a deep breath of air that smelled nothing like the last thing I remembered: the smoke and stench of charred flesh and death. The musty, foul scent of the ship Attes had shadowstepped us onto.

That was the last thing I remembered.

That and the explosion of pain along the back of my skull the moment Attes released me.

Which likely explained the throbbing headache. Traitorous bastard. Only the gods knew how long he'd been working with Kolis.

I vowed to myself that I would see him dead before I took my last breath, but how I would accomplish that was yet to be seen. There was a far more pressing concern at the moment.

The air I breathed as I lay on something *decadently* soft carried the scent of vanilla and…and lilac—stale lilac.

I was no longer on the ship, and I feared I knew exactly where I was.

My eyes felt glued shut, much as they had when I awoke from my brief stasis, but it took far greater effort to pry them open this time. And that was yet another concern to add to the already overflowing list of them. Many were for me, but also Ash…the others.

Had Attes honored his vow and stopped the attacks? Were…*our people* safe? Orphine and Rhain? Rhahar and the others. Was Ash? I knew he would survive the dakkais, the Cimmerian, and anything else thrown his way, but he *had* been wounded. Maybe even enough to need to feed—something he'd likely resist doing. He'd be weakened. And look what had happened to Veses. She'd gone into stasis. The same could happen to Ash.

I stopped myself before I began spiraling and lost whatever calm I had left—which wasn't much. I needed to find a way back to Ash. He needed to take the embers, and I…

I needed to see him one last time. To say goodbye. To tell him that I…that I loved him. I'd been wrong to not tell him before, out of fear it would cause him guilt. My chest squeezed. I didn't think that now. He needed to know. I needed him to know.

And I had to get out of here. Which meant I couldn't lose it. I had to keep my senses sharp because my time was limited. I felt that in my bones. So, I forced my eyes open.

And saw nothing.

Only deep, dark utter nothingness. Pressure rose to settle on my chest. I swallowed to take a deep breath—

Something tightened around my *throat.*

Icy fear punched into my chest as I lifted a shaking hand to my neck. My fingers met a thin, cool metal band at the base of my throat, below my pulse. I dragged my fingers across it, finding a thick hook in the center, and....

A *chain*.

Panic exploded as I gripped the chain, jerking up so fast my heart seemed to whoosh and then stutter. Dizziness swept through me. Hands trembling, I pulled weakly on the chain, jumping at the loud rattle it made against what sounded to be stone floors. The length was long, and no matter how much I pulled, the chain met no resistance, but that didn't fill me with any sort of relief.

Because there was a godsdamn shackle around my neck.

The pressure continued tightening around my chest as I struggled to control my breathing and not let the panic take complete hold. But I was chained, and—

Lights flooded the space, sharp and bright.

Blinded, I threw up a hand to shield my stinging eyes, dropping the chain. It clanged off the floor, hurting my ears.

"You're awake."

The voice.

It wasn't Attes or Kolis, but it was familiar.

"You've been out for two days," the male added.

My chest seized. *Two days?* Had I gone into another stasis and somehow survived?

"We were beginning to worry," he said with a laugh. "Attes wasn't supposed to hit you *that* hard, but he's...as some would say—and that *some* being me—all looks and little thought."

Slowly, I lowered my hand and blinked open watering eyes. The first thing I saw was the golden, shimmery swirls on my right hand. The *imprint*. The comfort that brought vanished as I lifted my gaze.

I went cold inside.

Numb at what I saw.

Gold bars spaced about half a foot apart. A cage. A gilded *cage*. Horror clawed its way through me, leaving me frozen, hand still half-raised.

"He should've been more careful. After all, you are technically just a mortal. Isn't that correct?" he continued. "Not a god on the verge of their Culling. Not even a godling. But a mortal with embers of life inside them."

A tremor started deep in my chest, where the embers remained unnervingly quiet. I turned, my gaze flickering over chests of varying sizes, a round table, a chair, a gold-toned divan, and a thick rug of fur. All items in the cage with me.

Then I saw him.

Golden hair.

Golden mask.

Pale blue eyes lit by the faintest wisps of eather. Eyes I had believed belonged to a god. But Dyses had the same eyes, and he was something else entirely.

A Revenant.

I'd seen this male in Dalos, only a bit of his profile. He'd been in the hall, waiting for Davon. But that wasn't the first time I'd seen him.

I'd seen him in the mortal realm, in my kingdom, and that was why the gold-painted wings had kept striking a chord of familiarity. He'd been at Wayfair, speaking with my mother. Ezra had told me his name.

Callum.

He stood a few feet on the other side of the cage, but it was the only other thing in the space that occupied the otherwise dark chamber that caught my attention. A single elaborate, gold-adorned chair.

A throne.

Bile rose, and I choked it back as I lowered my hand to the soft blanket on the *bed* I lay on.

The same taunting, half-formed grin I'd seen that day at Wayfair appeared now. "Hello, Seraphena Mierel. It is so lovely to see you again." His head tilted, and he smiled, causing the edges of the painted wings to lift across his cheeks and above his brows. "Do you remember me?"

"Did the…" I cleared my throat, wincing as the band momentarily tightened. "Was the attack stopped?"

"Attes gave you his vow. Kyn's forces pulled back." His head straightened as I glanced down at the hilt of the sword strapped to his back, and the dagger secured to his thigh. He'd gotten rid of most of the golden attire. Only the embroidered tunic was the sunny color. The pants were dark. "You didn't answer my question."

"I remember you." My fingers dug into the blanket as I steadied myself, lowering my feet to the floor—my *bare* feet.

I looked down, and this time, I flashed hot before going cold again as I saw *gold*. I no longer wore my pants or even my shirt and vest. I wore a golden sheath of nearly sheer, gossamer fabric.

"You were covered in filth and stank of the Shadowlands and the Primal there," Callum explained.

My head jerked up. "The only stench I carry on me is that of this place."

Callum's grin kicked up a notch. "I would warn you not to let His Majesty hear you say that."

Anger simmered through my veins, a red-hot fury. "Fuck His Majesty."

The thing before me chuckled. "And I would strongly advise that you don't let him hear *that*," he said. "Anyway, you were bathed and given cleaned clothing."

Bile rose once more at the knowledge that I had no idea who had taken care of that. I couldn't dwell on those things, though. I *couldn't*. I glanced around the chamber, spying one door and what appeared to be a sliding partition wall, both currently closed. "Do you expect me to thank you?"

"I would expect no such thing." He drifted a foot closer to the bars. "But it would be nice."

I sneered as I glanced at the dagger on his thigh again. "You were speaking to the Queen—"

"Queen Calliphe? Your mother, you mean," he interrupted, and I stiffened. "Though I got the distinct impression that she wasn't much of a mother." He shrugged, and...good gods, wasn't it telling that even he had noticed that. *Gods.* "But, yes, I was speaking to your mother. I spoke to her often." His chin lowered as those pale, pale eyes glinted with *mischief*. "For many years."

I jolted.

Callum came a bit closer. "Have you ever wondered how a mortal came into possession of the knowledge of how to kill a Primal?"

"Let me guess," I hissed. "You?"

He angled his body slightly and bowed with a flourishing sweep of his arm as his gaze met mine. "Me." He winked and then straightened, his smile fading as his eyes widened. "What? You seem shocked to learn this."

I *had* wondered how my family could've learned such information, but I had assumed it was a Fate or maybe even a *viktor*. But this? Knowing that the knowledge had been gained only during the last two decades? It wasn't hard to believe that my mother had lied, but that someone of Kolis's Court had shared the information with her? Possibly even one of his Revenants? Never.

It didn't make sense.

"Why would you do that? Why would he—?" I jerked again,

stomach dipping as disbelief rose. "Kolis knows."

A slow smile tipped up the corner of his mouth. "Of course, he does. He is the King of Gods." He spoke gently as if conversing with a child. "His Majesty learned of it the night of your birth when your father summoned the Primal of Life to make another deal."

Every muscle in my body stiffened. "What?"

"What was his name? Ah, yes. *Lamont.* Poor King Lamont had no idea that Eythos had answered his ancestor, so he spoke openly and freely with His Majesty. Asked for—no, *demanded*—that another deal be made, one that freed his newly born daughter from any obligations promised during the original deal."

Reeling, I couldn't move. I could barely breathe. The news that my father had tried to undo the deal—for me—left me stunned.

"He was quite insistent. Desperate, even. Unfortunately, one cannot simply undo deals made by a Primal." Callum's lips pursed. "Either way, the deal was of great interest to His Majesty. After all, he knew that his brother must have done something with the true embers of life since they didn't pass to His Majesty upon his brother's death."

My lips parted. That meant…gods, that meant Kolis had drained his brother of his lifeforce. His *own brother.* Sickened, I gripped the edge of the bed.

"He spent many years searching for wherever his *graeca* had scampered off to." Callum laughed. "*Scampered.* I do love that word."

Graeca.

The word had two meanings. Love. And life. But when Taric had fed from me and said that he wondered what the *graeca* would taste like, I'd thought he'd learned about the soul inside me. But he hadn't. Taric had tasted life. *Graeca* had always meant life—the embers of life.

"His Majesty knew that Eythos had to have hidden them somewhere." Callum tilted his head. "Then, enter your father and the discovery of the deal. So, yes, His Majesty has known since your birth what you carry inside you."

Good gods…

I rose without realizing it, without even understanding why, I only knew that I couldn't remain seated as shock rolled into confusion and then gave way to anguish.

"No," I stated, flinching at the sound of the chain rattling against the floor as I stepped forward.

"Yes."

I didn't want to believe it. Not because I couldn't understand how

Kolis had known this entire time and proceeded as he had, and not even because Kolis surely knew how to remove the embers from me. But because everything...

Everything Ash had sacrificed had been for *nothing*.

Kolis had known about me and the embers. He had always known. And there had been no reason to keep me undiscovered and safe. For others to have given up their lives to do so. There was no reason for Ash to have made that deal with Veses.

Callum eyed me. "You seem upset."

Upset? I shuddered, seizing the anger instead of the sorrow. One strengthened me. The other would destroy me.

He shrugged once more. "It was quite clever of Eythos, though, wasn't it? To take the last of those embers and hide them in a simple mortal, where no one would think to look—a mortal he insured would belong to his son. Very clever."

As Callum spoke, I realized that Callum had not once mentioned Sotoria's soul. That was something neither King Roderick—who made the deal—nor my father would've known about.

And neither did Kolis.

"If he knew I had Primal embers in me, why wait?" I asked, tucking the piece of knowledge about the soul away. "Why let me be taken into the Shadowlands? Why let it get to—to this point? People died and—" I sucked in a sharp breath. "He could've taken me at any time. Why wait?"

"*Blood.*" Callum inhaled deeply. "*Ash.*"

Something about the way he said that shook free a memory of the night the draken had freed the entombed gods. Veses' guard had said something similar after he scented my blood. He'd said—

"Blood *and* ash."

I stiffened to the point where the shackle around my neck threatened to cut into my throat. My heart fell and tumbled as I turned to the partition wall. It had opened, letting a bit of the rare hours of night seep into the chamber. I could make out the shadows of tall leafy trees behind...

Kolis.

At that very second, I realized I hadn't thought of what I'd been groomed to do since birth. What Holland had prepared me for. Not once since waking up.

Become his weakness.

Make him fall in love.

End him.

Kolis.

Not Ash.

And here I was, with him, yet fulfilling my duty was the furthest thing from my mind as I fought the urge to take several steps back from the false King. He was dressed as he had been when I saw him in Dalos. Loose linen pants. No shirt or boots. He bore no crown tonight as Callum faced him, bowing deeply.

"I'm glad to see you're finally awake," Kolis noted.

Breathe in. The embers remained silent as Kolis strode forward, but there was still a burning in my chest. Terror and fury that were *only* partly mine. A sense similar to déjà vu swept through me. I hadn't been here before, caged and chained.

But Sotoria had. When Kolis brought her back to life.

I wanted to run. I wanted to rage, but a lifetime of being taught to never show fear—to never show *any* emotion—filled me. The veil settled over me as I held Kolis's stare.

Kolis inclined his chin. "You do not kneel?"

"No," I bit out. "I do not."

Kolis laughed, low and soft, as Callum stepped to the side of the gilded cage. "Still incredibly brave, I see. Just as you were when you took the dagger handed to you." He placed his fingers on the bars. "Then again, how brave were you when you planned to betray me the moment you left? Using what does not belong to you to snatch away the life owed me?"

I clenched my jaw shut to stop myself from saying something incredibly foolish and keep my teeth from chattering. "Blood and ash?" I repeated. "What does that mean?"

Kolis trailed his hand over the bars as he laughed again. A look akin to respect flickered over his too-perfect features, and then his gaze lowered. I could only be grateful for my loose hair hanging in tangled curls over my chest. "It is the name of the prophecy."

My thoughts immediately went to the one Penellaphe had shared. "A prophecy?"

"No. I speak of *the* prophecy. The last dreamt by the Ancients. A *promise* only known by a few. Dared to be spoken of by even fewer." His fingers danced over the bars as he began to walk, to prowl. "And only repeated by the descendant of the Gods of Divination," he said. *Penellaphe.* He spoke of her. "And by the last oracle to be born."

The god, Delfai, had mentioned the last oracle, too, hadn't he? An oracle born of the Balfour bloodline. What were the chances that it was a coincidence that Delfai had mentioned this oracle?

None.

Kolis's grin was slow and cold. "But my dear Penellaphe didn't receive a complete vision," he said.

I tensed.

"Lucky for her, Penellaphe believed I had no knowledge of the vision. Those who do seem to meet untimely deaths," he said, and Callum chuckled. "My brother knew." He gestured at me. "Obviously."

I turned, following him as he stalked the length of the cage.

He stopped directly across from me. "Prophecies often come in threes. Each part seemingly unrelated until they're all pieced together."

The nape of my neck tingled. Penellaphe...she had said that. That they often had a beginning, a middle, and an end, and they weren't always received in order or completely.

Kolis's golden-flecked gaze shifted to Callum.

He stepped forward. "*From the desperation of golden crowns and born of mortal flesh, a great primal power rises as the heir to the lands and seas, to the skies and all the realms. A shadow in the ember, a light in the flame, to become a fire in the flesh,*'" he recited. "*When the stars fall from the night, the great mountains crumble into the seas, and old bones raise their swords beside the gods, the false one will be stripped from glory until two born of the same misdeeds, born of the same great and Primal power in the mortal realm. A first daughter, with blood full of fire, fated for the once-promised King. And the second daughter, with blood full of ash and ice, the other half of the future King. Together, they will remake the realms as they usher in the end.*'"

"*And so it will begin with the last Chosen blood spilled, the great conspirator birthed from the flesh and fire of the Primals will awaken as the Harbinger and the Bringer of Death and Destruction to the lands gifted by the gods,*'" Kolis continued for Callum. "*Beware, for the end will come from the west to destroy the east and lay waste to all which lies between.*'"

Kolis pressed his forehead against the bars. "I'm sure you've heard that before."

The fact that he'd known Penellaphe had spoken to us unsettled me greatly.

"And what do you think of it?" he asked.

I forced a half-shrug. "Nothing much except that it's clear to me who the false one—the great conspirator—is."

Kolis laughed. "Your attitude amuses me."

"Happy to hear that."

"But not *that* amused." His eyes flashed an intense shade of gold and silver. "But, yes, I do believe it was referring to me. Now, the two daughters? That has always confounded me. Still does a little, but I do believe it's Mycella. She was, after all, promised to the once King. My brother." He tapped his chin. "The second daughter? *You*. You are promised to the future King—or who would've been the future King once Eythos entered Arcadia, and Nyktos Ascended to take his place.

"Three parts. The beginning. The middle," Kolis continued before I could wrap my head around the fact that Ash and I had believed the middle part was some time in the future. "And then the end. There is more to that prophecy."

"Of course, there is," I murmured.

"There is the end." Kolis smirked as he gripped the bars. *"For the one born of the blood and the ash, the bearer of two crowns, and the bringer of life to mortal, god, and draken. A silver beast with blood seeping from its jaws of fire, bathed in the flames of the brightest moon to ever be birthed, will become one,'"* he said, and my skin chilled. "That would be you again, in case you're not keeping up with things."

My pulse thrummed unsteadily as my thoughts whirled. "My...my title. The born of blood and ash part. The...the brightest moon."

"Yes. Your title, bestowed on you by my nephew." His smirk deepened. "'Blood and ash' is something the draken like to say. It can mean several things."

I folded an arm across my stomach. "That's...that's what he said."

"He spoke no lie, at least not then." A hint of his fangs appeared, turning my stomach. "Blood. The strength of life. Ash. The bravery of death. Life and Death, if taken literally."

Suddenly, I remembered Keella's reaction to the title and how she'd asked what had inspired it. *My Consort's hair.* That had been an honest answer. I knew this, felt it in my bones and heart, and Keella had...she had said it made her *hopeful*. Just as Delfai had said after referencing the brightest moon upon Ash not killing him. Could they be the few who knew of the complete vision? Keella was nearly as old as Kolis, and the gods only knew how old Delfai was. Then there was Veses' guard. He knew what he'd sensed when he scented my blood. And Veses' reaction to learning what I carried. I was betting she knew, too.

"You carry the Primal embers of life. You have from birth, thanks to my brother." The golden flecks stilled in his eyes. "And now you are the bearer of two crowns."

Two crowns.

I inhaled, chest tightening. The crown of the Consort and the crown of a Princess. "That was why you waited. For me to be crowned?"

"Yes."

"Then why did you delay—?" Bringer of life to mortal, god, and draken. My stomach cramped. "You needed me to restore the draken's life."

That smile of his returned and sent a dual bolt of dread and anger through me. Because Attes had been playing us even then with Thad's life.

"I needed to make sure the embers had reached that point of power. That you were at the point the prophecy referenced for the rest to take place."

What had Kolis said when I demanded to know what taking Thad's life would give him? He'd said it would tell him everything he needed to know. And it had. "Is there more to the prophecy?"

Callum's laugh echoed behind me.

Kolis nodded. "'*And the great powers will stumble and fall, some all at once, and they will fall through the fires into a void of nothing. Those left standing will tremble as they kneel, will weaken as they become small, as they become forgotten. For finally, the Primal rises, the giver of blood and the bringer of bone, the Primal of Blood and Ash.*'"

My lips parted as my eyes widened. "The Primal of Blood and Ash…" A shudder of disbelief coursed through me. A being that should not exist. "A Primal of Life *and* Death."

"Clever girl," Kolis remarked.

"I'm not a girl," I snapped, my arm falling to my side. "And one does not have to be that clever. It's literally said right in the prophecy."

"No, you're not a girl," he purred, sending a curl of disgust through me. "You are the vessel who will fulfill what the Ancients dreamt of. Who will give me what I want."

"And that's…to do what? Rule over Iliseeum and the mortal realm?" I laughed. "Sounds to me like it will only give you what you deserve."

"And that is?"

"Your death."

Kolis's still eyes met mine, and several seconds ticked by as tiny bumps spread across my flesh. "You would think that. Perhaps that is what it originally foreshadowed, but I suppose the Ancients never thought I'd try to change it. That I'd dare to do so. Apparently, it was acceptable—even foretold—that Eythos set things in motion." A sneer accompanied the mention of his brother. "But me?" He laughed coldly. "No, they thought I'd just stand by and do nothing. They should've foreseen that, but even in their dreams, they underestimated me. What I will do to not only stay alive but also get what I want. And that is to be *the* one, Seraphena. The beginning and the end. Life and death."

His eyes began to glow. "There will be no need for mortal Kings. There will be no need for any other Primal. Not when a Primal of Life and Death has risen."

A new horror descended over me. "You...you want to kill all the Primals?"

"Most of them. Yeah. What?" He snorted. "You look surprised. Come now, you've met a few of them." He shook his head. "You've seen firsthand how fucking annoying most of them are."

Well, I couldn't argue with that, but...

"Whiny, sniveling brats who have forgotten the way things were. When we were respected and feared by not just mortals but also by the gods. When even the draken bowed to us." His lip curled. "When power actually meant something."

I took a step forward. "Do you not already have enough power? You've crowned yourself King of Gods. You already usurp any mortal ruler, as do the other Primals." Anger flooded my senses. "Why would you need more power?"

"Why? What a silly fucking question," he replied, and Callum laughed on cue. "One only a mortal would ask. Besides the fact that if I do nothing, I die? Power isn't infinite or limitless. Another can always rise. Power can always be taken, leaving you weakened and incapable of protecting yourself or those you care for."

"As if you care for anyone but yourself," I snapped.

His eyes flashed pure gold, then he was *inside* the cage. With me. He remained several feet from me, but I felt his hand on my throat, squeezing tighter than the band there.

"As if you know a thing about me that hasn't been told to you, Seraphena." He took a step, the edges of his body blurring. "You think I'm the villain?"

I breathed in, but the pressure sealed off my throat. My hands flew to my neck.

"You think I'm the *only* villain in this tale? That the other Primals deserve to continue when they did nothing to help me when my brother ruled as King? Not one of them? That the mortals who carry wealth and prestige are innocent, worthy of life despite their many wars and lack of empathy for their brethren? You think I'm the only one who seeks absolute power? If so, then you're not as clever as I thought you were."

I couldn't breathe.

He took another step forward. "Every mortal wants it. Every god. Every Primal. Even Eythos. What do you think he was setting up his son to become by putting the embers of life in the mortal promised to him as a Consort? *'A silver beast with blood seeping from its jaws of fire, bathed in the flames of the brightest moon to ever be birthed will become one.'* Emphasis on the will-become-one part. Eythos put those embers in you so his son could take them—something Nyktos would've done the moment he knew he was ready, if he'd been aware of what it meant. He wanted Nyktos to be *the* Primal—the silver beast. To not only overthrow me and end me, but because Eythos knew his days were numbered. After all, the Ancients dreamt of just such a powerful being as the Primal of Blood and Ash. He knew what that meant for him, but he also knew that once his son took those embers and Ascended, Nyktos could even raise him."

I wheezed, shaking.

Eyes burning like pools of gold, he dipped his head. "Eythos always hated me. Do you know why? Because he loved Mycella, and Mycella loved me. It didn't matter that I didn't return those sentiments. That I never acted upon what she felt. He still hated me, and that was why he refused the only fucking thing I ever asked of him." Kolis's chest rose sharply. "If he hadn't, it wouldn't have changed any of this. The Ancients still had their dreams. Their visions. He still would've needed to die, but he could've saved the lives of so many others, including his precious Mycella—and all the lives his son had to take in place of him."

I clawed at my throat, my veins bulging as my vision darkened—

The pressure released suddenly. I sagged, falling to my knees and palms. Gagging, I dragged deep gulps of air into my aching throat.

"But here we are." Kolis knelt. "Just as promised." He cupped my chin. Even though his handling was gentle, I flinched as he tipped my head back. "Do you know what's about to happen, Seraphena?"

My throat was too raw to form words as I met his stare, but I knew exactly what would happen.

"I am about to drain you. I will take every drop of your blood. Even the last," he said softly. "Then I will take the embers of life, and I will rise. I will complete my final Ascension. I will become the Primal of Life and Death. Those who do not bow to me and relinquish their Courts and kingdoms to me will die." He leaned in, stopping when his face was mere inches from mine. "And I think you know what that means for my nephew."

I shuddered.

"Yeah, you do." His thumb swept over my cheek. "I will have what I want. What I deserve. Finally. Because…nothing"—he began to rise, forcing me to my feet—"absolutely *nothing* will be forbidden. Impossible. Not even what has been hidden from me."

Sotoria.

He spoke of her.

"Seraphena Mierel," Kolis murmured, bringing his mouth to my temple. "You kept the embers safe. You dared to use them. You made sure they were ready for me. Words can never do justice to the gratitude I feel. But thank you."

Kolis struck.

There was no other warning.

He turned me so my back was to him, and then his fangs were at my throat, tearing into my flesh just above the band. A scream tore from me as pain exploded. My body went rigid, eyes wide, and the pain…good gods, it was absolute.

I clawed at the arm around my waist—at the air. Kicked at him, at nothing. The agony was too much. With each deep draw he took, a fire ripped through me, tearing my bones from my skin and leaving flames in their place. Spasms of agony seized my chest, my throat, and this—oh, gods—this was it. This was how I would die. He was going to drain me and take the embers. I would be the first to burn, and then the rest of the realms would follow.

I *was* dying.

I wouldn't get a chance to say goodbye to Ash, to tell him that I loved him. There was no saving him or any of the gods or realms. I wouldn't fulfill my destiny. I jerked, my fingers curling inward, nails digging into my palms—into the imprint—

Ash could sense my pain. Feel it. Gods, could he feel this from where he was? He would know, though, when the imprint vanished from his palm. He would know then.

Kolis's chest swelled against my back as he drew even harder, deeper—

Heat poured into my chest as the embers began to flare faintly, weakly, but the heat kept building and building. And that presence seized me again. That awareness. That voice. The voices.

No. No. No. No.

It wasn't just my voice screaming. It was *hers*. Sotoria. All the lives she'd lived. And it was ours that moved my tongue.

"*You're killing me,*" I slurred, eyes heavy. "*You're killing me again, after all these years.*"

Kolis's head jerked up. "*What?*"

My tongue felt useless. Bulky. The ceiling flickered in and out. There was no pain. The only thing I felt now was *her* anger—*our* rage.

"What did you just say?" Kolis turned me in his arms. His face blurred. Blood smeared his lips, his fangs. He shook me, rattling my head. "What the fuck did you just say?"

"*It's me...*" A laugh that didn't sound like mine at all parted my lips. "*Sotoria.*"

Kolis went completely still as his eyes searched my features, looked over my hair, my body. He shook his head, his lip curling, mouth dripping with blood. "Liar," he snarled.

"It's...not a lie. Eythos had her soul..." My heart felt as sluggish as my words. "And he placed it with the embers, to be...born again in me. I'm her."

"There is no way." He gripped my hair, jerking my head to the side. "Clever lie, though."

"Your Majesty," a voice interrupted. Attes. When had he arrived? "A moment please."

"Are you fucking serious right now?" The tension on my neck didn't let up as Kolis barked out, "One *second.*"

"Keella," Attes said.

Kolis went rigid once more.

"You know that Keella helped Eythos capture her soul so she could be reborn." His voice was closer. "You know she's out there, and you haven't been able to find her, even though you have taken every Chosen—every mortal who bears an aura. Could it be because she has not been reborn in all these recent centuries?" Attes questioned. "Could it be that you have finally found her?"

"This is a trick," Callum snapped. "Do not trust her, and do not trust this Primal."

"I know how to kill you, you shit," Attes growled. "Speak of me again like that, and I'll prove it."

A tremor ran through Kolis's arm as he lifted my head, forcing my face to his. He stared down at me, his eyes widening, the eather swirling and then stopping until only gold flecks were present.

"Think about it, Kolis," Attes continued. "Your brother was very clever. He could've taken Sotoria's soul and placed it with the embers to protect her and to fuck you over. You know he would."

Kolis shuddered.

His arms loosened, and I started to fall. He caught me before I hit the floor, going down on his knee as he lifted me to his chest. He cradled my cheek with a shaking hand—then cradled me to him, letting my head fall to the side of his arm. I shriveled at the feel of him, shrank inside myself at the sight of the *horror* etched onto the false King's features as he realized who he held in his arms—as he realized who he'd have to kill.

Again.

Kolis shook. He rocked as my gaze drifted to the open doors and the shadowy leaves swaying in the balmy breeze. To the—

To a wolf.

A wolf crouched at the trunks of the trees. A wolf more silver than white.

A silver beast.

Bathed in the brightest moonlight.

Ash.

Author's Note

Sera is a creation of my imagination, but her thoughts, her feelings, and her actions regarding what she admitted at the Pools of Divanash are something very real. These are complicated emotions and actions I've experienced myself. Because of this, I know they may strike a certain chord in readers. Not all of us have a sage, ancient draken letting us know that they're there for us when we need someone, but if you've had the same thoughts as Sera, as I have, there are people waiting for when you're ready to talk.

Here are some resources that are available all day, every day.

The National Suicide Prevention Lifeline
The National Suicide Prevention Lifeline provides free and confidential emotional support to people in suicidal crisis or emotional distress.
Telephone: 1-800-273-8255
For Deaf & Hard of Hearing: 1-800-799-4889
Online chat: suicidepreventionlifeline.org

You are not alone.

Discover More From Jennifer L. Armentrout

A Shadow in the Ember
Flesh and Fire Series
Book One

Available in hardcover, e-book, and trade paperback.

#1 New York Times bestselling author Jennifer L. Armentrout returns with book one of the all-new, compelling Flesh and Fire series—set in the beloved Blood and Ash world.

Born shrouded in the veil of the Primals, a Maiden as the Fates promised, Seraphena Mierel's future has never been hers. *Chosen* before birth to uphold the desperate deal her ancestor struck to save his people, Sera must leave behind her life and offer herself to the Primal of Death as his Consort.

However, Sera's real destiny is the most closely guarded secret in all of Lasania—she's not the well protected Maiden but an assassin with one mission—one target. Make the Primal of Death fall in love, become his weakness, and then…end him. If she fails, she dooms her kingdom to a slow demise at the hands of the Rot.

Sera has always known what she is. Chosen. Consort. Assassin. Weapon. A specter never fully formed yet drenched in blood. A *monster*. Until *him*. Until the Primal of Death's unexpected words and deeds chase away the darkness gathering inside her. And his seductive touch ignites a passion she's never allowed herself to feel and cannot feel for him. But Sera has never had a choice. Either way, her life is forfeit—it always has been, as she has been forever touched by Life and Death.

From Blood and Ash
Blood and Ash Series
Book One

Available in hardcover, e-book, and trade paperback.

Captivating and action-packed, From Blood and Ash is a sexy, addictive, and unexpected fantasy perfect for fans of Sarah J. Maas and Laura Thalassa.

A Maiden...

Chosen from birth to usher in a new era, Poppy's life has never been her own. The life of the Maiden is solitary. Never to be touched. Never to be looked upon. Never to be spoken to. Never to experience pleasure. Waiting for the day of her Ascension, she would rather be with the guards, fighting back the evil that took her family, than preparing to be found worthy by the gods. But the choice has never been hers.

A Duty...

The entire kingdom's future rests on Poppy's shoulders, something she's not even quite sure she wants for herself. Because a Maiden has a heart. And a soul. And longing. And when Hawke, a golden-eyed guard honor bound to ensure her Ascension, enters her life, destiny and duty become tangled with desire and need. He incites her anger, makes her question everything she believes in, and tempts her with the forbidden.

A Kingdom...

Forsaken by the gods and feared by mortals, a fallen kingdom is rising once more, determined to take back what they believe is theirs through violence and vengeance. And as the shadow of those cursed draws closer, the line between what is forbidden and what is right becomes blurred. Poppy is not only on the verge of losing her heart and being found unworthy by the gods, but also her life when every blood-soaked thread that holds her world together begins to unravel.

A Kingdom of Flesh and Fire
Blood and Ash Series
Book Two

Available in hardcover, e-book, and trade paperback.

Is Love Stronger Than Vengeance?

A Betrayal...

Everything Poppy has ever believed in is a lie, including the man she was falling in love with. Thrust among those who see her as a symbol of a monstrous kingdom, she barely knows who she is without the veil of the Maiden. But what she *does* know is that nothing is as dangerous to her as *him*. The Dark One. The Prince of Atlantia. He wants her to fight him, and that's one order she's more than happy to obey. *He may have taken her, but he will never have her.*

A Choice...

Casteel Da'Neer is known by many names and many faces. His lies are as seductive as his touch. His truths as sensual as his bite. Poppy knows better than to trust him. He needs her alive, healthy, and whole to achieve his goals. But he's the only way for her to get what she wants—to find her brother Ian and see for herself if he has become a soulless Ascended. Working with Casteel instead of against him presents its own risks. He still tempts her with every breath, offering up all she's ever wanted. Casteel has plans for her. Ones that could expose her to unimaginable pleasure and unfathomable pain. Plans that will force her to look beyond everything she thought she knew about herself—about him. Plans that could bind their lives together in unexpected ways that neither kingdom is prepared for. And she's far too reckless, too hungry, to resist the temptation.

A Secret...

But unrest has grown in Atlantia as they await the return of their Prince. Whispers of war have become stronger, and Poppy is at the very heart of it all. The King wants to use her to send a message. The Descenters want her dead. The wolven are growing more unpredictable. And as her abilities to feel pain and emotion begin to grow and strengthen, the Atlantians start to fear her. Dark secrets are at play, ones steeped in the blood-drenched sins of two kingdoms that would do anything to keep the truth hidden. But when the earth begins to shake, and the skies start to bleed, it may already be too late.

The Crown of Gilded Bones
Blood and Ash Series
Book Three

Available in hardcover, e-book, and trade paperback.

Bow Before Your Queen Or Bleed Before Her...

She's been the victim and the survivor...

Poppy never dreamed she would find the love she's found with Prince Casteel. She wants to revel in her happiness but first they must free his brother and find hers. It's a dangerous mission and one with far-reaching consequences neither dreamed of. Because Poppy is the Chosen, the Blessed. The true ruler of Atlantia. She carries the blood of the King of Gods within her. By right the crown and the kingdom are hers.

The enemy and the warrior…

Poppy has only ever wanted to control her own life, not the lives of others, but now she must choose to either forsake her birthright or seize the gilded crown and become the Queen of Flesh and Fire. But as the kingdoms' dark sins and blood-drenched secrets finally unravel, a long-forgotten power rises to pose a genuine threat. And they will stop at nothing to ensure that the crown never sits upon Poppy's head.

A lover and heartmate…

But the greatest threat to them and to Atlantia is what awaits in the far west, where the Queen of Blood and Ash has her own plans, ones she has waited hundreds of years to carry out. Poppy and Casteel must consider the impossible—travel to the Lands of the Gods and wake the King himself. And as shocking secrets and the harshest betrayals come to light, and enemies emerge to threaten everything Poppy and Casteel have fought for, they will discover just how far they are willing to go for their people—and each other.

And now she will become Queen…

The War of Two Queens
Blood and Ash Series
Book Four

Available in hardcover, e-book, and trade paperback.

War is only the beginning…

From the desperation of golden crowns…

Casteel Da'Neer knows all too well that very few are as cunning or vicious as the Blood Queen, but no one, not even him, could've prepared for the staggering revelations. The magnitude of what the Blood Queen has done is almost unthinkable.

And born of mortal flesh...

Nothing will stop Poppy from freeing her King and destroying everything the Blood Crown stands for. With the strength of the Primal of Life's guards behind her, and the support of the wolven, Poppy must convince the Atlantian generals to make war her way—because there can be no retreat this time. Not if she has any hope of building a future where both kingdoms can reside in peace.

A great primal power rises...

Together, Poppy and Casteel must embrace traditions old and new to safeguard those they hold dear—to protect those who cannot defend themselves. But war is only the beginning. Ancient primal powers have already stirred, revealing the horror of what began eons ago. To end what the Blood Queen has begun, Poppy might have to become what she has been prophesied to be—what she fears the most.

As the Harbinger of Death and Destruction.

On Behalf of Blue Box Press,

Liz Berry, M.J. Rose, and Jillian Stein would like to thank ~

Steve Berry
Doug Scofield
Benjamin Stein
Kim Guidroz
Chelle Olson
Hang Le
Camille Fabre
Michael Pearlman
Social Butterfly PR
Chris Graham
Jessica Saunders
Dylan Stockton
Kate Boggs
Dina Williams
Kasi Alexander
Malissa Coy
Erika Hayden
Stacey Tardif
Jessica Mobbs
Laura Helseth
Jen Fisher
Richard Blake
and Simon Lipskar